REVOLUTION

REVOLUTION

A Novel of Russia

Barnaby Williams

S I M O N & S C H U S T E R

LONDON·SYDNEY·NEW YORK·TOKYO·SINGAPORE·TORONTO

First published in Great Britain by Simon & Schuster Ltd, 1994
A Paramount Communications Company

Simon & Schuster Ltd
West Garden Place
Kendal Street
London W2 2AQ

Simon & Schuster of Australia Pty Ltd
Sydney

A CIP catalogue record for this book is available from the
British Library.

ISBN 0–671–71818–5

Typeset in Garamond by
Hewer Text Composition Services, Edinburgh
Printed in Great Britain by
Butler & Tanner Ltd, Frome and London

For my wife Anne, with all my love.

In memory of all those who suffered and died.

With thanks:

To my courageous and skilful publisher, Nick Webb, for letting me do it, and for all his advice and help. To my fine editors, Daphne Bien and Jenny Olivier, for all their work.

To my marvellous agent, Anne Dewe, for everything, and to Debbie.

To my mother, for forty-six years of faith.

To Susan and Peter, for much encouragement.

To Jean and Jim, for finding obscure books, and sending them off to obscure places.

To Chris Donnelly, for much gathering from library shelves, and phone calls interrupting his fishing.

To my daughters Abbey and Philippa, for being who they are.

1

Bolsheviki

Tsarskoye Selo, Petrograd, August 1917

THERE was something wrong with the photograph. On the right it seemed conventional enough, the young men and women of the class sitting and standing formally, the girls in their high-necked, fitted white blouses and ankle-length skirts, the boys in the suits made by their fathers' tailors behind the Liteynyy. But their faces were too set: the pretty young women were gripping their parasols like pistols, the boys were looking at their classmates on the left from the corners of their eyes. A trickle of blood was running out of Piotr Pavlovich Sadovsky's hair, and down his temple.

On the left, the carefully posed photograph had disintegrated. The young men and women grinned disrespectfully and destructively at the lens. They were dressed in a variety of fashions, all shocking. Coarse military clothing vied with anarchist black. A shock-headed young man stood in a grey German soldier's tunic, shorn of badges. A sailor in round cap with a bandolier wound over his chest, gold against the blue of his uniform, was looking at the finery of the walls, at the glittering chandelier on the ceiling. The colour red was much in evidence, in scarves and huge handkerchiefs, carelessly tied about the neck and hair. They were very red, these bindings, more scarlet than the blood seeping out of Piotr Sadovsky's head.

The magnesium flash bloomed in the great room, sending white light and shadows racing over the porticoes and pillars, and they all blinked. Their wide-eyed young images rested, sealed, upon the roll of film in the big box camera and outside the white night of the past two months was over: dusk was gathering.

The two groups moved apart.

'Where is Madame Dumaine?' a slim, blonde girl asked. 'Oh Piotr, you're bleeding!'

Sadovsky dabbed at his head with a handkerchief.

'She got out, I should think, Yelena – and I don't blame her. Some oaf threw half a brick at me as I was driving out of Millionnaya to get here. Do you know what he yelled at me? *Boorzhoi gavno.*'

He looked at her, his face still shocked.

'Excuse my language, Yelena. But some bit of dirt I wouldn't let chop wood calls me bourgeois shit . . . and throws a brick at me?'

'*They'd* probably kiss him on both cheeks,' a voice said acidly. A tall, striking girl had come up and was staring at the swirling, laughing rebel camp through angry blue eyes.

'Hullo, Verochka. Have you seen Anna?'

'I think she went to get her things, Piotr,' said Yelena.

'What's *he* doing here?' Verochka demanded, pointing at the boy in German uniform. '*You've* brought him, haven't you, Shapiro?'

'He's a comrade!' yelled a young man in a Russian soldier's tunic, bereft, like the German's, of all markings. He wore round, steel-rimmed glasses. 'One of us. A Bolshevik.'

'A deserter, you mean!' Verochka sneered. 'Like you. Why aren't you at the front, Shapiro, instead of creeping back here with the enemy?'

'Israel Shapiro is dead,' said the young man, very seriously. 'He was killed in the bourgeois war. The man you see here is a new man – *he* is Leon Krivitskiy.'

'Is Leon Krivitskiy still a *zhid*?' asked Verochka nastily.

'Verochka . . .' Yelena murmured. 'Don't say things like that.'

'Let her, Yelena,' a slim girl in soldier's clothing called. A scarlet scarf blazed like fire at her throat and glossy, curly black hair bobbed as she bounced about. 'She's the stupid one. She doesn't know that there is a new world coming, filled with new people, when the revolution comes. No Jews, no gentiles, no bourgeoisie. Just new people.'

'I don't want a new world, Ruth,' said Yelena, distressed 'I am happy with the old one. And we have had a revolution already.'

She turned away. There was a big, glass-fronted display case by the wall. In it were all the exhibits of the class in their final year, carefully laid out by Madame Dumaine before she had slipped away on the train from the Finland station. Ruth had been Yelena's friend since they were little. Growing up was supposed to mean learning how to be adult, in an ordered world. The problems of life should have been about wondering which handsome young officer the *dirigeur* would allow over, as the ball orchestra waited to play the mazurka. Good girls, *baryshni*, did not dress up as soldiers and affect scarlet scarfs. Next to Ruth was that strange, intense girl, Nadezhda. Yelena blamed her for leading Ruth into all this. The Alliluyevs were all revolutionaries.

'Kerensky?' she heard the boy in the grey tunic say mockingly, in his strange accent. 'He is no revolutionary, just the last of the old guard. *We* are making real revolution.'

'Well, I don't think we need Germans here to make trouble.' Yelena snapped, turning back. 'We have enough of our own doing that, thank you.'

'But my dear Countess, it is an *international* revolution,' said the German. 'All over the world the proletariat will rise up, and throw off the yoke of their oppressors, the bourgeoisie. Here and in Germany, in Britain, America and France. Everywhere.'

'You tell her, Manfred,' a tall boy with over-long hair and giant red scarf laughed.

'You keep out of it, Konstantin. I am not personally aware of having ever oppressed anybody,' Yelena snapped.

'You function, because you are.' Manfred said elegantly. 'You are bourgeois, so you oppress.'

They all cheered, including Ruth, as though he had said something clever, and Yelena turned away again.

'You're all stupid,' she muttered. She looked at Konstantin, lounging against the display cabinet. 'You've always been stupid, Konstantin, but you're an artist. *They* ought to know better. Do you want your drawings?'

They had done *The Cherry Orchard*, and there they all were, in striking caricature. He reached inside the case for the sheets of paper, tearing them across, and throwing the pieces to flutter like feathers in the air.

'Why did you do that?' she demanded, angrily.

'The same reason I'm a revolutionary,' he said, moving away casually. 'To execute the past.'

'Is that why you came for the photograph, too? You could have stayed away, you and your nasty friends.'

'We thought we would,' he said, pushing his long hair off his face. 'You're the old world, we're the new. Shall we march? Left, left, left. *Who moved his right*? Left, left . . .'

A striking girl with auburn hair and dazzling green eyes came by carrying some books. The young artist was hopping in a circle on his left boot.

'I like your scarf, Konstantin,' she said, grinning.

'Don't encourage him, Katia,' said Yelena. She glanced across at the rival group. 'What's Savinkov doing here? I thought Madame Dumaine dissmissed him for being a subversive.'

'Now there I agree with you,' said Konstantin, tiring of his hopping. 'He goes about posing as the great Marxist thinker, just because he knows Lenin. Shapiro, or Krivitskiy, he calls himself now, wanted him with us. I think he just wants to get his hands up Ruth's skirt.'

'He'll get frostbitten fingers if he does,' Katia giggled. 'Ruthie's only hot for the revolution.'

They were joined by another girl, also carrying books, thin and studious.

'What were you talking to the sailor for, Katerina?' Katia demanded.

'He looked so out of place. He's from the fortress in Kronstadt and they treat the sailors very badly, you know. They aren't all madmen like Lenin, you know. They just want a better life.'

'I want a better life too,' said Sadovsky, rejoining them. 'I want people to stop throwing bricks at me in the street.'

Vassily came by with Zhenya. He took his book of poetry which had been bound for him in leather, and they hurried away to his car outside, together with Nadia and Valerian, who had produced the play. Verochka, who could sing, like a bird, was waiting there for them and they all crammed into the Renault. Yelena saw Vassily drive them away.

Anna had joined Sadovsky and the little group stood by the display cabinet. Yelena tucked her book of pressed flowers under her arm. There was a whole year there, with notes in blue ink on each page. A copy of Davydov's *Elementary Algebra* lay abandoned on the floor and she went over and picked it up. Someone would need it again soon, when things were back to normal. When Madame Dumaine returned, when the war stopped, when Leon Krivitskiy went back to calling himself Israel Shapiro, when Ruth put on a proper dress, when the man in the street tugged his cap as Piotr Sadovsky drove by, when the world was back to normal.

She put it up against some others on the shelf.

'Nobody's going to be reading it any more, you know.' Ruth had come over and was standing there in her ridiculous soldier's clothes.

'Of course they will,' Yelena said shortly. 'When classes start next term.'

'We shall write a *proper* maths book,' said Ruth. 'New, exciting, and the truth! Not that imperial rubbish.'

'Oh, yes?'

It was all too much to bear. Ruth was pushing her unpinned hair back with her hand.

'Oh, yes?' Yelena demanded again. 'A revolutionary maths book?

"If three revolutionaries have five bombs between them and each kills eight people how many does each bomb blow apart?" Is that it? Is it?'

Ruth tossed her curly black hair.

'Oh, if you're going to be silly about it – '

'Algebra is algebra, Ruth. You can't get revolution into it.'

'You're *wrong*, Yelena,' her once-friend cried passionately. 'The revolution must enter into *everything*.'

'It entered into my father,' Yelena said evenly. Her grey eyes looked over the group. 'People who looked like you, talked like you, shot him.'

Ruth suddenly flushed, embarrassed, and, as quickly, was angry with herself.

'Oh, well, I couldn't expect you to understand. Anyway, those people ... you know, the ones who ... the ones with your father, they were anarchists.'

'You're all scum,' Yelena said bitterly.

'We aren't like that! We're *Bolsheviki*, we don't kill people!'

'Scum,' said Yelena, and Ruth suddenly turned her back, running across the room to the noisy crowd. Yelena tucked her book of pressed flowers under her arm and gripping her parasol, went out through the white-and-gilt French doors into the pillared and paved courtyard. Sadovsky was standing there with Anna next to him, and Katerina and Katia by his car. He had a little model aeroplane in his hand, a Nieuport, a pretty biplane of wood and tissue paper, gaily painted. With his long, delicate fingers, he could make anything. His Mercedes was standing there in the last of the evening sun, and an ugly truck which the revolutionaries had arrived in. They were now all streaming out of the classroom, clambering into the back like apes. Ruth and Nadezhda were clinging on to each other like best friends.

Sadovsky was winding the rubber motor of the little aircraft.

'Want to see it go?' he asked

He put it down on the paving, holding the little wooden propeller and then let it go. It whirred through the air and across the courtyard like a bird, bouncing to a stop near the gate. The truck started with a belch of blue smoke, moving off with a rattling crunch from the gear box. They were singing some revolutionary song, and waving their red scarves. It passed through the gate and, on the paving stones, there were just scraps of wood, and paper fluttering like ruined feathers.

'Oh, Piotr ...'

Sadovsky shrugged, pretending indifference. 'It's not the right day, is it? Don't worry, I'll make another, some time.'

Anna looked at the wreck unhappily. 'It was so pretty . . .'

'Come on, I'll take you home, girls. What about you, Yelena? Want me to drop you at your house?'

'I'll walk across the park,' she said. She watched them get in, Katia and Katerina in the back, Anna by Sadovsky. They waved as they went off down the road towards the city. The school was quiet and empty. She snapped open her parasol, giving it a defiant twirl.

She paused by the bandstand in the dusk. Its rococo shell was empty. The Cossack band played martial airs there from eleven to twelve and they had come there the bright Easter morning the boys were to leave, the two counts splendid in their guards uniforms; trousers striped scarlet, gold braid on their shoulder boards. Now her brother was dead, and she waited, like so many other girls, for her fiancée to come back. Mikhail had taken his English Purdey shotgun to the front, for it was, he said, the only weapon for a gentleman to use. Her brother Alexei had taken his as well and they had sent it back with his body, its stock smashed by the rain of bullets coming from the Maxim gun that had killed him in his glorious uniform.

She closed her eyes briefly and said a prayer for the soul of Alexei and for the safety of Mikhail. God listened, she felt sure.

She set off again. The dark was gathering, across the lovely lawns and, through the trees, the lights of the houses glittered gold. The flowers that loved the dusk were pouring their perfume into the air and, in the distance, she saw the white forms of some people leaving the park, moving like moths.

As she went over a delicate ornamental bridge she heard the ducks splashing quietly, the soft sound of their voices, an echo of her foosteps. She went along the path where the rose bushes had dropped a fine carpet of white petals and glanced behind her. Something dark slipped over the bridge, crouching low, like a beast.

She gripped her parasol, and stepped out determinedly. Going under the pergola she looked around again, but the path behind her was empty. The lights of the houses ahead shone large and bright, and she hurried towards them.

Foaming pink hydrangeas glowed in the gloom and behind them a waterfall of jasmine let its scent flow down the path in a sweet river. He came from between the dark bushes like a wolf and knocked her flying.

She drew breath to scream and a fierce blow to her stomach held the air in her throat. The air was suddenly cool on her legs, the skirt of her dress high around her waist and she shrieked soundlessly as he hit her between her thighs. She was drawn up in a ball, trying to protect herself as he tore off the top of her dress. Savage hands crushed her breasts as the breath returned to her lungs and she screamed.

He was on top of her, his knee in her stomach, both hands on her neck. Her nails dug into them and he hissed in pain.

She heard the bang through the drumming in her ears and suddenly the pressure was gone. A huge figure stood tall above her, a crutch swinging from one hand. Her assailant lay unconscious on the grass.

The man bent down beside her, favouring his good leg.

'Countess,' he said, lifting her. 'Are you hurt?'

'Ivan Ivanovich!' she gasped thankfully. 'Thank God.'

The young giant turned her attacker face up on the grass. He was small, his hands still outstretched like claws and they stared at him in amazement.

'It is Rykov,' she said.

There was a man in the room. A board creaked and her waking moments were filled with terror. She moved in the bed, and pain stabbed through her from a multitude of bruises.

The morning sun was shining through the light French silk that curtained the windows, and he stood at the foot of the bed.

'It is only me,' he said softly. 'Don't be afraid, Yelena. Ivan Akulov told me what happened.'

She reached out her arms to him and he came and kissed her, sitting on the edge of the bed. His Guards' uniform was muddy, and torn, here and there. His hands bore deep scratches.

'The wire,' he said apologetically. 'The shells are supposed to cut it, but they don't. But what has happened? Why did this man attack you – and are you hurt?'

'I am stiff and bruised,' she said, 'but that is all. Who attacked me? His name is Oleg Rykov, Mikhail. I employed him here as a footman. I have kept only a small staff since mother died. Mania the cook, Olga my maid. Your peasant boy, the groom, Ivan Akulov came back from the front, wounded. He had been taught how to drive a truck out there, I made him chauffeur of the Renault. Then this Rykov appeared. He was respectful, and it has been so difficult to get young men with the war ... I needed a footman. A week ago I woke in the night. Someone was in the room, moving towards the bed, very quietly. I screamed. He ran, but Akulov sleeps by the stairs.

He caught him. It was Rykov. I bade Ivan Ivanovich throw him out. Last night I cut through the park to come home from the photograph at the Lycee, and I was attacked. By Rykov.'

She was quiet for a moment.

'His hands were about my throat, and then Ivan came. He knocked him out with his crutch and we took him to the police. He's in the jail. I made a statement, and so did Ivan. He's up before Grigoriev the magistrate later today.'

She reached out and rang a little bell on the French table beside her bed.

'Olga will bring some tea. I haven't been to the English shops since the troubles began because it isn't safe. But we still have some tea. But Mikhail, how are you here?'

'The front's collapsing,' he said grimly. 'The army's finished as a fighting force.'

'What is going to happen?' she asked quietly.

'Someone's going to have to make a peace with the Germans.'

'Kerensky still believes in fighting the war,' she said. 'He makes so many speeches to the troops they call him the "Supreme Persuader-in-Chief".'

'I know,' said Mikhail dryly. 'I heard one. The troops were very good; they waited until he'd gone before they deserted.'

'So who will make peace?'

'The Germans are sending huge sums of money to Lenin. They sent him here, after all. *Revolutionierungspolitik*, they call it. They sent him here like a typhoid bacillus, and he's given us the disease. A *coup d'état*. And he'll make peace with the Germans, give them everything they want.'

'And after that?'

'Civil war,' he said, his face grim. 'The better of the Tsar's generals will raise forces and fight Lenin. Who will win I cannot say.'

'I want to get away, Mikhail. I do not want to stay here.'

The peasant girl brought tea in a pot, English Wedgwood china, and poured into the delicate cups.

'Ask Ivan to come up, Olga,' Yelena ordered. 'Then draw my bath and put in a lot of the salts – I am stiff.'

The girl bobbed, her grey and white uniform rustling, and went out.

'I don't want to stay either,' Mikhail observed. 'The deserters are looting houses in Petrograd. They get drunk and go looking for an *ofitser* to kill. Where shall we go?'

'Porechie. The old estate. I haven't been down there since the war began. Everything's under dust sheets but we'd be safe there, it's a long way from the front, from here. Just peasants and woods, and rivers.'

There was a knock at the door and Ivan came in, hopping on his crutch.

'Ivan, the Count and I are going to Porechie. I want you to get the bags ready and take us, this afternoon, to catch the night train. You'd better go this morning and arrange for my carriage to be attached to the train.'

'Very good, Countess,' he said respectfully. 'May I ask when you will be returning to the house here?'

'Not for a long time, I think,' she said quietly. 'Not until the troubles are over.'

He stood silent for a moment before speaking.

'Then may I ask leave not to accompany you, Madam?'

She looked at him in surprise.

'You want to stay here?'

'Yes.'

'What on earth for? There's nothing here but trouble.'

'I have . . . things to do.'

Count Mikhail sat on the edge of the bed and eyed the peasant boy from his estate shrewdly.

'And what will you do once those things are done, Ivan?'

'Go home, sir,' Akulov said steadily.

'To my lands.'

'A new world is coming, sir. Not all the lands will remain yours. Those who work them and sweat on them shall have them.'

'Don't be ridiculous!' Yelena said sharply. Her teacup clattered as she put it down on the saucer. 'You talk like one of these frightful *Bolsheviki*.'

He looked her in the eye.

'Yes, Countess,' he said plainly. 'That's what I am.'

The sound of breaking glass underlay the shouting. Rykov paused in the park, looking at the great palace. Dead leaves swirled about his feet and crowds of people swirled in the courtyards, on the marble paths. They bore off paintings, chairs, tables, icons and rugs. The exquisite glass of the windows they poked out, and it fell tinkling in a glittering carpet below.

Rykov watched only briefly, then went off across the bare park. Of what use were paintings and chairs with curved legs? In the distance smoke rose in a dense column from the jail. Burning in it were the

records. The Bolsheviks had done it, for in the new world there was
to be no need for prisons.

Rykov padded along the paths, moving quickly to keep warm in
his striped convict clothes. He paused for a few moments by a bed of
hydrangeas, where brown stalks still supported faded flower heads.
A strange, excited feeling surged through his stomach, and he hurried
on, small and quick, sharp-eyed, a stoat. He felt something in the air,
an electricity, and he liked it.

He stopped to look at the house. It was tightly shuttered. A truck
was going by, on the road to Petrograd; as it passed, he ran behind
it and heaved himself up over the board.

The streets of the city seemed rather empty, although he saw a few
unkempt soldiers. There were no policemen. He jumped out as the
truck slowed near the Liteynyy Bridge. As he stood on the pavement
something in the house caught his eye, a bourgeois middle-aged
woman staring fearfully at him from a window, his convict's uniform
a further and worse indication of the steady breakdown of her world.
When she saw his cold eyes she jumped back into the room and the
curtain fell still across the window.

Rykov looked hungrily about him. There was something in the air,
a feeling, a smell, a knowledge; there was something coming – and he
liked it. Like a wild dog, he moved towards the Neva Quay, where
the great granite steps led down to the big, cold river, all his senses
keen and alert.

Shops were along there. Some were closed and dark, like missing
teeth. Most of the others had fitted heavy iron grilles to their windows.
A woman's clear voice rang along the street, haranguing a small crowd
of loafers gathered about the box she was standing on. She was in
soldier's clothes which she had had altered by a tailor to fit her. A
young woman, with a *boorzhoi* accent and a red silk scarf about her
neck, proclaiming the glories of Communism.

Rykov came up to the edge of the group.

'Capitalism is dead, comrades,' she said in ringing tones. A faint,
wolf-like smile came over Rykov's face as he watched the young
woman identifying herself with rabble.

'Capitalism loots from the people. All goods, all houses, all lands
are the property of the proletariat. When the revolution comes the
people will take back what has been looted from them. *Krasnyi!* Red
justice for the people!'

They were all looking her way. Most of the men because she was
a pretty girl, and they wondered what she would look like without
her soldier's fashion outfit on. Rykov looked about him, always, so

he saw the man's head poke cautiously round the door of his shop to see if the coast was clear. A small, balding shopkeeper, with the delicate hands and eyes of the watchsmith. He had a black leather coat on against the cold.

'There!' Rykov shouted suddenly. 'There he is! There is your capitalist, your enemy of the proletariat, creeping like a rat.'

He had their attention, they whirled to stare like a pack of dogs. The shopkeeper turned fearfully in his doorway, fumbling for the keys he had just used.

'Come, comrades! Let us take what he has looted from the people!'

They rushed at him as he tried to get inside and shut the door. They poured in, snatching at the watches and fine clocks in the window, and the man cowered in the corner. They were all busy filling their pockets as Rykov slipped through. He smiled menacingly at the watchsmith.

'Your coat, comrade,' he said, and the man took it off and handed it to him. Rykov put it on.

'Comrades!' he shouted. The little shop smelled of cheap vodka. The demobilised soldiers were half-drunk.

'This exploiter has leeched on the people, has sucked their blood.'

They turned, hands full of shiny things, and crowded about him.

'It's not so,' the man protested. 'I have never harmed anyone . . .'

Rykov laughed aloud.

'Let us see *his* blood!' he howled, and they fell upon the shop owner. Rykov picked up a slim ladies watch, golden on a slim lizard strap, and strolled outside.

The young woman was there, standing in alarm as the shopkeeper screamed. Rykov handed her the watch.

'Here,' he said. 'The property of the proletariat.'

'I didn't . . .' she faltered.

'But you did!' Rykov beamed. 'See what an orator you are. The enemies of the people are crushed at your very word.'

The screaming had stopped; there was just the thudding of boots and fists.

'Tell me,' he said. 'What is your name?'

'Ruth Gunzburg,' she said. The men came out, laughing, their hands bloody, pockets clinking. As she looked at them Rykov detected a faint undercurrent of fear in her, a child on a horse that she could not stop. He found it most attractive.

'What kind of Communist are you?' he asked.

'A Bolshevik.'

The name was a talisman, as she said it he could see her confidence return, her certainty of a new and perfect world.

'I, too, wish to be a Bolshevik,' he said. 'Will you take me to join?'

They went down the street together and now Rykov knew what it was that was on the air, what it was that was coming. It was a glorious thing, a world made for him. His hands were spattered with the shopkeeper's blood. He held one out in front of Ruth, grinning.

'*Krasnyi!*' he said.

25 October 1917

She sat outside the cafe, the scarlet scarf Konstantin the Futurist had given her blazing in its lights. Inside it was warm, and the patrons grinned at the intense young girl with her revolutionary paper and dress sitting in the cold, and went back to their cards, gossip and drink. The government was changing, the war would soon be over, things would soon be back to normal.

Ruth chose to sit outside in order to see better. The cold didn't bother her; revolutionaries didn't feel the cold. She had not wanted to be there, staring down the bridge towards the Winter Palace every time a vehicle came down it, she had wanted to be at the Congress of Soviets being held in the great white ballroom of the Smolny Institute, the former school for aristocratic young ladies. There, with perfect symbolism, something created useless was being transformed into something of incalculable value as the people of Russia democratically decided their future. As one who had helped bring that future to the people of Russia she had wanted to be there and a small frown of irritation creased her smooth, unmarked forehead.

However, Shapiro who called himself Krivitskiy had asked her to come to this cafe by the bridge and watch. She had asked why, when the new goverment was taking over and he had said that Kerensky still had the Winter Palace. When you were engaged in a *coup d'etat* you could not allow those you were taking power away from the possession of key points, lest they use those points to rally their forces against you. Ruth had not seen the relevance of that, since they were engaged with the remorseless and unstoppable forces of History that were propelling the proletariat towards its inevitable triumph, according to scientific laws of society. Details as to who was sitting in which obsolete bauble of the dying capitalist state as it did so were irrelevant. So he had simply said it would be for the good of the Revolution if she did and, as she would do anything for the Revolution, there she was, sitting in the cold reading *Rabochii Put'* in the gaps between the cars, her trousered legs apart, in a manner that would have appalled her mother, smoking a cigarette and carrying a gun. Revolutionaries had guns and so she had made Krivitskiy give her a revolver before she would go. She touched it from time to time under her black sailor's jacket like a talisman, and a small, childlike smile of delight lit up her face.

She had read through the Bolshevik newspaper twice. The editor, Josef Stalin, was calling for a soviet government, which put him somewhat behind the times, since there it was, taking shape over at the Smolny.

Big headlamps shone over the bridge, and a limousine came towards her at speed. Her eyesight was good and she stared intently into the interior as it shot by, registering the passengers. It was an American Pierce Arrow flying the American flag; she got up and hurried inside to the bar. She paid to use the telephone, and a man picked it up at the other end. She was lucky, she got Krivitskiy first time.

'Room seventeen.' In the background she could hear voices shouting.

'It's Ruth,' she said importantly, her young face very serious. 'I've just seen Kerensky in an American Embassy car. He's heading out for the Pulkovo highway, going towards Pskov.'

The earpiece clattered as Krivitskiy put the telephone down. She jammed it up against her head, stuffing a finger in her other ear as she listened to what they were saying, over in Trotsky's command post in the Smolny.

'Kerensky's run! Heading for the front.'

'He'll have no joy there.' That was Lenin, she knew his voice. He sounded pleased.

'What of the Palace?'

'It is not yet ours.' That was Trotsky.

'Order the attack.'

The telephone on the bar rattled as at the other end Krivitsky dropped the mouthpiece on to its receiver, but Ruth was gone, hurrying down the street and over the bridge towards the palace. In the middle of the Neva the dark bulk of the old cruiser *Aurora* loomed. In the square she could see hundreds of Red Guards and sailors clustering, their arms spiky, bandoliers creaking. She pulled out her own revolver, waving it high in the air. It exploded in her hand, and the bullet howled as it ricocheted off the stone.

'Little Countess, little Countess,' a voice said admonishingly. A figure came out of the darkness by the wall and gently removed the gun from her grasp. It was Pavel, the revolutionary sailor from Kronstadt. He shook the remaining bullets into the palm of his hand and gave the gun back.

'You can kill people doing that,' he said. She must have looked abashed, for he peeled off a bandolier and put it around her, heavy, machined and revolutionary. 'There. Have you come to see us go in?'

'No, I have come to go in with you.' She swelled with importance. 'I have just been talking with one of Trotsky's commissars in his command post in the Smolny. The attack is imminent.'

'Well then, come with us. Some of your friends are here.'

By the wall she saw Konstantin in the glow of his own cigarette. His red scarf was about his neck, his worker's hat tipped back on his head. A bottle of wine was in his pocket and he had a machine pistol in his hand. He grinned.

'I am composing a poem. Tomorrow I shall stand in the middle of the Prospekt and declaim it, to the wild cheers of the people.'

The German, Manfred Liss was also there. He had a black leather coat, now. She saw Savinkov in a doorway and he nodded towards the Palace, where hundreds of windows looked out like dead eyes.

'The death rattle of imperialist capitalism,' he said, and she thought that as wonderful a poem as she would ever want to hear.

In a moment of silence she heard a gun go off and, a second later, a purple flare burst high over the Palace. From the other side of the Palace came the heavy crump of a naval gun as the *Aurora* fired. Inside the palace someone screamed.

'Fix bayonets, lads,' Pavel ordered, and all along the wall metal clattered as the men slapped home the long swords on to the muzzles of their Nagants. Behind them, Savinkov pressed himself a little further into the safety of his doorway. At Pavel's side, Ruth felt herself on fire.

Savinkov saw them trot forward in a steady, trained run. There was some loose firing from the cadets at the barrier and the sailors replied with a volley. There was a ripping of cloth as Konstantin loosed off a magazine from his machine pistol, and Savinkov saw the bullets strike the stone of the palace like fireflies, climbing ever higher.

Then they were over the wooden barricades with one shouted

hoorah. He heard Ruth's contralto shriek of ecstasy, saw the pistol waving in her hand like a flag.

He slipped across the square in their wake. By the commander's gate abandoned rifles lay like spillikins and he picked one up, adjusted his worker's hat on his head to a rakish tilt and went in.

Ruth stood in a backwater off the Tyemny Corridor, where generals of old stared grimly down at the people. The people were behaving much as they, the imperial generals, would have expected. Red Guards, workers, Pavlovskys, sailors from Kronstadt, children, prostitutes swirled through the halls and corridors. She had heard one of the Red Guards shout: 'Comrades, don't touch anything. This is the property of the people!' As he'd moved on, the people seemed to have agreed with what he had said, and were relocating their property from the home of the Romanovs to theirs with a will. Brass clocks from the White Hall, exotic finery from the wardrobes, silver monogrammed candlesticks and plate from the store rooms, green vases from the Malachite Chamber . . .

Ruth did not think that it mattered. There was no room for relics of the old world in the new. The people would clear the palace and throw all into the Neva, raze the vast symbol of oppression and, under their own hands, a new, shining building would emerge, perfect in every way, the first of millions all over the world.

In the short corridor Konstantin was removing pictures from the wall and stacking them in a rough pile. He had found some cans of paint in a storeroom, and had lined them up in a row. Now he opened them. He took a swig of wine from the bottle in his pocket and offered some to Ruth. She shook her head and he put it on the mantelpiece of the corridor fireplace. Wine fumes were swirling through the corridors and, down from the cellars, came the steady clinking and tinkling of glass as the people drank like Tsars. She needed no alcohol, she was already intoxicated. She was a part of the new world, at its birth.

Manfred Liss came down the corridor, a bottle of wine in one hand, and the bottom of a young sailor in the other. The couple paused by a door and peered in. A huge four-poster stood inside.

'A dead cathedral of art,' Konstantin said dismissively, his long hair falling over his forehead. He dipped a decorator's brush into scarlet paint and applied it to the silk wallpaper with swift, skilled strokes. A rhomboidal woman with triangles for eyes and several breasts in different places began to appear.

'We shall create a living factory of the human spirit,' he said.

The door was open and, in the bedroom, Liss and the young sailor were taking it in turns to swig from the bottle and kiss each other. Ruth could not help looking, feeling rather shocked. It wasn't proper. The revolution was supposed to be pure in mind and body. Now they were rubbing each other's trousers . . .

'They've arrested the ministers,' an excited voice called. They turned to see Savinkov, clutching a rifle. He waved it in the air. 'I was there. Look, I got their last minutes.'

In his other hand he clutched a leather-bound black jotter. Konstantin put down his paintbrush and took the rifle. He shifted a lever.

'It's all right to look like a revolutionary, Sergei,' he said. 'But keep the safety on when you're near genius.'

Savinkov angrily snatched his weapon back.

'Get on with your daubing!' he said sharply. 'Some of us have a revolution to run.'

He went off down the corridor, pushing through the crowds.

'He's in a hurry,' said Ruth.

'Hoping to get to Lenin with his pad, before anyone else does,' said the artist. 'An apple for the teacher.'

'How can you say that?' she asked hotly. 'He was a revolutionary when we were in the Empress's school, learning our multiplication tables.'

'Have you seen his tongue?' Konstantin asked. 'Brown from all his arse-licking.'

He began breaking up the frames of the canvases and piling them into the fireplace.

'I'm cold . . . People want revolutions for different reasons, join causes for different reasons,' he observed. He lit a match on the leather sole of his boot and applied it to the cracked, ancient oil of a canvas. A saint began to burn. He sniffed the aroma of the paint in pleasure.

'Me, I joined for a new world.'

In the bedroom, Liss had bent the sailor over the bed. Their *trousers* were down. It was disgusting . . . Ruth turned her back, trying not to look shocked.

'Of course. So did I,' she said. 'So did Pavel, so did Sergei and all of us.'

From somewhere came the shattering of glass and a falsetto screech of terror that left only its echo as the body hit the ground.

'What was that?' Ruth said in alarm.

'There is no beauty without struggle,' he said, his brush creating an insane square, attacking his rhomboidal woman. 'No masterpieces without violence.'

In the fireplace the gilt wood burned brightly, hundreds of years having dried it to perfection.

'I joined so that the revolution would give me a new world,' he said. 'One that looks only to the future. Constant change. Raw art, raw words, raw deeds. Violence, the compulsory eradication of the past, the recognition of no authority save myself.'

He took the bottle from the mantelpiece and drained it, his adam's apple bobbing. He threw it on to the flames, where it began to shatter in small explosions. Manfred came out of the bedroom, his eyes glazed with pleasure, pulling his coat about him.

Konstantin looked at her with glittering, intoxicated eyes.

'That is what I want from my new world,' he said. 'It is not to say it is what Pavel wants from his, what Manfred wants, what you want. Pavel wants land, Manfred wants little boys, you want – what do you want, Ruth?' He smiled faintly. 'More important, what does Lenin want?'

She was ravenously hungry. Her soul had fed on the events of the previous day, now her body demanded sustenance. In the spacious, low-ceilinged refectory she handed in her two-rouble ticket at the head of the long table and the party worker sloshed a good ladleful of cabbage soup into a tin bowl, green and steaming. She took a slab of *kasha*, coarse black bread, oily to the touch, and a greasy wooden spoon from a basket. As she sat down at the table she eyed the spoon doubtfully. Her mother had always taught her that cutlery should be clean . . . A hungry proletarian sat down opposite her and gave his spoon a preliminary wipe on his sleeve. Relieved, she did likewise, and began to eat. It was but one more absurd *bourgeois* ritual to be junked in the new world that was coming to glorious life. The worker bent over his bowl, shovelling the boiled pulp through his beard with spoon and bread, and so she did the same. It was just like being in a new school, that was all.

He was finished well before her. He looked up, bellowed a coarse greeting to a friend, stood up, releasing wind from different parts of his body and left, wiping his face on the other arm of his jacket. She blushed, and was annoyed.

'Ruth . . . *Ruth!*'

It was Nadezhda.

'He's coming,' she called, and Ruth bolted what was left of the soup, and put the bread into her pocket to eat later, when her jaws were feeling stronger. She wiped her mouth on her cuff, revelling in her new freedom, and the peasants eyed her breasts as she bounced from the room.

The two young girls hurried excitedly along the corridors to the south wing. On the doors she passed effete enamelled signs proclaimed the rooms within to be Ladies' Classroom Number 6, and Teachers' Bureau, but over these, hanging from nails banged into the white-painted wood with a proletarian thump were crudely-lettered signs, evidence of the vitality of the new order: 'Central Committee of the Petrograd Soviet' and 'Bureau of Foreign Affairs' and 'Central Committee of the All-Russian Trade Unions'. The long, vaulted corridors were thronged with hurrying soldiers and workers, the sound of their heavy boots an incessant, rolling thunder on the wooden floors. On every landing they passed were workers behind tables piled high with pamphlets and literature of the various parties of the new democracy taking shape, colourful and vibrant with ideas for the future. Ruth hurried alongside Nadezhda, the excitement inside her almost overwhelming. She gave a skip, her hands high in the air, and gurgled with joy, her dark hair bouncing, her face alight.

They came to the great hall, the former ballroom. Nadezhda had the passes because Josef, her fiancée, had given them to her. They took up a position on a ledge, where they could see what was happening. The vast, lofty white room, lit by immense glazed white chandeliers holding hundreds of ornate light bulbs was filled with the delegates to the soviet. The air was thick with the smell of the smoke drifting from their cigarettes and the stale sweat from their unwashed bodies and clothes. Ruth breathed it in rapturously. In the old order people bathed simply in order to fill in the interminable boredom of their pointless lives; here were people so busy constructing the new they had no time to. All about were men who were unshaven, filthy even, men who were living prodigies of sleeplessness and work, men with burning eyes, driving towards their fixed purpose on engines of exaltation.

There was so much to do! She knew it, she was a part of their struggle. Take over the Government, run the city, fight the Duma and the Committee for salvation, let alone the Germans and Kerensky, inform the provinces of what was happening, spread the truth from Archangel to Vladivostok, struggle against Government and Municipal employees refusing to obey their commissars, against the post and telegraph refusing them communication, railways ignoring their lawful requests for trains . . . and against them the crowned and uncrowned hangmen of the bourgeoisie, all over the world. But *with* them the soldier-masses and the workers, their ultimate victory certain.

A rumbling thunder of applause signalled the arrival of the praesidium, making their way to the great dais where once had been banked the brilliantly-coloured military and ecclesiastical uniforms of the old regime on festive occasions. The men shoving their way through were drably-clothed, but within them burned a fire no former general or bishop could match, the leaders, portfolios bulging, arguing, explaining, giving orders even as they walked, surrounded by friends and lieutenants. And there he was among them, the man they had come to see, a short, stocky figure, with his big head set down upon his shoulders. Shaven from his escape and hiding, his chin was once again bristling with the coming beard.

First, the lesser men. Kameniev, to read the actions of the Military Revolutionary Committee: abolition of capital punishment in the army, restoration of the right of free speech, release of officers and soldiers arrested for political crimes . . . enormous applause.

Someone less popular. The representative of the *Bund*.

'The uncompromising attitude of the Bolsheviki will mean the crushing of the Revolution.'

They began to shout him down.

'Therefore the *Bund* delegates must refuse any more to sit in the Congress.'

'Go, go!' they shouted. 'We thought you left yesterday.'

Ruth and Nadezhda booed and hissed with the rest, waving their small fists in the air. Fools! Obstacles in the path of democracy.

The Mensheviki, bleating.

'We consider it dangerous and perhaps even mortal for the Revolution to transfer power to the Soviets –

They shouted him down, too.

Then he came, he whom they had been waiting for, gripping the edge of the reading stand, his little winking eyes running over them as they applauded, on and on, and afterwards wondered why their palms were sore. He held up his hand, and they were silent.

'We shall now proceed to construct the Socialist order,' he said simply, and they roared for the words of Lenin, so loud it seemed the very roof would come off.

'We shall offer peace,' he said, when the tumult had finally died down. 'Peace to the peoples of all the belligerent countries on the basis of the Soviet terms – no annexations, no indemnities, and the right of self-determination of peoples.'

Her palms adding her worth to the grave thunder of applause,

Ruth burned to help the oppressed. Now that the workers and peasants of Russia were free, it was time for the rest of the world to be liberated.

'Revolution will soon break out in all the belligerent counries; that is why we address ourselves to the workers of France, England and Germany . . . the revolution of 6 and 7 November has opened the era of Social revolution . . . the labour movement, in the name of peace and socialism shall win, and fulfil its destiny . . .'

They spoke quickly then, the leaders, one after the other, with rising enthusiasm; the Left Socialist Revolutionaries, the Social Democrat Internationalists, Ukrainian Social Democrats, Lithuanian Social Democrats, Populist Socialists, Polish Socialists . . . there was a fire within these men. They spoke of the 'coming World-revolution, of which we are the advance-guard', of 'The new age of brotherhood, when all the peoples will become one great family . . .'

The cards swept up into the air, and it was unanimous . . .

They found themselves singing the *Internationale*; men were crying as the anthem of hope soared through windows, through doors, through the very roof to reach out to the peoples of the world.

And then the Funeral March, for the comrades who had died for liberty, the chant, slow and melancholy, but Russian and triumphant:

> You fell in the fatal fight
> For the liberty of the people, for the honour of the people.
> You gave up your lives and everything dear to you,
> You suffered in horrible prisons,
> You went to exile in chains . . .

Ruth drew in her breath in sobs, tears streaming down her cheeks, as she made her promise. Next to her, Nadezhda was crying too.

> Farewell brothers, you chose a noble path.
> At your grave we swear to fight, to work for freedom and the people's happiness . . .

As the rough, strong voices died away, Ruth felt, clustering about her, the presence of the thousands – the tens of thousands, even – who had died in the prisons of the Tsar, in a cold exile, in a Siberian mine. She felt them there, brave and noble. Their day had come, tyranny had fallen, and the people had risen up, free at last.

Half-heard conversations from her childhood, her parents talking of the need for reform. What had *they* known about it? *Here it was.*

The revolution of the people, coarse, strong, contemptuous of table manners and the formulas of the *intelligentsia*. The simple bursting of bonds, a great shout of triumph.

She wiped her wet face with her palms, and she and Nadezhda embraced each other. Lenin was reading the Decree on Land.

'One. All private ownership of land is abolished immediately without compensation.

'Two. All landowners' estates and all lands belonging to the Crown, to monasteries, church lands with all their livestock and inventoried property, buildings and all appurtenances, are transferred to the disposition of the township Land Committees and the district Soviets of Peasants' Deputies until the Constituent Assembly meets.'

The debates were to begin. Someone was pushing his way through the crowd, throwing people out of his way and illegally clambering up on to the dais. A peasant, long-haired and booted, wild-eyed in his sheepskin coat.

'The Executive Committee of the All-Russian Soviets of Peasants' deputies protests against the arrest of our comrades, the Ministers Salazkin and Mazlov!' he shouted. 'They are in the Peter-Paul fortress. We demand their instant release! You sit here and talk about giving the land to the peasants, and you commit an act of tyrants and usurpers against the peasants' chosen representatives!'

Ruth felt an instant dislike for the man who was pushing his way forward and marring – however slightly – the holy occasion. She was glad to see Trotsky get to his feet, his rich voice ringing throughout the hall.

'Yesterday the Military Revolutionary Committee decided to release the Socialist Revolutionary and Menshevik Ministers, Mazlov, Salazkin, Gvozdov and Maliantovich – on principle. That they are still in Peter-Paul is only because we have had so much to do . . . They will, however, be detained at their homes under arrest until we have investigated their complicity in the treacherous acts of Kerensky!'

She felt a fresh burst of indignation. The man was representing traitors! She shrieked her approval as someone pushed him off the stage and he vanished into the crowd, to be given a good kicking.

It was time for a short break. The cabbage soup she had eaten hours before now fermented uncomfortably in her stomach. In the press of humanity pushing for the doors an enormous, rattling exhalation of gas rose up from her boots. A worker next to her guffawed and clapped her on the shoulder with a cracked and reddened hand in rough and honest approval. How far removed it all was from the foolish, dead *minutiae* of teacups and cakes, light opera and chatter at her mother's salons.

It was two thirty in the morning; the little people had had their say and now it was time to read the decree of the Constitution of Power. They were quiet as Kameniev stood up at the lectern.

'Until the meeting of the Constituent Assembly, a provisional Workers' and Peasants' Government is formed, which shall be named the Council of People's Commissars.'

In the silence he read out from his hand-written list the names of the men who would run the country.

'President of the Council. Vladmir Ulyanov.'

A roar of approval for Lenin.

'Interior: A.I. Rykov. Agriculture: V.P. Milyutin. Military and Naval Affairs: A committee composed of V.A. Avseenko, N.V. Krylenko, and F.M. Dybenko . . . Foreign Affairs: L.D. Bronstein.'

Another roar for Trotsky.

Kameniev was squinting at his sheet of paper, attempting to decipher the hurried scrawl at its end.

'Chairman for Nationalities . . .'

He turned to Trotsky, sitting close by.

'Leon, who's this?'

Before he could answer, Nadezhda, beside Ruth on the ledge, filled her lungs.

'*Josef Stalin!*' she shrieked. 'My fiancée.'

Urbane and charming, Trotsky looked at her with amusement.

'It must be Stalin,' he smiled. 'The pretty lady says so.'

'But they're Bolsheviks,' a man next to Ruth muttered angrily. 'Lenin's taken the government for himself.'

She turned to him. 'My dear man.' she said icily. 'Don't you have ears? Did you not hear Comrade Kameniev announce a *provisional* government, to rule until the elections for the Constituent Assembly can be held, and it meets to accept power? Who better to look after us for the time being than those who made the freedom of the people possible?'

His comrades laughed and nudged him, hearing him so rebuked by a young girl.

'I remember how the Bolsheviks have behaved in the past when they were the majority,' he said, in a surly voice.

But another troublemaker had got up. She knew him, Avilov, a smart young man, a journalist on *Novaya Zhizn*, looking out of place in his frock coat, *bourgeois* and *intelligentsia* amongst rough honesty.

'We must ask ourselves where we are going ... The ease with which the Coalition Government was upset cannot be explained by the strength of the left wing of democracy, but only by the incapacity of the Government to give the people peace and bread. And the left wing cannot maintain itself in power unless it solves these questions.'

'He knows what he's talking about,' the agitator next to her said, irrelevantly.

'As for peace, that will be even more difficult. The Allies refused to talk with Skobeliev. They will never accept the proposition of a peace conference from *you*. You cannot count on the effective help of the proletariat of the Allied countries, because in most countries it is very far from the revolutionary struggle. No one party can conquer the enormous difficulties we face. The majority of the people, supporting a government of Socialist coalition, can alone accomplish the Revolution.'

'The Revolution has been accomplished, you fool!' Ruth shrieked, and there was applause.

But another of them, another young man, Karelin, of the Left Socialist Revolutionaries, stood up.

'Our party has refused to enter the Council of People's Commissars. We cannot sustain any government except a government of Socialist coalition. We protest, moreover, against the tyrannical conduct of the *Bolsheviki*. Our Commissars have been driven from their posts and our only organ, *Znamia Truda*, the Banner of Labour, was forbidden to appear yesterday.'

'Really,' Ruth said exasperatedly to no one in particular. 'He seems to think the Tsar is back!'

'The Central Duma is forming a powerful Committee for Salvation of Country and revolution to fight you. Already you are isolated, and your Government is without the support of a single other democratic group ...'

But Trotsky was on the tribune, confident, powerful, the man who had overthrown Kerensky, his mouth a sneer for the puny efforts of the youngsters.

'These considerations on the danger of isolation of our party are not new. On the eve of insurrection our fatal defeat was also predicted. Everybody was against us. How is it that we were able to overturn the Government almost without bloodshed? That fact is the most striking proof that we *were not isolated*. In reality, the provisional Government was isolated; the democratic parties which march against us were isolated, are isolated and are for ever cut off from the proletariat!'

As he destroyed them, the great veteran revolutionary pointed to them with one scornful finger.

'These little men, Avilov and Karelin, accuse us of repelling an agreement with the other democratic parties. But is it we who are to blame? No, comrades. Is it not Avilov and Karelin who have gone over to the enemy? It is *they* who have declared pitiless war upon *us*. As for Avilov's threat of a peace – out there where the bourgeoisie still tramples upon the workers – a peace at our expense, I simply say that if Europe continues to be ruled by the imperialist bourgeoisie, revolutionary Russia will inevitably be lost. *There are only two alternatives.* Either the Russian Revolution will create a revolutionary movement in Europe, or the European powers will destroy the Russian Revolution!'

They came to their feet and their voices almost lifted the roof away, the champions of mankind. She was swept away on their ardour; she made a commitment to the centre of her soul, not to rest until the whole world was free.

The far light of dawn was brushing the sky with pink as they came out of the Smolny into the clean fresh air. They poured out of the great gate, under the vast, carved imperial insignia, to the streetcars of the Street-Railway Workers' Union, where the conductors and motor-men rose, yawning, ready to take the delegates home. Squeezing aboard with Nadezhda, Ruth found herself humming.

They heard her, caught the tune and broke once again into song.

> 'That time is near; when tyranny falls the people will arise, great and free!
> Farewell brothers, you chose a noble path.
> At your grave we swear to fight, to work for freedom and the people's happiness . . .'

2

Chekisty

December, 1917

THE tall windows were streaked; the revolution left no time for cleaning. Blurred through them Krivitskiy could see the smoke-blue cupolas of the Smolny Convent, outlined in gold. Down on the cobbled street, where dirty snow lay, something was moving. From its lack of speed and the groaning it made as it hauled itself along he knew it was the streetcar, coming to the end of the line. He took off his steel-rimmed spectacles and polished them on his shirt-tail, but the window was still blurred.

The tall doors were shouldered open and they all came to their feet as Lenin came in, small, moving quickly, followed by the tall, lean figure of the Pole, Dzerzhinskii. They climbed up on to the stage, standing in front of an unfinished backdrop. Krivitskiy thought that he recognised something from Pushkin. The corseted teachers and their girls at the Smolny had believed that the rituals of their life would keep the devils at bay. They had been wrong; now the devils stood on their stage, stood in their theatre, packed it tight in their Caucasian greatcoats, fur hats, purple felt cloaks, black leather jerkins, galloons, daggers, black moustaches, and their smell of horses, gun oil, nicotine and sweat.

'The revolution is in danger,' Lenin intoned.

'In clear and present danger,' said Dzerzhinskii, standing like a monk in soldier's uniform at Lenin's side, and they all felt a prickle of adrenalin running under their skin as Lenin looked down upon them.

'Much has been done,' he said. 'We have control of the press. We have closed the papers that have libelled us, and removed the editors. The people of Petrograd and Moscow are able to read the truth from *Pravda* and *Isvestia*.

'You, the commissars, have taken control of the physical apparatus of power on our behalf. All organisations from factories to trams

have held soviet-style elections under our guidance. Elections have
been held for the running of housing, trade, industry and municipal
services. Company after company, enterprise after enterprise have
become Bolshevised, and delegates acceptable to us democratically
elected.

'Governing by decree, we have given our control the support of
law. The Table of Ranks has been abolished. House searches are
authorised. Fur coats banned!'

That raised a chuckle, the thought of the bourgeoisie shivering, and
Lenin smiled. Never let it be said he had no sense of humour.

'All schools have been removed from the control of the Church
and handed to the state for correct running. The state has acquired
the monopoly of all banking activity, and all industry, under its
new Bolshevik management, is subject to workers' control. We have
introduced a new law code for revolutionary courts. Within the
next few days we shall nationalise all factories, we shall cease the
corrupt payment of interest and dividends, and severely curtail bank
withdrawals. The funds of the people must remain for the people.
The inhabitants of the cities now carefully study our new decrees,
still wet from paste, stuck up on the walls. They have come to terms
with the government, early in the morning they search through the
paragraphs to ascertain the form of the new order.'

Lenin spread out his arms. 'And yet I said to you not a minute
ago that the revolution was in danger, and Feliks Edmundovitch here
supported me. It is in clear and present danger.'

He looked to the very corners of the room as if in search of the
source of that danger.

'Danger from what? From whom?' he cried, and then answered
himself in a voice like granite.

'From our *enemies*!'

Krivitskiy bared his teeth in agreement amid the rumble of approval
from the fifty-odd men.

'The bourgeoisie, the landowners, and all the rich classes are making
desperate efforts to undermine the revolution. They seek to drown our
glorious achievement, to drown the workers and peasants in blood.
From outside they menace us with armies; from within, whole classes
of their agents seek to undermine the fabric of our society. Have
you not seen them on the streets? Criminal plunderers, saboteurs
and degraded elements. Idlers, swindlers, speculators. Prostitutes,
hoarders, bagmen . . .'

Lenin paused to let his men run a mental eye over the picture he
was painting. Dzerzhinskiy stood patiently by a painted flower bed,

its canvas dusty from waiting for young aristocratic ladies to say their lines in front of it.

'What can we do? We turn to Marx and, as agents of History, we look to the past for guidance. Have others been in our predicament? Why yes. The French before us overthrew their tyrants. You have all heard of Robespierre. Let me quote you from memory his words: "The attribute of popular government in revolution is at one and the same time *virtue and terror*, virtue without which terror is fatal, terror without which virtue is impotent. The terror is nothing but justice, prompt, severe, inflexible; it is thus an emanation of virtue."'

Again, Lenin paused, to let them take aboard the concept, to arrange their mental furniture so that they were sure of the righteousness of what they were to do. For an impatient man, he was prepared to spend a lot of time getting the details right.

'Let us turn to Marx. Marx gives terror his own, holy, specific endorsement: 'There is only one means to *curtail*, simplify and localise the bloody agony of the old society and the bloody birth pangs of the new, only one means – the revolutionary terror.' It is an inadmissible weakness to even think, as some woolly-minded people do, that a revolution can be accomplished without shooting. What of these enemies of ours? Idlers? Apply the terror, shoot on the spot one out of ten. Takers of bribes, swindlers? Arrest and shoot. Decree-breakers? The terror for them.'

Krivitskiy felt his heart thudding in his chest, as it had in the filthy trench, waiting for the whistle to blow.

'Who is to do this? You are. Feliks Edmundovitch has asked the Sovnarkom for an organisation for taking revenge in the name of the Revolution against any that would seize it from us, and they have agreed. *You* are its first agents. It is the All-Russian Extraordinary Commission to combat Counterrevolution and Sabotage, the *Vserossiiskaya Chrezvychainaya Komissiya po Borbe s Kontrrevolyutsiei i Sabotazhem.*

'Now, that's a fine title, but a long one. By the time you tell some bourgeois scum who you work for he could be half-way to the Finland station!'

They chuckled.

'No,' Lenin said merrily. 'Let's take the initials, it's the VChK, or Cheka, and you're Chekisty. You'll work for Feliks. There is no one better, a staunch Jacobin, an iron revolutionary.'

Dzerzhinskii stepped forward and looked over his men. He was tall and thin, with a pointed beard. Even from his viewpoint near the window, Krivitskiy noticed his eyes. They stared, frighteningly, the eyelids unblinking.

'You must expect not to be understood,' he said. His voice was calm and measured. 'We are in the front line of battle, and those in the rear will fail to understand correctly the character and task of our Commission. They think of the struggle with counter-revolution and speculation on the level of normal state existence. There will be screams for courts, for guarantees, of inquiry, of investigation, etcetera.

'Don't they know the times in which we live, in which the bourgeoisie are trying to snuff out our very existence? No, we shall leave such bourgeois things to the bourgeoisie, and continue with our task of protecting the Revolution. We represent in ourselves organised terror and this must be said very clearly. If there is one of you here not prepared to live with that, then let him leave now.'

He paused, but his audience was only waiting for him to continue.

'Such terror is now very necessary, and will become more so. Our task is the struggle with the enemies of Soviet power. We shall terrorise the enemies of Soviet power in order to strangle crimes in their germ.

'We shall have to move quickly. There are more henchmen of the bourgeoisie out there than there are defenders of the revolution. I don't want any more than twenty-four hours to elapse from the time of arrest to a decision. When pressed against the wall by the evidence you will find that the criminal in your charge will admit his or her crime. And what argument can have more weight than the confession of the accused?'

'Your tasks will be many,' said Lenin. 'Those of the bourgeoisie not actively engaged in counterrevolution we shall make use of for labour. Camps will have to be prepared to keep them in. We shall need to set up a nationwide intelligence service, to gather information about organisations and persons whose activity is directed against the revolution. We shall have to practise counter-intelligence against our enemies at home and abroad.'

'Our mission is holy,' said Dzerzhinskiy. 'We cannot afford the luxury of soft, humanitarian thoughts. My own thought induces me to be without pity and there is, in me, an iron determination to follow my thought to the end. It is our task to better Russia's future. If ever you doubt, if ever you flag, think of your children. Concern for your children is one of the best ways to wipe out counterrevolution.'

*

There was a smell of leather in the room because the score of new trainees had been given their black jackets. They listened carefully and respectfully, as Krivitskiy spoke.

'Listen to me, lads. You leave the theorising to the highups. They've read all the books. But down here, you boys want to know what the rule of thumb is. It's simple. We aren't waging war against individuals. No, no. We're exterminating the bourgeoisie as a class. During investigation, do not look for evidence that the accused acted in word and deed against Soviet power. The first questions that you ought to put are: To what class does he belong? What is his origin? What is his education or profession? And it is these questions that ought to determine the fate of the accused. In this lies the significance and essence of the Red Terror.'

Krivitskiy was a busy man. The Cheka was expanding as fast as it could. There was an incredible amount to be done and, like Dzerzhinskii, he resented the time in sleep or eating spent away from his job. He turned to the instructor, the trainees' superior by only weeks.

'Carry on,' he said. Rykov smiled deferentially, and then turned to his class as Krivitskiy went out.

'We'll go and do some real work now. But listen to me. The high-ups like Commissar Krivitskiy, they all theorise too much. What purpose is served by all these questions of origin and education? All you need to do is go into the kitchen of the accused and look into his soup pot. If there's meat in it, then he's an enemy of the people. Stand him up against the wall!'

Rykov grinned at them, and the faces of the young men brightened.

January 1918

She always volunteered for the dirty jobs, the ones that kept her out late, or in the cold. She did it because words were not enough, you had to get out there and *do* if the new world was to be made, and because it set an example. There were some comrades only too willing to shirk their duties and that hurt her. Ruth felt that if they saw her ready to take on the heaviest burden it would shame them. She was often disappointed, and that, too, was painful.

It did not stop her, however, and she was there in the pale dawn light with her rifle slung over her shoulder, waiting for her first squad of bourgeois to be brought along for their re-education, to be made fit for a world without class or prejudice. The snow was thick on the Petrograd streets and by the wall where the other guards stood huddled by the brazier were shovels and picks. The cold drew the skin tight on her face, made her green eyes shine.

There they were, shuffling cautiously along the icy road in their polished shoes and striped trousers, their fine coats and French silk scarves, a band of the upper classes come to learn how a world worked where all were ready to work for all. They were under the command of a small young man in a black leather jerkin. He had a revolver in a holster on his hip and black leather gloves on his hands. The bourgeois did not look at him directly, only from the corners of their eyes, and fearfully. Under the crack of his voice they took the shovels and began to work. Ruth watched them in stern approval. It was good for them.

'Well, hello,' she called, and he turned to look at her. 'You're Rykov, aren't you? Remember me?'

Rykov smiled. 'Why yes. My orator.'

There was something about the way he was wearing his clothes.

'What's this? A new uniform?'

'We're at war.'

'War?' she said, startled.

'Lenin has told us so. Counter-revolutionaries are seeking to destroy the Revolution. We have to seek them out wherever they may be.'

'Why yes, of course. But who are they?'

'Prostitutes, work-shirkers, bagmen, speculators, hoarders. Lenin has decreed that the agencies of the state must purge the Russian land of all kinds of harmful insects.'

'Are you doing this?' she asked, bewildered.

'The Revolution must have protection,' he said coldly. 'I work for Dzherzhinskiy with your pal Krivitskiy. We are the All-Russian Extraordinary Commission for Combating Counter-Revolution and Sabotage. We call ourselves the Cheka.'

A middle-aged woman rested, wheezing, on her shovel for a moment. With a swift blow of his foot he kicked it away and she fell heavily on to the ice. She looked fearfully up at him, her face bleeding. Ruth took half a step forward, her hand instinctively reaching out to help the woman, then stopped herself. She bit hard on her lip.

'On your feet,' Rykov ordered. 'You know what happens to work-shirkers.'

An old man offered her his hand and she heaved herself up. Rykov turned back to Ruth.

'Something the matter?' he asked, looking closely at her.

'Of course not!' she said quickly.

'A collection of the best, here,' he said. 'Bankers, aristocratic idlers, Jews. Make them sweat.'

'Yes. Yes, I will,' she promised nervously. 'When shall I let them go?'

'Go? No, these are criminals. They're to be made to work every day. We have a camp outside the city for them.'

'They have been tried?' She was surprised. 'Who by?'

'By us. We have the authority from Lenin. We try those who oppose the authority of the Workers' and Peasants' Government and we judge them according to the dictates of the revolutionary conscience.'

A man was looking at her, from the very corners of his eyes, his head down, pushing snow. A man past middle age, in a long dark coat.

'They will be re-educated then, in the camp?'

Rykov smiled.

'I must get on. They breed everywhere, these insects. Yes, yes, we re-educate.'

The woman near him had stopped shovelling again. She held on to her spade to stand up, the breath gargling in her chest, her face a fearful puce.

Rykov pulled the revolver from its holster and, before Ruth could move, or protest, fired. Blood spouted from a gouge in her neck. She staggered, still standing. He jumped forward, putting the muzzle to her head, and fired again. The body fell, a spray of gore staining the snow, and Ruth screamed. Rykov whirled on to her, his gun still in his hand.

'Something the matter?' he demanded again, his eyes on her like a hunting dog.

'It was the noise,' she choked. 'The noise. It was so sudden.'

'For a moment I thought you didn't like revolutionary justice,' he said dangerously, and she heard him through ears ringing from the shots. 'We shoot idlers. Idlers, speculators, swindlers, enemies. We are the will of the Revolution.'

He turned and walked away down the street.

'Guards will come for them later,' he said over his shoulder.

She watched him go, her fist jammed into her mouth to stop the scream that was welling up from coming out. When he turned the corner out of sight, she unslung her own rifle. The old man was weeping. Next to him was the man in the black coat and, by him, a woman with her hair tied up in a yellow silk scarf.

'You and you,' she said. She pushed at them, almost in panic.

She herded them down the icy road with the point of her rifle. As they turned the corner she glanced back. Two of the old men were carrying the body of the woman to the side of the street. One slipped, and all, dead and alive, tumbled to the ice.

'Ruthy, Ruthy,' the woman at her rifle point whispered. 'What are you doing with these madmen?'

'It is just a terrible mistake, Mama,' she said, her voice high, hysterical. 'I shall find someone, now, this minute, to have it seen to.'

'You are in the company of murderers, my darling,' her father said, softly as he trudged along, his polished black shoes becoming sodden. He had his hand on his wife's arm, helping her along.

'The revolution needs no murder – it hates and abominates murder!' she shouted, and her voice echoed from the buildings.

'Do not make so much noise!' her mother beseeched. 'More of these maniacs may be about.'

They were on Nevsky Prospekt and she could see the high spires of the Admiralty building, the vast statue of Peter the Great.

'The house will not be safe now,' her father said. 'But we have the apartment.'

Ruth realised that her father had led them to the fine block where they had their rooms. He pulled her in off the street into the archway with its twin double doors. Her breath was coming in deep gasps so he slapped her on the cheek, not hard.

'Calm yourself, darling,' he urged. 'Can *you* get to the house? We cannot move on the streets because it is not safe for us. The slaughter of the aristocrats is beginning – and rest assured, when they have done with us they will begin on their own kind. Get food and money from the house, Ruth. We must get out of the very country.'

'I'm not leaving!' she shouted, and her parents darted anxious looks about the street. 'I am a *communist*. You could not get me to leave what we are making here. But I could not expect you to understand that, you've *never* understood.'

'I understand that Irina Alexandrovna lies dead on the street because of your disgusting revolution,' her mother said bitterly. 'And that you are a foolish and ridiculous young girl.'

Her breath was coming more easily now.

'We are the future,' she said unsteadily. Sweat was beginning to freeze on her face, and she wiped it away with her hand. 'I'm going to get someone to arrest Rykov.'

She slung her rifle over her shoulder and set off down the street, walking as though she were drunk, her carefully tied scarlet scarf blazing in the winter sunlight. Her parents shuffled inside, and the big brown doors clunked shut.

From down the street a small figure in a black jerkin stepped out of a doorway. He came down the road and paused outside the big, balconied apartment building. Alert as a hawk, Rykov studied the names on the polished brass plaques.

The parliament building. It was the sixth of January, and inside were the 375 members of the Constituent Assembly, elected by the people back in November. They were there, meeting for the first time. There, among the Social Revolutionaries, the Mensheviks, and the Bolsheviks she would find someone in authority, someone who could take charge for her. People were standing about in groups outside. Sailors from the Baltic Fleet, heroes of the revolution, stood symbolic guard on the doors, as was proper.

Ruth went across the snow-covered street, her scarf blazing, and up the steps. A sailor stood there, stolid and indifferent to the cold, his rifle by his side. As she went to go in through the doors he blocked her way.

'Comrade, I need to go in,' she protested. 'I am a revolutionary.'

'It is closed,' he said shortly.

'No, you misunderstand,' she said, making herself speak clearly. He was a typical peasant, illiterate, with a thick Ukrainian accent. 'I have business to conduct with someone in government. I am, as you see, a Party member.'

'The Assembly is closed,' he said again.

'But how can it be?' she asked. Panic was rising up again inside her; nothing was working as it should. She forced herself to smile at him as she explained.

'Inside,' – she pointed – 'are the democratically elected delegates of the Assembly. If it is closed, there is no government. So don't be silly; be a good man and let me in.'

From down the street came the sound of people singing. Glancing over her shoulder she saw a crowd marching towards the building. They had banners but at that distance she could not read them.

'The delegates have been sent home,' the sailor grunted. 'They are not needed here.'

'Who says so?' she asked angrily.

'Lenin. This was not a people's democracy but a bourgeois one. So it is closed.'

The procession had arrived. They drew up below the steps. Behind her the doors were suddenly opened, and sailors lined up. From the crowd a group of five appeared, three men and two women. They bore armbands proclaiming them to be Social Revolutionaries and Mensheviks. They carried sheets of paper in their hands, and climbed the steps with them. Behind Ruth an officer waited, one who a few months before had been but a sailor. The group stopped in front of him.

'We bear here the signatures of thousands, demanding the reopening of our democratically-elected parliament,' said the woman in the centre, holding out a pile of paper.

The officer reached out as if to take it, and instead shoved her hard. She tumbled backwards down the steps with a shriek, the sheets of paper flying in the air. Rifle butts flailing, the sailors clubbed her companions and they, too, tumbled down the steps.

There was a bark of command, the rattle of oiled bolts sliding in the receivers. Ruth howled, and her voice was drowned by the first ragged volley.

Then she was on her hands and knees on the steps. Below people were running, leaving others lying on the bloody snow. She shrieked in anguish . . . and nobody heard.

Porechie, March 1918

'You are welcome to stay, Countess.'

Yelena stared with cold, aristocratic grey eyes at the man standing in her drawing room his cap held politely in his hands. His name was Koulakoff and he could pole a punt. When the river flooded the land about the great house he would be waiting at the railway station up on its ridge for them to arrive from St Petersburg. In a shining, distant world she heard the clop of the pole as she sat on the embroidered cushions, the sun running across the water as they glided over the sunken fields towards the square white house, the chuffing of the locomotive going away in the distance. But that had been a thousand years ago, when she had been a little girl, and the world a certain place.

'I am to be given permission to stay on my own property?' she asked icily. Her back was to the fire because it was still cold. She pushed her blonde hair out of her eyes. Without the maid it did not behave as it should. Koulakoff met her gaze steadily.

'Those who work the land own it now, Countess. There is a new government out there, a government of the people. We peasants know how to work together and we will run our own lives now. But we do not object if you stay here in the house.'

'Your goodwill I do not need,' she said, her head high.

Koulakoff nodded to the bronze bust that sat on its plinth in the corner of the room under the lines of sealing-wax red leather-bound books, a scroll in one hand, a starred sash across its chest. Had he been alive, this would not be happening.

'There are those of us who remember your father,' the thickset peasant murmured. 'He was on the *zemstvo*, he worked to help us. Yet the landlord Kaletsky, whose lands are over there, was a hard man, and cruel. Yesterday his peasants burned his house to the ground, and whipped him through the snow into the forest. They, like us, wish to order their own lives. We have what is called a Soviet, and organise our affairs in a decent manner.'

'I am familiar with Soviets,' she said haughtily.

'We have heard that the government is sending envoys out into the lands. Now all the peasants will be able to be free.'

Koulakoff bowed and turned to go from the room.

'You are still welcome to stay,' he said, and went out, his heavy boots leaving prints on the dusty parquet.

Yelena was still standing by the fire when Mikhail came in. His boots and jacket were dusted with snow and he smelled of gun oil.

'I got a couple of pheasant,' he said, pulling two soft, golden birds from his inner pocket, and putting them on to a curved whist armchair. 'We can have supper. And there's still some Lafitte and Yquem in the cellar.'

He hesitated for a moment, and then fished inside his jacket.

'I walked as far as the station. They had some copies of this rag. Communist rubbish, *Pravda*, Truth, they call it, which it isn't, but it seems the war's over. The Bolsheviks have signed a peace treaty with the Huns. The only thing is, they've given them most of the Ukraine, my estates included. I'm afraid you're engaged to a landless aristocrat with no knowledge of how to earn a living. Not unless you count knowing how to shoot, or my way about a wine cellar.'

She smiled, then.

'You sound a pretty good catch, for a landless Countess.'

He frowned, puzzled.

'I've had Koulakoff here. The peasants have formed a Soviet and they're going to run their own affairs. On *my* land. And the Bolsheviks are sending out what he calls envoys into the countryside. They are expecting Bolsheviks here. Koulakoff says he doesn't mind if we stay on in the house.'

Mikhail laughed shortly. 'The Bolsheviks will. We'd better go. But where, is the question.'

'England. London.'

He looked at her in amazement. 'We're *Russian*.'

'So's Lenin. It's *his* Russia, for the moment. But there's a lot of men with guns who'd have it for theirs. Civil war is coming, Mikhail. I'd rather sit it out abroad.'

'I have no money.'

'*I* have, Mikhail. When my father was assassinated my mother said revolution would come, one day. She knew the Tsar's world was rotten, at the core and with her own hands she built a small cave in the wall of the cellar in the house. She lined it with brick and I helped her to do it. Inside she placed gold and jewellery. Then we bricked it up and plastered and painted, until it could not be seen. She said it would be our passport to safety, if the world fell apart. Mikhail, it's still there. It means going to Petrograd, but only briefly.'

'We can wear peasant clothes,' he said, thoughtfully. 'And with gold we can get across the border into Finland then down into Sweden and a steamer to England.'

'Tomorrow, then,' she said, and they grinned.

She walked around the room, fingering the books in the shelves.

'I had an English governess, a Miss Harding. Ruth had a French one and it was she who filled her head with the talk of revolution. Miss Harding told me about England and they don't think much of revolution, over there. It seemed like a fairy-tale land. She brought lots of English books for me, I loved them. Kate Greenaway, *The Wind in the Willows* . . . Oh, we'll like it in England, Mikhail.'

He watched her, as she wandered about the big room.

'We used to play a game, Alexei and I,' she said, 'when it was time to leave, and go back to St Petersburg. We'd say goodbye to all the most familiar things. I would say "Goodbye chair" and kiss it, and then "Goodbye stairs" and kiss the railings. And Alexei would say "Goodbye piano", and I'd quickly say goodbye to the stool that stood in front of it, so that it wouldn't be offended. It wasn't really a very sad goodbye, since we were excited by the prospect of the journey, and we knew we'd be coming back.'

She paused by a table, and picked up a photograph in its frame.

'Oh, look, here's Ruth and me, when we were eleven. Her daddy was off in Europe all summer helping corner the silver market or something and she spent the whole summer with us here. We had a wonderful time . . . look, we've got the bikes Piotr Pavlovich's father made for us in his factory. We were true tomboys.'

She turned to him, and her mouth puckered in regret.

'I miss her awfully, you know. She got the revolution, just like you catch the flu – she got scarlet fever, if you like, and I didn't know her any more . . .'

She picked up one of the pheasants and sat down with it between her knees. She began to pluck the feathers, her blonde hair gleaming in the firelight. Dark canvas portraits of her ancestors looked down at the last of their line from the walls.

I don't think I'll say goodbye to anything this time,' she said. Then, shrugging, 'Let's have some Yquem. No point in leaving it for Koulakoff!'

Tsarskoye Selo

They were grimy from the long journey and now they sweated in the clammy cellar, knocking a hole in the wall. Streaks of dirt ran across their faces where they had wiped it away. They unwound the cloth wrapping and gold, diamonds, emeralds and pearls shone in the candlelight as brightly as they had when she had sealed them up as a little girl.

They went up the steps and into the house. It was lit by candles and they had left the shutters tightly closed. Mikhail ran some water from the tap, and it was warm. He had fired the boiler – they had both acquired new skills, without servants. Yelena searched through the cupboards, her slim hands deft.

'Here,' she said, laying out her haul on the table. 'From the English shop. Tinned chicken breast in jelly, bottled baby peas, new potatoes. Stilton cheese in a jar, waxed Cheddar, biscuits. All from Fortnum and Mason. And a box of chocolate mints.'

They began to gnaw on some lumps of the Cheddar and some Bath Oliver biscuits. She held up a large photograph in an ivory card frame with her free hand and her eyes were shining.

'Look what else I've found! The class photograph from the school.

Samarin, the photographer must have delivered it while we were gone. Before the revolution came . . . Oh, look, Mikhail.'

He stood next to her as she ran a fingernail over the young faces in the group, the new lines on her own softening.

It was a bit of a mess . . . look, there's that sailor Konstantin and Savinkov brought along . . . and Ruth looking like a revolutionary. Her father spoiled her so . . . they went to America and she met Alexandra Kollontai. My dear, to meet a real aristocrat who'd thrown the whole thing over for revolution! From that moment she could think of nothing else but doing the same . . . Always reading subversive literature by Rosa Luxemburg and the like. She couldn't bear seeing suffering. I remember riding in a carriage with her, and she wouldn't let the coachman whip the horses . . . When she went wild on revolution her mother came round to see mine – she was in despair – but Ruth's father said to leave her be, that she'd grow out of it, the more they disapproved the more attractive it would be . . .

'Who else is there . . . look, there's Zhenya. Isn't she so pretty? And here's Vasilii. Always writing poetry. About her, some of it. How he adored her! And if you want another beauty, look at Verochka. She could sing, like a nightingale. She and Ruth couldn't stand each other . . . Here's Valerian, he was always with Konstantin, planning some new play. That's Nadia – I always thought she and Valerian would marry. He had pots of money, or his father did. He made shells, and rifles and things like that, for the war. And look, Katerina, she was the most sensible of us all. Not like Katia next to her, she was all bubbles. She wanted to be an actress and her parents were *horrified*. There's Piotr Pavlovich, next to Anna. Someone had thrown a rock at him and you can see the blood on his head. There's Israel Shapiro. He'd taken to calling himself Krivitskiy.

'Oh, we'll have a reunion when all these horrible things have passed. That's what I want. We'll all get together again . . .'

She dusted off the crumbs of biscuit and cheese and held the photograph between her two hands.

'I want to keep it. I'll hide it here and collect it when we come back, when the Bolsheviks have gone. There's a secret cupboard here which looks like an ordinary panel, but if you slide it so . . . you can put things inside. It was a hidey hole of mine when I was little . . .'

She carefully put the photograph away behind the woodwork.

'There. It's safe. Now, what did you get?'

Mikhail held out a yellow-labelled bottle.

'More gold from the cellar. *Shampanskaye*. Some Klikofskoe from the Widow.'

'Papa *always* drank Cliquot,' Yelena said, approvingly.

'It's cold. Want some now? We can't move until its dusk. We'll eat all we can before we go, to give us energy when we cross the ice. But if we step out we'll be in Finland by dawn. I have my compass which is luminous, so we won't lose our way.'

Yelena was moving about the kitchen, gathering up tins and bottles. She began putting them inside the hidden cupboard.

'I'll not leave these for whoever comes in to loot. We can have a feast when we return. And I'll gather up some of my things – ornaments, photographs, books. We can save something . . . But, oh, we do need a bath!'

Yelena undid her jacket, her nose wrinkling. The journey had been very long because the railways were chaotic, the soldiers from the front hijacked trains, and made the drivers take them wherever they chose. There had been no personal coach this time, just wooden-slatted seats. When night came they had slept on them, lying on their stomachs so their belongings underneath them would not be stolen, keeping their boots on for the same reason.

'We pass for a couple of peasants,' she said. 'Papa always told me not to pass downwind of them, especially after winter. I never thought I'd end up smelling like one. Let's have a bath, and champagne in it. A bath . . . champagne . . . God, how wonderful!'

For the last two days of the journey they had existed on tea, made from dry leaves they had brought with them. Boiling water could still be found at the stations, if you had a kopek. The Tsar had provided it free. They had drunk the tea like the poor, from a tin mug, sipping it through a lump of hard brown sugar held between the teeth.

The water steamed gently and the air was perfumed with French bath salts. Mikhail poured champagne into flutes and they took off their clothes, leaving them in a pile, and climbed in. The wine was bubbly, cold and scented with flowers. They lathered each other with cologned soap, dried themselves standing together inside one huge soft towel imported from Paris. He carried her to the bed and, afterwards, they finished the champagne.

Outside, the light was dimming around the edges of the shutters. She got up and looked through the wardrobes, the candlelight shining gold on her body.

'You'd better use Alexei's old winter clothes,' she said. 'You were the same size, he and you.'

He got up then, from watching her move about the room. He stopped to kiss her as he went to find his clothing.

'I love you,' he said.

They had padded clothes and felt boots with waterproof bottoms to them; they had eaten, and had food in a pack Mikhail carried; they had gold and jewels. Yelena paused to blow out the candles as he opened the door.

They stood in the dark porch.

'Ready?' he asked.

'Let's go,' she agreed.

From the darkness came the rasp of a flint. Flame flickered from a lighter, and a lamp glowed. Men seized their arms and Rykov came forward out of the night. He had a revolver in one hand and he smiled triumphantly.

'Are you ready for the ball, Countess?' he cried. 'Someone saw you coming through the station, you know. We look out for the tall ones, we know they're *boorzhoi* shit.'

He whistled, and from the street came the clopping of a horse, the groaning of wheels. A black maria, cramped and narrow, came into view, and stopped.

'Your carriage awaits,' Rykov said triumphantly, and they stumbled down the path towards it.

She always volunteered for the dirty jobs, the ones that kept her out late, or in the cold. It was both when she left the party offices. The Cheka had taken over the house next door and the snow was stamped down and bloody across the pavement where they dragged in enemies of the people from their black marias. They kept them in the cellars.

A black maria was standing outside in the dark, its coachman hunched on the top, trying to keep out the cold. She did not know whether it was one that had brought prisoners, or was waiting to take the dead away. The cellars were very crowded, damp and cold, some people died from it and other things, she knew.

A face was pressing against the bars as she came by and she turned her head away. She did not want to see.

'Ruth!' came the voice. '*Ruth.*'

She stopped, staring, her mouth slightly open.

'Ruth, it's *me*. Yelena. I'm in here with Mikhail.'

The coachman turned and crashed a whip down on the roof.

'You keep quiet, *svoloch* scum.'

Ruth cracked then. She stood on the bloody snow, looking up at him, her face suddenly hard and aristocratic.

'*I* am speaking, comrade,' she said icily. '*You* will be quiet.'

It was soon enough since the slaves became masters, he knew

an aristocrat's voice when he heard it. He responded, like a dog, muttering something unintelligible and turning himself away from her gaze. She went back to the small barred door at the rear.

'How are you here, Yelena? What have you done?'

'Done? What does one need to do to be arrested in this madhouse except be oneself? But listen, Ruth, it's Rykov who has us. Do you know him, Ruth? He's mad. He hates me. He's gone in there to get a room.'

'I know Rykov,' she said slowly.

'Ruth, he's going to kill us. He tried once before. Can you get us out?'

She thought quickly, standing there in the cold gloom.

'I'll be back,' she said, and ran the way she had come, to the Party headquarters. She was in luck, few people were there, but he was, the huge young man in his army tunic, his baggy trousers tucked into knee-high boots.

'Do you still want Tsarist officers?' she said abruptly, rushing up to him.

'*Voenspets*? Why yes. We are making a people's army, but the workers and peasants have had little practice at being leaders. We need some real ones to show us how.'

'I have two. Well, one, but the other is a woman who is as good. A Countess.'

The big young man looked at her curiously.

'Who is she?'

'I went to school with her,' Ruth said softly. This was dangerous ground, but she had gone too far to back out. 'Her name is Yelena Nikolayeva Isakova.'

'And mine is Ivan Ivanovich Akulov,' he murmured. 'I was her chauffeur, not long ago. Yes, I will take the Countess and Count Mikhail, if it is he.'

'There is just one problem,' Ruth said anxiously. 'They are outside in a black maria. The Cheka has arrested them. Rykov has them.'

He moved quickly, running down the corridor, his heavy boots pounding. He stopped at the doorway, peeping round the jamb, and she caught him up.

'They are still there,' he whispered. 'Go talk to the cabman.'

She strode down the snow and stopped beside the carriage.

'So you're still here,' she said hectoringly. The man flinched at the sound of her voice.

'*T'otchen*,' he muttered, the peasant's unquestioning response to an officer's enquiry. 'Quite so.'

He had no time so say any more, for a giant leaped up behind him out of the dark, pitching him from his perch into the dirty snow of the street.

Akulov cracked the reins with skilful hands and the horse jerked forward in its harness. By the time the winded coachman had staggered to his feet the black maria was turning the corner out of sight. A hand was waving from the grille, and Ruth raised her own.

'*Where have they gone?*' a voice shrieked in fury behind her, and she turned. Rykov was on the path that led into the Cheka building. The coachman blenched in fear and ran towards him.

'It was not my fault, sir!' he babbled. 'Someone pulled me off. Someone stole them as this woman talked to me.'

Rykov smashed him across the face with the revolver in his hand and he fell into the bushes and lay there, groaning.

Rykov stood very close to her, and she looked down at him.

'Yes?' he said. There was a fleck of spittle at the corner of his mouth.

'You had a Tsarist officer, there,' she said calmly. 'Trotsky wants Tsarist officers for our new army. I've sent him one.'

She looked into his eyes. For a second she thought she saw something like a furnace door opening; a brief, incandescent fury, and then it was gone.

'I picked them up for routine questioning,' he said indifferently. 'So you did well. Let Trotsky have them.'

He put his revolver away in its holster and put his free hand about her waist.

'We don't see enough of each other,' he said. 'Why don't we get together one night?'

She forced herself not to shudder at his touch.

She smiled brightly. 'Why not? When we aren't working so hard for the revolution.'

He took his hand away, smiling, and she had a sudden insight that she did not interest him sexually. It was something else . . . and she forced herself to be unafraid. As a young girl her coachman had taken the wrong turning. Caught in a tangle of wagons and carriages she had seen some slum children with a cat. The leader of the band was tying a paraffin-soaked rag to its tail. He had a lit taper and he took a long time to light the rag, for he liked the cat to be afraid.

'I must go,' she said pleasantly.

'I'll see you soon,' Rykov promised. She wondered if it had been he, running the taper over the cat's fur as it struggled.

As she turned the corner she heard the coachman scream. The cat had shrieked, too, blazing like a comet . . .

Moscow, August, 1918

Konstantin gave the black door a push with his foot and it shuddered in a swollen jamb before swinging in with a creak. A scrawl of red paint gave its name, the Poets' Café. He stood in the alley in the summer sunshine with Krivitskiy, two young men looking in.

'I loved this place,' he said. 'I loved them all – I went to the Red Cockerel, The Forge, The Tenth Muse – they bloomed like flares in a midnight sky, after the revolution.'

'And went out as quickly,' Krivitskiy said, smiling.

'Yes, everything was so new that even what happened last week seemed far away. But this one lasted.'

He went in, stepping over something that had gone in there to die on the floor. Black paint had been smeared over the walls, and on it purple bosoms fought for possession of the space with multi-limbed horses' rears, green, yellow, and red stripes. Bulging, detached eyes watched the two visitors as they walked around. Konstantin shook his long hair back, at home.

An orange stage commanded one end of the long narrow room, and crude wooden tables still stood on the wooden floor.

'This was the best,' said Konstantin. 'You got everybody here. Poets like me, artists like me. Journalists, soldiers, sailors. Bourgeoisie who hadn't had their throats cut yet. Guns and grenades and bandoliers everywhere. The anarchists used to come in – they had their headquarters just down the street – all dressed in black, with bandoliers emblazoned with their slogan – 'Death to Capital!'. They'd have a breather and watch a show before going out for another street battle.'

'Gone now,' said Krivitskiy. 'I was there, we smashed them.'

Konstantin glanced sideways at his former schoolmate. Krivitskiy's steel rimmed glasses glinted in the dim light.

'You were a quiet little sod. Bookish,' he said amiably. 'I never took you for a man of action.'

'I still read. When there is time. But yes, I do whatever is needed to protect the revolution. Including busting heads.'

'You'd have liked it here. All the best performers – Klimov and his girls sang, Vladmir Durov was the king of clowns. Prokofiev played his own compositions. Maiakovskii recited poetry. A couple of times *I* recited poetry. I helped him put up *that*. That's the revolution . . .'

Konstantin pointed to a line of poetry scrawled on the wall.

'"I love to watch children dying,"' Krivitskiy read aloud. 'I must ship Maiakovskii out to the front, he will be delirious with excitement . . .'

Konstantin was lost in memories.

'The walls here, Burluik did them. That's Cubist art. He used to get up on stage sometimes – nobody was going to stop him, he started the club – he wore full make up and a lorgnette, and he'd look out at us and say: "I am fond of pregnant men." I was seventeen and I thought it was the wittiest thing I'd heard.'

Konstantin was eighteen, but he spoke as though ten years had passed. Krivitskiy felt a puritanical desire to bend Burluik over and push the barrel of his Mauser up the appropriate part of him as far as it would go before pulling the trigger. The rabbi had always condemned pederasty as being against God's law. But he smiled.

'No time for that now,' he said pleasantly.

'No,' Konstantin muttered. He pushed his long hair off his face as he looked about the room. 'No time for a lot of things now, is there? Where did the revolution go? This was what it was about, being at the cutting edge of art, about solving the riddles of the Sphinx before it ate you.'

He turned. 'Guns and sweat and violence and women,' he muttered. 'Dazzling poetry jumping in your head, your hand twitching with visions to put on paper. I feel it now, but where is the revolution? Where's it gone?'

They went outside into the sunshine and went back along the alley to the boulevard.

'It's out there,' said Krivitskiy. 'And the past's trying to kill it. The *ancien régime*'s advancing on us; the Whites, the British, the Americans. The revolution's fighting for its life. And fighting back. We're all fighting, the people you know. Remember Ruth Gunzberg and Sergei Savinkov? They're on the Comintern's General Staff of World Revolution. When the capitalist war finishes out there they're taking the revolutionary bacillus to them. They're giving me an armoured train, soon, and I'm off to smash the Whites. We have to protect the Revolution until the battle's won.'

In the distance stood the Kremlin.

'We've killed the Tsar,' Krivitskiy said quietly.

Konstantin stared at him. An emaciated horse clopped slowly by, carrying the corpse of another on a waggon, taking it to the market.

'No going back now, then,' he said.

'The past doesn't exist. Only the future.'

'So what I am I to do?' Konstantin asked.

'We're teaching the people to read and write. They're mostly illiterate, you know. That's why the Tsar fell; he didn't communicate with the people. He couldn't. An illiterate person stands outside of politics. First you teach him his ABCs. Without it there are only rumours, fairy tales and prejudices, but not politics. We have literacy squads working in the barracks. Two days with pencils, a week with bayonets! We're printing our own primers – communist primers – so that they learn communist morality from the start. But it will take time, perhaps more than we have. And we need to reach the common man, too. The man out there. We need his support, we need to send him a message. We can't do it if he can't read, only if he only *half*-reads.'

'Cartoons!' Konstantin said instantly. He fished in his pocket for pencil and paper and, resting on a wall, drew a picture with swift, sure strokes. As Krivitskiy watched, a vivid picture of a booted, triumphant, rifle-wielding worker appeared. His boot thrust a grovelling, effete Tsar into mire.

'Cartoons. *Big* cartoons. Use the empty shop windows in the towns and cities. Call it . . . Cartoon Windows. Or Windows of Satire. Let *me* do it. I know all the artists and satirists who matter. We'll send out cartoons, we'll cut stencils and send them out on your fighting trains. Have a two-line caption to support the visual message.'

'You do it,' Krivitskiy said softly. 'You do that for the revolution.'

'That's cutting edge,' said Konstantin. They were by the Kremlin walls. Still there were the vivid violet, blue, brick red and crimson paintings of the previous May Day. Demented squares battled with rhomboids for possession of space, and faces with triangles for eyes leered down at them. The paint had been good, the efforts of the removers had been only partly successful.

'I don't see what Lenin objected to,' Konstantin complained. He wanted Moscow different, and we did.'

'When the revolution's safe, you can come back and finish it,' Krivitskiy said soothingly. 'When the revolution's won there'll be *nothing* you can't do.'

3

Krasnyi

Moscow, 30 August 1918

THEY needed good party members who could speak foreign languages. Ruth's father was a banker; his interests spread to London, Berlin and Paris and she had learned French, German and English as a matter of course during holidays spent in elegant apartments and the rebellion in her that had led her to Bolshevism had made her have the chauffeur teach her to drive, so she was behind the wheel of the bus as it ground down the streets of the new capital city.

Savinkov's father had been a diplomat; his son had learned German when he had been in Potsdam, English in Mayfair. He couldn't drive, so he talked to the foreigners while Ruth did. Far away the war that had toppled the Tsar was coming to a decision. Other great empires would crash to ruins at its end, and the workers of the world would emerge to take what was theirs, by right. The leaders of the first communist state in history wanted to help them do it. Ruth and Savinkov wore in their lapels special, rare enamelled brooches that the foreigners eyed with awe. They were *krasnyi*, the colour of magic, they were red. She and Savinkov were emissaries of the first revolution; they were from the Communist International, the Comintern. They were on the general staff of world revolution.

In the bus they had English, French and Germans, a handful of them, not separated by the conflict their governments were engaged in but bound together by the thought of the coming world utopia. They had smelled its sweet perfume blowing from Russia, they had come long miles to see for themselves, and Sergei Savinkov was delighted to show it to them.

They went round Arbatskaya Square and, as they passed Arbat Street, Savinkov pointed out the tired, defeated men and women holding bunches of artificial flowers, evening dresses, medals and uniforms. They had been there all the long day.

'Jetsam,' he said, steel grey eyes looking out contemptuously.

'Members of the *ancien régime* washed up on the shores of a new society. Soon we shall send them into the countryside to learn the wonders of honest toil, of a world free from exploitation.'

An Englishwoman behind Ruth brayed with approval.

'God, how marvellous! I wish we could do that at home!'

'You will,' Savinkov assured her. 'The revolution is coming to all countries and *your* Dukes and Countesses will have callusses on their hands and dirt under their nails.'

'My parents would do to begin with,' the Englishwoman said malevolently.

Ruth wondered why he didn't mention the others. The ones in the shabby clothes with hollow faces, bartering things of slightly better value than gowns for balls that would never come, uniforms for offices abolished. They traded in hard spiky crusts of stale, black, rationed bread, in lumps of dirty, unwholesome brown sugar and blemished apples. The ones with the one-ounce packets of coarse tobacco could always do a deal – it took the hunger away.

She knew why he didn't mention them, it was because he did not see them. Until recently, she had not noticed them either, for they could not exist in a perfect world. Driving up the empty, dirty street she saw them in her mirror, staring after the bus with sunken eyes. She wished they would go away.

'I would like soon to see some peasants,' a German man in steel-rimmed glasses announced, and there was a buzz of approval from the others.

'Oh, God yes,' said the Englishwoman. 'I love real people.'

'Ruth will arrange it,' Savinkov assured them.

'On the train here I travelled through miles of golden corn,' the German said. 'Back home in the Kaiser's society people are starving, but here in the new world there is plenty for all.'

Ruth wondered where to get some peasants. These foreigners could not possibly be allowed to meet any real ones. They had tasted the revolution, and had not liked the flavour. It was, she knew, an acquired taste. She decided to talk to Krivitskiy; he could get some out of jail for her, suitably prepared.

She saw him as she turned in at the gate of the Mikhelson Works. Some Renault trucks were in the courtyard, drab and muddy, and he was with a group of party workers, leaders of the twenty-five odd teams of factory workers who stood by the vehicles. The leaders had maps, their men rifles slung. In the trucks were piles of sacks.

As she got out, the group broke up, and they began to mount up. She heard Savinkov behind her.

'These members of the proletariat are going out to meet with peasants,' he said. 'To help them.'

'Why do they carry their rifles?' asked the German voice, interestedly.

'Symbols of their revolutionary ardour,' Savinkov said grandly. 'We are building a new world, one in which we shall end discussions and disputes. They are for counter-revolutionaries! As Lenin says, it is better to discuss with rifles than with the theses of the opposition.'

She heard them break into a kind of cheer as she went over to see Krivitskiy. He still looked like Israel Shapiro, in a black leather jerkin, to her. The trucks were grinding into smoky life.

'The last lot of bastards just got drunk on potato liquor when they got there,' Krivitskiy said savagely. I've told them, I don't mind how they get the food out of the stinking peasantry, but I want it back here. The people in the city are starving. I shot one of the commissars in front of them a few minutes ago, before you arrived, so they get the message.'

'Don't do it in front of my foreigners,' she said nervously. 'They won't understand.'

'Might be good for them,' he said. 'We were all wet behind the ears once. You have to learn it takes blood and steel to make a perfect world.'

She decided not to ask him for peasants.

'Is he here?'

'Lenin? Yes, he's addressing the workers.'

'I'd better go with my lot – I feel like a kindergarten mistress!'

He smiled, and for a second he looked like the young Jewish boy who had sat next to her in class.

'You don't look like you're eating enough,' he said. 'Come by and see me tomorrow – I'll put something good by for you when the lads get back. Some smoked ham, maybe.'

'What will the peasants eat, this winter?'

'These are kulaks,' he said dismissively. 'Exploiters. We're redistributing their wealth for them. Lenin's decreed that vanguard party fighters get improved rations.'

'We can't enter the kingdom of socialism in white gloves on a polished floor,' she said.

Krivitskiy ran a hand through his hair. He looked tired, like all the rest of them.

'Exactly.'

'*Ruth*!'

She turned and saw Nadezhda smiling at her. She had come from inside the factory.

'Darling, how lovely! Are you with him?' Ruth asked.

'Yes, I'm to work on his secretariat. Congratulations!'

'What for?'

'Don't you know? The war's coming to an end out there and you and Savinkov, you're off to Germany to bring them the torch. All Europe will be ablaze! And Lenin wants you to meet Rosa Luxemburg.'

She felt her heart suddenly sing, and Nadezhda grinned happily to see her joy.

'That's wonderful . . . And Rosa Luxemburg . . . !'

Nadezhda linked her arm through Ruth's, squeezing affectionately. 'Isn't it marvellous? Come on, let's see what Vladimir Ilyich has to say.'

They followed the group that Savinkov was leading. Ruth fingered her Comintern badge, stroking its smooth, cold surface, the raised metal star. Rosa Luxemburg . . . These were incredible times. Mighty, almost mythological figures had come alive, moving events like giants. In the great machine hall a group of greasy men and women stood about a platform. There he was, balding, bullet-headed, his fist striking down on the rail like a pile driver, his flat cap gripped in the other. One of the giants. She saw the Englishwoman looking about in wonder.

'You run such a factory with so small a workforce? You really are making a new world. In Britain we could never do this.'

'You should see how they work after Lenin has spoken,' said Savinkov.

'What are they making?'

'Hand grenades.'

'Oh, how marvellous. The very symbol of the proletariat's destruction of the bourgeoisie!'

Ruth stood with Nadezhda on the edge of the crowd. The foreigners were goggling in awe and the harsh voice and its rolling Rs echoed round and round, bouncing off the walls of her brain.

She saw another young woman, not far away, standing by a huge, dusty machine. She too was staring at Lenin with big, dark eyes, her black hair pinned back behind her ears. She was smoking cigarettes, one after the other.

It was her calm that caught Ruth's attention. She looked as Ruth still sometimes felt, wholly certain.

'What is the difference then, between the dictatorship of the proletariat and the dictatorship of the bourgeoisie?' Lenin demanded.

'It is this. Wherever democrats are in power, you have real, barefaced robbery, and the bourgeoisie endeavour to delude the masses with empty promises of equality and fraternity. All workers, workers like you, must join in the struggle to make a workers' government a reality in which all who work have the right to enjoy the benefits of life. Your commitment cannot be half-hearted.'

Ruth found herself shaking her head in agreement. She felt ashamed, that she ever had doubts. When you got close enough to the leader you realised how strong your faith should be . . .

'In the battle against the predatory bourgeoisie, who have condemned millions of workers to unrelieved destitution under the guise of parliamentary democracy, there are only two alternatives.'

He banged the rail with his fist, and glared down at them.

'Victory or death!' he bellowed, and they roared their assent.

He came down from his platform, and walked out through the cheering crowd. The plainly dressed woman Ruth had noticed had vanished.

Outside, the courtyard was in shadow. Lenin's Mercedes was waiting near her bus. Her foreigners were close, anxious to catch the smallest nugget of gold that might drop from his lips. They left room for him to get into his car and then suddenly the woman was there, only feet away, a revolver in her hand. She fired, and the impact of the bullet rocked Lenin back on his heels. As she fired again he put his hand up to ward off the bullet. Blood spattered the side of the white door as he slumped back. By her side, Nadezhda screamed in anguish.

Krivitskiy was there, with Lenin's bodyguard, holding him up, helping him into the rear. The chauffeur was revving the engine, his face white with shock, and Krivitskiy hung on the running board.

'Stepan, Stepan!' he yelled. 'Don't take him to the hospital. The SRs will kill him if you do. Get him to the Kremlin and we'll get a doctor, one of ours.'

He jumped off as the big limousine raced across the courtyard.

'Quickly, Ruth, your bus,' Krivitskiy ordered.

She jumped in, starting the engine, and crunched into gear, jerking round in a tight circle to leave the yard. She saw the Englishwoman screaming hysterically, heard her words,

'They've killed Jesus!'

Then they had left the wailing, were on the street.

Krivitskiy was next to her, his black leather jacket slick with *his* blood, bright red on his hands.

'She can't have got very far,' he said. 'Look out for her.'

Ruth saw her on the street. She was leaning against a tree, her chest heaving. She pulled up beside her, and Krivitskiy got out. He dragged her to the door and threw her in.

'To our new building,' he ordered. 'In Lubyanka Square.'

Ruth put the bus back in gear and jerkily turned around in the street.

'Are you an imperialist agent?' he asked harshly, and Ruth heard the woman gasp in pain. Her voice, when she spoke, was calm, however.

'I am one who was for the Constituent Assembly that Lenin killed,' she said. 'And I still am.'

'Who has paid you? The British?'

The hard rubber tyres of the bus squealed on the cobbles as Ruth rounded the square by the great high insurance building. Cheka guards were outside.

'Lenin has killed all the revolution stood for, so I have killed him. If he had lived, there would have been no end to the killing.'

She stopped outside, and Krivitskiy hustled her through the doors into the building. The Cheka had their new sign up over the doorway, a shield and sword, the one to protect the revolution, the other to smite its enemies.

Behind the wheel she fumbled in her pocket for her flat case of cigarettes and lit one with shaking fingers. On the pavement a small boy of three or four stared intently at her as she drew upon it. The inside of the bus stank of blood and the tobacco was sweet in her head.

Someone was banging on the side of the bus. It was one of the Cheka guards, ordering her on. She threw the cigarette away, half smoked. In the mirror she saw the little boy run into the street to pick it up . . .

Tsaritsyn

Rykov was in the grip of an emotion. He was not sure what it was and it was disturbing. It surged within him, made him think, brought out new qualities and abilities that he had not known he possessed.

He had first been aware of it the day he was out collecting food.

He was in charge of the *prodotryad*, one of the teams that fed the Fifth Red Army holding Tsaritsyn. On the other side of the Volga, coming up, was Krasnov and his White Cossacks.

The summer was over and the harvest was in; they had arrived at the right time. They were in the village at the right time too, before dawn, so that the peasants emerging on their way to the privy were unprepared. Not that they wouldn't have hidden the crop – peasants had a folk memory of the requirements of armies that went back thousands of years before Marx, or Bolsheviks – but Rykov had them lined up in the street as the sun was crawling up the sky. He liked to make a joke about saving them the cost of transport to market, because the market had come to them. He had a sense of humour the same as theirs, sly, knowing, cruel. They knew each other, the small, quick young man in his black leather jacket, and the enduring peasants.

The theoreticians in Moscow had passed on detailed instructions as to the formulation of peasant society, with low, middle and kulak classes, and from somewhere in a high building they had identified a village proletariat, with which the Chekists were supposed to ally, but Rykov knew that they couldn't tell cow dung from pig, which he could. Peasants were peasants, and a pistol shoved into the ear of the prettiest of the little girls normally got a father's tongue wagging. He called his Mauser the Orator – it could persuade anyone to agree with his views.

Rykov was a happy man. He liked his organisation to run efficiently and he considered himself fair. He told the team what he wanted and when someone didn't perform, he shot him, and the others made sure they did. At the end of the day he issued some of the spoil as reward.

He was putting some bottles of vodka into his car for distribution later as he watched his team bringing in burlap sacks of grain from some of the outlying farms, driving pigs, carrying chickens and leading horses. The peasants still stood in a row against the wall, their faces as immobile as any other beasts of burden.

'Any good?' a soft voice enquired. He turned, vodka bottle in hand. A short man, about his own height stood there, moustached, his trousers stuffed into his boots in the peasant fashion. A car and driver stood some distance away. Two other men stood watching the arriving team.

'I don't know,' he said casually. He twisted the cork and pulled it, offering the bottle to the stranger. The man took a swig before handing it back. Yellow eyes appraised him carefully.

'You in charge?'

'Yes.'

'You know, you look like a criminal to me.' The yellow eyes were watching him, assessing his reaction.

'I was,' Rykov said levelly. 'To those who served the Tsar.'

The man smiled then.

'Me, too,' he said. He fished in his pocket and brought out a packet of real *Herzegovina Flor* cigarettes and offered it. Rykov noticed that his left arm seemed to be stiff, hanging from the shoulder.

'I've always liked criminals,' the man confided. 'I've been in exile – in the Tsar's time – and I used to hang about with them. Good fellows, salt-of-the-earth types. We'd share our last kopek and drink together. When you offered me that vodka, I knew you were one of us.'

He glanced across to the other men standing by the car.

'You know who I can't stand? Politicals. And so-called experts. We had a lot of rats among the politicals, back then. Still have. See those over there. One's fresh from Moscow, his mouth dry from spouting theory. Aksov's his name. He was sucking on his mother's tits when I was fighting the Tsar. The other's an army officer, worked for the Tsar. Mamontov. Trotsky sent them. I don't need either. Who needs these experts? You can make a new one out of a good ordinary boy in a week – and one who thinks like you.'

'Wasn't that what the revolution was about? We got rid of the bastards.'

'Yes. But I've got a few left.' He stared at the men. 'You ever hear of Trotsky, fellow criminal?'

'I had two prisoners, once – aristocrats. He stole them for his army.'

'What does Trotsky know about armies?' the man muttered. 'Pretty boys can't fight . . .' He looked at the arriving horses. 'I need cavalry,' he said. 'I'll take those.'

Rykov smiled. 'We're the Cheka, we usually do the taking.'

The man smiled. 'I'm your boss,' he said, and held out his hand, the right one, the good one. 'Stalin, Josef Stalin.'

He looked at the peasants standing along the wall. 'I'll take the men, too,' he said. 'All between sixteen and sixty.'

Rykov barked the orders and his chekists quickly separated them out.

'You're in the army now,' Stalin said jocularly.

A woman broke away and threw herself at his feet.

'Your honour, how shall we live, with no food, and no men-folk?'

'We are communists. By next year there will be food and plenty for all.'

The woman slowly picked herself up. 'By next year we shall be dead.'

'Then the grain you do not eat will help the revolutionaries who are not,' Stalin said, with equanimity.

The woman spat at his feet, and Rykov shot her. Then they got on with the business of getting the supplies out, living and otherwise. There was another village further towards the river and Rykov wanted to get there while the peasants were sleeping in the afternoon.

But he was off the *prodotryad* now, and on to more useful work. The Director General of Food Supplies in the South of Russia was holding a dinner. On one side of Stalin sat Aksov, on the other the *voenspet* Mamontov, wearing his drab proletarian uniform as easily as he had his glorious 3rd Cavalry Corps of scarlet and gold. Bottles of Georgian wine and vodka littered the table and, as Rykov watched through the half-open door, Aksov slithered down in his seat and vanished under the table, his eyes rolling back in his head. Stalin and Mamontov roared with laughter.

The party was breaking up. Stalin himself saw Mamontov to the door, embracing him with the bonhomie of the drunk.

'Sleep well,' he said. 'Get ready to fight.'

'We're all Bolsheviks here,' Mamontov assured him. He went out, down the corridor, and Rykov, in his rifleman's uniform, slipped after him. The grounds of the magnificent villa Stalin had taken for himself were filled with the scent of flowers. In the half light, Rykov caught Mamontov up.

'Colonel,' he hissed urgently. 'Colonel Mamontov.'

The officer turned and stared down at the little man from an aristocrat's height and eye.

'Who are you?' he asked coldly. His pointed cap with its red star formed a peak in the moonlit sky. Rykov whipped his off, holding it obsequiously across his stomach with both hands.

'Rifleman Rykov, Colonel.'

'What do you want?'

'Stalin is going to kill you,' Rykov whispered fearfully. 'I work by his office and I heard him discussing it with Yagoda, his Chekist. You're Trotsky's man and he hates Trotsky.'

'Infernal rubbish!' snarled Mamontov. 'I'm a socialist the same as he is – we're all working for the same end.'

'You do not understand the nature of communism, Colonel,' Rykov suggested.

'I understand a troublemaker when I see one!' the big man growled. An arm like a hawser reached out and grabbed Rykov by the shoulder. 'You come with me. We'll see what Stalin has to say about you and we'll have you flogged in the morning.'

He marched back into the villa, half-carrying Rykov. The Colonel learns fast, Rykov thought to himself.

Mamontov stopped suddenly in the dark corridor. The double doors were back and the dining room still glittered with golden light. By the table Stalin was standing with Voroshilov, the metalworker turned general who commanded his troops. With them was the balding, spindly Chekist, Yagoda. An assistant in a chemist's shop before the revolution, he was another for whom its arrival had brought secret, furtive fantasies into glorious, bloody reality. There was no bonhomie about the trio. All, including Stalin, were sober. Voroshilov was holding a telegraph.

'Orders from Trotsky,' he said. Stalin took a pen from his pocket and bent over the table.

'To . . . Be . . . Ignored,' he said as he wrote, and handed it back to Voroshilov with a grin.

Yagoda kicked the inert body of Aksov, lying at his feet, his boot making a squishing sound.

'What about this sack of shit?' he said.

Stalin glanced down at the political expert. 'Shoot him with the others in the morning,' he grunted.

'You still want to go ahead with shooting Mamontov and his staff?'

'Rykov felt Mamontov's grip slowly bite into his shoulder like iron.

'Yes, yes, do it.'

'I got an order from Moscow this morning concerning the military specialists, insisting on further investigation.'

'What investigation? They're all guilty. They're all plotting, against me, against the revolution. Shoot the bastards!'

'It may cause problems,' Yagoda demurred, as if questioning a prescription.

Stalin looked across at the secret policeman in the soft, golden light, his face unemotional.

'Death solves all problems,' he said. 'No man, no problem.'

'Okay, boss,' Yagoda said cheerfully, assured that the dosage was correct. 'I'll have them set it up early and we'll come for them before dawn. I'll have the boys drag this one out in a minute.'

'He'll have such a hangover in the morning he'll probably *beg* us to shoot him,' Stalin joked, and they all chuckled.

Carefully, stealthily, Mamontov backed away down the dark corridor, taking Rykov with him. Out again in the garden, he muttered to himself, 'What the hell am I to do?'

'Krasnov's only thirty miles away, Colonel,' Rykov said softly.

'Krasnov? What do you mean, Krasnov? Krasnov's the fucking *enemy.*'

'Wrong, Colonel. The enemy's in there, in the villa.'

'Thirty miles . . .'

'There is a car. Over by the depot. The driver sleeps in it and he's drunk . . .'

Rykov found himself flung to one side, and the big man vanished into the darkness. A minute later he heard the clunk of a starter crank, and the solid beat of a Renault engine. Gears grated, and then he heard the car going off down the road. The lights came on and he saw the trees illuminated as it swept towards the Volga, and the approaching White forces. Rykov turned, and went off to bed.

He was up early. He put on his black leather jerkin and took some bread and cheese to chew on. Outside in the field they had Mamontov's men tied to posts. The political expert Aksov was there, too. He appeared to have vomited over himself.

Stalin stood waiting with Yagoda and Rykov had a chance to finish his breakfast.

A car was coming up the road, a green Renault. It squeaked to a stop and a man was flung out. He pushed himself to his hands and knees, very wearily, and the two Chekists behind him grabbed him, dragging him over to the post that was waiting for him. It was Mamontov, his face bruised and swollen. Rykov went over to help them tie him to the post.

'See, Genrikh?' Stalin shouted to Yagoda, who had moved to supervise the squad of men behind the machine guns. All about could hear. 'See what kind of men Trotsky is sending me? *Traitors and spies*! Investigate, they demand! Very well, send them the details of our investigation. Tell them how these good Bolsheviks caught Trotsky's man five miles from the enemy, going to him at full speed! Tell Moscow how honest Bolsheviks protect the revolution here!'

Rykov secured Mamontov's big hands behind the post with wire. His shoulder was bruised where Mamontov had gripped him and he gave the wire an extra twist with the pliers in his pocket, so useful for persuading still tongues to wag. Mamontov winced, and turned his head.

'You little bastard!' he said hoarsely.

'I said that you did not understand communism, Colonel,' Rykov said cheerfully. At the next post Aksov whimpered.

'You cannot do this,' he protested. 'The Moscow committee forbids it.'

'Death solves all problems,' Rykov assured him. 'No man, no problem.'

He strolled back, past the machine gunners setting up their weapons. Stalin caught his eye and he went over. The boss squeezed his shoulder approvingly.

'Well done, little jailbird,' he said softly. 'I'll not forget you.'

Rykov felt himself warm with pleasure. He stood back, where he could see both Stalin and the show. He looked at his boss, an older, more experienced, more capable version of himself. Already he had learned so much from him. In the years to come there would be so much more to imbibe. Yagoda murmured the instructions, his eyes gleaming. Rykov shivered with a sudden *frisson* of lust. The cocking levers gave out a precision clatter and as Stalin stroked his moustache in anticipation, Rykov stroked his.

A wave of that unfamiliar, disturbing emotion surged through him again. The guns fired in their staccato bursts, bits of blood and flesh flew in the air, and Rykov wondered if it was love.

Moscow

Ruth had a room in the Luxe Hotel, just off Tverskaya Ul. Savinkov lived there, as did some others in the International. It was an easy walk for her down the cobbled, twisting boulevard to her office in Strastnaya Pl., on the other side of the square to the old Strastnoy Convent. She stopped on her way at *Gastronom*, Food Shop No.1, and the doorman in his red scarf let her in in hers just as he had when he had worn full Tsarist rig, and she had accompanied her mother in theirs, and the Number One food shop had been Yeliseyev's. She'd found one of the old tailors, and he'd done her a new military outfit in soft cloth, it looked wonderful. She had her glossy hair pinned up in a scarlet brooch.

It was wonderfully uncrowded and she strolled easily across

the tiled floor, through the magnificent pillared and gilt hall. She remembered the scrum there used to be, in the old days. Fadeyev had her parcel ready for her, smiling and beaming – she didn't even have to show the Party card that authorised her to be there. She took it and exchanged a few pleasant words as she liked to. It was rude to be abrupt, especially with those of lesser station in life. Then she strolled out again, under the fabulous chandeliers, and on to the street.

The Tverskaya was Main Street; any signs of life returning to the corpse of the capital would appear there. The public baths were open, though the water was cold. Outside a pretty girl watched for the presence of someone connected with the party with the eye of a hawk searching for mice.

In the square, the workmen were busy taking things out of the Convent, useless icons and statues of Jesus and his mother, and putting up the new signs. They had the nuns digging trenches somewhere on the outskirts. Ruth was pleased to be working close to the Central Museum of Atheism; its presence was symbolic of the Revolution transforming yet another useless artefact into something vibrant and purposeful.

They were waiting for her in the corridor, sitting on the bench. They stood up quickly, when they saw her coming and Verochka took the lead.

'Good morning, Ruth,' she said, smiling nervously, and Valerian and Nadia echoed her.

'Good morning, good morning!'

If it had not been for their welcome faces that she knew so well – had she not sat in the same classroom with them for years? – she would hardly have recognised them. Verochka seemed to sense it, and smoothed the badly-cut velvet skirt over her thighs.

'All our things were stolen,' she said. 'We had to cut up cloaks and curtains and things.'

'You look like a lot of refugees,' she said cheerfully, unlocking her office. 'But don't worry, I'll take care of you.' Going in ahead of them she did not see the expression of fear on their faces begin to wash away. She filled the kettle at the sink and put it on the ring to boil.

'No stupid samovars in the new society.' she said.

'How is Comrade Lenin?' asked Nadia.

She was both pleased, and surprised. Nadia had always made such fun of her revolutionary beliefs.

'Why, thank you, he's going to be fine, he's going to live.'

'That's marvellous . . . I mean, we're all Bolsheviks now, aren't we?'

'Wonderful,' muttered Valerian. His father had owned mines, she recalled. From the look of him his son didn't own much more than he stood up in. Someone had told her the father was in Paris, penniless.

'Give us a scale, Verochka,' she said casually, clinking with the cutlery. Verochka had had it all – looks, poise, beautiful voice; she had gone about the school like a princess. Memories of past roles made her flush at the tone of command but the spirit of survival got her to her feet and she opened her throat like a nightingale.

Valerian gave an excellent extract from one of Lenin's speeches – he had the declamation off pat, the gestures and grimaces. Nadia danced as the kettle boiled, light on her feet as a bird. All the boys had wanted to dance with Nadia. Not boring, committed, revolutionary Ruth, pretty though she might have been.

'Lovely!' Ruth poured the tea, dark and strong, in mugs, and put the chocolate biscuits she had got from Gastronom on to a decent, thick, proletarian plate.

'Help yourselves,' she said, and they shovelled sugar into the tea, and tried only to nibble the biscuits, affecting not to be hungry. It was polite to offer refreshment, polite to put it down between small bites, they all knew that.

'It's wonderful that I've got hold of you,' Ruth said, getting down to business, and the three pushed the biscuits into their mouths, assured that she would be doing the talking.

'I – we – have a small problem. It's a temporary one. But I've been told to solve it. What's happening is that here we have the world's first society devoted to freedom and the people's happiness. The imperialist exploiters have been overthrown and the peasants and workers rule. Now that is the most wonderful and amazing thing that has ever happened in the history of the world. And people who want the same to happen in their countries, people who long for freedom themselves, are coming here to see what has happened. The revolution is going to spread throughout the world, like the wave of a mighty rock hurled into a capitalist pond. They will come and they will take the fire of the revolution home with them.'

She put some more biscuits on a plate.

'Help yourselves, by the way. Our problem is that we haven't completed everything. Aren't we still fighting the exploiters? We have capitalism floored, but still not throttled. And while we're doing this we can't implement full communism. The perfect society we are going to create is just around the corner – a matter of months away, a year or two at most. But the people are coming to see what we have wrought! And for the sake of a few ridiculous months we can't show them. And we can't, can't, *can't* let them go away disappointed.'

She sat back in her chair and pushed the hair back out of her eyes.

'I've talked with Savinkov, who's on the general staff of world revolution as I am, and this is what we're going to do: we're going to be as Lenin. He brought about the revolution by means of *vanguard fighters*. So that's what we're going to do, create a vanguard of peasants, a vanguard of workers. New, wonderful, communist peasants; new, wonderful communist workers; efficient, powerful, handsome, happy and singing with the love of communism.'

She stared at them, and they stared back.

'Wonderful,' said Valerian.

'Yes, wonderful.'

'Wonderful.'

'We're going to start with the peasants,' Ruth enthused. 'We have a village not far from Moscow that we're going to use. Konstantin's out there now – remember him?'

'He used to work on the plays with us,' said Valerian, brightening.

'That's right. He's getting it . . . right. It wasn't very good when we got it, wouldn't do at all. Horrid, squalid, mud floors and manure heaps. There are *no* manure heaps in a communist country! Anyhow, he's making it *much* better.'

'What about the peasants?' Verochka asked, puzzled. 'You want us to go and train them to sing, or something?'

'Oh, darling!' Ruth said laughing. 'No, of course not. No, we want you to *be* the peasants. You see, they just won't *do*. I know once we've had the chance to show them, to instruct them, then they'll be fine. But have you *met* any of them? Honestly, we can't let any of our foreign visitors near them. They're very smelly, apart from anything else. They wash about once a year and can only talk about seeds and pig manure, if you can get them to talk at all. No, so that's why we need you to organise things.'

'Like a play,' Valerian said, catching on.

'That's it. We're writing a script, Konstantin, Savinkov and I. You can extemporise from it, of course, and I'll send you along some more actors. Obviously, you'll all be acting yourselves, but I want you to direct, Valerian. You, Nadia will be in charge of the choreography. These peasants are *happy*: when the day's work is done they dance for the love of liberation and freedom. They also sing. Verochka, you're in charge here. Konstantin's writing some marvellous peasant and proletarian songs and while you're in the fields sowing and reaping and things you'll be singing them. When you come home from the fields, you sing for the love of freedom.'

She smiled. 'Obviously you don't have to do this all the time. We'll give you warning of when the foreigners are coming. We'll park the tour bus a little way off, so that they can get out, and, as they walk up through the lovely, tended paths they'll gradually hear the wonderful sound of peasant voices in song, as you move gracefully about the fields, happy and contented. That was Savinkov's idea. He has a terrific sense of theatre – he has some marvellous ideas for spreading the revolution to the workers in Germany and France. We're going to wait until the wind's blowing right and release a million toy balloons, each hung with quarto handbills calling them to arms, to overthrow their exploiters. Bang. A million revolutionaries on the streets.'

'I can direct and produce the peasant drama,' Valerian said firmly. 'Leave it to me. How long do you think we'll be doing it?'

'Oh, not long at all. I mean, that's how it will be, just as soon as we can defeat the exploiters for once and for all, and actually get out into the fields ourselves, to bring communism to them. But while we're still struggling, we need this for our foreign comrades.'

'It sounds marvellous,' Verochka said. 'What about food? Do these peasants eat well?'

'Of course. Simple fare but good. You'll be expected to entertain our visitors while you tell them how good life has become, and how terrible it was, in the old days.'

'Can we eat what's left when they've gone?' asked Nadia.

'Of course! Don't worry, there'll be plenty of food. Once the revolution's won there'll be food for all, as much as anyone can eat. We'll be exporting the surplus to the poor of the world and we'll give it to them free from mighty red granaries. We'll see to it that you don't lack.'

Valerian was anxious to get his stage-setting organised.

'What about the fields? Personally, I couldn't tell one end of a plough from the other, let alone what to do with it. This village has to burst with crops. There has to be wheat waving in the wind, rows of green-topped carrots and potatoes and things. Fat cows with swaying udders, woolly sheep grazing, brightly-coloured hens pecking. Trees laden with fruit. Luscious vines.'

Ruth looked at him in admiration.

'I *told* Sergei – Savinkov – that you would be the one. Don't worry, it's a good village. Some nice orchards because a lot of the peasants invested when Stolypin was trying to make them capitalist. We've got some people who actually know about seeds and fertiliser and things, and milking cows – though you'll have to learn how to do that, yes, brimming milkchurns . . . happy milkmaids . . . They have some British tractors and steel ploughs and things the landowner imported and we're putting some nice red stars on them.'

'Um, Ruth . . .' Nadia asked nervously. 'What about children? Babies . . .'

'Oh, yes. We must have those. We're putting a clinic into the village, to show how communism has advanced, over the old order. Why, don't tell me, have you a baby, Nadia?'

She blushed. 'Yes. My sister Anna's looking after him. Petrick, he's called. He's very little.'

'But how wonderful! He's a new man, darling, a creature of the new society. But I didn't know you were married.'

'We're not,' said Valerian, simply. 'We've been . . . surviving.'

'We were trying to keep warm . . .' Nadia said, with a smile. 'One thing led . . . to another.'

A wave of contempt for the empty-headed creature swept over Ruth but she hid it with a generous smile.

'Oh, you must take him with you! You can breast-feed him in the fields while you're gathering in the harvest.'

'What about the peasants? Will we have to instruct them, too?' asked Valerian.

'Oh, no. I told you, we'll send along proper actors and actresses. We thought of it, but it's no good, they've very slow, resistant to new ideas . . .'

'Where are they?' asked Verochka, casually.

'Oh, they've gone off,' Ruth said vaguely. 'Tilling the fields somewhere. Very well. Are you in agreement? *Wonderful.*'

She took some forms and wrote on them, then stamped each one with her official seal, moistening it well on the ink pad so that the lettering stood out well. She handed them out.

'You all look like you need new clothes and some *food.* We're having your peasant clothes made up, but these forms will get you clothes to wear today, and improved rations. Take them to the *Potrebitelskoye Obshchestvo*, the Co-operative in Myasnitskaya. Come and see me tomorrow about midday and I'll make the arrangements for you to get to the village, and begin rehearsals.'

'Thank you.' They got to their feet. 'Thank you, thank you.' Ruth held up the thick pottery plate. 'Here, take these with you.'

She got up, putting her arms about them as they went to the

door. 'It's wonderful,' she said sincerely. 'We're making the future together.'

They went down the stairs and out into the square. Over at the Convent the workmen were removing a statue of its founder, the Tsar Aleksey Mikhaylovich from the plinth upon which he had stood for the past two and a half centuries, and preparing the site for the founder of Soviet Atheism. Vladmir Iliych Lenin stood, partly covered by a sheet, gripping a scroll and marching into the future, fist upraised, his raincoat furling in the wind of History.

Verochka bit a knuckle to stop herself from crying out in frustration.

'*Yob, yob, yob*,' she sobbed quietly. '*Fuck* this revolution. I'm a *countess*. For that I have to be handed biscuits and given a job as a peasant by a rotten little Bolshevik *zhid* like Ruth de Gunzberg?'

Her companions clustered about her in horror.

'Hush, Verochka,' Nadia said fearfully. 'Someone will hear you and they'll tell the Cheka. Look, have one of these nice biscuits. We'll need our strength if we're to queue up all day for clothes and some rations, and what about me? I've got to dance the *gopak* with my blouse up around my neck and little Petrick getting his lunch.'

Verochka gave a watery smile and wiped the tears away.

'At least we'll eat and be warm,' said Valerian. 'The winter's coming, remember? Now come on, let's eat our biscuits.'

'I'll be all right,' said Verochka. 'I just felt that there was more to life than hoping for a set of someone else's old clothes and a biscuit.'

'It can only get better, now.' Nadia said comfortingly and they went up the street, munching their biscuits.

In the Lubyanka they brought Fanya Kaplan out of her cell. She was all in black, black hair, black circles about her eyes. Krivitskiy was waiting for her at the end of the corridor, by the lavatory. He had hung his black leather jerkin on a peg.

She was very calm. 'Did I do it?' she asked. 'Is the monster dead?'

'No,' he said. 'We have saved him.'

'You'll be sorry,' she said.

He stuffed her head into the bowl of the toilet, and put a soft-nosed .32 bullet through it with his small Walther pistol. The two Chekists took her back down the corridor and threw her on the pile in the yard with the others.

In the lavatory Krivitskiy flushed the blood and brains away, and washed his hands with soap.

*

The big sign outside the gate still said Sadovsky Aircraft Company. As the peasant's cart came creaking through the long grass of the smooth runway, the horse paused to rip mouthfuls of food on its way, and its master let it. The runway was free.

The factory owner leaned against the wooden hangar door with his workforce, watching the slow arrival of his customer, and made a pyramid from his long, sensitive fingers.

'If the horse shits before it leaves we're level,' Piotr Sadovsky observed. Animal dung was fuel, you could burn it, and the winter was coming. 'Any bets?'

'On its way out, down in the grass where we can't find it,' said Andrey Stukalov. Lean and Jewish, with a mop of dark hair, he was responsible for the customer being there at all. Only when the world ceased to turn on its axis would there be no deals.

'I think it'll do it on the hangar floor, just to show us,' said Piotr.

Boris Fedin, squat and round faced, a miner's son from the Donbas chuckled.

'You don't know peasants,' he said. 'He'll have it trained to crap outside the gate, and *he'll* pick it up.'

Piotr turned to the fourth member of the team.

'Anna?'

'I think you're all quite vulgar,' Anna Suvurova said. She tossed her glossy black hair. 'In our house we were told never to mention the *room*, let alone what happened in there.'

Fedin laughed again. 'Where I was brought up, Miss, we didn't *have* a room. We had a pot, and carried it outside to fertilise the field in the morning.'

'Your field must have been very smelly.'

'You get used to it,' he said, philosophically.

'At last,' Piotr said, as the horse meandered off the grass on to the concrete outside the hangar.

'Bring your cart in,' he called. 'It's inside.'

The peasant grunted inarticulately from within the wild scrub of his beard, his greasy sheepskin coat wrapped around him.

They accompanied the cart inside. By the door a large brown mongrel opened one eye to look at them, then went back to sleep. The peasant peered suspiciously down at a framework of tubing supported on two rubber tyres, holding a shining, curved moldboard set behind a disc colter. He grunted. Piotr turned to Fedin.

'What's he say, Boris?'

'He says it's not strong enough, that it'll break.'

The man from the mines of the Donbas leaped up on top of the plough and jumped up and down with all his might.

'Special metal, you silly bastard!' he yelled. 'Light and strong, to make an aeroplane. You'll get rich, using this. It won't break.'

Shrewd eyes peeped out. Boris was burly, heavily set. The plough simply bounced on its pneumatic tyres. He grunted again, but this time, it seemed, in agreement. Fedin climbed down.

'He likes it,' he said. Along the hangar floor there was an assembly line of them. Where Nieuport fighter aircraft had once inched forward, advancing from frames into fully-fledged machines, now ploughs in various stages of completion stood.

From under some hay in the cart the peasant handed down some sacks.

'Potatoes, wheat, turnips,' said Piotr, stacking them. The smell of damp earth was pleasant.

A sack moved, clucked with grievance.

'Chickens.'

'Eggs,' said Anna, clutching them carefully.

'Three bottles of home-made vodka.'

'A ham.'

The parties all beamed at each other, and they helped carry the plough up on to the cart, and fix it with cord. Then the cart clopped away, making slow progress across the runway to the gate. Outside, it paused. They saw the peasant get down and scoop the deposit from the road. Boris laughed.

'I told you.'

They stood around the supplies, admiring them. Piotr glanced up at the sky; there was daylight left.

'Want to take some to your parents?' he asked. Anna nodded.

'Please.'

A little cart made from the same materials as the ploughs stood by the door. It already had some firewood stacked in it, and they loaded up some of the food.

'Trotsky! Come here, boy.'

The dog opened his eyes and obediently trotted forward to be harnessed up.

'Where are they living now, Anna?' Andrey asked.

'At our old house,' she said quietly. 'The new occupants let them stay in the old gardener's shed. But it's better than living in the city.'

'Try again to get them to move out here,' said Piotr.

'They are proud,' she said. 'They will not move from what they feel is theirs.'

She looked out over the rolling countryside, through the pines towards Moscow. The fine villas that had belonged to the rich were not far away. She reached up and buttoned the top of her workman's blue boiler suit.

'Do you want Boris to go with you?'

She shook her head. 'I'll be all right.'

It was a different world to the one they'd known: no carriages, no dancing, no fine clothes. A coarse overall, a little cart and a mongrel called Trotsky.

'Get back before it gets dark.'

'I will. Come on, Trotsky.'

Piotr watched them go down the runway, then went inside. They began to assemble another plough from the piles of materials in the store rooms.

'I was thinking, if we could get some truck tyres from somewhere, we could make some big trucks, or buses. There's a dozen brand-new water-cooled Gnome-Rhone engines in there.'

'They're six hundred horsepower. You could make armoured cars,' said Stukalov. 'I'll see what I can dig up.'

The three men worked on the ploughs. Then, in the distance, they heard the noise of a lorry. It came closer, and stopped outside. Piotr went towards the door, then halted as two men came in. They wore red stars on their peaked caps and the dark uniforms of Party commissars. They were young. One was a roundfaced peasant, the other wore steel-rimmed glasses.

'I've got a train,' the man in the glasses said flatly. He also had his badge of office in his hand, a Mauser machine pistol. Piotr suddenly recognised him as Israel Shapiro, and began desperately to try to remember what he had taken to calling himself.

'It hasn't got any armour, and it hasn't got any guns. They sent me someone to fit them. The concrete fell out and the guns don't turn. I shot him this afternoon. So you come with me and fit them.'

'Of course, Commissar,' Piotr said obsequiously. 'When would be convenient?'

'I'm late!' Krivitskiy yelled. 'If I don't pull out on Friday, *I'll* be shot. I want you on the train, you know how to fix things.'

'But we are making ploughs! Lenin is giving the peasants their land and they are buying ploughs.'

Krivitskiy raised the muzzle of the Mauser and squeezed the trigger. Nine-millimetre lead screamed off steel, whining about the hangar. He stared at Piotr with insane eyes.

'Fuck the peasants! The revolution needs a train.'

The peasant boy – a little older, in his twenties – suddenly came forward, grinning cheerfully.

'You wait outside, boss, while me and the boys get things loaded up.'

He turned Krivitskiy around, easing him out of the door. Then he was back, pushing his round and now unsmiling face into theirs.

'Listen, when the *vlast* says dance, you dance. The *vlast* says armour the train, you armour the train. Quickly now, take tools, load up that food.'

They began to scurry in and out, loading up their boxes of tools and supplies. Fedin seemed to understand the peasant commissar.

'He's from the Donbas,' he grunted to Piotr. 'He's all right.'

'What's his name?'

'Nikita Sergeyevich. Junior commissar Khrushchev.'

As they threw the sacks into the back of the Renault truck, Piotr remembered what Israel Shapiro was called.

'Commissar Krivitskiy, my fiancée will be back in a few minutes. Anna Suvurova. Can we wait for her?'

Krivitskiy stared through the flat glass of the windscreen at a future of his own devising. The smell of gun oil and propellant oozed out of the cab from the machine pistol on his lap. His nostrils flared as he inhaled it, as though it was the perfume of flowers.

'She won't be long,' Piotr said desperately. 'You remember Anna. She needs me to look after her. It is not safe.'

Krivitsky turned, he looked straight through him.

'The Revolution cannot wait.'

They drove off down the runway and on to the road. When Anna Suvurova came back with the dog trotting at her side she found the hangar empty and echoing, the door unshut . . .

4

Wider das blut

Breslay, Germany

'HAVE you ever been in prison, my dear?'
The little woman in the balloon-backed armchair cocked her
head on one side to look at her pretty young visitor, papers and a
fountain pen in her lap. Ruth sat in the visitor's chair, her feet on the
rug that helped keep the cold of the floor out.

'Only like this . . .' she ventured. It was strange, one came
expecting them to be giants, and they weren't. Lenin was small,
almost insignificant, until he began to speak, and the huge sense
of purpose, of will within him was transmitted. The woman in the
armchair was the greatest Marxist thinker of her time, and it enveloped
her; she was tiny, her face aged beyond her years, her hair white.

'You expected to see me as I was,' Rosa Luxemburg said, and
Ruth realised she could read her mind. 'Prison makes you old. I'm
a subversive, so they say, a danger to the safety of the Reich. I am a
social democrat! So I am here. You will never go to prison, for you
come from that wonderful land, Russia.'

She smiled, an enchanting smile that lit up the whole lined, tired
face, and Ruth fell in love with her.

'It's so good of you to come to see me. A real, successful
revolutionary. What a comic *change de places* February last year
was! All my good Russian revolutionary friends were let out of jail
over there, and here, in this backward place, I was kept in!'

She glanced at a posy of flowers in a vase, and bent her nose
to them.

'I'm in what they call protective custody. But it's really to break my
psychic resistance. You won't need to know, my dear, you'll never be
in jail, but you have to fight back.'

Dark, intelligent eyes like a bird's watched Ruth. 'Fight them,
because they will attack you. Watch out for the end of your
sentence. If they wish to destroy you they will extend it – at

the last moment, when you have planned your release, in detail. Be prepared.'

'She laughed merrily. 'But here I go again! Telling you things you don't need to know. We ought to be talking about the revolution. They tell me you were there, at the Winter Palace itself.'

'Yes,' Ruth agreed, eagerly. 'We stormed it – it was the last stronghold to fall.'

'It was very violent, then?'

Ruth hesitated. She couldn't bring herself to lie, to pour out childish boasts, not to this woman.

'Well, not really,' she said, and smiled sheepishly. 'Everyone expects you to say it was a great battle, but when we got over the barricade we found it wasn't manned. The biggest problem we had was finding our way in! It's a very big place.'

'I'm so glad. A revolution shouldn't involve bloodshed. When the old order is decayed, it should just fall like a rotten trunk, leaving the sunlight and air for the thrusting new growth to take its place.'

Ruth waved a hand, to indicate the world outside. 'We're ready! The old order is dying here, too, the war is being lost. That's why the International sent me, to take part.'

She was careful not to use the word communist because she knew Luxemburg insisted upon the definition of socialism. It was an old argument, an argument with Lenin that went back almost to the beginning of the century, one of the definition of revolution, and of the dictatorship of the proletariat.

'What is happening?' Luxemburg asked eagerly.

'The German summer offensive collapsed. The troops are retreating and the High Command has recommended the end of the war.'

'And who are they blaming? The *Junkers* in their uniforms who started it all?' she said, astutely. 'Who do they *blame*?'

'The talk is of a . . . *Dolchstoss.*'

'A stab in the back.' Luxemburg said quickly. 'And who is wielding the dagger?'

'Socialists, communists, liberals, pacifists . . .'

'Anyone else?'

'Jews,' Ruth said uncomfortably.

Luxemburg shrugged. 'You and I are both Jews, but we know it's not important. So many people spouting Yiddish and calling for attention for the special suffering of the Jews! What of the Negroes suffering in colonial Africa? The *pogrom* is a thing of the past, Russia has shown that. There's no anti-semitism there now, not now the people are in charge.'

'Lenin calls it the socialism of fools.'

Luxemburg smiled. 'Vladimir Ilyich has a way with words. But he's right. The bourgeoisie are responsible for the ills of the world. If a Jew is a member of that class then he is to blame, but because of *that*, not because he is a Jew. However, the *Junkers* will find it an attractive idea. The scapegoat phenomenon, so typical of modern civilisation. The Italian in Western Europe. The Jew in the East.'

'There's a book that's simply selling out in Berlin. It's called . . . *Die Sunde wider das Blut*,' Ruth said carefully.

'Sins Against the Blood,' said Luxemburg. 'What is it about?'

'It's a horrible book! About these wealthy Jewish men and this Aryan woman. They . . . do things. To her.'

Ruth blushed, and was annoyed with herself.

'But the Germans will believe it,' Luxemburg said. 'Not the workers – the others. They're so backward. *Learn from the Russians*.'

They will. Very soon.'

'They will,' agreed Luxemburg. She looked at the pink young girl in slight amusement. 'And what of you, my dear? Surely so pretty a girl is not unattached?'

The colour in Ruth's cheeks, which had been fading, came rushing back.

'Oh, I don't have time for that sort of thing. I'm a *revolutionary*.'

'But love and revolution go hand in hand!' Luxemburg laughed. 'When I was but eleven Sofja Perovska and Alexander Zheljabov, lovers to the end, were hanged side by side for assassinating the Tsar. Two years later Aleksandra Jentys and her lover, Ludwik Warynski, the founders of the first Polish workers' party, Proletariat, were incarcerated together in the terrible Tenth Pavilion in the Warsaw Citadel. I was there in the city and their very presence was a constant excitement. And Jogiches and I . . . we have struggled and loved together all these years. And now Paul and I . . .'

She looked across at Ruth and her eyes twinkled. 'You see how we revolutionaries never grow old. Love is always present!'

'Well, I'm sure I'll get around to it,' Ruth said lamely. 'When I'm not so busy.'

'What of Comrade Savinkov, with whom you have come?' the older woman said slyly.

'Oh, no! I *respect* him, of course. He's older, more experienced. He's a. . . . mentor.'

'Jogiches thought he was *my* mentor. Men like to think they are in charge, my dear, and it does us no harm to let them believe it.'

They smiled conspiratorially at each other, women together.

'A harmless untruth,' whispered Luxemburg, and they laughed. 'I'm glad the revolution was nearly bloodless,' Luxemburg said artlessly. 'The bourgeoisie just gave up.'

'Well, there are some . . .' Ruth said uncomfortably. 'Not all give in immediately. And now there's the Whites.'

'And a police, a secret police?' Luxemburg asked softly.

'The Cheka . . . yes. Against counter-revolution.'

'Of course . . .'

Behind Ruth the cell door opened, and a female warder put her head round it.

'*Herr* Savinkov is here,' she said.

'Ah. Ruth, my dear, I must have some words with him. I'll ask Anna to give you some coffee. The turnip gives it its colour, and, I am afraid, its taste, but it is at least hot. Coffee beans are rather rare at the moment. What was I going to say? Oh, yes, Soap. When you're in jail, if you can stay clean and smell nice, it is such a help in keeping your spirits up. But there I go again. Soap's lovely at any time. Listen to me, my Ruth. I shall soon be free and I am going to Berlin. I came to it to change the world twenty years ago. I anticipated history then, but now the time has come. Will you come with me?'

'Oh, yes!'

'We shall be like mother and daughter,' Rosa promised, and Ruth found tears pricking at the back of her eyes. She bent, and kissed her idol, and then ran from the cell, almost bumping into Savinkov, coming in. The wardress looked up from a small canteen along the corridor and smiled at her.

'You will want some coffee,' she said. 'The turnip gives it its colour, and – '

'Also its taste!' Ruth cried. 'I *know*.'

Rosa heard her laugh, and smiled briefly. It vanished as Savinkov eased himself into the chair Ruth had left.

'Get back to Lenin,' she said coldly. 'We need no Commissar for Bolshevism here. We have *our* revolution planned. The Bolsheviks are welcome to keep their tactics to themselves.'

'I haven't come from Lenin,' Savinkov protested. 'I'm from the International. You should be pleased to see a fellow worker.'

'Children think puppets move of their own accord,' Rosa said acidly. '*I* do not. But tell me, fellow worker, what do you want?'

'To offer what help I can, obviously. Whatever you may say, Russia is the only country where the workers have thrown off their chains, you can't let us not help. But look, let's not argue so soon. What do you think of my lovely comrade, Ruth? You are her great heroine, you know.'

'She's a lovely young girl. Fresh and unspoiled.'

'You mean naive. Why were you talking about soap?'

'Advice,' Luxemburg said evenly. 'To survive in jail.'

'Jail? Why would she go to jail? You mean if the Germans get her.'

'No. If the Bolsheviks do.'

'She *is* a Bolshevik.'

'Precisely. Do certain types of revolution not devour their own children?'

'You've got our conversation on to terror,' Savinkov said mildly. 'It's not what I came to talk about.'

'It is what needs to be talked about. But very well, what is it *you* want to talk about?'

'We're worried about your articles. The ones in *Spartacus Letters*. You're criticising us.'

'I am criticising the current Russian *leadership*. The Russian *people*, with their indomitable spirit and devotion to socialism have my greatest admiration and I make that clear.'

He shook his head. 'But the Russian Revolution faces great dangers from its enemies. To openly criticise – in print – Soviet Russia is to join forces with those enemies.'

He reached inside the leather briefcase he had brought with him, taking out a slim volume.

'Last month's,' he said. 'What title does it have? "The Russian Tragedy". When you write this kind of thing you simply support the forces of reaction. Treason to the Tsar wasn't a crime. Treason to the Party *is*. And they say you have written another article.'

'I have.'

'You have analysed the October revolution, I understand. Will you tell me what your conclusions are?'

'Yes, I will,' she said calmly. 'I am a Marxist. Marx evolved a theory of human societies which is true for all time and all place. He laid bare the scientific laws which govern the evolution of all human societies in all epochs, from the most primitive to the most advanced, from the earliest of times to the latest. His work is *scientific*. My analysis is scientific, since I follow him.'

Luxemburg glanced out of her curtained window. Some women prisoners were taking exercise in the yard.

'So,' she went on, 'where then does the Russian October revolution fit into the development of history towards the more advanced, more democratic society postulated by Marx? First let it be said that the Revolution was the most significant development of this World War, leading as it will to the overthrow of Capitalism in all the developed countries of the world. Furthermore, the party of Lenin, the Bolsheviks, were the sole party in Russia that grasped the true interests of the revolution in that first period. However, I believe the methods used by Lenin and by Trotsky, which involve the complete elimination of democracy, to be catastrophic.

'Let us take what they have done, Savinkov, what they propose to do. With the overthrow of the landlords the distribution of their land will create a powerful mass of new property owners who will become potential foes of the Revolution.'

'The peasants are a problem that will have to be organised after the civil war is won,' said Savinkov, dismissively.

'How?' she said quickly. 'By historical forces, or by Lenin's forces? Brutality and terror?'

'Terror has been applied to the enemy of the proletariat, the bourgeoisie. You cannot believe that communists would do it to their own kind. That *would* stand Marxism on its head.'

Belief and fear struggled briefly on her face.

'Let us move on then. Lenin's dissolution of the Constituent Assembly has deprived the masses of their most fundamental democratic institution. The abolition of universal suffrage and the destruction of the most important democratic guarantees – the freedom of the press and the right of association and assembly – have prevented the development of a healthy public life.

Socialism, by its very nature, cannot be introduced by command . . . Lenin is completely mistaken in the means he employs: decree, the dictatorial power of a factory overseer, draconian penalties, rule by terror. . . . Without general elections, without unrestricted freedom of the press and assembly, without a free exchange of opinions, life dies out in every public institution and only bureaucracy remains active . . . Slowly, public life falls asleep, and a few dozen party leaders command and rule. In reality, power is exercised by a dozen outstanding minds, while the elite of the working class are now and then invited to meetings to applaud the speeches of the leaders and to approve unanimously approved resolutions. In fact, then, it is a clique – certainly a dictatorship. It is *not* the dictatorship of the proletariat, however, but that of a handful of politicians.'

The papers in her lap crackled as she gripped them, and the pen slid on to the rug. Savinkov bent forward to pick it up.

'I know you're busy,' he said, considerately. 'Can you see why I urge you not to publish your article? The revolution is fighting for its life. In such times, with such enemies, to criticise the world's first proletarian democracy at all is to ally yourself with those enemies. When the battle is won, all your worries will be for naught.'

'Is that the only reason you have come?' she asked. 'To dissuade me from criticism? Or have you brought other messages from your master?'

'The revolution will come here. Very soon. You cannot dissociate us from it. To push us away is to be an enemy. You must let us take part . . .'

'Tell that to the social revolutionaries, to the social democrats. Where are they? Where are those who were elected to the Constituent Assembly? Has Lenin got them locked up, or are they dead?'

Savinkov got up and paused by the door. 'Solidarity, Rosa,' he said softly. 'We have to maintain solidarity.'

5

Grazhdanskaya Voyna

Perm

IT was a quarter of a mile long and contained a printing press, a library, a tailor's shop, a kitchen, an armoury and four hundred soldiers. It consumed several trees a day and it had been made in 1903 and was surrounded by two inches of armour plate and a foot of concrete put on in 1918. It rolled down out of the Ural mountains towards the hidden town as silently as it was possible for such a monster to do.

Mikhail was in the bridge of the dreadnought. The trees still held their autumn leaves. The town was close, for as his great train rumbled down the track they passed a siding where dead locomotives lay, rusting pipes trailing from their guts, cannibalised to keep fitter engines running. The factories that had made the parts weren't working any more. The siding was a graveyard of Tsarist rolling stock. Russet leaves drifted about the rust red rails.

The line they were on showed signs of maintenance for the sun's light brought out a sheen on the rails. Ahead of Mikhail were two armoured carriages, sprouting round casemates like carbuncles. From each protruded the barrel of a military field gun. At the controls of the locomotive was the designer of the train. Piotr Sadovsky. There two stokers kept the boiler supplied with fuel. From Mikhail's post he communicated to the driver and gunners by means of voice pipes snaking away through the floor.

They rolled around the last curve and the town lay before them. He stuffed his pointed cloth hat with its red star into his pocket and put on his old one from the Guards, resplendent in red and gold, which had been made for him by Obolenskii's on Nevsky Prospekt. Beside him Krivitskiy's mouth tightened in disapproval.

'It's lucky, Commissar,' Mikhail murmured. 'Even revolutionaries need luck.'

'No,' said Krivitskiy. 'They only need to believe.'

Their scout had been correct, the White train lay in the station, and smoke drifting from the locomotive showed that steam was up. In the vastnesses of Russia, fighting trains had the power of armies, but the style of warfare was naval. Like a battleship or cruiser, they had the power to subjugate enemy ports.

Mikhail uncorked a tube. In front, the casemates were turning as the gunners brought their weapons to bear.

'Bring her to a stop,' he ordered, and the brakes squealed on the track as Sadovsky twirled his controls. The whirring of the hand cranks inside the gun turrets ceased and the barrels were steady.

The corks dangled on their cords.

'Open fire!' Mikhail shouted. 'Open fire.'

The six guns exploded in a volley. As the smoke cleared in the breeze they could see fires burning in the town where the shells had landed. The turrets echoed to the clang and clatter of ejecting shell cases and Mikhail and Krivitskiy scanned the town through binoculars.

'Here they come,' Mikhail murmured. 'Like a nest of ants.'

He bent over his tubes.

'One more at their backs,' he called, and, on the train, the guns traversed once more.

'*Fire!*'

Down in the station men were pouring on to the train. As the shells arrived they redoubled their efforts. Smoke poured from the high funnel and a field gun puffed. The shell howled over their heads and the White train came out of the station into combat.

'*Retreat!*'

The driver had been waiting for his order; the wheels jerked on the rail and they began to move back up the mountain. They escaped around the curve and shells exploded in the trees about them. Earth and branches showered the train. Mikhail hung out of the side of the bridge. A figure in uniform was waiting by the track, the points lever pulled hard over. It was Yelena. As the armoured train swung into the siding of wrecks Mikhail looked down, and she up. They grinned as they passed.

Their train came to a halt among the rusting locomotives, one of many. Swinging back, Mikhail saw Yelena running along the track. Another set of points was there. She crouched down by them as the White train approached and heaved the lever over. With a rumbling rattle, travelling at speed, the train was forced up the spur. Mikhail sat head-on as his enemy was made to expose its full flank.

Yelena was running for the safety of the ditch.

'It's called crossing the T, Commissar,' Mikhail said happily.

'Open fire!'

Yelena tripped, in the line of fire.

'Nelson did it. You know, the British admiral,' Mikhail said calmly.

'*Fire!*'

She was up, scrambling. Krivitskiiy rammed the barrel of his pistol into Mikhail's neck.

'Open fire!' he screamed.

She vanished, like a rabbit down a hole.

'Lead the target, and *open fire*!, Mikhail called.

The guns fired as one, and the train bent at its joints, blown from the rails. A great cloud of steam hid the wreck from sight momentarily. Then, as the noise of its explosion reached them, they could see it on its side in the trees. The soldiers hidden by the track opened fire while others, frantically-waving white vests and handkerchiefs, sprouted from the wreckage. The firing ceased, and men began to stumble and limp, hands high, from the destroyed carriages. At their backs smoke from the spilled coals wandered through the trees. The victors began herding them together. Yelena appeared from her hole and reset the points.

'Do that again and I'll have you shot,' Krivitskiy said grimly to Mikhail.

'But then what good would I be to you, Commissar?' Mikhail drawled, annoyingly. 'Lenin and Trotsky know you cannot win without such as we. This is *grazhdanskaya voyna*, a civil war. Be nice to me. Here is one more town for you, won for the glorious proletarian Red Army.'

Ahead a man in sweaty shirt and breeches had emerged from his turret and was peering out at the arriving, defeated troops.

'Good shooting, Boris,' Mikhail called. 'We'll make a pheasant-plugger of you yet.'

Krivitskiy grunted in annoyance as Sadovsky's assistant Boris Fedin smiled in pleasure and Mikhail turned to him.

'I know, I know,' he said. 'In the glorious new age no one will shoot pheasants. I know.'

Yelena had joined the men herding the White soldiers. They bore a collection of weapons, Nagants and Lee-Enfields, Brownings and Colts. She was unarmed.

'Hurrah for the Railway King!' she shouted, and they cheered. Mikhail took off his Guards' hat and waved it, grinning in acknowledgement. Krivitskiy got down from the train and walked over to Yelena.

'I'm going into town to take over.'

He cast his eyes over the Whites. There were about sixty of them, dazed, shocked, the uninjured supporting the wounded.

'Usual conditions,' he said. 'Those who are willing to change sides can join. You're in charge. Shoot the rest.'

She stared at him levelly.

'I already did,' she said calmly. 'They're all Bolsheviks now.'

'Just like you,' he said, caustically.

'Just like me.'

She infuriated him, she always had. At school he had desired her, and said nothing, for such as he were not for such as her. And here she was, in a war, still calm, still elegant. He knew she was thinking of him as Vladimir Shapiro, the Jew, and it infuriated him. A desire to maim her overwhelmed him.

'Then shoot every tenth man!' he snapped. 'Yourself. Decimate them. Choose them yourself. *Yourself.*'

'It's a waste of troops,' she protested.

'Trotsky's own orders,' he countered triumphantly. 'The survivors know they have to fight to the death.'

She turned. 'Leon, Alexei, Pasha – form them up in a line.'

As the rest of the troops climbed aboard the train, the three young men lined the Whites up. Krivitskiy climbed up into the bridge. The whistle blew through the trees and the train moved, rolling down the hill into town, taking its new king with it. He looked back and saw Yelena moving along the line, pulling out every tenth man. He felt a vicious satisfaction, to know that she had become like him.

Six young men stood ahead of the line. In a different age, they would have come to tea, bought her posies of violets from the flowergirl's stall at the ball, their names filling out her finely-printed card of dances.

'Tie their hands,' she ordered, and Pasha moved behind each, securing their wrists with cord.

'I'm going to take them over by the others,' she said. 'It will all smell bad enough in a few days, and we have to come by this line. March the others into town and give them uniforms, treat their wounds.'

'Don't you want some help?' Alexei asked.

'The Commissar has ordered me to do it myself, and so I shall do it myself,' she said steadily. 'Take the others into town as I say.'

Alexei had grown up on an estate where the mistress of the house talked like Yelena; he moved.

'Let's go!' he shouted. 'Move along.'

The column shuffled off along the line and Yelena addressed the six.

'Over there,' she said, and indicated the wreck with her gun. They began to move.

As Alexei went around the bend he saw the six young Whites kneel down in a row.

Yelena stood behind the first. He felt something cold on his wrists, then the easing of his bond. The cords fell away.

'Go to the wreck,' a steady voice said at his ear. 'Fetch me six of your fellows that are dead. Put them in a row.'

The young man scrambled to his feet and hurried into the destruction. He emerged, dragging a body.

'You can get up,' Yelena said to the others. She moved along the line, cutting the rope.

'Get some cord,' she ordered. 'Tie the hands of these poor bastards.'

The corpses were set out in a line.

'Thank you!' they chorused, clustering about her, looking at her like men who had seen the presence of angels.

'You'd better get away from here,' she said. 'Buy me some flowers when this is all over, when we dance the *mazurkha* again.'

They slipped away through the trees, going away from the town, picking up weapons and what food they could find in the wreck as they went. Yelena watched them go, standing by the dead men, her Mauser in her hand.

As Krivitskiy dismounted from the train at the station, he heard, in the distance, six measured shots from the hillside, and he laughed . . .

It was getting dark by the time Yelena trudged down the track into town. The great armoured locomotive stood at the station. Piotr Sadovsky was at its side, tending some shining part. Wisps of steam drifted about him. He looked up as she came along the line.

'I knew one of those boys,' he said quietly. 'Nikolay Feodorovich. His papa bought one of my papa's aircraft; we used to play together.'

'Krivitskiy about?' she asked, coming close.

'The miserable bastard's gone into town.'

'Then you still know Nikolay Feodorovich. I shot six corpses up there,' she said softly, triumphantly, and he grinned savagely.

'Where's Mikhail?' she asked.

'In town. He went in with Krivitskiy. They were having an argument, Yelena.'

She frowned with worry, and hurried from the station. She found them in the best building, the old Duma Hall, yellow-painted in the square. Mikhail had found a bottle of wine and sipped some from a crystal glass with his polished, hand-made boots up on a table to annoy Krivitskiy. She stopped appalled in the doorway. He was aristocratic, superior, infuriating.

'You leave the fighting to me, Commissar,' he drawled. 'And you get on with making your new world.'

She was alarmed. This seemed to be a second round of whatever contest was in place. Soldiers were standing about the walls listening and Krivitskiy's Chekists stood behind him in their black jackets, holding their Mauser pistols. The deputy commissar, Khrushchev, was there, too.

'You take orders from me,' Krivitskiy said coldly. 'The Party rules.'

'The Party will get our arses shot off,' Mikhail said and grinned. The soldiers laughed. He held up his medal between finger and thumb.

'The Cross of St George, Commissar. Stick with me and you'll be safe.'

'A Tsarist order,' Krivitskiy said dangerously. 'Remove it.'

Mikhail looked at his award. 'I don't think so,' he said. 'The Tsar was as good a judge of courage as Lenin. Better, I'd say. He actually went up to the front. Now, you see, your sort, you and your Trotskys, you don't find you in the thick of it. Just behind, shooting brave men.'

Krivitskiy's eyes glittered with rage behind his glasses.

'Me and Trotsky? Why don't you say it? Jews. *Zhids*, that's what you want to say, isn't it?'

'I couldn't care less if you're an Armenian negro,' Mikhail said indifferently. 'I just don't want you getting us all killed with your Party notions of how to fight a battle.'

Krivitskiy sprang forward in fury and hit him in the face. Mikhail fell backwards and, picking himself up, flattened his opponent with one giant kick of his boot. The Cheka guns came up and, from the floor, Krivitskiy wiped blood from his mouth.

'Seize him!' he shouted. They grabbed him, and tied his hands.

'You'll be shot in the morning,' Krivitskiy said savagely. Yelena opened her mouth to protest, then she saw that he had seen her and remained quiet.

'The Party is sacred,' Krivitskiy stated quietly in the still room. He wiped the imprint of Mikhail's boot from his jacket. 'Those who would damage her must suffer.'

He took two rifles from the soldiers and gave them to a pair of his Chekists.

'Smash his feet,' he ordered.

Boris Fedin was there, standing near Khrushchev. He stepped forward. 'Look, boss, don't we need him? He knows how to fight.'

His eyes glittering behind his spectacles, Krivitskiy took back one of the rifles and thrust it at Fedin.

'*You* smash his feet,' he whispered, his face deadly. As Fedin hesitated, Khrushchev shoved him forward.

'Do it!'

Down at the station Yelena found Piotr Sadovsky in the cab of the locomotive, lying in a sack he had made out of greatcoats, sewn together. It was warm in there, near to the great boiler. He was eating some bread and cheese as she climbed up out of the dark and poked her head in. Inside it smelled of goat's cheese and burning wood.

'Can it go?' she asked.

'Someone came by, said Krivitskiy was shooting Mikhail in the morning,' he said, looking up at the metal roof.

'Can it go?' she repeated.

'If I give it more fuel.'

'Then do. And undo the carriages.'

Piotr sat up and pulled himself out of his bag. 'I never liked that *nedoyobysh* Krivitskiy,' he said. 'Not even when we were at school.'

She threw up a sack. 'There's food in there,' she said.

She went back into the town through the dark. A light was shining in the Duma Hall and she peeped through the window. A single guard was dozing at a desk. She slipped inside and, as he looked up sleepily, she pointed a revolver in his face.

'Count Mikhail,' she said clearly, quietly. The man got up and led the way to an office. In the light that streamed through the door she could see Mikhail, his hands tied, lashed to a radiator. His boots were bloody and torn and sweat streamed down his face. He was semi-conscious.

'Undo him,' she ordered.

She gagged the guard and tied him to the radiator, then began to drag Mikhail out, with her hands under his shoulders. He was heavy, and as they bumped down the steps, he cried out in agony.

'Who's that?'

A match scraped on a boot and she saw Akulov looking at her.

'Where are you going, Mistress?' he asked steadily.

'I was taking Count Mikhail to the station,' she said wearily. 'In order that Krivitskiy might not shoot him in the morning.'

The match waved sharply and went out. She felt his huge hands lift Mikhail from her.

'*Graf* Mikhail is too good a soldier to be shot like a dog,' he said.

Sadovsky was in the cab. Akulov lifted Mikhail up and looked about him.

'Is steam up? Then take it to Segezha,' said Akulov. 'You'll be safe there. Have a driver bring it back.'

'I'll bring it back myself,' said Piotr. 'Krivitskiy can't have *me* shot – nobody else knows how to make the train work.'

Akulov vanished into the darkness. Sadovsky twirled a shiny wheel, steam gushed through the pipes and the train moved out of the station.

Berlin, November 1918

Ruth sat forward in her seat, entranced, oblivious to the smoke of the charcoal fumes blowing in from the back of the stuttering Opel cab. Petrol was a forgotten commodity, along with coffee, cigarettes and beer. Savinkov had taken the trouble to obtain supplies before they had left, exerting the power of his low-number Party card, so now he sat back in his seat and chewed on the tinned breast of a chicken, washing it down with a bottle of real beer.

'I don't know how you can guzzle at a time like this,' she said, her pink lips pursed in disapproval.

'The wise revolutionary eats when he can,' he said. 'You never know where your next meal is coming from. Keep an eye out for Manfred.'

'Poppycock! The revolution is *here*, Sergei. In just a day or two the streets will be overflowing with food and drink, free for all. Just look around you!'

The cab pushed its way along the wide thoroughfare of the Chausseestrasse, packed with boisterous, excited crowds. From the buildings, red flags were flying, snapping in the breeze. Ruth bounced on the seat with delight and Savinkov sat back, admiring her breasts.

'It's happening just the way it did in Russia,' she crowed happily. '*Exactly* the same. Their Emperor has gone, just the same as ours.

No more Wilhelm II, no more Tsar Nicholas. The sailors have rebelled against their masters. For us, Kronstadt, for the Germans, Kiel. Democratic workers' movements have sprung up everywhere. Soviets for us, republics for them. Sailors have taken over the Reichstag, just like Pavel and his comrades took the Winter Palace. The revolution is happening, Sergei. First Russia, and now Germany. Next the world! Oh, I just hope the trains run fast enough for me to keep up with it.'

Her small hands beat a tattoo of excitement on her knees. Her face was prettily flushed, and her eyes sparkled. Not for the first time, Savinkov wondered what she looked like without any clothes on.

'There couldn't be a better time to be alive,' he agreed.

'See how the laws of Marx are cast in steel,' Ruth said. 'When history decrees that the old order shall fall to the new, it happens in exactly the same fashion. Scientifically, as he ordained.'

The young could be extraordinarily pompous, thought Savinkov.

'Why do we have to have Manfred Liss?' she asked, suddenly discontented. 'The revolution is *pure*. People like him just *sully* things.'

Savinkov laughed. 'So he's a bugger. But he's a German, he knows his way about here. And, let me tell you, when it gets down to hand-to-hand, you need everyone you can.'

'There won't be any *fighting*. Don't be silly.'

'There he is. We're here,' he said, and opened the door. The cab had stopped outside a small lane off the street, and Manfred Liss stood there, waving. He had discarded his soldier's jacket in favour of a long black leather coat, under which were knee-length boots and black riding breeches. His shock of curly hair was stuffed under a peaked leather cap. Savinkov paid the driver. Ruth had ignored Liss and was staring at a large poster, that bore a skull with a bloody knife between its teeth and a gallows in the background.

'The Danger Of Bolshevism!' howled the headline. 'German Women! Do you know what Bolshevism and Spartacism threaten? Women will become the property of the people. Any man who wants to use that communal property needs a permit from the Workers' Committee . . .'

It was signed by the Union to Combat Bolshevism.

'That's disgusting,' Ruth called to Savinkov. 'How can they believe that? We'll soon have that kind of filth off the walls.'

Liss took her elbow, steering her towards the lane. Passers-by had stopped to look at the angry young woman with her strange voice.

'Not so loud,' he murmured.

'What do you mean? The workers are in charge now.'

'*Juden*,' a voice said derisively, and someone spat. Liss and Savinkov took her along the lane. A handwritten sign on a door identified it as the editorial offices of *The Red Flag*.

'Hullo, Manfred,' said Savinkov. 'Listen, Ruth, we're going to find out what's happening on the ground. I'll pick you up later.'

She went through the door and up some dusty, worn, wooden stairs. In a small room a small figure sat at a table, a pen in her hand. She looked up as she heard the light, quick footsteps. It was Rosa, and she beamed in delight.

'Ruth!' she cried, and came limping across the bare floor to embrace her.

'I've come to help,' Ruth said simply.

'Oh, that's wonderful! You've come at just the right time, we get so busy with everyone later.'

She seized a few pages of folded type from the table. A splash of red blazed from the head.

'We've done it,' she said proudly. 'The only socialist paper in Berlin. Getting the printer was the thing. I must have been to *dozens*. I began to think the only red flag I could get would be the one flying on my grave, but we got one in the end. I spend most of my time here, and go and sleep for a few hours in whatever hotel I can get to put me up for the night. I feel like one of Moses' Israelites, trailing about the desert!'

'Lenin himself had to hide here, there, and everywhere before the revolution came,' Ruth said comfortingly. 'He even shaved off his beard.'

'He probably looked the better for it,' Rosa said briskly.

She looked up at the taller, younger woman. 'Will you write?' she asked. 'I need a good Marxist writer. I've asked Franz Mehring for critical comments – he's a veteran socialist here – and Clara Zeitkin's going to contribute. The shortage of paper's a terrible problem, so we all have to be as concise as we can. But good writing! Life and passion! The workers thirst to be educated! When the paper shortage eases I want supplements – for women, for the soldiers, for the children. But, for the moment, we have to mobilise everyone's energies to continue the work that has just begun.'

She held Ruth's arms, just below her elbows, and squeezed them affectionately.

'Oh, I look at you and you remind me of myself when I was young! So full of idealism, of love for the people. I saw you come in and I knew you thought the revolution was already won. It's started, Ruth,

but we can't rejoice or triumph yet. Our accomplishments are meagre
and here we struggle in one room, the only socialist paper in Berlin.
Are you surprised? A reactionary country like this cannot turn into a
revolutionary republic overnight. And it has been at war, its soldiers
have been killing their brothers from other countries. Will you write
an article for me? We must blend idealism with pragmatism. Since I
am old I shall provide the pragmatism. You are as filled with idealism
as a flower with light and scent. We shall marry the two.'

'I could never be more idealistic than you, Rosa,' Ruth said simply.
'But give me some paper, for I have a pen.'

All through the day she sat on a chair in the corner, chewing on the
cap of her pen like a schoolgirl, sometimes calling out to Rosa, trying
out the phrases in her mind, fitting them together into a coherent
whole. Visitors came and went; Clara Zeitkin brought an article; Paul
Levi came and they talked quietly by the window, kissing before he
left. Slowly, the words went down on her pad, fighting for the soul
of the German workers.

The creation of a revolution was a formidable task. Not to be
achieved with a few decrees from above, but by the conscious
action of the workers. Free will, and spiritual maturity, not orders
and force, would bring about social change. That was the idealism.
Practical, too. They demanded that a world congress of workers
be convened promptly in Germany – what was wrong with that?
Did it matter where the spirit burned? A proletarian Red Guard
and workers' militia, stern and incorruptible, had to be formed, to
guard the revolution. Dynastic wealth and landed property should be
expropriated immediately to put an end to hunger – here she washed
down a dry crust of black bread with turnip coffee, and wished, not
without humour, that it could happen soon. Fresh elections should
be held for new local Workers' and Soldiers' Councils, to replace the
ones that had sprung up in the first chaotic days.

In the early evening, Savinkov came in with Manfred. Ruth was
tired, Rosa almost exhausted, but both were happy.

'The new issue can go to the printer,' Rosa said proudly. 'We have
it done.'

Savinkov read Ruth's article. 'It's good,' he said, and passed it to
Manfred. 'You turn a nice phrase. But are you sure they'll read it?'

'Of course they will!' Ruth said hotly. 'Under capitalism, human
labour – essentially creative – becomes an ordeal and a burden for
it is used to satisfy artificially generated needs. We are offering a
socialist society, in which the workers will work with joy, for they
will recover their creativity.'

Rosa smiled through her weariness, hearing the fire in Ruth's voice.

'I, too, read Marx,' Savinkov said. 'But sometime we all underestimate the power of a plate of hot food and a stein of lager to the weary workman.'

Manfred put the article back on the table. 'Or things like property, nationalism, religion,' he said quietly.

'Bourgeois baubles!' Rosa snapped.

'You're a cosmpolitan. Do you know what the day-to-day existence of the worker is like? And you've missed something out. Two things, in fact.'

'What?'

'Someone to blame. The *volk* have been beaten. My *volk*, you understand? The German people. They have been told for generations that their armies were unconquerable. In this war the people did not experience gunfire, trenches or battlefields. They were told that victory was certain. Suddenly, they have been defeated. *Someone must be to blame.*'

He looked at the two women. 'Do you know who they say is to blame?'

'Me,' said Rosa wearily. 'And others like me.'

'Right. Bolsheviks and Jews. Bolsheviks who *are* Jews.'

'I am not a Bolshevik! The Socialists are not Bolshevik. The Spartacists are not Bolshevik.'

'They are all on the left. And have Jews aplenty at their head. And is Trotsky not a Jew named Bronstein? Yes, he is. So Lenin becomes Issachar Zederblum, also a Jew.'

'How can they say these lies?' Ruth demanded angrily.

'They are engaged for the battle for men's souls, just as you are,' said Savinkov. 'But listen. They do not have mere words. The Chancellor has a direct telephone line to the chief of staff, Groener. They talk each day. They are moving up ten divisions of troops.'

'Kerensky talked each day too,' Ruth said impatiently. 'Much good it did him, the great persuader. He had to run away dressed up as a woman. No troops followed *him*. The troops will come over to *us*, to the workers.'

'*Will* they, though? Noske isn't using regulars anyway. He has a new force of ex-officers and *frontkampfers*. Stormtroopers. A Volunteer Corps, a *Freikorps*. They have no badges of rank, they elect their own officers. They hate leftists, whom, they say, caused their defeat. They hate Jews.'

'We have history on our side,' Rosa said certainly, and Ruth felt comforted. 'We are socialists. Ruth tells me in the Winter Palace the rifles were lying about in piles. When proletariat and soldiers unite, these fanatics will vanish as snow in springtime.'

'I'm staying with Rosa, at her hotel,' said Ruth.

'I said that you had missed two things,' Manfred said, from his corner. He picked up Ruth's article, and then dropped it again. 'Lovely words. But you talk about the workers, the international proletariat. The workers don't give a stuff about the international proletariat.'

'*How can you say that?*' Ruth shouted furiously. 'That's not what you said in Petrograd.'

'That was there. It is the party line. This is here. I tell you, the workers are German first and last. We have just fought a great war to prove it. German workers thrust their bayonets into the guts of British workers, and got shot by French workers. If we want power here we had better remember that.'

Petrograd

The pale, grey blue Volga had frozen into bluish white ice not unlike the colour of what was called milk, if it was available, and if people were registered to get it. It normally was not, even if they were, along with most other forms of sustenance. The lack of calories produced a strange flowering among the artistic folk of the city. Schools of literature sprouted, with the Communist Futurists battling the Prolekults, the Fuists the *Nitchevoki*. On the boulevards, in unlit rooms called clubs and cafés where frost gleamed on the walls, on icy factory floors and freezing railway platforms, poets stood up and howled, in the manner of the day, creative verse. And the people stood about and listened to them. It took their minds off the pain of their hunger.

The hunger was very bad. People attempted to ignore it by clinging to the ritual of better times. Those of the bourgeoisie still in possession of their goods and property dressed and sat down for dinner, eating with good cutlery from fine china. They found that if it was possible to heat the thin millet gruel or thin potato soup very hot it gave the illusion of eating a meal. The professors at the university made their way to the faculties' dining room every day from their homes at various places in the city, carrying their soup dishes and spoons with them, like the beggars at the church door in olden times. One of the scientists there calculated, while waiting in line, that they had all expended more energy in travel and wait than they received in calories and vitamins from the food. However, they all agreed that the words 'dinner', and 'I have dined' had a pleasant sound, and gave a sort of impression that they were still getting something to eat, so they continued to do it, politely taking their leave of each other with the words, 'Goodbye, I hope you will be alive tomorrow'.

As the weeks of hard winter passed, fewer and fewer were. The professors had little to sell apart from their intellect, which could not command a high price in the black markets. Those with goods, or youthful looks, fared somewhat better, although the law of supply and demand bred a new law of mathematics that decreed that prices would rise faster than the ability to pay.

The mere rumour that the corpses of horses, dead themselves from starvation, had arrived at the food distribution centres, was enough to produce a mile long queue at the desk that issued passes entitling those registered to do so to move on to the queue for the ration of rotten horsemeat. Supplies were short, so those in charge – the radish communists, red on the outside, but white and corrupt within – invented new rules to take up people's time, so that they would simply give up. No one had to be in the know, to spot a radish. They could quote Marx, and their good warm clothes fitted them snugly.

They kept a look out, those who were in the know, for the rare trains that came puffing and grunting up from the south bringing food. Several of them spotted the one coming up through Detskoye Selo; they saw the three long freight cars marked: FRESH MEAT, DESTINATION PETROGRAD and, by the time it clanked into the Baltic station, a mob had gathered.

Rykov saw them, on his way to the Smolny. He stood in the great hallway as the mammoth's howl of wind blew the snow in from outside, and the train's wheels cut twin black lines through its carpet between the platforms. Strange, capering, desperate people in flapping clothes attacked the doors. There was a short, abruptly-ended shriek as someone fell under the still-moving wheels. Crowbars flailed, hammers clanged against the latches. With a savage roar of success the doors rolled back.

Rykov noted the howl that went up. Horror should have been there. But it wasn't. Despair was on the faces of those straggling away through the flying white snowflakes. Resentment at the expenditure of so much precious, husbanded energy for nothing.

Rykov went closer, his strong boots crunching the snow underfoot.

The freight cars were stuffed with corpses. Naked men, wearing only caps with the star on, Red Guards, frozen solid. They had been placed in obscene positions by those who had killed them, on whatever battlefield of the war that had claimed them, and sent home, marked FRESH MEAT.

Rykov glanced at his watch, and retraced his steps. He did not want to be late. Dzerzhinskiy worked eighteen hours a day for seven days each week; if a man was late when he called a meeting, it was because his revolutionary ardour was cooling. Rykov vanished into the snow, moving smartly.

He was there, on time, in his chair with all the other Chekists when Dzerzhinskiy entered the lecture hall and took the rostrum. He was even thinner than before, his features sharpened by age and the power of life and death over others.

'The war against the Whites is almost won,' he said, and the features of all listening stiffened into attentive immobility. If it was necessary to show respectful belief while a purveyor of *pokazukha* was indulging in *vranyo*, how much more important when he was not just feeding you bullshit, but lies.

However, all listened attentively, for if indeed it was *lozh* that the war was not yet won, their attention had been gained, they would now be told *why*.

'In our Red Army we have created discipline,' said Dzerzhinskiy. 'Discipline that is winning the war. As we now turn to the reconstruction of society we, the Cheka must become the weapon for creating the sort of discipline that we have been able to establish in the Red Army in society as a whole. Our leaders are drawing up the unified economic plan. First and foremost will come the improvement of transportation, shipment and storage of essential grain reserves, fuel, raw materials. The economic reconstruction of Russia will proceed by firm and logical steps. Production of machines for transportation and for the production of fuel, raw materials and grain; intensified development and production of machines to produce consumer goods; intensified production of consumer goods themselves. Modern schools, hospitals and housing must be constructed. The realisation of this plan will be made possible not by means of the separate, one-time heroic efforts of the advanced elements of the working class, but by dogged, systematic and well-planned labour that draws into its sphere ever increasing numbers of the toiling masses.'

The spectacle of the horde of staggering, skeletal figures in the station, all wrapped in rags, suddenly went through Rykov's mind.

'But comrades,' the thin man above them said softly, 'things should already be better than they are. You and I, we are on the streets every day, we know that things are not working as they should. Why? Clearly, having lost the military battle, our enemies are turning to another form of combat, and our own struggle against them must change. Our enemies are trying to worm their way into our Soviet institutions, so that once they have infiltrated our ranks they can sabotage our work. It is our task to catch them. We, the organs of the Cheka, must become an instrument for realising the centralised will of the proletariat.

'Search in government offices, trades unions, factories. Along the frontiers, waterways and railroads. Within cities, villages and party offices. The White Guardists, saboteurs and shirkers are there. *Find* them! It is in a man's nature to do evil. Ask him who his parents and grandparents were, how they were employed. Where and how did they live? Who did they entertain? What did they say? These things are important. Always search for undiscovered crimes. Never confront him with material evidence convicting him of guilt at the beginning of an interrogation. It is important to ascertain first other participants in the case, and the possibility – the certainty – of other, as yet undisclosed crimes.'

The head of the secret police glanced at his watch. His time was up.

'Always remember,' he instructed, to finish, as he always did, 'a good Chekist has a cool head, a warm heart and clean hands.'

His men stared back at him with impassive faces.

The snow had stopped by the time Rykov walked back through the streets to his office. He walked, like everyone else, in the road. There was no danger of being hit by anything larger than one of the little sledges people had made to pull firewood, paraffin or millet or a bag of frozen apples, black potatoes.

In Narvskaya Place he saw someone he had never met coming round a snowdrift. He knew who she was, because he had seen her photograph. He owned it. He had it up on the mantelpiece of his apartment on Lesnoy Prospekt, where he lived alone. Often in the evenings he would take it down and look at it, and the fresh young faces would look back at him from the celluloid. Hers was in the front row; she had been wearing a pretty summer dress, long, with a round straw hat.

He had found it the day he had gone to the big apartment building in Nevsky Prospekt. They were still there, the old couple, living in one room. While his lads had taken them down to the waiting black Maria, he had had a look through the place. He'd found it on the mantelpiece, its ivory card surround slightly grubby, as though it had been gently handled, many times. It bore the coat-of-arms of the Empress's School, in Tsarskoye Selo.

He had expected the daughter, Ruth, to be there, once he had realised what it was, a class photograph. And the sight of the woman who had been his employer filled him again with a desire to beat her, to crush her nipples, hit her between her thighs. Yelena stared out from the picture, slightly angry, her grey eyes cold.

The chaos of the approaching revolution had communicated itself to the photograph. An unknown Kronstadt sailor stood to one side, almost out of picture, rifle over shoulder, cigarette in mouth, apparently in conversation with an older man. Rykov recognised Savinkov – he had seen him with Lenin. The artist, or poet Konstantin was there with them, his worker's cap pushed back on his head, a scarf, presumably red, tied in a big knot about his neck. The daughter, Ruth, wore one too, looking out with excited eyes. Next to who? What was Krivitskiy doing there?

He had taken the photograph and rested it above his mantelpiece. He took it down, from time to time, to look at it. It drew him, like a drug. He could not explain its fascination, not even to himself. He felt, somehow, that he should have been there in it. Sometime he dreamed, while he was asleep, of being there, among the strange, privileged young people who were just his age. Then he awoke, and when he looked at the photograph it was always just the same.

She came round the snowdrift. She liked clothes, he knew that from looking at her in the photograph. There she had worn one of her best dresses, a light, striped fabric, tightly-waisted in the fashion of the times, high necked but showing off her figure. Her straw hat had had a gaily-coloured ribbon about it.

It was not easy to dress well, that winter, but she had done her best. A soldier's greatcoat had been cut into a ladies' garment and on her head she wore a smart green hat, made from the baize of a billiard table. She carried a carpet bag, a piece of Tsarist luggage. In a city where people wore dresses made from loose-covers and curtains, and coats made from carpets, she did not look out of place.

He wondered what her name was. The photograph bore only the coat-of-arms of the school. The young people looked out of its frame, anonymous.

She crossed the square, going under the trees where icicles grew as winter leaves, and he followed her. She was a lady, he could tell that, carefully picking her way through the piles of refuse that littered the streets. The city cleaning services had not worked since October 1917 and Rykov had made a mental note to have himself transferred by the time the thaw came. Frozen rubbish, broken pipes of frozen ordure did not smell, would not produce disease. In the spring it would be different, people would smell Petrograd fifty miles downwind.

She was making for Sadovaya, where the black market operated. Unless you were a Party member, you could not live, even if registered with the Commissariat of Food Supply, on what that office provided. To survive, you had to buy on the open market. Rykov wondered what she had in her bag.

The crowded market made no distinctions. Proletarians jostled with aristocrats, Communist bargained with bourgeois, peasants sold to intellectuals. There you could pick up a Bokhara rug or a Ming vase for a relative song, but there were few takers, nor for Tsarist left-overs such as silk underwear and French make-up, although soap had value. The really valuable goods were such things as butter, eggs, flour and vegetables.

When the young woman made her way to the stall of a broad, seamed peasant woman, wrapped like a cabbage in different layers of clothes, Rykov could see that she had been astute in her choice of payment, for the bag contained sawn lengths of wood. From their irregular shape he took them to be pieces of furniture. Dry, seasoned wood like that burned beautifully.

She was able to make her deal quickly. The logs slipped into the woman's cart, potatoes, dried turnips, butter and barley into the carpet bag, and the young woman left the market. Rykov followed her, at a distance.

Near the Fontanka River she went by the ancient church of St Simeon and St Anna. The windows were dark, the doors closed. Someone was waiting for her at the entrance to a courtyard, a young man in a torn sheepskin coat. He, too, carried a bag and his gaunt face lit up in a smile as he saw her coming. Rykov knew him. He smiled out, younger, less troubled, less thin, from the photograph above his mantelpiece.

They embraced, talking animatedly, their heads close together, clearly comparing notes of successful shopping expeditions. Clutching their bags, they picked their way through the rubbish piled up in the courtyard, and vanished into the Empire-style building.

It took Rykov about an hour to get back to his offices and return, with a couple of his lads.

Inside the building, he knocked on the first door he came to. An engraved plate from before the revolution announced it to be the home of someone called Egorushka. A shuffling announced the approach of the inhabitant, and the door opened to reveal a woman wrapped in a bearskin rug. Her pinched features lost the little colour they had as she saw the men at the porch.

'A young couple. A girl and a boy,' Rykov said pleasantly.

'They don't live here,' she babbled. Her voice betrayed her as bourgeois. 'Upstairs. The room on the right.'

'Thank you. What are their names?'

'Maslov. And Paustovskii. Zhenya Maslov. He's Vasilii.'

'You've been most helpful, *mamashka*,' said Rykov, turning to go up the stairs. The woman Egorushka, if it was she, was shaking all over; she could hardly take hold of the handle to shut the door. He made a note to send a couple of lads round that night to see what she was hiding.

As they went up the stairs he spoke to his two men, Kudrya the Cossack and Gaidouk the Latvian.

'Let's be polite, now,' he said, and they grinned. It was a paradox, that when you opened your door and the devil came in, he was more terrifying, not less, if to begin with he had no horns or tail, and spoke to you pleasantly.

Outside the first door on the right was a rare, exotic smell. Food cooking. Rykov knocked twice. It opened, after a few moments, and the young woman looked out. Like everyone else in the city, she had remained fully dressed inside the house.

'Hullo, *devushka*,' he said. 'Mind if we come in?'

He did not have to say who he was.

There were two rooms, but they were living in one. It was smoky in there. A bed took up one wall, it was made, and had a thick rug on it. There was a wardrobe, a small table and chair, some paper and pencils. On the floor was a small, rusty, pot-bellied stove, a *burzhuika*. The man, Vasilii, was crouched by it, feeding it with the pages of a book. A black iron pot was on it. Rykov opened the door to the other room. It was empty. Some stalagmites of ice were growing from the bare boards.

Turning back to the room he lifted the lid to the pot. An emaciated, but genuine chicken sat surrounded by pieces of potato and turnip, and grains of barley. Golden globules of butter separated and reformed in the simmering stew.

'It's his birthday,' the girl, Zhenya said quickly. 'It'll be the first time we've eaten anything hot for months.'

Vasilii had a bottle in his hand. He was still wearing his town coat.

'*Vodochki?*' he asked. 'Would you gentlemen like a drink? The man I got the chicken from had some vodka.'

'Why not?' said Rykov. 'Since it's your birthday.'

The glasses were crystal, Vasilii filled them hastily and gave them to the three Chekists. Rykov held his as he wandered about the room. He opened the wardrobe. It was empty except for two sets of clothes. A good, bourgeois suit, with waistcoat, top hat and shoes. And a wedding dress, with silk underwear, veil, train and shoes.

'You are married? Or about to be?'

'Soon,' said Zhenya. 'When it's warmer. You couldn't get married in this cold.'

'No . . .' Rykov said absently. He looked up. 'It's Vasilii and Zhenya, isn't it?'

He saw the flash of fear in their eyes.

'I couldn't help noticing you at the market, Zhenya. Wasn't that wood you paid with? Now, where would you get that?'

'My mother gave it to me. As a present for Vasilii's birthday. It was a chair.'

'Of course. And what about you, Vasilii?' he said amiably. 'Where did you go?'

'To the village. There's a peasant there . . . my father died from the cold, I sold him his boots, and a cloak.'

'Everything has its use, doesn't it?'

He tipped back his vodka. His two men had drunk theirs. He threw the glass into the dead fireplace, and theirs followed. He saw the pain in the eyes of the two young people. In a world where everything had a use, three glasses might buy the same number of eggs.

He sighed. 'I'm sure everything is as you say it is.'

They looked puzzled, behind their scarves, and relieved. Everything was what? But the terrifying little secret policeman was happy with what it was, so that was all right.

Rykov sighed again, and rubbed the tip of his nose with his glove. 'Still, better safe than sorry, I say. It's my paperwork. I tell you what, let's just go down to the office and sort it all out. It won't take long. What do you say?'

They went out. Rykov left the door open and, as Kudrya and Gaidouk took them down the street, he knocked again at the door marked Egorushka. The woman was still wrapped in her rug. She peered out at him in fear. He smiled pleasantly.

'Thanks for your help. They'll not be back and there's some food up there. It doesn't do to let things go to waste.'

An expression of total desire dominated the woman's face. He could see her begin to salivate.

'Good day,' he said, and behind him he could hear the frantic slapping of the woman's galoshes as she hurried upstairs.

It was a half hour walk to the Shpalerny prison where he operated. On the way he turned to Gaidouk.

'Where we've just been – that woman downstairs. Bourgeois, I'd have said. A profiteer, no doubt. A hoarder. Probably has things she shouldn't. Go back and see.'

'Yes, boss,' the Latvian said obediently, and set off back the way he had come.

The square was deserted as they trudged across it. No citizen voluntarily went near it. He led the couple inside. Going down the corridor towards the newly-constructed cells he thought he heard singing, and glanced at his watch. Yes, it was the right time. He took them by a route that led to one of the inner courtyards. The high walls reverberated with noise. A lorry was parked in one corner, the driver revving its engine up and down. By the wall stood three people, two men and a women, singing at the tops of their voices. They sang about a coming revolution that would make all men free.

They were half-naked. By each was a small pile of possessions and their outer clothes. A man was staggering, drunk, across the courtyard. He wore a smock, filthy and stained, a revolver was in his hand, knives and an axe hung from his belt.

'*Shut up, you bastards!*' he screamed.

They sang, their heads held up, staring ahead of them at the coming golden age. The executioner thrust out his gun, ramming it into the elbow of one of the men, and pulled the trigger. The singing became mixed with frightful shrieks of agony as the victim clutched at his shattered joint. Beside Rykov, Zhenya began to sob.

The man paused to take a pinch of something from a silver snuff-box. It glittered in his hand.

'Old Maga does like his cocaine,' Rykov said amiably.

Maga fired again, through the back of the second man's head, and his face vanished in a spray of gore. Then he shot his first victim in the knee.

'We'd better not cross,' Rykov remarked jovially to his two prisoners. 'When old Maga gets going he sometimes can't tell the difference. Why, Popov the Commandant himself was here the other day when he was going through a score and Maga tried to kill *him*! His enthusiasm just runs away with him . . .'

Maga reloaded the Colt when he'd killed the second man, and used it to blow bits off the woman.

'I think we can go now,' said Rykov. Vasilii had been sick and traces of mucus coated his chin. The girl's eyes were blank with horror. In the courtyard, the headsman saw them coming, as he collected the effects of his victims. He waved his gun.

'Hey, *starik*, Rykov. Some more bastard socialists for me?'

'I'm not sure yet. I'll let you know.'

They passed him, his bloodshot eyes followed Zhenya and she shook with fear. Fresh gore, brains and bone spattered his smock, his arms, his beard.

'I'll be waiting,' he promised.

Rykov put them in two separate single cells.

'Nothing to eat or drink,' he told the warder. On his way out he met Gaidouk, bringing in the woman Egorushka.

'An enemy of the people, boss,' he said happily. 'I found her eating chicken.'

'*Chicken?*' said Rykov, in simulated horror. 'While the people starve?'

'But you –' the woman began.

'Yes?'

'I meant nothing . . .'

'Put her in. I'll deal with her later.'

He went down to the refectory in the basement. The lads in the larder office had got a couple of good new trucks and were able to get further afield so they'd found some more hoarders in the villages. He helped himself to some good chops; he was partial to pork.

After his early supper he went home and had a nap by the fire. When he awoke in the evening he took his photograph down from his mantelpiece, and sat looking at it, for a long time. Then he went out, taking it with him.

He had it on his desk when they brought Zhenya and Vasilii in. It was midnight. He sat in his thick jacket, and they shivered before him.

'There are messages in code on the papers we found where you live,' he said.

'They aren't messages –'

'They make no sense. Of course it is a code. You work for the Whites, don't you?'

'It's poetry!' Zhenya burst out. 'Vasilii writes poetry. He gives recitals in the cafés, they pay us with a little food. Sour milk . . . some lumps of sugar, sometimes.'

'It's code,' Rykov said certainly. 'Your neighbour, the woman Egorushka says people come to your room. She hears them. Your agents. She hears them giving you intelligence about us, to send to the Whites.'

'Friends come to see us. In the cold, it helps . . . we huddle together and talk.'

'Friends . . .' Rykov said softly. He turned the photograph face up so that they could see it. 'Are these your friends?'

'It's our old school photograph,' Zhenya said in bewilderment. 'How did you get it?'

'We know everything,' said Rykov. He produced a pen. 'Write down for me, if you will, the names of each person, underneath.'

Zhenya bent over the desk, her chilled hand slowly and carefully writing out the names.

'This was a school for the sons and daughters of those who crawled for the Tsar. Clearly, you are all members of a White spy ring that seeks to overthrow the revolution.'

'Sir, we are two people only trying to stay alive,' Vasilii said humbly.

'You will be in your cells for a few days,' Rykov said. 'I want you to think carefully about how the spy ring was formed, whose idea it was. Who recruited whom. How you gathered the intelligence, and who you give it to. Perhaps a foreign power is involved? How they pay you. I'd like it detailed, please. Oh, and your mother, Zhenya. Her address. She is *clearly* involved; someone is supplying her with firewood. A foreign agent, no doubt. When you're ready, tell the guard, and we'll have it all typed up for you to sign.'

He beamed at them. 'Then you can get married,' he said.

He was busy after that. The files that were being built up were most useful. He found two ice men in the cells, skilled in the art of cutting great ingots of ice from the frozen river, for use in the ice houses of the rich in Tsarist times. They promised him that their hands had not lost their cunning. A sculptor was more difficult, but he found an artist who knew one, waiting in the death cell for Maga, and he postponed the man's appointment temporarily while he sent Kudrya the Cossack round to get him. Musicians, yes, there were plenty of those.

He went out with Gaidouk, the ice men and the sculptor in a wagon. They travelled out of the city and took a track down through the larches and pines to where the river lay flat and frozen before them, and he told the men what he wanted. They had their saws, the sculptor his tools. He provided food and tea. They were warmly clad, and Gaidouk set to building a fire.

It was Christmas Eve when the black Maria came clopping back along the path. It was dark, but on the ice something beautiful shone in the light of oil lamps. It was a house, a single-roomed house. Pillars of ice stood either side of the door, frozen walls supported cunningly-carved tiles of ice covering the roof. It glowed from lights within.

Rykov got down as the wagon drew up outside. On a silk cloth on an icy pedestal a big bouquet of white flowers rested. He unlocked the small door, and Zhenya and Vasilii climbed out, moving stiffly from the cold. They wore their wedding clothes and looked fearfully about them. Rykov picked up the bouquet and gave it to Zhenya. She gasped as she took it. The flowers were carved from ice. From inside the house music came, a wedding march, and Rykov led them in.

The room was lit by the candles on a pine Christmas tree. In one corner a three-piece orchestra played, the prisoners dressed in the tails of the old era. Their faces were blank, their eyes elsewhere as Rykov led the young couple in. Gaidouk and Kudrya were waiting, their vodka fumes tainting the air. In the middle of the room stood a huge, elaborately carved bed. Icy posts supported a canopy, ice pillows lay upon an ice mattress.

'You may consummate the marriage,' Rykov said softly. Gaidouk and Kudrya began stripping them of their clothes. The Latvian folded the white silk carefully as he took it off the girl, hanging it over his arm. He liked to dress up in ladies' clothes.

Naked, they climbed on to the bed, moaning softly in their pain. They lay, as they were told to, in each other's arms. Kudrya took a metal watering can that stood by the bed. A drum of water stood outside, kept from freezing by a brazier. He ran it to and fro, and a fan of light rain fell on to their bodies from its rosette, and froze.

The girl, Zhenya, was underneath. She was blue, her beautiful body matching the colour of the ice that she lay on. Breath seemed only to flicker within her and she could not close her eyes. The steadily falling rain froze upon them . . .

Rykov squatted down next to them. He thought that Vasilii could still hear him.

'We had a custom, back where I come from,' he said quietly, in the boy's ear, while Bach sang from the icy walls. 'In the winter, we'd come into a town, in a troika, and wait. We'd wait for a merchant, a rich, fat merchant, to waddle out from the hotel, where he'd been drinking. Fat and happy. Warm. Swathed in furs. Out he'd come, and we'd whip up the troika. Come out of the night at him, whooping and howling with delight. Lasso him with our ropes, tow him down the ice as helpless as could be, as fast as we could. Stop in some remote place, strip him of everything he had. Then cut his throat.'

Vasilii's head rested on the dead face of his fiancée. Breath still groaned in a death agony as the rain fell upon him.

In his apartment he had crossed neatly through the first two names below the photograph.

'We are the revolution,' Rykov said softly.

Berlin, Christmas Eve, 1918

From the window they could see the street below glittering in the dusk. The shop windows glowed with light, people hurried home clutching their bags, stopping off to bargain with a street vendor, adding a trinket, a twist of red-berried holly, darting into a café for an ersatz beer before pushing their way home. From a hundred apartment windows little Christmas trees glittered with candles.

'Now,' said Savinkov. 'The moment has come.'

Rosa gestured towards the street. They were in her old apartment. Paul Levi had gone out to try to find some wine not made of beetroot. In the corner Manfred sat quietly and Ruth was curled up in a chair, simply too tired to sit like a revolutionary.

'You see revolutionary masses?' she asked. 'I see celebrating capitalists.'

'Ruth,' said Savinkov. 'You were out in the city, the day we took the Winter Palace. What was it like?'

'It was like this, Rosa. The shops were open, the trams ran. The Social Revolutionaries were somewhere, having a conference. Salvation Army bands were playing on street corners. The cafés were full. Contant's restaurant was packed and I think Chaliapin was singing at a concert.'

'*And we were about to seize power,*' Savinkov said intensely. 'Lenin had recognised the moment. He told our Central Committee: "The crisis has matured. The whole future of the revolution is at stake." *And he was right.*'

'Lenin is a political Jesuit!' Rosa spat. 'He believes that only he is able to interpret Marx. He's a *heretic*. What do his "Vanguard fighters" have to do with the inevitable triumph of the proletariat? He claimed that consciousness had to be brought to the proletariat from without, by these vanguard elements. You cannot short-circuit history in this fashion.'

'He rules Russia, in the name of the proletariat,' Savinkov said softly. 'You can do the same here.'

'He *rules* the proletariat,' Rosa muttered.

Manfred leaned forward. 'All you have to do is say the word,' he said. 'You can say the word, others will do the work.'

'Whatever you think, the Revolution has happened in Russia,' said Savinkov. 'And Lenin and we Bolsheviks are the only ones with the will to defend what the proletariat has won. When the victory is secure, then the kind of measures necessary to win a war will be abandoned, and true proletarian democracy allowed to reach its full flowering. But none of us wants the triumph of counter-revolutionary bourgeoisie.'

'And shall I be Germany's Lenin?' Rosa asked. 'Shall I seize power, and dissolve the Constituent Assembly?'

'*Someone* has to,' Manfred said intensely. 'If not now, later. But now is the time, Rosa. We have a source inside the army. Groener, the chief of staff is panicking. His ten divisions have got out of hand and there are almost no troops in the capital. Assemble your men and we can take the key points, topple the government.'

'Sergei is right, Rosa,' said Ruth. '*I* was the one who saw Kerensky flee. Krivitskiy had put me there. I didn't understand why then, but I do now. It was a *coup d'état*, that's what he told me. But the timing is everything. We *walked* into the Winter Palace.'

'Your men could walk into all the key offices tomorrow,' said Savinkov. 'Leave it a week to try it and they'll be shot down in the street, massacred. Get the Spartacist leadership here, arm the teams.'

'They are busy,' she said. 'I cannot interrupt them.'

'What can be more important than this?' Savinkov cried. 'What are they doing?'

'A crisis has come over the party. With the results of the elections now clear our problem is whether or not to secede from the Social Democratic Party, to found a separate party, and if we do, should it be called "socialist", or "communist"? I believe we must, despite my fears of what capital those who hate me will make of it.'

Down on the street a man was putting up a new red and black poster. His paste brush swept on to the boards a caricature of a hook-nosed, evilly-smiling dwarf reaching out with claw-like hands towards a prostrate Germany in the form of a beautiful princess. It was possible to recognise Rosa. Underneath the slogan read: 'Judah is reaching out for the crown.'

'I shall be labelled a Bolshevik, which I am not. I am a Marxist,' she said, despairingly.

'Do as we say, and it will not matter,' Manfred said. 'You must decide. Now.'

'Rosa looked at him angrily. 'I do not have to do *anything* you say! And the German workers are not ready to take over the government.'

'The triumph of the proletariat is not a Darwinian process of evolution!' Savinkov cried.

'You are urging me to become a dictator. To destroy the pure, scientific laws of Marx, to break their truth, to take power through the use of naked force. What truth is that? One who brings truth all masked and painted to humanity may well be truth's pimp but truth's lover he is not. Lenin is truth's pimp. *I* do not wish to become the same.'

'You want to *talk*,' Manfred said, suddenly derisive. 'Power goes to those who *act*. Afterwards, you can call yourself Jesus Christ, if you like.'

In the street two lean, unshaven men with the look of former soldiers passed the poster, glancing up at it. One made the gesture of wringing a chicken's neck.

'If you won't be dictator, then someone else will,' he said contemptuously.

He went out of the door and they heard his feet clattering down the stairs. Savinkov shrugged wearily, and went over to the table, helping himself to a bottle of brown beer. He sat drinking it from the neck while Ruth sat under the light, and took some paper, composing her new article. Rosa was quiet, sitting with her eyes shut.

The words would not come. Ruth pushed the paper to one side, and stood up, stretching. She wondered if Paul Levi had found any wine. She felt, rather suddenly, that she would very much like some wine, to see things as they should be, instead of as they were. She went to the window, and peered out.

'Rosa! Sergei!' she hissed. '*Freikorps*. They are in the street.'

Savinkov peeped around the curtain.

'They're coming for us,' he said positively. 'They're looking at the numbers. Quickly, Ruth, take Rosa over the roof. I'll try to delay them on the stairs.'

The two women found themselves on the flat roof of the building. A chill wind was blowing and they pulled their coats tight about them. They could hear the noise of the troops in the building.

'We can't hide up here, Rosa,' Ruth said. 'They'll see us.'

She helped the older woman to limp over the ridged lead and found an unlocked door that went down into the next block. It was quiet as they crept down to the street. In the dark hallway Ruth pushed Rosa behind the door.

'Let *me* look.'

She opened the door and stood in the porch. The street was quiet. From windows little candles were burning on the Christmas trees.

There was a clatter of boots, only feet away. She quickly tugged at the buttons of her blouse then they were upon her, two *Freikorps* Volunteers, in grey army tunics without badges. She smiled invitingly, and held the front of her blue coat open.

One of the men leered, and put out his hand towards her breasts. She let him squeeze them, still smiling, and then held up her hand, rubbing finger and thumb together in the universal sign for money.

'*Roschen*,' he said in disgust. 'A bloody whore!'

There was a commotion from the doorway along the street, and more men streamed out. As they passed she saw Savinkov in their midst, his arm jammed up behind his back, struggling to keep his balance as they forced him along.

She heard them go and, when it was quiet, they slipped away through the darkness.

Berlin 12 January 1919

There was a Spartacist sniper on the roof of the police headquarters. From inside the little room they could hear his deadly tapping as he fired on the men coming up the street. Men in grey, moving in swift, practised and co-ordinated rushes, their own rifles in their hands. Peering through the grimed window, Ruth could see them, tiny figures across the bare park. The rifle fire made the pane vibrate like a child's triangle and when the artillery went off dirt came away from the jamb, floating dustily down to the bare boards. Rosa sat huddled in a chair. She seemed even smaller than she really was. A volume of Goethe's *Faust* lay open on her lap which she read from time to time. She was alone with Ruth. Paul Levi was in jail, with Mathilde Jacob and a dozen more of the Spartacists who had thronged the office of *The Red Flag*. Jogiches, the long-time lover of the woman in the chair, was on the run. Ruth wondered where Liebknecht was, since he had started it all. Maybe in the building, under the sniper. Across the park, men in grey were bringing up some kind of cannon.

'The old Rosa stands victorious over the corpse of the new,' she said bitterly. 'I have said for twenty years that we socialists must be united, that any split in our ranks will prove fatal. Yet I stood up at the founding Congress of the Communist Party of Germany not two weeks ago, and supported them. And I had to; Liebknecht was right to distinguish the heirs of Marx from the Social Democrat thieves who would present themselves as the representatives of the people. In my speech I pointed to the way forward as one of intensified economic struggle and the workers' participation in a national assembly. The notion that the German workers are ready to take over the government is a dangerous illusion.'

From across the park came the dry crackle of machine gun fire.

'As that proves,' she said. 'All my life I have stated that there is no socialism without the support of the majority of the proletariat, yet I know the majority supports *them*. Those out there in grey. I have always insisted that socialism cannot be implemented by the use of force. Liebknecht armed the workers and I supported him and the end of five days of fighting is this. The old Rosa has won.'

By her chair was a scattered pile of thin, crumpled papers, bravely emblazoned with red.

'Neglected Duties!' her headline cried. 'Don't talk! Don't consult! Don't negotiate! *ACT!*'

'After twenty years, you cannot accuse me of not knowing my comrades,' she said sadly. 'Savinkov was right – if you are going to do it, you have to *do* it. What did Liebknecht do? Formed a Revolutionary Committee to handle the uprising. Admirable. What did the Committee do? Voted to seize power. Very good. Next it created several commissions. Very well. And what did they all do? They spent their time doing what they were good at, *they debated*. And Noske and his *Freikorps* got on with doing what they are good at, which is smashing opposition, killing people.'

'I don't understand where they have come from,' Ruth said quietly. 'We did not have them, these *Freikorps*, in our revolution. There is nothing in Marx to say they should be there.'

'They are the last, virulent flaring of the dying bourgeois era,' Rosa said wearily.

'Manfred said they are something new, something born out of the wreckage of the war. Something terrible, that hates us.'

'Certainly they hate us,' Rosa said. 'We are the avenging sword of the proletariat, we smite the bourgeoisie.'

'He said they're *not* bourgeoisie.'

'Then Liss is not a Marxist!' Rosa said irritably. 'The interpretation of human society is only possible by careful study of the laws of Marx. Liss is not a Marxist any more than Savinkov. Savinkov knows that. He is a skilled persuader. That's why Lenin sent him here, to persuade us to be Bolsheviks.'

'Perhaps if you had been,' Ruth said gently, 'then this revolution would not be ending as it is.'

'Lenin wanted us to be part of some sort of colonial communist empire, run from Moscow,' Rosa said tiredly. 'You can see the judgement of the people on that, out there.'

The boom of the cannon rattled the glass in its frame. A great cloud of dust erupted from the roof of the building and masonry tumbled through the air, falling into the street. As the wind blew, Ruth could see a gaping hole, like a missing tooth. The sniper was silent. The sounds of fighting were dying away and Ruth could see men straggling hesitantly from the building, their hands held high. Some still wore splashes of red and the men in grey clubbed them to the ground.

'Order reigns in Berlin,' Rosa said sarcastically. She roused herself, reaching for her pen. 'Some paper, Ruth. *The Red Flag* shall continue to fly. Yes, Order in Berlin. That shall be the title.'

She wrote, the nib scratching gently in the strange silence. There was a sudden crash from the door, the sound of heavy boots. Someone kicked in the door to the room and it smashed back against the wall.

'There's the bitch!'

Ruth threw herself in front of Rosa and a terrible blow buckled her in half. She lay, helpless and winded, clutching her stomach, and heard the men dragging Rosa away. There was the sound of a car engine, of doors slamming.

The pain in her stomach eased and breath dragged back into her lungs. She pushed herself to her hands and knees, the air rasping in her throat. The front door was open, a wind was blowing. She got up, pulling on her coat as quickly as she was able, and went out on to the street, walking away from the house.

'*Ruth!*'

It was Savinkov. He was in the trees of the park, she hurried across the road to him.

'*They've captured Rosa.*' She said urgently.

'I know. I escaped. I was coming to get you.'

'Manfred was with them. Manfred Liss. He told them, he said, "there's the bitch".'

'I know.' He took her arm. 'I saw him. Ruth let us get away from here.'

They hurried through the darkening park towards the station.

'I'll get you out to Poznan,' he said. 'You can get home from there.'

'What about you? It's finished here.'

'There's another way,' he said. 'You'll see.'

From through the trees came the clink of metal, the tramp of boots, the gruff chant of a military marching song. Ruth grabbed Savinkov's arm in terror.

'*Freikorps!*' she gasped, pulling at him. 'We must run.'

He held her steady, looking through the trees at the approaching column.

'People who run get shot,' he said certainly. 'Quickly!'

He pushed her up against the bole of a tree by the path, his hands tugging at the buttons of her coat. She felt the cold air on her thin shirt, his hand on her breast.

'We're *lovers*,' he hissed. 'Love laughs at locksmiths – and war, too.'

They kissed and she clung to him as she would have a raft in a drowning sea. The tramp of boots, the hoarse singing, came nearer. The chorus faded, leaving just the thudding of their feet, the sound of laughter, and then someone broke into a new song, and they roared it out with gusto. She did not have to peep over Savinkov's shoulder to see the thrusting rifle barrels and grinning faces to know that it had to be obscene. Without breaking from his embrace, Savinkov waved an upraised arm in comradely acknowledgement.

They heard them going on their way but Savinkov's hand was inside her blouse, her mouth was still locked against his. She burned all over. She opened her mouth to him, felt his hand pull her skirt up around her waist. Her leg pulled him to her. Across the park, the soldiers bellowed out one final chorus . . .

6

The Midwife of History

Moscow, March 1919

R UTH climbed down from the filthy carriage, her frozen feet stumbling as they hit the platform. It seemed to her that she had been cold for eternity. Getting off at the Finland station, Petrograd had howled with wind, icy gusts off the sea knifing through her clothes as she went through the empty streets. On a child's hope she had gone to her parents' apartment on Nevsky Prospekt: it had been shut tight. Peering through the keyhole she saw it dusty and empty, charred cabriole chair legs and smashed inlaid drawers littering the gilt hearth where someone had made a fire.

She had trudged over the dirty snow to the station, waiting interminably for the train to Moscow. It came, in the end and she huddled on a slatted seat as close to the vent as she could get. It dispensed wisps of warm air and, after a time, the frozen tears melted and trickled down her cheeks. She dried them with her dirty scarf which had once been blazing scarlet.

The train started with a slam of worn-out buffers, sending her head smacking against the wood of the seat, and she tried not to think of the carriages she had ridden in as a child, with their soft rugs and furnishings, playing cards with her mother on the sofa by the fire as the rolling fields of corn passed by outside on the way to Moscow, the rythmic clicketty-clack of the wheels tapping gently through the springs, reading books with her father by the window and the clinking of the arriving trays of china bearing tea.

The train had broken down in the middle of nowhere, in the middle of a vast field where rotting, snow-covered vegetation stretched towards the horizon. The wisps of heat had vanished and, as somewhere up in front the noises of men hitting metal parts with hammers indicated repairs, she had stared over the great field. Rusty stalks poked through the snow, a shrill noise like a million crickets all around indicated the presence of the owners, more mice than the corn field had ever seen. The remains of the vast harvest they had eaten stood in the snow. Soon the mice, too, would die, starving to death after plenty.

Rosa would be cold, lying on her bed of earth. The Landwehr canal must have been cold, too ... Irrationally, she hoped that Rosa had been dead before the *Freikorps* soldiers had thrown her in. Beaten, shot and bleeding, she would have drowned horribly, in the freezing water.

Her stomach ached, but she knew it was simple hunger. The train had finally clanked to life and she had sat by the vent with her arms about her knees as she had once sat by the feet of Alexandra, witty, aristocratic Alexandra, wishing she could be like her. Well, so she had, if one frantic coupling against a tree with fear driving desire qualified as the emancipation Alexandra had somehow married to Marx. It had made sense, then, part of a new world where all the old ills were to be banished by the magic of words.

She closed her eyes. There were plenty of words to describe her situation. Her mother could have used them – and would have done. Old words, describing very old ills. Unmarried. Illegitimate. Bastard. Stupid. Pregnant.

She got down from the train on to the freezing platform and made her blue hands open, stiff in the cold, to carry her bag. She stumbled along, her ticket in her teeth.

A voice was calling.

'Comrade! Comrade!'

She looked behind her, but the handful of passengers had left her staggering figure well behind. The plaform was empty.

A man's voice. A man waving from the barrier, pushing through with authority. A small man, smiling.

A stab of fear went through the ache in her stomach. Rykov!

But he was smiling, taking her bag.

'But you're cold,' he said, and took off his own coat, putting its thick wool over her shoulders. The black leather jerkin she remembered was gone and he was wearing a knitted army jersey.

'They told me you were on your way,' he said, 'and so I hurried down to meet the train.'

'They did?' she said, puzzled.

He looked at her reproachfully.

'You didn't think that one on the General Staff of world revolution could come back to Moscow without being noticed, did you?'

The ringing phrases echoed in her mind, like the trumpets of a soon-to-be defeated army on its way to the battlefield.

'We lost,' she said dully. She had come back to be condemned, she knew it.

'Lost?' he said, wide-eyed. 'Did the revolutionaries of a hundred and five lose? No, they won in seventeen. We, the proletariat, won.'

'We shall win,' she said eagerly, hope suddenly returning to her. 'Out there, in the world. It will happen. We shall overthrow the oppressors. We shall bring the new world to the old.'

They stopped near the entrance. Drifting from the shelter of a pillared portico was the smoke of a little *burzhuika* portable stove burning its scraps of wood and paper and the scent of tea in a battered samovar. The old man knew there were still those with coins in their pockets and the pain of the freezing journey from Petrograd in their limbs. He knew Rykov it seemed, for he came hurrying with a tin mug in his hand, steaming in the freezing air.

'Here, comrade,' he said, holding it out. He seemed to be bending, as if to make himself not taller than Rykov. He did not ask for payment.

'For the lady, comrade,' Rykov said softly. 'You are with a hero of the world revolution.'

The greasy cap was swept off his head, and she felt the metal of the mug hot in her hands.

'Here,' Rykov said. He had a polished silver flask in his hand. It was like the one her father had had, aeons ago, out shooting with his Purdey. He poured a golden liquid into the tea. She drank, and it exploded hot in her stomach, running through her veins like fire. After being so cold for so long the heat stunned her senses, and it was some moments before she realised that Rykov was talking.

'Back from the front,' he said softly, modestly. 'Down south, at Tsaritsyn. In Petrograd, for a while. They sent me back to Moscow to train up some more lads. I've got them ready to go, to fight.'

'You're still with the Cheka?'

'Yes, yes, the Cheka. We look after the souls of our revolutionaries, don't we? We keep them free from error. A bit like priests were thought to keep the souls of men free from sin. But perhaps I shouldn't say that. Lenin might not approve.'

'You must be careful not to stray into God-building,' she agreed. It was strange. but pleasant to be discussing the scientific laws that governed man's behaviour on a windy station. And with Rykov. The hot tea and liquor had stimulated her. She smiled.

'You would be the one in error if you talk about God – and your Cheka friends might have to take your sins away!'

Rykov beamed pleasantly at the idea.

'Talk of Gods and devils is but intellectual necrophilia. I have myself read Lenin's work on the subject, *Materialism* and *Empiriocriticism*. If you are training your young men they should read it.'

Rykov continued to smile.

'But look,' she said, 'I'm keeping you. I must get on.'

Rykov's smile died away. He took off his cap, holding it in his hands, looking rather embarrassed.

'No, I'm afraid I'd like to keep you, if I may. You see, I have a problem. It's with these lads I've been training. You hit on it just now. I knew you would.'

He stood looking at her expectantly.

'Religion? Lenin?'

'That's it. And Marx. What he taught. I'm just a simple boy, I haven't read like you. I can't instruct these trainees – good lads every one – not like you could. I can tell them what to do, out at the front, but not how Marx put it.' He thumped his chest with a small fist. 'My Marxism is right here, like a hot coal, but I can't express it. Not like you could. I remember you.'

She longed to get her filthy clothes off, to get into a hot bath, to find some food, a bed. To sleep.

She smiled. 'You want me to have a word with your young men?'

'You're back from the revolution in the world. You could give them your blessing, so to speak . . .'

Her parents' summer house had had its own chapel. Gold and incense, the priest's incantations, the warmth of the people all about one. The presence of God. Comfort . . .

'I've got a little truck,' said Rykov. 'I'll take you to where you want to go afterwards.'

If you wanted someone to stay late, someone to do the dirty jobs, someone to go into the cold to push the wheel of revolution one more turn, you knew you could count on Ruth Gunzberg.

'Of course I will,' she said.

The Lubyanka building was warm, the parquet flooring still shiny, the smell of Tsarist polish still in the air. He opened the door for her deferentially. A half-dozen youths lounged on benches set by worktables. A couple wore black leather jerkins, the others had theirs slung on the tabletops. Eyes like flint ran over her and for a second she felt as though all her clothes had been stripped from her body, and then they were scrambling to their feet, standing to attention as they saw Rykov coming into the room behind her.

'Good, good,' Rykov murmured. 'All right, boys, sit down.'

He went with Ruth to the front of the classroom. The six youths sat on their benches, backs straight, watching Rykov attentively, warily.

'I have a special treat,' said Rykov. His hand on her elbow guided her to the solid oak table at the front of the class.

'This is Comrade Gunzberg, who was a Bolshevik even before I was.'

He smiled, and in the light she could see his teeth were yellow, like a wolf's.

'That's saying a lot!'

They laughed, all six watching him closely.

'Yes. Commissar!' one called. Rykov smiled again, like a dog-handler watching his charge perform as it should.

'Comrade Gunzberg is on the General Staff of the world revolution. She is just back from Germany.'

They applauded, their palms clattering in the room. Rykov raised his hand slightly, and they stopped. He turned to Ruth, still deferential.

'You know so much of the teachings of Marx and Lenin that you could speak to us for days, and we would still be here, attentive to your every word. But the revolution awaits, and we have to get to the front, to fight the agents of counter-revolution. The old order. The foreigners who encircle us, those imperialists making war upon the new world.'

'The last phase of capitalism,' she agreed.

'That's it. I knew you'd know. When the war is won we'll come back and sit at your feet. But this time, shall I put the questions, on behalf of these lads?'

'Please,' she said, slightly uncertain of what was going on.

'Who are we? You, me, my boys here?'

'We are Bolsheviks.'

'Who do we represent?'

'We represent the proletariat.'

'We represent the proletariat,' Rykov said quietly after her. He raised his hand and she could hear the youths chant the words, softly.

'Who commands us to?'

'Marx and Lenin.'

'Marx and Lenin.' Rykov paused. 'You're back from Germany. Has the revolution succeeded? Do our brothers in the proletariat there enjoy freedom and happiness, as we do here?'

'No,' she said. 'We failed.'

'Why?'

'The forces of counter-revolution were too strong.'

'Then we shall return, stronger than ever, until we crush them.'

'We will,' she said fervently. 'Oh, yes we will.'

'Are we communists special?'

'Of course!'

'Can we accept only part of Marx and Lenin, or is what they taught a whole?'

'It is as a cast ingot,' she said proudly. Savinkov had taught her that. 'It is of a piece.'

'Who do we represent?'

'The proletariat.'

'We are fighting a war for them. Is it violent?'

'Yes.'

'Of course. What is violence? What does Lenin say it is?'

'The midwife of history.'

'Violence gives birth to revolution, to freedom. Who do we apply it to?'

'Our class enemies.'

It was quiet in the room, just the faint creaking of leather from her side. She turned to see Rykov sliding his black leather jerkin over his shoulders.

'It is holy, our task. We are commanded to protect the proletariat from all those who would injure her. To ensure her victory, to rule in her name. We are commanded to use violence against those who would damage her.'

He opened a cupboard by the wall. Inside were stacked some rifles, brown and blue. The scent of gun oil pervaded the air as Rykov tossed a weapon to each of his men.

It was suddenly cold and she found herself outside in a courtyard. By the wall stood two bent figures, black hoods over their heads. The snow about their feet was dirty and dark with old blood. She had a rifle in her hand, Rykov had put it there. They pushed her in line with them and she could feel Rykov behind her, smell his fresh sweat.

The couple by the wall shivered in their thin clothes.

'Kill our enemies.'

Rykov's voice was hoarse with desire and the rifle exploded in her hands . . .

Savinkov found her down by the church. Not one of the big ones, not like the great Church of All Mourners that stared across the river at the Kremlin, where the metropolitan presided with his teams of black robed priests. Worshippers it had, however, and had for centuries. The stone of its pillars was darkened by the soot of the priests' incense and the myriad tapers lit for the souls of those present and departed.

He found her outside, the priest standing nearby, his lips moving in prayer. Two young Chekists stood by the door and laughed at him. From the archway came a bar of light, and a voice calling commands, and others, replying. The lamps lit up the stained glass; Christ held up his hand in benediction over the small Moscow street.

Savinkov's boots crunched on the snow, and he stopped by her. 'The foreign delegates are here,' he said. 'Aren't you coming?'

'What delegates?' she asked dully. 'We picked them from the hangers-on we have here. Most of them have never *been* to the countries they're supposed to represent. Some of the parties they are supposed to represent do not exist.'

'The Bolshevik party did not exist once,' he said softly.

'And you have never been to America, but one day you will help make it a democracy of the proletariat.'

She did not reply, but continued to stare at the church.

'I hurried back for the International,' he said, 'but someone said they had seen you heading this way. One of the foreign "hangers-on" who will one day bring freedom and happiness to all.'

He produced a folded newspaper from inside his coat. A brave splash of red was at its bannerhead. 'I brought you this. *The Red Flag*. Jogiches reconstructed the murder. He named the names and they're coming up for trial, the ones who killed Rosa.'

She took the paper. 'Thank you,' she whispered.

He looked about, half-smiling. 'You've come to see the show?'

'I came to pray,' Ruth said. 'But they were already here.'

'Pray? To what?' Savinkov asked softly. 'There is no God, you know that.'

'I do not know anything, any more.'

'Of course there is no God! Without God, all things are permitted.'

She raised her eyes to look at him. 'That I know. Here, in this place we have made, there is nothing that is not permitted. I am evidence of that.'

Savinkov looked quizzically at her, standing so still and sad in the snow. 'What is wrong with utopia?'

'This is utopia?'

'It is coming. Soon there will be freedom and happiness for all. But not until we defeat our enemies.'

Her face contorted, as if she had been struck. 'You cannot accuse me of not believing!' she cried. 'I was with you before the revolution, I am an old Bolshevik.'

From within the church came the tapping of mallets.

'You as me,' said Savinkov. There should have been comfort for her in the certainty of his voice. It did not come. 'It is not given to all to be in the army of the proletariat. We who are in the vanguard of that army are fashioned of special stuff. We have no higher honour than its membership, no higher calling than that.'

'Rykov was waiting for me,' she blurted. 'At the station. He wanted me to talk to some young men he was training. Ones like those over there.'

Savinkov glanced over at the two Chekists on the door, grinning in at one of the workmen inside, their hands stuffed in the pockets of their jerkins. He nodded in an understanding way, urging her to go on.

'I told them who we were, all we communists.'

It came out in a rush, colour suddenly flooding her pale cheeks.

'That we fought for the proletariat. And inside I was thinking, and I thought, *what* proletariat?'

She gestured wildly about the street. 'Where are they, Sergei? Who do we represent? The factories are empty, there are no workers.' Tears trickled down her face. 'I've had doubts, Sergei,' she whispered. 'It's so difficult to believe. Everything gets stood on its head. Before the revolution, we knew from reading Marx that afterwards the state would wither away; on the very day we came to power, the bureaucracies, the armies, the police, all would disappear.' She pointed to the two secret policemen as mute evidence of the opposite. The nails on her hand were rough, chewed.

'You thought that all we had to do was have a revolution, and all the ills of the world would suddenly go away? As if we had waved a magic wand?'

'Yes,' she said.

'It isn't like that. The revolution has to be won, every day. And where do we get the strength to win it? From our faith. We came to communism as people to a spring of fresh water, and we drank.'

She was aware of his steel-grey eyes staring at her from beneath his brows. She had seen him do it to others.

'Is there still exploitation on this earth?' he asked softly.

'Yes.'

'Do our class enemies hate us? Have they sent armies? Are there British and Americans, Czechs and Japanese on Soviet soil?'

'Yes.'

'Do they seek to deny the fruits of communism to the proletariat of the earth?'

'Yes,' she whispered.

Then until we defeat the exploiters, we have to keep our weapons sharp. Our armies, our workers, our police. All tireless, all vigilant.'

'There is the killing,' she said, and she winced, as though the word itself was a knife, cutting her mouth.

'We *have* to kill them. They would kill us.'

'Our *own*. Krivitskiy sends Cheka teams to get food, and they kill the peasants. Before the revolution did we not represent the peasants, too?'

'Darling,' Savinkov said gently. He put his arm about her. 'We do. The ones Krivitskiy kills are the kulaks. When the revolution came the rich peasants seized the land from the landlords. They stole the people's birthright for themselves. Now they hoard vast quantities of food and deny it to the people. They stand in the way of the revolution, and, like a mighty locomotive of history, it crushes them.'

'Rykov kills, too.'

'Like Krivitskiy, he administers justice on behalf of the people,' Savinkov corrected her.

'He had two people waiting outside . . . against a wall. They had hoods over their faces. I was there. Somehow I had a rifle in my hand. Rykov had put it there. We stood in a row. Rykov was behind me. My rifle went off and the man flew back against the wall. He cried out. And then they all fired. There was smoke in the courtyard. Rykov took me over, he pulled the bags off their heads.'

She looked at Sergei, and tears were running slowly down her cheeks. Her eyelashes were frozen with them.

'It was my mother and father, Sergei. I killed them.'

There was silence for a moment, just shouted orders inside the church, the running of feet. A number of men came tumbling out to join the Chekists, who had moved away. The priest stood nearby, still in prayer.

'But what are you, Ruth? You are a Bolshevik, as I am. We are making a new world. We are made of special stuff, we have the highest calling of all. We fight. Who do we fight?'

'Those who exploit us. Our class enemies,' she said, like a child reciting a rhyme.

'Some of us will be called to make the greatest sacrifice for our calling. Some of us will choose to die for the proletariat,' he said softly. 'Some of us *have* died. I will die if I am called. Will you die?'

'Yes,' she whispered. 'I suppose so.'

'Others have. Jogiches is dead. They captured him. They took him to a room full of *Freikorps* officers. They beat him for an hour, until he was dead. For telling the truth about Rosa.'

'Rosa is dead,' she whispered again, into the icy breeze.

'Did you love her?'

'Yes. She was like a mother to me.'

'Who killed her?'

'The Germans.'

'There are good, Communist Germans, our comrades, who are dead, or in hiding, or in jail. Who killed her?'

'The imperialists. The exploiters. The murderers of the working class.'

'*Who killed your mother?*'

She stared at him. It should have worked. She'd seen him do it to others. A spark should have ignited within her, lit a burning fire of faith.

'I did,' she said, through grey lips, leaden words falling into the cold. '*I* killed her. I killed my father, too. Nothing is worth that, Sergei. Not to kill your own parents, no. No cause.'

His mouth twisted in disappointment.

'You have failed the test,' he said, and his voice was chill, had lost its friendship. 'You should be a daughter of the working class, a daughter of poverty and struggle, of unparalleled privation and strife. You should shine like a beacon to all, clean and pure. But you cling to the relics of the past. Remember the words of Lenin. A good communist is a good Chekist. You will be tested again. You must not fail the next time.'

From within the church came muffled explosions, and the eight-hundred-year-old roof folded inwards, almost in slow motion. Dust and debris roared high through the roof as the incense-blackened pillars crashed down.

'I am being tested already,' she said. 'I'm pregnant. I'm having your baby.'

'He will be a new man. Born a communist. *He* will have no doubts,' said Savinkov certainly, cruelly.

'I want a drink, Sergei.'

He took her arm and they stepped down the street. As the dust began to clear from the ruin they saw the priest dead on the snow, crushed by a falling statue of Jesus.

'You see?' said Savinkov. 'There is no God.'

The dance floor was cleared; they had pushed the sofas and chairs to the side of the room. Outside the mansion the bushes and beds were bursting into leaf and flower, shaggy, untended, overgrown, but the new life of spring was fresh and vigorous, and after the long, cold, dark winter they felt its renewal. Bulavin had his accordion out; his big hands squeezed it, fingers moving and Ukrainian folk music filled the room. Rykov had requested it specially – he hoped it would make the young woman preparing to dance feel at home.

The boots stamped on the floor and they sang out in approval as she whirled in the middle of the ring of men, nearly ten of them, her plaits flying, arms outstretched to keep her balance, crashing from one to the other as they bounced her within their circle. Standing by Bulavin, Rykov clapped his hands as they stamped their feet. They had brought the revolution and it was time to celebrate.

Fragments of cloth flew up in the air, one after the other, as the men gripped hold of her maid's dress before sending her spinning across the ring, ripping it away in pieces that they threw triumphantly up at the ceiling. Her shift and bodice became visible, then they too, were torn away.

With a final crash and whoop the dance came to an end. She was naked except for her shoes and they spreadeagled her across the wide arm of a sofa and grinned at their boss. Rykov let his coat drop to the floor, and went slowly across, his victim's eyes following him fearfully the whole way. She had known what he was from the moment the Cheka truck came up the overgrown drive of the delapidated country house. They had heard rumours, of the revolution, of civil war, but they had not thought such evils would come. not out there.

As he violated her, Gaidouk rolled up her little finger. squeezing it horribly at intervals, making her scream. He understood his boss because he enjoyed the same things. Rykov kept a stubby screwdriver in his pocket for interrogations; now it was in his hand. He found a rib with its blade and raked it up and down. The girl howled in agony, and it was done.

He went upstairs to look around while his lads continued to celebrate. The sounds of the party filtered up through the boards. They would use the house as their headquarters. The stink of Petrograd and Moscow was far behind, they were back with the war, behind the troops.

A gargling shriek of horror penetrated the room, along with a gust of laughter. Rykov wondered what Gaidouk had done to the girl. The problem with Gaidouk, with all of the lads, was that they lacked imagination. He, Rykov did his best with what he had. Always, he felt that things could be improved upon. It was like food. Anyone could eat lamb – it was only when there were the herbs, the spices, the charcoal fire, that it became *satsivi*, that it came live in the mouth. Rykov wanted the spices, the colours, the strong sensations. He did his best to add spices to pathetic things like the little creature downstairs.

Outside, from a cherry tree coming into bloom, the old woman whose house it had been flapped weakly from the branch where she hung upside down. Rykov looked down at her from one of the bedroom windows. A bag sat on the bed, Gaidouk's. Something white was inside, he saw a sleeve spilling out. He pulled at it, and it slipped on to the bed in a sigh of silk. It was a wedding dress. The dress the girl had worn in the house of ice he had built for her, on the river. He stroked its soft folds and felt a stab of real excitement.

Below, the lads spilled out into the garden. Gaidouk was riding something, slashing at it with a riding whip. It was the girl. who went staggering about the garden under her burden, in a dying frenzy of fear. She collapsed, and he kicked her to get her moving again.

Rykov picked up the dress, folding it carefully. He realised that he should not have given it to a pig like Gaidouk. Not something precious like that. It had been worn by one of the young ladies in his photograph.

He felt certain that Gaidouk had counter-revolutionary tendencies. He would have to pay for having sullied the beautiful dress. Rykov stroked the fabric. It had been made for an aristocrat. Soon, he was sure, an aristocrat would wear it again. There were several, smiling out at him from his photograph . . .

7

Krasnyi Krym

The Crimea, June 1920

THEY lay on the reverse slope. When the whistles blew and the officers rose, jogging forward over the brow they got up, too, a long, thin line of men. The machine guns were popping in the tree line and they bent forward with their rifles held across their bodies, like men walking into driving rain.

The air above howled and the tree line erupted into gouts of flying brown earth. Green leaves floated like a carpet, and the torso of a man, still uniformed, tumbled over and over in the air before hitting the ground.

On the ridge Yelena saw it and, in a momentary silence in the shelling, she heard the thud as it hit the hard ground. Engines roared in her ears and she rolled to one side, still clutching her pack, as the Renault armoured cars came through. The men heard the crack of their four-pounder guns, low over their heads, and the thin line began to bunch, like chicks clustering about their mothers. Their backs were straight now and they covered the last twenty yards at the run, their bayonets glittering, small black balls rising in the air to fall into the trenches with so many poppings like small fireworks. The cavalry swept across the battlefield at the gallop, and Yelena went forward.

It stank, already. Later, it would smell worse, but the reek of blood and entrails, the stench of the slaughterhouse mixed with the acrid gag of explosive made her retch.

She found her first man fifty yards into the field. Smoke was drifting across from the line and her eyes were watering. He held his knee, and blood squirted through his fingers.

'God bless you! God bless you!' he exclaimed hoarsely, seeing the red cross on her armband.

She cut away his British uniform trouser leg and staunched the wound, binding a pressure pad over it, and immobilising the shattered joint with a splint. She gave the boy a small white cloth.

'The stretcher bearers are coming,' she promised him. 'When you see them, wave your flag.'

She worked her way forward. Near the line of the hastily-dug enemy trenches she found a young soldier kneeling, as if in prayer, his head resting on the ground. She put her hand on his shoulder and he crumpled slowly. His head moved, dislocated from his shoulders. One side was quite intact, like a shutter just detached from its hinges, the other was quite gone, and she could see inside the empty cranial shell.

'He doesn't need your help,' a voice called, 'but my comrade does.'

Looking up, she saw the back of a man's head in the trench, bending over.

'I'm coming,' she called. She slithered down the earthen side. The remains of a dugout was there and baulks of black timber lay scattered like spillikins. A soldier lay pinned beneath one by the leg. His comrade struggled to pull it off him, but it was wedged fast in the ruins. He looked up as she climbed over the wreckage.

'We are men of the Red Army,' he said directly. 'But will you help us?'

'I tend the wounded,' she said. 'I don't ask what colour, red or white.'

She bent over the trapped man. He was unconscious, but breathing.

'His leg is almost off,' she said. 'The timber is acting as a tourniquet. I shall amputate it and we will take him to the ambulances waiting in our rear.'

'Do what you must, Countess,' the man said quietly and she looked up in surprise. A smile appeared in his smoke-blackened face. She saw that he was a sailor for he had a greasy round cap on his head with the lettering of the Aurora still just visible beneath the dirt.

'You know me?'

'I am Pavel from Kronstadt. Your friends brought me to your school before the revolution. I remember you all, countess.'

The wounded man's thigh bone was shattered and she sawed its jagged stump smooth. Pavel passed her what she needed from the roll she laid out on her pack.

'We thought you were defeated,' Pavel said. She took a scalpel, and began to cut through the muscle and connective tissue, leaving the pulped, filthy, flesh and bone behind.

'We are recapturing the Crimea,' she said. 'Join us, Pavel from Kronstadt. We are not as we were. I am not a countess. I am just a nurse. Wrangel is giving the peasants their land and he will give you yours. You will not get it from Lenin or Trotsky, I promise you.'

Pavel stroked his cap in a familiar gesture. 'We are the heroes of the revolution,' he said proudly. 'Trotsky told us so. He will not betray us, not after all we have done for the people.'

'None of us have done much for the people,' she said bitterly. 'It were better that none of this had happened.'

She took a length of catgut and deftly drew it tight about the big artery with her forceps. The blood ceased spurting and she wiped the back of her hand across her face to get rid of the sweat and replaced it with blood. She cut the skin and folded the flap down over the red stump, tacking it closed with a line of fast stitches.

'I did not know you were trained,' Pavel said admiringly.

'You learn,' she said shortly. 'I went to Madame Chatillon's sewing and embroidery classes. When you are a lady, you learn these things.'

She put her things away, and Pavel reached out with gentle hands, lifting his unconscious comrade up over his shoulder.

'We have fought many battles, Timofey Iakovich and I,' he said. 'I thank you for saving his life.'

'The ambulances are at the rear,' she said, weary now. 'Carry him there for me.'

Steps were cut in the fire wall. Pavel mounted them with his burden and they began walking back over the battlefield, leaving the sounds of pursuit behind them. Smoke drifted, reddening in the afternoon sun. Scents rose up from the wild plants and flowers that they crushed with their feet.

An ambulance waited on the far side of the ridge, a converted Morris bus. A cluster of stretcher bearers and wounded and bandaged men were about its rear door and a tall man in a Guards hat and padded boots stood nearby.

'Mikhail!' Yelena called. 'Is there room for one more?'

He looked up and smiled. 'One more, for you.'

Pavel eased his comrade down on to a slatted wooden seat. 'Take care of him for me,' he said.

'Take off your hat and stay,' Yelena urged. 'Wrangel is taking Bolsheviks into his army, if they wish to fight for us. Do it. *We* are the real Russian army.'

Pavel smiled. 'I am a hero of the revolution. Heroes cannot change sides.'

Then he was gone, jogging through the smoke for the trees. The stretcher bearers went back up the slope to the battlefield, and Mikhail prepared to shut the doors.

'We'd better get them to the casualty clearing station . . .'

His voice faded as he stared at something in the bus. A small soldier sat huddled on the floor. His cap was pulled down over his face, his mouth and jaw obscured by a bandage. The battledress was soaked in blood over its chest and moving to one side he could see the gaping hole of an exit wound in the cloth at the back. But the man's shirt was white, and unmarked. Yet it was a killing wound that the owner of the battledress had received.

Mikhail looked at Yelena and she nodded. A deserter. Mikhail reached forward and seized him roughly by the shoulder with a powerful hand, dragging him out of the bus.

'Hey, you. Get out of here! This is for wounded men, not cowards.'

He cuffed him angrily, and the cap tumbled from his head. The little man reached inside his battledress like a snake striking, and pulled out a Mauser machine pistol. He dragged the bandage from his face.

'Oh, God!' Yelena said softly. 'Rykov.'

'Does Wrangel enlist Chekists, Mistress?' Rykov asked savagely.

'We hang your sort,' said Mikhail coldly. 'Trying to run away, Rykov? Here to shoot the ones slow to go forward, were you?'

The Chekist stared at both of them. 'Get in,' he ordered. 'And drive.'

They sat along the bench seat of the cab. Mikhail at the wheel. Yelena next to him and Rykov by the door. He pushed the muzzle of the machine pistol into her side.

'Bit of a shock being on the losing end of a battle, hey, Rykov?' Mikhail drawled. 'More fun shooting our wounded and frightened young kids, isn't that right?'

Rykov stared out of the window. In the distance cavalry was moving, Wrangel's Cossacks. He was very pale, his breath coming in short gasps.

'Frightened, Rykov, old fellow?' Mikhail asked mockingly.

Rykov dug the pistol barrel into Yelena's side and she gasped. 'Drive,' he ordered. 'Drive away from those troops or I'll shoot her now.'

Mikhail started the engine and the bus vibrated with life. From behind them a weak cheer came from the unknowing, wounded troops. The bus wheeled around on the slope, and took the dirt road towards the sunny, tree-covered hills.

'I was there when Semenov had the Kharbin Cheka hang themselves,' Mikhail commented. 'Swinging like corks down the main street, they were.'

Rykov said nothing, just sat staring through the glass of the windscreen with narrowed pupils. As they made their way from the battle area he began to relax.

'We have to get these men to the hospital, Rykov,' Yelena said quietly.

'*Graf* Mikhail will have me hanged,' he said grimly. 'We will go to *my* hospital. Here, take this left fork.'

'We are near the lines,' said Mikhail. 'The Reds are not far down that road. You can get out and make your way from here.'

'Go down this fork,' Rykov repeated, and jabbed Yelena with his gun.

A mile down the path they saw a roadblock set up between the river bank and the wooded side of the valley.

'I'll shoot you both,' Rykov warned. 'Them, too.'

They drew up and dust from their passage blew in on smoky air through the open window.

'We're taking the long road,' said Mikhail. His voice sounded weary. 'The Reds cut the route to the hospital.'

'Better be careful, sir,' said the guard. He was young, in a pair of imperial cavalry trousers and a British army battledress. 'Keep right round the hill. Zhloba's said to control the area to the north.'

'We shall be careful.'

'You might to better to go back to the fork,' the boy suggested helpfully.

'*We have wounded men here!*' Rykov screamed. 'Move the barrier.'

'Move the barriers,' Yelena said quietly.

Mikhail put the bus into gear and they ground forward, carrying their load of injured.

At the crossroads they stopped again.

'Straight on,' Rykov said.

'As you said, we have wounded men on board,' said Yelena. 'Won't you let us take them to one of our field hospitals? You are safe, now.'

'I can shoot you and *Graf* Mikhail now, Mistress,' he said unemotionally. 'And take myself through our lines. I know how to drive. But I will not do so unless you make me. I am taking you and these men to one of our hospitals. So drive on.'

They looked at him doubtfully. Then Mikhail put it into gear once more with a crunch, and they headed north.

It was dark by the time they arrived. They had followed the river up into the foothills from whence it came and, in the glow of the headlamps they could see grey stone walls pocked by small windows. A plain stone cross stood outside.

'Let's get out,' Rykov suggested. He tapped on the glass of the bus with his pistol.

'Just going to get help, lads,' he called, and a faint, and aching cheer came from inside the packed vehicle.

They went through the tall doors. A Cheka guard was there. He knew Rykov, and grinned. A dreadful smell was in the air; it hung in the tall, bleak stone hallway like a pall. Jesus hung on a cross from the wall, looking down upon them in his agony.

'What is this place?' Yelena whispered.

'A hospital, I told you.' He turned to the guard. 'Where's Zemliachka?'

'Here!' a woman's voice called hoarsely. Rykov smiled.

'Let's go and see the matron.'

They went down the hall, their boots echoing off the stone flags, worn smooth from centuries of shuffling, praying monks. They went into some kind of changing room. A long cupboard occupied a wall, made for vestments. A woman of middle age sat in an armed carving chair set on the stone. The cupboard seemed hung with chains, axes, knives and tools. She wore black leather from the boots over her riding breaches to the peaked cap on her head. A dreadful odour filled the room, both pungent and putrescent, and it came from her. She looked up at them through bloodshot, malevolent eyes.

'Well, what have we here?' she rasped.

'Patients,' Rykov said mockingly, and she smiled, revealing tobacco-yellow teeth. 'I caught them on the battlefield.'

Mikhail grunted contemptuously, and Rykov stamped on his foot.

'How did it go?' Zomliachka asked. Mikhail staggered against the wall, and she ignored him.

'Bad. They fought like rabbits. We shot dozens, simply to get them to fight. I'll have to go over to headquarters to find out what's going on. We may have to move if Wrangel's lot are on the way.'

'We must get busy in the morning, then.'

The prospect seemed to please the creature in the chair. She stretched, and small clouds of dark dust puffed out of her uniform.

'I'll go now,' said Rykov. 'Listen. Keep these two for me. Put them in a cell somewhere.'

Zemliachka nodded. Her flushed eyes were hooded, as if she looked into some strange future.

'We brought a bus full of patients with us,' Rykov said. 'I'll just take them to the ward.'

They heard his boots going away down the corridor, heard him exchange some quip with the guard, heard them laugh.

'We are both trained medical attendants,' Yelena said clearly. 'We are willing to help you look after your patients, if this is a hospital.'

The eyes came into focus and she looked up at Yelena.

'Yes, this is a hospital,' she whispered. 'A hospital where we cleanse, where we eliminate sickness, where we purify. This is the hospital of the punishing, merciless sword of Red Terror. *Krasnyi Krym* . . . we are making the Crimea red . . . Here we purify the worker-titans of Russia of the hangmen, enslavers and tormentors of the working class. And, no, we do not need medical attendants of your class here.'

'Your class, too,' Yelena said softly. 'You are no peasant, no worker-titan, no more than are Lenin or Trotsky.'

The bloodshot eyes looked at her with pupils that narrowed to pin-points.

'Very clever, we are. Yes, I am Rozalia Zalkind, but I am called Zemliachka. Yes, I was born into wealth, but I am a vanguard fighter, one of the *zakalennye bolsheviki*, a bolshevik as hardened as steel. Unlike you, I reject the past, and embrace only the future. But stay, I may have work for you after all . . .'

She put her head back and yelled, '*Scum*! Come here, scum.'

From somewhere nearby there came a slapping of feet, hurrying along at the command of the voice. Something came into the room behind them and they turned.

'Here it is, Scum. Once it wore fine clothes, robbed from the sweat of the workers; once it rode in a carriage while they suffered. Now it is here, where it belongs. Scum, handling scum, wading in scum, dripping with scum.'

A creature stood in the doorway. From its rags, from the rotten mat about its face that was its hair, it was covered in putrescent, dark slime. Only two blazingly-green eyes in the terrible face indicated that it was human.

'I found it,' Zemliachka said softly. 'It is one like you are, an oppressor of the workers. I found it pretending to be one of us, so now it works for me, it helps me purify the Russian people. It may be I shall put you to the same work.'

She yawned, then yelled once again for the guard. 'Stick them in a cell. I'll leave them there until Rykov comes for them . . .'

They were herded up the corridor towards stone steps. From behind them came a thud and a crash. Glancing back Yelena saw that the Chekist had kicked the creature over with a boot. It was human, bright red blood streaked the stone.

They were put into a tiny monk's cell. Mikhail went to the window as the door clashed to.

'That thing.' Yelena said quietly to him. 'The one that woman called scum. That's Katia.'

He looked down from testing the bars. 'Your schoolfriend?'

'I'd know those eyes anywhere. And she looked at me – she knew who we were, Mikhail.'

'There's Rykov,' he said suddenly, and Yelena peered out. They could see the bus, see Rykov in the yellow light of its headlamps, saw him put down a big can on the ground. There was a glow in his hand, and then a sudden flash of light that ran along the side of the bus, licking upwards. The cell window was barred, but without glass. The quiet of the night was shattered by screaming, by shattering glass.

The vehicle burned rapidly and it lit up the inside of the cell. A crutch smashed through a window and two, and then three terrible, burning, flapping things fell out, rolling over and over. They blazed until they were still. A man clawed his way to the window in the bus, heaving with one hand as his hair, his clothes, his bandages burned. Rykov watched at a distance, his hands on his hips, and they saw his teeth gleam in the firelight. The breeze blew smoke across the monastery, and the cell was filled with the acrid smell of charring pork.

The lock on the door grated, and Yelena came awake. She shook Mikhail. They were huddled together in a corner for warmth. A tiny light outlined the door and they saw it swing open.

'*Yelena*,' a voice hissed. The door moved shut, a candle-stub cupped in a hand came across the cell. It was enveloped in a terrible smell of death.

'Katia!'

'Are you both awake? You must be very quiet, and come with me. I can get you out.'

'How?' Mikhail whispered quickly.

'I have a key, I stole it. I keep it . . . where they would never look. In a horrible place . . . It opens some of the doors inside, but none outside.'

'What does that thing make you do, Katia?' Yelena asked. There was anguish in her voice. 'Why are you covered in . . . all that . . .'

'She kills, darling.' Her friend's clear voice in the dark was as though she was still at the *Lycée*, on stage, with their parents applauding in the audience at the end of term.

'She kills everyone like us she can find. They all do. This is a *lager osobogo naznacheniia*, one of the camps of special purpose. Its purpose is to murder all the Bolsheviks' class enemies. And I . . . I have to dispose of those she kills. She finds some sort of pleasure in watching me like this . . . But enough. *Listen* to me, I will take you down by a back stair. I will put you outside, in the courtyard. There lie the bodies of those she killed yesterday. I will put you in the pile and you must lie very, very still. Later, in the morning, I will load some of the dead on to a cart that is drawn by a donkey. The gate will be opened for me, and I will lead the donkey out down to the river, where I will tip the bodies in. You will be there and you can float away downstream with the dead.'

'Can't you escape, too?'

'No,' Katia said flatly. 'I am watched.'

'But won't she know you have helped us escape when she finds the cell empty?'

'She will not remember that you are here in the morning. She kills so many, and she takes cocaine. When Rykov asks where you are she will simply assume that she slaughtered you like the others. Now come, we don't have time to waste.'

She opened the door, cupping her hand so that the candle flame was but a glow, and they crept out and down a small and winding stair.

'Through here.'

They went through a door and Katia pushed it closed. She put down the candle and, in its sudden light, Yelena stuffed her fist in her mouth to stop herself from crying out.

They were in a chapel. Over the altar Christ looked down from the cross. The baptismal font had been dragged over to the altar and brimmed with a hideous soup. The floor was inches deep in a dark slime. Dead bodies lay jumbled everywhere, many mutilated, missing parts. The last to die hung over the altar, his brains in the font. The crowbar that had performed the deed lay on the stained altar cloth.

'This is where I live,' said Katia. 'She keeps me here.'

There was another door and she worked its lock and blew out the candle. They heard a scraping, then she opened the door, and cool, fresh air came into the stench.

She led them out. There was only starlight, but she found the pile by touch.

'Quickly, now,' she whispered, pulling some bodies down. 'Get on!'

Yelena and Mikhail clambered up amongst the dead, who moved in a rubbery fashion. Katia dragged some corpses over them.

'You must look like them so do not cry out now. I must make you like them.'

Yelena shut her eyes, and cold, terrible slime poured over her face. She ground her teeth in horror, and whimpered inside her head.

'I'm going. I'm going now, darling. Stay still, both of you. Stay very still and I will take you to the river . . .'

The clean scent of burning charcoal penetrated nostrils clogged with the stench of death. Mikhail breathed it in, lying amidst the dead in the pile. There were hoarse shouts of command, the shuffling of feet, the thudding of repeated blows, the whimpering of pain and fear.

The gore that coated his face was congealed and glued his eyes closed. After a while one came partly open and he peered past the spikes of dark red lashes into the courtyard.

A crowd of people stood huddled by the wall, guarded by Chekists swinging heavy clubs, crowbars and axes. In the shade of the wall a bed of charcoal glowed. Iron stands were at each end. As he watched, Zemliachka came out of a door. She was dressed as the day before, in black leather. She stood in front of the group of people, men, women and children who shivered with cold, hunger and fear by the wall.

'*Boorzhoi*,' she said softly. 'You are bourgeois.'

She licked her lips almost painfully, as though tasting something foul.

'You have come here to die. We are those sent by the worker-titans of the world to cleanse it of your presence. We wage pitiless, unceasing struggle against your very existence.'

Three figures stood in front of the mass, separated by the guards, two men, one old, wearing a military uniform, one middle-aged and a young and beautiful woman in yellow silk. The middle-aged man was dressed in the remnants of a black suit of tails and a ruined top hat had been placed upon his head. Now Mikhail heard him speak.

'We are human beings,' he said, speakingly clearly and bravely. 'As, I suppose, you are. What right do you have to appoint yourself murderer of those who dress differently to you, who speak differently to you?'

'We are those appointed by the working classes of the world. For us the old systems of morality and humanity invented by the bourgeoisie for the purpose of oppressing and exploiting the working classes do not exist. To us, all is permitted, for we are the first in the world to raise the sword in the name of freeing all from bondage. We are the *zakalennye bolsheviki*.'

The old man, who wore a faded general's uniform, snorted contemptuously.

Zemliachka went up to him.

'Did you not slaughter thousands of workers in your army?'

'Peasants,' he said shortly. 'The workers were in the factories. And they fought for the love of Russia and the Tsar.'

'*Liar!*'

She slashed him with something in her hand and he stood with blood streaming down his face, his head high and military, still staring at her in contempt.

'Bring the barrel!' she shouted. 'As you cut the workers to death, so shall you feel *their* sharp steel.'

Guards rolled a big wooden barrel from the wall and bundled the general inside, banging on the lid. Mikhail heard him grunt in agony, heard Yelena whimper through clenched teeth. They were holding hands amongst the corpses and he squeezed hard, and she was quiet.

Zemliachka turned to the man in his old suit of tails.

'And you,' she said softly. 'What crime did you commit against the workers?'

'I was an industrialist,' he said levelly. 'I provided work for them, and paid them wages, so that they might feed and clothe their families.'

She hit him, too, and blood fountained from his face.

'*You drank their blood!*' she screamed. 'You ate their flesh!'

'I understand that you intend to murder us,' he said, his voice shaking slightly. 'But spare the children. They have done you no harm, however you may think. Let them go free.'

'Let them go? When you put the torch to lice, do you spare the eggs? Would they not grow up in our new world and appear like us? And all the time, beneath the skin, they would be *boorzhoi*, scum. Traitors to the working class. Working once again to enslave us. No, no!'

Her arm snaked out into the crowd pressed back against the wall and dragged a woman from it. She was pregnant and she cradled her round stomach in terror, trying to move away from the woman in her dreadful black uniform. Zemliachka pointed a blood-encrusted claw in accusation.

'There it is,' she whispered. 'There is the enemy.'

Her blade flashed in the summer sunlight and the woman's dress was suddenly scarlet. She fell to the ground, clutching her stomach. The industrialist struggled with Zemliachka as she went after her and a Chekist smashed him in the kidneys with his rifle. Zemliachka dragged the woman over on to her back as she begged her to stop, and the knife rose and fell.

When she stood up fresh blood streamed from her, and she was breathing hard. She held up something pink, like a rabbit.

'There it is,' she said in triumph. She dashed it against the wall. 'There is the enemy!'

She looked down upon the industrialist, who lay gasping on the earth. 'Peg him out!'

The guards ripped his clothes from him and lashed him to pegs set in the earth. A Chekist appeared with a small bird cage, and another with a copper bowl. Inside the cage was not a bird but something else, something that chittered angrily. Zemliachka held the cage close to the industrialist's face, and he saw the rat.

'This is what you are,' she whispered.

They took the rat out, and imprisoned it under the copper bowl, which they placed upon his stomach. Then they brought coals from the bed of embers, and laid them on its upturned bottom.

Finally, Zemliachka stood in front of the young woman. Blonde hair fell down over the canary yellow of her dress, and she stared at the hideous creature in front of her in terror.

'And you . . . the worst of all.'

'I have done nothing,' the girl protested.

'Nothing?' the Chekist asked mockingly. 'Did you not live in a fine house? Did you not eat fine food? Did you not go to the best school, wear the best clothes? Are you not beautiful?'

'It is not a crime,' she said bravely.

'Oh, but it is. Beauty is for the idle. I have never been beautiful, because for all my life I have struggled for the victory of the working classes. Beauty is disgusting, beauty is a crime. We shall stamp beauty out.'

She sidled up to the young girl, who could not help cringing away from her.

'What is it like, being beautiful?' she whispered. 'What is it like, knowing that all men who see you wish to possess you? You could have any man you chose, could you not? And breed more of your kind, to oppress and enslave. That is what your beauty would do.'

They tore the dress from her so that she was naked, and the guards raped her as she screamed, one after the other. Zemliachka laughed, for the first time that morning. Then they lashed her to a long iron pole with wire, and placed it on the stands at each end of the bed of coals. Her long blonde hair hung down and it caught fire and she shrieked over the laughter of the guards. They began to turn the spit.

Two guards began to roll the barrel about the yard. It glittered strangely in the sunshine, and soon it oozed blood through its strakes.

Stretched out between the pegs, the man with the copper bowl on his stomach gasped, and then moaned in pain.

Zemliachka took a shiny silver snuff box from her pocket and inhaled some pinches of the white powder inside.

'Into the chapel with them,' she said casually, pointing at the remaining prisoners. 'Let them pray.'

She went over to the spit, where the girl turned and roasted, groaning in her agony.

'You are not beautiful now,' she said, with satisfaction, then she put back her head, and yelled.

'*Scum!*'

Through his one eye Mikhail saw Katia hurry from the chapel door where the crowd of victims stood waiting to die. She stood by the executioner in her stinking rags.

'It's time to get rid of them, scum. But first, you should have something to eat.'

The knife flashed in her hand and carved the blistered, charring body in front of her. The girl was still alive and she thrashed convulsively. Zemliachka held out flesh . . .

A donkey stood between the shafts of a cart, his nostrils flaring, his coat twitching from horror. A woman prisoner joined Katia, and they began to load the dead up into the cart. They took Mikhail's arms, one each, and heaved him on top of the corpses. More slid over him.

The cart began to move towards the gate. They went by the barrel, and he saw that hundreds of nails had been driven through its sides, the heads gleaming in the sun. The industrialist lay still, spreadeagled between the pegs in a spreading pool of blood and the rat poked its nose through a hole it had torn in his body. It slithered through, slimy with blood, and ran away across the yard.

As they went through the gate, its shadow fell across the cart. There was the bang of a rifle and the prisoner fell back dead among the corpses. He heard a man laugh.

He could hear the splashing of water, the rush of the river going down from the mountains to the sea.

The cart stopped and he heard the crash as the tailgate went down, the explosions as bodies began to fall into the river. He felt Katia's hands on his leg as she pulled him from the tumbril and through his one eye he saw the blood of the woman in the yellow dress fresh on her mouth, saw her green eyes, completely blank as she dragged the corpses of the murdered ones into the stream. Then he was gone, floating away amongst the dead.

He found Yelena where the river made a little bay.

She knelt in the water, frantically rubbing herself with handfuls of sand, her blonde hair dark and congealed. She tore at herself, ripping her own flesh until she bled.

'Come on,' he said gently, pulling down her hands. 'We have to get away.'

She allowed herself to be helped to her feet. 'I shall never be clean again,' Yelena whispered. 'Never . . .'

A lorry was coming down the road, one of theirs. The driver stopped as they waved their stained Red Cross armbands.

'Get in,' he said. 'There are five Red armies coming down the road.'

They stared at him. 'But we're winning the war,' said Mikhail.

'The Poles have left it,' the driver said shortly. 'They signed an armistice. Now the Reds are coming for us. We're falling back to the peninsula.'

There was a tortoiseshell comb on the dashboard. Mikhail took it, and slowly, carefully, drew it through Yelena's hair, freeing the hideous debris.

8

Gaspodi, Pomilui, Umershikh

The Crimea, November 1920

T HE *Red Banner* was a train. Its powerful locomotive had hauled armoured flatcars set with gun emplacements earlier in the war, fighting Denikin and Kolchak along vast stretches of railway line. Now it pulled even more impressive weapons. The big carriages were emblazoned with slogans and heroic, brightly-coloured paintings of soldiers, peasants and workers striving and struggling together, building a new world of social justice and social equality. Konstantin had perfected his stencils, and the artists aboard the train could stamp their message upon a town or camp in half a day, making it communist. The carriages contained a printing press, stacks of books, brochures and pamphlets. simply and attractively written, and an array of specially produced films bringing Russia's new leaders and way of life to the people and the troops. Flatcars carried automobiles and trucks to carry the message out to villages or camps away from the railway line. And it had entertainers, musicians and singers, to lift the hearts of the people. They called it an agit-train. The Reds had beaten the Whites in the field, and also in men's minds.

The *Red Banner* was moving along the line, a stop a day. Over one hundred and eighty thousand of Frunze's Red soldiers were massing for the final attack on the forty thousand Whites behind the Turkish Wall that protected Sevastopol. Frunze had captured thirty-six thousand tons of White grain in his advance and the trains – the *Red Banner* one of them – had brought new greatcoats and felt boots by the truckload. There were enough machine guns on the front to provide the lead echelons with fire from one for each squad of twenty. The White prisoners they had taken were in ragged summer uniforms. stuffed with straw and moss. It was almost November 7. Frunze's troops included the *Konarmiia*, the Red Cavalry, and Bluiker's Fifty-First Division. They were the Eagles of the Revolution and, as its third anniversary approached, their generals had promised Lenin final victory. And the entertainers from *Red Banner* had arrived.

The troops packed the frozen ground in front of the big, floodlit stage. They were warm in their new clothing and boots and the cooks had provided hot and plentiful food. They were ready and receptive to be told what they were fighting for, and why.

They enjoyed the revolutionary poetry. The poet on the stage might not be Mayakovskii or Blok, but he knew their verse. The soldiers, who had won the revolution, could identify with Blok's patrol of twelve brave Red Guards, with Wrangel's ragged forces waiting to be defeated, they knew who the mangy dog symbolised:

> So they march with sovereign tread:
> Before them a hungry dog,
> Before them, with a bloodstained banner,
> Unseen through the blizzard.
> Unscathed by the bullets . . .

They knew of Mayakovskii as the 'drummer' of the revolution, they roared out the words as the post began 'Left March.'

> 'Left, left, left . . .
> Who moved his right?' they demanded.
> 'Left, left, left.' they insisted.

There were dancers, there were musicians. And there was the Volga peasant girl, Verochka. She came on last, and they fell quiet, because her voice was like liquid silver, her hair like gold in the lights. When she danced she lifted her skirt and her long legs flashed. Her bosom was high, her skin like peach. They were all in love with her.

Trucks took the entertainers back to the train. It travelled during the night, so as to be ready for the next day's work soon after the crews rose in the morning at their new destination.

Verochka was the star and the party commissar had given her her own room at the end of the train, where it was quiet. She wore French silk underwear under the simple peasant blouse and skirt the soldiers loved and the army greatcoat she affected was lined with soft, warm fur. She ate fresh meat and vegetables, had yellow butter on her bread when millions starved. The new world was not as different to the old, she had found. There was everything for the few, and little for the rest. The only change was the necessity to keep what one had, concealed.

She opened the door to her room and went in, locking it behind her. Her maid had left an oil lamp burning, a glass bowl of water in front of it to diffuse the soft light, and the curtains were drawn to protect her privacy. The grumble of the artillery lobbing shells at the Sevastopol-Armiansk railroad and the counter-battery fire of the White armoured trains firing back from the north came through like a distant thunderstorm brewing.

It was not her night to entertain Stanislavsky, the Party Commissar. She slid her warm coat from her shoulders, hanging it on the back of the door from a scented, padded hanger. Stanislavsky didn't like the cold so he kept the whole train well heated with the coal from the *Red Banner's* bunker. Her room was pleasingly warm and she shrugged off the ridiculous peasant outfit that she loathed. A soft cough from the corner of the room caught the blouse and skirt still in her hand and she clutched them up against her body in alarm. A man was sitting there, his dark uniform blending in against the wood panels. A small man. He smiled politely.

'Who the hell are you?' she demanded nervously.

'I did not mean to frighten you,' he said apologetically. 'My name is Rykov.' He stood up, and offered her a bouquet of flowers. 'I found these in a bourgeois greenhouse,' he said. 'As one who would walk fifty versts in the rain to hear you sing, may I give them to you?'

One of *them* she thought and her confidence began to seep back. The silly saps infatuated with her beauty she could cope with. She took the flowers with a gracious smile. But how did he get in here? The station was guarded.

'I'm with the G.P.U.,' he said, and a fresh stab of fear went through her stomach. The Cheka was the Cheka, whatever it had taken to calling itself, and the gallows humour of the day said that G.P.U. stood not for State Political Administration, but '*Gaspodi, pomilui umershikh*', 'Lord have mercy upon the dead.'

The little man was obviously well-acquainted with the effect that the announcement of his profession had on people, for he smiled reassuringly.

'No, no, don't be afraid. We Chekists have off-duty interests too. I love your songs and I try to attend any concert where you are. I am, you may say, a *devot*.'

She smiled back, rather less certainly, still clutching her peasant clothing over her skimpy underwear.

'Now that the war is almost won, I am to make a collection of gramophone recordings of our great revolutionary songs. Real, 78 rpm records. I would be very happy to send you a set.'

'And I to receive them. I am, by the way, a friend of Comrade

Lunacharskii,' he said, naming the Commissar for Enlightenment. 'Perhaps you would care for an introduction.'

'I would, yes, please.' she said eagerly.

'You see, your *devot* come bearing gifts. I have one more. In the deserted bourgeois house where I found the flowers for you I discovered something else. As soon as I saw it I knew that it could clothe no other.'

From the arm of the chair where he had been sitting he lifted up a dress. It shimmered ivory in the soft light.

'It is a wedding dress, of course,' he said apologetically. 'But the cloth is of the finest, it could be altered.'

She rubbed the cloth between finger and thumb. Silk. The finest embroidery. You didn't see work like that now, not in these filthy revolutionary times.

'It is a lovely garment,' she agreed.

'The sort of dress you yourself would have worn to get married, had times been different?' he suggested.

'What do you mean. comrade?' she faltered. 'I am a poor peasant girl.'

'Surely not. It is *Countess* Verochka, is it not?'

She looked at him in the soft light as a large rabbit stares at a small, but deadly stoat, unable to run.

'I am correct?' he asked softly. 'You did attend the *Lycée*, the Empress's School in Tsarskoye Selo?'

'Yes,' she whispered.

He smiled pleasantly. 'I knew it. It is in the phrasing of your singing, you see. You have been trained, and peasant girls do not get trained.'

'No,' she said unhappily. He came up close to her and squeezed her arm.

'Don't worry,' he said reassuringly. 'Let it be our secret. Really, I don't care where you come from. I am just a *devot*. Look, why don't you try on the dress. I would love to see you in it.'

'Very well,' she said. She was trying to assess the situation. Did the little bastard mean what he said? Or was this some game, and goons were waiting outside to drag her off? Or did he mean to have her? The train would be moving soon, maybe she could stall for time.

She put down her peasant clothes and was reassured to see him keep his eyes scrupulously on her face as he held out the dress. She wriggled into it, sliding her hands down the long sleeves.

'Here,' he said. 'Let me do up the buttons.'

She turned her back and he carefully did up the long line of pearl buttons, sliding them into their loops. Then she felt his hands slide around her chest to feel her breasts under the silk.

'The train is leaving in a few minutes,' she said.

'Yes, I know. Then we shall not have to take too long.'

She was resigned. She bent obediently over the arm of the sofa, and felt him pull up the dress about her waist. She heard him gasping with excitement. She was relieved, in a way. He was obviously only what he said. She braced her long legs against his energy and his hands moved from between her thighs to her breasts, and up to her neck.

All his weight was bearing down on her and she put out her hands to support herself as his fingers bit into the soft skin of her throat. She jerked her head back, slamming her skull into his face, and he snarled in pain. She was strong. She reared up with him on her back and they crashed into the wall of the carriage. The whistle blew, drowning out her screams, and his hands found her larynx. In the sudden silence he took away her breath in a crackling of eggshells. The brakes squeaked, the carriage jerked, he stood back, blood streaming from his nose, and watched as she staggered, clawing at her throat, and fell. Then he knelt over her once more. The engine whistle blew, and he finished violating her as she died.

As the train left the station he dropped down from the rear platform of the carriage. He walked away, something white folded up under his arm . . .

The gleam of the rails behind them slowly dulled in the sunshine as the frost came stealthily back. The train stood quite still – a flyer, just a locomotive with its bunker of fuel and empty, waiting carriages behind. Huge red crosses marked their roofs and sides. In the distance the sky was dark with smoke and the air grumbled with artillery fire. At the end of the cold, frosted line, wounded men lay waiting for the train to come.

Yelena sat at the side of the locomotive, by one of the huge driving wheels. She wore a soldier's uniform and had a clean armband marked with a red cross. Two legs stuck out from underneath, ending in the loose, padded boots that Mikhail favoured for his crippled feet. From time to time she passed a tool in, and took another back. Finally Mikhail wriggled out and sat up, holding a shiny, heavy part in his hand.

'Wrecked,' he said bitterly. It bore the blue and yellow stains of great heat, a broken rod projected jaggedly from its interior.

'Can you mend it?' she asked. It looked hopeless.

'No, we need a new one from the works in Kiev, and they aren't making deliveries.'

'We'd better go, then. Make our way to Sevastopol.'

Mikhail stood up, moving stiffly.

'Alexander Borisovich!' Yelena called, and a greasy head poked itself out of the cab, the coal dust that coated it evidence of its owner's trade.

'The train can't be fixed so we're going to try to get to Sevastopol, to the evacuation ships. Count Mikhail can't go very fast; you go on ahead to look for some transport.'

'Very good, Countess,' the fireman said. As they walked down the length of the train, past the empty carriages, they saw him hurrying along the cold line ahead of them.

'We should have thought of bringing bicycles,' said Yelena, as Mikhail shuffled painfully along.

'Bicycles?' he smiled. 'For the railway kings?'

She laughed. The flat land stretched out before them and there was the glimmer of the sea, the darkness of woods ahead.

'I always thought we would win,' she said sadly.

They trudged along the line in the cold.

'Their Russia, now,' he said.

'We'll be in London,' she said. 'We'll read about it in the papers.'

'There's a church in Knightsbridge where my parents used to go on Sundays,' he said casually. 'We could be married there.'

She put her arm about him and he suddenly said, bitterly, 'It should have been the Cathedral of St Andrew. That was where my parents were married. The Tsar was there . . .'

'Your church in Knightsbridge will be good enough for me,' she said. 'What will we do, do you think?'

'If we can survive civil war, we can manage anywhere. Perhaps I'll join the railways.'

'I'd like a garden. Even a small one. The English are great gardeners . . .'

In the distance, a group of horsemen came out of the woods.

'Ours or theirs?' said Mikhail, stopping.

Half a mile away the small figure of the train's fireman suddenly crumpled to the ground by the tracks. A moment later the pop of a firearm going off came on the breeze. The horsemen rode up the embankment and they could hear the hooves drumming on the frozen ground.

The cold went through into his bones. His uniform, which should have kept him warm, was so cold the fleas had stopped moving in it.

The Sivash salt flat mud on it which had melted when they had burned the White soldiers up in the trench, now held it stiff like armour. He clacked dully and rythmically on his horse as he moved up the road by the garden of the house.

Akulov had fought too long to expect elation from victory. The small company of cavalrymen he shepherded along in the wake of Wrangel's retreating troops had been twice its size when they had attacked over the frozen mud flats, the foggy night illuminated by the yellow flares of the artillery behind them, and Kutepov's machine-gunners in front. When the wind had died down and the tide came back the water had covered over dozens of men he had fought with since the war began, killed on its last day.

There was nothing unusual about a Party commissar rounding up a group of soldiers to shoot – they had been doing it since the war began. They shot White ones for fighting too well, they shot Red ones for not doing it well enough, and the others tried harder.

There was a metallic clattering as oiled bolts pushed cold rounds out of their magazines and into the receivers of the rifles. The White soldiers stood still and erect among the frozen, frosted bushes in the old Tsarist garden.

She was standing there, a red crossed arm-band over her soldier's jacket.

He ran, his horse standing riderless behind him as he lunged across the line of fire.

'*Yelena!*' he bellowed, and the muzzles wavered like aspens in the wind, rising away from the prisoners. He crashed into her, his arms around her like a bear.

He yanked at the British army cap she wore and dirty blonde hair fell down about her face. He turned around, where both his own troops and the men of the squad gaped at him in astonishment.

'My fiancée!' he roared. 'They captured her and now she is found!'

He pulled her out of the line, one huge arm almost carrying her over the frozen mud. He beamed and, as they realised the import of his words, the simple men about him beamed back, chuckling and slapping their chilled hands together at such a chance.

'*What the hell's going on?*'

The commissar came running down the line of executioners, furious. The three stared at each other.

'Rykov,' Akulov whispered.

'Akulov!' Rykov looked from one to the other, fear and hatred mingled in his face.

'Put the bitch back, Akulov,' he said softly, the wind slicing up his words so that only the three of them could hear him. 'I'm going to shoot her and I'll shoot you too, if you try to stop me.'

'She is my fiancée,' Akulov said levelly. 'She is a Bolshevik and the woman I am to marry. The rifles of my men say so.'

Rykov's eyes flicked to the squad of armed cavalrymen at Akulov's back, and he whirled, turning to the group of captured Whites.

'So when did you *capture* this woman?' he demanded. A tall young man in an old Tsarist cavalry officer's tunic limped forward in loose, padded boots.

'Two days ago,' he drawled. 'We needed a cook. We are officers, and do not do such things.'

'You have a name?'

'Pokrovsky. *Count* Pokrovsky,' he said, and Akulov saw Yelena close her eyes.

'You are a peasant,' Mikhail observed. 'I had fields full of such as you.'

'Not any more,' Rykov said truly. He turned back to where Akulov and Yelena stood, and a strange smile lit up his face.

'We must celebrate the happy couple's good fortune, boys!' he shouted. 'Saved from the dead! I think they shouldn't wait any longer, unless they get separated again, don't you? Shouldn't they be married? What say you, boys? And we'll drink to them!'

The chilled and hungry soldiers cheered.

'I'm the representative of the Party,' Rykov said, staring at the couple in front of him. 'I have the power, and we have the witnesses.'

He turned towards the firing squad.

'Boris, I saw you stripping the dead woman yesterday. I'll bet she had rings; give me one.'

A gap-toothed peasant came over, grinning, fishing in a pocket with a filthy hand. Gold gleamed on the dirt of his palm.

'Hold hands,' Rykov ordered, and Akulov took hers, unmoving, in his paw.

'In the name of Lenin and the Party, I pronounce you man and wife.'

He handed the ring to Akulov, and he put it on to her cold finger.

'Kiss the bride,' Rykov said mockingly, and Akulov did so, feeling her lips as chill and unmoving as death. The soldiers cheered, and Rykov called for vodka.

The two tall aristocrats, man and woman, stood looking at each other through the curtain of rifles. Mikhail lifted his hand, saying goodbye . . .

The oily smell of the rough spirit was on the wind and colour came into the chapped, frozen faces.

'What are we thinking of, lads?' Rykov yelled, and they looked at him, the smart one among them, attentive like dogs. 'We've married them but they haven't time for a honeymoon because the war's still to be won and there's a revolution to be built out there.'

There was one quicker than the others. Boris, he whose thick fingers were nimble enough to slide rings off a dead woman's hands.

'The house,' he shouted. 'There's a bed in there – it's too big to carry away.'

They roared in approval; Rykov detailed some of his squad to remain on guard over the White prisoners and the mob of the rest swept Akulov and Yelena through the gap where the door used to be and inside.

It was only partly looted; the Red soldiers had only taken the smaller things that they could carry. Chairs and tables and picture frames, ragged edged with cut canvas, littered the floor.

'Start a fire with this junk,' Rykov ordered. 'Where's the bed, Boris?'

They stampeded up the stairs and into the bedroom. The rugs had gone, but the bed was intact. Big dark carved wood, it would have taken a squad to carry away. A thick quilt covered the mattress and Rykov bounced on the springing and it squeaked loudly. He grinned savagely at the men and they all roared in approval, flexing their arms lewdly. They looked at Akulov, grinning in approval: at Yelena, imagining themselves in his position.

Akulov gripped Rykov by the arm as he moved away.

'Let the White boys go,' he said softly. 'Wrangel's shipping them out. There's no need for more killing.'

'Is this not a war against the exploiters?' Rykov spat back. 'Has not Lenin said so? First here, and then in every country. Kill them now, to save doing it later.'

Then the room was empty, just the noise of the men clattering back downstairs to warm themselves in the fire of furniture, and to search through the place for whatever things of value that they could find.

The room was freezing, the glass of the windows rimed with frost. Their breath puffed white as they stared at each other and she spoke for the first time.

'Are you an officer or a soldier? Your horrible uniforms all look the same.'

'I lead, mistress. The *ofitser* is a thing of the past, I am the *kombat*, I command the battalion.' Akulov said quietly. From downstairs they could hear the noise of smashing furniture as the troops made a fire. 'I lead the men.'

'My brother led his men. He was tall and beautiful in his uniform. When they attacked the Germans his men crawled over the ground as he walked.'

'He is dead mistress. It's not good tactics to look like a peacock on a battlefield.'

'There is nothing beautiful in Russia now. I would rather have the peacocks.'

'We are making a new world. Those that once were nothing now will become everything. There will be neither tyrant nor slaves.'

Akulov bent to heave off his boots, and pull off his trousers. 'Get some clothes off, mistress,' he urged.

Her voice was as chill as the air of the room. 'I have no intention of getting into bed with you, whatever farce you and Rykov played down there.'

Akulov took a stride across the boards in his thickly stockinged feet and yanked her coat from her shoulders. It was padded with moss against the cold.

'I thought rape was Rykov's speciality,' she said proudly.

'Rykov's speciality is *shooting* people,' Akulov whispered intensely. 'He is a Party Commissar and he carries out Lenin's will.'

'No tyrant, no slaves?' she jeered. 'Is this the fruit of your new society, rule by Rykov the rapist, Rykov the murderer?'

Akulov's big hands pulled off her boots, undid her belt and took off her trousers. He picked her up and put her into the bed, then he took a pistol from his uniform coat pocket and climbed in beside her.

'Rykov wanted to shoot you. This is his price for letting me save you.'

Under the thick quilt where they were naked their bodies began to burn with heat.

'I stink,' she said. 'Almost as badly as you.'

There was a commotion of men coming up the stairs. From the garden outside came the rattle of bolts, the harsh bark of command. Along the little window above the door a line of grinning faces appeared. The springs of the bed twanged and they roared their approval to see the couple locked in embrace within.

The fusillade made the icy windows rattle in their frames. A man moaned in agony and there was a pause, then the flat bang of a pistol.

'*Gaspodi, pomilui umershikh*,' whispered Yelena.

'You're a *Bolshevik*,' Akulov hissed into her ear, lying on top of her.

The door crashed back and he rolled off to see Rykov there. There was blood on one glove, and a pistol in the other.

'Count Pokrovsky wasn't dead,' he said. 'But he is now.'

He looked at Yelena. 'Tears? On your wedding day?'

Yelena sat up and the men at Rykov's back goggled in approval as she tugged her shirt about her. She smiled brilliantly at them. 'Tears of joy,' she said. 'Long live the Revolution!'

9

Molot, Serp.

Petrograd, January 1921

THE room was warm, the layers of caked snow on his boots were beginning to melt, showing the cracked leather beneath. Pavel stood by the merry coal fire burning in the grate, while the man looked through his pay book. The place had been easy to find, in a silvery street where the buildings wore coats of ice it was patched from the warmth of the heated rooms within. A flag hung outside, red with gold. Under it, people queued on the ice, for permits to queue for train tickets, for permits to queue for clothing vouchers, for permits to apply for firewood, for permits to bury their dead. They queued for permits to queue.

Pavel had not had to queue for long; he had been invited in. While the people of Petrograd stayed out on the street and conducted their business with petty officials through small windows taken from ticket offices, he had gone inside, into the warm room, and he stood, watching ice from the Crimea melt to show the mud from the flats still staining his boots.

The man behind the desk was plump and pink, in contrast to the people outside, who were gaunt and pale, except for the livid, brick red scars of chilblain and frostbite. He was the official Kapustin and he fingered the pages of Pavel's red-bound pay book, slowly, carefully, a pink tongue running along wet lips, his breath wheezing through his nose. Like the flag outside, like the small flag on the desk, the paybook was decorated with gold, *molot* and *serp*, the hammer and the sickle.

'You are owed much pay, Sailor Volkov.'

'I have been too busy fighting to collect what I am owed, Comrade. But now the war is won, and I am going home. So I have come for my money.'

It was a very pleasant feeling, this warmth coming through the back of his trousers as he stood in front of this fire. It was a long time since he had not been cold.

'Also,' he said. 'My extra rations as a fighting soldier. I have saved them, for I am going home. Flour, sugar, butter and tinned meat. See, it is all there.'

The fat man nodded. 'Yes, it is all in order,' he said, yet he did not reach for the pad of *propusks* nor his pen by its inkwell, or the all-important stamp. 'You may find the food more valuable than the rubles,' he said. 'Things have become very expensive while you have been gone.'

'So I believe,' Pavel said stolidly. 'It is all the more reason for us all to get back to work to build our new, free society, now the war is won.'

'Yes, yes,' the official Kapustin murmured. 'Although our new society has much to recommend it already, does it not?'

'I am one that Trotsky called a hero of the revolution,' Pavel said gravely, 'I am from Kronstadt and I and my brothers raised the flag of revolution there. It seems to me that there is much to be done before our goals are achieved. But we have made a start. Now, I have far to go, so . . .'

'Of course.' Kapustin fingered the pay-book. 'You know, you will have much to carry. It will be heavy.'

'No man minds the load when it is for him and his family. I will bear up as best I can under it.'

'I could make it a little lighter for you,' Kapustin suggested.

Pavel said nothing, but reached for the bayonet in its sheath at his belt, and fitted the eighteen inches of shining steel to the end of his Dragoon rifle with a practised slap. With its butt on the dampening carpet by his boot, the blade gleamed silver by his eye.

'I want,' he said, 'what I am due. No more and no less, and you will give it to me.'

'You shall have it, Comrade,' Kapustin said hastily. 'Every sack, each can and bag. I was merely suggesting that I might provide you with some comforts before you go. Some . . . things you might not have had much of, so far away, fighting for our new society. The new society that would like to reward you.'

'What things?'

Kapustin smiled. It was an unpleasant sight. His wet lips shone in the light of the fire.

'I have said . . . this new society has much to recommend it. It is a better world we live in, Comrade sailor Volkov. Take me, a humble servant of the people. Once I worked for a cruel woman, one who tormented the toiling masses while she dressed in silk, and ate from golden plates. Yet however hard I worked for this woman she accused me of idleness, of laziness, and of being dishonest, and she threw me out of her great house here in this city, threw me out on to the street without so much as a backward glance.

'Then came the glorious revolution. Because I wished to serve the people I was given this job as a commissar here. And in the name of the people I sought out this woman who had been their oppressor. I found her, living illegally in the cellar of the great house she had stolen from the people, and I had her thrown into the street, and her goods confiscated in the name of the people. I saw to it that she was made to pay for all the crimes she had committed, that she had to live out on the street and starve in the cold, as I had done.

'And the day came when she had to come to me, to kneel before me and beg for my help.'

Kapustin paused, running his pink tongue over his thick lips, coating them with saliva at the memory. 'I agreed to alleviate her lot a little, under . . . conditions.'

Pavel cut him short. 'So you are proposing that this old woman gets on her back for me, is that it?'

Kapustin smiled. 'No . . . no. Not the woman. She had an accident, she slipped from an upstairs window . . . she is dead. But there is the daughter, who once rode in carriages, who danced at balls while the people starved. She is . . . very beautiful. She has to come here each week to receive her permits for food, for clothing, to be permitted to stay in the room I have given her.' The fat man's eyes glittered. 'It is enjoyable . . . thinking up new ways for her to amuse me.'

He looked up at Pavel. 'There is a room here you can use. A whole night of joy. She will do anything you desire. I assure you. All for very little – say, one third of a *pud* of millet?'

'She is very beautiful, you say?'

'And willing.'

'And I pay her a third of a *pud*?'

Kapustin looked shocked. 'Not her. *Me.*'

Pavel smiled. 'Well, you'd better sign the *propusk* and give me the money.'

The commissar leered back. Gold shone in his mouth. He busied himself with his forms and counted out rubles from a cash box.

'You can get your supplies from the depot in the next street, while I have her brought here.'

He gave Pavel the permit and his money, and lumbered out from behind the desk. He took his arm conspiratorially, and winked at him. 'You won't regret this, you know,' he wheezed.

'I know I shall not,' said Pavel.

With one strong, hard, callused hand he thrust into the voluminous folds of the fat man's trousers, seizing him by the testicles. He squeezed with all his might.

Kapustin squealed like a stuck pig, his eyes bulging from his head. Pavel crushed down with both hands and felt something burst like a ripe plum. Kapustin's shriek was coloratura and he fell to the carpet, vomiting.

As Pavel opened the door a young female worker was standing there in alarm.

'The commissar has been taken ill,' he said, slinging his rifle, and he saw a light of pure joy in the young woman's eyes as she looked down upon the writhing figure.

He went out into the street. It was getting dark and the line of silent, shivering men and women stretched into the gloom. Near the depot he traded some rubles for a small sledge a man was using to carry scraps of wood scavenged from the structure of a derelict building.

At the store he loaded up his little sledge with the goods he was due, stuffing them away out of sight in his big army pack, and began to trudge through the night to the Moscow Station at the east end of Nevskiy Prospekt. He had his rifle over his shoulder, its bayonet still attached.

Yellow street lamps illuminated the green façade of the terminal. New lettering proclaimed it to be the October Railway, but underneath the crude paint the raised glazed tiling of Tsar Nicholas's name was still visible. He passed the great, barrel-chested statue of Alexander III, still standing in the square where the crowds had brought Kerensky to power. A woman was hiding there in the gloom. She came out in front of him and he had to stop. She wore a long, fur-trimmed coat and she spoke in the manner of an aristocrat.

'The trains won't be running until tomorrow,' she said. Her voice was cultured, but he could not see her face clearly in the light.

'Then I shall rest inside and wait,' he said stolidly.

'It is cold there, and the platform hard. I can offer you a warm bed for the night. Not far from here. For very little. You have some food?'

'I have food. But I am used to discomfort. I can rest without a bed.'

He moved to go around her, but she darted forward again, blocking his path. The light was on her face which was thin from hunger and rouged. She undid the belt of her coat and pulled it apart to show herself. She was naked from the waist up.

'I come with the bed,' she said. 'It is I who will keep you warm.'

'I have already turned down the offer of one young woman this night,' he said. 'Now cover yourself, it is too cold for that.'

She pulled the coat back over herself. Her teeth were beginning to rattle. 'I am a countess. I will dress as one and you may do whatever you wish.'

'I know that you are an aristocrat, Countess Katerina,' he said levelly.

'You know who I am . . .' she said, her voice faltering.

'I am Pavel, from Kronstadt. I came to the school with Konstantin the poet, and with Savinkov, and Ruth de Gunzberg. I saw you there, Countess. There were those of your friends who did not care for the presence of a common sailor, but you talked to me.'

'There were injustices then,' she muttered. 'Although not as much as there is now.'

She turned away, her head hung in shame. 'You must be on your way. I would that you had not seen me like this.'

'These are hard days,' he said. 'But wait. Is there nothing else for you to do?'

'My parents are old and there is no work for them. They live in a single room and I am the only one who can help them.'

Pavel reached into his big pack and took out a bag of flour, some butter and tinned meat.

'Then give them this. It may help. And listen to me. Your friend Yelena is in the city, she has come with her new husband, Ivan Ivanovich Akulov, my comrade.'

'Yelena . . .' Katerina breathed. 'She was to have married Mikhail . . .'

'Count Mikhail is dead. I saw him die. Listen to me. You will find Akulov at the Red Army depot, the Kalashnikov grain exchange that was. It is not far from here. Akulov will take you to Yelena and she may be able to help you.'

Katerina took the food in her arms. 'Oh, thank you. Thank you, thank you.'

'Go now. Give the food to your parents and go.'

She turned to leave, and he called after her. 'And take the damned paint off your face, Countess. It makes you look like a whore!'

He thought he heard her laugh, as she ran across the square, vanishing in the darkness.

He went into the station. There was a train leaving in the morning. So he paid for a ticket. He found a corner out of the wind, and pushed his pack into it, sitting on it for safety. He wrapped his greatcoat about him and cradled his rifle in his arms.

In the gloom, something rustled. He took the bayonet off with a metallic snap, and held it in front of him.

'I am armed,' he snarled.

'I mean you no harm,' said a girl's voice. She came out from behind a pillar, a child of perhaps twelve, and thin. Her eyes were big and luminous in the half light. She lifted her skirt so that he could see her calves, then higher, to show her thighs. She pulled it up about her waist . . .

Kronstadt Naval Base, March 17 1921

Sasha brought up the last box of belts for the machine gun as the first glimmerings of sunshine appeared in the grey fog about them. Pavel fired it off in bursts, waiting for the booming *Hoorah* of Tukhachevskiy's infantrymen coming across the frozen ice of the harbour. By the time he could see groups of them moving through the thinning mist it was gone. They got up and left the weapon where it was.

He lost Sasha in the crowds near the great space of Anchor Square where they had proclaimed Kronstadt the Paris commune of 1871, reborn in 1917, where they had begun the overthrow of the Tsar. Heavy shells from the Krasnaia Gorka howled overhead, smashing into the inert hulls of the two great battleships, the *Petropavlovsk* and *Sevastopol*, still frozen into the ice. From behind him came the crump of grenades as the attacking troops began fighting house to house, and the rattle of pistol and rifle fire as the sailors used up the last of their ammunition. The fifteen thousand heroes of the revolution had fought continuously for ten days against fifty thousand enemy. There were women and children in the crowds of people trying to push their way through the dense Kronstadt streets, making for the Finland ice. The sailors were taking their families with them, as well as the spirit of the revolution.

In an alley a burst of gunfire mowed down the family in front of him, and he saw white-clad troops pushing up the other way. He loosed off three rounds from his Nagant revolver and they went for the ground. A door was at his elbow and he crashed through it, slamming it behind him, leaving just the white fog of his breath in the street.

Inside it was deserted. A rough table stood on the stone floor, empty shelves lined the walls. It was a store-room, the only way out the way he had come in. He tipped the table over on to its side and dragged it to the far corner, hiding behind it.

A heavy boot smashed the door back. Something clattered on the floor like an iron ball. He crouched down as low as he could get. The explosion beat on his flesh, stung him in a hundred places. But he sat up, and as they piled through the door he shot them, one, two and three.

A giant blotted out the light. The Nagant clicked futilely in his hand. He threw the gun at the bayonet, and it stopped in the air above his head.

'Pavel,' a voice growled through the ringing in his ears. 'What in hell are you doing here?'

He looked up at Akulov. 'I should ask you that,' he said.

Ivan turned and kicked the door shut, his boots slithering on the congealing blood on the floor. Pavel got up, looking down at the dead men. 'Who'd I get?' he asked.

'Tukachevsky's using Tatars and Bakshirs. Letts too. Ukrainian commanders like me. Chekist machine gunners to stop them retreating.'

'To kill Russian sailors.'

Akulov sat wearily on the edge of the upturned table, the Lee Enfield like a toy rifle in his huge paw.

'We left our start lines hours ago. There's under half my battalion left. Pavel, Pavel, why did you come here?'

'I went home, when the war was over,' the veteran revolutionary said levelly.

They stared at each other in the dark cellar, its dank air stinking of explosive.

'That's why *I'm* here,' Pavel said sharply, accusingly. 'Why are you?'

The noise of the fighting still rumbled and vibrated through the foundations of the building; they could feel it under their feet.

'There's no time for this,' said Akulov. 'Get yourself out, get across the ice to Finland with the others. There's no future for you here.'

Pavel tasted the gall of defeat. 'What of *your* future, Ivan Ivanovich?' he cried bitterly. 'What Leninist bauble will they hang on your chest for this service to the revolution?'

'There's no time!' Akulov said again. He pulled off the white sheet that covered his uniform, sodden with melt-water. 'Put this on and get down to the ice.'

He picked up the Nagant from the floor, and fished in his pocket for some loose rounds. He gave them to Pavel and peered round the doorway. 'Go on, now,' he said gently. 'Go.'

Pavel found himself on the ice, the city behind him. There was the rushing of an express train, a gigantic hand throwing him across the snow.

The sun pierced his eyes. He lay on a floe. A jagged hole marked the place where the shell had fallen short but the attackers had taken the island. Through the ringing in his ears Pavel could hear them dealing with the last of the defending sailors. The ice stretched ahead of him and he hurried away towards the safety of the Finland shore.

The fog was coming down again by the time he reached land. Buildings hung over him as he came ashore, the familiar streets he knew well, and he slumped to his knees, looking about him in despair. He had walked the wrong way. He was in Petrograd.

He was too weak to attempt the crossing back and he knew it. They had existed on mouthfuls of condensed milk and the odd slice of coarsely-tinned meat for days and simply crawling up off the ice on to the street had taken most the of the last of his strength. He needed to get inside, to eat something, to rest.

His Aunt Nina. She had a room near Sadovaya, one of the two she and his Uncle had had when they came to work in the munition factory. Now he was dead she let the other out, or had done. As he trudged through the streets their silvery coating of frost betrayed the lack of occupants in the buildings. The occasional and rare heated room showed up as a dark patch against the silver.

The summer gardens were bleak with bare branches and rime as he went by. He found the building, and went into its courtyard. By the stairway he saw a very thin man standing watchfully, a long thin knife in his hand. He stopped, putting his own hand inside his coat for his pistol.

'Don't mind me,' the man called. 'I saw a cat slip in here.'

Pavel staggered up the stairs, pushing past frozen refuse. It was dark and unlit and he found his aunt's door by feel. He thudded weakly on it with the butt of his gun.

'No use knocking there,' the man called up. 'The Cheka came and took her away. Last week.'

'Why?'

'She had some nephew, out on the naval base. So that made her as guilty as him.'

'Where did they take her?'

'Who knows?' the man said, still concentrating on what he was doing. He began to move imperceptibly forward. 'It won't make any difference – those they take you never see again?'

Something scurried desperately from the corner, and screeched as the man moved, equally quickly. The knife was thrust through the emaciated body of a cat and the man held it up in triumph. A door came open and a woman rushed out holding a pan to catch the precious blood. The couple dived inside with their spoils, shutting the door quickly against the possibility of Pavel trying to take a share, and he was left alone in the icy courtyard.

He forced himself to try and think. He would die if he stayed on the frozen street through the night; by morning what cats, rats or dogs that remained alive in the city would be chewing gratefully on his bones.

The girl, Ruth. The one who had so wanted to be in on it when they stormed the Palace, the one who'd nearly shot herself in her excitement, untrained, unversed in the use of weapons. He'd taken the bullets out before she killed someone, and let her wave the pistol about. Hadn't her parents had an apartment on the Prospekt? It was a bit of a joke that the revolution dispossessed the exploiters and gave to the proletariat, and Ruth Gunzberg kept the apartment in the family. Being a revolutionary.

He hurried along, making the best time he could. The entrance hall of the great Tsarist block was dark and cold, ice riming the mirrors, but up the stairs there was light filtering out from around the big double door, and he used the butt of his revolver to beat on it.

'Who's there?' A woman's voice. Alarmed.

'I'm looking for Ruth. It's Pavel. Pavel the sailor.'

The door opened a crack, and she peeped through. A heavy chain held it safe. It shut and he heard the rattle of the links as she took it off.

'What has happened to you?' she cried. 'Have you had an accident? You're covered in blood.'

He put up a hand and felt his face, encrusted with frozen gore.

He went in. They were using one big room. Where the Gunzbergs had received their glittering guests, standing on their priceless Bokhara rugs, their daughter had found newspapers to put down on the floor, to stop the cold driving through the marble. An iron stove burned by the ornate fireplace, its stack shoved up the chimney and pile of firewood stood in the corner. On the shelves where her mother's Fabergé ornaments and Chinese vases had stood, she had assembled potatoes, eggs, flour and butter. A pan stood on the stove heating. By it was one big bed, with real blankets. Tucked under them were two small children, a boy and a girl, sleeping. He looked around him, marvelling at the luxury.

'Have you had an accident?' she said again, anxiously.

'In a way . . .' he said. The warmth of the stove drew him irresistibly, and he went to stand by it. 'I went home,' he said. 'Home to the village, when the fighting was over, when we'd won, when we'd thrown out those who'd exploited us for so long. We've had sailors in my family for generations. Rebels, too. We could think for ourselves. When you live in a world where they forbid you to ride inside a streetcar, because of who you are, where they forbid you to walk on the sunny side of the street, because of who you are, where they put up signs forbidding you to enter public parks – you and dogs – you think about ways to bring a better world, a place where people can be equal, and free.'

'Why do you think I became a Bolshevik?' Ruth asked, passionately. 'I was a part of that order that exploited you. My parents rode on the backs of men like you. I rejected them and their world to create the new.'

'I fought for it,' he said simply. 'I was there, at the Winter Palace.'

'Yes, I too!'

He smiled, and little flakes of dried blood crumbled away from his face to float in the rising air from the stove.

'You were there,' he agreed. 'But are you a better shot now?'

'It was not the shooting – it was to take part, to make a commitment.'

'Commitment . . . yes, that too. I made mine, I fought. The pride and glory of the Revolution is what Trotsky called us. We saved him and Lenin in the dark days of 1918. We stopped Iudenich in the suburbs right here. We fought and died at Pulkovo, at Sviiazhsk and a hundred other battlefields. We did it to save the revolution, to save the democracy of the proletariat. We followed Trotsky to the Tauride Palace, to his cell at Kresty, we followed him to the walls of Kazan . . . we took his advice, took his orders . . . we thought he believed in a new world, as we did.'

A faint, slightly puzzled frown appeared between Ruth's brows. Pavel blinked, standing by the stove. After so many weeks of bone-numbing cold its heat was as intoxicating as alcohol.

'Where was I?' he murmured.

'You were going home,' said Ruth. 'To your village.'

'So I was . . . I went into the station and settled down to wait and a young whore approached me. Twelve years old. It was my younger sister, Mariya. She was without food, and I gave her some of my rations. Then I asked her why she was there. She said she had come from the village to seek work, because the villagers were starving. Our Aunt Nina took her in and got her a job at the mill where she worked. Then the Bolshevik Committee closed it because they couldn't keep the fuel coming, and cut the rations. From two hundred grammes of black bread to a hundred. Those who protested were beaten up by the *kursanty*. To feed them, Mariya sold herself.'

The stove was sending him to sleep. He stood, rocking, then forced himself to go on.

'But why were the villagers starving, I asked. She said the Bolsheviks had taken all the grain, all the horses, pigs, fowl. They took the horses and carts to take it away. Life in the country had become more terrible than death itself. Those who protested were shot by the Cheka. My family were still there, and I used my money – I had some gold rubles, not paper – to buy some sacks of grain and seed potatoes from the bagmen in the black market, and managed to get to the village. Only my father was still alive. My mother had died during the winter, my brothers vanished in the war. When we got there he was lying on his bed, too weak to move. He asked who it was who had come into the room. With tears running down my cheeks I knelt by the bed, saying it was his son, Pavel. "I do not see my son," he said. "I see only one of the oppressor class, a murderer of peasants."

'He would not address me again. I made soup and Mariya tried to give it to him, but he would not eat. He died the next day. In return for a share of the sacks of grain and seed potatoes the neighbours agreed to protect Mariya, and I left.'

'But why? Why did you not stay?'

'The Revolution was in danger,' he said simply. 'I had to return to Kronsdadt to protect it.'

Her eyes widened in understanding. 'You're one of the rebels!'

Pavel's knees were giving way. He knelt on the wadded newspaper, his eyelids closing.

'The Bolsheviks have destroyed the revolution,' he murmured. 'They have murdered what was pure.'

He slumped to the floor, asleep.

The warmth had opened up the cuts on his face again, the blood made him sick and the pain as they pulled him up off the floor awoke him.

'Hullo, Pavel,' said Krivitskiy. Ruth fed a log into the stove and its red glow shone from his round glasses.

'Ready to go?'

'A commissar,' said Pavel, slowly, 'I see you, Israel Shapiro. Trotsky promised to shoot us like partridges. Have you come to do his job for him?'

'Let's go. You lost.'

'We lit a beacon that will burn until Bolshevism is crushed,' Pavel retorted. 'The whole world knows that we, the heroes of the Revolution rose against you, those who have turned our country into a penal colony. We of Anchor Square, we of the *Petropavlovsk* and *Sevastopol* will be on everyone's lips today.'

Krivitskiy inclined his head and his two men walked Pavel across the room to the door.

'I have never heard of these names,' Krivitskiy murmured. 'Are you referring to the Square of the Revolution? To the glorious Red battleships *Marat* and *Paris Commune*? And what sailors? The Bolsheviks overthrew the Tsar, defeated the forces of oppression. They required no help from sailors.'

He nodded at Ruth. 'Thank you, Comrade. A good communist is at the same time a good Chekist.'

Ruth heard him chuckle as he closed the door, heard the echoing clatter of their feet as they went down to the Black Maria on the street. In her parents' day the grand staircase had been swathed in thick carpet, but people had stolen it to make trousers and coats.

She heard the sound of voices in song and hurried to the window. The great street was darkened by a pall of fog. Two streetlamps were visible, flickering yellow. A column of Tukhachevsky's soldiers came by, singing the 'Internationale'.

They vanished, leaving the lamps flickering in the fog. Suddenly she saw them as candles, flickering at the head and feet of a corpse.

There was a voice, a small, insistent hand, tugging at her sleeve.

'Mama, mama.'

She was on her knees by the window, her mouth still moving in prayer. She did not know how she had got there and she was begging forgiveness.

She picked up her child.

'Who were the men, Mama?'

Sergei was on the Committee. He had got a jar of the English drink, she put some milk in the pan to heat. The children woke when they were hungry. With food, Natasha would go back to sleep.

'They came to take someone. A bad person. Because Mama asked them to.'

'The little girl understood that bad people had to be taken away, she had seen it happening to them, many times.

'Because we're communists, Mama.'

'That's right, darling.' She lifted up the lid and sprinkled one spoonful of the precious malty powder on to the milk. The aroma filled the air.

'We're making a new world, darling. One where everyone is equal. But there are bad people who want to destroy our new world, and those we must get rid of.'

'Like the bad man.'

'Yes, like the bad man.'

The little girl began to drink. Ruth was desperately hungry but she would not eat that day. A good communist was at the same time a good Chekist. Lenin had decreed it so. But she had committed error, she had found herself in prayer, to a God who did not exist, and so she must do penance. It was not enough to be correct. To be a communist was to think. Perfectly. Or be punished.

She was still sitting by the window when Savinkov came back. He had a bar of chocolate and he offered her some. She took it but put it in her pocket to save for the children.

'I've eaten,' she said.

'I've been talking to Lenin,' he said. He began to pace about the room, as was his habit, and she had to remind him to take off his shoes, not to wake the twins. He tugged on a pair of thick socks.

'There's going to be a famine,' he said. 'There's precious little grain left in the granaries, let alone seed-corn. That's the cost of winning the war. I'm to start an international relief agency and Lenin's backing me. I'm calling it the Workers' International Trust – the Supply Column of the Proletariat. We'll raise money in Western Europe and America to buy food, we'll channel gifts of goods. But there's more to it than that. There's going to be no overnight revolution in the West. The time's passed. It's a long war now. Our aid campaign will be the beginning of the great proletarian struggle.

'I want to target those in the West who have influence. Writers, academics, lawyers. Actors and actresses. Scientists and doctors and singers. They don't believe in a God any more, but they want to believe in the future. They aren't communist, not yet, but they could sympathise. Especially with the proletariat.

Since they believe in the future, they are open to new ideas. *Our* ideas. We can get them to make a commitment. Even a small one. A day's pay. They are fellow-travellers on the journey to the future. The act of solidarity will give them a nice, warm feeling. We can enlist them. They can receive a shiny red badge, *molot* and *serp*, hammer and sickle, small, discreet, to wear in their lapel. They have become drawn in. We will have a club they can join, a newsletter, a chance to meet others. And then there are the vain, whom we can tempt with honours, and the sort of adulation they cannot get in their own country. And the corrupt, who wish to believe, but can do so even better for money, or women, or whatever vice they indulge. They are innocents, of course. The intellectuals are the easiest to manipulate, they are not above vanity or corruption, and their brains do not extend to politics.'

'I, too, believe in a utopia. Somewhere,' she said wearily. 'I, too, have a bad conscience. My brain does not extend to politics. But I am not innocent, Sergei. I will not do.'

He stopped his pacing. 'Those who run things cannot be innocent. We'll be working with Krivitskiy. You see, some of these innocents might be *really* useful. Not merely sympathisers, but agents of influence.'

'Where are we to spread these fishing nets of yours?'

'Berlin.'

'Not here.'

'No. Will you come?'

'Yes,' she said. 'Please . . .'

10

Back with Nina Petrovna

RYKOV came down through the wood, following the stream, his sack slung over his shoulder, his feet silent on the thick carpet of leaf mould. He was alone. The trees were thinning out and he could see the green of the meadow that led down to the lake, speckled with the wild flowers. He paused, hidden in the wood, watching, as the water gurgled down the hill. More flowers grew in the soft earth of its banks – the peasants of the village made herbal remedies and wines from them, the busy mothers down in the wood houses sent their young daughters out to gather them.

Rykov looked carefully about. By the stream, you could not hear another person coming, their feet soft on the leaf mould. Pretty Nina Petrovna had especially liked the flowers of the stream side, she had gathered them early, while the mist was still on the lake.

There was no one about, and he continued on down the hill. Where the stream flattened out, slowing its course, he paused again where the reeds were particularly green and lush, and then came out into the open. The meadow was overgrown, the cattle of his youth gone.

The surface of the lake still bore duck. Sleek, brown and green and white, pearls of water running from their crisp feathers. You could snare them if you were careful. He watched them, a faint smile on his face. His nostrils flared for a moment, as if smelling the kerosene. His eyes flicked to the sky, remembering the blossom of light that travelled up from the rag round its leg.

He walked around the lake. The racoons that hunted there were difficult to catch. But if you drilled a hole in a tree trunk, just big enough for its hand, and tapped in a few sharp tacks, pointing inwards, and pushed a delicacy in there, some crawfish meat, perhaps, then when you came the next morning, there it would be, held fast.

Rykov smiled at his childish memories. Then when you were finished having fun, the lake swallowed up all secrets. He frowned. All *small* secrets. Big ones floated. Big ones had to be buried.

Rykov slung his bag over his shoulder, and stepped out. It

was getting dark and he wanted to be in the village before night fell.

He came down the road. Weeds were encroaching on the track that had been kept clean by the traffic of horses and cart wheels. The air – that would have borne the scent of cooking fires and smoking pork and fish, the reek of distilling vodka – was fresh. The trees were still there, lining the road into the village, and, as he passed between the houses and huts he could hear chickens clucking, the snort of a pig and a horse's whinny.

She was there, at the front of the wooden house, yellow wool stretching from the spindle at her hand. She stared at him, all colour draining from her face, then ran inside.

His house was still there, the logs of its walls greyer than he remembered. The door was open, so he went down the path and went inside. A man was there, tending the wick of an oil lamp in preparation for the evening, he looked up at Rykov and his face was like stone.

'These are bad times,' he said. 'I had hoped you dead.'

His beard and moustache were iron grey, he had grown old while Rykov had been gone.

Rykov tossed his sack on to the bed by the wall.

'Don't be like that,' he said. He turned, and dropped the wooden bar across the door.

'The devil looks after his own,' the man said bitterly. 'He has treated us badly enough, here.'

'The place looks empty.'

'We have little left, so many times have they stolen from us. The young men are all gone for their war and the old died for want of the food they stole. And here you are, looking as though you have not missed a mealtime since you left.'

'A man has to look after himself. And I have brought you some food. Flour, butter, cheese.'

'I want nothing from you. You are not welcome here. There are still those in this village who know why you left.'

'Stories . . .' Rykov said easily.

'Where is Nina Petrovna?' the man demanded. 'Answer me that?'

'She ran away, to the big city, to wear a pretty maid's dress. I saw her, in Moscow.'

'Lies!' He shook his head bitterly. 'All lies, for the truth could not sit in your mouth without dying. And what of Margharita Fyodorovna, who cannot look at a man, because of you?'

'All tales.' Rykov smiled. 'You know how women are.'

There was a sudden banging at the door.

'Is he here?' a voice roared.

'It is Fyodor.' said the man. He raised his voice. 'Yes, he is here. It is none of my doing.'

'Send him out to me!'

'I'll be gone before dawn.' Rykov said quickly.

'He says he will be gone before sunrise.'

'Whenever he goes, he will find me here waiting for him.'

The man looked at Rykov with a glint in his eye. You'll get more than a thrashing before you get out of this village.'

'I have been thrashed before, have I not?' Rykov said indifferently.

'Not enough! The birch has not been made that could drive the evil from you.' He suddenly gripped Rykov by his coat, thrusting his face close to him. '*We know you.* And I saw the marks. I know what you did to Margharita.'

Rykov nodded. 'Yes, you do, don't you.'

The dirty window was dark. Suddenly, it flared into yellow light.

'What's that?' the man muttered, in alarm.

'Open the door, let us see.' Behind him, Rykov opened his sack.

He fumbled with the bar and dragged the door open. He stumbled a few steps out into the open before halting, staring in shock at the burning house, the fearful crowd of his fellow villagers, surrounded by the grinning young men in black, their shiny guns.

Rykov came out. He was dressed in his leather jerkin, his peaked black cap, his Mauser in his hand. He beamed at his men.

'Hallo, lads!' he shouted. 'Welcome! This is my home. What is mine, is yours.'

They worked quickly, expertly. They brought out chairs, setting them in two lines, each side of the street, under the trees. The rope they had with them, in the truck. They slung the nooses, and stood them up on the chairs, all the men and women, except the handful of girls.

They scoured the houses and brought out food and drink, and set it up on tables. The flames from the house were dying down, so they lit another, warming themselves by its blaze. They brought out the big wooden bed that Fyodor the carpenter had made for his bride so many years before and set it in the street. They stood chairs either side of it and put him and his wife there, one on each, with ropes round their necks and their wrists tied, and they stripped their daughter of all her clothes while she wept.

When he was done, Rykov stood her up on the bed, and tied the rope round her neck as she stood naked.

'You shouldn't have said all those things about me,' he said softly. 'It was wrong of you. You're a very bad girl.'

One of the lads was waiting with a brand for him, and he dipped it into the bedding. As the dry wood caught sparks flew in the hot wind, rising from the yellow flames that licked about her shrieking dance.

'All right, lads,' he shouted genially, and they turned the girls loose, pursuing them with merry cries as they ran howling through the dying village.

Rykov went down the line, tipping over the chairs and saying goodbye.

'You will be back with Nina Petrovna, now,' he told her mother.

Along the street, fresh flames sprang up, as they set torches to the houses.

There was just the one left, at the end of the row.

'Your mother died, birthing you. You were marked,' said the man. 'It is gone now. A red mark, the devil's mark. His seal to make you his own. That is why she died.'

'It is his world, now, father.'

Rykov tipped the chair, and strolled away down the blazing street, never looking back.

11

Novy Mir

Moscow, May 1921

PIOTR SADOVSKY, Andrey Stukalov and Boris Fedin had taken to lying in in the morning. Piotr had calculated the value of the food they had been given, and had eaten, as Red Army soldiers, and compared it to the rations they were getting now that they were not. It represented money in the bank. When it was spent, the rations represented only an increasing overdraft, so they took it in turns to lie in the cocoons he had made for them from army greatcoats he had taken from dead White soldiers, and cunningly sewn together, and conserved their energy. When they could, they acquired copies of *Isvestia*, *Pravda* or *Krasnyi Krym* and read them before putting them in the lavatory for use. They made them smile, sometimes. Piotr had some volumes of Pushkin and Dostoevsky that had escaped use as fuel, and they lay, quietly reading, the two whose turn it was, while the third went to queue. In the afternoons they went out, to see if there was work, or something to scrounge.

The knock at the door was authoritative, the summons of a well-fed man. None of their friends would waste that amount of energy on such a knock, and Andrey was out in the queues. Piotr got out from his nest, fully dressed, for that too saved food, and pushed his feet into his army boots.

When he saw the familiar leather jacket and Mauser pistol of the Cheka on the man at his door, he began immediately to speak.

'I have done nothing!' he cried hotly. 'You see before you a veteran of the Civil War, an honourable Red Army soldier, a man who has waged class-warfare for the Bolsheviks – '

The Chekist grinned, revealing himself as a young man much the same age as Sadovsky, and also someone who had not come to arrest, try or kill him.

'*I know*, comrade,' he said holding up his hand. 'Commissar Krivitskiy told me so.'

'Krivitskiy?' he said suspiciously.

'Yes. His watch has stopped. He says will you come to lunch and fix it for him.'

Lunch. Now there was a word that had lost its everyday meaning. Lunch. He rolled it about, trying to catch its flavour, and went over to a corner of the room, where he lifted a floorboard. He took a selection of small tools and implements from his improvised cupboard and wrapped them in a cloth, putting the packet into the pocket of his coat. He tied his shoelaces. Lunch. He caught a mute expression of appeal from Boris Fedin lying in his cocoon.

They went out down the road that led past the pale green building of *Savvinskoye*, with its tiered rows of arches, and tent-roofed silver towers. They cut through *Nezhdanovoy*, and went through the little park, where flowers were pushing up in the ruined beds.

Krivitskiy had a small office in the Lubyanka, overlooking the square. The square was clean, possibly the only clean part of Moscow. No one had dared drop refuse near the headquarters of the Cheka.

Krivitskiy had a watch, a pocket fob. He also had a pie. A real meat pie on a plate, and a bottled jar of whole pears, the kind that had stood in rows, in the English shop, along with tiny, sweet peas, baby carrots and raspberries in brandy. It looked as though the pears had been pickled in brandy. Piotr Sadovsky calculated that one half pear would make him merry, and a whole one very happy, if he was allowed a spoonful of the liquor with each.

'It just stopped,' said Krivitskiy. 'It ran – like a fine watch – all through the war, and now it won't go.'

Piotr spread out his clean cloth, placing his implements neatly in a row on the table, and took the round watch.

'Let's have a look.'

'Piece of pie?' asked Krivitskiy, holding a knife.

'Why not?' Piotr said, attempting to sound casual. His mouth was filling up, and he swallowed. He lifted the back off the watch expertly and looked at its works.

'Nice watch,' he commented. 'An English hunter. It just needs cleaning. I'll do it for you. Obolenskii's down on the Quay in St Petersburg used to sell them, remember?'

'That's right,' said Krivitskiy, pushing a plate towards him. He could see the fine meat, without gristle. The golden jelly glistened. Piotr put the watch down on the cloth, carefully, and picked up the pie. The pastry was crisp, the juices of the meat and its cooking burst into flavour in his mouth.

'It's my father's, actually,' said Krivitskiy, munching on his piece.

'You've hung on to it?' mumbled Piotr, through his pie. 'Do you know. I haven't got one thing of mine. Not even a photograph.'

Krivitskiy gestured at the expert array of tools. 'You have his knowledge,' he suggested.

Piotr looked at him, suddenly suspicious. 'Not really,' he said, firmly.

'But yes. You know all about machinery, I know you do. You were always hanging round your father's aeroplane factory. You loved it. Your father gave you toy construction sets and you were forever making things. Little nuts, little bolts.'

'You are mistaken. I am the son of a miner from the Donbas. I learned about machinery from tending the engines of the pit while I was a young Bolshevik.'

Krivitskiy stared at him in amazement. 'You've never been to the Donbas. And you were *never* a young Bolshevik.'

'Yes I was,' Piotr said stubbornly.

'You *weren't*. I went to *school* with you. You brought models to class that you'd made with your own hands. Little trains that worked, aeroplanes that flew. Little clockwork motors. Why do you think I picked you to work with me on the train? *I knew* how good you were with your hands, with machinery.'

'If you went to school with me, then if you denounce me, I shall denounce you,' he said cunningly. 'Then you, too, will be shot.'

'Nobody's getting shot!' Krivitskiy cried in exasperation. 'Look, finish your pie and I'll tell you what I want.'

Piotr pushed the plate away. 'It is too rich for me. I am the poor son of a miner from the Donbas. I am used to *kvas* and cabbage soup.'

Krivitskiy banged his fist on the table. 'You are Piotr Pavlovich Sadovsky, the son of the factory owner!' he roared. 'You, too, know how to run a factory.'

'*No I don't!*' Sadovsky bellowed. 'All the people who know how to run factories have been shot.'

'That's the *point!*' Krivitskiy hollered. 'The war is *won*. There is a new policy. Lenin has announced it. The New Economic Policy. We have to get the factories and farms working again. And we need people who know how to run factories.'

Piotr eyed the pie. He reached out for it. 'So they aren't being shot?' he asked, quietly.

'No.'

Piotr put the pie into his mouth and bit into it. 'Not even if they are the sons of factory owners?'

Krivitskiy sat back down and smiled. 'They can be sons of miners from the Donbas if they like. As a matter of fact, I want you to go out there. I'll tell you about it in a minute. Piotr Pavlovich, you have no idea how serious it is. We won the war . . . I don't know how we won it. We had to use everything, every time. Perhaps that's why it was so horrible, so cruel. For we knew if we did not win today, then we would not live to face the problems of tomorrow, that this *novy mir*, this new world we want to make, would simply be strangled in its cradle.

'We *had* to live in the present. The fact that we were using short-term solutions that were making long-term problems could not concern us. But here we are, and the long term is upon us. We tore down city houses for fuel, we ripped out the drive belts of factory machines to make soles for our boots. We used people as just one more resource. The country is ruined, and we must begin again.'

Piotr shook his head. 'You need factories, and people who know how to run them. I wish my father was here – you could make *him* Commissar for Industry. Listen, I have not had much to do, since coming out of the army. I lie in bed in the mornings to conserve my strength and I read, and I think. It is a little more than three years since the Revolution. I calculate that on average, going by the prices today, one rouble in November 1917 is worth about one hundred roubles today. Paper roubles are one of the few things not in short supply, and I think I may have found an explanation for this. I read in *Pravda* a description of the printing presses of the state mint. They are the "machine guns of the Commissariat of Finance pouring fire into the arse of the bourgeois system". Commissar Zinoviev, I read, claims that "we are moving towards the *complete abolition of money*."'

Krivitskiy looked uncomfortable.

'How will I pay my workers? With apples?' Piotr asked.

'Whatever medium of exchange is chosen, the workers will receive payment by piecework,' Krivitskiy said.

Piotr's eyes widened. 'Really? Who says so?'

'Lenin.'

'I recall, before the revolution, a man making fiery speeches, describing piecework as one of the worst forms of capitalist exploitation. I thought at the time that his name was Lenin, but clearly, this cannot be so.'

'Piotr, it does not matter who said what, we have to get things working.' He handed him the rest of the pie. Piotr took a bite and then, mindful of his friends, slid the thick chunk into his pocket.

'A man,' he said, 'whose name I have forgotten, heard one of Lenin's speeches. He walked up to my father outside his factory and shot him dead. My father, who was a capitalist, knew how to make money, and how to make things work. All you have in his place is his son, who goes about pretending to be a miner's son from Donbas. There is something else I read in the paper. Lenin gave a speech, all about how to get things working again. He said – not once, but several times – that it was to be done by "strict accounting and control." It occurred to me then that our leader had probably spent more time outside factories inciting the workers to murder their employers than inside, seeing how it was done.'

The pie was finished, Krivitskiy opened the jar and tipped pears and juice on to their plates. They began to eat them with tin spoons and the liquor made Piotr's eyes water.

'It is probably best to keep such thoughts to yourself,' Krivitskiy suggested. 'But Lenin has done *some* things that will help you run your factory. All workers must be in the union, and the union has made strikes illegal. No strikes may take place in Soviet Russia. You have the threat of starvation to whip them into line. Lenin himself has said it. "He who does not work, neither shall he eat." If you have any trouble with undisciplined workers or hooligan elements we in the Cheka have work camps to re-educate them.'

He spooned the last of the juice into his mouth.

'You should be grateful to Lenin. He's on your side.'

Piotr could feel a pleasant numbness in his cheeks. 'My father will be very pleased to hear it,' he said politely. 'But listen to me, it won't be enough to intimidate my people like this. I'll have to give them something, too. A bit extra. We'll have to have our own farm, so people can have food to take home. A potato or two, an onion, some eggs, a chicken on a feast day.'

Krivitskiy looked at him doubtfully.

'I'm right,' Sadovsky said stubbornly. 'You cannot just bully people into doing what you want – it is not efficient. I'll get more out of them if I can give them something.'

Krivitskiy shrugged. 'You handle the details as you wish. Just so long as you get results. You'll be running a truck company. But first, I want you to go to the Donbas. Those two mates of yours on the train, Fedin and Stukalov, they still with you?'

'Boris and Andrey? Yes, we're sharing a room.'

'Take them with you. Fedin was a miner, wasn't he? You remember Khrushchev, he was commissar with me? He's the Party boss of the pits down there. Sixteen of them, producing nothing. They don't know how to work the machinery.'

'There must be manuals.'

Krivitskiy sighed. 'Piotr, we went to the Empress's school, we can read. Them, the ones down the hole, they're peasants. They communicate in grunts. Khrushchev's hardly literate himself. He's good at kicking them into line, but he needs someone to get the machines going.'

'Doesn't he mind?'

The alcoholic aroma of the pears still filled his nostrils, it was most pleasant.

'Mind? Why should he?'

'He's one of them. Nikita Sergevich is a peasant. He worked down the mine. Now he's holding the whip.'

'He's the boss. He's with the *nachalstvo*. He doesn't lick anyone's boots, they lick his. They're all the same, Piotr. Give any one of them a nice uniform and plenty of power and they'll do anything for you. They'd have their granny down shovelling coal if you wanted. Nikita Sergevich has the right idea. They don't work, they don't eat.'

Piotr smiled slyly. 'What of the international solidarity of the toiling classes, then?'

Krivitskiy smiled enigmatically. 'Let's leave that sort of thing to Savinkov's Western intellectuals, shall we? So, are you ready?'

'Yes, I'll be ready. We'll need some food, though. We haven't had enough to eat for a while.'

'That's no problem. Lenin's set up a department to see people like us get what we need.'

'And I'll need another person on the team.'

'Whoever you want.'

'Anna Suvurova.'

Krivitskiy frowned, trying to match the name to a face. 'You mean the one in our class? The one you were soft on?'

'I was going to marry her, if things had been different.'

'Well, where is she?'

'I don't know. You press-ganged me to make your train, and when I came back there was no trace of her. But you're in the Cheka. You can find her.'

'Yes, but you're one of the *vlasti* now; you can have any of them out there, just for a few cans of food.'

'I don't want any of them,' Piotr said stubbornly. 'I want Anna Suvurova.' He smiled pleasantly at Krivitskiy. 'See how quickly things go back to normal? You give me what I want, I give you what you want. Junk all that stuff in the Manifesto. *That*'s how things work.'

*

Rykov was surprised. Waiting behind the curtains at the edge of the stage he seemed almost grey, simply another bureaucrat. He had an oilskin pouch and stood stuffing his pipe like an old man while the hall buzzed and clattered with people taking their places. Out in the killing fields, he had seemed alive, powerful. The yellow eyes, when they looked up at him from their work remained formidable, however, and Rykov remained standing respectfully at attention.

'Things are quietening down,' Stalin murmured, from around his pipe stem. 'War's won. Period of consolidation. Cheka's being reorganised, it won't be quite the same as in the war.'

Rykov knew. He resented it, bitterly.

'Not many of us, you know. Old Guard, I mean. Old Bolsheviks. We'll be in charge.'

Rykov knew. The man waiting to hand out the awards was one of them.

'Quite a burden. I myself have two Commissariats; a lot of positions to fill.'

'I am your man, Comrade,' Rykov said quietly.

'Good. You have many talents, I have noticed and I shall find you useful. But not perhaps yet. You lack some practical experience. Have you been to the *osobogo naznacheniia*?'

'I served a short spell with Zemliachka in the Crimea.'

'Useful administrative experience,' said Stalin. 'She's here, you know.' He looked at Rykov curiously. 'Was she really as good as they say?'

Rykov chuckled at the memories. 'She could invent ways of doing in scum you never dreamed of! Even I learned a few tricks in her prison.'

'I could give you one to run yourself.'

'The war is won,' Rykov objected. 'There won't be much to do up there. I hear the prisoners die off pretty quickly.'

'I think you'll find you won't lack for employment,' Stalin said. He sounded almost jovial. 'There are still enemies left to be uncovered.'

Rykov brightened. 'I wouldn't mind that.'

'It's settled then. I'll keep an eye on you. Report to me.'

He went forward on to the stage, and they came to their feet. Stalin checked his list at the podium while a secretary stood ready at a table with the little red boxes of medals.

She came at the end, dressed in new black leather, clean and unstained.

'Rosalia Zalkind, Commissar with the Eighth and Thirteenth Red Armies,' Stalin announced, and she ran up the steps. 'For her tireless, selfless, and energetic organisational and political work in the Civil War.'

She stood proudly to attention as Stalin affixed the award to her leather jerkin.

'For helping to bring about the final victory of the Red Army, the international army of the proletariat, the Order of the Red Banner.'

Zemliachka turned to wave as they applauded her, tears of pride springing into her eyes.

Piotr Pavlovich Sadovsky cut down through *Nezhdanovoy*, and through the park. Emaciated people were sitting on the wrecked benches, soaking up the sun. Its warmth was free. They looked at him in listless envy as he went by with the free-spending energy of a man who ate.

He went past the pale green of *Savvinskoye* with its rows of arches, and into the building. His key still fitted the lock and he went in.

She was sitting with her back to the window. There was a smell of paint in the air and she had a brush in her hand. He saw the flash of her eyes as she looked over a half-white round wooden table at him and he felt the adrenalin surge in his stomach.

'Hullo, darling.'

He pushed the door to behind him.

Anna was looking down at her work, she waved her free hand then dipped the brush into the pot and applied another stripe of paint.

'Krivitskiy told me he'd found you.'

She nodded.

He came closer, and put his pack on the floor. She was bending over the table and he could see that her black hair was shot through with white and silver. He reached into his pack and brought out a bottle of red wine from the Crimea, opening it with the corkscrew on his knife.

'I've got some wine.'

She pointed up at a shelf. Old tumblers were set out in a neat row.

'I've been in the Donbas. Khrushchev gave me some wine before I left. He was a commissar with Krivitskiy, now he's boss of the mines. He was with Krivitskiy when he came and took us to work on his train.'

He looked at the tumblers; they were shining bright. The shelf had been polished. He turned, and the whole room was tidy.

'You've been cleaning.'

She nodded again. She had put up curtains on the window. They did not match, but they were bright and colourful.

'Here,' he said gently. He gave her a glass. 'Here is some wine.'

They drank, but she kept her eyes away from him.

'What is it, darling?' he asked. 'Can't you speak?'

Then she did look at him. She was gaunt, her mouth twisted in anguish, trying to form his name.

'P . . . P . . . Pi . . . P . . .'

Then she stopped, and hid her face in her hands. He put his hand out to comfort her, but she flinched. He thought for a moment, then went to his pack. He had a blue bound exercise book, that he had used in the mines, to make his notes, to draft plans. He took it, opening it to a clean page, and pressed the carpenter's pencil into her hand.

'Why don't you write down what you want to say?'

She looked at the book and then took the pencil in her hand.

Piotr, my love, I have thought only of you ever since I came back to the airfield to find you gone. And now I cannot speak to you not since –

She began to complete her sentence, and then scrawled through it with a mess of dark pencil.

'What happened, when you found us gone?' he asked gently. 'We were kidnapped by Krivitskiy, to work on his armoured train.'

She gripped the pencil, and wrote again. *I waited. That night, the next day. I went back to see mummy and daddy. In the hut. Then to the airfield. One day Bolsheviks with trucks were there, taking away all your things from the store rooms, and I knew that you had gone. So I went back to mummy and daddy in the gardener's hut.*

Piotr was crouched down next to her, reading over her shoulder. 'It is lovely to see you,' he said. 'I feared you were dead.'

She nodded, and the faded hair swung. It had lost its fine gloss. *I prayed for you, every day.*

She sipped her wine, and looked into the ruby glass.

'What happened to our mutt, Trotsky?'

We ate him.

The pencil hesitated, and then continued to fill up the page.

That winter, when we were starving. And when there was nothing left we boiled his bones for soup. Then mummy gave me her wedding ring and I went into the city to try to exchange it for food in the black market. I was picked up by some Chekisty. I pretended to be one of the proletariat, but they laughed at me, because of the way I spoke. They stole my mother's ring and took me away for forced labour, digging ditches and defences, for the Whites were coming.

She stared into the glass, and Piotr reached over, tipping it gently.

'Drink,' he said, and she did.

They never came, though we heard the guns. After a few weeks I escaped, I made my way back through the snow to the hut where mummy and daddy were but they were dead. They were frozen. I could not move them. There had been a fire in the house and there was no one there. I lived in the cellar. I grubbed up things in the garden to eat. It was hard, because the ground was frozen. My hands . . . There were two warm days and I dug a hole and buried my parents. I was afraid the dogs would eat them. A little dog came round looking for something to eat. I trapped it in the cellar and killed it, though it bit me. I roasted it. When things started growing, I dug up flower bulbs and took them into the market. People bought them to eat.'

A colour had come into her pinched cheeks with the wine. *How did you survive, Piotr?*

'I kept Krivitskiy's train running,' he said simply. 'Now he wants me to get a factory started.'

You'll be good at that.

He moved to her side, and put his arm about her. She turned her face away. She gripped the pencil fiercely, and made herself write. *You won't want to touch me. I wanted to keep myself for you, but they caught me. They put me in the prison, that's where Krivitskiy found me. I was still pretty, and I was bourgeois.* Tears were rolling down her cheeks. *That's what they said, when they came into the cell. The guards, the Chekists.*

Her mouth contorted, and she spoke, for the first time. One word, harsh and filled with hate.

'*Boorzhoi . . . boorzhoi . . .*'

It sounded like metal rasping on stone, torn out of her chest as it was. She wept and the tears wrinkled the paper of the page.

All the time, as they hurt me.

He held her close to him as she sobbed. 'That is over now,' he said gently. 'We can start again. Everything is starting again. New factories, new lives.'

I can't go out. They are out there. She looked up at him like a whipped animal. She held up the page so that he could see it. *I can't go out.*

'The factory has a small house for the manager and his wife,' he said. 'It has a small garden with a wall round it.'

You cannot want me.

'I want nobody else.'

I cannot speak. I know the words, but they do not come.

'They will come. And the house is waiting.'

I cannot go out.

'Then don't go out. *I* will go out.'

She looked around the little room.

I have made it as clean as I can. I would make the house clean. I am not what you want, but I will be a good wife.

'It's all over,' he said softly, and they held each other in their arms. 'I will keep you safe.'

Valerian and Nadia conducted the foreigners along Petrovka Ul like two sheepdogs, one at the front, one at the back. They were similarly dressed, in well-cut blue dungarees and shirts, their sleeves rolled up, wearing strong polished work boots. They did not wear peasant clothes any more. The striking success of October Revolution, the model peasant village created by Valerian and Konstantin, had led to promotion. Valerian and Nadia were now in charge of the running of the tours for the specially-selected foreigners arriving to inspect the future. They stayed in the Metropole, the lovely Tsarist hotel, chosen for its ameneties and proximity to the street of Petrovka, the once-fashionable shopping zone, the Bolshoi Theatre, the Square of the Revolution, Red Square and the Kremlin itself. From the hotel they could be taken on carefully-conducted bus and rail trips to see the creations of the new state, the October Revolution village, and similar factories, schools and hospitals.

They were on their way to view a parade of returning troops. Among their number were Americans of the Relief Administration, British and American journalists and academics sympathetic to the Bolshevik cause. Savinkov had sent them.

Valerian was at the rear, with Cyrus Waldburger, of the American Relief Administration, a large, earnest and sincere man, a Christian appalled by the reports of the starving and dying in a country devastated by more than six years of war. From Savinkov in Berlin had come the Kollwitz posters of the huge-eyed, hungry child stretching out its hands for sustenance. The good had come, to see what they could give.

What the Russians needed was grain. In the countryside the peasants were making bread from acorns, weeds, the bark of trees and the manure of cows. They were dying. This meant that they had run out of grain, which meant there was none to take to feed the workers in the towns. The government was close to collapse. There was a New Economic Policy. But first, they needed grain.

'You've been to the October Revolution village,' said Valerian. 'You've seen with your own eyes what we can do once we introduce communism to the countryside. When we can spread that throughout the nation, why, we won't be asking for grain, we'll be *exporting* it to the rest of the world. But you have no idea of the devastation caused by the imperialist White armies as they retreated in front of our Red Army forces. Our soldiers reported total destruction. Fields and orchards burned, all food supplies – grain, cattle, pigs, everything – forcibly taken from the people by the Whites as they left. They were left to starve.'

'Monsters,' said Waldburger. 'Just monsters. I've come to know you, Valerian, in the few days we've been together. You're a Christian as I am. You Communists have, in fact, revived and applied what are, historically, essentially Christian ideas, and applied them where they always ought to have been applied, to society and our social duties. I know that in his way, despite all his irreligious jargon, Lenin is as much of a Christian as I am, and that's why I'm going to try to help you good people as much as I can. For the forces of Satan are still at large. When evil men leave women and children to starve, we must *all* hold together. I've seen your village, I've been to your factories – and wish we could attain that sort of efficiency in America. And you've fought a terrible war. Look at this wonderful city of yours. After six years of war you keep it clean and tidy. Your people are orderly. The hotel we're in runs smoothly. The cultural life of the city is alive and vibrant. You make New York look like Calcutta.'

The street was clean and washed. The former people did it when they were driven down it, and the streets and squares around the city centre, at night. They took away the corpses of the dead, and their guards any beggars who had mistakenly crawled there in the night.

'I only have to listen to you talk to me in such good English to know what your new state is capable of. You, a simple factory worker taken from your lathe so that we may meet real Russian workers and you can learn English like that! Now that's a marvel.'

'The dictatorship of the proletariat is a marvel,' Valerian said unctuously. His father had been an anglophile and they had spent two months every year in London, staying at Claridges. He had had an English governess.

'It sure is!' said the young man striding along beside him. It was the United Press correspondent, Johnny Nichols. His red hair blazed in the street as brightly as his enthusiasm for where he was.

'Back home, I come from a stinking tenement in Corlears Hook. That ain't the best part of New York, *tovarisch*. Old Cyrus here, he's a fat cat. But here we both are, helping the proletariat.'

America sounded not a bad place, Valerian mused, if a boy from the slums could rise to be a journalist. But he kept his thoughts to himself. He liked the Americans, with their touching certainty that the world could be remade, for the better.

Suddenly he saw something that sent every trace of complacency from him. Someone was missing. He dashed up the straggling, bumbling column.

'Nadia, Nadia!' he hissed, trying not to betray his alarm. 'The Englishwoman. *Pani* Webb. Where is she?'

There were two English academics, fearsomely productive writers, man and wife, deeply committed socialists. They were interested in the workings of Soviet trades unions. And she was gone. Nadia stared down the street in terror.

'Are you looking for my wife?' the man called, bespectacled, and thin. 'She went off down there, said there was something she wanted to see.'

Valerian ran back down the street. Down an alley, in the distance he saw her, her black hat pinned to her head, bent forward, peering at something, and he pounded down the way towards her. She shouldn't have been here. It hadn't been cleaned: as he ran, glazed, listless eyes watched him from filthy tenement doorways.

'*Pani* Webb,' he shouted. Anything to distract her from whatever it was she had found. 'Mrs Webb.'

She turned and smiled archly at him.

'How many times, dear Valerian? I am *comrade* to you.'

She was about sixty. She had placed herself in front of a great acreage of rubble. 'Now tell me,' she ordered. 'What is this?'

Our God in Heaven, thought Valerian. Why this? It was the site of several streets of tenement housing. The inhabitants had been driven out and their homes used for fuel. All that remained was the incombustible rubble.

'A palace,' he said quickly. 'Built by the Tsar for his chief minister.'

'Ah!' Beatrice Webb sighed with satisfaction. 'And now the site of new and glorious housing for the urban proletariat.'

'Yes. That's what it is. Housing. For the proletariat. Now shall we join the others?'

They began to walk back down the alley.

'If only we could follow your example. It is simply imperative that we demolish such archaic structures as the Houses of Parliament and such symbols of bourgeois privilege as the Oxford and Cambridge colleges. They must be razed, razed to the ground, just as you have done.'

In the alley she halted, and breathed in deeply as she looked about her. Valerian winced. The smell of ordure and rotting waste was appalling. A starving man began to crawl out of a doorway towards them and Valerian aimed a vicious kick at him behind her back.

'Wondrous!' she exclaimed, looking about at the decaying Tsarist tenement. 'If only we could have such city housing.'

'The Revolution is coming,' Valerian said weakly. He managed to get her moving again and he could feel his whole torso under his blue work shirt wet with sweat.

A man was coming down the alley. He wore no trousers under a torn and filthy coat and he was gnawing at a tired apple.

'Hail!' she said. beaming. 'Long live the Revolution.'

The man looked at Valerian. 'What did she say?'

'She asked how you liked the Revolution,' he said blandly.

The man smiled cynically. 'This is Paradise. Here men eat apples and go naked.'

'What did he say?' Beatrice Webb asked interestedly.

'He said he lives in Paradise,' Valerian replied, truthfully.

'So sensible of him, to eat fruit. A diet of fresh fruit, cereals and raw vegetables is both nutritious and satisfying. I expect Comrade Lenin will make it compulsory soon.'

'Now, come on, Comrade, we mustn't miss the military parade,' said Valerian.

'I know we have both been looking forward to seeing your young men on their way home from fighting for peace.'

They emerged again on to the cleanliness of Petrovka. Nadia had halted the group, and was staring back at them. She looked terrified. Valerian waved discreetly at her, and she relaxed.

'This is *wonderful*,' Beatrice Webb declared. 'We are in the future, *and it works*.'

'That's right!' shouted Johnny Nichols, the newpaperman, cheerfully. He capered up the street with his red hair blazing, in an impromptu dance, singing, '*Arise, ye prisoners of starvation, Arise, you wretched of the earth! For justice thunders condemnation. A better world's in birth!*'

As they went up towards the sound of the marching troops Valerian felt limp with relief. The sweat was drying on him. There was nothing to worry about.

12

Byvshiye

W HOEVER was playing the piano found their fingers now supple, they finished with the scales, and the sweet sound of the composer's concerto in B flat minor came on the air to her. She was standing by the window, and only half-heard the knock at the door. Then it came again, and, glancing at the sleeping child in the cot in the alcove, she went to open it.

A man both broad and tall stood outside. He took off his hat, and held it between his hands.

'Do I inconvenience you, Mistress?' Akulov asked.

'Did it inconvenience you to send me your salary?' Yelena replied. 'Come in. And I cannot be your Mistress.' She looked him firmly in the eye. 'We know each other much better than that.'

She smiled, and he smiled back, sheepishly. He wore scuffed, high riding boots over scarlet trousers with silver stripes down their sides, and the cavalryman's jacket of Budyenny's *Konarmiia*.

There was a tiny kitchen behind a curtain and she put water on to boil. She saw him standing by the window where she had been, listening to the music.

'Ruth Gunzberg that was had this place. She gave it to me. She moved out of the Hotel Luxe, where all the Comintern lot stay. She said they all spied on each other and she couldn't stand it.'

It was hard to find people who remembered what it was like, before the fighting. She talked, building bridges with the past.

'She said she loved it here because you could listen to them playing down there, in the Tchaikovsky Conservatory. She said that, when she was in pain, she used to stand at the window, and let it wash it away. I think I was the only person she could talk to . . . She is married, to Savinkov but you cannot talk to Savinkov for his whole life is persuading others to do what he wants . . . Though doesn't he do it well? All that money pouring in from the West to buy grain for Lenin. I got a letter from Ruth; she seems happier now that she's gone. I met her before she left and she brought me here. She said I could have it, for she was going to Berlin. It belonged to a Princess, before. She lives in a room downstairs now . . . There are quite a few of us like that, hanging on . . .'

She went into the kitchen, and returned with two cups of tea, piping hot, mahogany brown and sweet.

'Do you know what they call us, Ivan?'

'*Byvshiye*,' he said, shortly.

'Former people. That's right.'

'Is that why you dress this way?'

She ran her fingers down her plain clothes. 'It isn't wise, to stand out,' she said. 'You can queue for hours and have them run out in front of your eyes, if you stand out . . .'

'I'm not used to seeing you like this. It will be good when girls can wear pretty clothes again.'

'I have some pretty clothes. I brought them from the house,' she said artlessly. 'I could wear them for you if you like. It is just not a good idea to stand out, not out there . . .'

'I shall arrange for you to get army rations. I am a commander,' he said with quiet pride.

The room was simply furnished, but here and there were ornaments, a few pictures, a school photograph, rows of books.

'I can see you have things from the house in Tsarskoye,' he said. 'How did you keep them, all through the war?'

'I hid them. I had a special place in the house, and I put them there. I was with Count Mikhail . . . we were going to escape to Finland, but Rykov found us. You and Ruth freed us that night. I went back and collected them.'

Her face had become clouded with worry. 'Ivan,' she said, and clasped his sleeve. 'I went back one time before. In the war. After *Graf* Mikhail and I escaped on the train. We were in Petrograd, trying to find a doctor to mend his feet. I had hidden tinned food in the house, in my hideaway. Food, and warm clothes. I had skis, I skied down the Neva, thinking to get food from the house.

'On a remote part of the river, I found a strange sight. A small house, like a large room, but with a roof, with pillars, all made out of ice. There was a door, and looking through it I saw a dreadful bed, made out of ice, and frozen upon it was a couple, quite naked.'

Akulov's face wrinkled with dislike.

'Someone had poured water over them, so that they were encased within a block of ice. And I knew them.' She took down a photograph from the wall. 'This is the school photograph, this is my class. Here is

Vasilii, here Zhenya. They were the couple I saw frozen to death in the ice.'

'Many terrible things happened in the war,' he said. 'I, you, we saw some of them. Men and women tortured by other men and women for no more reason than the joy those doing it got from it. I have seen my share of horrors. For me, war is about fighting for communism, fighting the enemy. When I found filth like that, I shot them, whether they were on our side or theirs. What did you do?'

'Like you, I had become hardened by the war. The food and clothes in the house would help us live. I went to get them. The house was in a terrible state. Soldiers had lived there. They had locked the downstairs drawing room and cut a hole in the floor of the bedroom above. They had used it as their latrine. But although the house was gutted, my hideaway was safe. I collected the food, and left the belongings. Those I took from the ruin, on my way here. But before I left Petrograd I went about, asking questions. It is my home city and I know it well. I managed to find out where Zhenya and Vasilii had lived together. I found a woman who had lived below them. She was very afraid, and would tell me little. But she said a man had come and taken them away, and she had never seen them again. A small man, in the Cheka. A small man who made her terrified. Who do we know, Ivan, whom would that description fit?'

'Rykov is both small and terrifying. But there are others who would fit that description.'

'But my schoolfriends ... Me, he hates. I know that. I read of Verochka, in the papers. Found strangled in her train.'

'Verochka the peasant singer?' he said, in surprise.

She smiled, sadly. 'Verochka the countess, who would do anything to survive.'

'I saw her last concert,' he said.

'In the Crimea,' she said softly. 'I was captured there, only days later, and would, but for you, be dead. Because Rykov was there, too.'

He looked worried. 'It is not proof ...'

'It is proof enough for me. I am afraid.'

'I can tell you where Rykov is,' he said unexpectedly. 'He is in the north, running a camp for enemies of the people.'

'May God help them ... How do you know that?'

'Krivitskiy told me.'

'You move in good circles, young Ivan. What are you doing with Krivitskiy?'

'Germany is re-arming. They have ... companies, under false ownership. In Spain, in Turkey, in Sweden and Finland. To make guns, weapons, tanks.'

'My grandfather was a general. It is no use having the weapons if you cannot train the soldiers.'

'That is so. They are coming to train here. With us.'

'With you, Ivan?'

'There is a new kind of warfare out there,' he said passionately. 'I sense it. Like the tachankas, the machine-guns on the fast carriages. Overwhelming force, fast and applied in mass. Aircraft, tanks, guns and men. Moving at speed. We have to co-operate with the Germans. They have the best officers, the best general staff. The best industrialists. In return for room, they will make *us* the best.'

'What can be more strange than Prussian generals and Bolshevik cavalrymen?' she marvelled. 'And you are to be a commander in this new partnership.'

'It is a new world,' he said simply. 'I am a soldier.'

He got up, and ran his finger along the books she had placed along the shelves, and over the mantelpiece. 'Your house was full of books . . . and you were always reading. I do not read well, or write well, but these are two things I must be able to do, if I am to rise in the new army.'

'Then I shall teach you to do it better. But you write, I got your cards.'

Akulov looked at the cot. Outside the dusk had gathered, the notes of the symphony were tinkling to a close. 'May I see the child?' He went over and peeped in. 'A fine young boy,' he said. 'What is his name?'

'Alexei Mikhailovich. He is Count Mikhail's son.'

'Yes. How do you get pregnant in the middle of a civil war? We were starving, terrified, struggling to even survive. I would not have thought it possible.' He remained bent over the cot for some moments, then turned to her. 'Count Mikhail is not here to look after his son,' he said directly. 'What happened with you and I, when Rykov captured you; I would not hold you to that. But the boy should have a father. I will look after him, if you will let me.'

Yelena looked at him directly. 'Perhaps we can all look after each other. I would that it had been anyone else but Rykov conducting the ceremony, but I would not change my status. I am happy to be your wife, if you are to be my husband.'

'I shall be a good husband, and a father to the little one,' he promised, sincerely. Then he beamed. 'Then there is one thing I must do, as a good husband. You have to meet my family. It is something one usually does before one is married.'

She thought of the estates of Mikhail, the villages he had owned. 'I would love to meet your family,' she said.

Poltava, the Ukraine

'Who are you?'

The big man whittling beside the fire did not look up at him, but carefully cut the holes in the wood as Akulov had seen him do a thousand times. The room should have been filled with people, his mother, his brother and sister, their children. It was empty except for the big man.

'Who are you?' he said again, harshly. 'Who is it who comes in the uniform of a Russian soldier?'

'I am your son, father.'

The man still did not look up, but shook his head. He flicked a shaving into the fire.

'No, no. No son of mine would wear that uniform.'

'It is a new Russia, father. We are creating a new world.'

He laughed savagely, sitting by his fire. Through the window Akulov could see the yellow flowers patching the green of the water meadow, saw the river glittering in the sunlight.

'A new world of slavery! Are you one such, that uses the cannon of the Tsars against peasant folk, who murders them in the name of this Lenin?'

Akulov was quiet.

'*Answer me, boy!*'

'I have fought against rebels.'

'Rebels? Rebels against what? One who wishes to make us slaves?'

He blew down the tube to free it of dust and shavings, as Akulov had seen him do a thousand times before. Through the window he could see the herdsmen bringing long-haired cattle along the path through the greenwood, switches in their hands.

'The *vlast* we understood. *Graf* Mikhail took what he took, but he left us what we needed. It was not perfect, and when the day came we took the land of *Graf* Mikhail for our own. This Lenin said that we should not – that we needed his permission, all the way from Moscow. We do not need Russians telling us what we may or may not do, here in the Ukraine. This Lenin knew that, for he sent armies against us, men wearing uniforms like the one you soil my house with. Now we have a new *vlast*. This Lenin says we should all be Bolsheviks. He says that the land belongs to us, the people, but he means that the bread we make from it belongs to him. He says that the streams are ours, but he means that the fish we catch in them belongs to him. He says that the forests are ours, but he makes us cut down the trees and take them to him.'

'The people in the towns must eat, and be housed,' Akulov said.

'Very good. Then let them come with money, and buy.'

'It was the war, Father. Now there is a new policy.'

'Do not talk to me of policies. This Lenin will be back, whatever he says, for we know him. The only thing about him one may be sure of is that he tells lies. Lie upon lie.'

'It is not easy!' Akulov cried.

'You go and live in your new world. I will live in mine, the one I understand.'

'I have brought some things, Father. Food.'

The big man blew from the right end of the flute as Akulov had seen him do a thousand times, and a clear, pure note filled the room.

'No, no. We need no food here, food is what we grow. We have what we wanted, which is the land of *Graf* Mikhail. You have what you wanted, which is the woman of *Graf* Mikhail. We shall see who has the better bargain. Now leave. And do not call me father, I have no son like you.'

Akulov went out. The pony was standing patiently between the shafts of the cart with its carefully-stacked sacks and he lifted himself up in a practised movement and slapped the reins. As the pony clopped along the little lane of fruit bushes he heard the sound of the children as they were let out of the barn, and he brushed his face with his hand.

Where the lane led down towards the square a girl was waiting, sitting where the stream tumbled down the hill to the water meadow.

'I see you, Ivan Ivanovich.'

'I see you too, Masha.'

She was petite, with bright, glinting brown eyes.

'You have come back,' she said, 'as you promised. I knew you would, for you are an honourable man.'

Akulov was silent. From where he was sitting he could see the waving green leaves of the waterplants in the stream, waving like long fingers over the smooth, white stones. If you lay on the bank and lowered your hands into the crystal water you could find fish there, long brown trout with white flesh, and you stroked them like seducing a girl, before whipping them from the water. He could see that there was a little boy down there now . . .

'While you were away, all that time, Anatoly the son of Andrey would call, every week, asking if I would care to walk with him a way, but I said I would not. Ivan the son of Ivan is coming back for me, I would say, and he is an honourable man. And Anatoly would leave without bothering me further, for he, too, is an honourable man.'

Akulov sat up on the trap, and still said nothing. The boy's hands were in up to his elbows and he seemed hardly to move. Akulov had done that, his fingertips running softly over the smooth skin of the fish, as delicate as the very current of the stream.

'So where will you take me, now that you have returned for me as you promised?' Masha said mercilessly. 'Will you take me far from home, to live with your Russian masters, Ivan Ivanovich? Shall I work as their servant while you travel abroad for them, to do their killing? That is what you do, is it not? You wear their uniform, and you are an honourable man.'

'I have a wife.'

'We *know*,' she said, her voice very low. 'Did she not ride through the village with *Graf* Mikhail in their carriage, and did we not bow very low as they passed? Shall we bow to you as you pass in your Russian uniform, Ivan Ivanovich?'

'I am sorry,' he said. 'Things do not happen as one thinks they will, when one is young.'

'They can do. Were you here next week you could stand outside the church and you would see me come out with Anatoly Andreyevich at my side, for I always said that I would marry an honourable man.'

On the river's bank the water suddenly flew high in glittering droplets, and a fish flapped on the grass. The boy hit its head with a stone in triumph, picking it up with his fingers through the gills. Akulov clicked his tongue, and the pony leaned forward in its harness.

'Don't come back,' Masha said.

Akulov drew up outside the wooden house at the head of the water meadow. The barns where the cattle were in the winter flanked the yard. The air smelled of seed corn, blossom, drying manue and pigs. Through the green woods lay the road to Poltava. He climbed down, and went inside. The room was much the same as the one he had left, for his father had helped his brother build it. Yelena was sitting at a table, reading a book with a young girl of about five. She had plaited hair, and hung eagerly over the colourful drawings and pages.

'Uncle Ivan!' she called over her shoulder. 'She reads so that you can see!'

'I know, Tatyana, my sweet. She had a house filled with books.'

'I still have books,' said Yelena. 'I have lots I had when I was a little girl, and I'm going to send some to Tatyana. Would you like that?'

'Yes *Please!*'

A big man was sitting by the fire, in his twenties.

'Give me a hand with the sacks, Boris,' said Akulov, and his brother got up.

'I told you,' his brother said.

'You keep it. Try to slip some over to Mama when he's not about.'

They went out, and a thin figure scuttled from the cart, a bag in its hand. Moving with a speed and grace that belied his bulk, Akulov scooped up a stone from the ground and released it in a single, following movement. The youth howled, clutching his head, and the bag of sugar fell to the ground. He ran off as Akulov went to pick it up, stopping at a safe distance.

'Some things never change, eh, Timofey Vasilyevich?' Akulov grunted. 'Sheep bear lambs in the spring, honest folk work, Timofey Vasilyevich steals.'

The scrawny youth rubbed his bleeding head and spat resentfully on to the dirt.

'You'll get what's coming to you,' he said malevolently, and slunk off along the hedgerow. The two brothers began unloading the sacks and inside the house Tatyana laughed, and Akulov's brother smiled to hear it.

April 1924

The bell rang and Yelena heard the ripple of Alexei's running feet as he went to the door. He was now tall enough to open it, and proud did so whenever possible.

'Daddy!' he shouted happily, and he came into the room, riding upon Akulov's shoulders.

'You managed it!' Yelena said delightedly. Akulov put Alexei down gently, and kissed his wife.

'I'm away to Kazan in two days, to help set up the training school, so I insisted on leave. Where is Natalia? Where is my little girl?'

He went to look in the cot, and Alexei came with him. A little baby was dozing, dressed in a lovely, long, embroidered christening dress.

'She's so beautiful. She takes after her mama. Where did you get that dress for her?'

He reached out a great paw to touch it, reverently.

'Ruth sent it from Berlin,' Yelena said happily. 'I wrote to tell her, and this parcel came. She's so kind.'

'Is she well?'

'She sounds it. I'll show you her letter later. She was disappointed that last year's crash didn't produce the revolution they all seem to be waiting for. She was annoyed, actually. The only good thing, she says, is that some lunatic called Adolf Hitler who was in charge of some socialist gang tried to set himself up as boss of Bavaria with that ghastly man from the war, Ludendorff. Anyway, they settled his hash and he's in gaol, and you won't hear any more of him or so she says. She loves Berlin. She says if the left haven't won power yet they've certainly won the cultural war. Honestly, the things she says go on! Lenin wouldn't approve. I can tell you. She takes the *Weltbuhne* and goes to the theatre a lot. She's reading Freud.'

'All beyond me,' Akulov said smiling. 'My reading wouldn't suit Ruth. Too dry and technical. I've been reading Triandafillov. And I've got something good – in English – will you translate? By an Englishman, Liddell-Hart. It's a technical article. He believes in the tank, as we do.'

'We'll look at it tonight,' she promised. 'When the children are in bed. How are you getting on with the Germans?'

Akulov was changing into his best uniform. Happy that his parents were together, Alexei was playing on the floor with a wooden armoured car that Akulov had made for him.

'Well, I like them because they're real professionals and we're working out something special. Look, I meant to tell you. I have to go to a Staff course in Berlin – as a Bulgarian! Mustn't upset the British and French or they'll think the Germans are planning a new war. You could come. Would you like to?'

'I'd love to see Ruth again. But I couldn't leave the children. When they're bigger.'

'You're right. You don't look Bulgarian, anyway.'

'I'll tell you who is going to Berlin,' she said. 'Katia. Savinkov's starting his own film company, *Russ* and she's going to star in *Aelita*, I think she said. He's got the best Russian *avant-garde* directors and actors – Protozanov, Otsep, Pudovkin. She says there'll be talking films soon. Can you imagine that? Being able to hear the actors. She's going to be at the christening. She's bringing this American Negro she's having a fling with. You know, one of the boys they have over here at the Lenin Institute as a symbol of the oppressed races. Leroy Smith, he's called. Do you mind?'

Akulov chuckled. 'I like to look at them. So black, like ink.'

'That nice Johnny Nichols is coming. You know, the United Press correspondent.' She pointed to a horn gramophone and a pile of paper-cased records. 'Look, he's lent us a whole lot of music. We can have a dance, later. Konstantin's coming, too. Oh, my darling, he's written a poem for Natalia! Now is that an honour?'

'I'm glad you're seeing your old schoolfriends again,' Akulov said quietly. He was buttoning up his high-collared jacket. 'Are they all well?'

Yelena looked quickly at him. Alexei was playing on the floor, untroubled.

'I . . . made efforts to find out what had happened to them. You know why. Petr and Gleb died in the war. In the fighting. Yury, Nikolay and Irina are in exile in Paris. Zhenya and Vasilii, and Verochka, those are the only ones.'

'You see, it was the war.'

'Yes, you were right. I was so frightened. I couldn't see things clearly. Look, now, come next door.'

There a table was set with plates over which white cloths had been placed. He lifted a corner and peeked in.

'*Zakuski*,' he said reverently. There was plate after plate of the special *hors d'oeuvres*. Marinated mushrooms, black caviar, salted herring, sliced salami, brown bread, pickled cucumber, black bread, cold tongue, boiled eggs, red beet salad, scallions, cheeses.

She looked at him anxiously, wanting him to approve. 'Will it do?'

There were bottles at the side, of vodka and wine.

'My darling, it is wonderful!'

She smiled with pleasure. 'And look.' She lifted another cloth.

'Cream cake!' he said in delight.

'People can eat again,' she said. 'Things are getting back to normal. I heard from Tatyana, did I tell you? Look, here is her letter. Doesn't she write beautifully? I send her books, you know. She's such a bright little girl. She talks about the planting, and the harvest . . . Your mother sends her love, Ivan. And she says that Masha has had a baby boy.'

'My mother wished me to stay in the village and marry Masha. I am a great disappointment to them all.'

'Your mother sends her love,' she said gently. 'See, Tatyana says so.'

'She says nothing of my father.'

'Give him time. He will be proud of you one day. *I* am. Oh, I must tell you something funny. I found Katerina! Look, here on the school photograph. Isn't she pretty? She's coming to the christening, too. You know what she's done? Got married.'

'That is good,' he said gravely.

'To an army officer. One just like you. A Cossack.'

'You see, the ladies cannot stay away from us.'

'It's just our way of winning the revolution,' she said.

'We're going to teach you the *mazurka*, it's been decided.'

She hesitated a moment. Darling, you remember when she came to us, right at the end of the war, we gave her a hand. Things were very hard and she was looking after her parents. She had to sell herself, but it wasn't her fault, there was nothing else she could do. You won't say anything, will you? She's got a new chance, now.'

Akulov put his arm around her and squeezed. 'I liked her very much. And I know nothing of her past, only that she was a schoolfriend of yours.'

Yelena kissed him, then went to the mirror, and made final adjustments to herself.

'Alexei, come and let me put on your coat!' she called. From the window came the sounds of a musician at practice.

'The orchestra will be playing this afternoon,' she said. 'I went to see. We'll fling the windows open while we're having the celebration.'

In the room, Akulov had picked his baby daughter up, holding her carefully and gently in his huge hands. Yelena carefully wrapped her in a lace shawl, and he cradled her in the crook of his arm.

'They'll be gathering at the Arbat,' she said, and they went out into the sunshine.

Moscow, December 1927

Yelena came down the cream and gilt corridor, her feet revelling in the sensation of walking on thick pile carpet. She knew the door – the hotel had changed not at all – and she tapped on the tall, ornately-carved wood, and a soft, cultured voice called from within, the right kind of voice for such a place.

'Come in, please.'

She opened the door. The suite was the same – one entered a fine reception room, with regency-stripe sofas and chairs, a card table or two, a French pedestal desk by the window where he sat writing. They had even found fresh flowers to place in the crystal vases. He stood courteously as she came in.

'Professor Bekhterev,' he said and she offered her hand.

'They have given you my mother's room,' said Yelena. 'This is the suite in which we would stay, when we came to Moscow from St Petersburg.'

'Of course.' He indicated the sofa, and sat down opposite, sweeping the tails of his frock coat around. 'Christmas shopping, a visit to the theatre?'

'Yes. We went to the Maly, sometimes the Bolshoi . . . and the shops, oh . . . they were like Aladdin's cave, to a child.'

He nodded sympathetically. 'I know . . . Your mother, she . . .'

'Countess Ivanova. We had a house in Tsarskoye Selo. Near to the Empress Catherine's school.'

'I remember her. You would have the title now, of course.'

'Not now, Professor,' Yelena said levelly. 'Were I not married to Ivan Ivanovich, who was a Bolshevik in the year seventeen, I should be one of the *byvshiye*, and not exist at all.'

'Yes,' he said quietly. 'Many changes, for us all . . .'

He reached out for a buff medical folder that lay on a small, round yew table. 'Now, about these headaches of yours . . .'

She held up a hand. 'First, please do let me apologise to you for taking up your time like this. I know how busy you have been with the international conference. It is just that I never get to St Pet – to Leningrad, and Dr Andreyev thought that as the nation's leading doctor of neuropathology . . .'

He smiled understandingly. 'Piotr Alexeyevich was one of my own students. And if I suffered from the kind of headaches that you do, I too would badger anyone to attempt a cure. They sound very nasty.'

Yelena nodded with feeling. 'They are. It is not just that the whole of one's head feels like a drum, inside which malevolent demons are poking with sharp knives, it is also the flashing lights behind one's eyes, and the moving battlements. Also the nausea.'

'Horrible . . .' he murmured sympathetically. 'Do they occur at random, or are they associated with anything, have you noticed?'

'They come with difficulties . . . with frightening situations. I had them when both my children were born, I am afraid to say. My husband went missing on an exercise once, and when he was found I had one that lasted two days.'

'Have you had them always? When did they start?'

'Not always,' she said quietly. 'Only since the war.'

'Of course. A terrible time. I myself nearly died in St Petersburg, in the bad winter.'

He glanced over at the desk, where another buff folder lay, the one he had been writing in when she had arrived.

'Some conditions simply appear, I am sorry to say. Conditions in earlier life provide a kind of breeding ground, and then some event or other acts as a trigger, releasing the syndrome, which then may reappear again and again. I saw a patient . . . or no, well, not a patient, but I was asked to see a man – a very important man – just recently, I was filling in the notes when you arrived, who suffers from a different condition, but one which only became fully apparent in middle life, and is now an integral, and dominant, if encapsulated, part of his personality. I'm trying to decide what to do about him.'

He paused, thinking, a worried frown biting into his forehead, and then looked up again. 'But yourself,' he said, bringing himself back to the situation at hand. 'Can you identify any particular event that triggered these very violent headaches?'

Yelena sat staring at him for several moments. 'Perhaps,' she said uneasily. 'So many terrible things happened in the war.'

'Have you talked about it to anyone?'

'Others suffered worse than I. I do not seek to bore people with my troubles when they have their own and I have much to be grateful for – I have two beautiful children, and a fine husband.'

'And terrifying headaches,' he observed.

'I thought, perhaps, there would be a powder to take . . .' she hedged.

'It might help to talk about it,' he suggested. 'Is there anything in particular that might have triggered the headaches?'

'We were in the Crimea,' she said reluctantly. 'Mikhail and I. We were Red Cross, for Baron Wrangel.'

Mikhail, he is your husband?'

'No. *Graf* Mikhail was shot . . . I heard the sound. But he was alive at the time I am thinking of . . . he was with me in the slaughterhouse . . .'

They arrived, in a terrible rush, were all about her. She put up her hands to her eyes, to block them out, but they came from within. '*They are here!*' she cried in horror. 'The d- the d- the d- dead people . . . b-b-blood . . . lying there wh- while sh- sh- she murdered them . . . b- b- blood and their b- b- brains . . .'

Bekhterev put out his hand quickly and held hers. 'Enough . . . enough!'

She fought to control her mind. 'Please . . . something else. Not this. Anything. Your other patient. Tell me of him. He has headaches?'

'No, not headaches.'

The feel of the dead bodies all about her, the cold, congealing gore in her eyes, in her nostrils, in her hair. The agonised shrieking of the tormented.

She reached to her hair with a frantic hand, expecting to feel the dead. 'Please, tell me about him,' she said urgently. 'Anything, please, help me make them go away . . .'

Bekhterev gave her an experienced glance, and rose, moving to a fine tantalus on an oak sideboard. He poured a large shot of brandy into a tumbler. 'My patient . . . yes. If things were different, a most interesting case.' He handed her the tumbler and she clutched it without drinking.

'What is the matter with him?' she muttered. Her eyes were closed, as she fought demons in her head.

'He is paranoid,' Bekhterev said. 'Severely so. Do you know what that is?'

'Greek . . . *para noos* . . . beyond the mind? He is mentally ill?'

'It can be. It can also be an abnormal state of personality in which the person who displays these psychopathic traits remains competent, knows what he is doing and is responsible for his actions. It is the latter which my patient is suffering from.'

He watched her closely, seeing the contortions of her face as she struggled to bring herself back to sanity.

'That's interesting . . . go on. What traits are these?'

'The symptoms associated with paranoid states are normally chronic suspicion, jealousy, self-absorption, hypersensitivity and megalomania.'

'I don't think I want to meet your patient!' She said. 'Are these people easy to recognise? I'd like to know, so I could keep out of their way.'

'I wish we could . . .' Bekhterev said strangely. 'They are not always easy to spot, if you are not trained. They become very good at concealing their true selves. This man is. Very good. He appears calm, reasonable, moderate. Underneath seethe delusions of grandeur and the conviction that he is the victim of persecution and conspiracy. These delusional beliefs are unshakeable and systematic, the victim constantly works significant details into a logical pattern that is continuously capable of ingenious adjustment to protect its credibility. The result is extreme suspiciousness and distrust of others, producing an eagerness to srike at enemies, whether real or imagined, before they can injure oneself.'

Yelena shook, as if with ague. Her face was slick with sweat. 'He must be a Bolshevik, this man. Lenin saw enemies everywhere.'

Bekhterev looked at her, startled. 'He is . . .' he murmured. 'The delusions become worse the more there is an element of fact to build on. Revolutionary politics is, almost by definition, a bitter, factional and conspiratorial affair. It becomes all too easy for the paranoid to detect or manufacture potential threats to his being or cause, and to act to forestall them.'

'What are you going to do with him?'

'I don't know,' Bekhterev said quietly. 'He is not, you see, one of the *byvshiye*. He is a *very* powerful man. I am hoping that I concealed my realisation of his condition from him. And did not join the list of enemies.'

She opened her eyes.

'Are they gone?' he asked.

'Yes.'

'How do you make them go? When they come.'

'I distract myself. I perform mental arithmetic or plan the garden I shall have one day, in detail, while they rave about me. As they begin to retreat I think of pleasant things, beautiful flowers and little children.' She took out a small sheaf of much read letters and opened one, finding comfort in the rounded handwriting. 'I read my niece's letters. Tatyana is her name and she writes to me from my husband's village, in the Ukraine. She understands figures. They're planting less grain next year, the official prices are too low, and there's nothing to buy, she says. It's sensible, she says. Her father says he's going to spend more time fishing. I haven't drunk your cognac. Won't you join me?'

He went to the sideboard, and she put the letters away. 'God save the Tsar,' she said.

'Oh yes,' he murmured. 'But not here.'

They drank. Bekhterev carried her buff file over to the desk. He scooped up the one he had been writing in and put them both away in a battered black case. He wrote upon a small white notepad with his fountain pen, and waved the piece of paper in the air to dry the ink.

'I shall return your file to Doctor Andreyev. I'm afraid that there is little I can recommend though you are suffering from an injury, just as much as though you had been in a car accident, or a train crash. It is possible that the symptoms may lessen with time. With regard to the headaches, I have known the painful effects be alleviated through use of a herbal tea. I used to know a shop that would have made up the mixture for you, but that was before . . . This is the recipe, should you be able to obtain or grow the ingredients.'

'Thank you! I really am so sorry to have taken up so much of your time. Will you send me your account?'

'No charge, Countess,' he said gently. 'Your mother was kind to me, as a young man.'

He held her coat for her, and came with her to the door. As he did so, the telephone rang, through in his bedroom.

'Do answer it,' she urged. 'I'll see myself out. And thank you, again.'

'It has been a pleasure,' he said, moving across the room. 'I hope we shall meet again.'

She heard him pick up the telephone as she dabbed her mouth with her handkerchief and put the herbal prescription away in her bag. Then she opened the door.

She heard a soft chink of glass. Someone was coming up the stairs. A servant . . . she saw his white jacket and gold braid moving through the banisters. He was carrying a tray with a bottle and champagne flute.

She was still in the doorway, forewarned by some strange knowledge. He paused at the head of the stairs, and checked something in his top pocket. He was small and neat. Rykov!

She backed into the room, panic flooding into her. She closed the door. Bekhterev was talking in the bedroom and she stuffed her fist into her mouth to stop from crying out. Rykov must not hear her as he went past.

She stood by the door in agony, waiting for the soft footfalls to go past. But stopped. There was a knock on the door.

Heavy curtains of dark velvet hung to the floor by the windows. Frantically she scurried across the room, stuffing herself inside the great folds. She heard Bekhterev call, 'Who is it?'

'Room service, sir.'

The old curtain was decaying at the seam and she found herself peering through a small gap of frayed thread. The neurologist stepped across the room, and opened the door. Rykov stepped inside.

'A gift from your comrades at the international conference, Professor, sir,' Rykov said deferentially. Holding the silver tray expertly, he closed the door behind him. 'Would you care for a glass, sir?'

'Not just now, thank you. Put it over there.'

'Yes, sir.'

Rykov put the tray down gently on the sideboard with white gloved hands. He took a fat fountain pen and a pad from his top pocket.

'Would you be so good, sir?' he said, holding them out.

'Of course.'

Bekhterev reached out, and Rykov held them forward. Yelena saw him move suddenly, like a snake striking. The pen was in Bekhterev's face and there was a sudden soft explosion of air. Rykov had a handkerchief over his mouth with his free hand. Bekhterev gasped, clawing at nothing, spinning slowly on one heel, his head back, his face contorted, suddenly purple, and he fell to the soft carpet with a thud, and did not move.

Rykov stuffed the pen inside the handkerchief, moving rapidly away from the dead man. He was holding his breath. He went straight to the door, poking his head out like a weasel emerging from a rabbit hole, and then he was gone, the door closing quickly behind him.

Wrapped in the curtain, Yelena let out a muffled sob of terror. Blood was dripping over her fist where she had bitten a finger to the bone.

She came out, making herself wrap the wound in her handkerchief before hurrying over to where Bekhterev lay. A bitter smell of almonds was in the air and his face was flecked with blue and he was quite dead, his eyes staring open at the ceiling.

Every instinct urged her to run, but she stood for a moment, and then went over to where the battered black bag stood by the desk. She pulled out the thin wad of buff files and stuffed them under her coat. Then she went to the door, looking out anxiously before slipping away along the corridor, away from the stairs.

13

Poetry in the New World

Moscow, July 1929

Evening light filled the room. Through the tall windows Katia could see the domes and spires of the cathedral in the distance, all different shapes, sizes and colours, like a collection of exotic fruit. The setting sun gleamed on Konstantin's shiny, shaven head as he stood by the window.

'I like your new studio,' she said.

'I'm an important man, so I've been told,' he said, without a smile. 'The state looks after its important people.'

The big room with its high ceiling was sparsely furnished. An easel stood near the window and the lectern that he used as a writing desk was in one corner, looking out.

'Have you been painting?'she asked

'No.'

'Writing, then?'

'Yes.'

'I've interrupted you.'

He smiled, and stopped looking out of the window, throwing off his gloom.

'What I was *doing*, was waiting for someone to interrupt me, so I could drink with them.'

He went to a small cupboard and took out a bottle of Georgian red wine and two tumblers. He extracted the cork with a single pull, and poured.

'They're selling all the paintings,' he said suddenly.

She swallowed the rich, blackcurrant-flavoured wine. 'What paintings?'

'Rembrandts, Rubens, Franz Hals, Van Dycks, Raphaels, Botticellis, Titians . . . you name a great artist whose work is in our galleries, they're selling him.'

'To whom?'

'Western millionaires. Someone called Mellon has got the best. He's given Stalin six million dollars for them.'

'Why does Stalin need six million dollars?'

'He's broke. He hasn't been paying the peasants the right price for grain, so they haven't been planting it. Last year he sent the goon squads back to steal it, just like in the war and so this year they've planted even less and he hasn't got enough to bribe the workers, let alone to export. It's a fuck up. If he'd just paid them to begin with, everyone would have been happy.'

'That would be far too easy. Not revolutionary at all. But does it matter? About the paintings?' she asked gently. 'Didn't you used to say that only the future mattered, that the past should be eradicated?'

Konstantin drained his glass and refilled it. 'I have talked a lot of shit in my time. Once I painted the line "I love to watch children dying." on a café wall.'

He smiled crookedly at the beautiful young woman with her long auburn hair. 'I cannot even stand the sight of blood!' I wanted the Revolution because I thought it would be exciting, shock people, just like my stupid poem. In the café people came because they'd been told I was an artist. I used to refer to them as "bourgeoisie who hadn't had their throats cut yet". Anything to annoy. When I was being annoying and young my grandmother said to me, be careful what you ask for in this world, you might get it. Well, I have what I wanted – the past is being eradicated and the great artists are going to the West.'

'And it's important?'

'Yes!' he cried. 'Because they all painted a thousand times better than I do. Forget triangles with fishes' eyes – Lenin didn't like us doing that anyway. But it was better than heroic workers erecting electricity pylons marching away into the future. It was certainly better than painting happy, plump, smiling peasants in sunlit cornfields!'

'I've just finished,' she said. 'Playing a happy, smiling peasant.'

'Filming's over?'

'Finished. I thought I'd celebrate. I thought I'd take a shave.'

He looked at her, puzzled, his mind distracted from its worries and she giggled.

'So I thought, who's got a razor? And I thought Konstantin will have a razor, *and* a bottle of wine.' He looked at her glorious hair. 'Your hair? Me, I was going bald anyway, it seemed a suitable gesture, the sort of thing the old Konstantin would have done.'

'Not my *head*, Konstantin,' she said patiently.

'Oh . . .' he said. 'Oh, I see . . .'

She giggled again. 'I've always wanted to try it. Be as smooth as a baby. So where's the razor, Konstantin?'

'In the bathroom. Over there.'

She put down her glass. 'I won't be long.'

He was still standing by the window when she came back. She had taken off her long skirt and wore a pair of snow-white pants under a blood-red shirt. She smiled enigmatically at him and sat down on a sofa by the wall, folding her long legs under her.

'How does it feel?' he asked, curiously.

'Different,' she said, and took a small bottle from her bag. The contents showed through the glass, it was red.

'See? I'm a good party member,' she said. 'Even if it is French.'

Papers, and a pencil lay on the lectern.

'A poem? Or the script? Eisenstein's given me a part, you know,' she said, polishing a nail in preparation for paint. He left the window and picked up the paper.

'No. I can't get to grips with what Eisenstein wants,' he said distractedly. 'He wants this central character, whom he calls a *Koolack*. He wants him really horrible, a monster – fat, gluttonous, lazy, brutal. A vile, sort of oppressive landlord type who exploits the other peasants. The problem is he doesn't exist. I must be one of the few Bolsheviks who actually knows something about the countryside and the peasants, Katia. I went there as a young man with some other idealists, we were going to "socialise" the peasantry. A complete waste of time. They were polite to us and thought we were buffoons. Most of the activists wound up *hating* them. There they were, ready to jump out of their skins to bring them the benefits of socialism and they wouldn't even thank them. But I went there. They're different, is all. They just want to be left alone. This *koolack* of Eisenstein's, he doesn't exist. I think I'll ask Eisenstein to get another writer. I'm a poet and an artist, anyway.'

'So what were you writing?'

An expression of worry went over his face, and he flapped the piece of paper. 'Someone came round, someone from Stalin . . . a small man, name of Rykov. He understood, he said, that writers had a way with words, and that I was a writer.' Konstantin glanced back up at the great cathedral in the distance. 'He frightened me,' he remarked, absently. 'He seemed to like that.'

'You don't have to be frightened, Konstantin. Nobody does.'

'I formed the impression that making people afraid was this Rykov's job in life, as it is, as he sees it, mine to produce this.' He held up the sheet of paper. 'Shall I read it to you? You must sit quietly, quiet as a buttercup. That's what I used to say, in the café, when I read my latest poem. And they would sit there, in the dim light and cigarette smoke, some of it mine, and I'd read, with a worker's cap on and a red scarf tied in a big knot about my neck. The Revolution was coming, it was going to be a different world . . .'

His eyes refocused, and he looked back down at his piece of paper. 'Here it is. Poetry in the new world. Stalino, Staliniri, Stalin-Aul, Stalinissi, Stalinsk, Stalinsky, Stalinogorsk, Stalinabad.'

He raised his eyes from the sheet. 'What do you think of it so far?'

'What is it?'

One hand of nails was gleaming red. She blew on the wet paint, carefully.

'Names. For cities and towns to choose from. When someone like Rykov arrives with the list, they can choose. There's some more. The Man of Steel. The Iron Soldier. The Brass-hard Leninist. The Granite Bolshevik. The Universal Genius. It's his birthday in December, he's going to be fifty.'

'Do you want me to guess who it is?'

'No. You know, Katia, back in 1917 when the revolution was coming towards us, like a great waggon rumbling down hill, I wrote a poem about how it would smash the dead, mummified hand of religion along with all the other things one's parents did that one objected to. I'd be ashamed to read it to anyone now. And now I'm writing liturgy. Would you like to hear some more? Here it is. "If you meet with difficulties in your work, or suddenly doubt your abilities, think of him – of Stalin – and you will find the confidence you need. If you feel tired in an hour when you should not, think of him – of Stalin – and your work will go well. If you are seeking a correct decision, think of him – of Stalin – and you will find that decision."'

'I think you have the metre just right,' she said gravely. 'It is indeed a prayer.'

'There's more . . .' he muttered.

'Konstantin, put your paper down and pour me some wine,' she ordered. 'I'm getting thirsty over here.'

'Yes, of course . . .' the bottle clattered against the glass.

She unfolded her legs and stood up by the wall, holding her hands up in the air, her scarlet nails drying. 'You'll have to hold it up for me.'

He put it to her lips and tilted it carefully.

'Now you.'

As he drank, she looked into his dark eyes with her own, glittering green. 'I've made a mistake, Konstantin. When you shave, you have to put on cream afterwards. It's in my bag, I have a jar.' She waved her scarlet nails. 'I can't do it.'

He opened her bag, and found the expensive French jar.

'Open it.'

Fresh fragrance of flowers surrounded them.

'If I don't put it on, I shall get sore,' she said. 'And I can't.'

She held up her hands. 'You'll have to do it for me.'

The white silk slid over her hips, and she leaned her shoulders back against the wall.

'It's cold,' she said. She undid his belt, her nails leaving scarlet scars on the leather. He slipped his hands under the blood-red shirt and she was naked beneath. She put a long leg around him, pulling him into her. He picked her up, carrying her over to the sofa and he lay back with her hands above her head. The shirt pooled like blood about her white neck, and her nails splashed the wooden rail she grasped with scarlet.

They lay together as the dusk rubbed the colours away from the room.

'I've loved you for years,' he said. 'Since we were at school.'

'I *know*,' she said. 'So why didn't you do something about it?'

She stirred, the silk whispering in the dark.

'Too shy,' he said quietly. 'Too afraid.'

'Konstantin the poet? Konstantin the great lover?' she asked, laughing gently.

'Konstantin the bullshitter,' he said. 'I've been full of *pokazukha* all my life.'

They got up and he lit an oil lamp and opened another bottle of wine. Through the window they could see that lights were on inside the cathedral.

'They're clearing it,' he said. 'They're going to use it as a grain store.'

She had dressed, but the scent of far-away flowers still hung in the air. She had a glass in one hand and with the other she picked up the sheet of paper he had been writing on.

'What are these?' she asked. '"Regrettable lapses from Soviet legality. Slipping into the methods of War Communism. Competition between grain-collective organisations".'

'I did not write that,' he said. 'Rykov had a list of phrases. Writers had a way with words, he said, so possibly I could think up some more.'

'Did you?'

'I thought of one. "Administrative mistakes." I got it from Trotsky, actually. Lenin complained that Trotsky was over-concerned with the administrative side of things.'

'And what would it mean?'

'It would mean what you wanted it to mean. Rykov understood that,' he said carefully. 'But administration, to Trotsky and to Lenin, meant Terror . . .'

14

Schutzstaffeln

Berlin, July 1930

MANFRED Liss had the windows of his apartment open and the curtains back and the room was lit by the blaze of white light from the nearby Kurfuerstendamm, restaurants, shops and cabarets pointing like a sword at the great Tiergarten park. Sitting in the room, Savinkov and Krivitskiy could smell the breath of its horse-chestnut trees, overlain with the electricity of the trams rattling along the street below.

At the door, Liss took the tray from the waiter, and handed over some money.

'There's the gravel, Hans. I'll ring down if we need some more. When are you off? At ten? Come up and we'll have a tankard.'

In the room he put down the tray on a table and poured nutty brown beer from a jug into three steins. He gave them to his companions. 'Here's to us,' he said.

'Why aren't we down in the beer hall?' Savinkov enquired.

'Maybe he doesn't want to be seen with us,' Krivitskiy suggested. He sipped the beer. 'The lager's good, though.'

'And why are you wearing a raincoat? It's summer.' Savinkov said.

'You'll see,' Liss said enigmatically. 'And I want to talk to you alone. It's been what? Almost ten years?' The shock-headed revolutionary they had known was balding, leaving a foaming rim of curls around his ears, but he still fidgeted with energy. 'I have a proposition for you. For you both.'

The window tinged itself green as the traffic light below changed on its thirty second cycle and the waiting tram whined forward.

'A revolution's coming,' he said quietly, significantly.

'I think you're right,' said Krivitskiy. 'I think the communists will have power here, in a couple of years.'

'Let's just say the old order is through,' Liss said carefully. 'Are you still a Party member, Leon?'

'Me?' Krivitskiy said casually. 'No. I've left all that stuff behind. I'm just a businessman, these days.' He took a pull at his beer. 'I'm more interested in the bottom line than the Party line now,' he joked.

'Strange, for one of Lenin's own Chekists,' Liss observed. 'But you'll remember enough to know what's happening here. Weimar's going, just as the Tsar was, in sixteen or seventeen. It's just a question of how to shove it over the precipice. And who to do it. You agree, Sergei? Weimar's finished?'

'It's certainly vulnerable,' Savinkov said cautiously. 'Because of the Depression. Mass unemployment, salaries and wages slashed, businesses and farms going bankrupt . . . You have fertile soil here, to be sure. But don't think you can repeat what happened in Russia, back in eighteen. The Germans are too educated – they wouldn't let you get away with a *putsch*.'

'We understand that,' Liss said mysteriously. 'Here, you have to come to power legitimately, through the ballot box. The *revolution* takes place afterwards. Once let us in, they'll have to carry us out of office feet first. And we'll make sure they never can do that.'

'You sound as though you're involved,' said Krivitskiy. 'It must be you who's a Party member.'

'Oh, I am. A Party member. We could use you,' Liss said quietly, in the half light. 'You actually did it. And you, Sergei, to help get us there. Now's the time; the catastrophe has happened as he said it would. Now's the time to grasp people's emotions. Isn't that right, Sergei?'

Savinkov looked across at him, curiously. 'That's right,' he agreed. 'It's the psychology. The *economic* factors – the unemployment, lack of money, the bankruptcies – are a new, and even more terrifying shock to a German people who have already suffered a whole series of shocks.'

'Hold on a moment,' interrupted Krivitskiy. '*Who* said the catastrophe would come? Who are you talking about?'

'Wait a second,' said Liss, holding up his hand. 'Finish, Sergei.'

'The German people are in a state of psychological shock. It began with the defeat of the war, after horrific losses. Then came Versailles, and the reparations. The collapse of the Monarchy, revolution, near-civil war and massive inflation. Then, a brief period of recovery in which they began to rebuild their lives – like survivors of an earthquake. And now – all snatched away again! Recovery an illusion! A cruel trick! People to whom this has happened are not rational. They are prey to virulent fears and resentments, they entertain fantastic hopes. They will support people that in other times they would never look at . . .'

'If this was the year seventeen, I would have said that the proletariat will rise up,' said Krivitskiy. 'And embrace communism.'

'They won't, you know,' Liss said softly. 'Not that there's anything wrong with communism you understand. But it's *impersonal*. It's a cause. The Germans are waiting for a *leader*. With a *vision*. A hero, the bearer of godly power of destiny and grace. He cannot be made, cannot be selected. He comes like fate, like lightning, terrible, sudden and compelling. Now is his hour.'

'What the hell are you talking about?' asked Savinkov, startled.

'Who. *Who* am I talking about. I am talking about the leader, the *fuhrer* who is come to show us the true way. It is Adolf Hitler.'

'*Hitler?*' Krivitskiy choked on his beer. 'You're a fucking *Nazi*, Manfred?'

Liss stood up, unbuttoning his raincoat and dropping it to the floor. From a darkened table he picked up a cap, and donned it with a flourish. He stood in the light of the window, where they could see him.

'There,' he said simply.

'Mother of Jesus,' Savinkov muttered. 'Are you allowed to go around like that?'

In the street light it was the silver death's head on the cap that glinted, the rest was black as night. A black-edged scarlet armband glowed like blood, the ebony spider of a swastika crouching at its centre.

'Yes, I'm a Nazi,' Liss said proudly. The leather of the black accoutrements of his uniform creaked satisfyingly as he moved. 'The distance is not far for a communist to jump. You could do it, too . . .'

'The Nazis are our enemies!' Savinkov protested.

'Simply because only one of us can have the power. What, really, separates us in essentials? Very little. We are both radical movements. We both hate the established order, and wish to destroy it and all its principles, moral, social and religious. We both have powerful ideologies and dominant Parties. In power, we will both require the services of a secret police to buttress that power and Party, as has been proved in Russia. *There is almost nothing to separate us*. In a contest, whichever side wins will incorporate the essence of the other.'

'But you have better uniforms,' Savinkov joked, still mesmerised by Liss's outfit.

'I am SS, *Schutzstaffeln*,' he said proudly. 'We are at Hitler's side.'

Liss held up his stein. 'Why don't you join the winners now? Join us, both of you. I can promise you both rich rewards.'

'What power do you have, Manfred?' Savinkov enquired cautiously.

'I am authorised to approach you both *by Hitler himself.*'

Krivitskiy drained his stein and stood up. 'Look, fellows,' he said apologetically. 'I thought this was just a few beers to talk about old times. But if you're serious, I'd better leave. The little lady has dinner waiting . . .'

'I didn't know you were married, Leon,' said Savinkov.

'I live with a fine German lady, Marthe. Although we are not yet married. Listen, it was good to see you both. But I have to meet with some Hamburg merchants in the morning, so . . .'

He went across the room and they heard the clatter of his feet on the stairs, the bubble of noise from the bar downstairs as he left.

'Is he really a businessman?' Savinkov enquired curiously. 'He had blood up to his elbows, in the civil war.'

Manfred laughed. 'Can the leopard change his spots, the nigger the colour of his skin? No! He has a business. It takes him all over Germany. He lives with Marthe and her young daughter Elisabeth. Marthe is a member of the KPD, the German Communist Party. We think that Krivitskiy is the illegal *rezident*, the underground intelligence boss for the Soviets.'

'I'd buy that. He likes power too much.'

'What about you? We need a propagandist. A genius. We have Goebbels, but you're better . . . *Reichsfuhrer-SS* Himmler himself wishes to have you with us.'

'He does . . . and Hitler would really have me on board?'

'He doesn't hate communists. Not like he hates the social democrats. Don't forget, he's a socialist too! The Nazi Party is a socialist party.'

'I could do it . . .' Savinkov said softly. He sat in the darkness, thinking about it. 'I suppose Himmler wants me to oust Goebbels, there's politics here. And that's what I don't have to worry about where I am, outside, the circling of the kites about each other . . .'

'It's an easy jump,' Liss urged. 'It wouldn't bother you.'

The bell of the tram clanged below, its motor hummed.

'Remember, you've done it before,' he said softly, in the darkness. 'When we were making revolution here, and the *freikorps* got you. I had already joined . . . You sold Rosa Luxemburg to us, the leading Socialist of her time . . .'

Savinkov sat silent for a moment, reliving the past. 'I know I did . . .'

He was silent for a moment. 'Lenin wanted her done in, if she wouldn't come aboard,' he said quietly. 'It had to be our revolution, not hers. So I told the *freikorps* where she was . . . He was pleased, when I got back . . . he gave me my charter.'

'You saved the young girl,' Liss observed. 'Ruth.'

'There was something really touching about her complete naivety. It was like having a beautiful idiot child about. You could tell her anything. . . . And anyway, I wanted to fuck her. There's something about the release from danger that makes women quite passionate . . . Hell, Manfred. I *married* her. She got pregnant. She's not so naive now, of course. Just a bitch like all the others . . .'

He drowned his muttering in a swallow of beer, and Manfred returned to his subject.

'So what about it, Sergei? Come on board . . .'

'Look, Manfred, one man, one great man like Hitler, I'd be submerged. That's what's so good about communism, we don't allow one single leader to emerge. No Bonaparte for us. Our great leader was Lenin, and he's dead. And I have my charter from him. My *signed* charter to spread the word . . . because I got rid of Rosa. She knew him for what he was, you see, Manfred. No Committee can tell me what to do, because I've already been told . . . It gives me a lot of freedom, Manfred. No, I think I'll stick to what I'm doing. Maybe I'll regret it. It's a hell of an opportunity you're offering. But I think it would choke me.'

He drained his stein. 'I'll see you on the streets,' he said.

The door shut quietly behind him and a few moments later Liss heard the buzzing of voices and clinking of glass as the door to the beer hall opened.

He got up and shut the windows, drawing the curtains. He put on two small lamps. There was a tall cheval mirror in the room and he stood in front of it, admiring himself in the SS uniform. He was still trim and his stomach flat; if his hair was receding you didn't notice it under the cap.

He wanted changes and he'd bring them to Himmler's attention once he had them properly worked out. His critical eye ran over the outfit. The brown shirt had to go. White was necessary, and white gloves, to contrast with the jet black, from peaked cap to glistening black boots. Black, picked out with silver for the death's head, silver runes, silver edging, silver leaves of rank. A new knightly order . . .

He was breathing heavily, his black breeches bulging. He picked up the telephone.

'Hans? You free yet? Well, come on, then.'

He heard the thump of the boy's feet on the stairs and stood, head back, arms akimbo.

'Manfred, you look marvellous . . .' the young man breathed. Blond, blue eyed, he put the jug of beer down, eyeing the uniform in awe.

'What about me?'

'I think I may be able to help you. Maybe . . .'

Hans knelt, undoing the buttons of the breeches. 'What about your friends, are they coming back?'

'They're communists, give them time, they'll come round.'

'We thrashed a couple of commies on the street last week and yesterday one walked in! Asked if he could join!'

'See? But I think you need to move from those nasty SA boys, Hans. I'll see what I can do for you.'

Aluminium-edging for the collar, twin brilliant mirror-wires, four-cornered starlets . . .

The youth worked at his task with the same zeal with which he whipped communist boys of his own age on the street. Liss felt himself as hard as a rod of iron.

The telephone rang.

'Manfred.' Krivitskiy's voice came down the wire. 'I saw Savinkov leave. Listen, I can't join you. It wouldn't be right.'

'Whatever you say, Leon.' Liss held his voice steady. 'You know where I am.'

'That's right. I'm based here, you know. Let's not lose touch. We're old friends, after all.'

'We think the same, Leon,' Liss reminded him.

'We're old friends,' repeated Krivitskiy. 'Let's stay in touch.'

Liss put down the telephone and bent the youth over the arm of a chair in triumph . . .

15

Gaspodi, Polilui, Umershikh

Moscow April 1931

'Nikolai!'

From the doorway of the Pioneer hall Nikolai Savinkov saw his friend Alexei waving to him from a mass of children. Red scarves and hammer-and-sickle badges blazed under the lights.

'I didn't know you were back.'

'Mummy brought us,' said Nikolai. 'Daddy's busy in Berlin. This uniform's stupid.'

Alexei Mikhailovich Akulov glanced casually around. There was a hubbub of noise.

'I know. But just don't say so, Nikolai.'

'Natasha likes it – she's been wearing hers since she got up.'

Alexei noticed the knapsack on his back. 'You didn't . . .'

Nikolai nodded, his eyes gleaming.

'*Real* ones?'

'Yes. Darts and everything.'

'Is Natalia here?'

'She's over there somewhere.'

The noise suddenly died down and there was a shuffling of feet. A woman, very tall and old to them, stood smiling down at them from the stage with its white film screen. Her hair was grey and she was dressed in a strange black uniform of leather trousers and boots, a leather jerkin. It was stiff – they heard the leather creak as she came down amongst them.

'Hello, children. I am Comrade Commissar Zemliachka.'

'Good morning, Comrade Commissar,' they chorused.

The old woman took a wooden chair and sat down on it.

'Gather round me, children.' She held up the sleeve of her jacket. 'This is an old uniform isn't it? Do you know when I wore it?'

Nikolai saw his sister Natasha's hand go up. Her blonde hair was shining in the lights. The curtains of the hall were drawn.

'Yes, what is your name?'

'Pioneer Savinkova,' she said proudly. 'And that is a uniform of the Cheka, so you must have been in the great civil war, Comrade Commissar.'

Zemliachka smiled in approval. 'Very good, Pioneer Savinkova. I was in the civil war. Do you know what I did?'

'Caught enemies of the people.'

'I did. Many, many of them. All those who tried to enslave the proletariat. But the proletariat knows no chains, which is why we have our wonderful, first communist nation. And now this uniform only hangs in my cupboard, except when I put it on to show brave young communists like you. Here, would you like to touch it?'

She held up her arms, and the children clustered round, patting the dry leather with little hands. Nikolai saw hard, observant eyes under hooded hawk lids above the smile, felt Alexei pushing him forward, and reached out with the others, saw the eyes checking all the children, each one.

'There has been blood on that uniform,' the old woman said. 'Blood of the enemies of the people. Does that bother you, children?'

'No!' Natasha cried, and others echoed her.

'Good,' said Zemliachka. 'For there is something else you should know about enemies of the people. Do you know what it is?'

They frowned, confronted with a new sum in arithmetic they had not been told about.

'They never go away,' Zemliachka whispered, looking around, catching the eyes of the children in turn. 'Oh, yes, you can find them, you can kill them, even. But soon, like rats breeding in the sewers, they come back. You cannot change them, you see, children. A rat is always a rat, it can never become a rabbit. When it breeds, its children are rats, not rabbits. The child of a *boorzhoi* is *boorzhoi*, not a proletarian titan. The child of a kulak is a kulak.'

Natasha Savinkova frowned from amongst many other puzzled little faces. 'What is a kulak, Comrade Commissar?'

'An enemy of the people.'

Zemliachka looked about the children, making sure they met her gaze. Nikolai felt it on him, felt it hot, like the eye of a dragon.

'It was my task to crush the *boorzhoi*, who sought to enslave the people. Now a fresh enemy has arisen and it is your task to help crush him. He is the kulak. Have you not seen the people who queue for bread in the streets? They queue because of the kulak. Does your own home lack for plentiful food provided by the state? You lack because of the kulak. Have you heard little children cry because they are hungry? They cry because of the kulak. Who is the kulak? He is the rich peasant. He sits astride his lands while poor peasants toil to pay him in gold. He hoards vast mountains of grain, tub upon tub of butter and cheese, barrels filled with apples and fruit. Whole barns are filled with the beef and pork he withholds from the starving proletariat. He is evil, he is the enemy of the people.'

The dark eyes were glittering now. 'Would you like to see him?'

The lights went down and the screen began to flicker with light as the projector rolled.

In the countryside, a band of men.

'See his rolling estates, stolen from the people.'

They were digging, a great wain stood nearby, laden with sacks.

'This is how they hide food from the people.'

Bloated stomachs, thick, leering lips.

'See the evil ones.'

The men were runing for cover, hiding in the bushes. Someone was coming.

'Here they are, brave komsomols.'

A teenaged couple, boy and girl, in their Party uniforms, standing shocked by the hole, piled with sacks.

'They have discovered the enemy. Look out!'

The evil figures were about them, beating them down. Their dead faces, close up.

'The kulak will do anything to starve the people. But see, justice is coming.'

Through the trees came banners, and a great column of children.

'See how they catch them.'

The children held them down, struck them with their own spades.

'They demand to know where the food that belongs to the people lies.'

Brave, smiling children, carrying away the sacks. The dead couple smiled down upon them from a sunny sky as the kulaks were led away in chains.

The lights came on.

'There, children. There is your enemy,' Zemliachka said softly, and Nikolai saw his sister's eyes shining.

Zemliachka stood up. 'Now, before you go out to play, let us sing to him. The one who keeps us safe, who looks down upon us. Let us sing the song of the Pioneers.'

Her hoarse voice began, and their little ones joined in.

'Oh, Stalin, the sunshine of springtime is you . . .'

Then they went outside, where the real sun was out.

'Let's play at catching enemies of the people,' said Natasha. 'Who's going to be the kulak? Let's have Ivy.'

'No . . .'

Alexei nudged Nikolai. 'Come on. Let's go in the woods.'

The trees were not far away, they slipped towards them.

'Hey, wait for me.'

By the fresh green bushes Alexei turned round. 'This isn't for girls,' he said importantly. 'We're going to have a battle.'

His younger sister ignored him. Her eyes gleamed.

'Did you get them, Nikolai?' Natalia asked eagerly. 'Alexei's been talking of nothing else for days.'

Nikolai opened his knapsack. Inside were two dark, shiny blue pistols with wooden grips, a packet of circled paper targets and a round tin.

'Real Webleys,' breathed Alexei.

'Two twos,' Nikolai said proudly. 'Mama didn't mind. She even bought a pistol herself. A proper one, with bullets, but she wouldn't let me use it.'

Didn't you get me one?' asked Natalia reproachfully.

'Girls don't need guns,' said Alexei.

'We can share,' said Nikolai. 'Let's get into the wood before that witch asks us what we're doing.'

They put up a target on the trunk of a birch tree, and loaded their pistols with fabulous shiny silver darts, with fluffy scarlet and green tails. They fired, the pistols making soft belching sounds.

'Mine's closer than yours,' said Natalia.

'Just luck,' Alexei said loftily. 'Anyhow, you'd better go back now, because me and Nikolai are going to have a battle.'

'So am I! I'm on Nikolai's side, aren't I, Nikky?'

'You can be on my side.'

'Go on then, Alex; you go off and we'll hunt you.'

Grumbling, but reverently carrying his air pistol, Alexei went off into the wood. After a minute they heard him call, 'Ready.'

The two children stood whispering together for a moment and then they giggled. They set off towards the sound of Alexei's voice, spreading apart.

Nikolai crept along, moving from one clump of bracken to another. He paused, crouching down in the curling green foliage, and cupped his hands. 'Cuckoo.'

A moment later, further into the wood he heard Natalia. 'Cuckoo.'

He ran across a little clearing and heard Alexei's pistol break wind, heard the tiny thud as the dart hit the tree trunk. From within a thick

clump of bracken he heard the clicking as Alexei compressed the
spring and reloaded. He jumped forward, out into the open, and put
up his hands.

'Don't shoot!' he shouted. 'I'm unarmed.'

Alexei stood up in the bracken. 'How can we have a battle if you
aren't armed?' he demanded.

There was a short rasp behind him and he suddenly yelped, holding
his backside. Nikolai heard Natalia chortling with glee, and she
emerged from behind a tree.

'*She* is,' Nikolai said reasonably.

'Very clever,' Alexei grumbled, pulling the dart out. 'Ow!'

'A great soldier you are,' jeered his younger sister. 'Getting shot
in the bottom!'

Through the trees they could hear the other children.

'We'd better get back.'

'We can have another battle behind our house. Where the old
huts are.'

Nikolai found the dart in the tree, scarlet like a drop of blood, and
put it carefully away in the tin. They slipped back through the trees
and across the open ground to the Pioneer hall. In amongst the noise
of the children Nikolai heard a thin, terrified keening. In a corner two
girls were holding another. His sister Natasha was twisting Ivy's hair
and he could see the skin standing out by her ear.

'Dirty kulak! Tell us where the grain is.'

Briefly he saw the old woman Zemliachka standing by an upstairs
window, looking down. She was smiling. Then she turned, as if
answering someone else in the room, and was gone.

He pulled his Webley pistol from his bag, and pushed Natasha
aside, pulling Ivy away from the two bigger girls twisting her
arms.

'What are you doing?' Natasha demanded angrily.

'We're taking Ivy off for questioning,' Nikolai said. 'We're the
Cheka.'

'We had her first! She hasn't confessed yet.'

Nikolai waved his pistol in his sister's face. 'We're the secret police.
We've got the guns.'

He took the sobbing child in one hand, and began walking off with
her, followed by Natalia and Alexei.

'Come on Natasha,' one of the other girls said. 'Let's play
something else.'

'But that was a good game. I want to do it with *real* kulaks.'

Round the corner Nikolai put his pistol back in his haversack and

Natalia gave Ivy her handkerchief. The little girl blew her nose. The skin around her ear was bright red.

'I don't like it here,' she said. 'I don't like it at all . . .'

She waited by the tram stop, close by the shiny water of the *Chistyye Prudy* pond. Across the boulevard a great pile of earth stood behind the wooden shuttering of a building site where they were constructing one of the experimental Metro stations.

The tram came clattering up on its loop in the dusk, its electric motor whining, and pulled up with a squeaking of metal. On the kerb Ruth saw her waiting at the gate to get out. She looked much older than she remembered her, slightly hunched inside her high-collared coat. But she beamed as she saw Ruth waiting.

'Nadezhda!'

'Ruth! How marvellous. Shall we walk along? I don't want to be late for my lecture.'

The two women began walking down the boulevard, past the Ministry of Education. Ruth turned, looking quizzically at her friend. 'I was waiting for the Chaika, and you got off the tram.'

Nadezhda shook her head. 'I don't like all that. We didn't achieve the revolution just so that some of us could ride about in cars like the *boorzhoi* used to.'

'So you're a college girl! What are you studying?'

'Textile production. Honestly, it's very interesting. And I feel I'm doing something to help the people. Me, Nadezhda.'

'That's wonderful . . . what are the other students like?'

'They're really nice, Ruth. I didn't tell anyone who I was, for ages. I registered in the name of Alliluyeva, and everyone was good to me from the beginning. Of course, they found out who I was in the end, but they treat me just the same, just as one of the team. I've managed to help one or two a little. There's this lovely boy from the Donbas, Nikita Sergeyevich, he carries his engineer's tools about with him – so sweet – but he's a first class Party organiser, he'll go far, and I've introduced him to one of Josef's men, Kaganovich. He's taken him on as his assistant.'

'They're all high-flyers, aren't they? All the ones selected for the Industrial Academy.'

'Oh, yes, they're all good people, good communists. All Party members, all with working class backgrounds, of course.'

'Of course. I'd better not apply, had I?' Ruth said dryly.

'Oh, darling, I didn't mean that! You're as good as any of us. You were a Bolshevik from the beginning. I just really like my fellow students – going to the Academy makes me feel like I used to, before the Revolution, all filled with hope. That's it. It gives me back my hope.'

'The world has a way of taking the rosiness out of one's dreams, doesn't it?' Ruth said wistfully. 'You realise that there's much more dirt to get covered in, more toads and fewer princes.'

Nadezhda looked sharply at her. 'How are things with you and Sergei?'

'Savinkov? I don't see much of him.'

'Do you mind?'

'Mind? No. He likes sandwiches, and I don't.'

'What do you mean, sandwiches?' Nadezhda said, puzzled.

'You know, the sort with a man in the middle and two girls each side. He proposed I be one of the slices of bread and I moved him into the spare bedroom. I think he has his gourmet experiences at work now.'

In the darkness, Nadezhda blushed, then, 'I have my own room, too,' she said, after a while, near the little yellow church of St Fyodor.

'Yours playing about too? They're all the same. It's the dangly bit – it leads them about like the ring in the snout of a pig.'

'No . . . it's not that.' She walked on a few strides. 'Did you bring it?' she burst out.

'The pistol?' Ruth asked, slowly. 'I wasn't sure if I should. But I did buy it, in the end. It was your letter. You sounded . . . desperate. But I want to know why you want it.'

'It's him,' she said starkly. 'I'm afraid. He isn't as I used to think. We – my parents, my sister and I – we knew him for years. I thought he was a hero, as a young girl. A real, live, revolutionary. He'd been in prison, in exile, and always fighting for the cause. He was respectful to my parents and he treated me well. I looked up to him. A hero . . . I married him when I was sixteen.'

'There ought to be a law about it,' Ruth commented sourly. 'Savinkov got me the same way. I was young and naive and he was my mentor. He had me up against a tree in Berlin, and I really thought we were making revolution. I thought he had all the answers there were, that he was pure, like a flame. I thought he *believed*, like I did . . . like I *do*. I don't think Savinkov believes in anything, not really. He gets some strange amusement from getting people to think the way he wants . . .'

'Oh, Josef believes . . . he believes in History. Which I am starting to think is a reason to be afraid of him.'

She slowed up. A big junction was ahead of them, some one-horse carriages were clopping past, she stopped outside a high block of flats decorated with strange animals.

'Eisenstein lives along here, you know. The Institute is across there. I don't want to stop outside and I don't suppose I can explain it all, Ruth. But I am afraid. I should have known, years ago . . . He changed, he wasn't the way he was when he married me. He puts on an act, Ruth, he fools people, but I know him. He was the one who got rid of Trotsky, because Trotsky was exciting. Trotsky had charisma and the people followed him, and Josef accused him of a cult of personality. He was jealous . . . And now it's Josef they call the Universal Genius, and he pretends to be angry, but he's not . . . Just after Vasily was born, he dipped his fingers in wine and let him suck them. A little baby . . . I was very cross, and demanded that he stop, but he did it again and again because it upset me . . .'

She turned to Ruth, standing by one of the strange beasts.

'He's *cruel*, Ruth. He *likes* inflicting pain. Sometimes he hits me . . . or we might be sitting, and he bends my thumb back, until I want to scream, but I dare not . . . there's a rage inside him, like a pot that's boiling with the lid on, so you can't see it, but touch it and it scalds you . . .'

'You want the pistol to knock him off?' Ruth suggested, almost jocularly. 'I thought of it once, with Savinkov, when I came back and found . . . he suggested I get in too . . . If I'd had a gun I'd have shot him.'

'No . . .' Nadezhda said quietly, sadly. 'Just as insurance. Just to protect myself, if it really comes to it. I left once, you know, but he got me back. He was good for weeks, and then he had that look on his face, very white, he locked the door first . . . I won't let him beat me like that again, I told him . . . But he's stronger than I am, I *need* a gun.'

Ruth had her hand inside her pocket. She brought it out holding a small black pistol.

'There it is,' she said. 'I told the salesman I wanted it against burglars. A Walther. It's not too big – here are some of the little bullets. He said the best thing was to point it at him and keep pulling the trigger until the noise stopped.'

Nadezhda slipped it into her own pocket.

'I don't know how to thank you. I'm sorry I had to ask, but it had to be someone he doesn't know.' She glanced at her watch. 'I must get to my lecture.'

She looked across the boulevard at the green Baroque building illuminated on the other side, and her face suddenly lit up with happiness. 'My friends are there,' she said suddenly and simply. 'Real, real friends.'

'Oh, my God!' The exclamation was out before she could close the door. 'What has happened?'

Akulov slumped down in the closest chair as though he had come a very long way, and could march no further. He looked up at her and she knew what he would look like as an old man.

'There is no God,' he said. 'Why do you call on him?'

'What has happened?' she repeated softly. She knelt down beside the chair. 'Tell me what has happened. Have you had an accident? Are you hurt?'

He looked at her with unfocused eyes. 'Hurt? It is not me . . .' His voice faltered and his lip started quivering, as if he were about to burst into tears. Then he gained control again, and began to speak.

'The call came through at the range in the morning. It was the OGPU district commander reporting heavy fighting outside Poltava, and demanded regular army reinforcements for his men.'

'Fighting?' she asked, puzzled. 'Who was attacking him?'

'White forces. We were the closest unit to Poltava and we had our BA-27 armoured cars.'

'White forces? Ivan, the civil war is over, the Whites are in exile.'

'We have been sent reports,' he said stubbornly. 'From the Kremlin itself, warning us of invasion.'

'It's just not so!' she expostulated. 'The Whites are all driving taxis in Paris. This is ridiculous.'

'We were sent the reports,' he repeated. 'The divisional commander put me in charge, since I knew the land. Poltava is where I was brought up as a child. As we left the training area I was able to navigate without a map, for these were my fields, streams, woods and roads. I was coming home. On the road coming out of the village we saw the first signs of battle, a wagon, and, around it, the bodies of several OGPU men – their border troops. They had been hacked to death. That was strange, for a start. You don't expect those sort of wounds on a battlefield. The wagon was loaded high with sacks of grain, which puzzled me too, but we could hear firing from within the village itself, rifle fire, so we slid our high explosive shells into the breeches of our cannon, and cocked machine guns. The BA-27 is meant to provide support for the infantry. It carries forty rounds for the Hotchkiss gun, and over two thousand rounds of seven point six two for the Degtarov. As we moved up to link up with the OGPU commander I think we were all wondering how our training would stand up to the real test of battle. The 27's meant to be able to handle light tanks; I felt sure that the Whites wouldn't have attacked without armour, and we were on the look out.

'I got the OGPU commander on the radio – he had a whole battalion there and he himself was at the rear, which didn't surprise me. He wanted our armoured cars to provide artillery fire as his troops went in, and to accompany them into the village itself. I split the unit into two, taking command of one half myself, giving Golitsyn the other, to come at the Whites from the rear as we engaged their front. It was a dull day, overcast, and we could see the gunflashes in the house windows as the Whites opened up with their rifles on the advancing border troops. Each time we saw that, we put an artillery shell into the building, and soon the front of the village was wreathed in smoke as the wood houses burned. The OGPU troops took casualties early, but the White fire diminished as we shelled them, and we advanced to provide mobile artillery within the village itself. I was worried that the Whites would have sited their artillery within barns, camouflaged, and cut us up as we crawled up the roads – we were sitting targets.

'Because I knew the village so well I detailed Kruglov to lead a platoon round through the water-meadow and take the road into the main square from there, attacking them from the side. Then we went in. I pushed Merkulov on to the loop and took the main road myself. As he went by the Orlov's barn they got him, jumping down from the hay loft. They had bottles filled with petrol and wicks and they tossed them in through the vision ports and the car went up. The OGPU troops with him wiped them out with machine gun fire; they got Merkulov as well as he was getting out. The car crashed into the barn, and it began to burn.

'It's on a hillside, the village. As we came to the crossroads a cart loaded up with rocks came thundering down. It got my car, knocked it over on its side – that's where I got these cuts and bruises.'

In his Moscow chair Akulov looked at his marked hands, brushed the healing scar on his head. He looked at Yelena, still kneeling beside him.

'Do you know, as I crawled out, all I really felt was admiration! Those White boys were fighting so well!' His face clouded again. 'But I also couldn't understand why they hadn't made use of their artillery, or machine guns. All they had were rifles, and bottles of petrol. The cart had squashed one of the OGPU soldiers like a bug and I took his rifle. The rest of the crew had got out and I told them to retire to the rear and followed in the wake of the OGPU troops. I went up the lane that led to our house. Do you remember it, Yelena? It

was still lined with the fruit bushes my mother planted. My father
had got around to putting down stone paving against the mud, so
that the carts could move and pigs were grunting in the sties. I could
hear the cows in the barn – they were frightened of the noise of the
firing and they could smell the smoke.

'I was afraid that the Whites might have captured my family so I
slipped down the lane with the rifle, and had a round in the breech.
There's a little path that leads by the barn into the vegetable garden,
and I took that. By the shed where my father keeps his tools, someone
rushed at me.

'He was big and he roared in his fury. He had a pitchfork in his
hands but I slipped as I turned and the tines of the fork went over
my shoulder and I shot him with the rifle. The impact blew him
backwards and he hit the side of the shed and slid to the ground.

'Suddenly there was heavy firing as the OGPU came up from the
meadow and the crash of Kruglov's cannon as he provided artillery
support. The house began to burn. As it blazed the occupants rushed
out. They were armed. A few of the men had rifles, the women had
kitchen implements, the children knives. They ran at the troops,
yelling with hate and they were slaughtered, all of them, shot down
like cattle. They fell. The wounded crawled, and the troops came up,
and finished them off.

'I looked down then at the big man I had shot. It was my brother,
Boris. He was dying, he spat blood at me . . . I dropped the rifle, and
ran towards the house. They were all there, my sisters, my younger
brothers. My father and my mother . . . My cousin Nadia was still
alive. An OGPU soldier was about to kill her and I rushed him. We
went down fighting, one of the others knocked me on the head.

'When I came to I was still lying with the dead in the courtyard.
All about me the house was blazing. I staggered out of the heat.
Blood was all over my face and they had left me for dead. Down
in the water meadow the OGPU troops had the survivors rounded
up, herded together like cattle. Old people were there, the babushkas,
the grandfathers. Old Kutyepov had his little granddaughter Olga in
his arms, others of the little ones clung to their mothers' skirts.

'The OGPU commander was there. He'd come up now the fighting
was done. It was Rykov, Yelena. *Rykov* was in charge. One of the cars
was down there – Kruglov's. I could see him shouting at Rykov. Then
two of Rykov's men seized Kruglov, and Rykov took out his pistol
and shot him. They had machine guns set up and Rykov gave the
command, and they opened up. Rykov was firing too, shooting into
the people. When they were all dead they left them there, they didn't

even bury them. Then the OGPU troops went through the village, looting it of everything. They put all the grain into carts, they filled their pockets with money and goods, they drove off the cattle and pigs, they wrung the necks of the chickens, they drank vodka and they set fire to the whole place. It was still burning when night fell, I know, for I saw it.'

'What did you do?' she whispered, cold with horror.

'I hid in the overgrown ditch by the water meadow and waited for them to go. That night, I walked out. If Rykov had seen me he would have shot me too, and then I could not have told anyone.'

Akulov began to weep, and tears ran down his big face, falling on his bruised hands. 'My brother Boris,' he sobbed. 'I held him as he lay dying, and he spat his death-blood on me, and called me his enemy.'

She folded him in her arms, cradling his head to her like a child's.

'When I got back I told the commander. He kept me in a room while he made telephone calls and when he brought me back he was very pale, and frightened, and he ordered me to say nothing. We brought back our dead and buried them out in the range. The relatives have been told that they died in an accident and I have been sent on leave.'

In a while he sat up and wiped his face with his big, battered hands. 'What am I to do, Yelena? Who am I to tell?'

'*Nobody!*' she said fiercely. 'There are the little ones to think of. Terrible things are happening and we must keep them safe. But listen to me, my darling. If you can bring yourself to, can you think of any there – your family – who did not die?'

'Yes,' he said suddenly. 'Tatyana. My niece, whom you send books to. She wasn't there.'

Yelena gripped his hands in hers. 'Then we shall pray to God for her safety,' she said certainly. '*Spasitel mira*, Saviour of the world. We trust not in princes, they are but mortal. Earth-born they are and soon decay. Their counsels come to naught. We place our trust in thee, Christ our God and Lord. *Spasitel mira, spasi Tatyana*. Saviour of the world, save Tatyana.'

She looked up at Akulov. 'Won't you pray?'

He looked troubled. 'I cannot,' he said. 'For there is no God.'

'Do you still believe, Ivan?' she asked sadly. 'Do you think that it works, after all this? After Rykov has murdered your family?'

'Rykov is not the revolution,' he said stubbornly. 'The revolution did not do these things. No. I cannot believe that.'

*

The director of the Sadovsky Truck and Tractor Factory mounted the platform. Below him, spread out in the great yard were his workers. He could smell them. Behind him, on the wall of the main building hung a great length of cloth. He stood next to the factory party secretary, and together they pulled the cord. The covering slithered down from the wall, to reveal a huge, new and brightly painted sign.

Piotr Sadovsky smiled as broadly as he could, gestured up at it and began to applaud. Andrey Stukalov, his deputy manager and Boris Fedin, his trades union boss, former miner from the Donbas, standing with him on the podium instantly joined him, as did the masses below. They clapped until their palms began to burn.

This was the tricky bit, Piotr thought. There had been instances of people applauding until they collapsed from exhaustion, and the first to stop was the first to go. Still beaming, still gesturing at the sign with his beating hands he edged along the platform under the gaze of the party men. He went down the steps with his team, and they formed a short line by the entrance to the factory.

'Back to work, Comrades!' Piotr shouted. 'Overfulfil! Overfulfil! Storm the thousand truck barrier!'

The workers streamed past them, and the noise of the applause died away as they drifted to their machines. Stukalov and Fedin kept up their applause as Piotr led them inside and up the steps. They finally stopped as the door to his offices closed behind them. Flapping his stinging palms Piotr peered around his curtain. The party officials were walking off.

'The bastards didn't get any of us today,' he said, in satisfaction. As he sat behind his desk, the others slumped into chairs, loosening their ties. Public acts of worship were always dangerous affairs. There was always the chance of acolyte being turned into sacrifice. Piotr picked up the telephone and dialled.

'Konstantin? It's you? Piotr here, out at the factory. I just wanted to let you know that we have your wonderful slogan here on our wall. I'm just back from attending the trial. If those wrecking fools had only followed your advice they wouldn't now be waiting to be shot.'

He had the telephone away from his ear, the others could hear the weary voice of the writer coming down the line. 'It's not my slogan. It belongs to *veliki i liubimi*, great and beloved Comrade Stalin.'

'Of course, of course,' Piotr said hastily. 'You simply have put his thoughts to words. *Veliki i liubimi*. Thunderous applause followed when we saw his words on our wall. Any more coming?'

'I am working on a novel,' Konstantin said. 'It is very exciting. The Party has formulated the true theory of correct, communist, aesthetic method for a writer to use. As you can imagine, it is wonderful for a creative person to work within such boundaries. And they have sent me a party official to help me with the content of the book. Rykov is his name and he works for the OGPU. He is here now, in fact. We are pounding out our prose with sledgehammers, and ironing it into shape with tractors.'

'Then I must not keep you. But from all our workers here, from all of us overfulfilling our norms, we thank you.'

Piotr put the telephone down. The office was on the corner of the building and from it he could see the vast new slogan. Immense, muscular men and women pounded out the future on a red-hot anvil: THERE ARE NO FORTRESSES A BOLSHEVIK CANNOT STORM.

'Poor bastard. Writing *agitka* with the help of the OGPU,' he said absently. 'I remember him when he was a revolutionary, a Futurist. He spoke to us of the need for no rules at all. Well, this is all our futures.'

'How was the trial?' said Stukalov, round-faced and bald. The three had aged since they had waged battle on the railway lines of Russia, but they were still members of the same platoon, only fighting in a new war.

Piotr took a bottle from his desk and three tumblers, pouring a large shot into each.

'Nasty,' he said shortly. 'They couldn't even produce Zayaitsky – remember him, he ran the machine works – his counsel said he'd gone mad. Leskov's twelve-year-old son denounced him. He didn't appear either, after the second day. He hanged himself. *They* said it was out of guilt. Pagirev tried to withdraw his confession and they took him out for a bit and brought him back a couple of hours later, white as a ghost and with a warder holding him up because he couldn't stand. I can't imagine what they did to him. Anyway, they all confessed to bourgeois sabotage and wrecking.

That bastard Ulrikh was the judge. Eight have been shot and the other five are on their way to the logging camps. There were about thirty of us there, directors. I think we all got the message. They were very nice to us, of course. Prosecutor Vyshinsky had us in for tea while they were doing whatever they were doing to Pagirev. He was pleasant as could be. He shouts at the accused in court, you know. Calls them 'stinking piles of human ordure' and 'decaying carrion'. There's never any evidence, just all this abuse. Yet he spoke like . . . a gentleman with us. He comes from a good family, they say. They handed us the new norms of the battle campaign as we left. I have our breakthrough targets for the transport and tractor front here.'

He gave a sheet of paper to Stukalov, who looked at it, then handed it to Fedin. Then all three drank.

'It's what we expected,' Fedin grunted.

'We made the last quota of the Five Year Plan by our fingernails,' Piotr said grimly. 'And we had to cook the books. Thank God and Lenin for 'strict accounting and control'. Statistics we *can* produce. There's no margin left this time. So you'd better tell me. How did it go? What do we have to work with?'

'We got to the signalbox and overpowered the signalman on duty at one in the morning as planned,' said Fedin. 'The freight train was late, but we stopped it successfully, running it into a siding. Two of the lads were on the line with warning lanterns and the driver, fireman and guard came down to see what the problem was and we overpowered them too. The road runs alongside the line, there, and our loading was as swift as could be expected. We had blocks on each end with lads in NKVD uniforms. It took us two hours to load up the trucks. What did we get? Two tons of sugar.'

'*Wonderful!*' Piotr exclaimed.

'It's distilling into vodka now,' said Stukalov.

'Bolts of cloth and canvas. Two freight cars full.'

'Good. I spoke to Prishvin, at the aircraft factory. He can't cover his aeroplanes. He's got a whole load of carburettors and magnetos he can't use. We can make a deal and we can fit them on the trucks, somehow.'

'The cloth's quite light. Shirt fabric. It might not last long on an aeroplane.'

'We all have our problems. Ours and his are to get tractors, trucks and aircraft out of the factory gates. If they break in the customers' hands, that's theirs. But keep some of the fabric – we can use it to make shirts for the workers. Do the poor bastards know they'll be doing an extra shift a day? Yes? Shock-troops for socialism! We'll try and make it as good as we can. Keep some of the vodka, too.'

He rubbed a palm over his face, up and down. 'You know, when the norms came in we used to begin the month easily, rest up a bit, ten days of *spyachka*, before getting down to it, getting hot, *goryachka*, and a final wild burst of *likhoradka* to get the quotas filled, and we'd be back to lying about and drinking vodka for ten days before doing it all over again. But this, this is *likhoradka* all the time. I think we'll all go mad. Get anything else?'

'Ball bearings,' Stukalov said in satisfaction. 'I'm placing them carefully because everyone wants them. But I've got a firm promise of tyres, and a building group has bid some glass and corrugated sheeting. Where they are going to place the ball-bearings I don't know, but they've got lots of glass and sheet.'

Stukalov was the *tolkachi*, the fixer, the man who knew who to call, the one who dealt in *kombinatsia*. Without him, the factory stopped.

'The designer came up with a modification to the trucks,' said Fedin. 'We can save nearly ten per cent on the chassis structure, and still put in for the old amount. It makes it weaker, but they aren't lasting long out there anyway. Let's face it, we're making *brak*. We can blame the state of the roads.'

'Good. What about the whore-house?'

'Almost done,' said Fedin, nodding in approval. 'Real quality. Thick carpets, fine sofas and chairs – and beds, of course. I put our best carpenters and seamstress on to it.'

'Put it in the books as a medical clinic.'

'I've done a deal with an American at their delegation – he works in their commissary. If we supply him with girls he'll give us whisky and gin, and things to eat – cookies and candy. I'm trying to make a deal with him for films, too.'

'I thought the NKVD were servicing all the foreigners?'

'He's got no secrets to give away! The Americans are naive, they don't see us as enemies.'

'Films would be very good. I have Remenik at the ministry of food and he's willing to slide meat and grain our way if we give him a really good time. Try your American with two girls at once in exchange for some Fred Astaire and Ginger Rogers. What about girls? Any good ones in the new lot of workers?'

'Olga's training them up.'

'They have to be good – some of these men who are coming can deliver. They know they'll get better rations, living conditions? We reward our shock-workers of the proletariat.'

'They seem happy.'

'They'll earn it,' Piotr said gloomily. 'I wouldn't care to *yob* with a pig like Remenik. Shock troopers indeed . . . But it's gone well. Have we rewarded our man on the railroad? Yes? We'll need him again.'

'Someone came round to see me a couple of nights ago,' said Fedov. 'He was waiting for me when I got back. Ropshin, Boris Ropshin.'

Sadanov smiled. 'The centre-forward with Dinamo? I'd like to see him play again.'

'You can see him any time you want,' Fedov said quietly. 'I gave him a job here.'

'Here? Why?'

'He can't play football any more. His knees have given out. He got the news last week, went home and found someone else moving into his apartment. I've got him a room here.'

'What's he doing?'

'Watchman.'

'Can't we get him anything better?'

'He can't read or write. They put him in the sports school and they don't teach them anything else there.'

'He played for the national team.' Piotr was shocked. 'I *saw* him.'

Sadanov's secretary put her head around the door. 'The teachers are here.'

'Good. I'll come out and see them.'

Five pink and aggrieved young women stood outside. One slightly older than the others stepped forward. 'Director Sadanov? Can you explain what we are doing here, please?'

'Certainly, lady comrades,' Piotr said pleasantly. 'You have, I am afraid to say, been kidnapped.'

'Kidnapped? Who by? And why?'

'By me. Oh, it's all in order, I assure you. I know the man at the ministry and he changed your documents for me. He . . . has dinner with me sometimes.'

'We are schoolteachers! What do you want with us?'

'I want you to teach but I'll make things as pleasant as I can, in terms of living conditions. You'll have to stay – you know about the new internal passport, don't you?'

He gestured down from the gantry at the great shop floor where the tractors and trucks were being put together.

'They can't leave without permission, which they can't get.

You can't leave either. Just think of it as a form of *kommandirovka*. Now, do you see that man over there?'

He pointed to a bespectacled man of about thirty standing at a blackboard in the centre of a group of seated workers in a relatively quiet corner of the shop.

'That's my chief designer, Mikhail Kaledin. He's a *very* talented engineer, and he has a very talented team working with him. He's supposed to be working on a tank that we have agreed to build for the Main Military Council. Very advanced, it will be. Modified Christie suspension, sloped armour. But he spends a lot of his time teaching the workers, as do his team.'

'But why?'

'I am sent as many workers as I need,' Piotr said levelly. 'But they are men and women straight off the land. Peasants. The best of them have perhaps three years of primary school training. If I find one with more than that I make him a foreman. Down there we have precision tools from America. They make gears, sprockets, bearings. The peasants do their best. They use their fingers to measure whether what they are making is the right size, because they cannot calculate, cannot read the instructions. I want you to take over from my designer, and teach them, which is your job, thus letting him get on with his.'

'*Our* job is teaching primary school children,' the teacher said acidly. 'And I can't think what will happen to the young people if we are taken away from them in order to help you.'

'As to the young people, I cannot say. But I know what will happen to me if I do not get all those vehicles down there finished and out of the door on time. Perhaps you would go down and introduce yourselves, and I will join you in a few minutes.'

He went back to his office and opened the drawer of his desk again. He poured another shot into his glass. At the trial there had been a young NKVD officer sitting in the front row, near the dock. He had been smartly dressed, with a pair of soft leather gloves he held in his lap. Whenever one of the men in the dock had faltered he would recross his legs, in their shiny jackboots, and put the gloves back on his thigh, arranging them with a slap. Then the prisoner would start again, with a jerk, eyes staring in his pallid face, looking anywhere but the man.

From the window he could see the little house where he lived, its neat garden tidy and colourful about it. Occasionally he would see his wife Anna there because she liked, within the garden walls, to tend the plants. He liked to watch, in the afternoon, his daughter Gaia walking home from school to join her.

Evidence was unnecessary. Vyshinsky had told them so, in his cultured voice, as he sipped the tea and nibbled the sweet biscuit that stuck in their throats like dry wood shavings. The law was the expression of the will of the ruling class, backed by force. Since the ruling class of a socialist state expressed the will of the revolutionary working class, it was the dictates of the revolutionary conscience that were of vital importance. Evidence was both superfluous and *bourgeois*.

He drained the vodka in a single gulp.

4 November 1932

The voluptuous elegance of the old Baroque room was swathed in red sacking, its voice of style gagged by gold and scarlet Party banners proclaiming the permanent victory of the proletariat. Where once there had been Christmas, now there was the Anniversary of the Revolution, and the Industrial Academy was suitably dressed for the part, a dowager uneasy in her strange finery.

The door of the classroom where Tsarist society had sipped tea opened, and the small, squat figure of Nikita Sergeyevich Khrushchev came in, carrying his black leather case. The room was warm, heat flooding from the huge and exotically-cast iron radiators, and he took off the jacket of his baggy grey suit, hanging it on the back of his chair.

He opened the case, and took out a blue-backed notebook then selected a pen from a small squad lined up in his breast pocket, and waited.

The door opened again, and the lecturer appeared, a small man with a neatly-trimmed black beard. He carried a sheaf of notes, and threaded his way through the desks to the podium, where a table and a blackboard had been set up. He spent an excessively long time arranging and rearranging his notes on the table. He cleaned the blackboard with a duster. He selected and put down chalk, then glanced at his watch.

'Let us begin,' he said, with his back to the room, and began to write on the blackboard.

There was a crash as the tall classroom doors slammed back against the wall.

'*Nikita Sergeyevich!*'

Khrushchev stared at the blackboard.

The room echoed to her furious footsteps and the lecturer scrawled illegibly on the board.

'*Look at me!*' Nadezhda screamed. She seized Khrushchev's face in her hands. 'Look at me, you bastard!'

He was sweating, his skin was slippery.

'Where are they? Where are my friends?'

'I don't know,' he whispered.

'The NKVD came for them. Each and every one. They have taken them. Where are they?'

'I don't know.'

'It was you!' She shrieked. 'You told him, didn't you?'

'He asked me. He asked who your friends were. He said it was to be a surprise . . .'

Tears were streaming down her cheeks and her nails bit into the skin of his face.

'You told him! You got every one, you didn't miss any out.'

Khrushchev gripped the hand on his chin and for a moment he shed his peasant's innocence.

'*Listen*. When the *vlast* asks you a question you reply. *Immediately*. Because you have nothing to hide. You don't ask why he wants to know. And you don't hesitate.'

They stared at each other.

'I was afraid,' he said, and the flat words hung in the air. Suddenly she let him go, and they heard the sound of her feet stumbling away, and of her weeping.

Nikita Sergeyevich Khrushchev sat alone at his desk on the floor of the room, with no one about him . . .

8 November

She heard the door of the Kremlin apartment open and a few moments later light streamed in as he came into her bedroom.

'We are celebrating the Revolution,' he said coldly.

Nadezhda stared at the ceiling and did not look at her husband. 'I am unwell,' she said. 'Celebrate without me.'

Stalin stood at the side of the bed. He wore a white tunic with matching trousers, which were stuffed into soft leather boots. The Order of Lenin was on his chest.

'Those who are friends of the Revolution celebrate,' he said, an edge of menace in his voice. 'When people stay away, others ask why.'

'I am the Revolution's friend,' she said. 'But are you? And I am still unwell.'

'Are you missing your little friends?' he asked mockingly. 'Are you worried for them?'

'*They* are true Revolutionaries,' she said bitterly. '*They* told me what you had done, what you made them do. Making them accomplices to your murder.'

'They told you lies! *They* were traitors to the Revolution. But don't worry. They'll be back in your precious Academy in a few

... weeks. They'll tell you a different story then, I promise you. Ask any of them, then. They won't repeat these lies about starving people. Now – '

His hand snaked out and gripped her by the wrist and he began to bend her thumb backwards. 'You can celebrate the Anniversary of the Revolution, or spend it having your bones set. Which is it to be, Nadezhda?'

They were all there, in the room the Empress Catherine had built, The cream of society. All eyes flickered towards the door as the boss pushed his wife inside.

The men were in uniforms and suits, the women in fusty dresses. A long bar decorated with red bunting was along one wall with waiters working the guests while next door the fine cutlery and plate of the Tsar was set out for the banquet.

Nadezhda saw Polina, wife of the small, thin-necked Molotov, standing by a pillar, and went over to her. She was the closest thing she had to a friend among the people there. A waiter in white jacket and gold braid came up to her with champagne and she shook her head. He came back with a flute of orange juice.

There was a banging on a table. Stalin was thumping it with a vodka bottle, and there was an instantaneous quiet.

'Now we're all here – ' he glanced sarcastically, almost savagely, at his wife '– we can toast the Revolution.'

The waiters scurried to charge glasses under the urging of Voroshilov, the host, tall in his military uniform. Voroshilov, the Red Army's First Officer.

All eyes were on Stalin as he held up a cut glass beaker of vodka. 'The Revolution!' he shouted.

'*The Revolution*!' they roared. There were a few seconds up gulping and gasping and then the buzz of conversation started up again until Stalin's bellow cut through it all, halting words in people's mouths.

'*Hey you!*'

Nadezhda flinched and looked up.

'Yes, you, you bitch!' He was striding over the inlaid floor to her, his boots clattering in the silence.

'Why don't you drink to the Revolution?' he demanded.

'But I did drink!' she protested.

'In orange juice?' he snarled. 'The Revolution was forged in fire, and tempered in men's blood. You don't drink to that in orange juice!'

With a sudden smack of his hand he sent the glass spinning from her hand to smash on the floor. Sticky juice splashed over her dress and he seized a tumbler from the bar, and upended a bottle of vodka over it, the liquor spilling over the tablecloth.

He held out the brimming glass.

'Drink to the Revolution,' he said, his voice very low and quiet. He was pale, almost as white as his tunic. Faint beads of sweat had formed at his hair line.

'Josef, I cannot drink that . . .' she pleaded.

He slammed her back against the pillar and forced the glass into her mouth, tipping the raw liquor inside. His hand was at her throat and she gagged and retched as he forced her to swallow. All about her, men and women stood as deadly still and silent as dummies.

He dropped the glass at her feet and it shattered in pieces over them. 'See?' he said. 'You *can* drink.'

He turned away. 'Kliment Yefremovich!' he shouted, with sudden bonhomie. 'What have you prepared for us, this evening?'

And Voroshilov, who had never been afraid in battle, suddenly bounded forward like a tame dog, beaming obsequiously and bending to make his height less, details of the menu falling from his lips.

By the pillar, Nadezhda retched, filthy oily fumes rising from her stomach. She stank of vodka – it was all over her.

'Do you want to change?' Polina murmured. 'I'll come with you.'

'No,' she muttered. From somewhere, she was possessed by a terrible rage. 'No, I don't.'

She looked around her. 'Some people are missing,' she said clearly and Polina looked at her in alarm.

'*Nadezhda,*' she protested.

'You leave me alone!' she told her friend, goaded beyond endurance.

From across the room, Stalin had seen her.

'Did you say something?' he yelled.

'*Yes!* I said, *some people are missing!*' she shouted. The vodka and rage roared in her veins. 'This is the anniversary of the Revolution, and some people are missing.'

There was again, dead silence in the room, only broken by the shuffling of feet as people distanced themselves from her.

'Where is the priest?' She demanded. 'We shall need him. Where are the pall bearers, to carry it out? Where the grave-diggers, to prepare its resting place?'

She whirled about, her eyes staring at them all. '*The Revolution is dead!*' she shrieked and she stabbed a finger of accusation at Stalin. '*There* is the man who murdered it.'

Yagoda was near to her, the pharmacist's assistant in his OGPU finery. He shifted away from her as one would from a leper, but her hand lashed out and gripped him by the lapel.

'Want to know how I found out?' she demanded. Across the room, Stalin slid from sight behind the bulk of Voroshilov.

'My friends told me. They were sent to the Ukraine as loyal Party members. They were sent to beat and shoot and steal from the peasants. To starve little children to death, to whip their parents on to cattle trucks. To plunder their homes. They didn't like it. They were true Party members and they didn't know why they should do this to their fellow citizens. And when they came back, they told me, because they knew I was married to *him*.'

Again, she flailed out an accusing arm. Stalin slipped out and behind a pillar.

Nadezhda let out a terrible laugh. 'They told me because *they thought he didn't know.*'

Yagoda was struggling to free himself from her grip, but the cloth was wound up in her fist. She looked up at him.

'But I don't have to tell *you* that, do I? My friends are with you, aren't they? Dancing some agonising dance while they learn a new song to sing. You know, don't you, Yagoda?'

She released him suddenly, and he staggered backwards.

'I tell you what we have got though. No priest, no gravediggers, no pallbearers. But we've got enough people for a trial.'

They all, silent and stiff as they were, cringed, wanting not to look at her, and Stalin stepped delicately behind the burly form of Vyshinsky, the state prosecutor, moving ever closer to her.

'Let's have the trial here.' She turned slowly in the circle of empty space that was all hers. 'What have we got? Is anyone missing?' She pointed to the hulking, shaven-headed Ulrikh. 'We have a judge. You always bring in the right verdict, don't you, Vasily? Guilty every time.'

Stalin bent down behind Molotov who was pleasantly smaller than he, and slipped across to the army commander, Tukhachevsky.

'Oh yes. We have a prosecutor. Andrei never loses a case. We have the policeman to bring him to court. And we have witnesses.'

She swayed slightly as she turned from one to the next. 'Shall we bring in the dead? No, too many to count. Let's have the witnesses. What about you, Genrikh?'

Yagoda cringed in horror.

'Your OGPU officers were there, and so were you. What about you, Kliment? Didn't your troops guard the frontier to keep them starving inside?'

Voroshilov looked nervously at Stalin hiding behind Tukhachevsky.

'And what about you, Vyacheslav? You were in charge of taking the grain away, *you* saw what happened.'

Polina Molotov went very pale, standing by her pillar.

'What about you, Nikolai?' she called to the diminutive, bearded Bukharin. 'You must have gone along with it. So, what will you do now? How will you protest, when he comes for you?'

She turned round and round, staring at all of them.

'What will you say, when he comes for *you*?'

Stalin was behind the dwarf, Yezhof, crouching down as he pushed him forward. Yezhof was smiling faintly. As she turned, Stalin struck her in the face with his closed fist, and she fell heavily on to the gleaming jasper floor. Polina Molotov pushed bravely through them, and began to help her to her feet.

'She's drunk,' she said calmly, to no one in particular.

'That's right,' Stalin said amiably. 'She can't hold her liquor.'

No one stopped Polina as she helped Nadezhda from the room. But Stalin stood by a window, looking out. He saw the couple emerge into the open air of the lit courtyard. Near the rubble of the Monastery of the Miracles, making way for the Military School, Nadezhda bent, vomiting over six-hundred-year-old stone, and Polina supported her. They rested for a while.

'Are you sure you'll be all right?'

Polina had put on the lights in the sitting room of Nadezdha's apartment.

'Are you sure you don't want me to stay?'

Nadezhda shook her head, bedraggled, ill and drained. 'I'm going to have a bath and go to bed. I'll be all right. I'll pack my things and leave in the morning.'

'Where will you go?' her friend asked anxiously.

'A long way from him,' she said simply.

Polina went to the door. 'Lock it behind me,' she said.

'I will. Thank you, Polina.'

The key turned in the door and Nadezhda stood listening to her friend's footsteps going away down the Kremlin corridor.

'How far is a long way from me?'

She turned slowly, too tired and bruised to move quickly. 'Can you not leave me alone?' she asked.

Stalin came forward from the darkness of the bedroom into the light. 'You said terrible things about me,' he said softly. 'Why did you tell such lies, Nadezhda?'

'They are *true*,' she said desperately. 'Everything I said was true.'

'You take the word of these friends of yours against that of me, your husband? Oh Nadezhda, I'll have Genrikh bring them over and they'll apologise for lying to you, I promise.'

'Yagoda is your torturer! Of *course* they'll say anything you want!'

'You're not being reasonable,' he said softly. 'If they say they lied to you, then they lied to you. What more do you want?'

'For you to admit the truth!' she said bitterly. 'If you can't admit to anyone out there what you've done, you can admit it to me. Because I *know* you. How many millions are dead?'

Stalin shrugged. 'Who counts the enemy? It is that they fall that matters.'

'*They aren't the enemy!*' she screamed. 'This is not a war. These are human beings you have murdered.'

He stared at her in the lights from under hooded eyes. 'I am their enemy,' he said. 'Which makes them mine. Did they not seek to starve the people? They sought to strangle the revolution with the bony hand of famine. Because they thought they could overthrow me that way. That's what they thought.'

'You stole from them,' she said wearily. 'First you would not pay them for their grain, so they planted less. Then you came with guns to take what little they had left, and they fought to protect their families. So you declared war on them.'

'You don't understand . . .' he whispered. 'Everywhere there are enemies. They seek to overthrow what we have built and without me, how will you recognise them?'

They were standing very close and she leaned forward in a last effort.

'They are *your* enemies, Josef – Nobody else's. And what they seek to overthrow is both morgue and torture-chamber. I gladly join with them in trying to pull down that.'

His fist came out of nowhere, cracking into her mouth. She staggered backwards, blood bubbling through her teeth.

'*No!*' she shrieked.

She whirled, running across the room to her writing desk.

'No!' she howled. 'I won't let you any more!'

Her hand fumbled at the drawer but he was on her as she pulled out the small black pistol. He struck her and it flew across the room. As she picked herself up, it was in his fist.

'You are one of them,' he said certainly. 'One of the enemy . . .'

*

They all came to see her, before they took her away. The dwarf, Yezhof, stood up on his toes to peer in. Bukharin was a little taller, he could see her from where he stood, and he kept his thoughts off his face. Khrushchev came and he had his carefully arranged. Stalin allowed him to wrap an arm over his shoulder and bury his face in his lapel for a moment.

'How could she have betrayed you?' Khrushchev asked, his naivety writ large on his innocent peasant face, and Stalin gave him a clap on the shoulder as he stood by the door.

Polina Molotova came, very pale when she entered and white when she left, with Stalin's eyes upon her the whole way around. Vyshinsky came with Ulrikh, from a courtroom they had adjourned.

'The balance of her mind was disturbed,' said Vyshinsky, not loudly, but clear enough to be heard, and Ulrikh nodded his shining skull in agreement.

'Suicide,' he said.

Then they went back, and had the accused up from the cells to be found guilty.

Her killer came last of all, and stood by the open coffin. The undertaker had done his work well and the appalling wound in her head had been made invisible.

He suddenly pushed his hand out at her, as if to ward her off.

'She left me as an enemy!'

As he left, they brought out the lid and screwed it down, then they took her to the Novodevichye cemetery, all alone.

16

Lishentsi

B EFORE the revolution the garden of the house had been a
thing of wonder and beauty in every season. During the twenties
the commissariat of education had put up a series of huts on it where
they stored documents. But the former owners of the garden, the
plants, were slowly demolishing the intruders with powerful green
fingers.

The terrace where the aristocratic owners had promenaded with
their guests before descending into the scented delights below still
remained. With positively pre-revolutionary communist egalitarian-
ism the occupants of the building had divided it up between them.
En masse they had removed the paving stones and rubble, which
they sold *na levo* to a Nepman builder. The money bought fertiliser
and seeds. Topsoil they hauled up from the shattered garden below,
a bucket at a time.

Now, on warm days, an old lady climbed up out of the basement
carrying an embroidered cushion, and sat on the broad step in the
sun amid the scent of the flowers, and the green of the leaves, and
dreamed of the days long past, when she had been a princess.

Yelena had a site she considered to be among the best. Although
set at the corner of two walls, and thus with a tendency to dry
out, requiring her to carry down buckets of bathwater on hot
days, it had the advantage of those two walls, against which she
could grow plants.

Upon one she grew a rose. It bore single pink, apple scented
flowers, from which, once they had opened, she picked the petals.
With them she made rosewater, and used it to wash her family's
hair, soaking a cloth in the fluid, and cleaning them until their heads
shone. Shampoo was a thing of the past.

Just before the flowers opened she gathered leaves from the plant,
drying them and keeping them in a jar, from which she made tea in
the winter. The children had a mug of it before going to school. The
sharply-prickled, arching stems bore bright red hips in the autumn,

and from these she made jam, which she used to sweeten the tea, and wine, which she gave to the children when they were ill, to help them sleep.

On the other wall she grew tomatoes, training them carefully in a dense carpet of leaves and fruit. When they were ripe they ate them. In the autumn she gathered the green ones, and made chutney, using it sparingly to flavour food in the winter, and give it the nutrients it otherwise lacked.

In her oblong of lovingly-tended earth she grew herbs. Russian tarragon was there, its flavour improving by the year, and she made a tea from its leaves, and they all had a mug in the evening. Scurvy was rife in the winter. She grew comfrey, too. They ate the leaves, and Yelena used them to make poultices to relieve sores, cuts and burns. She had garlic, and flavoured things that were otherwise unpleasant with it. She had rosemary, and used the narrow leaves to keep the moths away from their clothes. She grew catnip, and gave it to the children when they had a fever. From ladies' mantle and feverfew she made a tea and drank it as soon as the lights in her eyes began to flash, giving warning of the horrors of the jerking battlements marching across her vision, and the gathering storm in her head.

It was pleasant, too, to steal an hour working among the living plants, carefully weeding, looking out for aphids and blackflies, which she ruthlessly removed, applying little doses of fertiliser, pausing to watch a visiting butterfly.

She had straightened herself after applying a mulch of old tea leaves to the base of her rose when she saw two children coming down the thin lane, a boy of perhaps thirteen with black, curly hair supporting a girl of about his own height. They were familiar and it was the fact that they were together that delayed her recognition of them for a moment, and then she was running down the steps and opening the little door in the wall.

'*Tatya*! Tatyana darling, you're alive!'

She turned to Nikolai, as she picked the girl up in her arms. She was dressed in very dirty padded clothes that were too big for her.

'Where have you come from, Nikolai? Where did you find her?'

'The Ukraine. She was close to the border.'

Tatya was as light as a five year old and Yelena could feel her bones as she carried her up the steps. Her face was thin, the nose like a beak, the skin stretched over the skull. She smiled a little but she seemed too weak to talk.

'Here, Nikky darling, open the gate of the lift for me. That's it.'

They went up, and into the apartment. She lay Tatyana down

on the sofa she had made from a bed, and propped her up on cushions.

She had milk, and a loaf and she stood tearing the bread into little pieces as she warmed the milk on the stove. There was a lump of honey Ivan had brought from a tree near the range and she put two spoonfuls in, and stirred the milk golden. She sat on the edge of the bed, and began to feed the girl.

'Nikky, make us a cup of tea. You look as though you need one, too.'

Tatyana fell asleep as Yelena was scraping up the last of the sweet mess. She stood up, looking down at her. There was faint pink tinge to her yellow skin.

'She looks better,' said Nikolai hopefully. 'I was afraid she would die on the way.'

'She won't die. Not now. I'll look after her. But however did you find her? What were you doing in the Ukraine? I thought you were at school. Don't you spend the holidays in Berlin, and come here for your schooling?'

'They took us on a special trip to the Ukraine. We're all the sons and daughters of party officials and it's a special school. We're all Pioneers, and the older ones are Komsomols. Before we went we saw films, about evil people called kulaks. They steal wheat from the people, and bury it. A woman came to talk to us, Commissar Zemliachka.'

Yelena felt the shock of it drain through her body. 'Who, Nikky darling?' she whispered.

'Zemliachka. She was all dressed in black leather, from the civil war.'

'Yes,' Yelena whispered. 'She was . . .'

'Komsomols found the wheat in pits and the kulaks were hiding in the woods, and came out and killed the komsomols. We learned a song to sing: "We take the thieves to jail, to intimidate the foe. We guard the village soil, to let the harvest grow."

'She told us stories of children who had found their parents stealing grain, and had handed them over to the authorities. She said they were good, these children. I just thought they must be hungry, the people. I wouldn't denounce mama if she was hungry.' He shivered suddenly. 'Natasha liked it all, though.'

Yelena got up, and went into the kitchen. She fetched a jar.

'Would you like some sunflower seeds, Nikky?'

He took some and chewed on them, putting the husks in his hand.

'We were given clubs and rods to beat the kulaks with, and find the grain they had stolen. There were a lot of dead people in the first village, and they told us that they had died because the kulaks had stolen their food. They were lying in their huts. Some were still living, but blue, with big blisters all over them. We found a man gnawing on something and he could still move. They told us he was a shirker and Natasha and the others beat him with their rods, and chased him out down the street to work in the fields. A little way along he fell over and died.'

A sparrow landed on the windowsill and looked in at them. Nikolai got up and put a small row of seeds out. It flew back, and pecked one up.

'Mama says you're her best friend. She talks about you a lot . . . she says you are kind . . . When papa's away and – and she drinks she talks a lot about when she was at school, when the Tsar was on the throne. Natasha doesn't like that and she goes out, and mama talks and cries and drinks and, in the end, I help her to lie down. She gets up late the next day and then she's different; she talks a lot about Marx and the bourgeoisie, and the march of the proletariat. Natasha likes that but I don't, and I go out to play with my friends, because mama doesn't drink when she's like that, and she won't need me. But she's different on the other days, before she starts crying, and she talks about you. Of course, there are lots of days she doesn't drink at all, or only a little. Those are good days and we play hide and seek, and make things . . . we go fishing . . . sometimes go to the park, and fly the kite . . .

'They moved us to a big village where there were people still alive, although very weak. The other Pioneers were very happy, because they could march the peasants to the fields, and stand guard over them while they worked. We lived in special quarters, a barracks, like soldiers, and had plenty of food to eat. There were children without parents who watched us, with arms like sticks, and big heads. They begged for food. I asked the brigadier, Storozhev, if we could give them some, since we had enough. He told me they were the children of kulaks who had been taken away. I said they were only children, and he rebuked me, saying that they were members of a class we were waging war against. I asked if they were Jews and he said some might be, but that was not the point?' He looked at Yelena out of pain-filled eyes. 'In Germany it is Jews they talk about like this, I thought they might be the same . . .

'The brigadier, Storozhev, thought that there were workshirkers hiding in the woods, and organised us into search parties and we found some dead people. Then by a stream, we smelled smoke, and came upon a girl, very thin, who was smoking a cigarette she had made. There were some fish bones nearby because she had managed to catch a fish. My sister Natasha wished to arrest her for theft of communal property, this fish she had caught. But she could still talk and she said she was not a kulak, that she had papers. She said she was a messenger from the commissariat of agriculture in Kiev.

'I told the others that I would march her to the brigadier who would decide if she was telling the truth. I suggested that there might be others hiding in the woods and they were excited by this, and went off on their hunt so I set off back to the village with her. She told me that her name was Tatyana. I had a plan, I did not want to hunt for kulaks any more, and I told her I would help her get to Moscow.

'So I took her to Storozhev and introduced her as an important party member from Kiev who had been robbed by kulaks on her way to Moscow. Tatyana showed him the documents. This was clever, for he reads and writes with difficulty. I then told him that I would accompany her to Moscow as I had to meet my father, Sergei Savinkov, who was, as he knew, head of the Workers' Aid Trust, and an Old Bolshevik. Storozhev is very respectful when you talk about the aristocracy, and he had the clerk draw up the travel papers right there, and put on the stamps and signed them himself with a lot of here you are, Comrade, and anything else you need Comrade, and a cart took us to the station. I did not say goodbye to my sister. When we were on the train I asked Tatyana where she would stay in Moscow and she said with her aunt, the most beautiful woman in the world. She told me the address, and it was then I knew it was you and I was very happy for her.

'The train was stopped at the border with Russia, at Mikhaylivka, and the OGPU came on. They were very thorough; they found people hiding all over the train who had no papers and took them away. When we came into the station there was another train waiting that had come from Russia, and they were taking men off it, who were carrying sacks of bread that they had bought. The bread they piled up under guard and the Ukrainians who had bought it they took away. Then the train pulled out and took us to Moscow.'

Nikolai put down the jar of sunflower seeds.

'Mama's coming. Daddy's sending foreigners. I'm not going back. I don't want to go to Berlin, either. I've got English friends and I want to go to school in England. I'm going to tell mummy.'

'If your mummy's coming, I'll tell her.'

On the sofa, Tatyana stirred. Yelena got up and sat next to

her, holding her hand. She opened her eyes, sunk back in their sockets.

'They're all dead,' she whispered. 'all dead . . .'

The old ballroom buzzed with the chatter of imbibing and nibbling guests as it had been designed to. They circulated in their best, keeping a sharp eye out for those of better status than themselves.

A glass of sticky white wine clasped in one hand, Yelena beamed commandingly at the elderly man carrying a tray of canapés and he altered course as if directed by remote wiring.

'So nice to see a party here again,' she murmured, and his eyes looked up at her reproachfully. They were in the old Nobles Club, now the October Hall of the Trades Union House, and occasional courtroom.

She held his eyes with hers as she reached out for his polished oval tray. Delicately taking a tiny sandwich between forefinger and thumb she used her remaining fingers to scoop up a selection of the delights. As the old retainer went on his way, she casually dropped all the food inside the large handbag she was carrying. She had planned a feast for the children, that night.

The foreign guests were up at the other end of the room, with the *nachalstvo*. She could hear the braying. A long bar of white-clothed tables stood by one wall, laden with bottles. There was champagne, wines and juice. She could see some screw-topped bottles of concentrated, imported orange juice. Some of the foreign guests did not drink alcohol. She edged over. When she was close she speared the bartender with her smile.

'Oh, can you help me? I'm looking for Maxy. You know, Maxim. Comrade Litvinov, the Foreign Commissar.'

The presence of a beautiful woman capable of referring to the powerful commissar as Maxy galvanised the man. He craned his neck frantically, standing on tip-toe to be able to point him out. As Yelena leaned over the table to look, her hand snaked out and whipped one of the bottles from the table, dropping it into the capacious bag.

'There, Madame – '

'Darling!' shrieked a voice. 'How *wonderful!*'

She turned to see Ruth hurtling towards her, elegantly dressed in a black French silk dress with patent shoes and sheer American stockings. Gold gleamed at her throat and she had a silk shawl about her shoulders.

They embraced, then Ruth stood back, holding on to Yelena's arms to look at her.

'I'm so glad you could come! Sergei *will* be pleased. And you look well. So *slim*, my dear.'

'It isn't from choice,' Yelena murmured, keeping her voice even.

'No, of course not, you were always just naturally slender,' Ruth agreed pleasantly. She looked at her schoolfriend quizzically. 'Why were you stealing orange juice, Yelena?'

'It has vitamins in it,' Yelena said levelly. 'It is good for the children.'

'Oh, of *course*. I insist that Nikolai and Natasha take tablets. Cod liver oil is very good. At least I did. My dear, I have hit the age of rebellion. You know that the children have been taking their schooling here? Now Natasha says she won't come to Berlin for the holidays! She says she won't live *anywhere* that isn't communist. I've told her that the Depression signals the fall of the old capitalist order, that practically the next *moment* the whole world will be communist, but no, she won't listen. She's such a keen one, always out with the *komsomol*, the Red Pioneers and the young party organisations.'

'Yes, I heard . . .' Yelena said, trying to sound vague.

She saw Savinkov through the throng, attending to his foreigners. 'Having a father like Sergei will be important to her, of course. I see he's done so well.'

'Oh, he has new ideas all the *time*. I just can't keep up!'

'Ruth darling, while we're on our own,' Yelena said quickly. 'You couldn't ask Sergei to do me a favour, could you?'

'Of course. What is it?'

'We're still living in the apartment you had, over by the Tchaikovsky Hall. You remember Princess Narishchine, the old lady who told you about the flat?'

'Why yes, of course I do.'

'She's been living in the basement, in one of the old bathrooms. Just one room. But someone knew, someone sent an anonymous letter to some *sluzhashchik* and she was turned out. For living somewhere without a *propusk*, a permit. She's an old lady and she'll die on the street. I've taken her in and it's a bit crowded – we have some relatives with us as well as the children . . .'

Ruth looked at her in horror. 'You're all living in two rooms? Sergei and I have *six*, just off the Alexanderplatz. Sergei's talking of continuing the struggle from Paris now that Hitler's in charge . . .'

'Ruth, that doesn't matter. But the Princess has her pride. She wants to go back to living in her little room. Look, if Sergei just asked for it, for one of his companies. As a storeroom. Not mentioning her name! Please, no. But then she could be a watchwoman over it. Officially.

Once he had it. Why not? They have old Civil War veterans guarding rubbish dumps. She could guard the room.'

Ruth stopped a passing waiter, and captured a glass of wine. Was she listening, Yelena wondered?

'You remember, she told you about the house. *It used to be hers.* The whole thing. Do you remember the great hallway, with the carved fresco of cherubs? She had it done in the year ten. If I come in late I find her there, in the horrible light from one of pitiful bulbs they have, looking at it. *The cherubs were modelled on her children.*'

'I'll do it. Don't worry.' Ruth drank some of her wine.

'He won't object?'

'Savinkov will do what I tell him,' Ruth said coldly, the gay mask slipping. 'He owes me a debt.'

Yelena looked at her old schoolfriend with the experienced eye of a trader assessing the worth of a customer.

'Good. Because there's something else I want you to get Savinkov to do.'

'More Princesses?' Ruth asked, lifting an eye brow quizzically.

'A relative of yours.'

Ruth stared bleakly over her glass at nothing. 'I don't have many relatives left, Yelena.'

'You have your Uncle Isaak. He sleeps on my floor, under the table.'

'Why?' Ruth was bewildered.

'Because he has nowhere else to go. He's been graded *lishentsi*, you see, along with the other *byvshiye*, the former people. You know, darling, people like we used to be. I'm all right, I'm an honorary peasant, because I'm married to Ivan. But Isaak's not. When you're *lishentsi*, you don't exist. And if you don't help him, he'll die.'

'I'd like to help Uncle Isaak. If he will let me,' Ruth whispered. 'Tell me how.'

'Have Savinkov apply for him. To help him with his propaganda in the West. A special adviser.'

'I'll do it, Yelena,' she said, her voice firm.

'Ruth?' called an English voice. They turned to see an angular, bespectacled figure pushing her way through the people, clutching a glass of orange juice.

'Yelena,' Ruth said smoothly, 'do you know Beatrice Webb? She and her husband Sidney are writing a book about us. *The Truth About Russia*, it is to be called. A very big, scholarly work it is too.'

The woman smirked in approval. An arranged commotion was taking place at the end of the room, where a tall, bearded, elderly man was mounting the stage with his hosts and travelling companion, the aristocratic Lady Astor.

'Oh, splendid!' said the Englishwoman. 'George is to speak. *Happy Birthday, George.*'

The playwright waved amicably. His eyes twinkled merrily. In them Yelena detected the humour of a man enjoying a personal, and cruel joke. Shaw's picture had appeared in all the papers, both foreign and Soviet, applauding the efforts of the October Revolution collective farm, visiting the progressive prison at Bolshevo, commenting on the productivity of a factory, cavorting for the cameras on the Napoleonic cannon in the Kremlin. He was experienced in the arts of special effects.

He waved a sandwich at the assembled guests.

'You won't believe this. When my friends in England learned that I was going to Russia they loaded me up with all sorts of tinned food. Beef and chicken, smoked fish, game pie, fruits and jams. *They had been told that Russia was starving.* Yes. By the capitalist newspaper owners. And they believed it!'

He chuckled merrily down at his audience.

'You know what I did? I threw the lot out of my carriage window in Poland before I reached the Soviet frontier!'

They all, worker and intellectual alike, knew better than to cry out in pain. The worst of it, as it sank in, was the knowledge that it had been some lucky Polish swine who had gathered in the harvest by the railway track.

'They told me people were *starving*. That the system was close to collapse. What did I find when I changed trains – to a splendid, classless carriage that was waiting – but two healthy, rosy-cheeked waitresses behind a sumptuously-stocked table. Furthermore, these girls not only spoke English, but were familiar in detail with my works! In Moscow I invited them as my guests to the performance of my play that was being shown. The public – well-fed, healthy and happy – flocked to see it.'

He leered obscenely. 'Perhaps everyone's cheeks are padded out with india-rubber? But no, let us put this poppycock from our minds.'

The playwright put down his sandwich and a hundred and fifty pairs of eyes watched him do it. 'I've been over-stuffed since I came to Moscow,' he said playfully, and they all laughed, because they had to.

As he went on to extol the collective, the model prison, the factory and the proletariat, Yelena was aware of Beatrice Webb looking at her sharply.

'Is something wrong?' she asked.

'I think everyone is sorry that George didn't wait until he got inside Russia to throw away his food,' Yelena suggested and then attempted to turn it into a joke. 'If he had let us know what he was going to do, we could have stood by the track and caught it as it flew out of the window.'

The Englishwoman looked at her coldly, and waved a hand around the room. 'Where do you see any food shortage?'

Suddenly Yelena was tired of this supercilious fool.

'Perhaps you should talk to my neighbour,' she said sharply. 'She queues for four hours a day to try to get milk for her daughter, who is ill with stomach problems. She only succeeds sometimes. And the milk is sour.'

'Then she should feed the child herself. Breast milk is far superior.'

'Her daughter is eight!'

'What of it? Eskimos nurse their children until they are twenty.'

'Even if she wished to,' Yelena said precisely, through her teeth, 'she does not eat enough herself to produce milk in any quantity.'

'*Yelena*, don't,' Ruth hissed warningly.

'Her anorexia is then entirely her own fault,' Beatrice Webb said dismissively. 'If people will not eat in the midst of plenty they have only themselves to blame.'

'Do the people you see on the street in rags dress that way for fashion? Or are there no clothes, the same as there is no food?'

'We all place too much importance on clothing. The Hottentots go about naked, and are entirely happy.'

'The Hottentots have clearly had the benefits of communism for longer than we have,' Yelena said quietly.

'*Yelena!*'

Beatrice Webb's eyes were chill behind her glasses. 'You almost sound like a subversive,' she said softly.

'Yelena is an old friend,' Ruth said protectively. 'Of *Sergei's*, too. She gets carried away. She doesn't mean what she says. Do you?' She squeezed Yelena's arm very hard, and Yelena forced herself to smile.

'No,' she said.

Satisfied with her humiliation, the Englishwoman returned her attention to the stage.

'Don't make trouble,' Ruth whispered anxiously. 'These people are important. Stalin himself takes an interest and he wants them to see our country at its best. Let's just have a drink.'

Up at the stage, applause broke out as the speech came to an end. Under the lights they saw the English aristocrat, Lady Astor, push her way to the fore. She waved a peremptory hand for silence, and the striped paper of a telegram flapped in the air. She turned to Maxim Litvinov, whose fleshy expression of benign satisfaction changed to nervous alarm as she flung herself extravagantly upon her knees in front of him.

'As in days of yore, I present a petition to your government on bended knee,' she declaimed. 'Most humbly do I pray you in the name of humanity to save this suffering family. This telegram I give you is from a Professor Krynin, now resident in America. He seeks to be reunited with his family. He has applied for them to join him, but they are refused exit visas. In desperation, hearing of my visit, he has cabled me for my help.'

Litvinov, who could read English, quickly scanned the telegram, then passed it back, smiling pleasantly.

'But all Professor Krynin has to do to be reunited with his family is return to Russia,' he murmured. 'Now, I am afraid I am busy, and must leave you.'

Yelena saw the foreign newspaper correspondents clustering about Lady Astor, sensing a human interest story for their readers. A mop of bright red hair stood out, and she recognised Johnny Nichols from the United Press. Then they made for the door in a gaggle, and she realised that the desperate academic must have included the address of his family.

The posturin and playacting of the eminent foreigners had turned the small sandwich she had nibbled into ash in her mouth. She felt sick.

'I'm going to get some air for a moment. Ruth,' she said. 'And you may be gone when I get back so let me beg just one more favour of you. Let Nikolai go to school in England, Ruth.'

Ruth, shocked, spilled some of the wine she was drinking, and it ran down her chin.

'He came to see me,' she said and didn't say how or why.

'He hasn't been telling you these lies?' Ruth asked desperately, her eyes frantically looking to see if anyone was listening.

'They aren't lies,' Yelena said, looking her friend steadily in the eyes. Ruth turned away.

'Don't look at me like that! You accuse me.'

'Let Nikolai go to England,' Yelena said stubbornly.

'But isn't it full of people like this Webb woman and her husband?' Ruth whispered desperately. 'And all the other ones Savinkov uses?'

'Nowhere is full of people like that. They fester in Sergei's offices, filled with bile and wanting to remake the world. The English people do not want to remake the world. It is a place full of what they call "stick-in-the-muds". They like their gardens and places they call "pubs", where they drink beer. Johnny Nichols says their favourite expression is "we'll cross that bridge when we come to it".'

'How do they live without an ideology?'

'How do we live with one?' Yelena murmured. 'They mistrust people with "ideas". They think that "character" is much more important.'

Ruth smiled sadly. 'They would not like me, then.'

'Try them,' Yelena urged. 'Go with Nikolai. Can anything be worse than what you have?'

Ruth suddenly looked straight at her old friend and now there was only truth in her eyes.

'Some mornings I wake up and I know I'm mad, Yelena. Completely mad. There are two parts of my brain, and they are fighting, even while I'm asleep.'

'Then *go*. Try gardening and a beer in the pub.'

'Natasha will not come,' she said sadly.

'Have you lost her?'

Ruth nodded. 'She belongs to them – and it is all my fault.'

'No, not yours. Theirs. So go, and take Nikolai with you.'

She turned to go, and Ruth called after her. 'Give Uncle Isaak my love.'

'I will.'

'Ask him, if he can, to forgive me.'

Yelena left the ballroom. In the corridor a window was open. and she stood by it, feeling the sweat clammy on her face.

'What is the matter with you?' asked an unfriendly voice. It was Beatrice Webb.

'I get no pleasure from seeing a woman and her children sentenced to death. It makes me, but not you, nor your filthy companions, feel sick.'

The two women stared at each other in mutual loathing.

'The poor professor in America must be demented,' Yelena continued. 'Once these foreigner correspondents have gone the wagon will come, the Black Maria, and take them away. I rode in one once, you know, before the Civil War. It was a small affair, drawn by a horse. Have you seen the modern ones? You must look out for them, since you are writing about us. You must make sure you put them in your book. They are very big, and do not have windows, but only some perforations near the top that let in a little air. In the West they would be used to move large quantities of furniture. Here they are used to move large quantities of people.'

'Enemies of the people!' snapped Webb.

'Ah.' Yelena said. 'You *do* know what I mean. No, not enemies of the people. Just the people. The enemies are elsewhere.'

'Where?' she asked, dangerously.

'I'm not *that* crazy,' Yelena said shortly. 'You'd go running to Maxy or the GPU, wouldn't you? But you know, don't you? You and your horrid chums. You know about the killing. *And you don't care.*'

Beatrice Webb paused before she spoke, seeming to take what Yelena had said seriously. That isn't exactly fair,' she said quietly. 'You're talking about the collectivisation of the peasantry. A seismic shift in the structure of this country, but one so necessary for society. Yes, there have been casualties, but you have to remember that the enlightened rulers of this country are achieving all their goals in a very short space of time. Events that in Europe took place over centuries – the changes in the use of land, the industrial revolution – are taking place here much faster. And here, as in Europe, there have been casualties. But here, so much finer! A new world, ordered and clean . . . Yet I take your point. Strong indeed must be the faith, and resolute the will of the men who, in the interest of the public good, could take so momentous a decision.'

She wagged her head, and pursed her lips in approval.

'Did it take strong faith and resolute will for one man to burn another at the stake for belief in a God slightly different from that of his own?' Yelena demanded angrily, keeping her voice low. She glanced anxiously over her shoulder. This was dangerous. But she found herself unable to stop. 'Are we to approve even more when one madman here inflicts that suffering upon millions?'

'Let us consider whom we are referring to here,' Beatrice Webb said disapprovingly. 'We are talking of the worst elements in Soviet society, those not yet brought fully under its benevolent sway. The peasantry as a whole is characterised by the vices of greed and cunning, varied only by outbursts of drunkenness and periods of great sloth. Yes, and theft. In our travels my husband and I came across numerous instances of individuals and even whole villages manifestly guilty of sabotage of the harvest directed by the Soviet authorities. Individuals who, out of spite, took to rubbing the grain from the ear, or even cutting off the whole ear and carrying it off for individual hoarding, simply a shameless theft of communal property.'

'They took the grain they had sown on their own land to feed their starving families,' Yelena said quietly. 'They found it difficult to comprehend that their land had been taken from them, that they should work to feed others and not their own, for no reward.'

'Exactly,' said Webb. 'Greedy, cunning and dishonest. Is it not better that such as they should be transformed into public-spirited co-operators working upon a prescribed plan for the common product to be equitably shared among themselves? Listen to me. I come from the capitalist world of storm and stress, where morals have vanished, where science is baffled, production halted, poverty unchecked. And I come to the Soviet world of order and purpose, where the future lies before a child born today like a carefully tended path through a beautiful landscape. Lenin, and now Stalin, are artists who work in men as others work in marble or metal. So shavings and dross lie on the floor, but is not the product wonderful?'

Yelena was exasperated and frustrated.

'People . . . Cut them into new shapes, they bleed. Bend them into new forms, they break. Bolt and bind them, they scream. But they are told that it is being done for the good of the people.'

Beatrice Webb sighed. Blind are those who will not see,' she said.

Yelena forced herself to speak calmly. 'Mrs Webb, I'm sorry if I am annoying you. But has it never occurred to you that you – and George and all the others like you – are being deceived? That your visits here are about as spontaneous and free-ranging as a railway and its timetable? That you see what your hosts *wish* you to see, that you speak only to those whom your hosts wish you to speak?'

The Englishwoman smiled incredulously. 'What an extraordinary notion!' she said loudly.

Yelena glanced nervously down the corridor.

'What is the matter with you?' Webb demanded peremptorily. 'Do you have some nervous affliction?'

'Mrs Webb, you are not supposed to meet anyone the GPU has not arranged for you to meet. And I am *exactly* the sort they do not want you to meet. I am looking about because I don't want to be seen with you. It is dangerous.'

Beatrice Webb stared bleakly at her. 'Frankly, I believe that you are suffering from some sort of persecution complex. If I were you I should go to one of the fine hospitals here, confess your plight and seek medical assistance for your affliction.' She looked over Yelena's shoulder. 'Ah. Sidney, there you are,' she called.

She turned back to Yelena. 'We are being awarded the privilege of an audience with Comrade Stalin.' Her eyes twinkled maliciously. 'Shall I apprise him of the dissent within his bosom?'

Yelena went white. 'I would prefer that you did not.'

'No. Because you know that what I say is correct. Well it is always pleasant to wrestle with an unbeliever, to place the seeds of doubt that flourish into intellectual harvest. I shall supply you with one final refutation of your fears. Comrade General-Secretary Stalin – Steel is his name and steely his resolve – and we have met before. Shall I tell you what he said to us? "Man must be grown as carefully and attentively as a gardener grows a favourite fruit tree." Comrade Stalin is the embodiment of the communist ideal now being put into practice. He combines a deep theoretical understanding with an unfailing mastery of practice, and a deeply scientific approach to all problems with the deepest capacity for feeling. Now, I must be off. But do go and get medical help for your problem. Mental illness can be cured.'

The tramcar clanked by, taking with it the howl of worn bearings and its load of tightly-packed humanity, all indifferent to its pain. Yelena went quickly across the street, mud squirting up from the loose cobbles and holes. On the side of the building a vast billboard kept score: *Over There*: unemployment, strikes and Fascism. *Over Here*: new factories, shock brigades, full employment, hydro-electric dams. Behind it people lived in rooms made as dark as caves.

Soldiers with bayonets guarded the doorways to the public buildings, keeping out the spies, saboteurs, wreckers and enemies of the people who seethed everywhere, unseen until found by the OGPU. The entrances to the private dwellings were secured by locks and bars, and opened only after complicated and correct bell signals.

She remembered the code for Katia and after a few minutes, the door clicked and clanked, and a pair of green eyes looked out.

'Come in, darling,' Katia said warmly.

She had a room on the top, where they had slapped an extra storey on to the old eighteenth century building, a dowager given a cloth cap to wear. There was a view over the square where there were kerosene queues and bread queues, tramcar queues and queues for *propusks* to queue. The swarming people were the colour of dung, their clothes soiled, patched, drab, drained of colour, their skins the same.

'Are you working?' Yelena asked.

Katia lit a Herzegovina Flor cigarette and stood in a haze of its strong smoke. She waved it about her little room.

'Nothing but the best for an actress playing the lead,' she said. 'I'm a beautiful komsomol dedicated to fulfilling the five year plan in four. I fall from grace by falling in love with the *boorzhoi* Sasha. I abandon my lathe and the five year plan trembles. At the last moment I realise my errors, return to the factory in an explosion of red bunting and the five year plan is done in three and Sasha is reeducated to the value of selfless toil by helping build a canal.'

She shrugged. 'It's not so bad, Yelena. I'm not cast as the type who has to act to live. Not like poor Konstantin. He's written in as a poet through to his soul, and now he's composing stanzas in praise of Soviet mineral water and the OGPU.'

A faint frown appeared between Yelena's eyebrows.

'Mind you, he has to, with that creep Rykov about.'

'You have kept away from Rykov, haven't you, Katia?' Yelena asked anxiously. 'He's very dangerous.'

'I have. I minded what you said, as always. But you haven't come to ask me that, have you?' she said shrewdly.

She made tea, very hot, sweet and almost ebony.

'That . . . boy you knew, the American. The black one. Is he still about?'

'Leroy? Yes, I think so. Why?'

'I need to get in touch with his friend, Johnny Nichols, the journalist. He's back in Moscow, but I can't just go around, asking about a foreigner, especially one working for the press.'

'You're afraid to?'

'I certainly am.'

Katia shook her head, sitting down on her bed, gaily decorated with a rug she had acquired from the props of the studio.

'Konstantin's afraid too. He wakes up in the middle of the night crying, and I have to wrap myself around him. I tell him not to be frightened, but he is.'

'Aren't you afraid, Katia darling?'

She shook her head again, and the auburn hair swung in a glorious sheet. 'It's only a film, darling.'

'What is?' Yelena asked, disconcerted.

The cigarette described a circle in the air. 'All this. It's not a very good film, and we can all go and work in a much better one next time. But it's still only a film.'

Yelena looked uncertainly at her schoolfriend. 'So this is all a film? We aren't actually here.'

Katia laughed, and looked at her with the clear, certain gaze of the insane. 'Well, of course not. Do you know when I realised it? I played a scene in the Cheka slaughterhouse. You remember, you played it, too. A very bad script . . . one minute we were at the Lycée, the next I was captured, made to work where they killed people . . . A terrifying creature called Zemliachka, all covered in black leather and blood. What a part she had! I was real aristocracy and she made me work with her dead. I had to stand by while she tortured and murdered the prisoners and she seemed to need to think up new ideas all the time. She killed some by twisting their heads round and round until they came off. Some she flayed alive. Some she had dig pits. They had to get in while their families covered them over with earth, and were made to dance on the moving dirt. She had a barrel she'd had nails driven into. She liked to put people in and roll them about the death yard and I had to pull the meat out when she had finished.

'I didn't understand then . . . One day I was thinking of hanging myself as I waited in the chapel of the dead to be taken out for the fresh day's work. Then it came to me, like a great bright arc lamp going on in the studio, and I understood that it was a film, and that we were all just acting. *Everyone*! And when I went out and Zemliachka was gutting someone it wasn't real, just special effects. All just a film . . .'

'It's still running, then.'

'Oh, yes. You only have to look out there. Real *people* wouldn't run things like that. It's all rather tedious and I'd like to start a new one, Yelena.'

'I would too, darling,' Yelena said softly, her eyes shining with tears. 'Maybe we can. If I talk to Johnny Nichols we might start.'

17

The Road to Utopia

Y ELENA stood with her back to the red brick of the silver-
spired Historical Museum, watching the crowds moving in
Red Square. To her left, through the trees, she could see them coming
and going in the huge *Universal 'nyy Magazin* Department Store. In
the distance the gorgeous red, white and green onion domes and
chapels of St Basil's shone cheerfully in the sunlight but closer by
pedestrians walked through the gaping hole where the Shrine of the
Iberian Virgin had been ripped out.

That was the way he came, a *karakul* hat on his head, hiding his
red hair, a warm coat about him. Merry eyes smiled at her from over
the muffler about his face.

'Yelena! It's been a long time.'

'Johnny,' she said warmly. She began to move. 'Shall we see the
sights? They've changed a few things since you were last here.'

'Sure,' he said amiably. 'Lead on.'

They walked towards the Kremlin wall. Ahead of them, workmen
were busy amidst scaffolding. Glimpses of red, grey and black stone
were visible beneath.

'So you're back. You didn't want to stay in America?'

'Times are pretty bad over there. There's a real depression on, you
know. A slump, and our political and business leaders don't seem to
have the first idea what to do. Here in The Soviet Union there's an
amazing, and totally relevant, alternative.'

'You ought to write a book about it,' she suggested.

'I'm going to,' he said fervently. 'I've already begun. It's called
The Road to Utopia. There's a real feeling in the USA that we're
witnessing the death throes of capitalism and, at the same time, the
birth of a new age.'

'Wonderful,' she said blandly. 'I knew you would. So I thought I'd
help you. I've arranged for some friends to show you round. And I
want you to meet some children I know. The first generation of New
Men, if you like.'

His face flushed with pleasure. 'Why, that's just fine! How can I thank you?'

'Write the book,' she said pleasantly. They were passing the series of small black granite plaques, newly-set in the wall to commemorate leading communists of the world.

'Big Bill Heywood,' she said. 'One of yours, I think. Didn't he come here on the run from a jail sentence in America?'

Nichols chuckled from behind his scarf. 'Now there's the Yelena I remember. You still can't bring yourself to admit that communism's got some mighty fine stuff in it, can you? Okay, so there are some rogues, but Big Bill was a man of the people, through and through. Some of your own leaders are rough diamonds too, but no one can doubt their sincerity.'

The multi-coloured granite of the *Mavsoley Lenina* rose up above them.

'I preferred the wooden hut,' she said, 'if one has to do it at all. Lenin would not have approved, you know being stuffed full of embalming fluid and put on show to be worshipped. He didn't approve of gods.'

A group of large women in tweed suits was coming across the square towards the tomb, escorted by a sharp-eyed female guide.

'Ah,' she said. 'Foreigners.'

'What makes you say that?'

'They gush sincerity. They have become tired of attending church at home, but they have found a much better one abroad.'

The women were forming a semi-circle in front of the mausoleum. They looked solemnly at their leader, a large lady with a fine bosom and three chins. She cleared her throat, and began to declaim.

> 'Oh! Why are words so poor and weak?
> Hopeless to write and hard to speak.
> To tell of all that you have done
> Since your great Victory was won.
> Your children are a happy band,
> Knowledge and Freedom hand in hand.
> War Crime Disease will disappear
> For perfect Love can cast out Fear!'

Led by the guide, her companions burst into applause. Nichols saw Yelena's expression, and frowned with a sudden flash of anger.

'Okay, Yelena, so she's naive. At least she's on the right side.' He held up his hand. 'I know what you're going to say. That things aren't perfect here. I know that. Your leaders have had to make hard decisions. Bolshevik decisions. Maybe even ruthless ones. But it's for the good of everyone. Maybe one or two speculators and crooks have got their knuckles rapped, or a bit worse. Well, you can't make an omelette without breaking eggs.'

'No, indeed. Ah, here we are, Johnny. Your first guide. One of the eggs.'

A tall, thin man in his forties had come up. He was Jewish and wore a dark coat that had been fleecy and fine when he had been smooth and sleek. Now, it was threadbare and loose. He smiled, pleasantly.

'Johnny, this is Isaak Gunzberg.'

'I'm so pleased to meet you,' Isaak said in a cultured manner.

'Gunzberg . . .?'

'That's right. I am Ruth's uncle.'

'I'll see you later, Johnny. Isaak will look after you.'

She turned, and vanished in the crowds.

'Such a pleasant day,' Gunzberg murmured. 'Shall we take the air?'

He led Nichols across the square. 'Some interesting shops have opened since you were last here. If you are looking for some memories of the real Russia to take home you should do some browsing about.'

'I'm really more interested in people than souvenirs.'

'Oh, these shops are filled with pieces of people,' Isaak said softly.

Nichols began to feel irritated.

The giant GUM store occupied a slab of the side of the square. At each side of it enormous portraits of Lenin and Stalin hung down from steel cables attached to its roof. The one of Lenin was slightly smaller and looked across at Stalin as though seeking advice. Around the edges of the store, below the huge icons, were a fringe of people, silent and ragged. They stood, holding their hands out to beg, and Nichols saw that Gunzberg was leading him towards them. He was about to protest, when the Jew stopped by one of them.

'How are you getting along, Solomon?'

'Oh, *lootche tchem zahvtra*, better than tomorrow,' wheezed the man. Like Gunzberg, he had once been plump. Now he had the deadly colouring of tuberculosis.

'I'm showing Mr Nichols around,' Isaak said. 'He's an American.'

'A fine place, America. I used to trade with the Gottlieb brothers in New York, Mr Nichols. Remember Solomon Shafarevich to them, if you go that way.'

'I will,' Nichols muttered as Shafarevich coughed convulsively into a murky rag.

'Tell Benny he still owes me for the carpets!'

Nichols thrust a hand in his pocket and stuffed some roubles into the claw. 'For God's sake, get out of this horrible line!'

'Thank you.' The money had slipped away, vanished.

'Go on – won't you get something to eat?'

The man smiled apologetically. 'I'm keeping Isaak's place for him.'

Nichols looked in horror at Gunzberg. '*You* beg here?'

Gunzberg smiled. 'Come on, we shan't be long.'

'Remember, Mr Nichols,' Solomon wheezed, 'these are great days. The Russians have all become Jews. They, too, cannot eat pork.'

They moved on along the side of the square.

'What's he talking about? Your friend has a strange sense of humour,' Nichols said irritably.

'Yes, Solomon likes a laugh. I had a yacht – before the troubles, of course – and we used to go cruising in the summer. One day Solomon turned up on *his* yacht and it was three feet longer than mine!' He shook his head. 'I wonder where they are now . . . Here, this is one of the shops I was telling you about. There are some real bargains here. For *valuta*, for real money, dollars and pounds, of course . . .'

The shop window was stuffed with all kinds of expensive goods. Fine rugs, paintings, clocks and watches, crystal and china, silverware and gold, icons, chalices, jewelled crosses.

'What did you mean, the shop is filled with pieces of people?'

A ragged figure was shuffling along the pavement, clutching a silver candelabra. He turned into the shop. The rags seemed to be remnants of a Tsarist uniform.

'There he is, giving away part of his life.'

'Who is he?' Nichols demanded.

'One of us, one of the *byvshiye*, the former people.'

'Look, this just doesn't wash with me, Isaak. We have beggars at home, too. *And* soup kitchens.'

A gleam of interest came into Isaak's eyes. 'Soup kitchens? We don't have those.'

'You wouldn't *need* them. Not here. And we have pawnshops like this one.'

'This isn't a pawnshop,' Isaak said gently. 'You can't get anything back, and you don't get what it's worth, no not one tenth or one twentieth of its value. I was a merchant, I know the value of goods.'

'You have sold things here?'

'I needed money for my family.'

'Look, I understand that there's bound to be some suffering when the old world gives way to the new. But it's worth the price, for what's being built here.'

'To be sure. And *there* is the new world, Mr Nichols.'

A party official was emerging from the store, carrying a rolled, precious Bokhara rug over his shoulder. He seemed very pleased.

'Let us move on. It is not very safe, to be about here.'

'What do you mean, not safe?'

'To be seen selling *valuta* implies you might have more. It was my visit to this store that brought about our misfortunes.'

Nichols had stopped, and was looking in alarm at his hand. It was smeared with blood.

'Oh, don't worry,' said Gunzberg. 'It's not yours, it's Solomon's blood. He hasn't actually lost them yet but he bleeds from the fingernails. It's something to do with lacking vitamins, I believe. Though sleeping on the street cannot help.'

'Why does he sleep on the street?' cried Nichols.

'He's *lishentsi*, you see. When you're a former person you don't have rights. Your children can't go to school, you don't get rations, the *sluzhashchy* redefine living space so that it does not include you.'

He looked almost admonishingly at the American. 'Well, don't look surprised. Don't you, too, believe in the eradication of the bourgeoisie, like all the other good communists? But we don't just vanish, you know. We have to be eliminated. Blood, like that on your hand, has to be spilled.'

On the corner a woman was selling small bunches of flowers from a bucket. Gunzberg coughed delicately.

'I like to take my wife some flowers when I go to see her. I don't suppose you . . .'

'Oh, yeah,' he said shakily. 'Let me.'

Nichols reached again into his pocket, and paid for a posy of violets. He could not help peering at Gunzberg's hand as he gave him the money.

'Oh, I'm not bleeding yet. Yelena is so kind to me. She makes some special brew from her garden plot which she gives to the children, and spares me a spoonful every evening before I go to sleep.'

'You sleep at Yelena's apartment?'

'Yes. She was good enough to take me in and I try not to be a nuisance. I'm away early to beg, and when I come back I know some good stories to tell the children. I sleep under the table.'

'But why not with your own family?' Nichols cried in exasperation.

'Well, I'm not ready to sleep with my family. Not yet,' Gunzberg said strangely. They had left the great length of the square, where the afternoon shadows were advancing across from the Kremlin, and were going past a small, red and white classical church.

'They brought the rebel peasant Stenka Razin along here on his way to be executed in the square,' Gunzberg commented. 'It's still called after him.'

'Look, I don't get all this about your family. Are we going to see them? And what trouble did you get into going to sell things in the store?'

'Oh, yes. Yes, we are going to see my family. I married a second time, you know. I lost my first wife in the Civil War and I married Vera some six years ago. We had a child, David, the following year. It was a difficult pregnancy for Vera, she was often ill afterwards and it was to get her some medicine that I went to the commission shop. I had managed to save a few possessions from better times – some silver spoons, a rug, my first wife's wedding ring – and I took them there to sell.' He pointed with his little bunch of flowers. 'We must cut along up here.'

They crossed the boulevard and went along a small and winding street of old buildings.

'I did not receive more than perhaps one twentieth of the value, but I was able to buy some medicine. Unfortunately, I was not at that time aware of a hidden trap set within the store, until it came round that same evening and took me away. There is, you see, in each store, a man or woman from the OGPU, a *Chekist*, posing as a member of staff. One has to show identity papers before one may sell what one has brought, and so they know where you live. I was taken to the Lubyanka, and tortured.'

'This is preposterous!' Nichols exploded. 'Tortured for what? Selling some goods?'

'No, not that,' Gunzberg said gently. 'After all, they had already obtained those from me. No, *by entering the store with goods that could be sold for valuta – real money – I had given them reason to believe that I might have more.* So they brought me in to get it.'

'I'm sorry, I just don't believe a word of this,' Nichols protested. 'No government on earth behaves like this. Okay, so someone sweated you for money – they must have been gangsters. Is that it? Did you get into the hands of loansharks? And if you were tortured, where are the marks?'

'The marks, Mr Nichols, remain on the inside,' Gunzberg said gently. 'They torture you in different ways, you know. I was put into the *parilka*, the sweat room. Several hundred of us in a cell. No ventilation, but hot radiators. One bare bulb. You stand, all of you, while your feet swell, and the lice swarm over you, eating your blood. No toilets, so you stand in it. After a day or two in there they put you on the conveyor. You go from one interrogator's desk to the next, running along corridors, cursed, kicked, shouted at, beaten on the shins, threatened. They work in shifts and you keep going. It is finely calculated, Mr Nichols, calculated to bring the strongest, whether a janitor or a professor, down to a common level of slobbering fear. It takes very little time at all to forget that you are a human being, that there are others who are not wild beasts, that somewhere else there is music, food, wine and poetry.

'My problem was that what I had sold was all that I had. They did not want to believe me, so that after a week of this they put me into the *parilka* again, and this time brought in my wife Vera, and our son, David.'

They crossed over the street, and went towards a derelict church, its stained glass windows destroyed, its facade like a skull.

'On the third day I thought of a way to get them *valuta*. I have a cousin in Pittsburgh and I promised to write to him, begging for dollars. I asked to see my chief interrogator, but he had gone home to sleep after his shift. I saw him the next morning, but during the night David, who had caught the fever that was running in the *parilka*, died. My wife was allowed to take him away. She was herself very ill by this stage. Me, they kept, until the money came from my cousin, who is a good man and will surely rest with Moses in Heaven. Then they let me go. I went home. The neighbours told me that Vera had died and that the bodies of my family had been taken away on the refuse cart . . .'

They went through the door of the rotting church, and out into the graveyard. It was the only part in use. Large mounds showed where mass graves had been dug, and filled.

'I believe that they are in here. The OGPU uses the old graveyards for its victims; it puts them in a few dozen at a time, and pours on the quicklime.'

Gunzberg carefully placed his posy of flowers upon one of the grim piles of earth.

'Would you care to join me in prayer?' he asked gently. 'Then I will take you back.'

'I'm sorry. I don't believe in superstitions,' Nichols said.

'In God, you mean? How unfortunate for you. I now believe in no one else.'

They began to walk back the way they had come.

'The Bolsheviks promised a new world, Mr Nichols, and they have been true to their word. Where else can you find this new industry, gold mining in torture chambers?'

Walking beside him. Nichols had his head down, and said nothing.

'And socialist capitalism,' Gunzberg said mercilessly.

Nichols twitched, as though stung by a whip. 'What the hell is that?' he snarled.

'The people in the *parilka* with me, those who staggered ahead of me on the conveyor, or who crawled behind, not all had made my mistake of going to the commission shop. No.'

'All right, so how did they get there?'

'Denounced. By a relative, friend, workmate or neighbour. Informed upon for the crime of possessing something of value.'

'Why would people who knew them want to denounce them?'

'For *profit*,' Gunzberg said triumphantly. 'The state decree of the year twenty-nine promises a full twenty-five per cent commission, a quarter share of all money, valuables and other property seized by the government to go to the informer. Yes, if in Heaven, or more likely in Hell, the shades of Lenin and Marx are on speaking terms they have a most interesting and delicate problem of dialectic to argue over. The socialist profit motive! I feel they will need the talents of a Trotsky to square this one. Perhaps, as the informer acquires the quarter share of goods and valuables, he or she automatically then becomes a capitalist restorationist, rightist imperialist exploiter of the masses, and is thus ready for denunciation themselves. The process could clearly go on for some time.' His voice held amusement.

They were nearing Red Square again. A tall, blond man in the uniform of an Intourist guide was standing near the cathedral. He waved, and Gunzberg waved back. The man was holding a small cardboard suitcase and, as they came closer, he seemed familiar to Nichols.

'Say,' he said. 'I know you. Ah . . . Valerian, isn't it? You showed me round Moscow some years back.'

'That's right, Mr Nichols. I showed you some of Bolshevism's finest creations, did I not?'

'That's right!' the American said enthusiastically. 'The Red October commune . . .'

'The Butyrki prison.'

'What a model of reformation for the world that was!'

'What a model,' Valerian said, smiling.

'The nursery school . . .'

Nichols stole a triumphant glance at Gunzberg to see how he was taking the little parade of fine achievements, but saw him smiling like Valerian.

'Don't tell me,' he said wearily. 'Now you're going to show me something nasty.'

'Well done,' Valerian said sincerely. 'Shall we go along this way?'

'Yelena's got it in for me today,' Nichols said, with a certain stolid determination. 'Where are you taking me?'

'Have you heard of the *Dom Nochlyega*?'

'The House for a Night's Lodging? Why sure, I've read Gorky's *Lower Depths*. A Tsarist hell-hole, right? The end of the line, for people who have nowhere else to go.'

'Correct. Built in Tsarist times, still used in Bolshevik ones. Want to see one? You'll be the first Western journalist to do it. But I warn you, it's nasty.'

'I grew up on the lower East Side of New York, son,' Nichols said quietly, with a hard edge to his voice. 'I have first hand experience of flop-houses on the Bowery, stinking tenements, steerage holes. I am a tough cookie who believes in a better world, Valerian, because he's seen the bottom. Yes, I'll come with you. You seem to think I'm really naive, the pair of you. Look, I know not everything's perfect here yet, that you can see some things that aren't pretty, but that's because the Bolsheviks have had the guts to rip off the veneer and show it as it really is. No pretences. The sores you see are up front, not hidden away like in the West. Here they'll be cured.'

The two Russians smiled sadly and knowledgeably. Nichols saw it, his annoyance smarting.

They had walked back up the square away from the cathedral, and were entering Tverskaya, the road that led to Leningrad. Its twisty path was being demolished and rubble stood piled up on every corner. Scaffolding supported new buildings and huge placards bearing the magic symbols of $2+2=5$, the *Piatiletka*, the Five Year Plan in Four Years. The air was filled with the drumming of the Sadovsky pumps, compressors and trucks, and the street underfoot was filthy with the mud. Valerian turned to Nichols.

'Did you bring the money? The *valuta*?'

Nichols flinched, and found himself unable to look at Gunzberg. 'Yes,' he muttered. 'Yelena said to. I have dollars.'

'I've arranged for you to talk to a few people, but they'll want a little money. And perhaps some food, and tobacco? From *Yeliseyev's?*'

They were close to the old Tsarist food emporium, its new name of *Gastronom No 1* contrasting sharply with the gilt, stained glass and pillars of its frontage.

'I'll go in,' Nichols said.

'We'll wait for you here,' said Valerian. 'Russians aren't allowed in.'

Through the glass they could see the foreign diplomats, journalists and industrial specialists making their purchases, and Nichols went in to make his. When he came out with his parcel they continued up the street.

'They're calling *Tverskaya Gorkovo* now,' Valerian said professionally. 'After the writer, Maxim Gorky.'

'I know who he is,' Nichols snarled.

They picked their way around the vast pile of earth and rubble that was *Pushkinskaya* square. A gang of very weary and very dirty men were emerging from a hole in the ground. They carried shovels, picks, sacks and the bodies of two of their workmates, which they proceeded to drop.

Valerian saw Nichols' alarmed glance. 'Workers,' he said laconically. 'Making the Metro.'

Nichols saw the NKVD guards. 'What's happened to those two men?'

'Probably imperialist wreckers,' Valerian said casually. 'And found out by their comrades. Either that or their hearts couldn't take the pressure. They use compressors to keep the water out while the concrete sets. Our Metro system will be the wonder of the world, you know – and the entire nation is pitching in to help build it.'

They went on, and into a side street. The district became shabbier and they halted in a refuse-strewn alley.

'We have to change,' said Valerian. 'Someone will kill you in the night for that coat you have on.'

Wrapped up in some newspaper were some filthy, ragged clothes and footware. Feeling his skin crawl, Nichols put them on with Valerian, and Gunzberg folded their clean ones away in the case.

'I'll look after them,' he said. 'I'll see you tomorrow.'

Then he was walking away down the street. Valerian stuffed the parcel of food and tobacco under his shapeless jacket and led the way along the alley. Nichols stepped in a dirty puddle and slime came through the sole of his laceless boot. He felt things begin to move inside his shirt, and gritted his teeth. He clutched his roll of dollars inside his greasy trouser pocket.

The building was high, with the floors and windows of an institution. They went through an arched entrance in the wall, their boots slapping. A queue of ragged men and women were slowly passing through a door.

'I'll pay,' Valerian muttered. 'It's only fifteen kopecks each. Don't show your *valuta*, whatever you do.'

A vile stench came seeping out of the doorway and engulfed Nichols as they went inside. A man was taking the pitiful handfuls of kopecks at a desk set under a bare bulb, another in uniform was segregating the inmates with an experienced eye, sending them to corridors left and right, or up one of two different stone stairways.

'They do their best,' Valerian murmured. 'They try to keep the simply poor away from the criminals and the diseased.'

They were sent up one of the staircases, the guard giving Nichols a sharp glance as he followed.

'What's with him? he asked Valerian.

'You look wrong. Wrong colour, wrong face. You've been eating good food.'

They emerged on to a landing and the floor beneath their feet was wet and slippery with grime. The whole of one side was taken up by a barracks of hard cots, and on them were cripples. Men without legs and without arms, paralysed ones who lay in strange postures, blind ones sitting still, hunchbacks lying in grotesque attitudes on the planks. The groaning of pain added itself to the growling and cursing of the criminals below. Across the way was a similar long dormitory of women. Haggard things lay apathetic, half naked in rags upon the cots. Some had filthy babies at their breasts, and infants crawled amongst the refuse on the floor. Some younger women still possessed of a little vitality saw Nichols' shocked stare, and hurled abuse. Valerian led the way up a further flight of stairs and into a smaller room, where the inmates had pulled some of the cots together in one corner to form a platform, and were sitting about on it, leaning against the walls. Nichols saw them look up as they came in, with eyes as sharp as crows.

A pretty woman was in the corner, sitting between two young people, a boy and a girl, both teenagers. She was reading a book with the boy. With his journalist's memory Nichols recognised her – it was Nadia, Valerian's fellow guide, and the boy was clearly their son. The two were taking turns to read a page from the book out loud while the others listened. Nichols suddenly realised he was hearing the story of

Huckleberry Finn in Russian. When it came to his mother's turn to read the boy, blond and handsome, but thin, closed his eyes to shut out reality, and return to the raft, Huck and the Mississippi. The girl sitting next to Nadia kept her eyes closed all the time, screwed up as though in pain. She was strikingly pretty.

Valerian slid himself on to the platform with a strangely practised movement.

'Come and join us,' he murmured, and Nichols clambered up. The smell was gamey, but he fitted himself in between a long-haired peasant and an unshaven man in a manager's dark suit, marked with grease and mud. On the other side of him was a tall man in the coal-blackened trousers and jacket of one who rode the footplate on the railway. Valerian fished inside the bagged serge jacket and withdrew a long, hard-skinned black sausage from the parcel Nichols had purchased at Yeliseyev's. With a sharp knife he began to cut it into carefully-equal lengths, beginning by slicing it in half. All about him Nichols could hear a sudden gulping as of a number of frogs at a pond, and realised that they were all salivating and swallowing. Valerian handed out the chunks, and they started to gnaw. In the corner, Nadia took a bookmark and slid it betwen the pages before tucking the book carefully inside her coat. She caught his eye, and raised her piece of sausage.

'Long life. Mr Nichols.'

'These people will talk to you,' Valerian said quietly.

There were just the four of them, the peasant, the manager, the railwayman and the girl. The girl spoke first.

'My name is Zabierska and I am a Pole, I come from Minsk, where there are many Poles, as it is close to the border. I had a sister. She was older than me and when our mother died she looked after me. We joined the Party in Minsk because Anna said it would make it easier to get food. I was a Pioneer, she was a *Komsomolka*. A Party official came from Moscow. He was friendly towards us and asked why such good Party girls stayed in Minsk. He said he could arrange for us to go to Moscow, that he could get a job for Anna, that we could have an apartment.

'Anna said we should go. In Minsk we were often hungry, and there was little work, so we went to Moscow when he sent the papers. He kept his word. One day he invited us both to a celebration at the Party headquarters. There were about twenty men there, all Party officials. There was much food, and much to drink. And when they had eaten and drunk they raped us . . . Then they let us go. We had never been with men before. The next week the man ordered us to come again, and in the morning I found Anna dead. She had hanged herself in the night. I ran away, and now I pay fifteen kopecks a night to sleep here. When I have spent my money I shall have to sell myself on the street to live, for I am a person who does not exist. If I had money I would go to Poland, for I know the sisters of St Theresa, and they would take me in to be a nun.'

Valerian looked up.

'She doesn't mean roubles. Johnny. The rouble is a jolly currency to travel with, everyone laughs at it. She needs *valuta*.'

'How much?' he asked quietly. From the depths came the sounds of shouting and blows, followed by a gurgling shriek.

'A hundred dollars will get her to the border and across into Poland.'

Nichols reached in his pocket and peeled off the notes. The girl's eyes were still shut and he handed the money to Nadia, who gave it to her. Valerian produced a hard round cheese, and sliced it into segments.

The peasant propelled a chunk through his beard.

'I am a *muzhik*, I come from Mala Lepetykha which is in the Ukraine. People in my village gave me things – pots, some brass, a few coins, shoes, a coat – to carry and take outside for bread. I bought bread and put it in a sack but when I got to the station the guard would not let me take the bread. It was orders, he said, and they put me on the train without it. I went back to the village, but while I had been gone the *Buksyr* brigade had come and taken the very last of what we had, some grain for the chicken.

'My son, who was twelve, had fought them. And they killed him. My wife was already dead, for the head of the Soviet shot her one night while she was picking up ears of grain from the field. When I heard this news I returned the way I had come. I found the guard who had forbidden me to take the bread and bade him give it to me. He laughed at me, and had me thrown from the station. I waited until he left that night and I killed him as he walked home. I took his money and I was able to travel here where I beg on the street. If I had money I would go to the Black Sea. I met a man who lived in a village there. He said it was many *versts* from Moscow. A man with money could buy a small boat there and catch fish.'

'I don't understand this . . .' Nichols said in a bewildered voice.

The peasant made a noise that was wholly contemptuous, and he felt himself flush. 'He's foreign,' said the peasant. 'He knows nothing.'

Silently, Nichols peeled off dollars, and it vanished into the man's coat. With it secreted away he folded his arms, closed his eyes and went to sleep.

They were ready, each of them. By the side of the manager the man in the coal-dusted clothes brushed his hand over his face. It was big and bony, and the fingers were deeply stained with yellow nicotine, like those of the peasant. The skin bore innumerable tiny white scars, the marks of flying embers. He was a fireman, one who shovelled in the coal to feed the hungry boiler. He began to speak.

'I am Ioakim, who was called a hero of the revolution. My master, Trotsky, who was People's Commissar for War, gave me that title when he pinned the medal to my shirt. I it was who kept steam in his train. We travelled every length of track in the Soviet Union while my master won the war for the Bolsheviks, and these arms, these hands shifted the coal from the bunker into the furnace; these arms carried my master's train.

'When the war was won we were given good jobs, we who had served him. Much work was to be done, to repair what had happened in the war. I myself it was who commanded the crews who rebuilt the Odessa line. We were proud of our revolutionary heritage – that was what our master said – and each year we gathered here in Moscow to celebrate, all those of us who had been on the train, and each year our master Trotsky would join us in the fine restaurant he had arranged for us. The finest food and drink was there, for he knew of these things, and provided us with them.

'In the year twenty-seven we joined our master on the streets of Moscow to protest at the policies of Djugashvili, who calls himself Stalin. He used troops against us – we, who were heroes of the revolution. Him, who never heard a shot fired by the enemy. Our master was sent into exile, and those of us who had been with him on the train met only in secret. Last year when we met for our dinner we were few. The missing had gone, taken away by the NKVD. It was on the orders of him, Stalin.

'He went for the officers first, those who had been our master's handpicked men on the train, ready to take command of troops wherever we should halt. Then those who had served the radio, run the printing presses, loaded the ammunition, driven his car, manned the artillery and machine guns. They even came for his valet. One day I was walking to work and one passed me by, saying the NKVD were waiting at the works offices, and I did not go to work, but ran away, for he, Stalin, had come for me too. Now I hide in this place. They will find me, soon enough, unless I can escape. If I had money, I would go far away, *za-granitsei*, beyond the borders where my master is. I served him once, and would serve him again.'

Silently, Nichols counted out the *valuta* and handed it over. Like the peasant, the railwayman folded up his arms, and went to sleep against the wall.

'My name is Barshai,' said the manager. 'I am a Jew from Kishinev. I joined the Bolshevik Party in the year nineteen. Under the Tsar, we suffered and I learned to know what *Bei Zhidov* meant before I could say Mama. Crush the Jews, crush the Jews. My father was killed by a mob during Passover. They called it the *zhid*-hunting season. My mother and sister were raped by the mob the Bishop of Kishinev had blessed. My father tried to stop them and they cut off his balls and stamped him to death.

'The Bolsheviks made me a commissar in the civil war and they sent me back to Kishinev. When we were short of bullets I crushed the windpipes of my enemies with my fingers and they crackled like eggshells. When I found clergy, I cut off their balls. When the war was over I was sent to help in industry. It was the days of NEP, the new economic policy, and they needed specialists to make things run – party slogans alone did not do the job. The director put me at his side, because I understood figures, and he, a peasant, did not. "It's good to have a *zhid* about, Leon," he used to say to me. "*Zhids* know about money." He used the same word that those who murdered my family had used, for he knew no other way to say Jew.

'In the year twenty-nine we heard that it was the year of *perelom*, the year of the great break with the past. Comrade Stalin had decreed it so. Heavy industry was to be the key, the proof of the superiority of communism over the decadent capitalist West. We were sent instructions. It was not the task of we the managers to study economics but to change them. There were no fortresses which Bolsheviks could not storm. The new norms followed. It was to me, his *stolkachi* that the director turned, and I who fixed things for him. By reduction in the quality of the steel we were able to raise the quantity. By paying the workers less we were able to buy in more. Storm the two million *pood* barrier! Overfulfil! Overfulfil! It was I who arranged for a suitable shock-worker to produce two thousand tons of steel in a shift. We supported him with thirty other workers and he took the credit. They were pleased, in Moscow. They paraded him about and he died from drinking too much vodka.

'The time came when even I could not make the books balance, and I heard the director talking to the party secretary. They knew of the trials; they knew that they could save their skins if they found

Wreckers to blame. "Take the *zhid*," the director urged. "Blame it on the *zhid*." And I heard them preparing the charges against me. I was to be sacrificed for their special shops, their dachas, the special schools for their children, their automobiles, their privilege. I, the *zhid*. They murdered my family and they were going to murder me. Nothing had changed. I ran and here I am, in this place.'

It was dark in the room, Nadia had snuffed out the candle-stub and her son lay sleeping with her arm about him.

'If I had money I would be like him, this one who snores against me and shovelled coal for Trotsky, I would travel *za-granitsei* far across the borders, I would go to America, where they know that economics is economics, not bloody fairy tales.'

The notes rustled in the dark and Nichols felt the hand take them, heard the Jew settle himself as best he could against the wall.

'Valerian?' he called softly.

'Yes, Johnny?'

'Is that it? Can we go home?'

'This *is* home,' the Russian said softly. 'I, Nadia and Petrick spend our nights here. We are hiding, like all of these people. We are hiding from a man who wants to kill us.'

'Oh, Jesus . . .' Nichols found himself almost sobbing. 'If some-one's trying to kill you, why don't you go to the police?'

'The man who wants to kill us,' Valerian explained calmly. 'He *is* a policeman.'

18

Dom Leninskiye

IN the early light Nichols glanced back. People were seeping out of the institution, grey in the morning, moving listlessly along the street. An image of a great tank oozing effluent stuck in his mind and he turned and hastened away with Valerian.

Where they were making the metro, pumps and compressors were belching blue smoke into the air. A group of workers were silently hefting tools under the bleak gaze of their guards and Nichols looked at them with changed eyes.

'It's a chain gang, isn't it, Valerian? Who are those guys?'

'Peasants. Undesirables. Former people. People with an apartment, wife or job that someone else wants.'

In Red Square the beggars were lined along the GUM. They passed by, and Isaak Gunzberg smiled at him without speaking. Nichols felt Isaak was mocking him.

As they crossed towards the mausoleum in its scaffolding cladding they saw Yelena slipping through the shoals of official *sluzachy*, and the groups of wide-eyed tourists.

'Sleep well?' she asked.

'No,' Nichols said quietly. 'I did not.'

'I'll leave you,' murmured Valerian. 'Best not to hang about.'

He took the small parcel Yelena gave him and was gone.

'I was going to give him some money,' Nichols cried.

'Oh, you will,' Yelena assured him. 'Come on. As he says, it's best not to hang about where you can be seen.'

They started to walk, and Yelena paused to let a group of tourists through. They were led by a large, florid, mid-Western American in a dog collar, and they stood staring reverently at the tomb.

'We're here,' their preacher said earnestly. 'Here in Red Square, in Soviet Russia. We're here at a unique moment in time. They don't come very often – the last was almost two thousand years ago. Why the Lord God has chosen the Russians and their Bolsheviks this time and not we Americans is His mystery, just as much as why He chose the Jews last time. Forget all the irreligious talk the Marxists indulge in. That's not what counts. It's their philosophy of life, and here we have men creating a unified philosophy of life that a whole people can live by. While we Americans cast about in the dark, seeking the true way, the Russians and their leaders are working through the very tenets of the New Testament itself to create a new, and Christian world. Now let us bow our heads in prayer to Jesus and his new prophet, Lenin.'

Nichols felt Yelena's hand on his arm, and started to walk again. 'More of your extras, Yelena?'

'Not mine. They are here all the time. They are pilgrims and they delight in anything that they are shown. Earnest advocates of proportional representation eagerly agree with the necessity for the dictatorship of the Proletariat as soon as it is explained to them. Earnest pacifists watch military parades in delighted approval. Earnest clergymen carry home bagfuls of atheistic literature to distribute to their delighted congregation.'

'But they believe they are witnessing the birth of a new world, Yelena,' Nichols burst out. 'They *mean* well.'

'They are projecting the dissatisfaction they feel with their own society to unquestioning approval of anything that happens in ours,' Yelena said coldly. 'This country is mine and she is a woman. She lies naked, because she is forced to. These foreigners come here in their thousands and they think that she lies there for their pleasure and for hers, but she lies there in suffering and pain and the Bolshevik pimp is hiding behind the door and what is happening is not making love, but rape.'

'I realise that hideous things have happened,' Nichols protested. 'But it doesn't mean that under wise leadership a new and just order may not emerge.'

'You're doing what they do – saying that the glorious end justifies the Bolshevik means? You don't understand. There is no end, only the means. You haven't understood where you are, Johnny. You spent one night in the *Dom Nochlyega*. It is a terrible place – but we all live here in the *Dom Leninskiye*.'

She waved a small hand about her.

'Here it is, the house that Lenin built. It's bigger now, but he laid all the foundations. They are made out of bones and broken dreams, from layer upon layer of lies, from tyranny and terror without end. They support walls that bear pretty paintings on the outside, and gargoyles and demons within. Inside the house is vast and empty except for the gigantic altar, upon which human sacrifice is conducted day and night, without cease.'

She turned on Nichols.

'This is it,' she snarled. '*This* is what you hallucinate over. The house that Lenin built. There was never any chance that it would be occupied by the wise men of your babblings. Where would they come from? He and his heirs have killed them off, and we are left with the Zinovievs and Kamenevs, the Bukharins and Trotskys, the party bosses and moral relativists, mass murderers all. But we do not even have rule by one of these. No. It is Josef Stalin who is in charge.

'And Josef Stalin is mad.'

'The District Party Committee closed the school, and my father arranged for me to work for Stefan Lykashenko, who was a cousin in the Department of Agriculture in Poltava. He was pleased to have me, for although I was only fourteen I was skilled with figures.'

They were drinking a tea Yelena had made from various plant leaves gathered and dried for use. Tatyana cupped her mug between her hands as if still needing the warmth and the two fingers closest to her thumb that he could see were deeply stained with nicotine.

'Why did they close the school?'

'They said we were individualists, for we would not give them our belongings and join the *kolkhoz*, the collective farm. The village Soviet they abolished, for our families served there, and in its place they put Timofey Vasilyevich and the Committee of Unwealthy Peasants. They came in the night and stole cattle, driving them off to the *kolkhoz*, and the next day the women of the village, led by my mother, went to get them back. Without the cows the children would have no milk. The Party officials were afraid when they saw women with clubs and hid, and Timofey Vasilyevich and his unwealthy peasants ran away, for my mother was going to tie him to a donkey's tail and beat him. So we got the cattle back. But after that they called us individualists, and closed the school, and the postmen stopped bringing letters.'

Tatyana paused to sip tea, which she did with relish. Nichols had found his undrinkable.

'However, we were pleased with the *babski bunty*, the rebellions of women, and we hoped that we should be left alone. They came next with men from the Fire Brigade, and Timofey Vassileyvich and the Unwealthy Peasants, and began to set fire to the church. We drove them out, all of us, and put out the fire. But after that their corn mill did not grind our grain, and they came and took the blacksmith in the night. My father found me the job with Stefan Lykashenko. He was a good man, one of us, not a Russian. He told me the ways the Russians were using to force the peasants into the collectives; how they broke men by tax, demanding more than they owned. They did this to Anton Andreyevich, the husband of Masha. When he could not pay he was arrested and . . . disappeared. His house was taken by Timofey Vasilyevich of the Unwealthy Peasants. Rather than be with him Masha took her four children to the house of her aunt, and they lived in a barn.

'Decrees prohibited everything. They arrested the men who tanned skins and if you owned a hand-mill or a press they took you away and you were never seen again. Those who sang the songs of the Kobzars, the songs of the Ukraine, were taken away. One day I went home, and found our houses burned, and my family dead. They were naked, for the Unwealthy Peasants had taken their clothes. I wanted to bury them, for they were being eaten by the cats and crows, but I was driven away by Timofey Vasilyevich and his friends, who sat drinking vodka. They threw stones at me, and I went back to Poltava.'

She rubbed a red scar across her forehead.

'By the spring, the people were beaten. We gave up what we had left and went to the kolkhoz. We realised that we were to be serfs, as our grandfathers had been. But it was better than being killed, far away in the cold north. And, that year, we tried to make the collective farm work. However, the kolkhoz was run by officials from the party, and the Machine Tractor Station was in the charge of the OGPU. During the summer, all the chickens and half the pigs died. Many horses died, and the tractors broke down. But some fields were tilled, and sown, and crops grew. When the autumn came, the harvest was gathered in.'

Katyana looked up from her tea for the first time.

'I am interested in figures, Mr Nichols. I like to know how things work. With the harvest in, we found out how the kolkhoz works. No grain is kept for the kolkhoz workers until the government's share is given up and the government pays for this grain at its own price. Last year these were twenty-five times lower than grain prices on the free market. The government charges for the use of its tractors and grain mills, but these prices are not low, and are paid in grain.

'The kolkhoz is called an agricultural factory. The workers have to be paid. They are paid by "labour-days", an amount of work – the ploughing of a hectare of land, or the threshing of a ton of grain. Several real days of work are required to fulfil it.'

'Do you recognise this, Johnny?' Yelena asked mildly. 'It's called piece-work. Much inveighed against in communist circles. Before October 1917, that is.'

'The cost of the food ration is deducted from the "pay" for the labour days. When the harvest is finally in, the workers are paid. In kind, not money. A truckload of flimsy shoes and some poor cotton clothes arrives, after the grain has been taken away. There is no food available for the people once it has gone. Stefan took me out into the countryside and there were starving – and dead – people. People living on bark, grass and roots. For the grain that would have fed them had been taken away by the government.'

'Has Tatyana made it clear enough, Johnny? You do understand why it has been constructed this way?' asked Yelena. 'The peasant continues to do the labour of agriculture, but no longer has any control over the output. The new system is inefficient and expensive, and produces less, but the state is willing to accept this in exchange for total control over the crop and the people who produce it. Furthermore, the shrinkage in the crop size is made up for in part by not giving the peasant any of it. The peasants survive by cultivating their own small plots of land, which the government taxes both in money and in kind. The collective farming system has been imposed as a method of extraction by and for the state of grain and other products, combined with the enserfment of the peasant class, whom the Bolsheviks have seen as their enemies since well before the end of the Civil War.'

Nichols made no comment, simply shook his head despairingly, and Tatyana took up her story again.

'The OGPU came for Stefan at his home one night. They took his wife as well, and the children. I heard them and hid in a cupboard. When they had gone I decided to try to go to Moscow, to my Aunt Yelena. I took documents, and planned to say I was a messenger from the Commissariat of Agriculture. I had padded clothes and, as Stefan had been a fisherman, I took some hooks, and line.

'It took me a long time. The land was largely deserted, and weeds were everywhere, black and rotting in the winter. No smoke came from the chimneys of the huts, there was no vodka being made, no meat, no fish being smoked. The farmers lay dead in their huts with their families. Once I met a woman who was eating a child. It was her own . . . She offered to sell me some of the child, if I had money.

'I saw the grain that had been taken from the farms. It was piled up in great heaps at the railway stations awaiting transport. Barbed wire and guards surrounded it and they shot people every night, trying to get some. Often it steamed with smoke, from the fermentation inside, but even when it was useless, they would not let the peasants have any.

'In a village a woman approached me, a Party official. Although I was thin, I was not starved like the girls of the villages. She said that there was something I could do that would get me some food. Special foreign visitors were due to come that day, to see the local collective farm and they were short of people, for the farm workers were too thin to be put on show. I could go and receive some food for doing it. I was very hungry, and went. As we passed, they were gathering up the dead from the streets, and driving the beggars and starving away into the woods.

'We were to sit down in the dining hall which was finely furnished, with furniture from a theatre, someone said. There were splendid curtains and tablecloths and vases of flowers and we sat down among the party members and OGPU agents, who were dressed in farm clothes, along with the fittest of the workers. When the visitors arrived the meal was served, big pieces of meat, cabbage, potatoes, beet and gravy, with bread and beer. A man and a woman were shown around by the OGPU chief, who was presented as the kolkhoz director. They were English and very pleased and impressed by what they saw. They left to inspect the grain silos and the kolkhoz nursery school, where the children of the *apparatchiks* had been placed. But once they had gone the party men began loading up all the props on to trucks, to be taken back to Kiev.

'I was afraid to stay, for I had seen how the Party officials looked at me, and while they were taking the furniture away I slipped out through their offices. I found some tins of tobacco, which I took, together with some books. Then I set off through the woods. Outside the town I came across a barn. Inside were about two hundred children, like skeletons. They made a terrible sound, moaning for food. They were between two and twelve years old. A man was nearby and I asked what they were doing there. He said that it was the local orphanage. The Party sent a cart each morning, bringing children who had been gathered up, and taking away the corpses.

'I found another man by an old manure heap. He said that grains of corn could often be found, which had passed through the animals, and also earthworms. I found that he was right and so I survived into the spring. When I was very hungry I would make a cigarette from the tobacco rolled in a leaf of a book, and smoke it. It was better, then. I was close to the frontier, but it was guarded. I was surprised one morning while fishing in a stream by some young party *apparatchiks*. One of them was the boy Nikolai, who rescued me, and brought me here.' Katyana, her tale ended, looked directly at Nichols. 'Is there anything else you would know?'

Nichols had found her lack of emotion, her dry way of talking particularly terrible.

'How did you grieve?' he asked. 'For your family.'

'You cannot weep,' she said evenly. 'It attracts suspicion.'

Yelena glanced out of the window. The sun was shining.

'Go and join Alexei and Natalia in the garden. I saw two tomatoes that were ripe this morning so share them between you and then when I come down we'll all go to the station and meet your Uncle Ivan.'

Katyana went out, pausing at the bookshelf to take a volume with her. She took a home-twisted cigarette from her pocket and lit it and they smelled the coarse tobacco.

'She's very clever,' Yelena said proudly. 'I work with her in the evening and the weekends, the same as I do with Alexei and Natalia. They teach them ridiculous things at school, that all language is made up from the sounds *rosh, sal, ber* and *yon*, that there are no laws of economics, that you can turn a pine tree into an oak. I spend all my time trying to undo the damage.'

'She's an extraordinary young girl,' said Nichols shaken and profoundly moved. 'I couldn't have survived like that when I was her age.'

'You did understand what she was saying? This famine in the Ukraine is not an accident. It has happened because Stalin wanted it to happen, because he organised it to ensure that the people starved and died.'

Nichols sat silent.

'It isn't sane,' he said finally. 'All of this . . . these are the actions of madmen. There is no sense in it all . . . It's not even efficient, it's just mad.'

'That's right . . .' Yelena said softly. 'It is mad. All of it . . . What government on earth declares war upon its own citizens? Who will feel safe after this? When the ruler machine-guns whole communities, perverts the minds of children, wipes out the culture of centuries. The Kobzars, the blind bards are dead, you know, Stalin had them invited to a Ukrainian national convention and, when they were all there, had them shot. Millions have died from starvation. Millions more are crippled. And for what? He thinks that he can overcome all simply by making people live in fear, but fear is not a creative emotion. Fearful people will spend other people's lives to protect their own. Even the Mad Hatter would not be able to make sense of it. Although the Red Queen might.'

'*Alice in Wonderland*,' Nichols murmured. Through the open window they could hear the voices of the children below. 'But the Red Queen was mad.'

'Yes, Johnny. And so is Stalin. Forget all the talk of "leaders", Johnny. All the foreigners awash with delight for this new society they think we are building love to talk about "leaders". I think they believe the Kremlin is full of them, stern yet benevolent, wise and all-knowing, charting a course for this great ship of state. *Rubbish*. None of the old Bolsheviks were benevolent, and none of them could chart a course beyond next week for a revolutionary splinter faction, let alone a nation, and Stalin's seen them all off anyway. What you have is one man's rule and Stalin is insane.'

She went to a drawer of the table, and took out a thin buff folder. 'This is not simply my view.' She opened the file. Inside were some sheets of foolscap, covered with writing in black ink. 'These are the notes of Professor Vladimir Bekhterev, who was the leading neuro-pathologist of the Soviet Union. He came to Moscow in December 1927 for an international scientific conference. I saw him a few days after the conference, recommended by a doctor who had been a pupil of his. He agreed to see me in his hotel room as a favour to Doctor Andreyev. I suffered, and still suffer, from rather violent headaches, and we thought he might be able to help. But I was not the only patient to talk to him during his visit. As a result of questions he was asking me I had a turn, an attack, and, as a way of distracting me, he talked about this patient, although not by name. After I had recovered I had a drink with him, and prepared to leave. The telephone rang for him, and I let myself out. Coming up the stairs as I opened the door was a man called Rykov. Rykov is an officer of the OGPU, one of Stalin's personal gang. He *terrifies* me. In addition to his official functions as a secret policeman Rykov hunts and murders certain people for his own amusement. He is pursuing Valerian and Nadia and he has killed others of my friends.'

Her grey eyes looked searchingly at him. 'Do you believe me? If you don't, I won't go on, for there will be no point.'

'I believe you,' Nichols said sincerely. 'There is nothing you have told me that I don't now believe.'

'When I saw Rykov I ran back inside, closing the door behind me. Professor Bekhterev was still on the telephone and did not see me. Rykov, who was dressed as a waiter, knocked on the door. I hid, and Bekhterev let him in.

'Now, you may go and check the records. They will tell you that Professor Bekhterev suffered a fatal heart attack in his hotel room on that day. That may be so. I do not know how the poison he breathed in works, but it had the smell of bitter almonds and it came from the fountain pen Rykov held up to his face. He died on the spot. Rykov went out immediately and I did not call help, for the Professor was dead. I simply knew I must not be associated with him so I took my medical file – in fact, I took the handful there was in his bag – and ran away by the back stairs. Among the files was this one.'

She put the open file flat on the kitchen table, where Nichols was sitting. 'How's your Russian?'

'I speak better than I read, Yelena, You help me.'

Yelena pulled up her own chair and began to read the file.

'This morning I had an interview with Josef Stalin. My name had come to his attention following the praise heaped upon me by the foreign delegates at the conference and, in my conceit, I thought that in desiring to meet me he had merely wished to acquire a little of the glow that surrounds suddenly famous people. I now know differently. What I learned during the interview worries me so greatly I am writing up the notes, in the hope that the process will help me decide what to do.

'He is a small man and I believe this to be most important. He is unimpressive to look at, ungainly and with a stiff and shortened left arm. While his mind is alert he is not at ease with intellectual abstractions – strangely so for an Old Bolshevik, a group whose complicated and tortuous discussions of the finer meanings of Marx must resemble Mediaeval religious dogma more than scientific laws. Once again, I believe these things to be important. Stalin is a man who holds a grudge and acts of revenge are both very important and very satisfying to him. He told me so. A perfect day for Stalin is the detailed planning and meticulous execution of revenge for a long-held grudge, after which he would go peacefully to bed at home. Stalin feels keenly – to the point of misery and pain – those things in which he feels lesser than other men: his height, his build, his appearance, his intellectual powers. This gives him very many people against whom he is able to hold a grudge. If one adds to this list all those who, whatever their mental and physical capabilities, are able to conduct a satisfying social and family life, the list must be considered very large indeed.

'Stalin likes the company of criminals. He approves of their attitude of mind and he dislikes all those who adhere to the rule of law.

'He believes himself to be a man marked out from all living others by History. I say "living", for Lenin is dead, and this sense of being one of the chosen few, or the elect, which he tells me he has felt from a relatively early age, appears to have crystallised around the ambition to be, and be seen as, the successor and equal of Lenin.

'He combines a powerful will with an almost complete lack of human sympathy. He was able to survive three years as a Tsarist exile in the frozen wastes of Siberia with almost no human company. Any recognition that other people feel hope, love or pain appears to have been eradicated by this sense of mission that he feels. He is the agent of History and such a mandate justifies anything, and everything.

'In clinical terms, such beliefs clearly come under the headings of megalomania, and delusions of grandeur.

'Stalin is as firmly convinced that his enemies abound around him as he is of his role in History. He is chronically suspicious, and extremely ready to strike against those he feels are against him. Since many of those who have begun to suspect his true nature *are* against him, this provides the vital nucleus of fact with which to buttress his delusions.

'Josef Stalin is a typical case of severe paranoia and such people are extremely dangerous. They will strike against anything which disturbs the image of themselves they have constructed, and which threatens to cause painful emotions of self-questioning or self-reproach. Their delusional system is unshakeable – they *know* that God, or History, speaks to them and they listen. It is encapsulated, and does not impair other mental functions. Latent, and in the process of construction in youth, it appears in middle age. The particularly severe attacks that are so dangerous for others appear to be provoked by external situations and difficult situations, and follow a wave pattern, flaring up and then falling away again until the next wave arrives.

'The personal effects upon a severe paranoic tend to be displaced upon public objects. That is, other people. The paranoid person will attack other people. They commit murder. And the act does not necessarily come out of a clear blue sky. The paranoic *knows* what he means to do, and there are many instances of someone else knowing about it in advance, because the paranoic had told them about it.

'I am very fearful, and very worried. It appears to me that I am that person. Josef Stalin invited me to speak with him from a desire to tell someone about himself, to justify what he is about to do. Opposition, alternative views have to be crushed. Who better to crush than an intellectual whose whole field is the mind, and its pathology?

'It appears inevitable that such a man would be able to capture the leadership of the communist Soviet Union. Communism, as a system, is itself paranoid, its construction of Party and Secret Police is conspiratorial; it cannot exist without enemies. If it can cause these to exist, well and good, if it cannot, it will invent them – it invented the *bourgeoisie* – in order to continue its existence. It requires hate objects as much as human beings need food, water and air.

'Josef Stalin is about to commit murder. The wave is building. It may be a year, it may be two, but he will do it. Who the victim or victims will be I do not know. Once started, the cycle of murder committed by the paranoic continues, at intervals, until they are caught.

'But who do I tell? The lunatic is not in the cell, he is in charge. Who is to catch him? *Who do I tell?*

Yelena closed the file, and she and Nichols stared at each other.

'Bekhterev was the first victim,' she said. 'The peasants followed.'

'Who the hell do *we* tell, Yelena?'

'The West. You write your book and we'll tell them that way. It matters to Stalin what the West thinks. Truly enormous effort is put into duping the Westerners. They are shown elaborate stage sets and productions. Flaws in the system that cannot be covered up are shown to be the fault of wreckers and spies. While Stalin can point to the West's approval – all the pilgrims who come here – he can justify what he does. So we must tell them the truth. Before the next wave comes.'

'Good God, Yelena. Who's next?'

'Anyone,' she said bleakly. 'Everyone . . .'

19

Bezprizorny

Berlin, May 1933

THEY came down the Ku-Damm, the great White Way. In the morning light it was quiet, the famous neon lights that lit up the sky for miles dormant, the cabarets, clubs and restaurants tightly closed.

'We're not staying, are we?' asked Nikolai, sitting next to her in the Opel taxi.

'No, darling,' Ruth said patiently. There was a bottle of mineral water in the kitchen, only it held gin. She thought she might send him out to get a couple of *Amerikaners* for breakfast, the iced buns he liked. There would be time just for a glass, a small one, simply to settle her stomach.

'And we're not going back to Russia?'

'Darling, how many times? No, and no. We are going to live in London.'

'Then why are we here?' he asked, and smiled charmingly at his mother. 'Now we're here, you can tell me. It's not just to shut up the apartment.'

The terrible row with Savinkov. His shrug, and turned back, knowing she had won a final victory.

'If we want to go to live in London we have to get the money,' she said openly, and at last. 'Otherwise we live with daddy in Paris. Or become *bezprizorny*. We don't want to be waifs without a home, do we? The money's here and your father's afraid to come and get it, so I'm going to do it.'

'He's always talking about storming the Palace!' Nikolai said scornfully.

'He was there,' she admitted. 'He followed along behind somewhere.'

They turned on to Unter den Linden. Chestnut blossom and coffee laced the air.

'It's changed,' he said, as alert as an animal. She leaned forward in her seat, and reached in her bag for a cigarette.

'You're right, I think. But what makes you say so?'

'At the station, the brownshirts went past and people gave the Nazi salute. Not the sort you would expect.'

They had. Respectable people in suits. She had sensed fear behind the smiles of approval for the young men they regarded as scum, long-term unemployables recruited in the party soup kitchens and given uniforms and exciting power.

'They aren't here,' said Nikolai, looking about.

'Who?'

'Daddy's sort. The communists.'

'No . . .'

The windows were sprinkled with pink and yellow. *Jude*, quarantine stars.

'Let's have some breakfast at a café,' she said, and called the taxi to a halt.

'It's too early to have a drink anyway, Mama,' he said pleasantly, taking the bags.

'Darling, you are becoming much too clever for your own good,' she said, and led the way to the café. She ordered coffee, rolls, jam.

'Let me call Krivitskiy,' she said. As she got up, she glanced around again, struck by a strange sense of *déjà vu*. Then she had it: it had vanished from the streets, the *zivilisation*, the *Geist* that Weimar had permitted. Josephine Baker would not be dancing, the *Weltbuhne* was not on sale. The Jew Tucholsky was not jabbing with his pen, inciting the Easterners. The colourful people had gone like a lost tribe, just as the streets of Petrograd had cleared of the bourgeois . . .

When she came back to the table the breakfast had arrived.

'He wasn't there,' she said. 'I called the number where he was living with Marthe and her little girl. Elisabeth. Elisabeth answered the phone. The Nazis have been arresting all the communists. Krivitskiy was undercover, but two men from Goering's new police, the Gestapo, came and took him away.'

Nikolai frowned. 'I'm longing to go somewhere they don't come to take people away.'

'That was last week. Marthe went out the next day to try to find him, and Elisabeth hasn't seen her since. I've told her to come here.'

She came down the street like an animal. Nikolai knew the look, too well. He got up and held out a chair. She was young, only ten years old in a pinafore dress, Ruth ordered hot chocolate for her.

'Darling,' she said, 'your aunt Ruth knows just everybody in Berlin so I'm going to find out where your mummy is, and get her. I'm going to go to the bank and get some money, and then, while I'm finding out where your mummy is I want you to go with Nikolai and look for a car, a good second-hand car. A Mercedes. Elisabeth, darling, where did your mummy go?'

'Prinz Albrecht Strasse,' whispered the girl. 'They have their office there, where the old craft school was. I went, but the SA is outside, they chased me away.'

'Let me make some phone calls.'

She left them finishing breakfast in the morning sun, and went inside to the pay telephone. When she came back she smiled brilliantly at the little girl.

'I've found someone who can find your mummy. He's going to meet me here in a little while.' She glanced at Nikolai. 'Werner Hoffman. One of Diels' Prussian Justice Ministry officials. I know him because of his wife. She has . . . expensive tastes.'

She took some money from her bag and gave it to her son. 'Take a taxi now and go and look for a car. I'll meet you back at the apartment. But first I want you to take Elisabeth along to Wertheimer's. She looks as though she needs a new dolly. Don't you, darling?'

The little girl beamed. Her mother's friend, beautiful, capable, smiling, was some kind of goddess.

When the children had gone off Ruth walked down the tree-lined boulevard to the bank. They knew her there and she went down with the incorruptible official and opened the deposit box. Much of the money sent in solidarity with Russian and world workers had been spent, in one way or another that was beneficial to the world's first and only communist state; some of the rest had ended up here, like rich sediment.

It had been chosen for ease of movement. A handful of gold sovereigns, for liquidity. A gold cigarette case. A small sheaf of share certificates. A wad of large-denomination dollars and pounds. A washleather bag of cut diamonds. A short-barrelled Colt revolver and a box of ammunition.

She was able to stow it all away in her bag and went back to the café. Soon afterwards, a man got out of a taxi and joined her. He bowed, and kissed her hand.

'Countess,' he murmured.

She ordered a beer for him and another coffee for her. He was in his thirties, with the livid tribal markings of a duelling corps on his cheeks.

'I've been on holiday, Werner,' she said casually. She was playing with a jewel in her hand, dropping it from her fingers into her palm and picking it up again. The facets flashed in the sunlight and he watched it, discreetly. 'A lot of people seem to be missing.'

'Communists,' he said, easily.

'So easy to pick up the wrong person, with so many arrests . . .'

'You're looking for Marthe Kovacs, Ruth,' he said shrewdly. 'We don't have her. It's chaotic. *We're* Goering's secret police, but there's Roehm's SA, and Himmler's SS, and there's more of them, and they don't like us. They go out and arrest people independently from us, and put them in their own cellars and camps. It's a mess. In fact, the SA have her.'

'But Marthe's not a communist! I've come to take her with me on holiday. She's just been arrested by mistake.' She held out the diamond. 'What do you think? That would suit Ilse's hand, wouldn't it? You could get it mounted by Goldmann who'd be happy to do the secret police a favour.'

Her hand closed over it again and she produced a wad of notes from her bag, passing them discreetly under the table. 'I'm sure you can get her from the SA. With the proper warrant, and some armed detectives.'

He took the money. 'I checked before I came. We have a note on her, for another file. On a man called Krivitskiy, a Russian. We think he's OGPU. Your friend was living with him.'

'What better cover for him than to be with an honest German citizen?' Ruth cried, in mock exasperation. 'I don't care about this Krivitskiy – just get Marthe from these frightful people!'

Ruth completed her morning by purchasing a second-hand Mercedes tourer that Nikolai had found. Elisabeth had bought a Tyrolean teddy bear and they had a picnic lunch at the apartment and the little girl pretended to feed him. Not long afterwards, the telephone rang.

'I'm going to get your mummy, darling,' she told Elisabeth after it and watched the small face light with joy. She took Nikolai with her to the door.

'If I don't come back, take my bag,' she said quietly. 'The valuable things are in it. Take the train to Paris with Elisabeth and join daddy. He will look after you, my darling.'

Then she went down to the Mercedes and drove to Prinz Albrecht Strasse. Armed SA men were on the door, but so was Werner Hoffmann, now in a black leather coat. She wondered what it was, that secret policemen so liked leather uniforms. He took her inside and the air smelled of paint and there was the sound of saws and hammers.

'You're planning on a long stay,' she observed. 'Now the opposition parties are illegal, are you really necessary?'

He turned to her in surprise. 'We are here to suppress subversive tendencies and activities. Those will not go away. We will always be able to find dangerous elements.'

'Enemies of the state,' she said, blandly. 'But why keep the SA and SS in business? They're paramilitary. There's no one to fight any more.'

'Their value lies in the fact that they spread terror. That is a wholesome thing,' he said seriously.

They were on the first floor. He paused outside a fresh-painted door and turned to her. 'Ah, was there . . .'

She took the diamond out of her pocket. 'Here it is, Werner.' She kept her voice even, holding her feelings in rigid check.

He took it smoothly, and gave her a signed and stamped pass. 'That'll get you out of the building but it would be best if you get her out of the country, Countess.'

'I'm going. Today.'

He turned to go along the corridor. Then, 'Oh, she may need to see a doctor . . .' he said and, seeming suddenly ashamed, hurried away. She opened the door. Marthe was slumped over a table. A man's shirt had been put on her. The sleeves were blue, the back dark with blood.

'It's Ruth. Marthe,' she said softly, and helped her up.

Marthe lifted pain-filled eyes to hers. 'They *liked* it. Ruth,' she whispered. 'When they took my clothes off I thought . . . But they didn't. It was the whips they wanted . . .'

Ruth felt the skin crawling on her stomach. She put Marthe's arm about her neck as gently as she could, and they went out, and down the corridor. Close to the stairs, she glanced behind her. Bloody footprints marked the sawdust on the floor. A workman was there, paintpot in hand, peering at the doors. He pushed one open. For a second, before he backed out, she saw inside the room. Krivitskiy was standing there, with Manfred Liss. Liss was in a black uniform and they were there together. They had glasses in their hands and they were laughing!

Marthe stumbled and Ruth held her up. When she looked back, the door was shut again. She got Marthe downstairs and into the car, where the tortured woman collapsed across the back seat. The SA men jeered as Ruth drove off.

There was a Jewish doctor she knew and she drove straight to his house. She waited as he dressed the fearful lacerations that had torn

Marthe's skin from her neck to her buttocks and after he'd given her a bottle of medicine to ease the pain and she'd taken some, they put her across the seat again.

'I'm getting her out,' Ruth said. 'You'd better go too, there is no future here.'

'It's only another pogrom,' the doctor said phlegmatically. 'We Jews are used to that.'

She drove back to the apartment. Freed of the pain, Marthe had fallen into a deep sleep. By the double doors with their glass and brass fittings Krivitskiy was standing. He looked inside at Marthe.

'Thank you for getting her,' he said simply. He hesitated. 'We need to get out of the country.'

'I'm going to Switzerland. With Marthe and the children.'

'Can I come?'

'How did you get free, Leon?' she said casually.

'I managed to convince them it was a case of mistaken identity.'

He stood on the pavement, unharmed.

'I got Marthe from Prinz Albrecht Strasse. A workman opened a door and I saw you. You were talking to Manfred Liss.'

Fear sprang into the metal-framed eyes.

'That's how I got away,' he said quickly. 'I know him.'

'I know him, too. I know *everybody* who matters.'

'Ruth! It doesn't matter what strings I pulled. It's the people back in Moscow. They mustn't know,' he pleaded. 'It's dangerous enough just living abroad. They examine you for contamination by foreign ideas, every time you go back. If they knew I'd been arrested . . .' He gestured inside the car. 'Marthe and Elisabeth, they're coming back with me . . . If the men in Moscow know about this, they will shoot us all.'

Ruth turned away, suddenly disgusted. 'And you want to go back to that? I'm going to London – you should too. But come with us, by all means.'

They drove south, with the warm breeze flowing in through the windows. They stopped for *schinken* on warm bread with butter and Ruth filled her flask with coffee and sipped it as she drove on through the night, while the others slept.

She crossed the Danube at Ulm in the dawn and, in the morning light, they were drinking coffee and eating rolls on the shores of the Badensee as she negotiated for the hire of a sailing boat. She left the Mercedes ostentatiously on show. They carried no luggage – this was simply a boating trip.

The long hours of sleep had revived Marthe and she was able to

climb into the boat without help, and sat near the stern. The others
scrambled in, and the owner pushed them off with a boathook, his
scepticism turning to relief as he saw how Ruth gathered tiller and
sheets together like a good horsewoman with the reins.

'How do you know how to do this?' Krivistkiy muttered nervously
as the first choppy waves tapped the sides.

'My father had a country estate. It had a boating lake on it and he
had little sailing boats made. We had competitions and it was such
fun . . .'

The breeze caught the canvas as they came from the shelter of the
land, and foam hissed at the prow.

'Better for everyone had we all stuck to messing about with boats,'
she said. 'Nikolai! The foresail.'

Across the glittering water was Switzerland.

'I could do with a beer, over there,' she remarked, to nobody in
particular.

New York

They stood, very polite and patient, the two parents and the son, in
the big draughty hall. From where they had come came the salty,
decaying smell of the docks, and the arrogant cawing of seagulls.
The immigration official slowly went through their papers, his jaws
moving steadily, and when he had finished looked up at them in
bewilderment.

'What are you doing here, buddy?'

'Are the papers in order?' Valerian asked anxiously.

'Yeah, yeah. All in order. But let me get it straight. You left Russia
last year and made your way through Europe to England. You had
friends there, got some work, saved your money while you applied for
immigration papers to come to the USA. And now here you are.'

'That is right, sir,' Valerian said, not understanding.

The man spread his hands uncomprehendingly. 'Why here? You
leave Russia for this? We got the worst times anybody seen here. The
Depression's on. My brother-in-law's out of work – he's a trained
machinist. He saw an ad to go work in Russia and I told him to jump
at it. Never got it. Six thousand, they wanted, a hundred thousand
applied. That must be a mighty fine place, for people to do that. A
new world. And you come here . . .?'

A frown had appeared on the immigration officer's forehead. 'Say
. . . hold on a minute.' He riffled through the papers. 'This John
Nichols that's sponsored you to live here. He a writer? You knew
him in Moscow?'

'Yes, sir.'

'Well, he sure didn't learn anything. He wrote this book, all about
Russia, said some really nasty things about them. Turns out it was all
lies! And you know what he done, back in Russia? They want him for
fraud, embezzlement, forgery and rape.'

Valerian could feel the anxiety radiating from Nadia, at the level
of pain.

'It does not invalidate the document, surely?' he asked fearfully.
From where he was standing he could just see Isaak de Gunzberg on
the other side of the barrier. He was wearing a new warm woollen
coat, and his face was pink in colour. The man with him would be
one of the Gottlieb brothers. On the other side of the barrier there
was food, and warm clothes.

'I guess not . . . he ain't charged under US law. Not yet, anyhow.
All right, buddy, you're in.'

'Thank you, sir.'

Valerian reached down to pick up their suitcase.

'Where are you headed?'

'California, sir. To Hollywood.'

'Hollywood? You want to get into the movies?'

'Yes sir. My wife and I, we are illusionists. We create fantasy.'

London

'Ready or not, here I come.'

Hidden in the huge cupboard Nikolai grinned to himself. All about
him was a mixture of scents both old and new. The smell of Berlin,
from his mother's clothes hanging up. The new smell of London, of
the cupboard itself, the carpets, the curtains, the smoky air outside.

'I'm coming to find you, ready or not . . .'

He giggled.

'Is Nikky here?'

He could hear his mother's voice close by and a floorboard
creaked.

'No, not here . . .'

A door squeaked.

'Is he here?'

It squeaked back again.

'Not here.'

He heard her soft footsteps, the laughter in her voice.

'*But is he –* '

The cupboard door swung open and, as it did, he jumped out.

'Boo!'

They collapsed laughing against each other.

'It's a good place for hide-and-seek, isn't it?' she said. They started to walk about the flat. Through the windows they could see the shiny black taxis, the red omnibuses, the cars and the lorries all busying themselves along Knightsbridge.

'Do you like it?' she asked.

'It's great.' he said enthusiastically. 'Do you remember James, from the Embassy in Berlin? He lives round the corner. I've got quite a few friends, in London.'

'I thought we'd go down to the school tomorrow, have a look around. It's not far – near Windsor.'

'All right. Will we get a car, Mama? How about a Rover?'

Ruth adjusted some ornaments on the sideboard, and he began to unpack a model glider from a teachest.

'You know, you're my best friend,' he said.

Ruth was immensely touched. 'Why, that's a lovely thing to say, darling. Why do you think that?'

'You just are. You never mind doing nice things with me, like playing hide-and-seek, or going fishing . . . Daddy never has time. He gives me some money instead.'

'Oh, well, your daddy likes playing other sorts of games, darling.'

'I know,' he said and grinned wryly. 'I see the girls in the morning. They're never the same . . . Don't you want to have any men friends? I wouldn't mind, honestly.'

'Me, darling?' Ruth laughed. 'No, I don't want any men friends.'

'But you're pretty.'

'That makes *them* want *me*, darling. *I* don't want them. I'd rather play hide-and-seek.'

'You like playing games. Why?'

'It's lovely to be a child,' she said quietly. 'Better than . . . if you have . . .'

He saw her eyes suddenly flood with tears, and she turned away, wiping them with her hand.

'Oh, look, you know what we've forgotten?' she said, in a muffled voice. 'The flat's as dry as the Sahara. I'll slip down to the off-licence and get something. Do you want a beer, darling?'

'I'll come with you,' he said quickly, and she smiled, and blew her nose.

'Don't you trust your mama?'

'Of course I do,' he said generously. 'I just want to come with you.'

'I'll tell you what. We'll go down and get some gin, and a few bottles of beer, and we'll have a tiny drink while we get ready, and then we'll go out and find a restaurant. What do you say?'

'Oh yes! Can I have a steak?'

She ruffled his hair. 'You can have steak. And let's take the glider tomorrow. We'll find a hill to fly it from. Yelena and I had gliders, you know. Piotr Sadovsky made them for us. I bet I can keep it in the air longer than you.'

'What kind of glider?' he demanded.

'Oh, I had a Nieuport, and Yelena a Sopwith Camel.'

'They aren't gliders!' he cried. 'They're fighters, they have engines.'

'They flew, didn't they? That's gliding.'

They went down the stairs and out on to the street.

'Honestly, Mummy . . .'

Paris, June 1937

Savinkov took off his jacket, tossing it over the back of the chair. It slipped, falling to the floor, and a handful of little red and gold badges scattered on the boards, shiny as boiled sweets. He sank back in the armchair and loosened the blazing scarlet scarf about his neck as the two young women began to take off each other's white blouses. They left on their own red scarves, marks of their commitment.

His scarf drew the eye to it, the gold on his wrist and hands flashed against it in the spotlights. They had sat there, the sea of pale faces and hungry eyes, as transfixed as rabbits, their will taken from them into his grasp, wanting it so . . .

The girls' hands caressed their breasts and they kissed each other, pink lips and tongues eager; in the new world there were no taboos, he had told them so.

They had been eager, too, all those who had come to the hall.

They hungered to be seduced, too. In the new world there were no taboos, no impossibilities, only ultimate man, and the future. There new, unfamiliar and wonderful forms of democracy were in birth, there Jesus Christ walked the world again. He knew it was so; the Dean of Canterbury had been in the audience, with the scientists, the philosophers, the artists and the writers, the doctors and the lawyers, and he had told *him* so, as he had walked among them afterwards, his hands always ready with a little red and gold badge, the symbol of solidarity . . .

He demanded a commitment, they longed to give it. The two young women wriggled, their hands fumbling with the hooks of their skirts. The cloth pooled scarlet on the floor and they felt eagerly between their thighs. It was all a part of utopia, Savinkov had told them so.

They stood on the debris, among the ruins of the old order, the liberal world that had failed. To the east the new world shone like the sun. But between them and it was darkness, a hideous vale filled with monsters. There were the beasts who would destroy heaven on earth, there were the Nazis, led by the Anti-Christ himself.

Savinkov appreciated the power of amplification, the wonderful devilry of search and spot lamps. Like Hitler, he knew the value of *son et lumière*. He, too, believed in staging and effect. As one professional to another, he admired the German demagogue immensely. He understood, as Hitler did, that the masses came to part with their will, to surrender it to their leader, to their prophet, who restored it to them reinforced, who bound them to him, to the cause.

They had panted, in the audience. Hands raised involuntarily, as if to Heaven. Their eyes glistened. They were excited, they threw off their old philosophical clothing and helped dress each other in the new he gave them . . .

The girls fell on him, pulling at his clothing, their mouths meeting around him, hair and breasts bobbing.

Music supported him, Wagner for Hitler, Rachmaninov for the new world. The entire orchestra came to its feet in a crescendo of power and they had risen too, the pale faces now flushed, slippery with the sweat of desire.

One of the girls sprawled on the sofa, her legs apart, her partner kneeling between them. Savinkov pulled up his clothes, pausing to watch her. They were like that in the crowd, his words seducing them, stroking them, exciting the souls that they gave up like slaves. The girl arched in ecstasy, the scarlet scarf running down her body like blood, and he went out. The hall was empty, the committed had gone.

On the Parisian boulevarde he stopped at the *Chat Noir* café and drank a long, pale gold beer in a tall glass in the warm evening air. Red Renault taxis darted among the staid Peugeots and racing *traction-avants* like buzzing dragonflies. He smoked a blended cigarette as the sweat dried on him, enjoying the strong tar, and walked away home.

From his apartment on the top floor he could see over the rooftops to the Seine. The sun sinking behind the far clouds turned it to a stream of blood, to a scarlet scarf. He thought of the girls, of the people in the crowd, and he chuckled.

He was hungry now. He could not eat before he performed, and now he was ravenous. When he put on a show he always had the *femme* fetch a meal from the restaurant down on the street below. Infusing so many people with his will left him drained and he liked to dine alone.

The table was laid in the dining room. Half an *homard*, its red claw already cracked, resting on a bed of crisp green lettuce, set off by piped, egg-yolk yellow mayonnaise. Cold roast beef done rare, in the English fashion, served with a potato salad speckled with chives, glistening with oil. A fresh salad in a bowl. Asparagus. A small pot of melted butter. A slice of raspberry tart, shining fruit settled on soft yellow custard and flaking pastry. A small cheese board.

A bottle of Margaux was decanted; he poured some into a glass and held it to the light to appreciate its ruby clarity. A half bottle of sweet Graves stood opened on the cloth, to accompany his sweet and cheese.

He paused by the bookshelf and took down a copy of *The Odyssey* in the Greek to read as he dined. He lifted the wine glass to his lips to drink, and the doorbell rang.

He frowned, then shrugged, putting down the glass, and went out into his wide hallway with its tall, gilded doors, his shoes clacking on the patterned tiles. He opned the door. A small man stood outside, smiling, his hands in his pockets like a schoolboy.

'Hallo, Sergei,' he said cheerfully. 'I hoped I'd catch you in.'

Life, Savinkov understood, was a war zone. It did not matter whether one was feather-bedded in a chateau, or on a straw palliasse in a leaky hovel, revolutionaries could come up the drive or the king's pressmen kick in your door at any time. It was no use, as they strung you up from your own oak, or forced you forwards into the shellfire, complaining that you hadn't been expecting this. So Savinkov beamed, in well-simulated delight.

'Oleg! How wonderful! And I was just getting ready to eat alone. You couldn't have come at a better moment.'

Rykov grinned, and stepped in through the open door. 'I'm a bit peckish,' he confided. 'Don't mind if I do.'

He was still boyish; his thick brown hair fell forward over his forehead and Savinkov noticed with unease that he seemed to know his way about the apartment. He went into the dining room, and stood looking admiringly at the laden table.

'A banquet. You must have known I was coming.' Then he turned suddenly to face Savinkov. 'But first – '

His hand went into his pocket and Savinkov felt his hostly smile slipping from his mouth.

Rykov laughed ghoulishly with an executioner's sense of humour. He slapped Savinkov on the arm in a familiar fashion. 'No, no,' he chuckled. 'I've got something for you. Something *nice*.'

He took out a pretty red box and opened it. Inside was a shiny gold medal hanging from a scarlet ribbon. 'The Boss is pleased with you,' he said. 'Real pleased. Now, stand still a moment.'

Carefully, he pinned the Order of Lenin on to the fine light wool fabric of Savinkov's suit jacket. Then Rykov took a small scroll from the inside pocket of his own grey suit.

'See?' he said. 'Signed by the boss himself, for outstanding services to the party.' He reached for a chair, pulling it out, and sat down at the table. 'Matter of fact,' he said, 'that's what I've come to talk to you about. He – the *kinto* – has a new job for you. Here, sit down. Let's have some grub while we're talking. Got a glass for yourself?'

Rykov took a swig from Savinkov's filled wineglass and pulled the plate of beef towards him. 'These froggies know how to look after themselves, don't they? You'll have to get used to different stuff where you're going.'

Savinkov filled another glass, red wine slopping on to the tablecloth. His hands were beginning to shake. 'Where's that?'

He kept his voice as level as he could.

Rykov pushed a slice of soft rare beef into his mouth with his fingers. 'Spain,' he said indistinctly. 'We're backing the Republicans. The civil war's taking off and there's plenty in it for us. Their gold reserves for a start. But more than that. We'll be the people in the white hats. You know, in the American films. What are they called?'

Savinkov made himself fork lobster into his mouth. It was as dry as biscuit. 'The good guys.'

'That's it. We'll be the good guys. We want you to get all your fools in the West out there. You know, the writers, poets, all the ones with big heads. We're starting an International Brigade. Think you'll have any trouble?'

'For a Cause?' Despite himself. Savinkov's mouth curved cynically. 'No, no trouble . . . It's tailor made . . . glamorous, exciting . . . get them close enough to the fighting to hear and smell it, keep them out there long enough to give them a good thirst when they get back to the hotel and they'll be banging out prose about the deathly orgasm of the trenches before you can say Communist International. Crawl over broken glass for a good Cause, will your intellectual.'

Savinkov paused. 'You want me to go down from here?'

Back to Moscow first,' Rykov said casually. He spooned potatoes from the bowl into his mouth. 'The boss wants to brief you himself. We can leave in the morning.'

'That's fine,' Savinkov said, equally casually. He took a large swallow of wine to get the lobster down his throat. 'Will you excuse me a minute? Your arrival caught me on the way to the bathroom.'

'Don't mind me,' said Rykov. 'Have you finished with that lobster?'

'Yes. Help yourself.'

Savinkov went down the corridor to the bathroom and locked the door. His guts had turned to liquid and he tore at his clothing. He stood up when he had finished and secured his trousers. He hung on the chain and, as the water roared down from the high box, used its racket to pull up the window. Then he was out and running across the leaden rooftop. Behind him he heard the splintering crash as Rykov smashed in the door.

He tripped on a rib of the roof and went headlong. As he picked himself up he saw Rykov coming through the window, grinning like a stoat. There was a door set in a housing like a ship's foghorn and he crashed through it, his sweating fingers slippery on the key of the lock. He felt it click through as Rykov slammed into the panels. As he ran down the stairs, he heard Rykov laugh.

He came down through the common parts of the apartment block, hurrying on the soft carpet, round and round the central well until he pushed through the engraved glass doors and was on the street. A taxi was passing. He screamed for it and the driver pulled over to the kerb.

'Place de la Madeleine!' he gasped.

The driver looked at him strangely, and he made himself smile sheepishly. 'Her husband came home,' he said, and the man chuckled.

'*Bien*,' he grunted, and, moving into the traffic, began a long tale of one of his own *amours* that had run awry. Savinkov looked behind him, but saw only the traffic swirling along the boulevarde.

By the time they reached the elegant square his breath had returned to normal, although his heart was still thumping. He paid the man and slipped through the doors of the elegant, canary-yellow block. The porter knew him and called up, then indicated for him to take the lift.

On the third floor the butler had the door open and was awaiting him. He looked curiously at him, but held the door wide.

'Lady Webb is in the study, sir,' he said, and Savinkov went in.

Beatrice Webb was seated behind an inlaid desk, making notes in a book with a fountain pen. She peered in alarm over a pair of *pince-nez* glasses as he came in.

'Comrade Savinkov! What brings you here like this?'

Savinkov forced *bonhomie* into his voice. 'I'm sorry to disturb you – I wasn't sure if you'd still be here.'

'We don't leave for London until tomorrow.'

'That's it. I wondered if there was room in the car for me. You are taking the Rolls?'

'Of course. But this is somewhat sudden. You said nothing of this earlier . . .'

'It's my wife. I need to go and see her.'

Beatrice Webb frowned at him. 'Comrade Savinkov, you have lost a shoe, and there is blood on your face and hands. Why?'

Savinkov stared at her, his mind temporarily blank. 'A robber,' he said. 'Someone tried to rob me in the street.'

A cold glint came into her eye. 'To my *knowledge*, you are separated from and on bad terms with your wife. You smell strongly of wine and you are bleeding and in disarray. You are wearing the Order of Lenin and you are spouting some cock-and-bull tale about wanting us to take you to London. Now, are you drunk? Have you committed some crime, taken leave of your senses or all three? Inform me, pray.'

Savinkov sat down on the arm of a sofa. 'All right, then,' he said quietly. 'I'll tell you. I was in my apartment this evening when a man came to kill me.'

'A robber? An assassin?' She was sceptical.

'Oh, he's an assassin all right . . . but he wasn't to kill me now. He was to take me somewhere else, for the deed to be done.'

'And you ran away, as one would. Very well. This does not explain your presence here, rather than at the *gendarmerie*, nor your need to travel to London, nor the Order of Lenin.'

'It was he who gave me the Order of Lenin. It was to allay my suspicions, to get me to go back to Moscow. His name is Rykov and he is one of the *kinto's* creatures.'

Her brow wrinkled. '*Kinto?*'

'The gang-boss, Stalin. I've been told I am to head the propaganda team in Spain. I'm not. I'm to be put on trial with the others and shot.'

'Shot? Trial? You *must* be drunk. Or mad. If the Party needs you in Moscow then you must go. Go now.'

Savinkov shook his head. 'I would like to go to London. With you. Please.'

'What on earth for?'

'It's safe,' he said softly. 'The government does not come in the night to kill its citizens. There are laws. The police protect you, they do not come to kill you. Rykov is a policeman – he is a *chekist*.'

'What appalling piffle! Britain is the most reactionary country in the world. Oh, if we only had justice like you do in your brave new country. How I long for that day!'

'It's *me* you're talking to,' Savinkov hissed, exasperated. 'We can be honest with each other, we're in the same business.'

Her face froze. 'What business would that be, Mr Savinkov?'

'*We're in charge.*' He waved an arm. 'All of *them*, the fools, *they want to believe*. They want to be duped. They want to be told about the new world that's being created, how the rules don't apply, how we make the new ones. *You can get them to do anything.* They surrender their will to you.' He shook his head. 'There are two girls, I can get them to do anything, *in the name of the Party*. And they're only like all the others. You can stand them up in front of a Moscow slum and tell them it's new world housing and they roll their eyes and marvel. Blood leaks out from under the frontier and they think it's surplus fruit juice.'

He stared intensely at her. 'They think I'm some sort of angel,' he said clearly. 'They think I've come from Heaven with the word of God and I get everything I want. Only they have not understood; it is not God but Satan who is in charge. Rykov has come to kill me, and I am trying to run away. I *know* how it is done, I *know* what happens – and I like life too much not to want to escape. I'm not proud. I'm a liar, I've told lies, lived them for so long I have no pride left. I just want to live.'

His eyes were unfocused, seeing the past.

'I wasn't always this way,' he said quietly. 'You know, once I really believed there were such things as scientific laws of History.'

Beatrice Webb stared at him, speechless, an expression of stupefaction on her face.

'Don't look at me like that!' He brushed his face, looked at the blood smeared on his hand. '*You're* no different. You live like kings. You're high priests of totalitarianism. You have wealth, Rolls Royce cars and fine homes. You write garbage for the fools just as I have. The only difference is that your government makes your husband a Lord, mine has come to kill me.'

There was a creak as the door opened and the face of Sidney, Baron Passfield poked around it. 'Ah. Comrade Savinkov.' he said nervously. 'So you *are* here.'

'He is,' his wife said weakly, waving a hand.

'Ah. Um, Comrade Savinkov, I, ah . . .

The door pushed itself open and three men stood behind Sidney Webb. Two were large, and one was small, and they wore white coats.

'Doctor Rykov has – '

'*No!*' Savinkov screamed. He ran for the window and was tearing at the lock as the two big men seized him. They overpowered him easily, holding him down as Rykov slid the needle into his arm. His thrashings ceased, and he lay inert on the Aubusson carpet, his mouth open, eyes shut, blood streaking his face. Rykov stood up, pocketing the syringe.

'I am so sorry that you have been disturbed so, Lord and Lady Webb,' he said politely. He gestured down at Savinkov. The two big men had brought in a canvas stretcher on poles, and were strapping Savinkov to it. 'This is a very tragic case. A fine and tireless worker for the Cause, overtaken by mental illness. A complete breakdown. He has been working too hard.'

'He was saying things . . . that were completely mad. *Terrible* things.'

Rykov wagged his head solemnly. 'Yes, we know. We have been sent by Stalin himself to take him back to Russia for a full recovery.'

Relief flooded into her face. 'Oh, that's wonderful. You have the finest mental hospitals in the world.'

'We do,' Rykov agreed.

They had taken Savinkov out, Rykov gave a little bow, and followed them. The Webbs stood at the window, saw them put the stretcher into the white ambulance, saw it drive away.

'That poor man! Completely deranged. Oh, well, if anyone can cure him Soviet medicine can. He actually thought they had come to take him back to Russia to be put on trial and shot. Classic persecution mania.'

Sidney Webb watched as the ambulance lost itself in the traffic. 'Just say, if he is. When he gets back. Put on trial I mean. We do know that there *are* trials going on.'

'Of wreckers, and subversives. Exploiters of the masses.'

'Yes.'

'Well, then he is one, of course. Their system of justice is infallible. If he's tried he's a criminal, a traitor to the system.'

She turned and went back to the desk and resumed her work.

Windsor, England, July 1937

The wild flowers made the hedgerow like a glorious Indian carpet of colour. The tyres of her Morris ran over their shed petals and their scent filled the inside of the car. As she came close to the town larger cars passed her travelling the other way, bearing black-coated, exuberant schoolboys.

She navigated the maze of ancient buildings and parked her shiny-nosed saloon among a selection of gleaming Rolls, Humber and Lanchester limousines being loaded up with trunks, tuck boxes, cricket bats and schoolboys. She got out, and went across the courtyard. A scurrying boy came the other way, carrying a model of a sailing ship.

'Hallo, little Lord,' she said cheerfully. A pair of aristocratic eyes peered at her through the rigging.

'Good morning, Countess . . .'

The young heir to a fine seat in the country turned, abruptly. 'Sir, sir!' he called, to the housemaster, standing begowned on the steps, his white starched shirtfront and bow tie shining. 'Nikolai's mater is here, sir.'

The man looked up from his supervision and came down the steps to meet her. He looked worried, and she felt instant alarm.

'Is something wrong, Mr Roberts?' she asked anxiously. 'Where is Nikolai?'

'He's with his father, Countess. He received a letter from him two days ago, requesting him to join him in Paris for the holiday early, as they were to make a trip together. When Nikolai showed me the letter he assured me that this was as had been arranged. I recognised your husband's writing because he corresponds with Nikolai regularly. I thought nothing of it and gave Nikolai permission to leave. He told me that he would be letting you know what he was doing . . .'

'Yes. yes – ' she cried, in an agony of uncertainty.

'It was just when Lord Melcaster found this letter addressed to you left on Nikolai's desk in his study . . .' The housemaster reached inside his jacket, and took out a crisp white envelope, with her son's handwriting.

She opened the letter.

> Dearest Mama,
>
> I have received a letter from Papa, asking me to go to Paris to meet him. For the reasons I give below, I did not believe this letter, although he had written it. So I went to the town and placed a trunk call to the office in Paris. A man whom I did not know answered, and told me that Papa had had to leave early, but that he had left tickets and money for me to follow. I asked if he had gone to Moscow and, after a pause, the man said that he had. Then he asked if I would be coming to collect the tickets, and I said that I would.

Standing in the courtyard, amid a swirl of boys, chauffeurs, mothers and the paraphanalia of boarding school, Ruth bit on her knuckle in order not to sob, and Mr Roberts looked at her in alarm.

> Do you remember Mama, when I spent ten days in Paris with Papa last Easter? You picked me up, and we went skiing. Papa had a visitor one night at the apartment, and they sat up late, talking. I am sorry, to say – Mr Roberts would not approve at all – that I eavesdropped. (Mr Roberts does not understand the art of survival where we come from. He lives in a better world.)
>
> The man's name was Viktor and he was an OGPU officer in their Foreign Department and he was on the run. He told Papa that he had received a summons to return to Moscow. This was, he said, a sentence of death, as all operatives being recalled were being shot in the *Yezhofschchina*. He had bolted, and was trying to get out to the USA with his wife and daughter. This was why he wanted Papa's help. What frightened him most of all, he said, was that they would send men to kidnap his family, to make him give himself up.
>
> In the morning the man was gone, so I do not know what has become of him. But it is much better, Mama, that I go back to Moscow. My guess would be that Papa is to be put on trial, and that they wish me (Natasha, they will have no problem with) to denounce him publicly. They are very fond of having children denounce their parents.

I will survive, Mama. You would not. You know I am right, because of all the time we have spent together, all the things we have talked about. Stay here among the good English people and one day I will join you again, I promise.

Your loving son,
Nikolai.

Ruth stood in the summer sunshine, with tears streaming silently down her cheeks. Mr Roberts stood by her, unknowing, only comprehending that something dark and terrible had come into the ancient courtyard, and the mother of her son's friend came up, put her arm about her and led her away.

20

Yezhovschina

Peredelkino, June 1938

PIOTR PAVLOVICH SADOVSKY, Nikita Sergevich Khrushchev and Andrei Yanuarievich Vyshinsky peered over the ridge line. They made a strange trio, the industrialist, the Party boss and the state Prosecutor General, all watching the approaching train. The peasant Khrushchev and the intellectual Vyshinsky, descendant of Polish aristocrats, looked at the unfolding drama with equal, childish delight. Sadovsky, who knew what was to happen, expertly manipulated the controls.

The room they were in was large; it occupied half the top floor of his dacha. Moscow was just over twenty miles to the east and around them were the larches and birches of the forest. Set among them were the holiday homes of the well-connected and the powerful.

The train was an armoured one; it boasted guns, ammunition wagons, a sleeping car and a flat-bed upon which rested a Rolls Royce limousine.

'Kazan, on the Volga,' Savinkov intoned. 'It is the year eighteen. The Civil War rages. Everywhere the valiant Bolshevik forces are falling back, outnumbered a hundred to one by the imperialists and their lackeys, the Whites.'

Had he been looking, Savinkov would have seen a momentary flicker in the eyes of Vyshinsky. In the year eighteen Vyshinsky had been a Menshevik and ideological purity was like virginity. But the sensitive moment passed and, bending smilingly over the train set in his stiff white collar, checked tie and smartly-cut blue suit, he looked for all the world like a stockbroker home from the city, indulging his children.

'Kazan, the last important town on the east bank. The Whites capture the imperial gold and platinum reserves. Now only open plain stands between them and Moscow. The entire Bolshevik cause in the Civil War hangs in the balance. In desperation, Lenin sends the

self-proclaimed People's Commissar for War, Leon Trotsky, to save
the day.'

A flicker now appeared in the eyes of Khrushchev, squatting down
with his hands on his knees, watching the drama unfold. He had been
in the Civil War and the flicker in his eyes was of amusement. Fine
food, wine and plum brandy lay in his stomach, courtesy of his host,
now he was being cleverly entertained.

The train halted some way from the diorama of little buildings along
the edge of the river. Ramps fell down from the back of the flat car
and the Rolls Royce rolled off. From its rear seat a small figure rose
up, black-haired and in a leather coat. Tiny round pince-nez shone
on his nose.

'Trotsky,' said Sadovsky, his voice deep with contempt. 'Come to
save the day.'

From the town tiny puffs of smoke issued from emplaced cannon
and, through a hidden loudspeaker, came the sounds of artillery.

The model Trotsky sat down.

'Trotsky is saving the day.'

They laughed.

There was the sound of trumpets and over the cloth landscape came
galloping cavalry. Trotsky's Rolls Royce wheeled abruptly and drove
off the other way, vanishing behind a wood.

'Trotsky is saving his arse!'

They chuckled. The cavalry stopped and they heard sounds of
cheering.

'The White army has won and Trotsky has run away. The road to
Moscow and absolute victory lies open. Alas, poor Russia, will no
one save her from her fate?'

Sadovsky cupped an ear.

'Hush, what is that we hear?'

Through the speaker came the faint, but swelling sound of a
thousand voices singing the *Internationale*. From behind the trees
where Trotsky had fled a second train emerged. It was bright red.
Scarlet and gold hammer-and-sickle flags erupted from its length and
it bristled with guns. As it roared in towards the town they fired, and
over the singing came the howl of arriving artillery.

'Toiling masses! Worker-titans! You are saved!'

The lights began to dim. On the battlefield scarlet and white flashes
indicated the fighting.

'The struggle continues throughout the night.'

Cries of defeat, of running men, panicking horses.

'The forces of the Red Saviour prove invincible. Fresh from

victories at Tsaritsyn he has rushed to the aid of the Bolshevik armies abandoned by Trotsky. By his matchless example he rallies the troops. By his peerless military capability he commands them throughout the fighting. As the sun rises, he is, alone, master of the battlefield.'

In the darkened room, a round sun began to glow upon the far wall. It was the face of Stalin, beaming down upon a scene in which the Whites had run one way, Trotsky the other. The red train dominated the scene, and Stalin shone down upon all. Conditioned, Khrushchev and Vyshinsky broke into reflex applause. Slowly, Sadovsky allowed the lights to come back on, but the face of Stalin remained.

'Remarkable!' Vyshinsky said jovially. 'A wonderful and correct creation.'

'Thank you,' Sadovsky said, and smiled modestly. 'I owe it all to Comrade Stalin, without whose example I could never have created it.'

Vyshinsky straightened up. 'You did it all yourself?'

'Well, not all. I had the assistance of a comrade at work.'

He allowed his eyes to slide round to look at Khrushchev, and saw the infintesimal nod of the party boss's head.

'As a matter of fact, I am working on another project, Comrade Academician Andrei. One which may amuse you, since you are present.'

Vyshinsky looked up from the trains and smiled in pleasure. 'I? How is this?'

'We are making a courtroom. One that illustrates the eternal vigilance of the Party in seeking out and destroying the wreckers and spies within our midst. The defendants skulk in the dock, as evil as snakes, as treacherous as hyenas. The merciless avenging sword of the party exposes their sins. That is you, Comrade. You give one of your finest speeches. Comrade leader Stalin beams down upon you in approval. The judge passes sentence. The broken evil-doers crawl outside, where the firing-squad of proletarian justice awaits.'

'This is wonderful!' Vyshinsky cried, eyes sparkling behind his round glasses.

'I had hoped to present it to you today.'

'You did!' His face fell. 'Why not?'

Sadovsky sighed. 'A terrible mistake has occurred. My colleague, with whom I made this model, with whom I was making your model, has been taken in error by the NKVD.'

Vyshinsky's face was suddenly as watchful as a hawk. 'In error?'

'Yes,' Sadovsky said firmly. 'He is a loyal and tireless worker for the cause. He helped us storm the thousand-truck barrier. There is no more dedicated servant of the revolution than he. I believe that it is another Andrei Stukalov that our eternally-vigilant security forces seek, and that they have taken my colleague by mistake. My colleague, without whom I cannot finish the model of the courtroom, to present to you.'

Vyshinsky licked his lips, greed and caution at war in his face. 'Has he confessed?'

'I doubt it very much. He is an innocent man.'

'The confession is the proof of guilt,' Vyshinsky murmured. 'It is all the evidence one needs for conviction.' He pursed his lips, his ruddy cheeks flushing pink. 'When did you say he was taken?' he asked.

'Two days ago.'

They all stood in silence, considering how long the average person could hold out against the will of the NKVD.

'It would be worth investigating,' Khrushchev suggested. 'It would be a dreadful thing for a miscarriage of justice to take place in a perfect system.'

'Yes, yes.' The prosecutor seemed to make up his mind, and took out a small, leather-bound notebook, writing in it with a neat, legal hand.

'I shall investigate,' he announced. 'Now, Comrade Director Piotr. I shall leave you. I must be at my desk early.'

As they went down the corridor to the door it opened, and a beautiful young girl of around fifteen came in. Her blue eyes sparkled and the scarlet scarf of a *komsomolka* blazed at her throat.

'Hallo, Daddy,' she cried. 'We have been singing songs to practise for the revolution festival.'

'My darling, do you know Party Secretary Khrushchev, Academecian Prosecutor Vyshinsky? My daughter Gaia, comrades.'

She bobbed in a curtsey, raven-black hair swinging, white teeth smiling.

'What did you sing? Will you give us a song?'

'A song,' smiled Khrushchev. Vyshinsky beamed at the young girl like a stockbroker meeting one of his son's friends.

'Shall I sing? We sang a wonderful new song.'

Stalin, the freshness of springtime is you,
Oh, Stalin, the warmth of the sunshine is too,

When she had finished, they applauded.

'Get yourself off to bed now, darling,' said Savinkov.

He embraced Vyshinsky, and they kissed each other on their cheeks. 'My house is your house. Comrade Academecian Andrei,'

Sadovsky assured him earnestly. He waved, and waved, until the two limousines vanished among the dark trees.

He closed the door, and locked it, with hands that finally were shaking. He staggered the steps to his bathroom on knees that were stiff and fell over the basin vomiting, his entire body bathed in running sweat.

He felt hands helping him, bathing his face, supporting him as he staggered to the bedroom. They took off his clothes, damp with the sweat of fear and laid him down in bed. His wife Anna sat on the edge. She held his hand and smiled at him with love as his daughter Gaia sponged the the fever from his face.

Outside, the *Yezhovschina* howled. No locks, no prayers were protection.

'Daddy will keep us safe, Mummy,' Gaia said in certainty to the dumb woman. 'Don't worry, Daddy will keep us safe.'

Sochi, Azerbaijan July 1938

From his seat by the open window Krivitskiy could smell the acacias. Looking out over the park he saw fruit on the trees, golden oranges and tangerines, acid-yellow lemons, pink apples of paradise. Some fountains were playing, cooling classical statues that stood ankle-deep in the water with their fine spray. The only thing out of place were the two workmen, digging three holes in the fine lawn beneath. They appeared to be setting up some posts.

Krivitskiy was on the first floor of the villa. It was a magnificent affair, and had been built as the summer residence of a Georgian oil magnate. When the revolution had come to Azerbaijan, Ordzhonikidze, its embodiment in those parts, had had the man shot, along with his family, and it had passed into the keeping of the revolution. In due course the revolution had come to Orzhonikidze. But the revolution remained in possession. Krivitskiy looked out over a scene that had been created by the gardener of a Tsar, from a house built by his architect.

'You may go in,' the secretary at the desk said, without looking up, in response to some hidden signal, and he got up, and went in.

The office was huge, a former drawing room. Inlaid paddle-fans whirled from the ceiling, he walked across an immense and thick rug, its motif the coat-of-arms of the magnate. Among the portraits on the wall was his and he looked down in disapproval. Soft and comfortable Georgian *takhta* couches stood among stiffer imperial chairs, with high backs.

He stopped in front of the huge desk with its mandatory bank of telephones.

'I'm Krivitskiy.'

Chill, watery, greenish grey eyes assessed him through round glasses.

'You're Krivitskiy,' the man agreed. He leaned back in his chair and took a fresh white cloth from a small pile that stood on the desk, and wiped his hands with it. He was Lavrentiy Pavlovich Beria, and he was the embodiment of the revolution in those parts. He pointed to the chair in front of the desk, a carved balloon-backed dining chair, and Krivitskiy sat down. As he did so he noticed that its silk seat was stained. He sat, and a faint odour of old blood drifted about him in the soft breeze of the fans.

'I'm going to do something nobody does around here,' Krivitskiy said. 'Something no one has done for a long time.'

'You're going to sing *God Save The Tsar*?' suggested Beria.

'No. Something quite as dangerous. I'm going to speak the truth.'

'To me?' Beria arched his eyebrows.

'I have to. It makes little difference. If I had stayed in Moscow much longer Yezhof would have had me shot. If you do not like what I say, *you* will have me shot. But if you listen . . .'

Beria studied the bitten nails on his short fingers, then wiped his hands once again with the cloth. It was now completely damp, and he threw it into a waste basket, where it joined several others.

'Go on then,' he said, indifferently.

'I should explain that I am one who has been a Chekist from the beginning, whether the organisation has been called GPU, OGPU, NKVD or the original Cheka. I have also seen service within the GRU. Military Intelligence. I currently work in the INO, the Foreign Department of the NKVD and I am a law graduate of Moscow University. In the INO, the Foreign department, I have done tours of duty in Paris, Berlin, Switzerland, Washington, Prague and London. I was until recently the NKVD illegal *rezident* in Berlin. My experience intersects party, state and state security. I have run intelligence agents within Germany and I know more about what is happening there, and will happen, than anyone else.'

Beria seemed bored. 'None of this will save your miserable neck if you are guilty.'

'Ah . . . guilty. Guilty of what? But I agree. Yezhof has just had shot Marshal Tukhachevsky, and eight other senior commanders, and the Marshal was a far more powerful personage than myself. But what was Tukhachevsky guilty of?'

Beria yawned. 'Get on with it.'

'I parade my past before you not as some prisoner seeking alleviation of sentence, but to impress upon you both the breadth and depth of my experience. I am a professional revolutionary, and, of course, a Marxist.

'My belief in Marx does not prevent me, however, from losing contact with the real world. I believe, for example, that a bullet goes down the barrel of a gun because of genuine laws of physics. Yezhof does not appear to agree with me. He has just destroyed the Kharkov Physics Laboratory, which was possibly the best in Europe. He has arrested almost all its leading staff, and those not shot are in the camps. There, if something is not done, they will die in the near future. Did you know that it takes five years to train an engineer, but fifteen to make a physicist?'

'Is it important? A few physicists more or less.'

'It matters in general, and it will, I believe, matter in detail. Of course, when I say political leadership, or Yezhof, I do not really mean Yezhof, nor the politburo. I mean Stalin.'

The watery eyes widened behind the glasses. '*I* am minded that you will not leave here alive, let alone get back to Moscow for your execution.'

'I said I was going to speak the truth,' Krivitskiy said equably. 'And so I shall. To return to the point I was making, I am the intelligence equivalent of one of these physicists. I am both rare, and know of what I speak, both in depth and in detail. There are not very many like me – and at the rate Stalin is having Yezhof kill the others there will in the future be even less of us.'

'I have never been impressed by arguments for the preservation of endangered species.'

Krivitskiy looked at the professional murderer opposite him. 'I am aware of that,' he said quietly. 'However, there are other rare species whose members are subject to periodic culling, secret police chiefs being one of them. I hope by pointing this out to you to concentrate your mind upon what I have to say.'

The eyes narrowed. It had been a long time since anyone had spoken to him in anything approaching such a manner.

The strain of fighting for his life had given Krivitskiy a fearsome headache. At work he found winding a wet towel about his head helped, and a cold bath at the end of the day, but to show weakness here was lethal. It was especially important to show not a hint of pleading. There was always something foul on the breeze that blew from the Transcaucasus. The ordinary people were simply afraid, but insiders like Krivitskiy knew of the detail, the hideous, near sexual joy the man opposite him gained from having men beg for their lives, for the lives of the wives and children, unaware that each beseechment only made the death of all more certain, its manner more horrible. So Krivitskiy ignored the pounding in his head, and made himself stare Beria in the eyes with what amounted to indifference, as icy cold sweat trickled down his back.

'I am a Marxist, as I have said. But Marx's scientific laws were worked out for societies of people, and cannot apply when you have a single actor able to distort the system to the extent that we have here. I am referring to Number One, to the *kinto*, to the Boss. Josef Issarionovich himself. Comrade Stalin.'

Beria picked up another white cloth and began wiping away the sweat oozing from his hands. His silence was menacing, but Krivitskiy continued calmly.

'So we have to ask ourselves, what is he up to? We already live in a society that bears little resemblance to the one we dreamed of, as young, idealistic Bolsheviks.'

Beria looked at Krivitskiy pityingly, and he was aware that for the man behind the desk, what he had was what he had dreamed of, as an ugly, sweaty, nasty youth the pretty girls laughed at.

'Some of us, anyway. We did not dream we would be asked to fight a war against our own people. Not the Civil War. The war we conducted against the peasantry. We robbed them, we tortured them, we slaughtered them by the tens, by the thousands of thousands, and all who did it – and he made sure it was as many as he could – have become tainted, brutalised, and guilty. Having done it to others in the name of Communism, who now can stand up and protest, if the same is being prepared for him, whether he be Party worker, military man or NKVD? Was that not a most important by-product of what was done to the peasants, to destroy defences among the others, whose time is coming?'

Krivitskiy helped himself to a glass of water on the desk, and carefully omitted to thank his host. 'So what is the *kinto* doing, and just as important, *why* is he doing it? By the way, let me ask you a question. Who does the Boss admire most?'

'I was not aware he admired anyone,' Beria said, the words falling like lumps of metal.

'Wrong,' said Krvitskiy, smiling pleasantly. 'There is someone he admires a great deal, and who, in fact, admires *him* a great deal. His name is Adolf Hitler.'

He allowed what he had said to hang in the air, and then continued. 'We shouldn't be surprised that they admire each other. They both do the same job, they both want the same things, and they are willing to learn from each other. That Hitler learned from Lenin and Stalin how to set up a regime based upon unrestrained use of terror can scarcely be denied. His realisation that Lenin's and Stalin's destruction of the capitalist professional managers of industry and their substitution by party ideologues has crippled the Soviet economy and his refusal to allow his revolutionary elements to do the same in Germany is flawless. He has been quick to set up his own concentration camp system for his enemies, in imitation of our own. But Hitler is a talented man, he has much to teach, too. Take the regime he set up in January 1933. What, from his viewpoint as single, overall leader, as *Fuhrer*, was wrong with it?

'The answer is that it had one major force not completely under his control – the SA, or Brownshirts, under their leader Ernst Roehm. One million strong by the autumn of that year. And Roehm planned to make it the new, radical, revolutionary army. Which also didn't fit in with Hitler's plans. We now know how Hitler dealt with his problem. Having prepared himself with great thoroughness, he used Himmler to build up a political police force united under single control, and used this on 30 June 1934 to eliminate all his immediate political enemies at once. In addition to smashing the SA he was able to take out people like Gregor Srasser, von Schleicher, Ernst Klausener and many other either dangerous or inconvenient people.'

Krivitskiy drank some more water. From the garden below came the thumping of mallets and the scrape of spades.

'And he got away with it. With the German people, with world opinion. With his own colleagues and followers, and who did that impress most of all? Josef Issarionovich. I know, because while it was happening he called an emergency meeting of the Politburo. Do you know what he said? "Have you heard what's happened in Germany? Hitler, what a lad! Knows how to deal with political opponents." It was the first thing he said.'

'I think that 30 June 1934 is a watershed day, for several reasons, not least because of its effect upon our own leader, Comrade Stalin. It put two powerful ideas into his mind. It made him realise that he, too, could have unfettered power. Given the different circumstances he had to operate in, he could not move in as swift a manner because at the time he was restrained by the fact that he was, while the leader,

leader of a number of others who, far from wanting Stalin to have more power, wanted him to have less. Everyone was tired, even those who had most ruthlessly executed his orders against the peasantry. A period of normalisation was wanted, a time to relax. The idea among the top figures was that now Stalin could be moved to a more decorative office, and let Sergei Kirov take over as General Secretary, as head of a collective leadership. None of them seem to have realised that Stalin was, and is, just as likely to give up or share power as was and is Adolf Hitler. "Have you heard what's happened in Germany? Hitler, what a lad! Knows how to deal with political opponents."

'Kirov's dead. "Assassinated". Now Stalin's finishing off the others. Just like Hitler, only he's taking longer over it.'

Beria wiped his hands yet again. 'I see that your grasp of what you say is so complete that you will have little difficulty in writing it all down when we take you to the cells. I shall have great pleasure in forwarding it to Comrade Stalin, the Leader of Genius of the Proletarian Revolution, from whom nothing can be hidden.'

A faint smile cracked Krivitskiy's face for the first time. 'I see we do understand each other. I thought that we might.'

Beria understood perfectly. If a partly-crippled middle-aged dwarf gangster from Georgia, with bad skin, bad teeth and smelly feet could rise from little to be lauded as Theoretician and Genius Leader of the Toilers of the Whole World the possibilities for a more intelligent, younger man, Cheka boss of Georgia in his twenties, ruler of Transcaucasia a decade later, seemed obvious. The man who would be king glanced at his watch.

'Get on with it. I have an execution to watch.'

'Very good. Of course, you and I know that he's not right in the head. the Boss. Hitler only got rid of people who really *were* a threat; the Boss is killing everyone. Factory-like "extermination quotas" of "enemies of the people" are sent by telegram. By return must come back confirmation that the right number of people have been shot – two, five and ten thousand at a time. However, when it is complete, the terror will have established Stalin as sole ruler within the Soviet Union, threatened by no one, no one within. But was that its sole purpose? Why slaughter us, the NKVD? Why massacre the military? Hitler left the Gestapo alone, the Wehrmacht too.'

'Tukhachevsky was about to mount a *coup*,' Beria said levelly.

'He wasn't, you know. Stalin had the German Gestapo work up evidence of collaboration between Tukhachevsky and his army commanders and the German generals, but it was fake. However, Tukhachevsky *would* have objected to what Stalin is planning very strongly, and that's why he had to go. Just as my people in the INO Foreign Department would object, which is why we are being slaughtered.'

'So what is Comrade Stalin planning?' Beria asked.

'He has been working since 30 June 1934 to cut a deal with Adolf Hitler, his avowed enemy. You can forget all the vituperative abuse – Radek's running that, and he told me himself it was simply *ochkovtiratelstvo*, strategic eyewash for fools, that Soviet foreign policy is, in reality, bound to Germany. Radek was himself in contact with high German officials. Stalin believes that Hitler is a realist, that the two of them can slice up Europe between them.'

'He is the Supreme Genius of All Humanity,' Beria murmured.

'War is coming. Anyone who thinks that Hitler's programme of rearmament was put into effect to eliminate unemployment in Germany needs taking away. His new armed forces are there to be *used*. A deal will be struck. Hitler will get Austria, Czechoslovakia and some of Poland. Stalin will get some of Poland, Finland if the Red Army can get it for him without experienced officers. Romania perhaps, Latvia, Estonia and Lithuania certainly. The West – Britain and France – will screw themselves up to war with Germany. In return for this free hand Stalin will provide vast quantities of raw materials for the German war machine – oil, grain, cotton, chromium, manganese and so forth. His hope will be that Germany and the western powers will exhaust themselves in a war of attrition, leaving Stalin to collect the prizes at a later date.'

'As I said, the Supreme Genius of All Humanity,' said Beria. 'Now, are you ready to go down to the cells?'

'No,' said Krivitskiy evenly. 'Aren't you interested to know why I have come all this way? There must, surely, be something in it for me and, by implication, for you. I cannot have come simply to give you a lecture on the congruence of internal and external Soviet policy, pleasurable though it must have been for you to listen to.'

'Go on, then.'

'I've come to save your life. Mine too, for that matter.'

'How?' Beria did not hide his scepticism.

'When Stalin was considering Yagoda's replacement as head of the NKVD he had two names: Yezhof and yours. He chose Yezhof without hesitation. This can only mean that he intended to use Yezhof for the purpose of the current terror, to execute the orders and take the blame. Don't they call the terror the *Yezhofshchina*? Not the *Stalinshchina*.

'Once Yezhof has completed his task he will be replaced – by you.

You will be expected to fight for it because Stalin does not hand over great prizes on plates. My knowledge of the Moscow NKVD *apparat* is far more detailed than yours. I can provide you with intelligence to help you win smoothly.'

'I can out-fight someone like Yezhof,' Beria said roughly. 'This does not come under the heading of saving my life.'

'Someone's coming to kill you,' Krivitskiy said softly. 'His men will take especial pleasure in making your end as long and as painful as possible.'

'Who?' Beria shouted savagely. 'Who is this man?'

'Adolf Hitler. The *kinto* will get his deal. He will give Hitler everything he wants. And when Hitler feels strong enough he will come at us. He is not really interested in the West, as Stalin hopes he is. He is interested in the East. Here, he knows, is the centre of the Jewish race-poison, and of Bolshevism, which he believes are the same thing. Here in the Soviet Union are the vast open spaces, the *Lebensraum* that the German *Volk* requires as the Master Race. Here are the masses of Slav slaves who will labour for their German owners. Here are the Jews, the Gipsies, the Asiatic Inferiors and last, but certainly not least, the Communist Officials, all of whom must be exterminated. That last category includes you and me.

'You will recall that at the beginning I took care to point out to you the depth and breadth of my intelligence experience. I have worked in the GRU, in military intelligence. It is my opinion that if Hitler prepares himself properly he will win. We must hope that he does not. But we cannot count on that, and my assessment of the German Wehrmacht – especially its officer corps – is very high. *Our* officers are dead, or slowly dying in the camps while the Wehrmacht is receiving excellent tanks from fine designers, made by first-class engineers. It is supported by superb fighters and dive-bombers which come from fine designers and engineers. Our scientists, designers and engineers are mostly in the camps, slowly dying, as are the professional managers of the factories and enterprises that produce the parts they require. Stalin does not believe in professional expertise. He does not like people larger in any way than himself. But unless somebody ensures that at least *some* of our talent survives, then, when Hitler arrives in Red Square to watch Stalin being hanged, among those swinging from the nooses during the first act will be *you*. The laws of physics act on a rope, just as they do on a bullet.'

Krivitskiy pointed his finger at Beria. 'You will be head of the NKVD. *You* have to get the arms' designers, the engineers, the scientists, the military leaders and planners some protection. Set up design bureaus in special camps. But do not allow the *urkas*, the cold, the lack of food, the diseases and the mines to kill them.'

Beria looked out of the window for a long time. 'I had you investigated,' he said finally, 'when you requested to see me. You're a subversive, Krivitskiy. You think I was going to have you shot, out there on the lawn? I don't think that I will, not yet, anyway. I'll protect you, I'll see to it that you aren't killed by Yezhof. And when I have his job, I'll do as you say, with the weapons people.'

From the open window came the sound of voices, orders and replies.

'I am willing to go along with your assessment of foreign affairs. Until events prove you otherwise, if they do. However, your views on internal policy are entirely false. The killings that are taking place have nothing to do with Comrade Stalin's desire for supreme power. They are solely the manifestation of the huge numbers of spies and saboteurs who seek to destroy our society.'

The gibing, watery, chill eyes looked at Krivitskiy through the glasses. 'I myself have found two spies. Two German spies. Come.'

Beria led Krivitskiy over to the window. On the lawn below a woman and a girl stood, tied to two of the posts. They looked up at him in appeal. A small firing squad of four stood some paces away, under the command of a sergeant.

'*Your* spies, Krivitskiy.'

'If they are spies, then so must I be,' Krivitskiy said steadily. 'They are loyal German communists, toilers for the Party good.'

'Save the claptrap, Krivitskiy,' Beria said softly. He waved a hand, and the men lowered their rifles. The sergeant began to undo the bonds that held Marthe and Elisabeth to the posts.

'Very well. They can live. While we see if you're correct . . .'

Peredelkino

It was dark, the middle of the night. Someone was knocking on the door. A soft, insistent knock. He went down the corridor of the dacha in his slippered feet, his warm wool dressing gown wrapped about him, and peered through the small pane of glass. A man was outside. Against his will, he opened the door.

'Yes?'

'It's me,' the man said softly and he craned forward to try to see who it was. The moon came out from behind a cloud, and he saw that there were cars in his driveway between the larches and birches and uniformed men stood behind the man who had knocked.

'You stinking heap of shit!' the man yelled, and they rushed him, knocking him down. They held him as others rushed past, and he heard his daughter scream in terror as they ripped her from her bed.

Piotr Sadovsky woke up. He was drenched in sweat. It was dark, the middle of the night. He got out of bed, careful not to disturb Anna. He took a fresh pair of pyjamas from his chest of drawers and went to the bathroom, where he washed himself and got into his dry clothes. He wrapped his warm wool dressing gown about him and put on his slippers. He poked his nose round his daughter's bedroom, and she was tucked up, sound asleep.

He went downstairs and along the corridor of his dacha in his slippered feet, his dressing down about him, and peered through the small pane of glass. He could see nothing except the trees. He unlocked the door and looked out. Only the soft air and the scent of pine and flowers came towards him.

He locked up and padded back inside the dacha. Upstairs he had a little room, a model room where he planned his projects. He went in and switched on the light, having closed the door. He had a table where he could make designs and it gave him comfort. He sat down at it and thought about escape.

His nightmares visited him with increasing frequency. He glanced at the clock he had made with his own hands, where a priest sitting eating and drinking at a laden table got up on the hour and, propelled by clockwork, mounted a spiral staircase to emerge at the top and strike the bell with his tankard. He had nearly thirty minutes more gourmandising before his next trip because it was just past midnight.

Piotr Sadovsky thought about escape. His nightmares were not fantasy. One day, men in uniforms *would* come and take him away, and he would never see his wife and daughter again.

But it was not simple. One could not hide. One could not go to another city under another name. Strangers would be denounced. There were plenty of those who had denounced everyone they knew, and roamed the streets looking for those they did not.

One had to escape, which meant abroad. Which meant transport across the frontier. But people, whole families, did not travel across the frontier. Individuals did, on state business, and left their families behind, as bail money, to be forfeited should they fail to return.

Which left goods. Goods passed through the frontier, as a matter of trade. There was, for example, something sitting in his factory that had been constructed outside Russia, and brought in. A tank. A British Vickers. It had arrived, ostensibly to take part in a competition against an American Christie and a French Char, organised by the Military Directorate, but in reality to have its best design features stolen, copied and improved.

It was time for the Vickers to be returned to its owners, together with a letter regretting its lack of technical sophistication. He, the factory director, would accompany it on its way to be shipped from Leningrad.

He took a sheet of paper and quickly sketched the machine. The engine was large, an Armstrong-Siddely straight eight, housed in the front of the boxy machine. Removed, it would leave plenty of room for three people to hide as the tank was lifted by the crane into the hold of the freighter. Padding would make it comfortable and they could take aboard food and drink. Once on the high seas they could emerge, requesting asylum in Great Britain. There, he was sure, there would be work for a man like himself.

Anna . . . Anna would be a problem. Inside either of their two homes she felt safe. She made the short trip between the two in the sedan, the curtains drawn and her eyes closed. Her terror of the outside world had not diminished as he had hoped. She knew that out there, *they* lurked, ready and waiting to commit hideous harm to her.

Somehow, she would have to be asleep. He would have to get hold of sleeping tablets, to drug her for a day, maybe for two.

Outside, it was dark. He wondered if he should go back to bed. But he was begining to be afraid of sleep, afraid of the nightmares, afraid of the men who came in his dreams.

He switched out the light, and then he heard the knocking. A soft, insistent knock on the front door. He went to the window. There was a man down there, a dark figure. Sweat broke out all over his body, hot and prickling, then clammy cold. He made himself pull up the window.

'Who is it?' he called hoarsely.

'It's me, your friend. Academician Vyshinsky, Piotr. Did I wake you? I have your colleague Stukalov, I got him out of the Lubyanka. Can you come out and get him?'

'Of course, Comrade Vyshinsky, I am coming now.'

His heart was pounding as he went down the stairs and along the corridor in his slippered feet, his warm wool dressing gown wrapped about him.

He opened the door and he could see a van parked on the path between the larches and birches.

'I have him in the back,' said Vyshinsky, as they hurried through the darkness, their feet scuffling on the stones. Vyshinsky opened the rear door.

'Up you get,' he said to Sadovsky and gave him a helping push up inside.

It was dark, pitch black.

'Andrei?' Sadovsky called hesitantly. 'Are you all right? It's me, Piotr.'

There was a sudden loud metallic clang behind him as the rear door slammed shut.

'Hey!'

He fumbled at the inside, but it was smooth, without a handle. Through the window he saw Vyshinsky stepping back and the lawyer waved mockingly at him. The moon came out from behind a cloud and he saw the uniformed men crashing through the front door of the dacha, he heard his daughter shriek in terror as they ripped her from her bed.

Then the engine started, and the van rocked as it took off down the path. He reached out for support, and fell against something hanging from the roof. He fell to the metal floor in horror as the van swayed down the road, and the dead hands of Andrei Stukalov slapped his face . . .

Moscow

Through the window, the coloured onion domes of the cathedral shone like lollipops. Inside the room, Rykov ran his finger down the white silk of the dress on its stand.

'I hope you were going to invite me to the wedding,' he murmured.

'Of course I was,' said Konstantin. He was by the window. He washed his hands together nervously.

'That's good. I'm fond of weddings, I am.' He turned. 'This must be the beautiful bride,' he said and something strange glittered behind his eyes. 'I'm sure I've seen you somewhere before.'

'I'm an actress,' Katia said smoothly. She lounged against the wall. 'You've probably seen one of my films.'

'Before that, I think . . .'

'Katia's just leaving,' Konstantin said.

'Oh, so soon? Not now we've met, surely?'

Rykov was wandering about the room in short moves, picking things up and putting them down again. He was like a weasel that knew its prey was close. Konstantin, the large, transfixed rabbit, watched him helplessly.

'What's this?' Rykov had a slim pen. He drew a line with it on some paper, experimentally.

'Just a pen.'

'It's too thin to write with.'

'It's for fine artwork.'

'Why don't we all have a drink?' Katia drawled. She went to the cupboard and took out glasses. A bottle was uncorked and she splashed ruby red wine into them. Rykov put the pen back down, moving away from the desk and Konstantin sagged slightly in relief.

'Long life,' said Rykov, and smiled like a wolf. He drained the glass in one swallow. 'Well, I must be off,' he said. 'Lots to do.'

He put the glass down on the desk. Then he picked up the pen again. 'You shouldn't leave things lying about,' he said. 'Keep things tidy, that's my motto.'

He slid open the drawer and took out the documents inside. 'This must be the artwork you were talking about.'

He looked up at Konstantin, white-faced by the window. 'Very nice,' he said. 'Very nice indeed. But you're a good artist, Konstantin. I knew that when you did the boss's portrait. Genius, I said to myself. Who can this tall, powerful man with hands like a gorilla be? Who but our beloved leader. Yes.'

Rykov dropped the documents on to the desk. 'You'd hardly know which was the real one, would you?'

He went over to the door and, for a second, hope flickered in Konstantin's soul. Outside, two men leaned against the wall.

'Take Konstantin along with you, lads,' Rykov said affably.

He closed the door and, in the room, there was just the clatter of their feet going down the stairs.

'I really have to get back,' said Rykov. 'Young Yezhof keeps us busy, oh yes.'

He ran his finger down the white silk of the dress. 'So pretty,' he murmured and looked up at her, his eyes as sharp as a bird. 'Let's see you in it, then, love.'

Katia came off the wall, her russet hair swinging in a glorious sheet.

She was wearing a blue wrap-around skirt, and a blue-and-white striped man's shirt. She stood in front of him and unbuttoned it, from the top down. When the last one was done, she slid it off her shoulders, and it fell to the floor in a soft heap. She was wearing nothing under it. She undid the knot of the skirt, and it pooled about her ankles.

'Put on the dress,' Rykov ordered hoarsely.

'Who needs a silly dress?' she whispered. She took a step forward, so that she was almost touching him. 'Just do it to me.'

She rotated her hips, and ran her tongue over her lips.

'The dress!' said Rykov.

'Come on. You're in the Cheka . . . show me how big it is.' Her hand went out and prodded his trousers. 'I know you're hiding it in there somewhere,' she said, and smiled mockingly.

'People are afraid of me,' Rykov said slowly.

Her eyes widened in simulated amazement. 'It's *that* big?'

His hand whirled in an arc, and there was something glittering in it. Blood fountained from her face as she staggered back against the wall.

'I've never liked this film,' she said.

It was not cold in the cell, but Konstantin lay curled up on the plank bed, his knees pulled up to his chest. He heard the footsteps coming down the passage and he forced himself to sit up. In the half light, he could see Rykov who swayed slightly on his feet. He might have been drunk.

'My boots are dirty,' he said. 'I want them clean.'

Konstantin crawled on his stomach across the floor and licked the boots from toe to heel.

'I'll take you home,' said Rykov. In the corridor Konstantin wiped his mouth with his hand and, in the light of the bare bulbs, saw it was dark with smeared blood.

Rykov stopped the car. The lights of the cathedral glittered, not far away. 'You can get out,' he said.

'Why?' Konstantin whispered. 'Why?'

'I saw a cat with a bird, once. When I was young,' Rykov said affably. His breathing was quiet again, and he did not seem drunk, now. 'It had it in its paws and let it go, from time to time. It would fly, just for a second . . .'

Konstantin opened the door, and lurched on to the pavement.

'Take care,' said Rykov.

21

Parilka

THERE had been blood on the floor outside Krivitskiy's office,
a cleaner, a *babushka* as shapeless as a stuffed sack had been
mopping it up with a dirty grey cloth and a bucket when they had
brought him in. But he was unharmed, and so was Savinkov, sitting
next to him on the chair while Krivitskiy sorted out his papers.

'Sorry you've got caught up in all this, Piotr Pavlovich,' he said.
'I'll find the forms in a minute, Ah, here they are. Look, we'd like
to put you in with Sergei's trial, but it does mean you learning your
lines quite quickly. Sergei's been with us a while, of course and he
knows his.'

Sadovsky stole a look at Savinkov, sitting quiet on his wooden
chair. He was unmarked. He was very pale, and his skin was clear,
like wax. Sadovsky almost felt he could see right through it, to the
skull beneath.

'You can fuck off,' he said roughly. 'Why the hell should I? I've
done nothing.'

'There's no need to be like that,' Krivitskiy said mildly. 'I'm just
trying to help. Ask Sergei, here. He's going to say his stuff like a good
fellow and I'll see to it he gets a light sentence. A bit of work feeding
the pigs on a state farm and, before he knows it, it's back to Moscow.
I can do the same for you.'

'There's no need. I'll be walking out of here today. That bastard Vyshinskiy is the one who's fucked up. Once First Secretary
Khrushchev hears about it'll be Vyshinskiy on trial, not me.'

'Oh. Well, suit yourself then.'

He pressed a buzzer on his desk.

'Do you mind cooling your heels a bit while you're waiting?'

A guard opened the door. Outside, the floor was clean, just a
shining wet mark to show where the blood had been. As the door
closed, Sadovsky could see Savinkov still sitting silent in the chair,
staring at nothing.

Another door, the sound of music. It opened and he went in. A strange sight, a slender man doing pirouettes in the middle of a bare floor. A wind-up record player, a chair.

'Ah, a new student for the dance class.' The man beamed. 'Do you like dancing, Director Sadovsky?'

'I have danced the mazurka, from time to time.'

'Ah, the mazurka . . .'

The dancer performed some twirls across the floor, holding an imaginary partner. He stopped abruptly, in front of Sadovsky. 'Here,' he said, 'we do the *stoika*. Come.'

Along one wall, set on the floor, ran a slim, shiny rail, perhaps three inches in the air.

'Now, slip off your shoes and socks.'

Sadovsky did so.

'And stand like so. That's it. Face to the wall, and *up* on your toes. *Lovely*.'

Sadovsky stood on tiptoe, staring at the wall. 'Is this it?' he asked. The violins swept to a close and he could hear the dancer slipping the seventy-eight back into its sleeve.

'That's it. A rather dull dance. I'm afraid. Only one step.'

The needle hissed and another record came on. Sadovsky's calves began to ache . . .

It was dark outside. It was quiet, the needle of the gramophone lay inert at the middle of the record and there was just the regular breathing of the dancer resting in his chair, and the splatter of the sweat running from Sadovsky's face hitting the floor. His legs were on fire from his toenails to the small of his back and his breath came in deep gasps of pain. He peeked cautiously over his shoulder; the dancer was asleep. Grimacing with relief, he put down his heels.

The blow threw him up in the air. He crashed to the floor and the slim metal rod sent a second bolt of electricity through his tortured calves. Unable to control himself he thrashed on the boards at its command, his muscles contorted in cramp.

The pain stopped and he became aware that he was screaming. The dancer was looking down at him.

'I should have told you about the electricity.' he said. He dragged forward a wicker chair. 'Fancy a seat?'

'Please,' Sadovsky croaked. He crawled across the boards and dragged himself upright. The chair had no middle so he crouched on the rim. Almost immediately, the pain started.

'It's not very comfortable,' he whispered.

'I know,' said the dancer.

'Oh.'

The dancer was resting in an armchair.

'Look, couldn't I get off for a while. Nobody would know. There's just you and me.'

'That's it,' said the dancer, rotating an ankle in exercise. 'Either you or me. So it's you, I'm afraid. But I'll tell you what, how about something to eat to take your mind off it? I've got some sandwiches.'

'Yes, please.'

The dancer reached out. He had a packet wrapped up in greaseproof paper and he opened it and took out some thick-cut sandwiches. Sadovsky could see the ham. He tore into it ravenously and didn't notice how salty it was until he had almost finished.

The dancer was pouring himself a glass of water.

'Could I have some, please?' Sadovsky asked. The dancer shook his head.

'Sorry . . .'

The dancer yawned. The light was now washing the window a pale grey.

'Time for my bye-byes, I think,' he said. Sadovsky peered at him through swollen eyelids. He had a fever. Sweat had soaked his clothes and it was in his shoes. They squelched as his legs beat out a tremor on the chair that he could not control.

The dancer stood up. 'You must be bored, with just me for company.'

The door opened again and two guards came in. They lifted Sadovsky up off the chair and he screamed as the blood ran through his legs.

He could walk again, after a fashion, by the time they had gone down into the basement. It was gloomy down there, lit by small yellow bulbs hanging from the tunnel roof, and hot. An iron door was open and they were dragging people out into the corridor. With them came a terrible stench, of ordure, blood and death.

Some of the people were dead and they put them in a pile. A man stood gasping near Sadovsky, pulling the foul, hot air into his lungs as though it were coming off a mountain slope. His naked legs were swollen and dark and from toenails sunk into the flesh, black blood was oozing.

They were pushing the prisoners back through the door and Sadovsky was with them. Now the stench was all about him, hot and noisome like a dragon's breath. He was jammed up against people he did not know, his flesh burning as it touched theirs. Things were crawling upon him from them, biting him. They were in his hair and from somewhere in the dreadful room a woman was beginning to wail.

'It helps when they take the dead out,' someone said next to him. It was a woman's voice. 'It gives us a little more room,' she said. In the faint light filtering through the wire-glass window he could see her.

'Welcome to the *parilka*,' said Yelena.

'I've been dancing the *stoika*,' he mumbled. His tongue was swollen and dry in his mouth and he could feel things moving in his clothes. 'What the hell is biting me?'

'Lice,' said Yelena. 'Bedbugs. Fleas. There's a grille and they throw in a box full every so often.'

In the half-light from the window he could see her face was puffed with lumpy bites. Something moved on her temple and she caught it between finger and thumb, he heard it crack, smelled a foul odour.

'I'm used to them,' she said. 'I just hate them in my hair.'

'When did they get you?' he asked.

'A few days ago. The children are in Minsk, thank God – I got them out. Where Ivan is I do not know . . .'

The iron door opened again.

'*Prisoner Akulova!*'

'What now?' she said quietly. They began pulling people out so that she could squeeze through the press. In the half light he saw her suddenly smile at him.

'Do you know what I did?' she whispered joyfully. 'I sent a letter, denouncing Rykov! Not signed, of course. Maybe they'll come for *him*!'

He felt her squeeze his arm. 'Have courage, Piotr Pavlovich. This, too, will pass.'

She came out into the corridor and they were stuffing the people back in. The female guard clubbed her with a gloved hand.

'Up the stairs, filth.'

Someone was coming down, a woman being dragged between two guards. She struggled in a shapeless shirt of coarse cloth and her face was contorted in terror as she screamed in silence. Anna Sadovskya!

They were pushing the people back in and there was someone thrashing by the door as it closed. In the last bar of light Sadovsky saw Anna. Desperately, he began to push at the people hemming him in and they cursed him for it.

'My wife . . .' he gasped.

The light was filtering through the wired glass and through the weaving heads, the waving hands he could see her. Her eyes were

closed to keep the demons out and she was winding the arm of her
shirt around her neck.

'*Anna!*'

There was the scraping of iron from above and men and women
and children screamed and cursed and cried as flying, crawling, biting
insects showered down upon them from above.

'*Anna!*'

It was wound tight. She had her arm in it and was twisting it like
a tourniquet, round and round. He struggled to get through, his feet
slipping on the ordure that covered the floor. They hit him in their
anger and sharp nails opened up his face.

He was next to the window and through the dirt he could see
Krivitskiy. He beat frantically on its surface.

'*I'll do it! I'll do it!*'

Krivitskiy did not turn round. By the door, Anna's eyes opened.
She stared at nothing.

'Let me through . . .' he wept. 'Please, let me through . . .'

It was a courtroom, anyone could see that. The judge wore robes
and he and counsel addressed each other courteously. The seal of
the party was on the wall. There was a dock, a clerk of the court
and stern, uniformed warders to take the prisoners down. There was
a gallery, where the public could sit and see justice done. The dancer
looked down attentively from the front row as Sadovsky got up in
the dock.

Vyshinsky looked sternly at him. 'You have been charged with
espionage, wrecking, and spying for the British imperialists,' he
intoned. 'How do you plead, prisoner Sadovsky?'

'Guilty,' he whispered.

'Speak up, we can't hear you,' Vyshinsky ordered brusquely.

'Guilty. I am guilty.'

The floor her swollen feet shuffled over was polished wooden parquet.
So she was still in the Lubyanka. She might not have been.

It had been very hot in the *kartser*. Central heating pipes ran
through the small hole and a large bulb dangled from the ceiling. By
its light she made herself catalogue the different types of occupant:
One human being, thirty-six sorts of insect, all feeding on the first.
It was a way of staying sane.

It was hard to remember the days, they had kept her awake so
long. Smoke seemed to rise in front of her eyes. She had left the insects
behind, but still felt them on her skin. But the floor her swollen feet

shuffled over was polished wooden parquet, so she was still in the Lubyanka.

It was a different room but the powerful lights cut half of it off. A beautiful young woman was waiting for her. She was dressed in a shaped blue skirt and a white shirt. In front of her was a strong wooden chair.

The guards put her in it, and strapped her legs and arms to the wood. From behind the glare came a young man, fit, arrogant and heartless, the new breed of Chekist. They had shot most of the old ones. She had a feeling he had been a part of her first interrogation team, that his name had been Andrey.

'It is time for you to confess,' he said. He used the word *ti*, insulting and intimate and, irrationally, she was annoyed.

'Mind your manners,' she said sharply. He smiled at the young woman, who was preparing a small tray of instruments by the chair.

'There speaks an aristo,' he said mockingly, and the back of his hand smacked into her face. From behind the glare of the lights came a gagged, incoherent roar of rage, followed by the slap of a rubber truncheon on flesh.

'We're going to jog your memory,' he said. 'She's all yours, Natasha.'

The girl knelt down in front of Yelena. She had a white kidney-shaped bowl by her, and a pair of shiny medical forceps in her hand. She used them to grip the smallest nail on Yelena's left foot, and squeezed so that the catch engaged. Then she began to pull.

From behind the lamp came again the muffled sounds of fury, once more followed by repeated blows. This time she knew.

'Don't, Ivan!' she called. 'It won't do any good – they will only beat you.'

The nail tore from its bed and the girl dropped it in the bowl. Her hands were coated with a fine, bloody spray and she moved to the next toe on Yelena's foot.

'I know you,' said Yelena. 'Do you know me?'

The pain was excruciating and she gripped on to the arms of the chair with slippery hands.

'You are an enemy of the people,' the girl replied unemotionally. She pulled steadily and expertly, not allowing the nail to come free too soon.

'Is this where they promoted you to, Natasha? Did you take the grain from the starving children? Did you take their clothes, their last pot of borscht? Did you empty out the old folks' storage chests? Did you ignore their protests, ignore the crying of the little ones? And, in the spring, did you drive the dying out into the fields to fulfil the revolutionary sowing-plan, in shock-worker style? Were you so good that they promoted you here?'

The nail came free and Yelena's legs shuddered in a tattoo of pain. She ground her teeth together to stop from screaming.

'I performed my revolutionary duty. I, and those who sent me, knew better than the class-enemy peasants how they should live, what they should sow and plough,' Natasha said calmly. 'There, as here, we realise historical necessity. I work for the socialist Fatherland. *I* fulfil the plan.'

'I went to school with your mother,' Yelena said. 'Is she happy that her daughter is a professional torturer?'

'My mother, like you, is an enemy of the people. Any suffering I seem to cause, is, in fact, due to the machinations of the class enemy. I work so that the great and necessary transformation of society may be accomplished. I cleanse that society so that the people may be free and happy.'

She gripped one of Yelena's bleeding toes between her forceps and began to crush it.

'You must understand,' she said, 'that it is you who is doing this, not I.'

Yelena screamed, then, for the pain was worse than anything that had gone before. As she bit into her lip she could hear, from behind the lights, a man laughing.

'I wish to confess,' she said suddenly. Natasha looked up, and the pressure upon her toe eased. The man Andrey came forward from the wall where he had been leaning.

'I am a British spy,' she said. Andrey picked up one of the standard confession forms from his desk. Someone hissed angrily at him from behind the lights and he shrugged.

'Good choice, Countess,' he said approvingly. 'Spying for the British has more class, for an aristo.'

'First I must tell you who it was who recruited me, who made me betray the Party.'

Andrey's expression became weary and Natasha looked up, all attention.

'I suppose you must,' Andrey said reluctantly. 'And we go and arrest them, and *they* denounce twenty more . . .' He sighed. 'I'm not getting enough sleep . . . who is it, then?'

'His name is Oleg Rykov. He works for Stalin himself and it was *he* who made me betray the Party.'

Muffled sounds of agreement came from Akulov, behind the lights.

There was silence in the hot room, just the buzzing of the high-powered lamps. The two young interrogators stared at each other, and then at Yelena.

'Untie Pani Akulova,' Andrey said sharply.

'But . . .' said Natasha.

The guards bent to loosen the bonds and lifted her out of the chair.

'Take her back to the cells.'

It was quiet in the interrogation room. A chair scraped and a man came forward into the light of the lamps. It was Rykov. He stared furiously at the two interrogators.

'Bring her back!' he demanded. 'That was just the beginning.'

'She has confessed,' said Natasha. She looked at Rykov. 'And has implicated you.'

'Natasha, go and make us some coffee, there's a good girl,' said Andrey. She went into a small annex of the room and the two men heard the rattle of cups.

'Look, Comrade,' said Andrey, 'I just wouldn't recommend we bring her back. I know her sort. She'll implicate you again and there is that business of the anonymous denunciation of you we received . . . We're getting ready to change shifts, and the next is headed by Boyarsky. He doesn't have my understanding of these things. You made it worth my while and I let you have your fun. Natasha yanked out her nails and you heard her scream. But if we bring her back and she names you Boyarsky'll have *you* in the chair, close to Stalin or not, and if he says you're an enemy of the people Natasha will rip *your* nails out. My advice is leave it be.'

He turned back to his table and picked up his papers as Natasha came back with small cups of fragrant black coffee.

'See how they'll stop at nothing, these enemies of the state,' Andrey commented. 'They'll even try to destroy those in the trust of Stalin himself.'

At his name, Natasha felt her eyes prickle with love, and felt her resolve to root out all who would damage the state quicken again.

'Sometimes when I am tired I think of him, and then I find new energy again,' she confessed.

The two men looked at her expressionlessly. Andrey turned to filling in details on the forms. 'What about the sentence?' he said absently.

'What is usual?' Rykov asked softly.

'Well, tell the truth, Comrade, we've been shooting most recently. The overcrowding here's that bad we need the space.'

'I have the ear of Stalin. It was at his request that I came here, you understand. She has committed crimes I cannot tell you about. But shooting is much too merciful.'

'What shall we do?' asked Natasha.

Rykov switched off the arc lamps. In the light of the ordinary bulb they could see Akulov strapped to his chair, the gag biting viciously into his mouth, his face striped with fresh scarlet weals. Rykov absently slipped the rubber truncheon from his pocket and whipped him across his cheeks.

'Kolyma,' he said. 'Send them both to Kolyma.' He reached out and picked up the forms. 'Here, you get off to bed. I'll handle the paperwork for you.'

He went out. Andrey sat down at the desk, and began to work through his papers.

'I'm going to go and take a shower,' Natasha said. 'I'll see you tomorrow.'

She went out, and Andrey continued his work of sorting through the documents, his pen scratching in the quiet room, piling the forms in piles, those to be shot, those for the camps, those still holding out, those to be arrested.

When he was ready to go he noticed Akulov still slumped behind him, and picked up the phone.

'Send removal men, two.'

They unstrapped Akulov, undid his gag, dragged him to his feet. Between them, he shuffled painfully along the polished parquet corridor. He, too, had danced the *stoika*, day after agonising day. It was a long corridor. In the day well-groomed people tended their files and papers in the offices at each side. Now, as he pulled himself along, he heard the sounds of the night crew at work.

A young woman was screaming, 'don't you dare! Don't you dare!' she shrieked, and her voice splintered into a hundred notes. 'How can you?'

As he passed, a door was flung open by a sweating young man. Without looking at him he turned back into the room, where his colleagues were whipping a man with rubber hoses. Akulov recognised Savinkov, through the blood. His face was purple and he screamed 'Mama', 'Mama', over and over again.

A figure came out of a room, went away ahead of them.

'*Krivitskiy!*' Akulov yelled hoarsely. A truncheon dug brutally into his stomach and he collapsed on the floor. A pair of polished shoes came up and stood close by his face.

'Stand him up.'

They put Akulov against the wall and Krivitskiy waved them off to stand along the corridor.

'What do you want?' he said coldly. 'I can't get you out of this. Have you confessed?'

'I have done nothing but my duty as a Red Army officer. I shall not confess to anything else.'

A spasm of rage crossed Krivitskiy's face. '*Nobody's* done anything, you stupid peasant's son!' he whispered. 'That's the *point*.'

He moved, so that Akulov could see Savinkov inside the room. They had stopped whipping him and had him by the hands. He shrieked in agony and Akulov saw that they were pushing large, sharpened matchsticks under his fingernails.

'What do you think *he's* doing here?'

'You want him to confess to something he has not done.'

'You're a stupid peasant. He's already confessed. He's been tried and sentenced. They're shooting him in the morning.'

Savinkov lit up like a roman candle as the phosphorus ignited. Someone kicked the door shut, but it did not shut out the noise.

'*Why?*' said Akulov hoarsely. 'What is the point?'

'The boss prefers it that way,' Krivitskiy said simply, expressionlessly.

'Yelena has been taken,' Akulov said. 'She has been sentenced to Kolyma.'

'Then she, like you and like Savinkov in there, must accept her fate.'

'Rykov was there. He took the papers. He has her and she will not get to Kolyma. He will murder my wife slowly.'

'Kolyma will kill you slowly, too. That it what it is for, it is the *padezh*, the murrain to kill the cattle.'

'Not like Rykov will,' Akulov said desperately.

Krivitskiy shrugged, turning away.

'*Where did you go to school, Commissar?*'

Krivitskiy turned back, expressionlessly.

'Yelena thinks Rykov has a copy of your school photograph and you're on it. They're killing people like you, Commissar. It'll be in Rykov's apartment. It'll be there with my wife.'

The street was dimly-lit, the buildings old but solid. The boots of the two NKVD men echoed in the stone stairwell as they pulled Yelena up. Her foot left splashes of blood on every other stair. In the morning people would avert their gaze, the same way as they would pull the pillows over the heads, so as not to hear her screams.

Rykov had two of the old high-ceilinged, Tsarist rooms, big and airy, an entrance hallway, his own bathroom and kitchen. It was as much a symbol of his power as the dread silence of his neighbours.

They took her into the bedroom. The bed was large, fitted with spotless white sheets and pillows. Long white tapers burned on either side of its head and draped across its foot was a wedding dress. Rykov had heard the opening of the door and he stood waiting, smiling.

'Welcome, mistress,' he said. He was dressed in the black leather of the Cheka that she had not seen for more than fifteen years. He raised a hand, indicating his uniform. 'Good days, mistress, good days,' he said softly. 'Ones that are back again.'

She remained silent. She was very afraid, and knew she must try to control it.

'Here is your wedding dress. Won't you put it on?'

She looked at it, tired, stained and torn, but once, a thing of great beauty.

'It is not mine,' she said. 'It is Zhenya's. I was there when the seamstress came to fit it to her. And Zhenya is dead, frozen in a block of ice. The dress is ruined.'

Ryko nodded approvingly. 'Many have worn it. But none so suited, until now, as you. So put it on.'

'No!'

The two GPU men gripped her elbows and she had the horrible realisation that all three had played out this scene before, that she, like other girls, was the only one unfamiliar with the proceedings.

She was wearing the shapeless trousers and shirt of a prisoner. Rykov lifted the shirt. He had a knife in his hand and she felt the blade nick her stomach as he cut the string and the trousers fell to the floor. He cut the buttons of the shirt, one by one, and they pulled it off.

'Blood on white skin,' said Rykov, looking at her, 'is very attractive.'

The eyes of the two guards were elsewhere on her body. She wanted to cover herself, just as she wanted to beg for her life, but she knew that that was what Rykov wanted, too, and she forced herself to stand up straight. She said nothing.

'When it's just an ordinary one – we look through the cells for a nice aristo, don't we, lads?'

The two men chuckled, obscenely.

'When it's just an ordinary one, I let the lads have some fun first, because my fun is a little different, and there's nothing for the lads to have fun with afterwards. But this time, as it's you, mistress, I'm going to have you all to myself. The lads won't mind. I'll arrange a little treat for them tomorrow. So let's get you into the dress.'

It smelled as they pulled it on her, and it was stained with blood.

'Beautifully clean it was when Zhenya had it on, and young Verochka, too,' said Rykov. 'But that was a long time ago.'

Over the mantelpiece there was a photograph. It was the same as the one she had in her own home. Young men and women looked out, the anxiety or anticipation in their smiles reflecting their fears and hopes of their revolutionary futures.

'There you all are,' said Rykov.

'Why?' she asked. 'Why? What is the point?'

His eyes shone as he looked at her in the candlelight. 'That *is* the point, mistress. This is the revolution.'

'The revolution has been over a long time.'

'Oh, no. The revolution goes on forever. It never stops.'

'There is to be no peace, no normal life?'

'What is normal? *This* is normal, to me.'

'But all this? This dress, this horrible play you are making of me. That you have done to others.'

'You can shoot someone, mistress, and you never get to their soul, to where it is, and how it goes and shows itself. I found that out in the war. We had to shoot lots of people, to make the others fight. But if you weren't rushed, it was more interesting to shoot them a piece at a time, and that was how you got to know them. It's more interesting to hang a man upside down from a tree, and talk to him over a day or two. With someone like you, it is more interesting to put you in the wedding dress, and spend the night together, your last night, just you and I.'

He came over to her and put his hands on her, and she could not prevent herself from shuddering, her very skin crawling.

'That's good,' Rykov whispered. 'Very good . . .'

There was the tramp of boots outside and the crash of the door being thrown back. Krivitskiy came in, with three men at his back. He was in uniform, the lozenges of his rank on his shoulder-boards. He looked at the scene in the soft light.

'The train's leaving,' he said. 'Prisoner Akulova is wanted aboard.'

'So soon?' said Rykov. 'The Countess has been trying on new clothes.'

'The train!' Krivitskiy's voice was harsh.

'Very well.'

Yelena felt fingers at her back, undoing the buttons, and the dress slipped from her shoulders. Krivitskiy took a coat from one of his

men and she put it around her. They went outside and she gagged
on the stairs and was sick. She straightened up and Krivitskiy was
pushing the bent photograph inside his uniform jacket.

A car was waiting. It stopped streets away, to let Krivitskiy out
into the night.

'Keep the coat,' he said. 'It's cold in Kolyma.'

She pushed her hands into the pockets and found in one some
notes, wadded up. Surreptitiously, she rolled them together, and
pushed them up into her hair.

In his apartment Rykov was filling in forms. He wrote in Yelena's
full name, and the proven charge of spying. She was convicted
under Article 58 of the Corrective Labour Codex of the RSFSR.
Her category was sentence for Counter-Revolutionary Trotskyite
Activity. Its length was twenty-five years. He signed it, printing
his name and rank underneath, before affixing the correct stamps.
Rykov's paperwork was always impeccable . . .

The Lubyanka, Moscow

The door of the cell crashed as the guard threw it back.

'First Secretary of the Moscow *Obkom*,' he announced loudly,
and Khrushchev came into the room. It stank of sweat, blood and
malevolence. It was an unpleasant and unique odour, but he had
become used to it since inspections of the city's jails had been added
to his list of duties.

A man lay slumped on the stone floor, a very big man, his naked
body as striped and colourful as a Persian carpet, the bruises, lumps
and weals upon it every shade from yellow to vermilion. His wrists
and ankles were manacled. A young man and woman stood over him,
long black rubber hoses swinging from their hands. They looked up
and fell back as Khrushchev came in. The girl was quite beautiful, in
an icy fashion. She pushed her long yellow hair out of her eyes. On
the bloody floor the big man moved, slowly, and painfully.

'Any problems?' Khrushchev said formally. It was a part of the
job. The state had enemies, they had to be taken care of.

'A stubborn one, Comrade,' the young man said with a smile.

'Nothing we can't solve, First Secretary,' the girl agreed.

The tortured body was swollen and marked, everywhere but his right arm.

'Why that?' Khrushchev asked, pointing.

The young man smiled amiably. 'He's got to be able to *sign*, now hasn't he? Can't just make a mark, not an officer like this one.'

The big man had pushed himself to his hands and knees.

'Carry on then.'

'Wait. Nikita Sergeyevich, wait!'

It was the man they were beating. His deep voice croaked, his battered face was turned towards Khrushchev. With a thrill of horror, he recognised him.

'This is Divisional Commander Akulov!' he said to the two interrogators. He sounded shocked. 'What is *he* doing here?'

'Ah . . . he was brought in . . . he is charged with espionage . . .' The young man. Andrey, sounded flustered.

'I am guilty of nothing . . .' Akulov rasped.

There was a chair. Khrushchev indicated it with a flick of his hand. 'Sit him down.'

With difficulty, the two helped Akulov up and into the chair. There was a handtowel which they used to wipe their faces on the table. Khrushchev took it and put it over Akulov's lap.

'You say he is stubborn,' he demanded. 'What do you mean? He will not confess?'

'That's right, sir,' said Andrey. 'Natasha and I have been working for weeks now . . .'

The girl slipped past him. 'Excuse me,' she murmured. 'I'll be back in a moment.'

She went out through a side door, behind the powerful lamps and Khrushchev said something he had never said before.

'Perhaps he isn't guilty.'

Akulov looked up at him, and gratitude burned deep in his eyes.

'I am guilty of nothing but doing my duty as a Red Army officer,' he grunted.

'It is odd that he hasn't confessed,' Andey murmured acquiescently.

'Confession is all. Is that not what Prosecutor Vyshinsky says? Confession is proof of guilt. And here we have a man who has not confessed after weeks.'

'Perhaps he is not guilty,' agreed Andrey.

Behind the lights the door opened and there was the sound of people coming in. Natasha emerged into the glare but the other stayed behind, in the shadow.

'But he has to be guilty,' Natasha said softly. 'The Party has charged him, and the Party cannot, by its nature, make a mistake.'

Andrey had his back to the lights. His eyes were frightened and they tried to look over his shoulder. Behind the lights, a man coughed softly, tapped his fingers gently on the table.

The colour was slowly draining from Khrushchev's round, ruddy face. 'That is, of course, so,' he whispered. 'That is something we must never forget.'

The hope in Akulov's eyes died. Khrushchev found that he could not look at him.

'What should we do, First Secretary Khrushchev?' Natasha asked blandly. Behind her, the fingers tapped, a shoe scraped.

'You must obtain a confession. To prove guilt,' he muttered. He began to turn away, but her voice brought him back.

'But how? We have not managed it so far.'

'Beat him!' he choked.

'What if that doesn't work?'

'*Beat and beat again*!' he screamed. 'Isn't that what you do?'

The door crashed against the wall as he went out and they heard him hurrying away down the corridor. A foot emerged from behind the lights; it pushed the back of the chair forward with a savage jerk and Akulov fell to the floor.

'You heard the First Secretary,' Rykov murmured pleasantly. 'Carry out his instructions, Natasha.'

The young woman picked up her rubber whip joyfully and sent it whistling through the air.

'You fucking heap of cockroach shit!' she screamed.

Rykov turned to the ashen-faced man next to her. 'Andrey,' he murmured. 'Come with me a moment . . .'

Natasha Savinkova yawned. It was late, near the end of her shift. The door opened and a man came in with an official form in his hand.

'We'll have a bit of a rest this week,' he said cheerfully. 'They're having a clear out. Shipping them off to Kolyma.'

'Clear out?' she aded.

'Yes. The lot, confessions or not. Can't say I mind.' He looked about the empty office. 'Where's Andrey?'

'He was charged with espionage this afternoon,' she said with vicious satisfaction. 'With plotting to help prisoners escape.'

'Andrey?' the man said in amazement.

'He confessed,' she said precisely. 'I saw to it myself.' She frowned, looking at the paper. 'Here. Let me see that.'

The man handed it over. 'There it is. They're to be taken down to the railhead starting at five tomorrow morning. I'll be in my bed, lucky me.'

There it was, from the Party *gorkom* of Moscow *oblast*. Signed by First Secretary Khrushchev. She cursed, and got up, pushing the paper into the man's hands as she went out.

They had him in a cell, one of the small ones made for the big men. The bare bulb was on, as it was every hour of the day or night. He was covered by a thin cotton blanket and he woke and looked at her as the door banged open.

'They're shipping you out!' she hissed. 'You're escaping, you spying filth.'

'Shipping me where? To the camps?' Akulov asked. 'That is not escape.'

'You're escaping *me*, you syphilitic vermin. *I make everyone confess*. I am the will of the Party.'

She was white with rage. Suddenly, she reached down to the hem of her fitted blue skirt, pulling it up about her waist, standing over him with her legs apart. Underneath, she was naked.

'Take a good look. Where you're going you won't feel like fucking anyone.'

Akulov stared levelly at her from his battered, lacerated face. 'You are a nasty child, with nasty habits,' he said coldly. 'Now leave me in peace.'

He pulled the ragged blanket about him, and closed his eyes and she stood watching him in frustration. She looked like a spoiled little girl about to cry. The skirt fell about her knees, and she went out.

22

Padezh

Magadan, Kolyma

'YELENA. *Yelena!*'
She stood outside the long hut. When she had arrived she had
seen the sign above the door, which said Registration and Distribution. Over the gate she had come through with the others they
had seen the inscription: Labour is a matter of honour, valour and
heroism. But it was dark now. Her cheeks still stung from the blows
and it was very cold. The long, slow-moving millipede of grey
humanity had shuffled away into the maw of the camp and the dead
and unconscious had been taken up from the icy cobblestones of the
quay. The dying were stacked up like logs with the dead, the night's
chill to make both the same. A few thought worth saving had been
taken into the long hut next to the Registration section. And she stood
on her own outside, clutching her wet, ruined folder in her hands.
'*Yelena!*'
'Who is it?' she hissed back.
'It's *me*. Katerina.'
'Katerina! I can't see you. I'm blind in the dark. Where are you?'
'In the *slabosilk*. The infirmary. I'm to have my baby here. I was
pregant when the NKVD came for us . . . listen, the blindness is
because of the lack of vitamins. Lots of us get it in transit . . . you
need cod liver oil. Why are you standing out there?'
'I was ordered to. By one of the guards. A big woman with a
loud voice.'
'Gridassova! What did you do?'
'I dropped my file in a puddle. She says I am to stand here until
the registration section opens in the morning, to have it typed
out again.'
'Bitch! You've still got your coat, wrap it round you . . . how have
you kept a coat? The *urkas* stripped all us politicals of everything we
had on the ship when I came out . . .'

'Among our number was a woman called Tanya Shilova. she'd been a party worker, a foreman in a machine factory. She had hands like shovels and a voice like a volcano. When the apaché women descended on us in the hold she smashed one across the face with her hand, knocked her flying. She bellowed at them using their own language so they feared her and left us alone ... My papa always said, a lion among sheep, a sheep among lions. And then I told them stories, which kept them happy. Every day they came and sat in the horrible, stinking hold in the gloom, and I told them stories. They like *The Wind in the Willows* best. I had to tell the story of Badger and Mole and Ratty and Toad attacking the weasels lots of times.'

'Which ship?'

'The *Dzhurma*.'

'They still have the great tank in the hold? The one you squat on the rim of?'

'Yes. One of us had terrible diarrhoea, and she was found floating in there in the morning. They just left the body there ...'

There was a muttering in the dark.

'Yelena, darling, we're pushing a mug out to you at the end of a pole. We're at the window. Reach out your hand. Up a little. That's it.'

She felt its heat and she grasped it.

'It's tea. or what they call tea here. We've managed to put some butter in it, and some cod liver oil from the dispensary. We get good at stealing ...'

She drank and it was hot and sweet.

'Did they take Ivan?' Katerina asked.

'Yes.'

'You'll be fine, you'll see. You'll be together again. They shot Boris, but Ivan will live ...'

'Ivan will not confess. He still believes ... He will not confess to something he has not done.'

She finished the tea and the pole took it away again. It was very cold and she was starting to shiver, unable to stop.

'Katerina ... it's getting colder. The file has frozen stiff ... do you have anything I can wear?'

'Have you got any money? Anything of value? The trusty will sell us something.'

She reached into her hair, and found the tightly-rolled notes, greasy now, but still intact.

'I have roubles.'

The mug and pole came out again. and she thrust the money inside.

After a few minutes there was a thud close by, and something fell on her legs.

'Felt boots,' Katerina hissed. 'And a wool scarf. Wrap it round and round your head.'

Lights were flashing in her blind eyes, bright, lurid battlements jerked across her nerves and pain swept through her head like a thunderstorm breaking. She made herself put on the clothes. With the boots and the scarf she felt not warm, but less cold. She would not die in the long night. But now the money that she had guarded so carefully for the morning was gone. The long nail she had taken from the railway truck on the long journey to Vladivostok she had kept under her toes. Now it was in her hand. Carefully, stopping from time to time when the pain became too bad. she worked . . .

The morning came, in the end, and she could see. The skin of her brain was sore and pain ran across it like the fading sounds of thunder, going away in the distance. Someone like an old woman was looking at her from the window of the hut. She waved, and with stiff blue fingers Yelena waved back.

'Hallo, Katerina,' she croaked.

'Hallo, darling. I'm so glad you're still alive. They say here that God is on furlough, but He's not, you know. I can't talk long because the guards will be coming. When the baby's born I'll try and be with you but I must go now.'

People were moving about the great camp. A woman passed Yelena and unlocked the door of the Registration building and went in. Others followed over the next half hour. Then the first woman reappeared at the door.

'Come,' she said. Yelena shuffled after her, all her limbs stiff and unmoving from the cold that had gone all the way to the bone. The woman was dressed in a padded jacket and trousers, which she had kept on inside the building. She worked in a small office, at a table with a typewriter, and cast an experienced glance at Yelena.

'You can stand by the stove,' she said. She spoke quietly and quickly, with a good accent, of the old regime. She seemed about Yelena's age, although it was hard to tell through the damage.

'You'll have to learn quickly here,' she murmured. 'Dropping your file in a puddle is not clever.'

She fitted a fresh form into her machine and began to type quickly. 'You went to the Lycée. There's a woman in the infirmary expecting a child who went there. I did her form not long ago.'

'Katerina. I went to school with her.'

'Did you, now. My father used to say, sit in Chaliapin's long enough and you'd meet everyone you ever knew ... He hadn't been in a camp, of course,' she said wryly. 'Listen, if you are to have any chance of survival here you must get an indoor job. Last winter was very dangerous. Comrade Stalin ordered that the "coddling" of us prisoners had to stop. so if you're out there it's coats padded with paper and canvas shoes. It gets down to fifty degrees below freezing ... Maybe you'll meet someone you used to know, who can help you. If you get on to the logging teams you'll die ...'

Her fingers stopped working on the keys. 'Oh ...' she said flatly.

Yelena had been watching, intently. 'You've got to my category,' she said.

'Yes. You're KRTD, you're convicted of counter-revolutionary *Trotskyite* activity. Did your interrogator dislike you?'

'Yes. What, in real terms, does it mean?'

'Special instructions. During detention forbid all use of post and telegraph. Use only for the hardest labour, report on the conduct of the accused once every three months.'

'Do any last for three months?'

'Occasionally.'

'Six?'

'Never. That's the point of it. It's a passport to death.'

Yelena had her hand in her coat pocket, now she took it out and dropped a bloody, gold-crowned molar on to the desk.

'I dropped the file into the puddle because I meant to. Leave out the T. Then I'll just be a political.'

The woman stared at the gold, then scooped it up and put it into her own pocket. She started to type again. When she had finished she handed the damp, crumpled file to Yelena without looking at her.

'Put this rubbish in the stove,' she said. The little stove hissed as it consumed the wet paper and she looked up.

'You should have asked me to regrade you as a horse,' she said, with a slight smile. 'I'd be a horse, any day. I'd get good food. one day off in ten, only have to work according to my capacity and have my own warm stable and a blanket. But we're politicals, not as valuable as horses. Quickly now, what can you do? Anything unusual?'

'I'm good at gardening,' Yelena said, alert. 'Herbs. vegetables, fruit, flowers. The bosses must like to eat well, don't they?'

'They do,' the woman confirmed. She picked up a piece of paper, fitting it into the machine, and typed. 'Take this and go to Gumilyov at the farm. I'll show you where.'

'I have small hands,' said Yelena. 'I'm good with seedlings, if they have a greenhouse.'

'You do learn quickly. Very well. It's warm in a greenhouse.' She took out the paper and placed a stamp on it. 'Most of the guards can't read. If they stop you, hold this up. They respect the printed word.'

She passed it over, and said, 'I'll expect a bit of whatever you have. Herbs and garlic especially. I had scurvy last winter, nearly went blind, and a blind typist gets put on the logging team where you eat according to how much you work.'

'I will,' Yelena promised. 'An empty-handed gardener gets put on the logging teams, too.'

'I knew you were quick,' the other said and grinned.

Moscow, September 1939

'That the fresh batch?'

Krivitskiy took off his jacket and hung it over the back of his chair as he sat down. Marthe sat opposite, her pad ready to take notes.

They were in alphabetical order and the name on the first file caught Krivitskiy's eye immediately.

'Akulov,' he said. 'So he's still alive!' He opened it, and ran his finger through the reports. 'He's up in Kolyma. Hmm ... he wouldn't sign. That *is* unusual.'

'Is that the one who wouldn't confess?'

'Yes ... yes, it looks as though they couldn't break him. They got rather cross, it seems ... Let's see ... "Prisoner Akulov is stubborn and uncooperative. Under differing forms of pressure he refuses to confess. He maintains his loyalty to the Party and to the Red Army. When it is pointed out that all his fellow-officers confess when charged, sooner or later, he expresses amazement and states that clearly a mistake has been made. Too much time has been given to this prisoner and orders have come to clear the cells for fresh suspects so interrogation has now ceased. His circumstances – being in contact with agents of a foreign power – are such that contact leading to suspicion of espionage as defined by Article 58 took place and that a crime against the state has been committed. It is recommended that should the restriction on liquidation for his category be lifted he shall be shot." Yes, he *did* make someone cross. They don't like it if they can't break someone. I hope he isn't crippled – they did some nasty things to him.'

'What is his category?'

'Divisional tank commander. Do you know how long it takes to produce a man like that? Fifteen years of experience and training. Someone like Akulov is a national resource.' He smiled at Marthe. 'But don't say I said so.'

She smiled back, conspiratorially.

It was an added security, to have one's mistress as one's secretary. Krivitskiy could be sure she was not reporting back to Beria . . .

'Very well . . . what did they charge him with. Ah. He was one of the leading commanders in the joint Soviet-German tank school in Kazan. So they charged him with being a German spy. Well, in the light of the glorious agreement between our two countries, signed last month, pledging everlasting friendship, I think we can strike that out and put Prisoner Akulov to work.'

I cannot believe it,' she said softly, bitterly. 'I have devoted my life to fighting fascism, that is why I am a communist. To see Ribbentrop and those other Nazi swine here in Moscow, to see our leader Stalin embracing them . . . I could cry . . . I could.'

Krivitskiy shut Akulov's file and placed it neatly as the start of a new pile on his desk. 'Have the orders cut to send him to Unit 28,' he said.

He looked out of the window, over the square where black swastikas had so recently flown next to the gold hammer and sickle. The department responsible for the correct decoration and deportment of the streets on such international occasions had been caught completely by surprise. In desperation they had gone to a film studio where the equally-surprised director had stopped the production of his anti-Nazi propaganda epic and taken all the props.

'It won't last,' Krivitskiy said quietly. 'It will all end in tears. And worse.'

Kolyma

'*Katerina*. Over here.'

There was a small shed where they used to keep some carts. The vehicles had gone because the Ukrainians had burned them for fuel, but the shed remained, and you could hide out of sight. Katerina paused in her weary trudge and turned inside.

'Here,' said Yelena, pushing a length of sausage and two cooked potatoes into her hands. 'I traded some carrots for the sausage. It's got fat in it so it'll be good for you. Good for the baby. I did the potatoes on the boiler and they're still warm. Go on, eat some now.'

Katerina held the food listlessly in her hands. 'I don't need it any more, Yelena.'

'Don't be silly – '

'There's no milk,' Katerina said dully. 'They make you show them, you see. Poor Boris has been getting hungrier and hungrier and today there was nothing.'

'Can't we get cow's milk? I'll see what I – '

'*They've taken him away*. They let you feed your baby while you can. Then he's not yours any more. They told me so. They told me that I was an enemy of the people, and that Boris was no longer mine. That he belonged to the Security Organs, and that they would bring him up. He's *gone*. They've taken my baby to the *detpriemnik*, the NKVD children's home.'

She looked up at Yelena with terrible eyes. 'God will strike me down for saying this, but I would rather see him *dead* than be brought up to be one of them. To be spiritually destroyed, twisted and perverted into something that isn't human. In good Tsar Nicholas's day they took people like these away and locked them up. Now *they* are in charge and they take the children and turn them into monsters in their own image. I would wish Boris dead, sooner than know he has been made into a fiend!'

She turned, and shuffled away with her arms clasped about her shrunken bosom, her grey hair straggling in the wind . . .

The man looked like Sadovsky but he had done something to his hands which were wrapped in bandages. The truck stopped inside the wire and Akulov climbed down. It was much warmer here; the earth was soft under the tyre soles of his *Che-te-se* boots. In Kolyma it had been frozen solid and they had lifted it away in turves to be crushed, looking for the little fragments of gold. There was something about the earth here . . . he glanced down with a spark of old professional interest. It had been chewed up by tracks!

'Tanks, Ivan Ivanovich,' the man said. It *was* Sadovsky. 'They got you out in time.'

'I thought they were taking me off to be shot,' said Akulov. 'My team was dying off and we weren't making the norms. I couldn't even keep them going with tobacco pinches. What is this place?'

'Red Army proving grounds.' He began to walk towards the buildings and Akulov fell in beside him. 'We're *zek*-specialists. Engineers, designers, managers. And now a commander. We needed a driver. You can drive a tank, can't you, Ivan Ivanovich?'

'I can drive. But what are you doing here, Piotr Pavlovich?'

'Oh, I didn't come here from the factory. I was out at the camp on Kilometre Forty-Eight. That's where I went when they'd finished with me. Once I'd confessed to sabotage for the British. What did you confess to, Ivan Ivanovich?'

'Nothing. I had done nothing, so I wouldn't confess to anything.'

A glimmer of a smile crossed Sadovsky's face. 'Leathery skins, you peasants have.'

'How did they get you, Piotr Pavlovich? Yelena and I always said you'd be the last they'd take, because you had powerful friends. You were chums with Khrushchev.'

'He finished the Metro before time because of me and our machines and I let him take the credit. Nikita Sergeyevich isn't a man who suffers too much from gratitude, but it was enough. No, it wasn't him, it was Vyshinsky.'

'The prosecutor? I met him once – he was an arse-licker.'

'That's what I thought. He came to dinner with Khrushchev one evening and I showed them my model train set. I made it, and if you play with it right it shows you how the Kremlin bastard won the Civil War by himself. Trotsky runs away at Kazan and Stalin saves the day and the whole Bolshevik cause. It's a lie, of course. Stalin never went near the front, just shot people well behind it. At least Trotsky had guts and he really did win at Kazan. But it was another little piece of insurance I took out for us, me and my family. Arselicking by technology, you might say . . .'

The air was as soft as a blanket and Akulov allowed it to pamper his throat, raw from the alternation of the super-heated steam that thawed the frozen soil, and the sub-zero wind outside that had made it that way.

'I thought we had got through. Yezhof was gone and I thought we'd made it, but they came for us in the night, out at the dacha. I thought

I had made a deal with Vyshinsky but that *svoloch* bastard Malenkov came by the Lubyanka to watch while they beat me and he told me what had happened. Vyshinsky had my dacha. He hadn't risked freeing Andrei as I'd asked him in return for a courtroom model. He just took the train set, so he could crawl up Stalin's backside. He had it taken out and presented it to Stalin in the Kremlin and Stalin shows it off to foreign diplomats and other fools. Malenkov thought it was very funny. Rykov it was, who was Vyshinsky's removal man. Vyshinsky took the dacha, and he gave my daughter Gaia to Rykov. She screamed, Ivan Ivanovich.'

Sadovsky choked. In the gloom he wiped clumsily at his face with his bandaged hands. 'She screamed as they took her away, she was shouting *Papapapapapa*, and I could not help her. And now I do not know where she is, and my wife Anna is dead.'

'If we are alive, it may be so that your daughter is alive, too,' Akulov said gently.

'Anna was afraid to go out. The *Chekisty* caught her in the civil war and she was raped by them in her cell, again and again. She was damaged; she could hardly speak afterwards, a stutter. And she was afraid. She never went out, because *they* were out there. I always promised her I would keep her safe, she and our daughter Gaia. I promised Andrei and Boris that they'd be safe. In the van as they took me away Andrei was hanging from a meat hook. I got it wrong, Ivan Ivanovich. I got it wrong . . .

Sadovsky was weeping.

'I thought that Nikita Sergeyevich was in charge, that we had protection. I thought he had helped me to tie in Vyshinsky. He was First Secretary, but he did nothing to stop Vyshinsky . . .'

'Vyshinsky is the *kinto's* own,' Akulov said quietly. 'Do you not know the saying, "out of filth can you make a prince"? Those are the type he likes. Nikita Sergeyevich found me in the Lubyanka, on one of his inspections. He was about to have me released when Rykov came into the cell where they had been beating me. Rykov said nothing, merely stood behind the lamps. Khrushchev went white. In the end he ordered them to beat me until I confessed. Then he went out, and Rykov had them do as he had bid. They say that the first rule of survival in the Party is to abandon anyone calling for a lifeline, but before that, those boys have to learn how to crawl.'

They came to the door and Sadovsky opened it awkwardly, using both his bandaged hands. They were in a big shed. Inside a tank stood, sleek, compact and deadly, its wide tracks gripping the floor. The air smelled of oiled metal.

'Here it is. The new tank. The number Thirty-Four, the *Prinadlezhit-Chetverki*. It's very good. Say thank you to it, Ivan Ivanovich for it's saved your life and mine.'

In the light of the shed Akulov could see Sadovsky's hands. Under the bandages there were stumps where the fingers should have been. Only thumbs remained. Sadovsky saw him looking at them.

'Frostbite took the fingers at Kilometre Forty-Eight. I saved the thumbs by putting them in my mouth at night. Because I could not hold a pick they took me up the line with my mates, the sick and the injured. They took us to one of the killing stations, the abattoirs. They ran a truck engine with no silencer to drown out the screaming but when our lot got there the truck had broken down. I couldn't hold a pick, but I could use a spanner, and I fixed it. So they sat me in the truck and I revved the engine while they beat everyone else to death with crowbars. You don't have to be in the Party to know how to abandon your comrades, Ivan Ivanovich, nor how to crawl. I'm not like you, I'm not brave. I did that for three months, until they found me, and brought me here.'

23

SOE

London, September 1940

Ruth pulled back the curtains and the sun coming through the windows made a hatched pattern on the carpet. The glass was intact, striped with the tape she had carefully applied, according to regulations, after war had been declared the previous year between Great Britain and her Empire and the Third Reich of Germany.

She chose her wardrobe carefully. She had always appreciated the importance of dress in making an unspoken statement. For her purposes that day she picked a pair of the strong but smart brown shoes she used to wear when walking with Nikolai on the Downs. She had brushed and polished them the previous evening and she wore plain stockings and a suit of a light heather-mixture tweed, over a plain and sensible white blouse. She wore two rows of pearls about her neck, and dabbed on a small amount of French perfume.

She was ready. In her living room she kept a tantalus containing gin, whisky and brandy on an oak sideboard. Standing there, her hand went out to one of the cut glass decanters. She stood looking at it and, slowly, put it back. She took the case containing her gas mask with a hand that shook, very slightly, and went out.

Waiting for the bus the blue sky was discoloured with smoke to the east. The German bombers had been again in the night. Later the contrails would weave deranged patterns as young men tried to kill each other, miles up in the sky.

She got off the bus and walked the short distance down the street to the Northumberland Hotel. It looked drab, a dowager in army uniform with sandbags stacked in a wall about the entrance. She gave her name to the sergeant at the desk and restrained herself from making extravagant remarks to relieve her nerves.

She was taken upstairs, to one of the former bedrooms. A card on its door simply said Jepson. When she was shown in she found it completely bare except for two folding chairs on the floorboards.

A man was standing by the blackout screen next to the window, in a plain army battledress, and he turned as she came in.

'Selwyn, darling!' she cried. She could not seem too restrained, she reasoned, or else people would wonder if she was the same woman they knew.

'Ruth . . . Countess,' said the soldier. 'How nice to see you. Won't you sit down?'

She sat on one of the little chairs, crossed her legs and he lit one of her Sobranie cigarettes for her before sitting down himself.

'What a perfectly frightful room, Selwyn,' she said frankly. 'Do you work here?'

'I conduct interviews here.'

'With whom?'

'Different people . . .' he said vaguely. 'People like you, sometimes. But *you* asked to see *me*, so how can I help you, Ruth?'

She smiled. 'I have evolved a theory, darling, that something exists. Does that sound ridiculous? Ruth de Gunzberg, arch-chatterer of a thousand dinner parties has a theory?'

'I personally have thought you extremely astute, where people were concerned, for some time,' said Jepson.

'Ah, well, I have had a lot of *training*, you see. Working with Sergei, you had to be able to – let's say, fillet – fillet someone very quickly, without them knowing you were doing it. I did get quite good at it . . . with other people, that is . . .

'Anyway, I have this theory that something exists and I want you to tell me, if you can, where I can find it and, if you can't, where I should go to find someone who can tell me where I can find it. Colin Gubbins came to see me last spring, you know. I've known Colin for some time – he was in Russia in the Civil War, only we were on different sides. It was the Civil War he wanted to talk about, in fact. He said he was writing a little book for the Army about guerrilla warfare and there was a lot of that in Russia back then. He said that he'd been interested in the subject ever since the success of Michael Collins's gunmen in plain clothes in Ireland, in nineteen nineteen.

'I wasn't of much use to him on practical details, although I did pass on a few tips that my great friend Yelena told me – she fought on both sides all over Russia, you see, and I helped her escape the Cheka into the Red Army, but by the end of it she was with Wrangel – and so she knew a lot about it. I remember her telling me that if you wanted to sabotage a machine, or a factory, quickly, the best thing to use was a heavy hammer, because there were always essential parts made out of cast iron that broken, even on something as big as a locomotive, would render it useless. And if you wanted to sabotage several things – vehicles or machines – to break the *same piece* on each, otherwise the enemy could cannibalise one to mend another. Oh, and she won a whole battle for the Whites by mixing up sand and oil and putting it into the axles of a Red transport train. It seized up solid and not only did the troops on board not get to the fight, the train completely blocked the line, and the Reds surrendered and went over to the Whites. Yelena would never *kill* anyone, but she *was* good at sabotage. She was very tricky.'

She glanced at Jepson while she drew on her cigarette to see if she was establishing her credentials, but he was maintaining a mask-like politeness.

'Where I hope I *was* useful was in stressing the psychological element. That I knew about, because that was what Sergei's Workers' International was all about, establishing a sense of solidarity with our cause in people who might not otherwise have come over to us and making them, in the end, ours, body and soul.'

A bitter expression passed over her face, that he did not miss, but he said nothing. 'So, now, what of my hunt for this thing I am looking for? Here we are, the only country fighting against the Nazis. The disgusting Stalin has made a deal with the revolting Hitler, the French have fallen over in seconds and there is just us left. And we will fight. The brave fighter boys have shot Goering in the backside, and he is bombing London. But I spoke to Bobby Thomas, and he says that means Hitler can't invade, so we're going to be fighting on. And where? Well, *over there*. And I saw that photograph of darling Winston holding the tommy gun. He's a tough old man, isn't he? Sergei was an expert judge of character, and there *is* such a thing as national character. He said never to underestimate the British, that in peace they looked like a collection of stuffed shirts, but when it came to fighting, they played very rough. They invented the Queensberry Rules, he said, and were the first to give them up in a real contest.

'I saw poor darling Melanie, Colin's wife, and they've split up. She says he hasn't been talking to her, that he goes away for days at a time and can't explain where he's been. She thinks there's another woman.'

Ruth dropped her cigarette stub on the floor and ground it under the heel of her strong shoe.

'*I don't*. He's not with his regiment. He was doing something funny in the Norway fighting and now he's back, but no one sees him.'

Ruth lit another cigarette. 'What would I do, if I was darling Winston? He wants to keep the spirit of resistance alive in Europe among the people being occupied and the wonderful BBC sends out transmissions to every country and they listen. But you have to do more than that. You have to give them *hope*. They need, from time to time, to see a bridge blown up, a train grind to a halt, an oil tank set on fire. They need to see some dead Germans.'

She leaned back in the flimsy chair.

'I think Winston has set up such a thing. An organisation to go over into Europe, to send men and women over there to do nasty things to the Germans and give hope to the people. I think perhaps Colin, who talked to me about his little manual for such people, is doing something like that.'

'And if this organisation exists?' Jepson asked.

'Then I must join, darling. Of course I must!'

'Do you know much about fighting, Countess? About undercover work?'

'I, about fighting? My darling Selwyn, I stormed the Winter Palace! Rifle in hand we fought over the barricades. The blood flowed in rivers. Undercover work? I was the one who smuggled the NKVD's senior operative in Germany out of the country, mere yards ahead of the Nazis. Besides, I speak four languages fluently. And I know everybody. *Everybody.*'

'You do . . .' Jepson said thoughtfully. 'But tell me Ruth, how's the drinking?'

'Darling! What a perfectly foul question to ask a girl. Listen to me, if you had once believed in something as the salvation of all humanity as I did, and that something slaughtered, in different ways, your whole . . . family . . . among millions of others, and you realised you'd spent all your time living . . . *being* a lie, then you too would get drunk from time to time. Very well, so I woke up face down on my sitting room floor with an empty bottle beside me, many times. I admit it. But not now.'

He looked at her, and she made herself meet his gaze. 'You look happy,' he said. 'In the middle of a desperate war, you are happy?'

'Yes!' she said passionately. 'I was a communist. Always, we believed that we fought against the enemy. At first, the enemy was the bourgeois. Then the Mensheviks and the SRs. Then the kulaks, and then any peasant. And always, the counter-revolutionary elements, spies, saboteurs, wreckers hidden in society. And you wake up one morning and realise that there is no enemy, except for the Communist Party itself. And you reach out for the bottle. But now, yes, there *is* an enemy. It's over there, on the other side of the channel, and we can go and do something about it. And *I* can, if the organisation I think exists *does* exist.'

Jepson sighed. 'I usually do this in three meetings, if I like the look of someone, so that the prospective candidate can understand what is being proposed.'

Ruth smiled in delight. 'So I *am* right!'

'You seem to have leap-frogged the first two, so I will say only one thing. We estimate that for the people sent into Europe to do the kind of work you have described, the chances of being killed are very high, perhaps as high as one in two. Do you understand, Countess? Were you to join and be sent out to do nasty, not very Queensberry Rules things to the Germans, you would have perhaps only a fifty per cent chance of living to tell the tale.'

She smiled, brilliantly.

'No,' she said, shaking her head. 'I was a dead woman. I shall join, and I am Lazarus. I am living again!'

Moscow

Beria signed a form, added it to the pile in front of him and sat back, taking a short break from the load of administration that was much of his lot, day in and day out. He looked up at Krivitskiy.

'It's the man who can see into the future,' he said, not unpleasantly. 'If we go back to hating Germany again we'll have to send you back as *rezident*, and call you Cassandra. But what was it that was special about her, apart from seeing what was to happen?'

'She was condemned never to be believed.'

'That's it. We had a schoolmaster in Baku who talked about the Greeks. When I was in charge at Sukhumi he was pulled in on some charge or other. I had him shot. Anyone who knew that much about the past couldn't possibly be a good communist.'

He smiled at Krivitskiy. 'You've been right. The big boss got his pact with Hitler and he's very pleased with it. He's doing his very best to make it work, giving the Nazis all the raw materials they need. Very helpful to them, in their war in the West, I'm sure.'

He paused. It was cooler in Moscow, his hands did not sweat as much. 'Do you still stick to the rest of your views?' he asked quietly.

'Yes. Even though Hitler isn't going to succeed in invading Britain.

He won't try. The time for that was right after the Dunkirk evacuation. The British were totally disorganised and Paratroopers could have secured a bridgehead through which an invasion force could have been put. But not now. It is a mistake, mind you. The main obstacle to Hitler's winning his war is not Russia but Britain. His main opponent is not Stalin, but Churchill, for by surviving Churchill will bring Roosevelt and the Americans in against Hitler. But Hitler will turn East, for he believes it to be his destiny.'

Beria stared thoughtfully at Krivitskiy. 'We shall see. I've sifted out the prisoner specialists and they're back at work, designing and producing, they're just doing it in prison, that's all. Anyway. Enough gossip. For the time being the big boss wants the Nazi-Soviet Pact to work so everything must run smoothly. We're sending freight train after freight train of grain, oil, rubber, cotton, ore, you name it. The Germans send us the odd obsolete aero engine the other way, but – it's what the Boss wants! So we must make it work smoothly. Be a good lad; there's a special train leaving from the Belorussian Station. Rykov's taking it down as far as the Bug River Bridge in Brest-Litovsk and the Germans are picking it up there. Go to the station with him and check the lading bills, will you? Make sure everything's on that should be on when it leaves.'

'Of course,' said Krivitskiy. 'I'll go now, shall I?'

'Yes. Oh, there's one last thing. You're a thinker, aren't you? Remember that little creep Bukharin we shot a year or two back? He whined about our collectivisation of the peasantry. What was it the *svoloch* bastard said? That the mass annihilation of defenceless men, women and children was acclimatising party members to violence and brute obedience, transforming them into cogs in some terrible machine. What do you say to that?'

'Bukharin was shot for his views,' Krivitskiy said carefully. 'I don't have anything to say.'

Beria laughed, and pulled some more papers towards him. 'He seemed to think it was wrong,' he commented. 'I prefer Nechaev. You know what he said about socialism? "To become a good socialist, one must reject all tender, soft feelings of kinship, friendship, love, gratitude and even honour itself. He is not a revolutionary who pities anything in this world. Poison, the knife, the noose – the Revolution consecrates everything." I memorised his words some time ago because they seemed to be appropriate. The Boss read them to me – he has Nechaev's archive at his office. Report back about the train, will you? The Boss wants to be sure it all goes smoothly.'

Outside Krivitskiy found Rykov waiting, in NKVD uniform.

Rykov smiled pleasantly, and took him down to the Pobeda sedan that was waiting. They left the square where they had knocked down a big section of the Kitay-Girod wall and headed towards Ul. Gorkovo. The statue of Ivan Fyodorov looked down disapprovingly at the vandals beneath him.

In the car, Rykov was whistling a little tune quietly between his teeth.

'You seem in good spirits,' said Krivitskiy.

'I am,' agreed Rykov. 'I always enjoy meeting up with the German lads – I've even learned the language. Us and the SS, and Gestapo, we've been getting together off and on for a few years now, comparing notes. I was sent over to give them a hand with their camps – was up north for a number of years in the twenties, you know. The Boss sent me up there to get experience. When Adolf needed some technical assistance handling his filth he sent me along. We've got enemies of the people, he got *Zhids*.'

He turned and smiled amiably at Krivitskiy. 'Same thing, if you ask me.'

They turned right on to the great new boulevard, climbing up towards Sovetskaya. Rykov looked out at the vast eight-storey apartment blocks, newly-completed, vast and grey, their windows tiny, like cells.

'We go back a long way, me and the Boss,' he said.

Inside the station a table had been set up at the entrance to one of the quays. Two men were checking documents and there was a line of people waiting, under guard. The table was over by the high wall and the officials were sitting under a revolutionary icon, a great mosaic of Bolshevik leaders marching into History. It was mostly obscured. Kamenev, Trotsky and Bukharin peered out through the whitewash, Lenin was clean. A large section had been patched in, and showed Stalin leading the way.

'This is it,' said Rykov.

'What are they taking to Germany?' Krivitskiy said, in sudden alarm.

'Filth,' Rykov said casually. 'Adolf wants his German commies back. He's sending us the Ukrainian kulaks who ran over the border in thirty-two, and he's sending all our emigrés back – all the traitors who ran away after the Revolution. I went over to give Heinrich and his lads a hand rounding them up. What a haul! Whole families of aristos and *boorzhoi* we haven't seen since the war! Breeding away like maggots. A spot of chilly air up in Kolyma'll soon thin them out, and Adolf's new camps'll sort out his German traitors. He's got some advanced ideas, he has. We could pick up a few tips from Adolf, mark my word.'

He paused by the table. 'Here's Security Major Krivitskiy, Viktor. I'm going to check my train. You have any problems, refer them to the Major, he'll decide.'

'Very well, sir.'

There were ones he knew in the line, ones he had told to run, once it was clear their cause in Germany was finished, ones he had helped get through, to the Haven of the Persecuted, the world's first communist state.

He stared steadfastly across the great hall, feeling their gaze rake him like claws, heard the despairing shuffling of their feet as they were led down into the waiting train.

'Come on, move it now,' the man in front said. The locomotive let out a snort and steam rushed across the platform.

'Won't the Major check our papers,' she said in a level voice. 'There seems to be a mistake, the people here are Germans.'

He looked up, and she was looking at him with steady grey eyes. Elisabeth stood next to her, holding a small suitcase in one hand, clutching a Tyrolean teddy bear in the other.

'I was born in Austria-Hungary,' said Marthe. 'My daughter was born in Budapest. We should not be sent to Germany.' She pointed to the line on the yellow form in front of the clearing officer.

'But you took out German nationality,' he objected. He half-turned. 'Major?'

'Step over here a moment,' said Krivitskiy, and the two women broke from the line.

'Thank God you were here,' said Marthe. 'How did you know to come?'

'Beria told me to,' he said slowly. 'I had a meeting with him and he was quoting Nechaev at me.'

'Nechaev was a maniac, just the same as he is.'

'He approved of him.'

'Darling, let's got out of here,' she said anxiously.

Krivitskiy could see Rykov on the platform, neat in his long NKVD coat with its polished buttons and collar-flashes. His peaked cap was set back upon his head and he was smiling at him. Krivitskiy turned and went back behind the table.

'Send them through,' he said, without looking up.

He heard Elisabeth scream in fury as they dragged them down the platform. '*Fatherland of the Toilers, Bulwark of Freedom, Haven of the Persecuted.* That's what you told us you pig, you bastard!'

He heard her moan in pain as the rifle butt smashed into her kidneys and they dragged her on board. When he looked up, Marthe was staring at him.

'We'll live!' she shouted. 'We'll settle things with you.' Then they hit her too and the last of those he had known was going down the platform.

'I'll go now,' he said, to no one in particular. The doors were slamming, one after the other, like the measured shots from a hillside coming down on the wind. He stumbled on nothing as he went across the platform and almost fell. From the train he thought he heard the sound of laughter. He glanced back. A teddy bear was lying on the platform and Rykov booted it on to the rails.

Arisaig, Scotland, April 1941

Beyond the Major in his Argyle kilt and uniform the loch water glittered in the spring sunshine. He stood like a magnificent statue on the rise of the land, visible for a hundred yards all around, gazing at the loch as though assessing his chances of catching a salmon.

A fine sweet chestnut tree stood on the slope, decked in its fresh green dress. Ruth had used it as cover on her journey up from the big house of Scots stone. Now she hid behind it, taking a copy of *The Times* from inside her battledress jacket, along with some dry twigs she had gathered on the way.

Something moved among the bright green bracken and vivid yellow gorse. A girl, barefoot, slipping towards the Highland soldier. Behind her tree Ruth quickly crumpled up the paper, and set the twigs about it, starting the little bonfire with a whirl of her gold Ronson lighter. The flames burned bright and clean.

The girl, slim, her dark hair pulled back into a pony tail, was within yards. She ran forward, fast and low, and twitched the plumage of the kilt. The soldier turned, smiling. He seemed to be congratulating her. Ruth tossed a few handfuls of damp green grass on to her fire and shinned quickly up the trunk of the tree, where she crouched on a branch.

The girl produced a pair of sensible brown walking shoes from inside her battledress, and slipped them on and the couple began to walk up the slope, away from the loch. White smoke from her fire streamed across their path in the breeze.

'Hullo! What's this we have here?'

She could hear the burr of his voice as they halted, just below her.

'A wee fire,' he said. 'Red Indians, perhaps.'

She dropped from the branch right at the feet of the soldier, giving a terrible war whoop as she did so.

'Got you!' she cried triumphantly.

He smiled down at her. 'Verra good. Countess. A wee bit dramatic, and we could do without the sound effects, but verra good.'

'My teachers all complained I was dramatic,' she said, unabashedly. 'Now, I'm giving Joan boating instruction, Major, so may we go?'

'Aye. See you at the bar tonight.'

He strolled on up the hill, and Ruth took Joan towards a small jetty, to which were moored a number of sailing boats.

'And it'll be ten o'clock and he'll order a last round and then it's into a truck to be dumped in the middle of nowhere and find our way back!' said Joan. 'Honestly, I'd only just unpacked my bags last night.' She yawned, but looked happily about her. 'It's lovely here, isn't it, Ruth? What are we doing now?'

'Going for a sail. Fancy some salmon and a bottle of hock?'

'Oh, gosh yes. But how will we get salmon and hock, Ruth?'

Ruth reached in her pocket and brought out a small square of something like plasticene, smelling strongly of almonds. 'Here's my rod.'

'What on earth is it?' Joan asked.

'Plastic explosive. You chuck it in and, after it goes bang, you help yourself. The hock we get from a hunting lodge on the other side of the loch. I broke in last week with this.' She produced a strange knife, with a large selection of peculiar blades.

Joan giggled. 'You know, it's like being in *Swallows and Amazons*, doing all this. We're like a bunch of overgrown children, playing games with no rules.'

She looked out over the loch, suddenly serious.

'I say, Ruth. I only arrived yesterday and since then I have made my way across country by night after being filled with gin deliberately given to me by these very nice people here; I have played a funny game of hide-and-seek in which I have to touch someone without them hearing or seeing me; I am about to acquire the abilities of a burglar and a poacher and this afternoon I am to learn how to fire a pistol and, in general, learn to become something that would *horrify* Miss Trubshawe at the Academy for Young Ladies where I was educated. Would you tell me why?'

'You tell me,' Ruth countered, amused.

'That funny game with Major Watt . . . I suppose if I had had a knife in my hand, and knew how to use it, I could have stabbed him.'

'Well done! Silent killing – which is your first lesson tomorrow morning, with Major Fairbairn, actually.'

Joan giggled again. 'Do you know, I applied for a job as a bilingual secretary! Come on then, where's that salmon, I'm starved . . .'

24

Barbarossa

Baranovichi, Belorussia, 22 June 1941

His father would have disowned him for this and Marshal Tukhachevsky would have had him court-martialled and probably shot. But Tukhachevsky had had a drumhead trial and had been shot himself, and his father had vanished into the Arctic camps. Now Lieutenant Alexei Akulov sat dutifully in the turret of his T-26 light tank as it ground up the slope with the infantry, just as he had been ordered to. It was a very stupid thing to do, but he had no option. He went up the hill, his face tight with dread.

He was there to sit motionless and provide fire support for Lieutenant Barikov, who was in charge of the company of foot-soldiers. The two young men were of an age and the evening before they had been in Minsk, watching the popular comedy, *The Wedding at Malinkovka*. Nikolai Savinkov had been there, too, escorting his sister, Natalia, fresh from her school graduation ceremony. They had worn their dress uniforms and now they were in dun, he in his tank and Nikolai in his, waiting.

They had got to the top of the hill, and Barikov was placing his men. He had all the benefit of a five-month Lieutenant's training course for his tactical task. The division was commanded by Major Zigelya, and he was off on an intermediate military training course to fit him for staff command. Behind them Captain Alexeev was trying to find out where the artillery was. The general staff of the division had been trained by Tukhachevsky, and they were all with him, or with Akulov in the far north.

The two young men prepared their defensive position. Barikov was doing it by the manual, and the manual said to take and hold the high ground. It said to have a tank for fire support, and so there Alexei was. It was not Tukhachevsky's manual, and it was not Akulov's, for they had worked out the correct use of tanks in the twenties and the thirties, they knew that a tank force had to be massed, fast, hard-hitting and mobile, with a full range of vehicles and supporting arms and services fully integrated. They had hammered their doctrine out together with the Germans, with the likes of Guderian and Hoth in their clandestine joint training.

The terror had brought all that to a close for the Red Army. So Alexei Akulov sat in his single tank and waited for Guderian to come the other way and demonstrate how it was done.

It was a beautiful day. The summer solstice was just past and his light tank was hull down on the ridge. He and his two crewmen got out and collected brushwood to break up the lines of the turret. Then he got back in and reported to Captain Alekseev.

'C company in position.'

There was a pause, just the crackling of static, and he was about to try again when the captain's voice came on.

'C company in position,' he confirmed. Alexei thought he had gone, but then his voice came back, still disbelieving.

'There'll be no artillery support.'

'What do you mean, no artillery? Guderian's coming.'

'The boss doesn't want to upset the Germans.'

The clear summer's sky was getting dirty. Oily smoke stained the pure blue like a child's paintbrush muddying the jar. *Barbarossa* was coming.

Barikov's men were well-armed. They had long PTRS anti-tank rifles, capable of wreaking havoc with any tank unwise enough to come within a hundred metres. And *Barbarossa* was coming.

They were trained to take on tanks, not aircraft. One came at them so fast it was gone before they knew it. Small, venomous, greenish-blue, it emitted a ripping sound as it went. Alexei just had time to see the spiders of the swastikas it bore. It dropped two dark bombs and he crouched down in the turret but there was no explosion, just a deadly hissing, and yellow smoke began to drift across the position.

It rose in the air and through it things came howling, he caught a glimpse of one, bent-winged, shrieking as it dived on him. *Barbarossa*.

The explosions lifted his tank and banged his head against the sight; he felt blood running warm down his forehead. They were hammer blows, one after the other. Then they stopped. He put his head out of the hatch, very cautiously. The outside of the tank was covered in dirt and smoke and dust swirled about him. In it, men moaned in pain. Grit coated his teeth and, in the pale sky above, five bent-winged shapes climbed indifferently away.

As the air cleared he could see a plume of dust approaching. It came with incredible speed and he had little time to do more than to order the living to gather up rifles and ammunition from the dead and deploy in their trenches before they were upon them. Barikov was dead and he was in sole command.

The armoured car was travelling at forty kilometres an hour, festooned with tow ropes, picks and shovels, its eight tall wheels whipping the dust of the corrugations of the dirt road. In the distance he could see compact tanks and self-propelled artillery. He laid off in front of it like shooting quail on leave, and pressed the trigger of the cannon. The 37mm gun crashed.

He heard the clang as his shell bounced off the sloped armour. Smoke dribbled from his barrel and the turret of the armoured car swung on to him as Piotr, beneath him, reloaded. It fired on the move and the riveted armour of the light tank opened up like a can. It split back as far as the turret, its twisted plates coated with his driver's shredded flesh.

The reconnaissance vehicle did not deign to stop, dust spuming triumphantly from its wheels. In the distance the ground was pocked with sudden red flashes and the hilltop erupted about him.

He stayed in the wreck of the tank. As the armoured group passed by him he talked quietly in the ruined hull to Captain Alekseev, giving strength details. At least the radio was still working.

In the afternoon Alekseev suddenly went off the air in mid-sentence and it was now completely quiet, for the last wounded had stopped moaning and died. From down on the sunny road there came the tapping of a man kocking a signpost into the road. Peering through his vision slit he could see the machine-gunner of a motorcycle sidecar combination with a hammer in his hand. The twin cylinder machine thrummed away and he climbed carefully from the tank. The dead of the company lay scattered about like logs. He picked up an M1891 rifle and went back down the hill, walking in his tank tracks, dust sticking to the blood of his gunner on his boots.

The old man was in fine humour. His schnapps-red nose shone in the wild scrub of his beard and he grinned happily as he poured a big mug of water for Alexei from a pitcher.

'Now we're free, boy,' he said, standing outside his wood house as Alexei gulped. 'Jesus has sent his soldiers to rid us of that man. There'll be no more of his men here, talking of class war and taking our food, putting us into his collective farms, taking the young men and women to slave in devil factories. No, no. I saw the troops myself, I gave them bread and eggs and cheese. I've waited a long time for this.

They took my sons away when they declared war on us, those men he sent, the ones in the green caps, and I never saw them again.'

'The airfield is just down here, isn't it?' Alexei asked hoarsely. Dust and propellant were still in his throat, scratching like sandpaper.

'Yes, yes. But you take off that uniform now. No reason to fight for that man in Moscow.'

As if in confirmation the coarse racket of a PO-2 light bomber burst through the trees.

'Six took off this morning, but they haven't come back,' the old man volunteered. Alexei knew a few of the pilots; they'd let him get in when they pulled back.

'Yes, the troops of God are here now,' the peasant said happily.

'They're Germans!' said Alexei.

'They're *Christians*,' the old man said proudly. 'I saw the crosses on their mighty machines.'

Kuntsevo, Moscow, 29 June

Nikita Khrushchev got out of the Pobeda sedan. He was dressed in the uniform of a general, buttoned up to the neck despite the hot day. There was an NKVD guard standing by the mesh gate set in the high fence around the Number One dacha and Khrushchev went up to him like a small, belligerent tank.

'I'm Khrushchev. Let me see the boss,' he demanded.

The young Chekist shook his head. 'Nobody's to come in. Orders.'

Khrushchev put his round face close to the guard's. 'Son, I've just come from Kiev. My job is to defend the Ukraine, and the Germans are driving towards me at the rate of kilometres a morning. My people are dying like insects and I can't get any instructions from Moscow. I came to see Molotov and *he* can't get any instructions, because inside there – ' Krushchev pointed with a stubby finger '– nobody's picking up the telephone. Molotov's afraid to come out. So I said I would.'

The youth looked curiously at the burly, sweating figure in front of him. 'You aren't afraid, Comrade General?'

'If I can't get some decisions the Germans will shoot me from one of the tanks driving towards me at the rate of kilometres a morning. Not long after that they will arrive outside here and, instead of asking politely to be let in as I am doing, they will shoot you and, shortly afterwards, the boss himself.'

Khrushchev pulled his officer's Makarov automatic pistol from its holster and pointed it up the guard's nose. 'So, no, I am not afraid. And so, let me in and tell the boss I am waiting to see him.'

They went inside the fence and into the rambling dacha. Khrushchev put his pistol away.

'Wait here,' the guard said and went through a door. Khrushchev heard the low mumble of voices, then the door opened again.

'You can come in.'

Stalin was sitting in a corner of the room, by the window. It looked out upon the larches and silver-trunked birch trees. Shrubs were flowering in the sunshine, but he was looking inside the gloomy room. The curtains were partly drawn and he seemed aged and shrunken, his face covered in grey stubble. The room smelled of old sweat. He looked up at Khrushchev, furtively, and then resumed staring at the floor.

'You've come for me,' he muttered.

'The Germans are advancing on all fronts. We must begin to fight back,' Khrushchev said bluntly.

Stalin jerked half-upright from the cot he was sitting on. 'Take the offensive!' he barked. 'Throw them back with a single blow! Shoot those responsible!'

As suddenly, he collapsed, as though electricity had been turned off. He sat, breathing heavily.

'There is no organisation. No command structure,' Khrushchev went on. 'It's total chaos. We have to begin from the beginning.'

'It's me, isn't it,' Stalin said clearly, just as though Khrushchev had not spoken. 'I'm the one who is to be shot. It's my fault.'

It came, ready formed and polished, complete in structure, into Khrushchev's mind. *Shoot him.*

His hand twitched, by his opened holster.

Do it now.

'Molotov and the politburo are coming out,' he said. 'They sent me first.'

Stalin nodded. 'They'll want to see me shot. By God, has anyone ever fucked up as badly as me? I thought I had Hitler fooled. They sent me all the reports, saying he was getting ready to invade, but I knew he wasn't . . .'

'We have to have a command structure,' Khrushchev said, raising his voice. 'A plan. No claptrap, no *pokhazuka*, no bullshit.' He went to stand closer to Stalin. 'There are *real* enemies out there,' he shouted.

Stalin jerked like a puppet, nodding again and again. 'Enemies?

Oh, yes, I know. I've seen them for years. I know what to do with enemies.'

'*These are real!*' Khrushchev screamed. 'They're *Germans*. They're swatting us like flies.'

Something outside the window had caught Stalin's attention and he stared fearfully towards the gate. A small column of black cars had arrived.

'They've come for me,' he whispered.

Khrushchev reached down and hauled him to his feet. There was a small bathroom there and he propelled Stalin towards it. His body was slack, the feet moving out of time.

'Shave. Put on clean clothes,' he ordered. '*You* are the *vozdht*, the leader. We *need* you.'

Some semblance of understanding came into Stalin's face. Through the closed door Khrushchev heard water start to run. He stood outside, with his pistol now in his hand.

Do it now.

'The politburo are here, Comrade General.' The guard was staring at him anxiously, fearfully. The gun was at his side, out of sight. 'Shall I let them in, Comrade General?'

'No. He's getting ready.'

The boy vanished. He could hear the noise of voices outside. In the room, listening to the sound of Stalin clumsily washing, Khrushchev put the pistol back in its holster, strangely aware, in the electric tension of death, of emotions postponed.

Minsk, 28 June

Nikolai came down the street in the darkness. Stukas had bombed one of Pavlov's communications centres in the town and in the red glow of the fires a pair of traffic lights at the junction hung like bats in the torn tramway wires. A droshkie lay on its side, both horse and driver dead. Glass from the Rubens photography studio sprinkled the street and crunched under his army boots as he went up the narrow, steep side-street.

All the lights were out and he held up his cigarette lighter as he climbed the dark stair and knocked on the door.

'Who is it?' A girl's voice. Suspicious, alarmed.

'It's me. Nikolai.'

He heard the rattle of the locks and Natalia was embracing him. 'Nikky! We didn't know what to think . . .'

In the candlelit gloom, he saw Tatyana.

'You're alive! Are you hungry?' she asked.

'Starved! I've been walking for two days.'

They went into the kitchen and he propped up his rifle in a corner as Tatyana began mashing up some cold potato and cabbage to fry into cakes.

'What happened?' asked Natalia. In the gold candlelight she was very beautiful. 'There's been no news. The radio talks of throwing back the enemy, and yet the German planes bomb us as they want, and bleeding soldiers stream through the city . . .'

'Have you heard from Alexei?' he asked

'No . . .' She bit her lip. 'There has been no news.'

'The Germans will be here tomorrow, or the day after,' he said. It is only that they are mopping up what is left of our Western Army that I am here before them. Colonel Voronov shot himself on the third day and we had no tanks left so officers fought as infantry. I started marching that night and I was not the only one.'

Tatyana blew on the charcoal. It glowed and filled the air with the scent of heating oil.

'What are you going to do?' Natalia asked. She put a mug of sweet tea in front of him and he sniffed it eagerly.

'I'm going into the woods,' he said quietly. 'I'm going to take my tent, my fishing lines, my bow and traps and live out there until I know what's going to happen.'

Tatyana slipped a pressed cake into the pan, her back to him. 'Why do that?' she asked. 'Why not just wait until the Germans come through?'

'I don't think I want to be here when the Germans come through,' he said thoughtfully.

In the gloom, Tatyana seemed to shrug. 'So you lost. Men have lost wars for centuries. They come to terms with it.'

'I don't know. I thinks this time it is . . . different.' He began to undo his laces and ease his feet from his army boots. 'I was hiding in a ditch when some German fighting troops were handing over prisoners to men in black. They called for commissars, communists and Jews to come forward. They gave the clothes and belongings to any who denounced them, then the other prisoners were marched away to the rear. The men in black lined up the commissars, communists and Jews by my ditch, and they shot them. One fell on top of me, as I lay under the bracken.'

There was a silence. Then 'we are not Jews,' said Tatyana.

'It isn't usual . . .'

'*Isn't usual*?' Tatyana shouted. 'Is it usual for men to come to your village and kill everybody in it? *I'd* kill all the commissars and communists, too. I have nothing against the Jews, but obviously they do. Nobody is perfect.'

She put the potato and cabbage cakes in front of Nikolai and he began to eat. Natalia got up, and took some rucksacks from a cupboard.

'I start packing,' she said.

'You need take nothing for me,' said Tatyana. 'I shall stay here until the Germans come, and then I shall go home. Why don't you wait too, and then you can go home as well.'

By the cupboard, Natalia looked up at her in the candlelight. 'What do you mean, go home? I live here, I am a university student.'

'You're a *Russian*,' Tatyana said brutally. 'Same as he is. You're in a foreign country. To the south is another foreign country. My country, the Ukraine. Who killed my family? Russians. There is nothing we Ukrainians want more than that the Russians will go home. We don't mind if the Germans do it for us.'

'That isn't fair! My father is Ukrainian,' Natalia said.

'He is the Russians' man,' Tatyana said dismissively. 'And the Russians have rewarded him by putting him in the camps. You cannot trust a Russian.'

'You would rather trust the Germans?' Nikolai asked.

'They cannot be worse,' she said.

Central Command Centre, Kirov Street, Moscow, 15 July

The guard put his head round the door. He nodded at Konstantin and Krivitskiy, who got up from their seats in the corridor and went in. Stalin was sitting on a sofa under a mural of muscled, smiling men and women digging a tunnel with gleaming shovels and picks. The Metro station was underground.

He twitched a hand, indicating that they should sit. He was in a plain, military-style uniform and he looked dazed and exhausted.

'Comrade Stalin, this is the poet and artist, Konstantin Simenov. He has done much fine work and you yourself have read his poetry.'

Stalin peered at Konstantin, pulling him from his card-index memory. 'Yes, yes. I know you. You painted my portrait, and talked of Mayakovsky. You look older.'

'That's right,' Konstantin said genially. 'So do you.'

A sprinkling of surprise appeared in Stalin's yellow eyes. But he replied pleasantly enough. He had a peculiar, if uneasy respect for real writers, for their unique importance of power over the mind and he allowed them measures of liberty not given to others.

'These are bad times,' he said. 'They make you old.' He waved vaguely at the large map on the wall, where the Soviet Union lay slashed with Nazi arrows as long as scimitars.

'Retreat everywhere,' he grumbled. 'They used to talk of Russian gumption. Where is it now, that Russian gumption?'

Konstantin could have told him; it had been buried in mass graves and frozen in the camps. He opened his mouth and, sensing disaster, Krivitskiy kicked his ankle under the low table.

'Well, I have some good news,' he said briskly. 'And Konstantin has good advice.'

Stalin brightened perceptibly. 'Come on, then. All I've had this morning is Zhukov telling me we have to abandon Kiev. Abandon Kiev! Not an inch, I told him! Not one more inch of Soviet soil. I'll fire the bastard.'

He sagged back on the sofa, tired by his outburst. 'Give me the good news.'

'The Germans are advancing on all fronts. They occupy huge tracts of Belorussia and the Ukraine.'

Stalin's face began to flush with rage, and Krivitskiy hastened on.

'But Operation *Barbarossa* is not a normal war. Behind the regular fighting troops conducting this most successful *Blitzkrieg* move others, men of the Gestapo and SS, in charge of *Einsatzkommandos*. It is the task of these groups to find and execute all "Bolshevik bosses and commissars", the "Jewish-Bolshevik intelligentsia" and "all inhabitants who oppose the Wehrmacht". They have begun this task. This is a war of annihilation.'

Stalin nodded. 'Yes, yes.'

Konstantin leaned forward. 'Don't you see, They are making themselves hated.'

'Of course. This is normal.'

'My intelligence is that in the villages of Eastern Poland, in Belorussia and the Ukraine, the Germans were welcomed as *liberators*,' said Krivitskiy. 'The peasants hate the collective farms. They are deeply angry at the suppression of Christianity. They thought that the Germans had come to free them from communist rule. If the Germans had only *presented* themselves as liberators, the peasants would have joined them. But instead, they come as new slave-makers, with black-uniformed murderers at their backs.'

'Ahhh . . .' Stalin breathed. 'Of course. The Germans hate the bastards too!'

Konstantin had been watching Stalin.

'That's right,' he murmured. 'And now the trick is to get them to forget what *we* did to them, and concentrate on what the Germans are *doing*.'

Stalin nodded. Seeing that he had not taken offence, Konstantin continued, 'Now we have to present ourselves differently. You see, nobody, not the Ukrainian peasants, nor the Russian peasants, is going to fight for the Communist Party. Don't even think about it. They won't fight for you, either.'

Stalin's eyes widened slightly and he looked at Krivitskiy. 'Doesn't he care?' he enquired.

'Just listen to him, Comrade Stalin,' Krivitskiy said tactfully. 'He has some good ideas.'

'We have been invaded in the past, and fought off our attackers,' Konstantin continued. 'What, in past times, *did* the people believe in? They believed in God, the Tsar and the Motherland. You cannot bring back the Tsar, but you can give them back God – and you can give them *rodina*, the Motherland. And you can give them the war. Make it *their* war. *Their* war to save God, and to save *rodina*. Not to save the Communist party, not to save you. To save God and the Motherland. Bring out the priests from the camps, give them back their robes and holy icons. Open the churches. Find the Patriarch, be seen with him. Make speeches invoking the heroes of the past, embrace Peter the Great, and Marshal Suvurov. Give them *kvasnoi patriotizm*, blind patriotism, let them say, like Suvurov, *pust khuzhe, da nashe*, let it be worse, but let it be ours, and they will fight. You will find they will do anything, once they believe that God and the Motherland are in danger. Ask them to fight for the Party, and Hitler will be sitting in the Kremlin before the autumn leaves fall.'

There was silence in the room, only broken by the rumble of a Metro train beneath them and Stalin's heavy breathing.

'Yes,' he grunted, almost painfully. 'It is so. And that is the way.'

'I've written some speeches,' said Konstantin. He passed over a sheaf of paper. Stalin took it. He had an almost mystical love of paperwork: if it was written down, it was true. He ran his eyes over the words and nodded in approval.

'You haven't been writing like this,' he said. Konstantin opened his mouth to speak, but Stalin forestalled him. He clapped him on the shoulder, grinning. 'I didn't let you, did I! But we're all brothers and sisters now, oh yes!'

He turned to Krivitskiy. 'See he's taken care of,' he commanded.

'I will, Comrade Stalin. May I take the opportunity to bring something else to your attention.'

'Certainly,' Stalin said, peering good-humouredly at the speech Konstantin had written.

'I should like to point out that all my intelligence reports as to the intentions of Adolf Hitler towards us have been borne out by events. However as you know, all my reports – predicting in detail Operation *Barbarossa* – had to be submitted to you through the Intelligence Division of the GRU headed by General Gulikov, and the classification he gave these reports was that of 'Doubtful', and other reports which predicted no invasion as 'Reliable'. Thus vital information was hidden from you as head of state.'

The two men stared at each other. Konstantin was peering genially at the Party mural on the wall. Both Krivitskiy and Stalin were perfectly well aware that General Gulikov had simply been practising the three Us, *ugadat, ugodit, utselet*, 'sniff out, suck up, survive', news that Stalin had not wanted to hear leading to extinction of the last. But Hitler *had* invaded and the enemies were now real.

Stalin guffawed. 'I *know*! He always told me there was no danger of invasion! Well, I sent him to the front last week, to see for himself! They let him loose out there around dawn and a panzer ran him over, I'm told ... All right, Krivitskiy, you're getting promotion. You're a First Deputy People's Commissar and you report to me. *Direct* to me. You too, Konstantin. Your best work, both of you, now!'

They heard his voice as they went to the door and saw him smiling to himself. 'They hate the bastards, too ...' he crooned.

They found themselves back up on the street, and began to walk down Kirova to the shops.

'Here,' said Krivitskiy, passing over a red rectangle. 'Here's your new Party card. It's got a high *nomeklatura* number and it'll get you just about anything you want at the special shops.'

'Plenty of wine?' Konstantin enquired.

'Much as you want ... how much did you have to drink before we went in, anyway?'

'Just a bottle.'

'You'd have been shot, last month.'

'Not any more . . .' Konstantin said pleasantly. 'Listen, he said to take care of me and I want something.'

'What?'

The smile suddenly vanished from Konstantin's face. 'Rykov. Let me have Rykov.'

Krivitskiy shook his head. 'Sorry. If Rykov was up for offer, I'd have him myself. But he isn't, and you can't.'

Konstantin waved a hand out towards the horizon. 'Thousands are dying out there, and I can't have one little person of my own to kill?'

'Not Rykov. Rykov is valuable, Rykov has . . . certain talents.'

'I *know* what Rykov's talents are.'

'More valuable now than ever. Rykov can inspire fear – and that is a quality the Boss understands. You can't train someone to be Rykov, it's in there. This is a war without mercy so you need every Rykov you can get.'

Nagayevo Port, Magadan, October 1941

'Tea,' Katerina said wonderingly. She clasped her fissured hands, no better than claws, around the tin mug, absorbing its heat, holding it close to her nose to breathe in its smell and its warmth.

'Real tea. Now I *know* we've been freed.'

Yelena looked in equal amazement at the line of samovars, steaming like monsters in the icy air, at the NKVD guards actually serving up to the line of rag-wrapped skeletons shuffling towards them in their birch-bark shoes.

'It's probably a dream,' she said. 'One of those ones you get when it's really bad, and you can actually taste the food, feel it warm in your stomach. Then you wake up and it's the camp.'

'It's not a dream, Yelena, it's God. I've always believed in Him, even here, and He's always saved me.'

Katerina coughed, gripping her mug fiercely to prevent the precious fluid from spilling. It wracked her emaciated body, and traces of blood appeared on her lips. 'I wouldn't have made another winter, Yelena. I'd have been with the *dokhodyagi*, a goner all right. But we're going back to Moscow . . .'

At the dockside the bulk of a freighter loomed high above them.

'I never thought I'd be glad to see the *Dzhurma* again,' Katerina commented. 'They brought me here on that one and it took a month, because of the ice.'

'*Zhenskiy*! Ladies, listen to me.'

A big female guard had hoisted herself up on to a barrel, where they could all see her.

'Ladies?' Yelena muttered. 'Is that Gridas*sova* talking to us?'

The burly woman smiled down at them. 'Ladies, I'm sorry, but there's a fault in the *Dzhurma's* engine room. Now you're free again we want you to get home as soon as possible, so we're transferring you to the *Magadan*. She's docked just a few hours away, so if you'd all like to come with me we'll take you down there by barge.'

Yelena's eyes had widened behind her tin mug, opening in amazement. 'If we'd like to come? Gridassova hit me with a whip for not getting out of her way quickly enough last week!'

Katerina's jaundice yellow eyes were glittering with tears. 'Yes, but we're human beings again. All the guards think zeks aren't human beings. Slaves at best, animals otherwise. But now we're ladies again.' Her back stiffened in pride. 'It's that beast Hitler, you see,' she confided. 'Even that other beast with the moustache in Moscow knows he needs people like us now the Germans have invaded. It's all for the better, you'll see. The war will get rid of them both, and the Whites will come back.'

Suddenly she pushed herself forward. 'May this person speak?' she asked, in the manner they learned, in the camp.

Gridassova smiled. 'You are free, now. What do you want to say?'

'My son, Boris, was born here. I was pregnant when I was arrested . . . he was taken from me, to the *detpriemnik*, the NKVD children's home. Now we are free I ask that my son be returned to me.'

'Have no fears for your son,' the guard said reassuringly. 'The Party will restore him to you within hours. Now, ladies . . .'

The guards were forming up the column, and they began to shuffle slowly off at the practised slow march of the experienced convict without reserves to expend. The tin mugs rattled and clanged as they put them down on the long tables by the hot samovars.

'There'll be more tea aboard the barge, ladies,' Gridassova called cheerfully. 'And soup.'

The long barge was waiting beside the dock, attached to a beamy tug. Smoke was drifting from the stack and the prisoners were moving down the gangway and into the hold through the open hatches.

Someone was calling, 'Akulova! *Prisoner Akulova*!'

Yelena huddled among the others, her head down. It was one of the camp guards. Yelena knew her, the woman had bought needlework from her. But she didn't want anything to stop her going home, leaving this place, so she stayed silent.

Gridassova's suddenly hard eyes ran down the column. 'Akulova!' she barked.

Katerina gripped her hand. 'It'll be all right, Yelena. God will look after you, you'll see.'

Yelena stepped out of the line. 'Here,' she said. The guard was talking with Gridassova.

'I'll wait for you in Moscow,' Katerina called, moving away as the barge ingested the prisoners. 'You know where I am.'

Gridassova turned her normal chill gaze on to Yelena. 'It's back to the Lubyanka for you, Akulova. They're holding the mail plane at the airport.'

'Why?' she whispered.

'Fresh charges,' Gridassova said, turning away.

As Yelena walked away to the waiting truck she looked back. Katerina had turned and she was making the sign of the cross for her . . .

The fuselage of the Antonov was bare of seats and the copilot, not unkindly, told her to huddle up in the pile of empty mail sacks. He hesitated, then pulled out a thick black-bread sandwich from his jacket and gave it to her before going up to the cockpit.

The big radial engines turned, spurting smoke. It was blood-red in the light of the low sun hanging over the horizon. Yelena pulled as many of the sacks about her as she could, settling into the middle like an animal in a nest. She broke the sandwich in two and hid one half away inside her patched and mended clothing, where she had sewn a pocket in which she kept anything of value that she might be able to organise during the day.

She investigated the sandwich. The pilot, or his wife, had prepared it with real butter inside, and slices of salami. Very carefully, she began to chew.

It was worth looking out of the window to see Kolyma vanish, even if one was on the way to the Lubyanka. You learned in the camps that if there was any pleasure to be had, enjoy it at the time. She was warm, in her nest, there was food in her mouth and the promise of more in her pocket. And she had the view everyone yearned for, the sight of Kolyma vanishing under the aircraft's wings.

She looked out of the window. They were climbing out over the sea, the big radial engines roaring. Below, the water was unusually calm, blue-grey in colour. A small tug was heading back to port. The aircraft banked and, just for a moment, she could see clear down to the sea bottom, a few fathoms deep. Barges lay there, lying scattered on the floor like tombstones . . .

Moscow

The floor was polished parquet, so it was the Lubyanka. It was pleasantly warm, and the corridor smelled of carbolic and disinfectant. They stopped, and the guard knocked on the door. A woman's voice bade them enter.

She was sitting behind a desk with a folder in front of her. She looked up and Yelena's feet curled with fear inside her birch-bark shoes. Her nails had grown back, marked like flakes cut from a candle.

'Prisoner Akulova,' said Natasha Savinkova.

'Yes,' she said quietly.

'The Party is never wrong,' stated the interrogator.

'No,' Yelena agreed.

Natasha opened the file. 'This is your confession,' she said. 'It is lies. All lies.' The chill blue eyes looked up at her. 'What do you say?'

'Is your companion here?' Yelena asked. 'The one who interrogated me with you?'

'No.'

'If he was here, I would ask him what I should say.'

'He was found guilty of crimes against the people. He confessed, after interrogation.'

'Who did it?' Yelena asked softly.

Savinkova frowned. 'I did,' she said.

'So tell me what I should say.'

The interrogator stared at her and then, amazingly, her expression softened into a smile.

'You should thank the Party, which is never wrong. The Party which forgives. The Party which is always just.'

'Then I do,' she said slowly. 'Thank the Party.'

'Very good.' She pushed forward a sheet of paper with a few typewritten lines on it. 'Sign there.'

Yelena did as she was bid, and the woman carefully affixed the sheet to the file.

'Come with me, then, *Pani* Akulova.'

She went to the door, holding it open for Yelena. She eyed her as they went down the corridor.

'My, you are in a state,' she said. 'We'll have to see about some new clothes for you, you can't go about like that.' She laughed merrily. 'Why, you could be mistaken for a prisoner! 'But first, a bath, and some food.' She paused by a door. 'Oh, and something else.'

She turned the handle and, standing outside, waved Yelena through.

The door closed. Inside a big man got up from the couch on which he had been lying. He was as gaunt as a winter tree, and his general's uniform hung loose on him. He beamed, and there were gaps in his teeth.

'I knew you'd come!' said Akulov . . .

They stood at the window, looking out over Dzerzhinsky Square. Horse-drawn carts carried anti-tank hedgehogs one way, and people hurried the other, slipping on the early snowfall, carrying bundles and suitcases, making for the east-facing railway stations.

'The *bolshoi drap*,' said Akulov. 'The big scram. Most of the government officers have gone. Scurried off to Kuibyshev.'

'And you?' she said.

He pointed out of the window. 'Hoth's Panzers are only a hundred and twenty kilometres that way. He, Hoeppner and Guderian encircled over six hundred thousand of our men in less than a week. Captured over a thousand tanks and five thousand guns. The Germans are in Mozhaisk. That's one hundred and ten kilometres away. Napoleon marched from there to here in three days.'

'And will the Germans be here in three days?' she asked steadily.

'Not in three. The prospect of having done to him what he did to us has brought the *kinto* to his senses. They're getting all the professionals still alive out of the camps. Men like me. A zek one day, a general the next. Krivitskiy's handling it – he's here somewhere. And Zhukov's in charge.'

'And you?' she said again.

'I've been given the 5th Armoured Brigade. It's re-equipping with T-34s. I've been with the zek-specialists – the engineers, the scientists, the designers, the managers. Piotr Sadovsky was there with me and he's off to set up a tank factory east of the Urals, to get it started from nothing.'

'I'm staying in Moscow, if I can,' she said. 'Write, when you can, and shall we use the code, as before? Oh, Ivan, tell me where you will be, so I can think of you.'

He pointed once again out to the west. 'Hoth's coming. I'll be in his way.' He got up. 'I have to go, Yelena . . . But listen, when we were taken from the proving ground, when we were given our uniforms, I was brought here. Krivitskiy was waiting for me. After he had told me what I was to do I asked that you be found and freed from the camps. And he said he had already done it. And he had, because here you are, only hours later.'

He held her with his big, bony hands gripping her shoulders. 'This is to be a terrible war. It will be fought without mercy and human beings like you and I will count only in that we are considered a resource, one of some value. Those not of value will be abandoned.'

Tears filled her eyes. 'They killed Katerina and the others only yesterday. They sank them in barges, having told them they were free.'

He shook her gently. 'We will survive by being valuable. Krivitskiy must want you for something, for something for the war. So do it. Do it well, and we shall *both* live.'

Hot water came out of the tap, and she filled the bath. Bath salts were provided, together with scented soap and shampoo, and she lay for a long time in the warm, scented steam. The assault upon her deprived senses was almost that of a blow, of the drinking of wine, and when she got out, scrubbed and clean, every inch, she felt almost intoxicated.

Her clothes, dark and shiny with grime had been taken away and on the bed where Ivan had lain was an entire outfit. The labels were European and she dressed herself, marvelling at the softness and quality of the cloth and leather, at the strange feel of the smooth nylon stockings on her legs.

There was a knock at the door and a woman servant brought in food on a tray. There was a big glass of milk, a small steak with green vegetables, a pudding with rice and milk. She was finishing it when the door opened, and Krivitskiy came in. He was wearing civilian clothes and he sat down with her at the table.

'That's good,' he nodded, seeing the clean plates and glass. 'You must recover your strength.'

'What is it you want me to do?' she said directly.

'Good! We are at war. It is a war that some, like myself, saw coming. Also one which someone in particular chose *not* to see coming. Because of that we are worse off than we should have been. We may not win. However, Zhukov thinks we can hold Moscow. We have some other experienced commanders like your husband who have been saved from the wreckage and if we get time, the others, the younger men will learn. The new factories will come on line to produce the weapons. But we shall need that time. And help. Help from the West. The British and Americans have rushed a great deal of equipment to us. Tanks, fighters, trucks, food. We need more. Much more. Steel, aluminium, vehicles, armaments and food especially. Without vast material help from the West we shall not survive.'

'How am I to help?' she asked, puzzled.

'Our . . . image is important. To the West. The way they see us. They have something we do not have, an independent press. We have to manipulate them, to have them present us to their public in a very favourable light.'

'Lovable moujiks fighting for Uncle Joe,' she said bitterly.

'Something on those lines . . .'

'But you should get the best,' she said contemptuously. You need Sergei Savinkov. The Western intellectuals danced in the palm of his hand.'

Krivitskiy reached inside his jacket for a notepad. 'Where is he?'

'Which grave did you put him in?' she asked savagely, and he slipped it back.

'I remember the one . . . No, *you* must do. We do not have many skilled at talking to such people, but you know how. You speak English; you had many friends among the Western journalists. And you are an aristocrat. People like to deal with aristocrats. Churchill has made the mistake of sending us an ambassador who is a socialist! Cripps. An abstemious, teetotal, vegetarian ideologue! We sent all his kind to the camps long ago. We want an imperialist, someone we can respect.' Krivitskiy smiled. 'We have the problem in reverse. It is we who are imperialists, and cannot send one of our own to Washington. So we shall send you. A former person, an aristocrat.'

'An aristocrat who is not a communist! Are you sure I am what you need?'

'You think the people out there are fighting for communism? That was almost the first thing Stalin said, he said: "they'll not fight for us, but for Mother Russia." You'll be in good company.'

'I, too, will fight for Russia, I shall go. But understand, when I am there I must have freedom to move about, to talk to the newspaper men and women, to visit them, to take a drink with them, to eat in their homes. I cannot be chained to a political officer, nor read out prepared communiqués in the Embassy. I must be like Savinkov, before he was shot, I must have independence. If you cannot guarantee me that, there is no point in my going.'

'Very well,' he said easily. 'You shall have what you want, for as long as you perform as we wish.'

'And there is one last thing.'

Krivitskiy sighed. 'You want someone from the camps.'

'How did you know?'

He smiled coyly. 'It is everyone's request. Yelena Akulova, I don't have to tell you that for the Americans the camps do not exist. Any mention of them is a foul slander upon the Soviet state and its people. Who do you want?'

'A child. Katerina, who went to school with both you and with me was married to Boris Bulavin, a Cossack officer. He was taken and shot and she was sent to Kolyma where I met her. Their baby was born there. She is dead, murdered yesterday . . . the baby is in one of the ghastly orphanages you – the NKVD – run. I want him.'

'Why?'

'I would free them all . . .' She paused, recovering from the emotion which had swept her. 'Just him. It is something Katerina wished for him. I shall take him with me to Washington and he can attend an American kindergarden. The newspapermen will take photographs of him playing with the other children and he will become a symbol of American-Soviet friendship.'

Krivitskiy smiled. 'Very good! You are in your role already. Very well, it shall be done.'

He stood up and looked down at her. 'She did not want her son to grow up like me,' he said, and Yelena nodded in agreement. His face darkened with angry blood. 'I saved you! And your husband. Not everyone gets saved. You remember that.'

He went out. She was very tired and she thought she would lie down until someone came for her. By the bed, she knelt, and recited the prayer for the dead.

'*Gospodi, pomilui umershikh . . .*'

25

Frontoviks

THE car slithered over the hardening ground. *Bezdorozhie*, 'road-lessness', was coming to an end. Winter was coming, and the frost would release the tanks from the mud's embrace. Akulov was dressed like his men, in padded *telegreiki* jacket, fur hat and gloves, *valenki* felt boots.

A similarly-dressed figure was waiting for him, outside the hut among the green pine trees. Behind him in the wood monsters lurked, cold, hard, tracked.

He got out, and saluted. The young man in front of him responded by bounding forward and enveloping him in an embrace like a bear. Then he stood back, and formally saluted.

'Hullo, Dad,' Alexei said. 'You've come in time.'

Akulov gripped his son by the arm. 'This couldn't be better! We're together, Alexei and your mother's in Moscow. Natalia's in Minsk – I heard she was with the partisans.' Then he looked at his offspring. 'In time for what?'

'The NKVD is here,' Alexei said softly.

Akulov looked about him. The hut was his command post. 'Where are my staff officers?'

'With the NKVD. A man called Rykov came this afternoon.'

Akulov's very skin crawled on his flesh. 'Rykov's here?' he whispered.

'Yes. He's waiting for you. With the officers. Look, Dad, we're *frontoviks*, we've been in the fighting. We were with Yeremenko on the Desna river, we were to stop Guderian. The Kremlin bastard forbade him to group us into an armoured fist, to counter-attack in strength, and we were cut up in little packets.'

'The Kremlin bastard is better at killing unarmed, defenceless men,' Akulov said bitterly. 'That's his speciality. Though when we win the war they will say he did it. And I know why the NKVD's here.' He looked at the tanks hidden among the trees, wide-tracked, sculpted.

'Which one's yours?' he asked.

'That one,' said the young man, pointing. A young peasant stood up from where he had been patiently squatting.

'Very well, then. Where's Rykov?'

'In the clearing. Down the path. Igor, get ready.'

'Yes, boss,' said the peasant, climbing into the tank.

Akulov came out from the trees. On the other side of the open ground men in uniform were tied to tree trunks. In the middle was a line of four machine guns. Standing by them, arrogant and indifferent, were men in green hats. Troops were behind them, sullen and angry. But afraid. Of the power of the men in the green hats. Of the NKVD.

Akulov pushed his way through and came up to the guns. A man turned, smoking a cheroot.

'Welcome, general,' Rykov said sarcastically. 'Now we can dispense justice. Take note. This is what we'll do to you if you fail the Party, too.'

The men lashed to the trees were officers. Rykov swaggered across the grass and slapped one across the face.

'How much did you take to sell out, Judas?' he shouted. 'We have listened to your lies, traitor, now we will deal with you.'

The machine-gunners were taking last pulls on their cigarettes, preparing themselves for their routine work. Akulov stepped out in front of the guns, tall, his padded clothing filling out his emaciated frame. In the trees, a thirty-four tank engine grumbled to life.

'*Kal!*' Akulov bellowed. 'Don't talk shit, Rykov. No one here has sold out to anyone.'

'There was a stunned, shocked silence throughout the clearing. The eyes of the young NKVD men widened in disbelief.

'I'll have you shot too,' Rykov whispered furiously.

'You're shooting no one,' Akulov roared. 'These are *my* staff officers. Brave Red Army men, each and every one, who have been fighting for the motherland. You're shooting no frontoviks of mine.'

'The order came down from Stalin himself. Failed commanders and staff are to be shot,' Rykov hissed. 'Now get out of the way, unless you want to join them.'

'No,' Akulov said, his voice suddenly soft. '*You* get out of the way.'

The thirty-four's engine suddenly howled at full power. From the edge of the clearing it burst through the trees in a shower of pine branches. It went straight for the line of guns, and the NKVD men ran. Its tracks flattened the machine guns, picking them up between its treads and spitting them up in the air like so much scrap. It wheeled and came to a halt, the diesel grumbling. The hatch opened and Alexei appeared. The Degtyarev machine gun spat bullets at the feet of the NKVD execution squad.

'Be off!' Akulov bellowed. 'The next burst will be higher.'

Rykov was white faced. 'You'll pay,' he promised. 'I'll see that you pay for this.'

'Go hide in your hole,' said Akulov. 'Hoth is coming.'

He kicked Rykov with a heavy boot and he fell forward into the mud. With a bellow of joy, the troops seized dirt from the ground and pelted Rykov and his men as they ran up the path to their waiting vehicles. Akulov took a knife, and began cutting free the man Rykov had struck.

'Hoth's coming,' he said conversationally. 'We'd better be ready for him.'

Washington, D.C., April 1942

The big room was airy, the spring sunlight splashing through the windows on to the brightly-painted toys. The air was filled with the happy sound of the children at play as Yelena bent and kissed the little boy.

'Have a lovely time, darling, and I'll come for you after lunch.'

'Okay, Auntie,' he said, and rushed off into the scrum without a backward glance. She smiled, and let herself through the little gate that separated the room from the landing of the house.

'Hullo, Yelena.'

His hair was not flame red any more, it was dark, flecked with grey. But his smile was as she remembered it.

'Johnny! What on earth are you doing here?'

'Same as you. My daughter Karen is in the pre-school class downstairs. Is he yours?'

'Boris? No, I'm . . . looking after him for a friend of mine.'

'That's nice.'

'I persuaded them it was good for the image of the Soviet Union. It gets him out of the embassy and he meets American children and he speaks English, so it's good for him.'

'We all know of the aristocratic representative of the Soviet Union here. You're quite a star, Yelena. You give the place a good look, to the folks here.'

'Thank you,' she said quietly. 'I am doing my best to help my people in this war.'

'Probably paying back the debt,' he observed, and she said nothing.

'Say, I'm friends with the lady who does the meals and she lets me have a coffee. You want to come down and have one?'

They sat outside where the children came out to play, in a walled garden. Fresh leaves were on the trees, and flowers bloomed in the beds.

'What paper do you work for now, Johnny?'

'Oh, I'm not a hack any more. I decided I'd better stop writing about it and actually do it, before I lost all my self-respect. I got into politics.'

'I'm sorry our book didn't work out as we planned.'

'Well, in a sort of way it did. It got me to the attention of some people here who think the same way. There are things about the Soviet Union that worry us a lot. Remember the ones in Red Square that day?'

'The Westerners worshipping at Lenin's tomb? Yes.'

'We have them at high levels of government, too, unfortunately. And some funny things have happened. A few years back the Russian Division in the State Department was destroyed – the best intelligence unit we had on the Soviet Union. Just a part of the pro-Soviet bias of the White House in general, however.'

'What form does it take?' she asked, concerned.

'The general view amongst liberal opinion is that the Soviet Union is the natural ally of the USA, warts and all, and much closer to true democracy than the imperialist states of Britain and France. To me – a former liberal who has shed his rose-tinted spectacles – and to those who think like me, this is very worrying. We worry, specifically, as to what will happen when the war is over. Because the Allied powers will win, make no mistake. To use Winston's expression, all that is now required is the proper application of overwhelming force. But that force will leave most of Europe an ungoverned wasteland – and whoever holds the ground, will have the country. We don't want it to be Stalin.'

'No,' she said expressionlessly. 'How high does this pro-Soviet feeling go?'

'To the top,' he said softly. He drained his coffee cup and put it down with a quiet clink on the table. 'Right to the top. President Roosevelt wrote a letter to Prime Minister Churchill a few weeks ago. We got hold of a copy. In it he said: "I think I can handle Stalin better than either your Foreign Office or my State Department. Stalin hates the guts of all your top people. He thinks he likes me better, and I hope he will continue to."'

'He's met Stalin?'

'No. He said something else, too. He said: "I think if I give him everything I possibly can and ask for nothing from him in return, *noblesse oblige*, he won't try to annex anything and will work with me for a world of democracy and peace."'

'You're *sure* he wasn't in Red Square that day, bowing in front of the tomb?' Yelena asked.

'We think he just as well might have been. Do you see why we're worried?'

'Oh, I do. I do.'

'We think that Roosevelt is going to give Stalin all the help and material he can, and Stalin is going to use it to take the rest of Europe. We shall have defeated Hitler simply to put up a mirror image in his place. Frankly, there is something about the President that worries us deeply. He is not rational about Stalin. He seems to be craving his approval. He is . . . *courting* him.'

Her coffee was cold and she put the half-finished cup down on the moving dappled shadows of the leaves on the table.

'Why are you telling me all this?'

'Oh, because we go way back . . . the old Yelena would have been interested to know how right she was when she put a young fool straight about the revolution. I was in love too, like Roosevelt.'

He spoke without looking at her and from the house they could hear the voices of the children.

'The old Yelena is still here,' she said quietly.

'The old Yelena gave me information at the risk of her life.'

'My husband and my son are front line soldiers. *Frontoviks*. I am a kind of *frontovik*, too, Johnny. I am ready to fight for what I believe in.' She looked at Nichols with level grey eyes. 'When our Ambassador is adding up the casualties, he puts those of Britain and America in the same column with Germany . . .'

'Thank you,' he said. 'Shall we have coffee out here again? Say each Tuesday?'

'Each Tuesday, Johnny and there is only one condition. If, one day, I do not come to fetch Boris, take him home yourself. And keep him. The problem with *frontoviks* is that they get killed. He has no mother and no father and if I do not come for him, it will mean he has no aunt . . .'

Stalingrad, October 1942

They were the Fourth Tank Corps and they called themselves the *chetyretankovaya*, the Four Tanks. From the window of the house it was possible, if you wanted to get your head blown off by a German tommy-gunner very soon afterwards, to lean out and see the four tanks lying smashed amidst the burned brick rubble of the road they had pushed up. Akulov had had one of the tanks and the house they had fortified was known as his house, *Dom Akulovskiye*.

It had a smell, the house, though they had got used to it. It was a heavy, caustic stench of hot metal, burned brick, charcoal, explosive and propellant. Added to it, stronger by the day, was the cloying sweetness coming up from under their feet, where the dead lay rotting under the rubble. It caught in the back of the throat and would not leave.

The day belonged to the Germans. The bombers came and their observers and snipers made movement lethal. The Russians tunnelled, their sappers making trenches from which to attack German strong points once night fell, or simply to place high explosive underneath. Their snipers shot at Germans moving, and the Germans used artillery like giant sniper rifles, to blow their unseen opponents out of the tops of buildings. From the eastern side of the Volga *Katyushas* backed into the very water itself for maximum range, and loosed off salvos of rockets into the German assembly areas.

The city, in which hundreds of thousands of men were engaged in clawing, bludgeoning and burning each other to death, stretched all about Akulov and his house. His war was restricted to the building and the square it dominated, a place commemorating the heroic events of *Krasnyi Oktyabr* of the year seventeen. A fine statue of Lenin had been in its centre, set amidst a small park of trees. The trees had been the casualties of flamethrowers, the statue of Akulov's 45mm gun emplaced in the first floor. A German assault group had used it as cover and now they lay tumbled about its plinth while Lenin lay on his side among them, exhorting them to struggle for a perfect world.

The Germans held the house on the eastern edge of the square.

Darkness had fallen. Inside the house Akulov moved among his men. The house was stuffed with them. He had sent out soldiers in the night, illiterate peasant boys who had learned the topography of the ruined city as well as they knew their home marshes, woods and fields, and moved through it like shadows. They had harvested the men hiding in holes and under rubble and inside the house there had been *kasha* buckwheat porridge and tea from the samovar. Now they were assembled and, from a rag-bag of guardsmen, tankers, cooks, medical orderlies, trainee sergeants and others, Akulov had made a fighting force.

He called it a 'storm group'. In the dim room he went along the waiting line of its first element, the assault party. There were eight of them, all unwounded and the fittest of those he had, lightly-armed with Schmeisser and PPSh machine-pistols and sub-machine guns, grenades, fighting knives – and spades that had had their edges honed for use as axes in hand-to-hand fighting. He had Mahorka tobacco, dark and fragrant, in one pocket of his combat coat, and lumps of brown sugar in the other. As he went down the line he gave each man a twist of tobacco and a lump of sugar, popping both in their mouths, and they munched them up together. Then he clapped the man on the shoulders and went to the next.

Near the end he paused and fished inside his coat. He brought out a pamphlet and gave it to the soldier in front of him. The man smiled sheepishly and the others all laughed. He was a *politruk*, a political commissar. Akulov's men had found him with the remnants of a fresh infantry unit the Germans had successfully shelled almost to death on its way up to the line. When they had got to him he had been clutching his PPSh and a bagful of pamphlets entitled *How to Act in City Fighting*.

Akulov chuckled and gave him the tobacco and sugar. The politruk had taken his unit's annihilation personally, demanding to be in the assault team that night. In a world where generals commanded seventy men and their rule held sway over entire houses, he had seen nothing unreasonable in the request.

The last man was Alexei. He gave him tobacco and sugar and embraced him.

'What's the golden rule?' he asked his son.

The young man grinned. 'Plenty of women.'

'No, stay alive. But get the house, too.'

A cold flow of air indicated the open door and Alexei Mikhailovich led his men out, slipping into the darkness. Working like thieves, the sappers had cleared a lane all the way around the square that kept crouching troops invisible.

Inside the house Zharov the cook put a lid on a gently-steaming cauldron of kasha, and shrugged his way into the harness of a flamethrower, strapping its heavy tank to his back.

'Ready, Ivanych,' he said respectfully, and Akulov led the second component out into the darkness. They were the reinforcement party of a dozen. He had picked the biggest men, for they were loaded like mules with heavy machine guns, mortars, anti-tank rifles, crowbars, picks, flame-throwers and explosives. Their feet and the metal parts they carried were bound with rags and they followed the assault party down the trench in the dim orange glow of the burning city. Behind them the house was manned by the wounded.

They crouched behind rubble. Zharov, the cook, was behind Akulov; he could smell the sweetness of porridge on his breath, and the pungent odour of the oil dribbling from the nozzle of his flamethrower. Akulov reached in his pocket for a curl of tobacco, and chewed.

There came the sudden flat crump of grenades, the calico-tearing rip of the Schmeissers, the slower drumming of the PPShs. A green flare arced across the square and they were on their feet, running for the door that lay blasted from its hinges.

The politruk was dead in the doorway and they ran over his body. The air was full of plaster dust because the grenades had brought down the ceiling and it hung about them in a tangle of matted wood. Alexei was crouched by a door. He saw Zharov and called, '*Here!*'

Alexie had a cut-down sledgehammer in his hand. He smashed the hinges with two blows and, as the door fell in, Zharov poked the nozzle around the frame and the room filled with fire. As they moved on into the house things screamed behind them . . .

Something came at Akulov from the darkness and he knew it was a German because the smell was different. His fighting knife reflected the flames behind them and Akulov hacked the arm off with his spade and thrust the knife into his guts.

Zharov was ahead of him as Akulov trod on the chest of the dying man to pull out his spade. The darkness sparkled with bullets striking the tank on his back. Fire suddenly illuminated him, spreading over a whirling, howling thing in a hallway and Akulov threw grenades over him and shot him with his pistol.

Alexei was crouched by the stairway, setting explosive charges. All about them the house was blazing, fallen beams and planks incandescent in the plaster-dust fog.

'*Out!*' Akulov roared.

As they moved down the fiery corridor he saw something crawling. It was one of his own and he grabbed him by the webbing. They fell out into the cold air with their hair smoking, their eyes and noses streaming. Akulov pulled his flare pistol from its holster and a scarlet light arced over the square. Germans were at the windows of their burning fortress and a sudden storm of machine gun fire lashed the building from the support company as Akulov and his men pulled back.

Inside their own building all their innumerable small cuts, tears, burns and bruises began to ache and throb. The medical orderlies had been waiting and they began their work at once. Akulov ladled out kasha from Zharov's cauldron and, as he went to sleep in his corner, he could hear a man praying.

In the dawn, from the fourth storey, he could see the Stukas wheeling like hawks over the Volga, their strut-mounted sirens shrieking as they dived on the boats from Akhtuba bringing the Russian reserves into the city. The docks were on fire; smoke was pouring from the tractor factory, and he could see tanks moving along the railway line, the tommy-gunners like ants about them.

By the window Alexei lay, swathed in sacking, only the very muzzle of his Dragoon rifle on the sill. Across the square smoke drifted from the gutted house and things like charred logs lay scattered and broken on the rubble below.

There was a sudden bang from Alexei's rifle, and he rolled sideways to avoid counter-fire. From behind him in the room Akulov saw a man fall from the top of the ruin, tumbling down its ruined, wall-less sides. A projecting, sagging floor caught him, and he hung over its corner like a shot bird.

'Count Mikhail liked to shoot pheasants,' Akulov remarked. 'He said there would be no time for it, in the new world.'

He went down the stairs, to arrange another day in Stalingrad . . .

Washington, D.C., February 1943

'I'm sending Alexei some things. Can you make sure they get through? And you want to talk to General Anders,' Yelena said.

'The Polish commander?'

'Stalin let him out of the camps, like Ivan and the other military men, after the Germans invaded. The Polish government in exile has signed an agreement for him to raise a Polish army, to fight the Germans. He's been gathering up as many of the Polish officers and men who were put into the Gulag as he can, for his army.'

The day was crisp; frost still coated the grass and the coffee in their mugs steamed in the still air. From behind them came the sound of the children at play.

'Krivitskiy was in the Embassy and told me. Anders couldn't find his officers. He collected only about four hundred when he was expecting fifteen thousand.'

Yelena drank some coffee, wincing. 'I've got a hangover,' she said. 'I was drinking Tennessee whiskey with Krivitskiy until two in the morning . . . To continue, the officers have been missing since 1940. *Before* the Germans invaded. They're dead, Johnny. They were regulars, and reservists from the professions. Why kill them?'

'Take out the natural leadership,' said Nichols. 'It fits his patterns.'

'That's right. Since it was Stalin who captured them, Stalin must have killed them. Which means he intends to take Poland as a part of the Russian empire. Oh, my head . . .' She squinted at him in the bright sunshine. Johnny, are you able to get messages through to the Germans?'

'It could be done,' he said cautiously.

'You see, I know where they are, all those Polish officers. Krivitskiy told me, because he was there, and Rykov too . . . It was a lovely Spring day in April, he said, the sun was shining down in the forest and there was still a little snow on the fields. They're in a pit, Johnny,' she said, her eyes full of unending pain. 'A great pit in the Katyn forest, on the banks of the Dneiper, near Smolensk. Their hands are tied behind their backs and they have all been shot in the back of the neck. Tell the Germans where to look. When they find them, tell the President. Then maybe he'll see that what Stalin has on his hands is not perfume.'

Nichols was scribbling in a small pad. 'I'll do it,' he murmured. 'And was there something else? You're sending Alexei something?'

'A sleeping bag, some vitamins and things. I don't want them stolen.'

'I'll have them put in the diplomatic bag. I'll see they get there.'

'It gets cold,' she said, 'sleeping out in the open . . .'

Kursk, July 1943

Alexei zipped up his sleeping bag about him, settling himself against the bogie of the T-34. Rain was spattering on the tarpaulin he had carefully rigged above himself but in his little tent he was warm. It smelled of fresh paint from the new tank at his back and a thick yellow candle provided him with light.

From one of the eye bolts hung a gas mask. He took his pad of paper on his knee and his pencil stub in his hand. As he prepared himself to write, a horny and dirty hand thrust a metal jug inside the tent.

'Here, boss.'

'Good lad, Igor.'

The jug smelled of metal and fuel and he poured bright green glop into the gas mask. On the ground beneath there was a bowl. Alexei returned to his letter.

Dear Mummy,

He paused, licking the end of the pencil. He liked the taste. There was a plinking as the glop began to appear through the filters of the gas mask and fall into the bowl.

It was difficult, writing a letter. Images from the battle fluttered in his mind like sliced sections of film, unrelated and violent and he was quite unable to splice them together.

Thank you for the lovely gifts. They arrived safely along with about a hundred tons of Dad's armour-piercing shells. The sleeping bag is very comfortable, and I am taking great care of it. Thank you, too, for the Zippo lighter, which lights up in any weather.

. . . the German tanks came across the field of burning buckwheat like a huge black rhombus, a gigantic chunk of the forest that had somehow broken away from the main mass. The T-34 was hull down and he saw the immense Ferdinand self-propelled gun, its camouflage like a map of dark lowlands, brown zig-zags of mountains, yellow deserts and the spider legs of the swastikas proclaiming its nationality, and he fired, squeezing himself as far to the left as he could in the tiny, cramped turret. For a moment he had the sensation of being in a small ship hitting a rock in wild seas. Flame and dust and a lane of wheat suddenly ablaze along the muzzle blast.

He actually saw the shell fly off the sloped armour of the German machine, something black and misshapen tumbling through the air. There was the howl and whistle of arriving mortar shells and his vision port was blanked out by flying dirt. From somewhere outside he could hear infantrymen scream.

The Ferdinand fired, the huge 100 mm barrel opening like a scarlet cat's eye, the crash of firing and the crash of impact almost the same. A hurricane of noise, flame, sods and earth, leaves and burning air. His mouth was filled with dirt, his teeth jarring in his head. Furnace air rushed about him and he struggled up through the hatch. The T-34 had been turned half around and it lay beneath him, ripped open like the belly of a cow. In the air he could hear the roar of the approaching machines, the crashing of the guns and the clanging of impact.

The Ferdinand came up the hill through the smoke and he was very cross. He couldn't remember feeling so cross. He had grenades hung on his webbing and he crouched down in the soft dirt torn up by his own tracks. It came by, vast, like a ship moving on land almost twice his own height, the howl of its engines in his ears, the enormous gun dribbling smoke and he plucked the grenades from his belts one after the other, pulling out the pins and stuffing them between the enormous tracks and the whirling wheels.

He could hardly hear the explosions over the noise, but the breast suddenly slewed, almost trapping him against his own tank, sections of track spewing in the air. It stopped, track trailing, rucked and twisted like a length of intestine.

Smoke belched from exhausts like drains as the twin engines roared. The front drive sprocket whirred like a blurred top. Dead Russian infantry in their dun uniforms lay scattered about like logs and the German machine was suddenly silent, lying on the dirt like a metal fort.

He was cross. A dead soldier was at his feet, his tank of fuel on his back, Alexei dragged it off him, heaving on the harness. His Zippo cigarette lighter was in his hand, smooth and warm, and he turned the knurled knob of the flamethrower and whirled the flint. The air was hot; flame spilled out in front of him.

He clambered up on to the top of the machine, muttering to himself. He had a headache and the people inside the hulk seemed to him very unreasonable. He walked about on its surface, as broad as the deck of a ship. It was sealed up, tightly riveted, tightly closed. Through an oblong of thick glass he could see someone looking at him from the inside.

A hatch opened and a grenade tumbled out, tinkling on the armour. He kicked at it with a boot. There were more, and he danced on the armour, lashing them away. Fiery splinters clawed his back, and it made him even more cross. He squashed the grip of the flamethrower and fire engulfed the hatch. He heard someone scream.

Out on the field a comet came down from the sky, slamming silently into the burning wheat. As the smoke and flame billowed up he heard the crump of its dying. He stuck the nozzle of the flamethrower into an air vent and squeezed the grip.

They were scattered all about, six of them in their charred black uniforms. He thought that was all there was. They were lying about like half-consumed logs from a fire. He climbed up on to his T-34, leaving the flamethrower behind. His sleeping bag was still where he had left it, in the turret, and he tucked it under his arm. Flies, about a thousand of them, were walking and buzzing about a glistening dark red mass. They annoyed him, and he picked the flamethrower back up, hosing the great gash in the hull with flame. In the distance he could hear the battle as it drove into his lines . . .

Thank you for the bottle of Vitamin-C tablets.

Alexei sucked on the tip of his pencil, peering at the few lines of his letter. The glop was dripping into the bowl with a splashing sound and he tipped up the jug, refilling the gas mask.

They taste of oranges, and are very refreshing. I'm sure they will help keep the colds away, when winter comes.

. . . the crater caught him by surprise, it was a part of the secondary defence works, and the Germans had driven through it. His foot caught air as he strolled along, and he tumbled down the slope. As he picked himself up, somebody was looking at him. A soldier in grey, his leg roughly bandaged, blood still seeping from a wound in his hand.

He wasn't angry any more and he smiled. The German smiled, hopefully. Alexei beamed. His headache had gone. He gathered his sleeping bag up, and felt in the special sewn-in pocket. His bottle of vitamin pills was still intact. He produced it with the air of a conjurer performing a successful sleight of hand, unscrewing the lid and offering it to the soldier.

They sat in the sunshine, chewing on the bright orange pills like sweets.

'*Schon . . . gut.*'

The German produced a sausage, and cut off two hunks with his good hand.

'*Spasiba,*' said Alexei.

'*Blutwurst,*' the German said helpfully.

Alexei had a field dressing pack and he bound up the German's wound for him.

'*Danke, dankeschon,*' said the wounded man.

'*Dasvidaniya,*' Alexei said, climbing up the slope.

'*Wiedersehn . . .*'

The sleeping bag has come in very useful. It is especially good that it is waterproof outside. We were caught in a storm a few days ago and it kept me quite dry.

. . . they were pulling back. Scarred monsters bearing white wounds shining in the strange light of the approaching thunderstorm. Flecked with marks of machine guns, and the black burns of flamethrowers. Blood on their flanks, from the bodies of infantrymen. Monsters with their guns laid over their rears, belching flame in the driving rain, running tommy-gunners in black, wheeling SP guns and men with *Panzerfausts*. Orange and yellow fire, thunder and artillery. In the ditch he climbed into his sleeping bag, zipping it tightly over his head, pulling his knees up to his chest and, in the darkness, it was only a summer storm. In the morning it would be fresh and he could go out to play . . .

I have met a very nice girl. I think that when you meet her you will like her too. Her name is Anastasia Ivanovna.

. . . it was quiet in the gully; the soft green plants and bushes beckoned, the little brook babbled, ignoring the kerosene and propellant-scented wind that blew above. He slipped gratefully into its cover, sliding down the sides, explosions of scent all around him. The stream widened into a pool and he put his rolled-up sleeping bag down and knelt to drink, scooping up the cool water in his cupped palms.

He stopped, stiff, the water dripping half way to his mouth. On the other side, a German knelt, drinking from the pool, his face right in the water. Carefully, quietly, Alexei dropped his hands, letting the water trickle away. He reached for his Tokarev automatic.

The German in his grey uniform did not move. In the shadows, he saw a tank, a mottled green Panzer IV, backed into the trees. The sanctuary of the gully had attracted others.

The German still did not move, his face sunk in the water. Behind him there was another, lying down on the grass, as though asleep. A boy lounged against the turret of the tank, as though sunbathing in the shade but something dark stained his shirt black.

With his automatic in his hand, and his sleeping bag in the other, Alexei waded across the pool. None of the Germans moved.

The back of the man's head was missing. Alexei edged towards the tank. The driver's vision port was open a few inches, the metal was sprayed with blood. Insects moved in there, feasting.

Things howled about him, flying off the armour, and something stung his shoulder. He found himself crouching down by the track. A man moved above him on the skyline, a black outline against the sun, a tommy-gunner. Schmeisser fire tore about his hiding place, cutting down the plants.

The tommy-gunner pulled something like a potato masher from his belt, moving along the ridge to gauge his angle correctly. The grenade tumbled in a pretty arc and Alexei ran out into the open. The blast, as it fell where he had been, deafened him. He squeezed the trigger of his Tokarev and the hammer fell on an empty chamber.

The tommy-gunner stood at the top of the ridge. Then he fell forward, tumbling over in the air. Alexei heard his body crashing to the floor after it vanished from sight.

He was standing in the pool, his worthless pistol in his hand.

'Here,' called a voice.

He squelched out, still carrying his sleeping bag.

'Here,' said the girl, and he went along the gully, and up the side, his boots dripping.

'Here,' she said, and he crawled in beside her in the little cave, where they could see the whole little valley laid out in front of her camouflage screen of branches and leaves. The long Dragunov rifle with its huge telescope lay ready in front of her, its nose in the air, supported by its bipod.

She had green eyes, very clear, for looking through the telescope. She had dainty hands, neat and strong, for pulling the trigger. She had red lips, and white teeth, to call him with.

'I'm here,' he said . . .

The gas mask had finished its dripping. Alexei folded his letter up into the soldier's triangle, tucking it into his breast pocket. He heard someone moving, outside.

'Igor?'

'Yes, boss.'

The peasant stuck his head under the tarpaulin. Rain dripped off his nose.

'Here,' Alexei said, 'Get under cover. *Shampanskaye's* ready.'

Alexei had two tin cups and he carefully filled them from the bowl. The glop had lost none of its bright green colouration.

'Smells different, Igor, where did you get it?'

'Tiger tank. In the back, where the gears are.'

'Tiger transmission fluid, eh? Well, here's to us.'

They tossed it back and sat breathing fumes, their eyes watering.

'You know, Igor, my dad drank real *shampanskaye*. If things had been different, I'd have been a count. You know that? *Graf* Alexei. But I'm not. And here I sit, under my tarpaulin, drinking transmission fluid . . . You know, one day I'm going to get *bottles and bottles* of champagne, and *bathe* in it.'

The peasant held out his mug hopefully, and Alexei refilled them both.

'How many tanks this battle, Igor?'

'Two for me, three for you, boss. They did my leg up. I'm back now.'

'There's just you and me left, Igor. I hope we win this battle soon.'

'Another one after that, boss.'

The thunder rolled outside like artillery, and Alexei tugged his wonderful sleeping bag about him and drank deeply.

26

Dushegubka

The Kremlin, Moscow, May 1944

K ONSTANTIN stood very still amongst the marble servants of the tsars and the group of men passed him by in their foreign generals' uniforms, their footsteps tapping and clattering on the marble.

'Where's that Akulov johnny? You can never find him when you want him. I wanted him to put Stalin right about all that guff he was spouting and couldn't see him at all! The feller was hiding behind a pillar. So where's he gone now?'

They mooched off down the great hallway of marble and gilt and, in the emptiness they left behind, somebody moved. Akulov appeared from behind a great pilaster, and headed away in the other direction. As he passed, Konstantin stepped out.

'Hullo, Ivan. What *were* you doing behind the pillar?'

Akulov grinned. 'Hallo, Konstantin. What are you up to? Let me tell you, if any British general thinks I'm about to tell the boss he's not a military genius he's got another think coming!'

'What about a drink?'

'I don't think they have any bars around here. Where did you have in mind?'

The artist beamed. 'Konstantin's bar! Step this way.'

They went round the corner and Konstantin led the way around a screen, then through an arched doorway into a small courtyard where a fountain was playing.

'Most people don't know this is here,' he said. 'Now – ' He pulled up his sleeve and dipped his hand into the pool. 'Here we are!'

He plucked a bottle of wine from the depths. 'Nicely chilled. I had to go see the boss, too. I saw you and your lot going in afterwards and I thought I'd give you a drink. God knows, I always need one after I've seen him. The fountain here brings it to just the right temperature.'

Konstantin fished in the pool and extracted two tumblers which he rinsed before twirling a corkscrew into the bottle.

'I've got life worked out, Ivan, it's just a question of never being too far from a drink. I've got caches all over Moscow.'

'You like the booze, Konstantin?' Akulov said sympathetically.

'Like it? It's the only thing that makes sense of anything.' He filled up the tumblers and gave one to Akulov. 'I'm pissed all the time.'

He drank a good swallow. 'Ahh . . .' He looked at the big soldier. 'You going into Germany, Ivan?'

'We have to take Minsk, first.'

Konstantin felt inside his baggy jacket and pulled out a sheet of paper. 'You ought to be interested in this, then.'

Akulov took it.

'*Whirl, you demons. Rise up from your graves and whirl in your dance of death. The blonde hag is waiting. She is waiting for the fire, for the axe in your hand. Whirl, in your dance of ecstasy, for the hour of revenge has struck.*'

He looked up at Konstantin.

'There's more,' said the poet. 'The blonde hag is Germany, of course.'

'It is a war without mercy,' Akulov said, folding up the paper. 'But we know that anyway.'

'Oh, it's not my idea. It's his. The boss.'

'The Germans will suffer enough in defeat. My boys are good soldiers, *frontoviks*. I don't need poems about revenge.'

'*He* does. And anyway, it's not good enough – he said so. I have to go off and spell it out. He especially wants the German women to be raped.'

Konstantin tipped back his glass, and then refilled it. 'Raped and shot, is what he told me. So I'm getting pissed, and then I'm going off to write a poem about rape.'

'*I* shoot men who rape, in my army,' Akulov said darkly.

Konstantin looked at him with a sudden calculation in his drunken eye. 'I wanted to talk to you about that,' he said quietly. 'You wouldn't do me a favour, would you?'

'What can I do?' Akulov was wary.

'You could kill Rykov for me.'

'I have no objections to killing Rykov. Only in the middle of this war, at the loud end of an army, my chances of coming across him seem small.'

'You never know . . .'

'Why do you want him dead?' Akulov was curious.

'He is the *dushegubka*, the soulkiller. He has destroyed my soul
. . . but not for me, for Katia.'

'Where *is* Katia? Before they took me away, and to the camps, you
were to be married. I remember that.'

'They came and took me away, too. In the night, Rykov appeared
in my cell. There was blood all over him . . . on his boots . . . he said
if I licked all the blood off, he would let me out . . .'

Konstantin sat on the edge of the fountain, with unfocused eyes.
So he let me out . . . he took me back home, he let me out. I went
upstairs. Katia was in the bedroom, in bed.'

Silent tears slid down his cheeks.

'She was in pieces, Ivan, Rykov had cut her up into pieces. Her
eyes, her hair . . . all pieces . . .'

Akulov bent down, and cuddled the weeping man as he would
a child.

'I promise,' he said. 'I promise, if I can, I will kill him for you.'

Minsk, June 1944

'He's called "Blue Mist",' said Akulov. 'A blueish fog comes down
in these parts and they say he and his partisans move through the
woods and marshes just as though the mist's down.'

Through the pines came the distant grumble and crump of
Rokossovsky's Front grinding the 41st Panzer into the bank of
the Beresina.

'It could have been me,' said Alexei. 'I began the war not far
from here.'

He was tearing up a piece of *Pravda* into a squill, and filling it with
a line of dark Markhorka. He licked it expertly and was wreathed in
aromatic smoke.

They were at the tip of the advance. Through the woods came the
grumbling and squeaking of the thirty-fours, and the chopping and
crashing of Karkov's engineers turning trees into roadway. A group
of Germans sat sullenly nearby, under guard.

'What the hell is *she* doing here?' Akulov asked suddenly.

A woman had come out of the trees. She was young, slim and dark,
and a little child toddled beside her.

'Where did she come from?' Alexei muttered. 'Doesn't she know 20 Panzer is out there?'

The woman bent down and swung the child up on to her hip and suddenly Akulov was running down the forest trail, and she smiled to see him coming. Akulov turned, embracing them both, and tears were in his eyes.

'Come see your sister, Alexei!' he called.

'What are you doing here?' Alexei asked joyfully. 'And who is this?'

He beamed at the little boy, who, unmoved by the two big strangers, smiled back.

'This is my son, Ivan,' Natalia said.

'I'm a grandfather?' Akulov said in amazement. 'Where is his father?'

'He'll be here in a minute,' she said enigmatically.

'Look, here we are gossiping like *babushkas*, and Alexei and I have a battle to fight. We're waiting for a partisan leader, a fellow called Blue Mist, Natalia.'

She smiled. 'Here I am.'

All along the trail, men and women were appearing out of the woods, quite silently. They were all lean, their hair tied back or stuffed inside leather caps, armed with a catholic collection of guns, from captured Schmeissers to a PTRS anti-tank rifle.

'And here are my people, to take you through the marshes.'

'"Blue Mist"?' Alexei said in brotherly amazement. 'When I last saw you you thought Blue Mist was a French perfume!'

'Fifty thousand German marks and a dacha in the Tyrol for anyone who hands me in,' she boasted proudly. 'And more, with this one.'

Akulov looked at his grandson. 'A seasoned partisan, I can tell,' he said solemnly.

'A whole railway bridge to his credit,' she said. 'When he was only a few months old I took a basket of apples to market. We crossed the bridge and the guards took some of the apples and let me through. I stopped in the middle to change him, and clamped a time bomb to the girder. Then we went on to the other end. Those guards took some more apples and let me through. Three hours later the bomb went off. *With a train crossing.*'

Her eyes flicked to the group of Germans, some hundred strong, still sitting grimly in the trees, but she said nothing. A lean young man, dark-haired, came out of the woods, and she smiled. He came forward, and lifted up little Ivan.

'Here is Ivan's father.'

It was Nikolai Savinkov and Alexei greeted him warmly. A woman came forward too, in glasses mended with wire.

'Tatyana is also with us. But have you your map?' asked Natalia. 'You see, you are close to our base. I'll mark it. We have a bath house, if you want to steam afterwards! You can advance along here, and here. It looks as though you cannot, and the Germans believe it impassable, but with brushwood and logs the bottom is hard enough for tanks. Beware of here, though, for this they know to be passable, and have placed a minebelt.'

Akulov assessed his lines of advance expertly. 'We could hook round 20 Panzer's flank if we could use it,' he murmured.

'There's something else,' said Nikolai. 'We know where the command centre of their 9th Army is. It's in the rear, but we know the way to get through the lines. The Germans can't hold the marshes. If you give us some good men, we'll get them there for you.'

'I think I can find some men of the kind you want. Alexei, have Zakharov come up. Karpov, detail your men to go with the guides along these routes.'

Natalia was looking at the Germans again. 'Where did those swine come from?'

'We captured them this morning. SS troops getting out of Rokossovsky's way, at a guess. They put up a poor fight.'

'Of course they did,' she murmured. 'They don't like dealing with people who fight back, their sort. May I have a look?'

She and Akulov went over and he scanned their faces.

'You know any?' her father asked curiously.

She nodded. 'One or two. *He* was in charge of the team that took all the people of Lubova's village from their houses, the old people, the children, the husbands and wives. They took them to the church and locked them in. And then set fire to it. And *him*, yes, I know him, he was the one who Gartner detailed to round up and shoot 400 civilians at random. *That* was to announce Gartner's presence.'

Her eyes were searching the ranks. 'Gartner's not here,' she said regretfully. 'But you don't get his sort usually – they get out by the back way, before the fighting starts.'

'Who's Gartner?'

'The Gestapo chief for this area. The one who employs *Einsatzgruppen* – "Special duties" – Murderers. That's why they didn't fight well. They aren't good at anything except murder.'

Akulov eyed them thoughtfully.

A man had come up the track and was waiting. He held himself like an officer, but wore a plain uniform without badges of rank.

'This is Zakharov,' he said to Natalia. 'He'll go with you. We all have penal units attached to us, men who have committed crimes. They pay in blood, for they get to do the worst tasks. Zakharov commands ours.'

'What did you do?' she asked quietly.

'My unit was encircled at Stalingrad. We succeeded in fighting our way out and making our way to our own lines and the NKVD interrogated me. "How did you escape while so many did not?" they asked. "You must be a traitor." I knocked the man down. And here I am, commander of a different unit.'

He smiled crookedly. 'We are desperate criminals, each and every one. Are you sure you want to associate with the likes of us? Our ranks are filled with those who have done such things as call Stalin a murderer, and his secret police a collection of pigs' droppings.'

'You sound my kind,' she said, grinning.

'You're to attack 9th Army's command post,' said Akulov. 'Those who survive win back their good names, and former ranks. Tell the boys that.'

Natalia kissed her son and put him down. Tatyana was nearby, and she came over.

'Hold grandpa's hand,' Natalia instructed. 'Stay with him and Aunt Tatyana until I come back.'

Akulov watched her melt into the forest with Zakarov's men following. He hoisted his grandson up on to his shoulder, where he sat on a scarlet board of rank, well-pleased with his view.

The engineer was detailing his men.

'Karpov,' he called. 'I want a road on the third route. The one that goes to the minefield . . .'

Behind him the tanks squeaked and grumbled as they came up to the start line. From the rear, high in the air, came the sound of the Shturmoviks, the 'flying tanks' waiting in their cab rank for Akulov to summon them in to pound the German positions.

In front of Akulov were the two hundred-odd Germans of the Einsatzgruppe he had captured that morning. He leaned out of his BA-64 armoured command car and addressed them in good German.

'The Red Army does not want to keep you as prisoners. You are free to go.'

They stared at him warily. Experienced killers, they knew the look of the executioner.

'It's that way,' Akulov said. 'Across the open ground. Head for
the copse. Those of you who get there can go free. Stray to right or
left and these machine guns will cut you down. They'll fire tracer,
so you can see the limits of the lane.'

Reluctantly, they turned and began to move cautiously forward.
Akulov fired a burst from his sub-machine gun at their heels and
they began to run. The waiting tanks crunched into gear as the first
mines went off. Dirt and bits of flesh and bone rained down, and the
thirty-fours ground forward in the wake of the screaming men . . .

Lieutenant Pokryshin could dance the waltz and the mazurka. He had
been taught to as a cadet at his Suvorov school. Alexei marvelled at it.
The young man could also speak English and use the correct cutlery
to dine. He was an *ofitser*, and when not fighting in his tank wore
a Guards' uniform with Tsarist *pogon* shoulder boards. Army codes
of conduct promulgated by Peter the Great had come back in, and
the political commissars had gone back out. Lieutenant Pokryshin
expected rankers to salute him with as much punctiliousness as his
Tsarist grandfather.

Pokryshin's thirty-four wheeled in formation with Alexei's as
though the two were indeed dancing the mazurka together. They
fired simultaneously and red mouths of fire burst on the approaching
formation of Panthers and Panzer IVs. The thirty-fours streamed like
rats out of the trees, where the minefield was supposed to be. They
were festooned with infantry.

Something screamed. Alexei could hear it through his headphones.
It went on and on. Slim, winged shapes came over his head, three,
four, five, one after the other. Shturmoviks, so low that the wind of
their passage whipped the woods into a storm of fire and smoke. He
could see the helmeted pilots leaning forward against their straps in
their cockpits. They could concentrate on their job without worrying
about the Messerschmitts – the Yaks and Aircobras had taken care
of those. Shell cases streamed under their wings from their heavy
cannon and, in the distance, men vanished in clouds of exploding
dirt, and half-tracks erupted in flame. The Shturmoviks leaped high
in the air like flying fish, sunlight glinting on their wings as they left
the smoke below.

The thirty-fours were closing fast now, rocking over the bumps on
their strong suspension, the fighting troops on their decks clinging
on. They were in the dust and yellow smoke of TNT and they flung
themselves off as the armoured monsters clanged together in amidst
the trees and gullies. Alexei fired as a Panther loomed out of the

smoke fifty metres away and the turret flew off like a cap in the wind, tumbling over and over. The headless beast continued to crawl forward.

The dusty fog was suddenly blood red as his infantry swarmed on to the slowed German armour, the flamethrower operators sticking their nozzles into the air intakes to fry the crews alive. With an enormous crash the thirty-four collided with a bigger Panzer coming the other way. The gun barrels smacked against each other's turret and an infantryman leaped up on to the German machine and slapped an explosive charge over the engine hatch. As Alexei backed off in a screech of metal, the mine exploded. Smoke gushed from the interior and black-clad men tumbled from the turret like maggots out of a cheese. Emerging out of the man-made fog, Lieutenant Pokryshin cut them down with his machine gun.

Then Alexei was out in the fresh air again. Turning, he could see the machines of the German break-out formation burning. Survivors were scattered, running for the safety of the trees.

And the Cossacks were there. Over the crackling of the flames Alexei could hear the wild howls of the cavalry as they sabred the running men among the pines. *Ourrah! Ourrah!*

They flowed past him in an endless field-grey stream. The Germans were going to Moscow. There were some among them who had been close enough to see the Kremlin spires, just a few who had been with Kluge's 258th Infantry in the winter of 1941. The Russians had decided to let them see what they could not take. They were to march through Moscow and disinfectant trucks would spray the road behind them.

A group of dun-coloured men were coming the other way, and Akulov stopped watching the German 4th Army going off to die, and welcomed his men. The penal company was back. It was smaller than when it had left, but Zakharov was still at its head. In its middle it had an unusual figure in such a military setting, a civilian in a dark suit. 'We got the command post,' said Zakharov. A deep, dirty bandage was wound about his forehead.

'I know,' Akulov said warmly. 'They started running about like headless chickens.'

'The fighting was heavy, but fast. The Germans were surprised, for they had not expected to be attacked behind their own lines. When it was done your daughter, who led us there, asked if we were willing to conduct another operation. Since you had placed us under her command, I agreed. We sent the wounded back, guided and helped by some of her partisans. We took German uniforms and equipment and she took us through the forest hour after hour until we reached a road. It was the road that leads to Bialystok, the Vistula and Berlin. She had led us right behind the German lines. Here we rested. From time to time cars and trucks would pass, all heading west, to Germany. In the distance we could hear the noise of the battle for the city.

'She had a radio, your daughter, and she and the operator sat waiting, hidden with the rest of us in the thick bracken. In the end, it spoke. We went forward then, as she had instructed us to. She told me what to expect. I was dressed in the uniform of an officer. We pulled out the barriers that we had made from the trees, and set them up across the way so that it looked like a road block, a checkpoint. I stood in front of it, with some troopers in German uniform at my back, and three vehicles came down the road, a command car and a truck, with a black limousine in the centre. I raised my hand, and they came to a halt.'

The Germans continued to trudge by, baggy-trousered, helmetless and unarmed as Zakharov told his story and Akulov gave Zakharov a canteen of water and he drank from it.

'Thank you. I and the troopers who were with me shot all the men in the command car. They were SS men. As we did so, the rest of the men opened up on the truck. Nobody got out. And your daughter shot the driver and bodyguard in the limousine. She did it with a Schmeisser.'

Zakharov turned, and gestured to the man who stood, resigned, in their midst. He appeared exhausted, unused to the heavy march through wood and marsh. His well-cut suit was sodden and muddy and hung on him like an old sack.

'In the limousine was this one. We seized him and your daughter led us quickly away through the forest.'

'Who is he?' Akulov asked, puzzled.

'She would not say, only she seemed very pleased. I think she knew how much some of us hated the Germans and she feared that if she told us who he was one of us might see to it he had an accident on the way. A trip into a marshy pool, a knife in the ribs . . .'

'Where is Natalia?'

'She left us to come on, because she wanted to go to her partisan base to collect some of the others. She told us to come on, and to guard this one as though he were gold.'

'That we shall do, then,' said Akulov. 'Bring him to the house.'

Akulov had taken a big, square house in its own garden for his headquarters as they regrouped after the heavy fighting. Outside,

Tatyana was playing with his grandson. A toy bark boat floated in a pool they had made and she blew on its sail and it drifted across. The little boy giggled and Akulov ruffled his hair as he passed. He handed the German over to the guards.

'I want him kept safe,' he said. Then, to Zakharov, he said, 'I'll go and get Natalia myself.'

His lend-lease *Villis* jeep was waiting, and he hauled himself up to stand on the seat as he addressed the men of the penal company.

'You're *all* Red Army soldiers again,' he said. They stared at him with sunken eyes. They were the survivors of attack after attack, the ones not hung on the miles of electrified barbed wire, the ones who had escaped the flying splinters of the mines, the explosive of the shells and the mortars, the ones not ground up in the tank treads. A light shone now from every eye.

'There's food waiting,' said Akulov. 'And beer. You'll join your new companies tomorrow.'

They cheered, then. He got into the seat of the jeep and the driver took him bouncing into the forest.

He had the map with the reference Natalia had shown him and he had the driver stop.

'I'll walk down,' he said cheerfully. 'Wait for me here.'

He walked through the forest down the little path, the scent of pine in his nostrils, the needles springy under his boots. He was a country boy and it was good to get away from the stench of the battle, into the clean air.

His measured tread slowed and he stopped. His nose sniffed, he looked around. There was something wrong, he could smell propellant, blood . . .

He moved cautiously now through the trees. Ahead, the light was brightening as he came to a clearing. He peered through the pine branches.

They were in a row. Men and women, maybe twenty of them. Their hands were tied behind their backs and they had fallen forward to lie on the grass. He recognised some of them because they were the young men and women who had come out of the trees to guide his tanks through the marshes. A bloody leather cap lay tumbled by sightless eyes.

He rushed forward, seeking his daughter but she was not among them.

'Natalia!' he roared. 'Natalia, are you here?'

There was a noise, a faint sound in the forest, and he ran towards it.

He found her under a cut-down pine tree. A smashed Schmeisser lay there and pine needles clung to the blood that soaked her clothing.

'They were here when I returned, Papa,' she whispered. 'An army patrol. My people were happy, glad to see our own men. They were celebrating, for we had been fighting since the Germans came, and now we had won. They were relaxed.

'I came out of the forest and I, too, suspected nothing. I had my gun slung over my shoulder. The one in command, the officer, he turned to look at me. It took a second, a second too long, for me to know him. I knew his face, for Mama warned me of him, years ago.'

The breath shuddered in her body as she breathed and Akulov wiped foamy blood from her mouth with his hand.

'It was Rykov . . .'

The hand gripped the Schmeisser. Bullets had smashed the receiver.

'I went to cock the gun and he fired. He hit me and the bullets threw me back into the trees. The gun was broken and I ran. I knew the ground, they did not. I hid, and they thought that I had run away. But then they moved quickly. They shot Boris where he was, for he went for his gun, and then they made the others kneel and tied their hands. Rykov stood at one end of the line, and cocked his pistol. "You are all traitors," he said, and he shot Olga through the back of the head. "You are traitors to the Party," he said, and shot Vladimir. "You are traitors to Stalin," he said, and shot Ludmilla. When he had finished his eyes were excited, his face flushed.'

'He likes to kill,' said Akulov, brokenly. 'Rykov will come a long way from his office to kill someone.'

Natalia took a shuddening breath. 'then he and his men took their green caps from their sacks, the ones the NKVD wear, and they went away through the forest, laughing.'

'Let me pick you up,' said Akulov. 'I'll take you to the field hospital.'

'I'm dying, papa,' she said, sadly.

'No, you're not!' His protest was instinctive, angry. She was his daughter and he had only just found her again. How, then, could she die?

He picked her up as carefully as he could and she gasped with pain. He carried her across the clearing.

'There they are,' she whispered. 'He stopped half way through and he urinated on Sergei. Then he shot him. Rykov was right, of course. We didn't fight for the Party. We fought for a new world – that's why I got Gartner.'

'Who's Gartner?'

'The man I sent back. The one we captured. Gartner. The Gestapo chief. I brought him back, so we could put him up on trial, and show everyone we weren't like him. That the new Russia wasn't like the old . . .'

The jeep was visible through the trees. Once in it he closed her eyes and kissed her face, wet with his tears . . .

'Have a sandwich,' said Akulov. He gave Tatyana a length of fresh-baked bread spread with yellow butter and filled with slices of canned ham. He twisted the cap of a Thermos flask and poured two mugs of tea. They sat on the trunk of a fallen tree and watched the crews below servicing the rows of T-34s. They were fitting fresh, shiny engines, thick new tracks, replacing transmissions. Huge bowsers moved slowly along the lines, filling the fuel tanks with diesel. Ammunition trucks brought box upon box of 7.62 rounds for the machine guns, and shell after brass-cased shell of high explosive and armour piercing. More lorries brought new 85mm barrels for the main armament, to replace the worn-out ones.

'Thank you,' she said and munched on her sandwich. 'It's very good,' she said appreciatively. 'Where does it come from?'

'The cooks bake every day,' said Akulov, staring unseeingly at his army slowly rebuilding its strength.

'With what?' She was surprised.

'Flour, of course.'

'But where does it come from?' she said patiently. 'And this butter, and ham?'

'Oh, I see.' He made himself concentrate. 'The flour is American, Pillsbury, I think is the name. The butter comes from New Zealand and the ham from the American mid-West.'

'And our tea?'

'We get it from the British. From their colonies.'

'Your father, and my father, they did not grow tea, but they did produce grain for flour, and butter from the herd, and ham. We had whole sides, smoking for the winter in the smoke-house. That was when I was a young girl, of course.'

Akulov said nothing and Tatyana chewed another section of her sandwich.

'Now tell me, down there where the tanks are, what else to we receive from the West?'

'Why do you want to know?' he asked, rousing himself from the bruise of his pain.

'I'm an economist. I passed top of the class at the university and almost immediately, I became a partisan. Now I plan to be an economist again. With your help.'

'Down there . . .' he said. It was better to make oneself work. 'Down there, the Dodge bowsers come from America, as do the Studebaker trucks, the *Villis* Jeeps and the Harley-Davidson motorcycles. The medicines in the casualty stations and hospitals are American. My clothes are made from American cotton. I wear US boots, as does everyone else. What else? Half our tank engines are made from Canadian and British aluminium alloy, the shells use copper from the British Empire. My entire communications network is American and my supplies come up from the rear on an American railroad.'

'Anything else?'

'Our fighting and dying we do by ourselves,' he said dryly.

'Is there a lot of dying?'

'Yes,' he said bleakly.

'Too much?'

'Yes. The same result could be obtained for less expenditure of life.'

'But not so quickly,' she said wisely. 'Which would mean fewer peoples to be conquered, fewer slaves.'

She finished her sandwich and lit up a Lucky Strike cigarette. 'What happened yesterday?' she asked quietly. 'Was it a mistake?'

There was silence broken only by the clinking of tools and rattling of the sheerlegs below.

'It was Rykov,' he said finally.

'It might be policy,' she said and blew blue smoke down the hill.

'It was Rykov,' he said again. 'Rykov it was who killed our family.'

An exhaust belched fumes, and they heard the growl of a new V-12 engine on test.

'Do you know what was so good, being a partisan?' Tatyana said. 'Not the cold, not going hungry, not the fear, not the wounds. It was being *free*. Deciding for yourself. Not being forced into rituals of acquiescence. Not being told to believe what isn't true.'

She flicked some ash on to the grass. 'I could get quite addicted to these cigarettes,' she said. 'You see, I love the truth. The truth there is in cold figures. You can divine the future, from figures. I want to go to Nosovibirsk, in Siberia, to the Institute of Economics there. Will you arrange it, Uncle Ivan?'

They both knew of the debt he owed, as the killer of her father. He would never be free of it, just as she would never mention it.

'Of course,' he said. 'You wouldn't rather be in Moscow?'

'Too many Russians,' she said. 'I don't like the smell.' She stubbed out her cigarette, and stood up. 'But you seem to be able to stand it,' she said cruelly.

'Yelena is Russian,' he said.

'Yelena is different, Yelena is special. There are probably a handful of good people hiding from the Devil in the very corridors of Hell, undoing little parts if his work.'

'It was Rykov,' he said again. 'He is not the revolution. It was Rykov. Stay, and I will show you.'

27

For the general's eyes only

A FRESH copy of *Red Star* lay on the table, celebrating the victory. 'Party organisation is the real backbone of the Army,' the headline crowed. 'All the magnificent achievements of our Army are due to the fact that the Red army's military doctrine is based on the well-tested principles of the wisest doctrine in the world – that of Marx, Engels and Stalin.'

Nikolai removed the front page and tore it up into a squill, expertly filling it with Makhorka tobacco. He added a sprinkling of sugar and lit it. He wore the uniform of a Guards' officer because Akulov had taken him on to his staff.

'The NKVD's here,' he said expressionlessly.

They'd sent a captain who stood up when Akulov came in. The NKVD might rule, but a general had power, whatever the service.

'Captain Golitsyn,' he said.

'What can I do for you, Captain?' Akulov said. He dropped his big frame into his chair with a crash. Golitsyn looked at him disapprovingly. He was small and neatly barbered. Akulov looked as though he had slept badly.

'We read your report, General. We noted that you captured a number of SS men. We'd like them.'

Akulov eyed him. So many small ones among them, he thought. Rykov is small. The Kremlin bastard is stunted. Practically a dwarf.

'Why?' he said shortly.

Golitsyn smiled superciliously. 'You just keep winning the war, General Akulov,' he said condescendingly. 'Leave the planning of the time afterwards to us.'

'Oh, I will, I will.'

A steward appeared at the door.

'Coffee?' Akulov asked. 'We liberated mounds of it. The boys are eating tinned Portuguese sardines, Austrian chocolate and Italian pickled lemons.'

The delightful aroma filled the room, and Golitsyn took his cup with pleasure.

'Seriously,' Akulov said amiably. 'What on earth do you want with a bunch of SS men?'

Golitsyn smiled, thawing under the effects of the Italian ground coffee. 'They can help us in the new Europe, General,' he said vaguely. 'Rooting out the fascists, enemies of the people . . .'

'But the SS men are extermination types. Einsatzkommandos.'

'One shall not enter into the kingdom of socialism in white gloves on a polished floor, General,' Golitsyn said archly. 'I'm sure we can retrain them to our ways.'

'No doubt,' agreed Akulov. 'Well, then, do you want to take them away?'

Golitsyn seemed surprised that Akulov was being so accomodating.

'Why, yes. General Rykov will be very pleased. You see, the order has come down from Stalin himself, to begin gathering useful elements among the enemy for after the war.'

General Rykov is it, thought Akulov. How they love military titles. Doesn't the Kremlin bastard call himself Marshal of the Soviet Union now?

'Ah, well, it wouldn't do not to please the general, would it? Come on, then.'

He took Golitsyn outside to his jeep, and they drove off into the forest. A few miles on they stopped. There was a terrible stench in the air and by the road swollen purple and blue offal lay piled up like a butcher's shambles. Crows pecked arrogantly, poking their beaks into strings of gut. Flies buzzed black over the blood and maggots crawled in mens' eyeballs.

Golitsyn suddenly bent over the side of the jeep, and vomited sour coffee. The corpses still had the remnants of their SS uniforms.

'Here they are,' Akulov said cheerfully. 'I'm afraid they helped the glorious Red army on its way to Poland, Czechoslovakia and Germany.'

Golitsyn was silent on the way back and Akulov took him into his office and poured him three fingers of vodka in a shot glass.

'Here. That'll make you feel better. You mustn't mind me having my little joke. Look, though, I don't want to get you into trouble. SS men I don't have any more. They did too good a job of clearing the minefield for my tanks. But what about Gestapo men? Are they any use to you?'

Golitsyn's eyes were watering from the effects of the neat liquor.

He wiped them eagerly. 'Oh, yes,' he said. Even more than the SS types. We have a *very* high opinion of the Gestapo.'

Akulov looked thoughtful. 'I don't know if I really ought to do it, mind. You see, we caught a man called Gartner.'

The watery eyes widened. 'Gestapo *chief* Gartner?'

'Yes, that's the one,' Akulov said indifferently.

'General, you *must* give him to me! Oh, please, let me have him.'

Akulov shrugged. 'All right. He's no good to me. Orderly! Bring the German Gartner down, and put him in the back of Captain Golitsyn's truck out there.'

A minute or two later they saw him being led out and Golitsyn got hurriedly to his feet. 'I must take him straight to General Rykov,' he said.

'Very good,' Akulov said indifferently. 'Oh, he had this, too.' He picked up a black briefcase from beside his desk. 'Top secret stuff, all of it. Beyond your clearance level, Captain. For General Rykov's eyes only.'

Golitsyn actually saluted. 'Of course, sir,' he said, and took it.

Where are you based?' Akulov asked idly.

Golitsyn smiled. 'Chief Gartner will be going home. We've occupied his old headquarters.'

'Good idea!'

'Saves a lot of trouble to have it all organised for you,' the young man agreed.

Akulov watched out of the window as the truck pulled away, Nikolai at his side. They went out and Tatyana was by the door.

'Ready?' asked Akulov.

They all got in the jeep and Akulov drove. They headed into Minsk.

The truck was parked outside a handsome building, one of the ones to escape the destruction, and they pulled up some distance away. They sat waiting, their eyes fixed on the headquarters. Big red letter boxes had been affixed to the railings for people to drop in their anonymous denunciations and men in green hats were already bringing civilians in.

There was a sudden, dull crump from within the building. Glass blew across the street and smoke gushed out through the gaping windows.

Akulov started the jeep, and they drove away down the road . . .

Avignon, France, September 1944

'This is a good gun,' Ruth said. 'Not what you'd call a sniper's weapon, not really, but from where I am, I can certainly turn your desk into matchwood.'

The man behind the desk watched her, as she emerged from the cupboard, the short, ugly automatic Sten gun in her arms. He watched very attentively and kept quite still. A balloon glass of cognac that he had been about to sip stood on the inlaid leather.

'It also goes off rather easily. If you bump it,' she said.

He remained still, an artery pumping in his temple above the purple-ridged sabre scar.

Ruth steadied herself against the wall and felt the commando knife and the small, stamped-metal Woolworth's gun under her loose jacket press into her.

'But you're staying quite still,' she mused, 'so we should be all right.'

'What do you want?' he said, his voice hoarse, his mouth dry. Outside, the cicadas were creaking; the French doors were open to let in what air there was in. On the dark hills, a thunderstorm was grumbling, come to wash the summer dirt from the air.

'It's Rat Week, Colonel Frisch.' They were both speaking in German. 'We've come to kill the rats and you're the biggest one round here, you run the Gestapo. Do you want to die, Colonel?'

'No!'

'Why?'

'Life is good.'

She could see his mind working, see him make the calculations.

'If you have come to kill me, why have you not already done it?' he asked.

'Very good,' she said. The gun was steady in her hands and he was still looking down its stubby barrel. 'I'm prepared to let you off, this time. Just today. But tomorrow I may come back.'

'What do you want?'

'I want Joan. She was captured last week, betrayed. We've settled things with Michel – he's face down in a ditch. But Joan's downstairs in one of the cells you've made. Bring her up.'

'What do you want with her?'

'I'm taking her away, and you're going to help me. Now bring her up!'

He picked up one of the telephones on the desk, and spoke a few short sentences in German.

'They are bringing her up,' he said.

'Then I'll get back into the cupboard and you will stay behind the desk. Have them put Joan in the chair, there. And remember, I can still see you through the crack. The gun will still turn your desk into matchwood.'

She got back inside the old cupboard, where a leather dress coat hung next to a green felt hat, and a whip. She heard the knock on the door, saw two guards drag something in, and put it in the chair. Colonel Frisch sat, his back straight, immobile. He nodded at the men, and they went out. Moths and flying creatures from outside were whirling about the lamp, incinerating themselves on the hot bulb. Ruth came out of the cupboard and stood beside the chair. The girl slumped there cringed as she stood over her.

'It's me, darling,' Ruth said softly, and Joan reached out for her pathetically, like a hurt child grasping its mother.

'Careful of my gun arm, darling. I may want to shoot Colonel Frisch after all.'

She lifted her eyes from the mass of purple weals and burns that made up her friend's face, and stared chillingly at the German. 'Did you enjoy yourself?' she whispered.

'I was only following orders,' the man blustered. 'You special fighters, you make a lot of trouble for us, we have orders to stop you . . .'

Ruth's knuckles were very white about the gun and he stopped talking, staring fearfully at her.

'I have given you what you want,' he said quickly. 'Here is your comrade, a little damaged, perhaps, but alive. Here she is, take her.'

'The car in the courtyard. The *traction-avant*, the Citroen. It is yours, you have the keys?' Ruth asked.

'Yes,' He reached into his pocket.

'Careful!'

He put them on the desk and she reached forward and took them, putting them in her pocket. She picked up the balloon of cognac and gave it to Joan. 'Drink it, darling. It will help.'

She turned back to Frisch as the injured girl drank the soothing liquor. 'We're going in the car and you're going to drive. I'll sit next to you and Joan will be in the back.'

The glass was empty. Ruth took it and put it on the desk, then she arranged the strap of the gun so that it hung inside her coat. From the cupboard she took a little bundle of three sticks, with torches attached.

'You have an aircraft coming,' said Frisch.

'Are we going home?' Joan whispered.

'We're going home, darling. Now, Colonel, you help Joan over to the car, and I'll be right behind.'

He came out from behind the desk, but, as he reached to pull Joan up, she cried out, mewing with fear, reaching for Ruth. He stood back. Ruth's knuckles were very white, again.

'Very well . . . you lead the way, and we'll follow behind. Nice and slow . . .'

In the dark courtyard the oppressive heat wrapped itself around them like a blanket. They could see the low-slung, black Citroen in the light from the guardroom.

Frisch led the way. Joan was walking with difficulty, her feet stumbling on the cobbles, Ruth supporting her.

'Open the back door.'

He opened it and stood back. Ruth got Joan half on to the seat, working with one hand while the other gripped the Sten. At the window, a man in uniform was looking out, curiously.

'*Tell him what you're doing!*' she snapped.

Frisch stepped forward and suddenly, from the darkness, his boot slammed against the door, smashing it against her gun hand. He was upon her, then bellowing for help. The Sten was crushed between them, but under her coat she felt the cold metal of the Woolworth's pistol. She jammed it into his body as he forced her back over the car, and fired. The impact blew him backwards and he fell on to the cobbles.

From inside the house men were shouting. Joan had clawed her way on to the back seat and Ruth jumped into the front and found the keys, the four cylinder engine starting at a touch. Men were running from the doors and she poked the Sten out of the window and fired in short bursts, the muzzle flash lighting up the courtyard. She saw them fall and then she had the umbrella handle gearstick in her hand, and they were racing down the long, straight, tree-lined avenue in the moonlight, turning on to the road with a squeal from the tyres. In the mirror, she saw the lights of trucks.

Across the field where the lavender grew in silvery grey rows, coloured light arced towards her, increasing in speed as it came. The car was suddenly lit up and in the yellow and red flash shattering glass flew.

Blood was running down into Ruth's eyes.

'Are you all right?' she yelled, in the gale, and she heard Joan behind her say, 'all right.'

The Citroen clawed its way along the road on tyres that pointed different ways and she could feel rubber slapping against the mudguard but she kept her foot hard on the pedal. There was the lane . . . She turned down it, smelling the grass as the car pushed its way through. She drove it into the bushes in the copse, and switched off. It was silent for a moment; in the distance she could hear the grinding of lorries, and, from somewhere in the sky, the muted hum of an aircraft. As she helped Joan out of the back, the cicadas started to creak.

'This is the field, darling. I'm going to bring the Lysander in. Come on. Let's set up the lights.'

They pushed through the gap in the hedge, and went up the narrow field. It widened at the top and there was room for an aeroplane to turn round. Ruth let Joan sink to the ground, and quickly ran about, placing her sticks into the correct inverted L shape, and illuminated the torches. Then she stood, and began to flash her identification signal.

Something like a huge bat went across the moon but a mile away on the road lights were moving, coming towards them. Against a moonlit cloud she saw the aircraft wheeling on its approach. Others had seen it too, for she heard the crackle of automatic fire, like twigs burning.

'Darling,' she said urgently. 'The Lysander's coming, but so are the Germans. I'm going down to the end of the field to keep them off.'

She helped Joan up to her feet. 'You're on the right side to get in. When he turns round get in and tell him to go. I'll have them send another for me next week.'

Then she was running down the field. On the road she could see lights, hear men shouting. The Lysander came over the trees and she crouched down as its high wing passed over her. She felt its passage, heard the slow thrum of the prop, saw the RAF pilot guiding it down on to the grass. It touched with a thump.

In the lane there was a truck; she heard men shouting in harsh, hard voices. She crouched down and pulled the cocking lever back on the Sten. The truck crashed through the gate at the end of the field and came towards her, roaring, lights ablaze. She waited until the last moment, then stood up, firing into the cab. The lorry veered past her, crashing into the trees. Men spilled out of the back and she threw a grenade amongst them from the darkness.

They screamed, the wounded. Then there was a bellow from the top of the field as the big radial took the fuel. Men were firing and she slapped the next magazine into her Sten and shot at the gunflashes.

Something very heavy slammed into her and she lay on the grass, unable to move. There was blood in her mouth.

She was looking up at the sky. Something like a giant moth flew across the moon, climbing . . .

Washington, October 1944

He saw her coming through the trees. She was wearing a green coat set off by the drifting yellow and russet leaves.

'You told me the Fall was beautiful,' she said. As she came up to him he saw that she looked drawn and he stood with her back to the sun.

'Are you okay?'

'I have a headache . . . I get them sometimes. I could not sleep, knowing I was to meet your man today. It's so important . . . Can he really talk to Roosevelt, Johnny?'

'Sumner? He's the Secretary of State,' Nichols said simply. 'He can talk to him.'

'But why does he want to talk to *me*?'

'Harry Hopkins is Roosevelt's man. He sent him to Moscow as his envoy and Stalin gave him the treatment, the full works. He was very impressed – and *he* impresses Roosevelt. Sumner would like to damage this special relationship for reasons of his own and I told him I knew someone who might help him.'

He looked through the trees at the road, curling through the park. A big, dark Packard was pulling up and a sallow-faced man in a grey suit was getting out.

Nichols walked over, with Yelena following. 'Secretary Welles, Yelena. This is Mrs Akulova, whom I told you about.'

They began to walk through the park, the big limousine slowly following them.

'I guess it's a nice day for a walk,' Welles commented. 'Makes a change from holding meetings in the office.'

'It's safer, too. Mr Secretary,' Yelena said. The muscles of her neck were drawing in like hawsers, dragging pain across her skull, she twisted her head involuntarily, trying to release them.

Welles looked at her curiously. 'Talking out of school? Might lose your job, that it?'

'I might lose my *head*,' she said quietly. 'The people who run my country do not care for the truth.'

'You work for 'em,' Welles said jocularly.

'I was offered the job and they got me out of the death camp to do it. I was not about to return. Not after I had seen what happened to my comrades there. You know what they did? They put them on a barge and towed it out to sea. Then they sank it.'

Welles looked at her warily. 'But you escaped.'

'I was fortunate. Just lucky.'

'So what do you want to tell me about. Mrs Akulova?'

The battlements of light were beginning to jerk across her eyes and they were walking into the sun. Fresh golden beams swept through the branches, and she winced.

'Where shall I start . . . With the trucks? Yes. It would be better if you would send no more trucks.'

He looked at her bewildered. 'We think the trucks are pretty effective, here. They help the Red Army get a lot more bang for its buck. which means that fewer nephews of Uncle Sam get their butts shot off by Fritz, over there. We approve of the trucks.'

'The trucks are doing two things,' she said, forcing herself to concentrate through the pain. 'They are, as you point out, helping the Red Army to advance. Very fast. At great cost. At the cost of our boys lives at the rate of four to eight for each German killed. Because *he* orders it so. Stalin.'

Welles shrugged. 'I got to be honest, Mrs Akulova, better Russian boys than American.'

'You're missing the point!' Behind them, Nichols's feet crunched through the leaves, out of time. 'Stalin is buying *territory*. When the war stops, he will have most of Europe. It will be as though Hitler had never been gone.'

'When the war stops we'll all go home,' Welles said complacently.

'It is not a game of football! When the war stops you will leave Stalin in possession of the playing field. You don't seem to understand who you're dealing with!'

'My boss, President Roosevelt has a very high opinion of Marshal Stalin. He believes he will lead his people to democracy, with US help.'

'Then tell him what else Stalin is doing with the trucks,' Yelena said doggedly. 'He is using them to move peoples.'

'That's what they're for,' agreed Welles.

'Not people. *Peoples*. Whole nations!'

'Whole nations, hey?'

'About two million of them. When I say people I mean separate peoples. Peoples like the Russians, or the Americans. Or the Ukrainians, or the Poles. These were the Kalmyks, the Chechens, the Ingushi, the Karachai, the Balkars and the Crimean Tatars. The Volga Germans were done back in forty-one. These peoples, small separate nations were rounded up by the NKVD, stuffed into lend-lease Studebaker trucks, crammed on to trains and taken into the deserts and tundra of central Asia and Siberia and dumped. Half of them are dead. But don't go looking for them, because they do not now officially exist. They are not even on the list of Soviet nations. Their land has been taken from them and their songs may not be sung, their language taught or printed, their history remembered.'

'How do you know this?'

'Krivitskiy told me, and he was there. He was in the embassy, and he got drunk. He talked to me. We went to school together, you see.'

'Oh, you were classmates, right?'

'Yes. He told me about Katyn, too, because he was there as well. Why is there nothing being said about Katyn, Mr Secretary? Fifteen thousand of Poland's elite are murdered, shot in ditches with their hands tied behind their backs and nothing is said.'

'This is a dreadful war,' he prevaricated. 'Horrible things happen. But to start flinging mud about without evidence would be to offend our Russian allies in their current agony.'

'The agony has been going on a long time! Well before we became your allies. What about the Poles in *their* agony? They are a great independent nation, and are being freed from the hideous rule of Hitler to be given to the equally hideous rule of Stalin. Krivitskiy told me what Stalin said about the end of this war. He said "*cuius regio cius religio.*"'

'I don't speak Russian.'

'It's Latin. It's a maxim from the sixteenth century. "He who rules decides how his people shall worship." Stalin is deciding. What the Red Army occupies becomes his. What he has done to us, he will do to them.'

'We acknowledge Marshal Stalin to be a despot; however, we see him as an enlightened one, and a great leader of his people.'

'He is a madman!' she said, her eyes staring. 'A madman who has done nothing but enslave, torture and kill his own people ever since he came to domination over them.'

She saw Welles signal to his car.

'You must listen to me,' she said desperately. 'What I say is true. I know, I have Professor Bekhterev's file. Stalin is paranoid, you see.

Professor Bekhterev diagnosed him so. Stalin knew . . . that's why he had him killed . . .'

'I suppose you were there, just like your school pal Krivitskiy was there.'

'That's right . . . I get these headaches, you see, I went to him, that's when I saw Rykov kill him – '

But Welles was walking away towards his car, with Nichols running after him. Welles turned as he climbed in.

'Don't waste my time with fucking crazies, Nichols!' he snapped.

'I'm sorry, sir . . . But she is an expert . . .'

'Just take her down the bug house, Nichols. And don't waste my time again.'

'But . . .'

The big Packard turned in the road, the tyres squealing, hurrying back down the hill.

Nichols caught up with her, as she ran through the trees. 'Yelena!'

'Don't talk to me!' she shouted furiously. 'I am a madwoman.'

He held her by the arms. 'It wasn't your fault . . . I'll get to someone else, I promise.'

'I'm sorry . . . my head, it hurts so . . .'

'Yelena, this isn't the time . . . but we got some news. About Ruth.'

She stood still, her chest heaving, looking at him from behind the hand that shielded her eyes.

'She was working for the British, for their Special Operations outfit. They sent her into France and she got caught in some gunbattle. They think the Germans captured her . . .'

Budapest, October 1944

Holy talismans and magic rituals ensured survival. Anyone who doubted it, and there were very few, had only to look at such as Alexei Akulov, who had fought since the Germans first crossed the Bug, and Sergei Pokryshin, to see that. Alexei wore a holy medal of great antiquity on the ring of his braces, given to him by his mother, who had inherited it from her father. Its efficacy was proven by her possession of it in the firing squad from which his father had rescued her. In addition to the medal, he had a brassiere he had found tied to the radio aerial of a Panzer IV he had defeated. Overcoming such an opponent clearly meant the acquisition of all the dead men's luck that had reposited in it, and he kept it in his pocket, and patted it at moments of great stress in battle. He found that it helped clear his mind.

Sergei Pokryshin also had a talisman, and also a ritual. He had his grandfather's Tsarist *ofitser's* hat, and he wore it inside his tank in battle. Its power was proven, for his grandfather had *not* had it on when they had pitchforked him to death on Mogilev station in 1917. Had he done so, as Sergei pointed out, he would have been safe, and all who heard him agreed and nodded wisely. In addition, Sergei had an old wind-up gramophone, and a 78 rpm record. It was a British one, with a picture of a dog listening to a big phonograph on the label. It played a waltz and, before going into battle, he would put it on, and dance solemnly to its music, holding the woman of his dreams in his arms. They would ask him what she looked like, and he would always say she was a lady, an aristocrat. Then, with his hat on his head, and his dance performed, he would climb into his tank, immune from harm.

Both tanks and men were very tired. Akulov's advance west over the plains towards Szeged into Hungary had been fast, but bought at high price as the Germans fought at short range with dug-in Tiger tanks, tommy-gunners mounted in half-tracks and entrenched troops with Panzerfausts. As they halted short of Budapest, the tanks were in need of fresh, thick tracks to replace their paper-thin ones, new engines to replace those exhausted in the advance, and new gunbarrels to replace those the Tigers, tommy-gunners and bazookamen had worn out. The men, too, would have liked to have been replaced, for they, too, were worn out, but there was little chance of that. However, a rest, a steam bath and some new clothes, not to mention a whole night's uninterrupted sleep, or maybe two, would do.

Sergei was simply sitting, his back resting against one of the road wheels of his thirty four, when Alexei came up from the temporary command post, a Hungarian farm house, where his father had been briefing his officers. In his hand he had a glass and a plain bottle of spirit. He stopped before the younger man and smiled. Something glittered as he held it up.

'Congratulations,' he said. *Captain* Pokryshin.'

They crowded about him, clapping him on the back and shoulder. Alexei put the badge of rank into the glass. Then he fished in his pocket.

'Oh, and this,' he said casually. He held up the medal for all to see, and a rumble of approval came from the crews. The order of Suvurov

was only awarded for the most heroic actions, fighting and winning
in battle against superior odds. They all knew when it had been won,
for glancing at Pokryshin's thirty-four they could see the silver scars
of the Panzerfaust rockets and twisted and dented armour where the
Tiger had hit before being stalked, outmanoeuvred and killed.

Alexei put the medal into the glass along with the badge, and they
all watched with approval as he filled it to the very brim. The vodka
glittered as it curved to the edge of the glass.

Sergei bent and drank without spilling, his adam's apple bouncing
as he swallowed the neat liquor. Then it was all gone. He turned to
them, his eyes watering, a big grin on his face. The two awards were
gripped between his teeth. He hurled the glass, and it smashed, as it
should, on the rock.

Alexie helped him pin them on.

'That's the good news,' he said. 'But there isn't any more. We're
to take Budapest.'

They looked at their exhausted tanks through eyelids that twitched,
and their faces, tugged by varieties of tic, registered their disbelief.

'Your father knows we have to re-equip,' Sergei said quietly.

'Stalin called,' Alexei said. 'We are to go on to the offensive
tomorrow.'

'Why?' Sergei asked. 'What's the rush? We're *winning*.'

'So are the Americans, and British and they're on German soil. The
Americans are assaulting the Westwall.'

'I don't mind if they get to Berlin first.'

'Maybe the boss does,' Alexei said, shrugging.

Sergei got his feet and climbed up on to his tank. He pulled out the
gramophone and wound it up. He took his record. Black fragments
fell from the sleeve. He stared at them, lying on the armour, then put
the broken record back.

He climbed down and picked up the gramophone.

'Here,' he said, giving it to Alexei. He didn't look at him, simply
thrust it into his arms. 'I shan't be needing this again.'

The track snapped as he edged around the corner of the street and the
thirty-four slewed into the wall of the house. On the road behind him
the other two tanks of the section were burning in the pouring rain.
Poking his head out of the hatch he could see Alexei's tank getting
off the street, backing into an alley. The gun belched flame and the
front of a building nearby disintegrated. Men in black fell with the
rubble and Panzerfausts littered the streaming street like sticks.

Where was the infantry? All he could see were German soldiers.

At the other end of the street a whole window suddenly crashed out and a vast gun muzzle poked through. The flames at both ends of the street were as one.

All he felt was rage. He jumped out of the turret with his clothes singed and smouldering. A man with a Panzerfaust was looking up at him from the garden and he shot him with his PPSh.

He didn't feel the rain, nor pain from his burns. His grandfather's hat was on his head, and the long black rocket in his hand.

From his turret Nikolai saw him run up to the corner of the street. He crouched by the wall, the bazooka poking out. There was a blast of flame as the missile streaked up the streaming street, white fire blazing bright on the rain. The empty window exploded and black smoke roiled out of the room. Men jumped through the gap and Sergei cut them down with his PPSh.

Then there was a huge explosion and the street seemed to vanish in the billowing dust and smoke.

It was getting dark. Nikolai could see the figures of the bazookamen bobbing and weaving as they crept along in the cover of the suburban gardens. The tank reversed in a shower of bricks, and left the street to those still in ownership.

Behind him the dust settled like mud in the heavy rain, coating the cobbles, and the bodies that lay on them . . .

The woman was covered in mud. Alexei was chewing sunflower seeds because it helped keep the sweet, nauseaus smell of death out of his nostrils when it drifted out from some hole or ruin they passed. From time to time he took a little sip from his canteen. They had overrun a German supply dump and he found the thought that whole crates of schnapps were riding on the back of his tank along with fuel, shells and spare tracks most comforting. It had been a village and they could see the ruins of the razed buildings, the soot-covered chimneys still standing. The retreating Germans had not cared for their some-time Hungarian allies changing sides.

The woman was as covered in mud as a hog, thought Alexei as she came screaming through the ruins. He was sitting in his turret under a green ladies' umbrella he had found. It served well to keep the rain that was falling off him. The schnapps kept him warm, the umbrella dry, and Igor kept him on the road.

'Come!' she shouted. 'Come!'

There was never any telling how old the women were in the territories they liberated. They were all bundled up in threadbare rags, shawls pulled low over their eyebrows. But not always covered in mud. He grunted a command on the intercom and the thirty-four jerked off the dirt track that had been the village's main street.

A building was still standing, a large brick farm house. The tank halted by a rubbish tip and from the dirty bandages and used medical equipment piled up, the Germans had used the house as a field hospital.

The woman was scrabbling with her bare hands in a pit that had been covered over with soil wet from the rain. Alexei climbed down to see what she was doing. Then he saw that the soil moaned faintly. It moved and he dived down, shouting orders for the men to come to help.

Little children lay in the pit, eleven and twelve years old. Some still lived. He pulled a little girl out and laid her on the dirt. Her chest fluttered and he cleared mud from her mouth. The falling rain washed her skin, and it was dead white.

'The Germans had no more blood for their wounded,' the woman sobbed. Tears cut channels in the dirt on her face. 'They brought these little ones and took their blood. Then they threw them in the pit, because you were coming.' A thin shudder ran through the little body on the ground, lying there with her eyes closed and the fluttering in the chest ceased.

'Bring up the medics!' Alexei shouted. 'Bring blood! Some of the little ones may be saved.'

The woman was tugging frantically at his arm as the troops dragged the children from the pit, both dead and alive.

'They took others. Fifty, sixty, more,' she said desperately. 'I can show you the way they went.'

He hastily assembled a small force in trucks and *villises*, bringing his own thirty-four for fire support. The woman rode in the lead jeep next to Nikolai and she took them along a track.

They travelled for some ten minutes.

'They came, the evil ones, from the camp here,' she said. The road opened out and the column roared past the barbed wire and watchtowers of a prison camp. Skeletons in rags moved listlessly, then one saw the red star on the tank, and a hoarse, rising cheer went through the creatures behind the wire.

'Ours . . .' Alexei muttered. He stopped one of the *villises*, and told the driver to go back and report.

They caught the German column on a downhill slope. Alexei brought the tank forward and sent a shell from the main armament howling over their heads. Children and Nazis turned to look and began to run. The children knew the sight of the red star and knew

that they ran towards liberation. The Germans knew it, too. On a
slope without cover they slowly, reluctantly raised their hands in
surrender, throwing their arms to the ground. The children clustered
about the tank and, in his turret, Alexei shouted at them to go to
the rear. The Russians dismounted from their trucks and Jeeps. The
Germans had clustered together, staring balefully up the slope.

'Open fire,' said Alexei, and the main armament boomed amidst
the sudden clamour of their weapons . . .

The hat was clearly a commandant's hat. He had noticed it the
moment they brought the Russian in and stripped him of his uniform.
Although wet and muddy, the gold braid gleamed magnificently, and
the scarlet around the brim glowed. He had taken it for his own, and
had cleaned it carefully in his room.

He, Jan Dyuk was now commandant. His German masters had
promoted him and he sat in the commandant's office, with the key
to the commandant's liquor cupboard. A half-open bottle of Slivovicz
stood on the desk, and next to it was the hat.

It was time to walk about his domain, in which, up until that
morning he had been merely a guard. He drained his tumbler and
put on the hat.

He was in time to see some trucks and jeeps roar past, with a tank in
their wake. The tank wore a large red star, and he stared drunkenly at
it until it vanished through the trees.

He could not understand how a Russian tank was booming past
his prisoner-of-war cage. Slowly he became aware that the creatures
inside the wire had turned to look at him. For the first time, he
recognised them as human beings, for their faces held a very human
emotion, hate.

One emaciated creature came up to him, and took the beautiful hat
off his head.

'Mine, I think,' it said, and put it on.

Sergei Pokryshin stood by the gate with Iosif Wolff. Iosif Wolff was
a Jew and he had so far managed to conceal the fact from those, like
guard Dyuk, who would have beaten him to death for it on the spot.
He lived in fear of denunciation and when he saw the new young
officer arrive, fit and muscular, he knew two things: that Sergei,
left to himself was too proud to survive, and that no one would
risk denouncing him were Sergei his friend. As he tumbled down
the steps, his freshly-shaved head gleaming, Iosif stepped forward,
a chunk of precious salami in his hand and advice on his lips.

They were waiting now to be liberated. The *villis* had shot back the way it had come, and they were waiting for their comrades.

Two trucks came grinding down the dirt road and drew up. Men tumbled out. They carried and set up three heavy DShK machine guns outside the wire and pointed them at the Russian prisoners-of-war inside.

An officer got down from the cab of the lead truck. He wore leather gloves, and a green hat on his head. He came to the gate and they opened it wide for him. He stared coldly at them.

'You're scum,' he said. 'Filthy, surrendering scum. Traitors to the party.'

Sergei felt his carefully-banked emotions explode, and he stepped forward.

'I am an officer,' he snarled. 'I hold the order of Suvurov, and have surrendered to no one.'

The NKVD man's gaze flicked from the general mass of stinking prisoners in front of him to the angry young man advancing on him. Then the man was pushed aside by another, small and ingratiating.

'My friend is a hero, Colonel,' the man said in a wheedling tone of voice. 'When his tank was destroyed he continued to fight on foot. He personally attacked not one, not two but *five* enemy tanks with rockets. He was knocked out in the fighting and when he came to he had been captured. But surrender, never. He would never betray the party.'

The NKVD captain's hand was close to the Tokarev pistol on his hip. It was common to have to explain things by example. But he noticed that this lot appeared to have liberated themselves from the guards. Weapons were visible. The hero had a pistol in his hand.

'Very well,' he said, and attempted a smile. 'But you still have to aid us in our struggle. The fighting's not over yet, boys. We're uniforms for you, and guns.'

'And food,' said Sergei.

'Yes, food.' He looked at Sergei. 'You're an officer – you shall be in command.'

'I always wanted command of a penal company,' Sergei said wryly.

The captain pulled himself up on the truck so that the men inside could see and hear him.

'You're going into Germany,' he said. In Germany you may do what you will, take what you will. The dead march with you and they thirst for revenge. I see that you have your guards's weapons. Bring them out.'

They were a handful, the ones like Dyuk, who stood with the others the Germans had left behind. The prisoners surrounded them.

'Show me how you will treat the Germans,' the captain ordered, and they did . . .

Washington, April 1945

They went through the lobby where the string quartet was playing a selection from *The Pirates of Penzance*, and to the lifts. The doors slid expensively shut.

'Sixth,' Nichols said to the uniformed, middle aged attendant.

'Yes, sir. Fine day, ma'am.'

'It is,' agreed Yelena. 'It's lovely to see the blossom on the trees.'

'Nice to be warm, too. It sure get cold in the winter. Sixth, sir.'

They stepped out into the grand *fin de siècle* corridor, the carpet soft under their feet.

'Kolyma, wonderful planet. Twelve months winter, the rest summer,' Yelena said suddenly. 'Actually, although there were two months when the sun didn't come up at all, there *was* a sort of summer. The ground melted, and there were some flowers. We ate them. If you put a crowd of zeks through the park out there they'd strip it like locusts!'

She shook her head. 'Why do I talk about these things, Johnny? It just takes a remark, a smell, a noise even, and it triggers off these memories, they come flooding into my mind . . .'

They could hear the buzz of conversation from along the airy hallway.

'Shall we go?' She said.

'Down the stairs,' said Nichols, and she went with him around the sweeping stairway, slightly puzzled. They stopped outside a pair of tall, cream and gilt double doors.

'Isn't this where Mrs Eisenhower lives?' Yelena asked.

'That's right. She's out and she's lent her apartment to someone who's asked to meet you. He wants to ask you a few questions. About Stalin. I didn't tell you, in case you got another of your headaches.'

Nichols rapped on the door and a big man opened it. He nodded at Nichols.

'Go on through.'

The interior of the apartment was as spacious as the structure without.

'Who's *he*?' Yelena hissed. 'He looks like a guard.'

'Secret service,' Nichols said enigmatically. Yelena gripped his arm, holding him back.

'Who is it, Johnny?' she said in sudden apprehension. 'Who's here?'

'The boss,' he said gently, and smiled reassuringly. 'I got you to the top. It's okay. He wants to hear you.'

She found her heart thudding as he pushed open another high door and they went into a huge, airy room that overlooked the park and the city below. A middle-aged man in a dark suit got up from a chair and extended his hand courteously. He was short and wore glasses, but his handshake was firm, with a piano-player's grip. Yelena looked at him anxiously. This wasn't Roosevelt.

'Yelena, this is Vice-President Truman. Sir, Mrs Akulova.'

'Please call me Yelena,' she said nervously, and Truman led her to a wide sofa. Butter-yellow tulips were blooming on a table, the light from the great windows splintering along the cut glass of the vase. They sat down and Truman smiled at her.

'I hope this isn't too much of a shock,' he said pleasantly.

Yelena felt her hands becoming slippery. Her mind was racing. It was so important to have the right things ready to say. It was like taking an exam . . .'

'Meeting powerful people suddenly is always something of a shock,' she said. 'Especially in my country. But I am ready to talk to you now, Mr Vice-President.'

'I should explain, Yelena,' he said seriously,' that I shall shortly be President of the United States. President Roosevelt has left the capital, and has gone to Warm Springs to die.'

'I am very sorry,' she said formally, taken aback by his openness. Nichols sat down quietly in a nearby chair.

'I shall be acceding to power at what is a most important time of transition for our country. Foreign affairs dominate the agenda and they have not been my forté, but I intend to become expert – and I am a fast learner. The war against Germany is all but won, and the conflict against Japan will soon be over – sooner than expected. Which leaves us with the peace.

'Prime Minister Churchill has been complaining privately for some time that the real problem we in the West now have to face is Russia, but that he cannot get we Americans to see that. My problem, as the new man at the desk where the buck stops, is that when it comes to Russia, I get two very different types of advice. If I ask Ambassador Steinhardt he tells me that, at the most basic level, Stalin's men respond only to force, and if that cannot be applied, to straight oriental bartering. He mistrusts them and their motives, and plans, profoundly. If I ask his predecessor, Davies, he assures me that the Russians desire nothing more than world peace, and that we should disarm as soon as the war is over, unilaterally if necessary.

'Johnny here has been very helpful to me, as an expert on Soviet Russia in his own right. He's joining my staff and he told me that if I wanted to know about the Russians, I should ask you. He told me that not only were you uniquely knowledgeable, but that you were the most honest person he knew. Now, that's quite a recommendation. I don't know if you know it, but Diogenes had to carry a lantern in daylight to find an honest man. I wanted to invite you over to Blair House, but he persuaded me that were it known that you had met me your life might be in danger, so we have arranged this little subterfuge.'

'Thank you, sir,' Yelena said gratefully, warming to his directness. 'I shall be glad to answer any questions. And yes, I should be removed to Russia, and shot.'

'I should also probably say,' he said with a smile, 'that Summer Welles says that you are mad.'

'That will be for you to decide, Mr Vice-President,' Yelena said equably. Her head was clear, and there was no pain. 'Shall I begin with former Ambassador Davies? I met him once or twice before I was taken by the NKVD and put into a concentration camp.'

'What had you done?' he asked, intrigued.

'Nothing. Like everyone else,' she said shortly. 'But with regard to Davies, why don't you ask him about his collection of Russian icons and chalices? I believe their owner sold them to him very cheaply. He wrote a book called *Mission to Moscow*. Those of us who read it called it *Sub*mission to Moscow. And also, don't you give medals to those who fight for your cause? Davies is getting the Order of Lenin. I read the report at the Embassy.'

'You know what Winston says about Davies, sir,' Nichols chipped in. 'He said that after talking to him he needed a bath to get rid of the slime!'

'He lets me win at poker,' Truman said mildly.

'Not everyone who will tell you nice things about Stalin is corrupt,' said Yelena. 'Some are seduced by vanity, some are simply foolish, some are fired by idealism, and see communism as the only viable alternative to fascism, when it is but its alter-ego. Our government has proved exceptionally able at playing on the weaknesses of people it feels may be of use. I would introduce you to a man called Savinkov, who knew more about these subtleties than I, but Stalin had him shot.

'Sir, you should be prepared, once the fighting stops, for an intensive propaganda campaign aimed at the minds of the West, intended to convince them of Soviet goodwill, and the earnest desire of its government for peace and progress. Stalin had enormous success in gulling Western sympathisers in the thirties. He believes, perhaps with reason, that he can do it again. There are still enough socialists in the West who believe that the Soviet Union is superior because it is socialist. They should remember that Hitler's Nazi Party is socialist too. Nice words do not cancel nasty deeds, and dictatorships are not democracies.'

'Johnny tells me you fear a Russian domination of Europe after the war, Yelena. I should tell you that at Yalta, in January, Stalin signed The Declaration on Liberated Europe, which committed him to support the right of all peoples to choose the form of government under which they shall live.'

Yelena shook her head. 'Last month Molotov announced that the elections in Poland are to be held in the Soviet manner. Poland is already Stalin's, Mr Vice-President. Take a look at the government when it is announced: there will not be one politician, statesman or soldier there known to the West, only a collection of *apparatchik* nonentities, bowing and scraping to the Party line. Stalin had the rest shot at Katyn.'

Truman looked at her steadily. 'The Chiefs of Staff and General Eisenhower are agreed that they are loath to hazard American soldiers' lives for political purposes. That is, to occupy parts of Europe that will otherwise be occupied by the Russians.'

'The philistine does not understand that war is a continuation of politics. To neglect the demands of politics for purely strategic reasons is fraught with dangerous consequences.'

Truman looked enquiringly at Yelena. 'That sounds like a quote.'

'It is, Lenin said it.'

'Joe Davies tells me that he thinks we are hurting Stalin's feelings by suggesting that he may not be fulfilling his Yalta pledges. He wants me to be nice to him and I'm to meet him in Potsdam in July. Can I satisfy him, as Joe wants?'

'No, Mr Vice-President, you cannot.'

'What if we granted all the Soviet government's demands? Would that lead to an easing of tensions, and a post-war era of peace and goodwill?'

'It would lead to the West being faced, after a more or less short time, with the next series of demands,' Yelena said clearly. 'You are not dealing with a government, but only one man. May I recite a poem? All my life I have loved literature. In the camps I would recite poetry, to raise my spirits, and those of others. Happy poems, and beautiful ones. There is one I have memorised that is not happy, nor beautiful, but it is great poetry, and may help you in your assessment of Stalin. It was written by a man I knew, Osip Mandelstam. He was exiled for writing it, and was later sent to the camps. I don't know if he is still alive, or not. Anyway, it goes like this:

> "We live, deaf to the land beneath us,
> Ten steps away no one hears our speeches,
> But where there's even half a conversation
> The Kremlin mountaineer will get his mention
> His fingers are fat as grubs.
> And words, final as lead weights, fall from his lips,
> His cockroach whiskers leer
> And his boot-tops gleam.
> Around him a rabble of thin-necked leaders-
> Fawning half-men for him to play with.
> They whinny, purr or whine
> As he prates and points a finger,
> One by one forging his laws, to be flung
> Like horseshoes at the head, the eye or the groin.
> And every killing is a treat
> For the broad-chested Ossetian."

Truman turned to Nichols.

'Do you know that poem?' he asked.

'Yes, sir.'

'Write it out for me later. I want to read it. So what do you say, Johnny? Is Mrs Akulova mad?'

'Every word she has said to you is true, sir. I would stake my future career on it.'

'You just did, son.'

Truman stood and shook her hand again, and Nichols saw him to the door with his bodyguard. Then he came back.

'Well done,' he said. 'You just changed history.'

'I wanted to tell him that Stalin is mad, but I did not dare.'

'No.' He hesitated. 'We heard about Ruth.'

'Is she alive?' she asked eagerly.

'We don't know. They sent her to Ravensbruck. One of the death camps. It should be liberated by your armies, any day now.'

'I'll tell Ivan,' she said quickly. 'Perhaps he can find her . . . I must pray . . .'

She was standing at the great window, looking out over the blossom of the park, her face troubled. She turned to Nichols.

'Johnny, will you do something for me?'

Nichols beamed. 'After what you've just done? Anything at all!'

'Adopt Boris,' she said quietly. 'I want to leave him here in the West. They will be sending me home soon.'

'He's a Russian . . .' Nichols said tentatively.

'He's a Russian who has seen the West. It is enough to send him to the camps.'

'He's a child!' he protested, but then nodded, sadly. 'Yes, I see . . . Of course. We are Boris's friends already, we should love to be his family.'

Berlin, May 2 1945

The T-34 was halted, its long barrel dominating the street. From the houses that stood red flags were hanging limply, most with patches showing where the swastikas had been torn out. The pavement was littered with dirt and abandoned German uniforms. The house on Alexei's left was in the street in its component parts, showing where some German had kept his on. The Russians weren't sending men in after snipers; they simply blew their buildings into bits.

Through the gap Alexei could see the two great flak towers of the zoo. The green of the gardens was pleasant after the grey dust that covered the city but looking closer, Alexei could see that it, too, was a wasteland. A dead hippo floated in a pool, strange birds clustered in the trees, other animals lay in their cages, unmoving. The fins of a Lancaster bomber stuck up from the hole in the ground it had made.

The earphones in his rubber-padded helmet came to life.

'Hear that, Igor?' he called on the intercom. 'The war's over! Ceasefire. Hitler's dead!'

There ought to be a celebration, he thought. Dancing and bands. But he sat, slumped in his turret, resting against his sleeping bag. He unscrewed the cap of his canteen and took a swig of vodka. It was all too much effort. He was too fucking tired. He rested against his bag, closing his eyes.

It was the bang and whistle of shot that brought him round. The front of the tank was enveloped in a great cloud of black smoke and, as it cleared, Alexei could see a very small soldier standing there, in an immense helmet, and a coat down to his ankles. He was clutching an elderly rifle.

Alexei clambered out, communication cord swinging from his helmet, and slid to the ground. The soldier came up to his chest. The ancient black-powder Mauser carbine was taller than he was. Alexei reached out and took it from him, throwing it into the rubble at the side of the street.

The boy was about ten, and tears were streaming down his face. His helmet hung over his head like a small dustbin and his patched feldgrau coat dragged in the dirt. Alexei cuffed the side of the helmet and it fell off.

'Silly boy,' he said. 'Go home. Go away. The war is over. Hitler *kaput.*' He pushed him, and the boy broke, running away through the rubble.

Alexei stood on a bogie and climbed back up into the turret as Igor appeared from a side street.

'Hey, boss, you all right? You mind if I see what I can find?'

The three other crew members were missing, too. Alexei couldn't remember their names, he only knew the old faces.

'Don't go too far, old friend. Come if I call you.'

He settled himself in the turret again, and took another swig of vodka. He was closing his eyes, when he heard the bang, and the shrieking.

He slithered down the side of the turret and jumped to the ground. The ghastly, animal howling came from the side street. It was ablaze, something that flapped and jerked and screamed. From a doorway a woman came running; she threw a coat over the flames, and they went out.

The broken window was still on fire. He pulled the coat back and the purple and black thing on the ground was Igor. A Luger pistol was stuck to his hand, a wire trailing from the butt. He had stopped screaming but he groaned deeply from a charred hole that had once been his mouth.

Alexei looked up at the woman. She was young, in a grey nurse's uniform marked with a red cross.

'Help him!' he shouted, and she shook her head.

A fearful hand that oozed blood like an underdone steak came out from the coat. It grasped his leg, pulling at him in entreaty. He pulled out his pistol, gesturing at Igor, and the nurse nodded violently.

'Ja. Ja.'

He put the muzzle to Igor's head, and pulled the trigger. With the flat bang of the pistol the anguished groaning ceased. There was just a convulsion of the limbs and the sound of the nurse running down the lane. There was a hospital down there somewhere, he had seen it. He knelt in the road. The trapped house was beginning to burn. He picked Igor up under the coat and carried him down the little lane to the tank.

He laid him on the decking beside the driver's hatch, and pulled the coat over him. Russian soldiers were coming up the street. He knew them, not by face or name, but by type. He was a *frontovik*, these were the ones who came behind the fighting men. *Kosoglazyi* and *zheltoe gavnoe*, slant eyes and yellow shit. *Nerusskie*, not Russians. Unwashed and filthy, knives in their boots and their shirt-tails hanging out. Gleaming Mongolian eyes under fur caps. The houses in the street were relatively unharmed and the horde went in, seeing what they could find. Some were already back in the street, capering in women's clothing, eating canned fruit from jars and drinking from the necks of bottles, dousing each other with perfume. From the cellars, women began to scream.

Alexei felt very tired. The *Nerusskie* about him stank. He loathed them and despised utterly what they did, but he was too tired to do anything about it. He got into the driving seat of the tank, starting the diesel and crunching it into gear. He would go somewhere quieter, where a man could have a drink and go to sleep in peace. When he woke up he could think about what to do with Igor.

From the top of the hospital came a terrible shriek. He heard it over the engine. He looked up and saw a naked young woman sprinting along the flat roof. She was being chased by some soldiers who were brandishing bayonets and bottles. Their whoops of joy meshed with her howls of terror in a terrible melody.

The girl ran straight off the end of the roof. Her body fell down to the ground almost gracefully and now she had stopped screaming and she was looking at Alexei.

She had impaled herself on a length of broken railings with a hideous, ripping crunch, and hung there with blood spurting out over her milky skin. The soldiers stood on the edge of the roof, looking down at her in disappointment.

The girl was moaning, deep gasps of agony. She opened her eyes and he recognised her. It was the nurse.

'*Bitte* . . .' she groaned. '*Bitte* . . .'

He pulled at his Tokarev automatic and fired from the seat of the tank. A gout of mortar dust flew in the air. He fired again and again, and heard the soldiers above laughing like crows.

'*Bitte.*'

He got out, standing above the track and pulled the trigger. The recoil made him slip, and he tumbled to the ground. She howled in agony, and he saw that he had blown her foot off. Blood fountained over the filthy rubble and he picked himself up and put the automatic to her head. She closed her eyes in gratitude as he pulled the trigger.

The soldiers were silent and Alexei sat in the wreckage, weeping.

Ivan Akulov commanded his sector from a house in Potsdam. It was a fine building that had escaped destruction both from the Lancasters and Flying Fortresses above and the T-34s and KV-2s below. It had been the property of a wealthy Bavarian businessman who had been turned into ash in a trip to Dresden, but his family still lived there and Akulov allowed them to set up home in the summer house while he got on with the business of governing his slice of the city. He had his office in their old sitting room, with its fine view over the garden. They had dug some of it up earlier in the war to grow vegetables, in the darkness he looked out and could see the glow of the small fire they used to cook by, making potato soup. Their six-year-old son crept out through the fence at night, raiding ruined properties for firewood.

'You're good at getting on with people, Wolff,' he said and the small man stood at attention, looking watchfully at the broad back of the general in front of him. 'Now the fighting's over, the Chekists will be sniffing about. At least when we were fighting they kept away so they wouldn't get hurt, but now we'll have to cope with them again.'

From nearby there came a small fusillade of pistol shots. Half deaf from the constant noise of weaponry, and considering the sound a normal part of everyday existence, neither man took any notice.

'They'll be looking for spies on my staff so make yourself agreeable to them and let me know what's going on. I'll tell you what to say.'

There was another round of banging, and the noise of uproarious laughter. Akulov frowned slightly.

'I want to know if the NKVD bastards are getting together with the bastards who were in the Gestapo.'

More laughter, from within the building.

'What's going on?' Akulov demanded. 'You know, Wolff?'

Wolff grinned. 'Some of the lads are playing cuckoo.'

Akulov turned with a muttered curse and crashed from the room, followed by Wolff. A third, louder round of shots came from a room down the stairs. The door jamb was limned as someone inside switched on the light and, inside, men guffawed. Akulov threw open the door. Officers were in there clutching pistols, laughing, and the room stank of gunfire and vodka. A picture hung askew from its hook, its glass shattered by a shot. Akulov saw Alexei amongst them. A trickle of blood was running down his face from a splinter.

'Enough!' Akulov bellowed. 'Put the guns away.'

The young men began stuffing their Tokarev automatics into their holsters, still laughing.

'Just a little fun, General,' one of them said.

'Stupid children,' Akulov muttered. 'You can get killed playing that silly game. Shouting "cuckoo" in the dark and having the others fire at the noise. You can get killed.'

The young man smiled. 'Oh, yes. We know that, sir.'

Akulov pointed at Wolff, standing sardonically in the doorway. 'Does he play this stupid game? No, he doesn't.'

The captain patted Wolff on the head as he passed. 'No, Wolff's a survivor, aren't you, Iosif?'

'That's me,' the little Jew agreed.

'Come upstairs,' Akulov said to Alexei. 'I have some plum brandy. Have a drink.'

In his office, Akulov poured fiery liquor into tumblers. He dipped a handkerchief into his glass, and cleaned the gash in Alexei's face.

'Stupid children . . .' he murmured. 'Why do you do it, hey?'

'I'm a *frontovik*,' Alexei said. His face was puffy and pale and his eyelids sagged. 'Where's Igor, Papa? He went from Moscow to Berlin, too . . .'

Akulov laid his son down on the cot in his office, pulling off his boots. His eyes closed but he spoke once more.

'Where's Igor?'

28

Chuzhoi

Moscow, 24 June 1945

H E came at last, when it was getting dark. She had stood with the others as the regiments of the Red Army marched and rolled by, the steady warm rain muffling the tramp of the boots and the smack of the tank tracks on the cobbles of Red Square. She had stood as the battle standards of the Third Reich clattered to the ground at the feet of the man who stood alone above the Lenin Mausoleum he had had built, in an ever-growing pile.

She had waited, and finally he had come, marching at the head of his officers. His aircraft had come into Moscow Central Airport not long after dawn and he had gone straight to the form-up point.

It had been nearly four years.

'Are you an officer or a soldier?' she asked. 'I cannot tell without badges of rank.'

He smiled broadly as he took off his blue-grey greatcoat, with its magnificent scarlet embroidery indicating an officer of general rank.

'My father had one just like that,' she said. 'You must have borrowed it. And his sword.'

His Guards' dress uniform was glorious, his chest covered with the awards of the Tsars, the Tsar's scarlet *lampa* stripe running from hip to calf, disappearing into his polished cavalry boots.

He had a parcel and he put it down on a table and embraced her.

'You're still wet!' she said. 'Get this finery off!'

'I'm used to being wet,' Akulov said. 'We were wet all winter. Where is little Ivan?'

'In bed,' she said. 'Come see.'

Yelena took him through and he looked down at the little boy sleeping.

'Alexei is well. He sends his love. And this.' He reached in his pocket as she peeled off his jacket, and took out an old holy medal. 'He came through unhurt.'

'I wish he had kept it,' she said.

'He says his son may need it one day.'

'He'll have to meet a nice girl first,' Yelena said sadly.

They went through. Outside the night sky was flashing and sizzling, bright with the coloured lights of the victory fireworks. Akulov pulled the curtains.

'Do you mind? I see that and all I think of is artillery and flares.'

There was a tap at the door.

'That'll be Tatyana,' said Yelena, getting up. 'She's in Moscow.'

Tatyana came in and Akulov embraced her warmly. 'We need to celebrate!' he said, and opened his parcel, taking out a bottle. 'You will know what this is,' he said to Yelena with a smile.

'Bourbon,' she said immediately. 'American whiskey.'

He fished in the bag again and brought out another bottle.

'Ginger ale!' she said. She went to the cupboard to get glasses. Automatically, they had gravitated to the kitchen, and they sat about the little table.

'How did you get this?' she asked.

'From the Americans in Berlin. There's a lot more in there. Good food. We can have supper on it.'

Yelena began taking things from the bag. Tins of meat and fish, fruit and vegetables. Packets of chocolate and biscuits. Cake. Whisky and gin. Packs of wrapped cigarettes. Tea. Coffee. They seemed to alarm her and, as each emerged, she examined it anxiously.

Tatyana's eyes widened at the sight of the luxuries. 'You got all these from one of their *nomeklatura* perhaps?' she suggested.

'They don't seem to have such a thing,' said Akulov. 'Even ordinary footsoldiers seemed to be able to get anything they wanted. They have special stores, certainly, but not for the *vlasti* or *nomenklatura*, for all their troops.'

'Yelena told me that. She says there's no rationing in America.'

'Tatyana is interested because she's working for a team at the economic institute,' Yelena said. 'It was a good job you found for her.'

'What are you doing?' asked Akulov, interested.

'We are called consultants. We have been asked to consider the best way of administering the territories that your Red Army will have occupied when the war stops. Poland, Czechoslovakia, Hungary, half of Germany. Rumania, Austria and Bulgaria. Maybe Greece and Italy.'

'Who has asked you to do this?' Akulov could not hide his concern.

'The NKVD,' she said and her plain, metal-framed glasses glinted in the light.

'Why the NKVD?'

'The decision directly affects them. Direct control from Moscow would entail a huge increase in their area of responsibility.'

'And?' he queried.

'We recommend the Finnish model. No troops in the country, but their presence in Russia. Thus placing pressure on the government to conform with our government's wishes. Weak armed forces for them, and no alliance with the West but to be allowed to retain their national cultures. Trade agreements favourable to us, and no interference in their economies, so that they can produce industrial and agricultural goods for us, which we can pay for partly with raw materials. Such an arrangement would be very advantageous to us, would provoke little Russophobia in these countries and would be highly cost-effective. There would be a net flow of wealth from outside into the Soviet Union.'

Yelena was looking distractedly at the bright packaging of the various packets, bottles and cans that Akulov had brought. 'It won't happen,' she muttered. 'Ivan, darling, I'm going to have to burn all these Western labels. I daren't put them out with the rubbish.'

'Why?' he was astonished.

'And why won't it happen?' Tatyana chimed in.

'The NKVD aren't making the decision. It will be up to the *vozhd*, to Stalin. And you have to see it the way he sees it. If the Red Army is in Austria, in Czechoslovakia, in Germany – in Poland, even – what have the soldiers seen? *Riches.* The incredible wealth of the ordinary people. Some will have seen American private soldiers, like themselves, who live like *Grafs.* The ordinary ones will be seduced by the riches, the intelligent by the values of the West. This is dangerous to Stalin, it threatens his power, his principles.'

Yelena looked searchingly at her two companions. 'Don't you see? If the West is a threat, *they* are enemies. Everyone who has seen the West is an enemy. So he must seal off the Soviet Union from the West. He will take all these Eastern European countries over wholesale, see if he does not.'

She was gathering the labels and shaking biscuits on to plates.

'It makes no economic sense,' Tatyana objected. 'Instead of an asset, they will become a drain on all resources, and a weakness.'

'Did the terror make economic sense?' Yelena demanded. 'Or the murder of the peasants?'

'That was in the past, Yelena,' said Akulov, watching the pile of packaging grow in amazement. 'Before the war. The war has changed everything. My soldiers rode in American Studebaker trucks and jeeps. We ate American food. This uniform I wear is made from American cloth. Darling, you have been away for so long, you don't realise the changes that have happened, because of the war. We won, not just because of the Western trucks and food, but because we were all allowed to develop our own qualities. I as a general, my men as soldiers. We won because we outfought Fritz. We released the qualities of the soldier as an individual, his potential, his intelligence, his mother-wit and his courage. You cannot change that. And now that we have won, I can tell you, there is talk of a vast American aid plan to restore the economies of Europe. We are not to be excluded.'

'Being included would mean not being able to treat the West as enemies,' she muttered obstinately. 'And for him, enemies are as necessary as air. Don't you see? Everyone else is *chuzhoi*. Them. The enemy.'

She carried her collection of paper, card and plastic over to the fire, and began feeding it into the flames, her set face lit up with yellow and orange.

'You all think I'm mad,' she said. 'But I'm not.'

Alexei's holy medal fell out from the paper and she carefully picked it up.

'Alexei . . .' she said, suddenly fearful. 'Where is he? Why did he not come back with you?'

Akulov had come over, holding her glass of whiskey. 'Here, have a drink,' he said, seeking to calm her. 'Alexei's all right. He's a little tired, after all the fighting so I've given him some leave. He's gone off on a trip with Nikolai and another comrade. They've gone to get Ruth.'

'Ruth?'

'Your friend, Nikolai's mother.'

'But she was sent to Ravensbruck, Ivan. Johnny Nichols told me so.'

'So perhaps she is still alive,' Akulov said patiently. 'When I got your letter telling me where she was I told Nikolai. The war is over and he's gone to find her as he should.'

British Second Army HQ, Luneberg, Germany

There was a rattling from the lock on the door of his cell, a converted store-room in the villa, and Manfred Liss sat up on the iron cot on which he had been resting. He wore a British army uniform devoid of markings, in contrast to that of the man who came in, whose pressed outfit was decorated with shiny badges of rank and two rows of brightly-coloured medal ribbon. He carried a buff file, and went to stand by the window.

'Good morning, Colonel Fraser,' Liss said politely.

'Well, *Sturmbannfuhrer*, we have the result of the Russians' request to have you sent to the Soviet sector for trial.'

An attentive glint came into Liss's eye, but he continued to sit patiently. The British intelligence officer shuffled the papers deliberately and Liss ran a hand over his shiny bald head.

'Curious case, yours,' said Fraser. He shut the file and began fumbling in his pocket for his pipe and pouch. 'The Russians want you for war crimes. Very well, one might say. You were an officer of the SS. But that's not how I see it. You were *intelligence*. There's no evidence that you were one of those bastards involved in the killing of civilians, or running the camps. I think, if you were to stay here, you'd do eighteen months in a POW camp and be released.'

Fraser stuffed the bowl of his pipe and began to play a match across it. 'But here we are. The Russians say they want you for something I don't think you did and you appear willing to be handed over to them. Very odd, that. Most Jerries in your position are desperate to stay here, with us.'

He had his little bonfire drawing well, and sucked upon the stem in triumph. 'Want to know what I think? I think they're going to offer you a job. Y'see, I think that we've won this war against you lot, only to find ourselves with a new enemy at the gate, which is Uncle Joe and the Russkies. And the Russkies are recruiting talent. That's what I think. What do you think, *Sturmbannfuhrer*?'

Liss's stomach turned over, but he forced a smile on to his face, and shrugged.

Fraser tapped his file with his pipe stem, watching Liss. 'You were a communist once, weren't you, Liss? Find the change to being a Nazi difficult?'

'No,' he said, truthfully.

'No. I have advanced views on that too. I don't think there's much difference between a communist and a nazi.' Then he sighed. 'Too advanced for some, obviously. They're going to send you over there, Liss. Back to work, I should say.'

Liss simply smiled innocently.

'On your feet, then. They've sent a car for you.'

It was waiting outside, in the drive of the red-roofed villa, a big, captured Mercedes with a red flag on the wing where the swastika had flown. He got in, and Krivitskiy was sitting there, in the uniform of an NKVD general.

They drove down the street, the limes dusting the limousine with their leaves as it purred out of the town towards the pine-covered heath.

'Himmler's out there somewhere,' Liss commented. 'He took cyanide and they put him in an unmarked grave.'

The car picked up speed, driven by an MGB chauffeur.

'This is *schon*,' Liss said happily. 'What a car! You had to be a *gauleiter* to have one of these.'

'I think that's who had it,' said Krivitskiy. 'We shot him, anyway. But look – '

He leaned forward and opened a hatch in the walnut veneer. A light came on to illuminate a small bar.

'Drink? What will you have, schnapps?'

The scent of cherries blossomed in the cabin as Krivitskiy half-filled a shot-glass. 'Go on,' he said, and Liss's eyes watered with joy as the fiery liquor lit up his head.

'I haven't had a drink for six months,' he said hoarsely. 'Where are we going?'

'Berlin,' said Leon. 'We have our headquarters in Karlshorst.'

Liss turned suddenly to his old friend and seized his hand.

'It's good to see you, Krivitskiy. I didn't know if you'd find me, in all this rubble.'

Krivitskiy squeezed back, smiling warmly. 'Oh, I made sure of it. We're old friends and I'd not leave you.'

'I'd have come for you, you know, Liss said, 'if things had gone the other way.'

'I know you would.'

They were running along the road by the great Elbe river, passing drab khaki British army trucks with ease. The sun had come out and Liss sat back, enjoying the ride after his months of captivity.

'What do you want me to do?' he asked.

'We'll be holding elections and need experienced German Chekists to hold them for us. I want you to begin preparations.'

'Certainly,' Liss assented. 'What's it to be called, this Germany of yours?'

'German Democratic Republic.'

Liss laughed. 'Got a uniform designed yet?'

Krivitskiy smiled. 'Any ideas? Nothing in black, I think.'

Liss signed. 'I'll be glad to get this nasty rough serge off, anyway.'

'I'll give you one of our NKVD uniforms when we get there,' Krivitskiy promised.

'It won't be as good, you know,' Liss said, half-playfully. 'That's the one thing wrong with communism – no style. Lots of drab grey suits made out of felt carpet underlay. Well, that's how they look, isn't it. We should have kept Trotsky, he had style. Remember him, Leon?'

'I remember him. I borrowed his name, didn't I?'

'We could have made him minister for style. Appointed his tailor Commissar for Fashion . . .'

Liss drained the rest of the schnapps. 'I'd better not have any more or I'll be drunk. Yes, Trotsky, he knew how to look good . . .'

'He had charisma,' Krivitskiy commented. 'That's why Stalin had him killed.'

'Yes . . .'

Liss glanced across at his friend the Chekist general, almost nervously. 'Leon, I'm sorry about that women of yours, Marthe. I meant it for the best. When I saw her name on the list, her and her daughter, I had them taken in. The others all went on to the camps.'

'Yes, what happened about that?' Krivitskiy asked softly.

Liss had interrogated enough people to shift uneasily in his seat. 'I thought someone had made a mistake at your end.'

'Oh, they had. So you took them off . . .'

'I put them into a safe apartment I had. It was guarded, of course, only they didn't know that. That was the strange thing, they tried to escape . . .'

'Marthe had worked it out, Manfred. She was in the business, when she saw you, she knew what was going on. That's why she ran.'

'Well, it didn't matter,' Liss said hastily. 'Once I got your instructions I had her and the girl sent on to Ravensbruck anyway.'

'You should have shot them. Marthe *knew*. Don't you see that? It would have been the finish for both of us.'

'I didn't see that then . . . and you see, Leon, I had to follow the paperwork. I borrowed them, and the part of the SS I borrowed them from wanted them back. Anyway, don't worry, Ravensbruck did the job, I mean, that's what it was *for*.'

Krivitskiy slapped Liss' bald head, not hard. 'And you didn't like to think of shooting someone, did you?'

'I've never done it, Leon,' he admitted. 'I'm not like you, I don't like seeing blood . . .'

'I interrogated someone who said Himmler went weak at the knees when he went to the camps. Gutless bastard, Krivitskiy said.

'Hitler never went. Never even saw a Jew,' Liss volunteered.

'No . . .' Krivitskiy said quietly. 'Stalin doesn't, either. Ravensbruck, that's not far from here, isn't it?'

'North of Berlin, towards the coast . . .'

It was still bothering Liss. I could have kept Marthe alive, Leon. She was your woman; she wouldn't have told on us.'

'A tank is a tank, a car is a car. Manfred. You know what they will do. But a person is different. You cannot be certain what they will do. A person is a problem. But no person, no problem.'

Outside Neustadt they passed through two heavy sets of road blocks, manned first by British troops and then by MGB personnel. A few kilometres further on Krivitskiy tapped on the shoulder of the driver, pointing to a small, autumn leaved copse not far from the road, and the Mercedes slowed. He turned to Liss.

'Are you hungry? I've brought a hamper. We can stop here. If we go much further in the bombing's destroyed everything.'

They walked down a lane as the big engine of the car began to tick quietly behind them as it cooled. The driver stayed in his seat.

A wide sawn tree trunk lay in the sunshine in front of the wood. 'Sit there,' said Krivitskiy. He opened the wicker hamper and passed Liss a sandwich. 'I'll open the wine. We captured a whole cellarful.'

'Tongue!' Liss said joyfully. 'And mustard! You don't know *how* I've missed the good things. Good food and wine, a smooth young arse. It was bloody chaos at the end, you know. I'm lucky to be here.'

There was a metallic clicking behind him.

'Where's that wine, Leon?' he demanded. 'Oh, God it's good to be back with you. It'll be just like the old days. I helped you, and you helped me.'

There was a flat bang, almost by his ear. Something knocked him down off the tree trunk and he found himself on the ground.

'What the hell . . .' he muttered.

He pushed himself up on to his hands and knees. He felt strangely weak.

'Leon, give me a hand . . . what's happened?' Blood was spattering the dry leaf mould, it tapped on the tattered brown leaves like the first drops of a storm and, with difficulty, he turned his head to look up at Krivitskiy. He was standing against the sky, his automatic pistol in his hand.

'We're friends . . .' Liss protested. 'I helped you . . .'

He fell forward on to his face, one hand gripping the leaves. Krivitskiy looked up. The driver was walking towards them.

'He tried to escape,' he said, and the man nodded.

Ravensbruck Concentration Camp

Inside the hut, Nikolai opened his canvas knapsack, and took out a bottle. The man in the green cap stared suspiciously at the foreign writing, the strange label.

'What is it?'

'American whiskey. They call it bourbon. Here, try some.'

A tumbler was on the table; he opened the bottle and poured some of the brown liquor into the glass. From outside a brass band suddenly started up. When the tuba and bass drum came together a dusty window buzzed in time.

The NKVD guard sniffed the whiskey, and then tossed it back neat.

'Ahhh . . .' He looked at Nikolai with watering eyes. 'It's good!'

'Of course it's good. Here.' He put back the cork and handed over the bottle. The guard slipped it away inside his baggy jacket and wiped his mouth with the back of his hand.

'You can go in,' he said. 'What is it you want?'

'I'm looking for someone. We need to ask questions.'

Nikolai understood the mentality; the man nodded. It was reasonable that you came to get someone. He would not have understood *help*.

'I'm on duty into the afternoon.'

He opened the door and they went out into the warm sunshine. They were standing by the guard hut of the camp. The electrified wire fences stretched either side of them and still-manned guard towers looked down on the long huts, the parade grounds, the women who sat there on the ground, thick as insects. The high chimneys of the crematoria stood black and smokeless against the blue sky.

Over the road that led to the railhead that had brought the women to the Nazi camp they had erected an arch and draped it with flowers. The brass band stood by it, pumping out the patriotic favourites. Across the arch was written: THE MOTHERLAND WELCOMES ITS HEROINES. A little way off Nikolai could see his Jeep, with Alexei and Iosif Wolff. Alexei was beating his hand to time with the music and the green of Iosif's NKVD hat stood out against the wood. He wore the uniform to match. He was the man who could fix things, the *stolkachi* of their little group; he had gone off with some bottles of liquor and come back with a uniform, and a handful of stamped forms. All Nikolai had to do was find his mother.

'You've come just in time,' the guard commented. 'They're starting to move them out today.'

'Where to?'

'Home. Back to Russia.' He lifted the bar of the gate and pushed it open. 'Good luck,' he said laconically.

As Nikolai went in he realised why. Thousands of emaciated, shaven-headed women in filthy and ragged striped prisoner dresses filled the great compound. Some stood, some sat in the sunshine; there were drifts and flocks of them. He went away from the gate, suddenly aware of his size, the energy he had, his clean, bright uniform.

A group was nearby; they were swaying to the music of the band. Two of the creatures were shuffling about together, with their mouths open, and he realised that they were laughing as they danced. As he passed, one of the women reached out with a hand like a claw. He could not tell how old she was. She might have been eighteen or sixty and she was peering past him, beyond the wire.

'Is it true?' she asked. She spoke in Russian, but with an accent of the Ukraine. 'I can't see so well, not as well as when they brought me here. Is it a priest?'

He turned. On the road to the station, by the arch, there was a figure in his robes. Nikolai could see the glint of a gold cross in his hand.

'Yes,' he said gently. 'They have a priest.'

When he turned back tears were running down the furrows in the skin that covered the skull of her face.

'I heard . . . but you did not know what to believe. They said the priests had come back . . . oh, we're going home . . .'

'I'm looking for someone,' he said. 'But I don't know where to start.'

The woman wiped at her tears. 'Well, is she Russian, like you?'

'She is my mother.'

'Your mother?' The woman shook her head, wondering. 'I hope she's here . . . If she is, she'll be in this part of the camp.'

She touched the filthy red triangle sewn apex down on the left breast of her dress. 'She'll have one of these,' she said. The greens are the *urkas*. Oh, listen, they're playing *Volga volga*. Isn't it *lovely*?'

The women were swaying and singing and Nikolai felt drawn to help the little party along, to join. He fumbled in his knapsack. 'Do you smoke?' he asked.

'I did, once,' the woman said dryly.

He brought out a tin and took off the lid. 'Please, help yourselves.'

Within seconds the little group was wreathed in blue smoke. Other women came closer, to breathe in the scent.

'God's back, we're going home and I have a cigarette . . .'

The woman's eyes were watering again, from a combination of joy and the shock of the nicotine.

'Vera!' she called, and another skeletal woman looked around. 'Don't go off, they'll be moving us soon.'

'I won't, Irina.'

'We're among the first to go,' Irina said proudly. 'They came and selected us yesterday. I was a partisan, you know. I fought with Sidor in Putivt.'

Nikolai opened his mouth to claim kinship, and then shut it again. There was too much pain and he feared the memories that came with talking.

'Perhaps you know my mother? I am Nikolai Savinkov and my mother is Ruth.'

It was hard to see expression on the wasted face, but the woman turned away, drawing on her cigarette.

'No,' she said flatly. 'I don't think so.'

'You do, don't you?' he said, suddenly angry. 'Tell me where she is! I was a partisan like you. My mother fought in the Resistance. I have come a long way to find my mother. Thousands of miles and ten years. *Tell me.*'

'I don't know where your mother is,' Irina muttered, with her back to him. 'Ask Marthe. In the *revier*, the hospital hut. Over there.'

Nikolai walked through the clumps of women waiting in their groups for the gates to open. He went into the hut. It was gloomy inside and it stank. Dead women lay on filthy palliases that leaked wood shavings. Here and there, as his boots thudded on the plank floor, he saw the glimmer of an eye opening. Some were still alive.

'*Marthe*!' he shouted. 'I am looking for Marthe.'

Someone moved. A woman crouched by a mattress. Another woman lay there.

'Who is asking?' the crouching woman asked.

'I am Nikolai Savinkov. I am looking for my mother.'

The woman on the mattress was alive and her skin was not the blue of death, but was mottled red. Her breath bubbled wheezing in her chest, but she looked up at him with a seeing eye.

'I know you,' she said. 'But do you know me?'

The other woman stood up. In spite of their emaciation there was a similarity. They were mother and daughter.

'You rescued us from Berlin, you and your mother Ruth,' she said. 'I am Elisabeth. My mother has typhus.'

'Imagine,' said Marthe, and she coughed a dirty phlegm over her chin. Elisabeth wiped it with a cloth. 'Imagine, I survived all this time, and now I am dying, right at the end.'

Nikolai reached in his bag and took out a small brown bottle and a canteen. He shook tablets into his hand. 'The doctor told me what to expect here. He told me things like typhus were everywhere. Take these, they're British. M and B. See, it's written on the tablet. It's a wonder drug.'

Elisabeth took the pills and the canteen of water, but Marthe held up her hand. 'Wait. He wants to know about Ruth.'

'I met a woman out there,' he said, frowning, 'waiting to go down to the train. She knew of my mother, but said she did not.'

'You have to understand, Nikolai . . . those of us here who are still alive, we had to work together . . . We communists, we red triangles, we stuck together, we took control from the greens, the urkas. It did not guarantee you would live, and plenty of us went up the chimney, but it *helped*.'

She paused to cough again and Elisabeth gave her a little water.

'It *helped*,' Marthe repeated. 'You could not survive on your own. You had to have your family, if you like, to help. That is why Elisabeth and I are still just alive. We did not know Ruth was here because she stuck with the British and the French, the resistance types. She was very ill when the Russians liberated us. She survived; but when she recovered, she was with the Russian prisoners. The British and French had been transferred but someone had told the guards she was Russian and she found that they would not let her go. When she heard that the Russians were to be taken home, she tried to raise an uprising. She told the Russians that they would all be killed, that the guards were just the same as the SS. She wanted them to break out.'

'They were very angry,' said Elisabeth. 'This was just two days ago. In their eyes she became the enemy. She was not . . . *nash.*'

'Ours,' said Nikolai. 'One of us. No. She was *chuzhoi.*'

'*Chuzhoi!*' Elisabeth exclaimed. 'That was what they called her.'

'On the other side. The worst thing to be,' he said, bleakly.

'They attacked her, a mob of them,' Elisabeth said.

'Your mother has not been seen for two days, Nikolai,' Marthe said, from the dreadful bed. 'If I had been up I would have talked to her, persuaded her to stay silent.'

'Where is she?'

'We think she is dead. They were very angry . . .'

'Where is her body?'

'The camp is very large,' Marthe said simply. 'Now that you know, you had better have your special tablets back.'

'No,' he said. 'Get better, Marthe.'

As she swallowed the tablets, with difficulty, he went to the smeared window, looking out.

'Are those the huts where they lived?' he asked.

'Yes.'

He turned, and went to the door.

'Nikolai,' she called.

'Yes?' He turned.

'When you go back to Russia . . .'

'Yes?'

She licked her dry lips with a tongue that was mottled red. 'Don't tell Krivitskiy we're alive,' she whispered. 'Please . . .'

'No,' he said grimly. 'I won't do that.'

He went outside into the sunshine, and it felt clean. He lit a cigarette from his tin, and flushed his lungs with smoke. The gates were open, the women were filing out, going under the arch on the road to the station. They were singing as he began to walk along the lane that led between the twin row of huts. It was rough, simply ploughed up mud that had dried in the sun and he looked inside a hut and the smell drove him out again. It was empty, filled only with the stench from the stacks of wooden bunks and rotting mattresses.

On the breeze he could hear the sound of the band, the steady thump of the bass drum, the jingle of the cymbals. A shadow came over the sun and, looking up, he could see a big thunder cloud building, grumbling to itself as it climbed into the sky.

'*Ready or not,*' he sang. '*Here I come.*'

A glossy black crow was pecking at something nameless mixed up in the mud. It cawed at him, flapping up on to the roof of a hut where it watched him go by before dropping down to finish its meal.

'*Ready or not. Here I come.*'

He stopped, turning his head, but there was just the singing of the women in the distance. He kept walking.

'*Ready or not. Here I come.*'

He stopped again as his boots crunched on fragments of bone. What was that?

'*Come and get me . . .*'

There was a noise, a thud from under a hut. He scrambled on hands and knees, the floor beams knocking off his hat, pulling her hand, bringing her out into the bar of sunshine between the huts.

'Boo!' she said, and he clasped her to him.

'You are very thin, Mama.'

'A poor restaurant here, darling' she whispered. She held him very tight. 'No steak.'

'And you have a strange hairstyle. But you are still a good hider.'

She managed to sit up. 'I'm so stiff!' she said. 'I've been in there nearly two days. Have they taken the others away?'

'They're going now.'

'They wouldn't listen. They attacked me . . .'

'Can you walk?' he asked. 'I can get you out. I have a Jeep and Alexei is here.'

'I can walk,' she said proudly. 'When I parachuted in from the Hudson they dropped me in the wrong place and I walked twenty miles in the night . . .' With his help she stood up. 'I can certainly walk out of here,' she muttered. 'Though I doubt I could manage twenty miles . . .'

They began making their slow way back down the lane.

'Alexei . . . how is Alexei?' she asked.

'He's tired . . . he fought from Moscow to Berlin and he's very, very tired, Mama. I'm looking after him.'

'You always collected lame ducks, darling. Now you have me, too.'

'You'd never be lame, Mama,' he said lovingly.

A last squad of women were marching through the gate, singing happily, as they passed through in the dust. Alexei and Iosif were still in the Jeep.

'You found her!' Alexei exclaimed. He tipped back his tin cup and stuffed it into his sack. The smell of whisky was in the air and they clustered about, putting her carefully into the front seat. Ruth looked at Wolff doubtfully.

'You have friends in the Cheka, darling?' she murmured.

Nikolai shook his head. 'He's one of us, a soldier. But he got a uniform and it got us in here.'

'A *useful* friend,' she said, and smiled at Wolff. The camp behind them was quiet again. The gate shut with a creak and a crash and there was just the sound of the women's voices in song going down the path. By the flower-decked arch the priest was taking off his hat, wiping his forehead in the sultry heat. One of the NKVD officers clapped him on the shoulder and they laughed, walking together across the road.

'Do let's go, darling,' Ruth murmured, and Nikolai started the engine. 'Take the road that way,' Ruth said, and they drove quietly away through the pines. The road rose as they followed it round the hill, and they found themselves looking down a slope towards the railhead. A train was there, the locomotive gently leaking steam, a long line of wooden-sided trucks waiting behind it.

'Stop a moment, Nikky.'

He switched off the engine and they could hear an angry woman's voice shouting. They were down there in columns, their grey colouration dotted with the green hats of the NKVD.

There was outrage in the voice and Nikolai thought it sounded like Irina.

'They've realised,' Ruth said sadly. 'It's the trucks – they're the ones the Nazis brought us in.'

The fury of betrayal was punctuated by a lower snarling. Down at the head, the women were beginning to swirl. One stood out at the front then she crumpled to the ground. A moment later the flat crack of a shot came up the hill. Then they could hear the shouts of orders, the baying of dogs, the screaming as people were trampled underfoot, and the grey tide began to seep into the trucks, like porridge.

'They were captured, they were taken away. So now they are traitors, enemies of the people,' Ruth said quietly. 'I tried to tell them, but they didn't believe me.'

'They took Sergei,' Alexei said wearily. 'He got captured, fighting ... then he was liberated, he fought all the way to Berlin and the Chekists took him away ...'

'Let's get away from here,' said Nikolai. As they drove down the road, the train whistled ...

*

The thunderstorm broke over them and the dirt road turned to mud, the Jeep throwing up a red spray in the air. The rain whipping into his face woke up Alexei, in the back.

'Nikolai! We must be close to the line,' Wolff said, leaning forward. 'Let's leave your mother and Alexei under cover while you and I find out where it is. It looks suspicious, us carrying someone from the camp around.'

'Then wait for dark, you mean?'

Nikolai blew rain off his nose. He had put his hat over Ruth's head, but she was becoming soaked. An abandoned farmhouse was by the roadside and he pulled in.

'Alexei, we'll go to the army unit we saw back there and find out how close we are to the British lines.'

Alexei helped Ruth down and across the abandoned courtyard in the rain. She was shivering. As they went inside they heard the sound of the jeep going up the road.

They were in the kitchen. The house was simply abandoned, its owners having joined the great trek west, fleeing from the Russians. He broke up a chair and started a fire, putting Ruth close by. He was in his tanker's combat clothes and he had an axe on one side of his belt, pistol on the other. He took his axe and simply levered the kitchen door from its hinges, hitting it until the joints broke free and he could feed the dry, painted wood into the flames. It caught brightly and the room was flooded with heat and light as the rain swept across the road from the pines in white sheets, beating on the house, and running down the panes.

He sat down with her at the little scrubbed table by the fire and opened his pack, taking out an American aluminium canteen. As he unscrewed the cap, she suddenly smelled whiskey.

'Drink?' he asked.

'I'd better not. It might kill me if I did.'

Alexei smiled vaguely. 'It might kill me if I didn't,' he said.

He looked infinitely tired. His face had crumpled in upon itself along creases, scars and fold lines. He splashed some liquor into his tin cup and she reached out and held his hand with her claw.

'Are you all right, Alexei, darling?'

'No,' he said truthfully. 'I'm tired. I'm tired all the time ... I remember to drink, but I forget to eat ... I wake up in the morning and I don't know where I am ... I was all right while we were fighting. I was, really. I had the tank and Igor ... Now I seem to be in pieces, and I can't put them together again ... Nikky looks after me ...'

'You have green teeth, too,' she said, and smiled gently at him.

'I know,' he said and suddenly grinned. '*Shampanskaye!*'

'Champagne?'

'German champagne. You open the gearboxes of German tanks, and transmission fluid comes out. It's green, very green.' He looked at his pack, trying to remember something. He opened it. 'That's it . . . food. Nikky put in some chocolate biscuits. American. Want a biscuit?'

'Yes, please. And Nikky . . . is he all right? So many years . . . I see him for a few minutes and he has gone off again.'

'He lost his wife. Natalia, my sister . . . Rykov killed her.'

'Rykov,' she said, her eyes suddenly alert, glittering like a bird. 'Nikky was married to Natalia?'

'They were partisans . . . and there is a little boy, Ivan . . . We killed Rykov with a bomb, I was there . . .'

The rain was easing and she could hear the water splashing down from a broken gutter. The fire no longer lit the room so brightly.

'Have you seen my girl? he asked. He had a small sheaf of letters and photographs and he held them up tenderly.

'She's pretty,' Ruth said.

'Anastasia . . .'

'She has a gun, Alexei.'

'She's a sniper.'

When she looked up, Alexei had gone to sleep, slumped against the wall. She put the photographs back with the letters.

An old tarpaulin lay in a corner, the colour of dung. She was uneasy in the room and she picked it up, slinging it round her shoulders like a cape, and went outside in the drizzle. The sun had come out again and the warm, glistening road was beginning to steam. She walked out from the farmhouse, crossing the road to stand in the grass among the dripping wild flowers. There was just the sound of the rainwater splashing down through the pines. And an engine.

She looked along the road, through the green saplings and mist. A jeep. No, a jeep and a truck. Not Nikolai and Iosif.

She had been trained. You simply did not stand out in the open, and she slipped backwards into the wood, crouching down among the bracken with her green cape about her. She waited for the convoy of two to go by.

They came growling down the road in low gear. The Jeep was being driven by one man and she could see his green hat behind the flat windscreen. He slowed and stopped outside the farmhouse. He got out. And it was Iosif in his NKVD uniform . . .

She drew in her breath, as though to call, and then held it. The truck was stopping, too. A big, muddy American truck with a red star on the door.

NKVD troopers jumped down from the back and Iosif Wolff led them into the house. Someone was thrown out from the truck. He landed heavily in the mud, his hands tied behind him. It was Nikolai and he was bleeding, his face splashed with blood.

As they dragged Alexei from the farmhouse a creature climbed down from the cab. They threw Alexei down and a handful of letters and photographs scattered on the mud like playing cards. The thing moved stiffly, holding on with one hand, the other immobile, cork inside a shiny black glove. She could see the gold insignia of an NKVD general at its throat, below the livid red scarring of its mutilated face.

It was Rykov.

29

Shpionam

Moscow, August 1946

THE class of young men and women in the Lubyanka lecture room came to attention as Natasha Savinkova came on to the stage. Her eyes were the colour of steel and her long yellow hair was pinned up on her head. She wore a fitted blue skirt and white shirt with a red tie at her throat. The Order of Lenin glinted on her bosom.

'You may sit down.'

Her voice was level, a voice of authority. They knew who she was. She was a legend.

'We live in wonderful times,' She began. Under the rule of our *Khoziain*, our wise and strong leader Comrade Stalin, the Soviet peoples have, unaided, defeated the fascist Hitlerite menace of Germany. In Hitler's capital statues of our glorious leader now stand. And yet the traitorous forces of the West still seek, like hyenas, to tear off a piece for themselves. In Berlin, captured on the order of Stalin himself, Western forces now stand. I tell you this so that you understand that we, the world's first communist state, are always threatened by our enemies. No sooner do we defeat one, than another springs up in its place. Vigilance must be eternal.'

Her gaze swept across the young faces of the secret police trainees, noting with approval the rapt attention, the partly-open mouths.

'That's right. Our enemies are everywhere. Who protects the toiling masses of Soviet Communism? *We* do. We, the servants of the *Ministerstvo Vnutrennikh Del*, the MVD, under the all-seeing guidance of our leader, Comrade Stalin. Our enemies work unceasingly for our downfall and we are beholden to be vigilant, to work night and day for their defeat.'

She allowed a smile to spread over her face. 'But I can say again, these are wonderful times. Every area of our lives is now bathed in the radiance of communist thought. The very sciences bow to the superiority of Marxist thinking. Just as communism has made a New

Man, communist farmers, under the guidance of Comrade Lysenko, are about to grow New Plants. The very plant world has become submissive to the orders of the Party. Soon we shall enter a world of plenty.'

The smile faded, and she frowned. They frowned, too.

'Do not imagine that the capitalist Western powers will give up their evil struggle easily. Their world is on the point of economic collapse. In the streets of London starving children are machine gunned. In New York they work eighteen hours a day, for no wages, in Jewish sweatshops. They send their spies here to us, to attempt to steal our secrets.'

She leaned forward on the podium, and they leaned forward in their seats. 'Spies are everywhere,' she whispered. She stood up straight. 'You will soon be fully-fledged officers. Yours will be the responsibility of monitoring, of keeping safe every aspect of Soviet life. Concern yourselves! No detail of anyone's life is beyond your reach. Look for spies. And how will you find them? In deviation of thought and deed. Is there music that cannot be whistled by a worker? If there is, it is bourgeois. Strike it down and find the man who wrote it. Is there writing without Marxist principle? Root it out and put the alien who wrote it to work. Let them scrub floors with their bare hands, and do good for the Soviet people! Look out for those who came into contact with the West during the war, listen for tales of the wealth in the West. These people are infected! They are diseased and they must be put into quarantine. To the camps with them, to be re-educated! They have not understood the sacrifices made by the people of the Soviet Union for freedom. And do not let your searching gaze rest only upon them. Seek out their relatives. The bacillus of decadent Western thought is a virulent one. Let suspicion be your guide. Cleanse our society. Sweep them away. Do not let sentiment affect your judgement. We are the guardians of the Party. Let the words of our founder Dzerzhinskii be your guide. "A good Chekist has a clear head, clean hands and a warm heart."

They sat looking at her in awe and a timorous hand went up. A young girl in her late teens, with short blonde hair. Looking at her Natasha felt a wave of almost maternal feeling sweep over her.

'Yes?'

'What do we do if we cannot find proof of guilt? But if we suspect someone of treachery?'

She smiled affectionately at the girl. 'That's a very good question. What is your name, Comrade?'

'Olga Konstantinovna, Comrade.'

'Do you love our Party? Do you love our leader, Comrade Stalin?'

'When I am unsure,' Olga Konstantinovna said, 'I think of the Party, and am sure. When I am tired I think of our *khosiain* Stalin and I am refreshed.'

'Would you do anything to keep them safe?'

'If my grandmother said bad things about them I would denounce her to the proper authority,' Olga said proudly.

Natasha smiled approvingly. 'You are a fine person, a New person. Never forget the words of Lenin. "A good communist is a good Chekist." Well, Olga, some spies hide themselves well. They may seem honest citizens, may actually *be* Party members. They could even be among our own numbers. Yes, they might even be Chekists. We have to fall back upon proof of guilt and for that, we need a confession. How do you obtain a confession? That, my fellow-Chekists, is the subject of our lesson tomorrow morning.'

Olga Konstantinovna looked up at her in adoration.

The four men stood in the dark outside the tank factory, their coat collars turned up against the wind.

'Ready?' asked Piotr Sadovsky.

'Yes, switch it on,' said Khrushchev.

Standing on the platform of the modified searchlight, Sadovsky threw the switch. Electricity poured through the heavy cables, arcing in front of the giant mirror, and light stabbed upwards to the racing clouds above.

A gigantic Stalin leered down at them and they all stared up at him in horror. His entire visage wobbled grotesquely as the clouds whipped by.

'Turn the fucking thing off!' Krivitskiy snarled, and the light suddenly snapped out.

'You see what I mean?' said Sadovsky, stepping down from the control platform.

'I think we do,' Akulov agreed.

'Let's go inside,' Sadovsky said. In his office the lamps were lit.

'I saw an American film with some funny men once,' said Akulov. 'They were in a . . . a fun fair. There were amusing mirrors that made them different. It was like that.'

'That – Krivitskiy pointed savagely to the window. 'That is a free trip to the camps. *Smert shpionam.*'

'Ivan's right,' said Sadovsky calmly. 'Using the irregular horizontal surface of the clouds as a screen on which to project a picture will work like a distorting mirror. We need a flat surface, preferably vertical. I'm going to try a tethered dirigible.'

'Why should that be a free trip to the camps, Commissar?' Akulov asked softly. 'Didn't we fight the war at such cost to put an end to all that? Didn't we defeat both the Nazis and the terror? Weren't we fighting for a better Soviet Union, too?'

'No,' Krivitskiy said shortly. He took off his steel-rimmed glasses and began to polish them.

'My soldiers thought that they did,' Akulov said harshly.

'Then they'll soon find out that they were wrong,' Krivitskiy shouted. 'Just like your son!'

Khrushchev watched the two closely.

'Alexei? And his comrades? Yes, they're in the camps. But that was Rykov. My fault, my fault . . . I'd forgotten the little bastard was so short. Most of the blast went over his head.'

Khrushchev looked at Akulov in horror, while Krivitskiy actually grinned. Sadovsky was drawing a plan on a sheet of paper, not looking up at any of them.

'*You* blew up Rykov?' said Khrushchev.

'I did,' Akulov said coldly. 'He killed my daughter. I'm only sorry I didn't do a better job. I maimed him and he trapped my son. Who is in the Gulag.'

'He'd have been there anyway,' Krivitskiy said, sombre again. 'Didn't your lot meet the Americans on the Elbe?'

'Yes.'

'Contact with the West is contact with plague,' Krivitskiy said succinctly. 'The camps are quarantine.'

'No new world?'

'Those who have served their time and released are to be rearrested,' said the secret policeman. 'They're still guilty, you see. Maximum sentence is increased from ten to twenty-five years. A new category of camp to be introduced. "Strict regime". No blankets, and chains. And there are . . . other things. Things you don't need to know about.'

'What's happened?'

'He wasn't right in the head before the war, but he is worse now,' Khrushchev said softly. 'Sickly suspicious, enemies everywhere.'

Akulov looked directly at Krivitskiy. The room was quiet except for the rubbing of Sadovsky's pencil.

'Can you get my boy out? Him and his two comrades?'

'It's no use,' said Khrushchev. 'I already asked. I have two uncles, an aunt and several cousins there. *I* can't get them out, either.'

'He does the same to his own,' Krivitskiy said unexpectedly. 'He's had his own taken away too. And shot.'

'My daughter Gaia is there somewhere,' Sadovsky said quietly from his desk, still without looking up, his pencil trapped carefully between the side of his palm and thumb. 'But nobody will tell me where.'

'I've told you, Piotr Pavlovich,' said Krivitskiy, almost kindly. 'Don't go making trouble. It doesn't do. Beria beat Kalinin's wife unconscious when he was told to, and sent her to the camps. He told Kalinin about it over dinner at the Boss's place, because Kalinin was worried, didn't know where she was, she hadn't come home. Kalinin's head of State, for what it's worth, and Poskrebyshev's wife is up there, too. She'll be shot. *He* has only been the Boss's secretary the past twenty years. It's no good, any of you. Let's stick to ways of sticking the Boss's face on to clouds, or barrage balloons. It's safer.'

He got up to go.

'You could do something for me,' Akulov suggested quietly. 'Rykov got at my boy through a comrade. A little runt called Iosif Wolff. Rykov won't have much use for him now. He's a Jew and Rykov doesn't like Jews.'

'*I'm* a Jew.'

'We're all things we pretend not to be. I'm a Ukrainian pretending to be a Russian. Piotr Pavlovich is a former person pretending to be a Bolshevik. Nikita Sergeyvich goes about pretending to be a peasant. I haven't seen you down the Synagogue lately. So send this Iosif Wolff up to the camp as a guard for me. Somewhere up where my son and his comrades can see him.'

Krivitskiy gave a rare smile. 'Next time, remember that Rykov's small. Smaller, now you took half his scalp off.'

'You can rely on it,' Akulov said.

Krivitskiy turned at the head of the stairs. 'Your wife,' he said to Akulov. 'She was friends with Ruth Gunzberg. Tell her Ruth's in England.'

'England?' Akulov repeated, astonished.

'She walked across the zone at night. Tough bitch.'

Krivitskiy went down the stairs, followed by Khrushchev, and they heard the sound of their Chaikas driving away.

'Want a lift, Piotr Pavlovich?'

'I'm not going anywhere. Ivan Ivanovich,' Sadovsky said quietly. 'I live right here. There, that should work.'

'Here?' Akulov looked about the spare office.

'There isn't any point, going anywhere else. No reason. Nothing. Nobody.'

'You keep any vodka here?'

'Vodka? Of course. Fire extinguisher. I use it against my dreams.'

'Come on. I'll split one with you before I go. You know, in Stalingrad we drank aircraft coolant. Filtered it through gas masks.'

Sadovsky poured two shotglasses, and finally looked up. 'It isn't easy, is it, Ivan Ivanovich. Having to talk to them. I danced the *stoika* for Krivitskiy and he put Anna into the *parilka*. Now he calls me up, and has me design new icons of worship.'

He tossed back the glass and refilled it with watering eyes. 'We wouldn't have let Krivitskiy into the club, in the old days.'

'No,' said Akulov.

'Not the right sort.'

'No,' said Akulov. 'Not the right sort.'

The students crowded into the small room and settled themselves on the wooden chairs with the same prickle of excitement that trainee doctors felt arriving for the first time in an operating theatre, or would-be lawyers coming into court. They were secret police, and this was a holy place.

It was a torture chamber.

A heavy curtain was drawn across an alcove at the other end of the room. Large arc lamps stood, unlit, pointing its way. The door opened and an MVD officer came in. He walked through them with a curious, shuffling gait, and put his green hat down on a table where a few innocuous tools such as a plumber might use lay.

'Good morning,' he said. 'I am Captain Petrovskiy. Andrey Petrovskiy. I'm here to give you a lesson about the art of extracting a confession.'

In the front row, Olga Konstantinovna, dressed in a fitted blue skirt and crisply-ironed white shirt with red tie felt a pang of disappointment. She put up her hand.

'Please, Captain Petrovskiy, where is Comrade Savinkova? She told us yesterday that she would be giving this section of the course.'

Petrovskiy smiled pleasantly. 'That's right; she'll be taking part soon. I'm going to give you the introduction.'

Satisfied, Olga sat back again in her chair.

'I know a great deal about interrogation,' Andrey Petrovskiy said. His face had become sombre and he looked over each of them in turn. 'I really mean that. I know more than you would believe.'

He raised one leg from the ground, and slipped off his shoe and sock. His pale foot ended in a purple mass of scarring. There were no toes. He put his covering back on.

'I lost them in Kolyma,' he said. 'That's why I walk in a funny way.'

'Were you a guard. Captain Petrovskiy?'

'No,' he said. 'I was a prisoner.'

They looked at him, completely bewidered.

'Want to know why? I'll tell you. About eight years ago I was an officer of the NKVD, working here in this very building. It was a time of great activity, when we unearthed many, many spies of the Western powers. It is always possible, of course, that in such times an innocent man, a good and faithful Party man might be swept up by accident, along with the filth. It was, of course, my duty to see that if such a thing happened that justice should triumph, and that he be returned to his duties unharmed.'

They all nodded solemnly, sternly, approvingly.

'I came across one such case. An army officer of high rank. My doubts were raised because together with a colleague – one I thought was a colleague – I interrogated the officer over a period of weeks, and was unable to obtain a confession. He firmly maintained his innocence and he had a fine record so I became convinced he was innocent, and suggested this to a superior in the Party.'

His gaze swept over the spellbound teenagers.

'That very afternoon I myself was arrested.'

They gasped, all of them.

'I was charged with being a British spy and interrogated. Knowing myself to be an incorruptible servant of the Party, I maintained my innocence.'

Fierce indignation began to burn in Olga Konstantinovna's shapely chest. It was monstrous!

'It was my own colleague who had denouced me. My fellow officer who tore out my toenails, and, when I stoutly proclaimed my innocence, crushed each of my toes with pliers, one after the other.'

Olga silently beat a fist on her knee.

'In the end, unbroken, I was shipped out as a criminal to Kolyma. There I lost my pulped toes in the frost. But – ' Petrovskiy held up a clenched party hand in the air. 'But, I was still an officer of the NKVD in my heart, still a devoted servant of the Party. The Fascist Hitlerites invaded, and the Party had need of me. During the war I worked for SMERSH, *Smert' Shpionam* – Death to Spies. When the war was over, I was able to return to my case. I had been right: the army officer we had interrogated had been innocent. He was cleared of all charges and returned to active duty to fight the Germans and he became a general. So, what of my colleague who had so falsely denounced me?'

'It must have been he who was a spy, not you!' Olga shouted excitedly, and there was a rumble of agreement.

'You're right,' said Andrey Petrovskiy. 'But I had to have a last piece of evidence before I could, in my own turn, interrogate my former colleague and obtain a confession. And just a few days ago, I found it.' He turned, and gestured towards the curtain. 'Behind there is the culprit. In a moment we shall begin the interrogation.'

They glared furiously at the curtain, rage in their hearts.

'What did I find?' Petrovskiy asked. 'I found that my colleague had a brother and that the brother had been arrested for helping with the escape of a spy.'

He spread his hands with a smile. 'Well, it isn't that easy, you know, spiriting a spy away to the West from under our noses. No, you need help.'

He leaned forward towards them, and they to him. 'We have to find out how it was done,' he whispered.

He went to the curtain and whisked it away. There, secured with heavy leather straps to a strong wooden chair, was Natasha Savinkova. She was gagged and her eyes bulged in terror. She was completely naked except for her Order of Lenin. It had been pinned through her breast . . .

'Here is the traitor,' said Andrey. He picked up a pair of pliers. 'Shall we start?' he suggested.

A wild hatred that she had never conceived of burst from Olga Konstantinovna's heart, and she leaped to her feet.

'Let me!' she cried. She dragged the gag from Natasha's mouth and knelt down by her feet as she wailed.

'You fucking heap of refuse!' she screamed. Flecks of spittle covered the naked feet in front of her and she took a toe between the pincers of the pliers and squeezed as hard she could. Blood spattered up as she crushed it again and again.

'*Talk, you pile of cockroach shit!*'

They had real coffee in the commissary. Captain Petrovskiy bought her a cup and sat with her as she drank it. Her colleagues sat nearby, looking at her in covert admiration. Her white shirt was stained and splashed with the blood of the traitor. She never washed it, but kept it sacred, a talisman from her first confession . . .

Kolyma, October 1946

'Savinkova? You're Savinkova?'

Natasha looked up from the shirt she was ironing. A woman prisoner she did not know had come into the laundry room.

'Yes?' she said coldly. She still had friends. While they, that criminal horde she despised were driven out into the black frost to saw and axe and log, it had been arranged that she should work in the warmth of the laundry. She did not know who had done it, but it was a sign. Someone up there knew that she was still one of them. She only had to wait.

'A delegation has come to see you,' the woman said timidly. 'From Comrade Stalin.'

Triumph exploded inside her. She tossed the flat iron on to the board in contempt. It slid off and fell to the floor, but she left it.

'See?' she cried, to no one in particular. 'See? He has come to my rescue. I served him and he has come to see that justice is done.'

The other women looked at her silently, and then began to go on with their work.

'Don't just stand there, you miserable heap of shit!' she snapped. 'Take me to them.'

'Yes, of course,' the woman murmured. She turned, and led the way. Natasha Savinkova followed her, limping. As always, her feet sent stabbing reminders of what had happened to them.

'Oh, how I'll make them pay now!' she howled victoriously.

They went out and towards the better-made brick buildings of the administration. The woman opened a door and they went in.

'We'll cut through here.'

They went down the corridor and through another set of doors. The outside air was freezing and the heat, the smell of burning coal came like a blow. Piles of coal stood all about and some filthy women were feeding it into a furnace that fed the boiler of the administration's hot water system.

'What the fuck is this?' Natasha snarled. 'Where's the delegation from Stalin?'

'We're here, Savinkova . . .'

She whirled. Women were all around her.

'We're here,' one said, and they all growled in agreement. 'Stalin sent *all* of us here.'

'Let me out of here!' she said, suddenly terrified, and they all smiled.

'Don't you know us?' they cried.

'No!' she shouted, and they grinned even more. Their hands grasped her, led her to a long plank of wood they had found.

'Oh, but you do,' they assured her. 'You do. We're all old friends.'

They nailed her to the plank and stood it up against a pile of coal.

'You know me,' said one. 'You tortured me and made my husband watch.'

She had a piece of broken ripsaw blade with a chunk of a branch as a handle, and she hacked off the fingers and the thumb of Natasha's left hand and tossed them into the furnace and all the time Natasha screamed.

'You know me,' said another. 'You laughed when I begged you to let my son go. He died on the train . . . he was three.'

She did the same for Natasha's other hand. The walls were thick, the furnace roaring. Her screams were not loud, in comparison.

'You know me. You said I could keep my baby as long as I could produce milk. It wasn't long,' said a third.

She had a knife made out of the metal of a tin, sharpened on a stone, and she sliced off both Natasha's breasts.

They helped a woman across the littered floor.

'You know me,' she said. 'You beat me until I was blind.'

She reached up to Natasha's face, with hands like claws.

There was one more.

'You know me,' she said. 'I was pregnant and you kicked me until I lost my child.'

She buried the tin knife up between Natasha's thighs, as far as it would go.

When all was done, they picked up the plank, and fed it slowly into the furnace.

Pechora River, October 1948

Two hundred feet below ground, Sergei's ears were very cold. All of him was cold, for the hole in which he worked, from which he hacked frozen coal, was frozen. It was always frozen down there. Up above, in the summer, the surface of the Urals softened and produced a miserable flowering of lichen and moss, but down in the mine it was frozen.

It wasn't summer now. Up above the *khanovey*, the king of winds, was starting to blow. It cut through the rags the *zek* miners wrapped themselves in like a scimitar. Those born in the warm south it killed in weeks.

Sergei's ears were cold and he resented it. His head was cold too, for most of his hair had fallen out, along with his teeth. He resented that, too. He was a man who had always enjoyed the use of a warm hat or cap.

Iosif Wolff had a hat. It was made of lambskin with the wool on the inside, roomy, to fit over the entire skull down to the nape of the neck, and with large woolly ear-flaps that could be tied down over one's cold ears. Wolff had knee-high boots lined with dog fur, fur gloves and a *telogreiki* padded jacket that kept out the *khanovey*. Sergei knew this, for Wolff was at pains to tell him so. So warm was Wolff's clothing, in fact, that he had hung his jacket up on a peg as he watched the *zeks* slowly dragging the coal from the face in their trucks. Sergei coughed in the freezing damp and grimaced, spitting dirty phlegm on to the ground. It was tinged with blood.

The hooter brayed dismally down the shafts, and he hefted his pick, trudging up to where Wolff stood with his warmly-booted feet apart by the main lift. Two enormous tree trunks from the lumber camp to the south propped the entrance, and he stood in front of one.

The coal was so cold it took a special swing of the pick to break it up. You had to put all your body behind it. Sergei had his pick up on his shoulder and both hands were required.

Wolff took no more notice of him than of any of the others, although he had known him once. They all looked the same, coal-encrusted wrecks of men, one no different from the next. Sergei swung his great hewing helve with all his strength.

It did not make the hard crunch it did when it struck coal; it was more the sound of something smacking through a sack of wet sand, a gritty sound and a wooden thud like an axe as the pick bit through Wolff's stomach and into the tree trunk behind, transfixing him like a moth on cork.

Wolff could no more than gargle hoarsely as Sergei took the fine wool hat off his head. Then Sergei quickly stripped Wolff of his warm boots and trousers before they could become bloodstained. Wolff's bulging eyes looked at him in horrified disbelief. He began to gurgle noisily, blood spilling out of his mouth, congealing as it ran over his naked chest. Sergei put on the padded jacket and, picking up the PPSh sub-machine gun, found that he had no more use for Wolff.

Men were coming down the shafts. There was Alexei, a bloody spade in his hand, and Colonel Karpov, tugging on a guard's padded jacket like the one Sergei wore. Nikolai Savinkov was there, the plaited cloth rope he had used to strangle his guard a noose in his hand.

They slapped Wolff on his bare head as they climbed into the lift, and left him dying, down there in the darkness. They stood at the front of the great platform as it rose to the surface and the latticed gates clattered back as they rushed the idly waiting guards, hacking at their heads with their shovels – they did not want to damage the warm clothes.

They marched in to the camp as they always did. At the first checkpoint, Samsonov was waiting. They halted and dropped some lumps of coal, gleaned from the mine, as they always did. Most for the guards, a little for the *zeks*, for the stoves. Samsonov bent to gather it up as the column moved in and Alexei, in the rear file, decapitated him with one stroke of his shovel. They were all delighted with that; it was good to see Samsonov shorter by a head, leaking his life's blood into the snow.

Sergei had gone ahead and was climbing the ladder into the watchtower. The bored guard hardly looked round and Sergei opened him up from ear to ear with the jack knife he had found in Wolff's pocket. There was a fixed heavy DSHk machine gun there and he took out the three other towers with it in swift bursts of fire. When the guards came running out of their quarters, the *zeks* had manned the other guns. They massacred them out on the parade square, and then hunted the few survivors down.

When they were done, Alexei, Sergei and Nikolai had a bath. The guards had had a steam bath, all of their own. They sat in the wonderful hot, humid air, and watched the sweat run black out of their very skin. Alexei had found a bottle of vodka, and they drank, from steamy glasses.

'We'll go and liberate the logging camp,' said Alexei. 'Then march to Kotlas. There's an airfield there. And a railway that goes all the way to Moscow.'

'We want to go to Moscow?' asked Sergei.

'Of course. We must split up, to give us the best chance. I'll go by air and you take the train. Sergei. What about you, Nikky?'

'I'll walk. I'm a partisan and I'm good at walking. What shall I do when I get to Moscow, Alexei?'

Alexei got up and tossed a bucket of water on to the red hot coals. A fresh blast of steam enveloped them and from within the fog they heard his voice.

'Well, if I haven't done it, Sergei must when he arrives. And if he doesn't, then when you get there, you do it.'

They heard a cork pop as Alexei opened a new bottle.

'Do what?'

'Why, kill Stalin, of course.'

Nikolai had killed the commandant of the logging camp very carefully, slipping up behind him silently as he stared in horror from his bedroom at the attacking soldiers. He had slit his throat and as the commandant died, Nikolai had examined the nails, and been pleased to find them, as he had hoped, long and polished, those of a cared for man. Using a scalpel he had taken from the infirmary, he began to cut them away from the dying man's fingertips.

While Alexei and Sergei scoured the camp for provisions and fighting supplies, Nikolai took a razor and soap from the commandant's bathroom. In his wardrobe he found a thick raincoat, trousers, shoes and shoe-polish. He put these, together with notebook and pen, matches and tobacco, a black-stemmed pipe and a geologist's hammer into a rucksack, together with some shirts, socks and fresh underwear.

In the infirmary he found a pair of tortoiseshell glasses in a case, and these he took as well, together with as much money as he could find. Then he went and had a bath, a long one, in water scented with bath salts. Then, very carefully, he began to glue the commandant's well-tended nails over the stumps of his own, ruined in the mines.

When the soldiers left the camp, heavily-armed, he was already on his way. He travelled away from the sea, towards Yakutsk, going along the deer paths and horse tracks.

When he came to the settlement he paused to open his rucksack, and then entered the police post. The rural policeman inside looked up, and then rose in respect.

Nikolai peered over his glasses at him amiably, and continued stuffing his pipe with tobacco.

'Yanovsky,' he murmured, in cultured tones. 'Professor Yanovsky from the Academy of Sciences in Moscow. I have been sent on important – secret – work. I am a geologist and I shall require your help in recruiting a few workers to dig some trenches for me . . .'

'Of course, Comrade Professor . . .' the policeman said eagerly. He fumbled in his pocket for matches, and held them out. They went outside, and Nikolai lit his pipe, sending precious fragrance into the air.

From the distance came the faint sound of a storm brewing. The policeman took no notice. Nikolai knew that it was the sound of gunfire and he smiled pleasantly, smoothed his barbered chin with a polished nail and gestured with his pipe stem for the man to lead on.

Alexei and Sergei were on point, the bare mountains behind them. They slipped through the lumber with those who had worked it coming behind. The logging camp was occupied only by the corpses of those who had run it, guards and *urkas*. They were only military, those who marched down towards the town. They had as many guns as they could find and axes, bayonets, Molotov cocktails and sticks of blasting gelignite. Alexei also had a full canteen of vodka at his hip.

'It's no good thinking you can just hang around Red Square with your tommy-gun and blaze away at him when he comes in for work,' said Alexei. 'You have to know where he's going to be, and that takes intelligence. Also the right weapon. Nikolai always liked a bomb. He got General Schmidt that way; put a bomb in his bed. He was with his mistress at the time and he probably thought that he was the world's greatest lover for a second.'

Wintry smiles cracked their faces. They emerged from the trees and began crossing a tract that had been cleared.

'Your papa is a general,' Sergei suggested. 'He could get intelligence. He thinks the same way as we do. And we need someone to stand up when its done, just someone to say it doesn't fucking well work, it hasn't worked from the moment Lenin started calling people comrade, and we want another way. If all the people got on to the streets and demanded it, all the NKVD men in the world couldn't stop it.'

'That's right . . . what's that, Sergei?'

There was a faint buzzing in the air.

'PO-2!' Sergei snapped. The sound, like a demented coffee-grinder was unmistakable.

'Take cover!' Alexei yelled. They were out in the open, and behind them men sought ridges and holes where tree stumps had been. Sergei heard the revving of the truck engines, saw Alexei bumping back towards the tree line.

Then the light bomber was overhead. Peeping up from behind twisted roots Sergei could see the pilot circling round, the little biplane clear against the grey sky, saw him talking on the radio. He hung about, out of range, and soon they heard the deep drone of big radial engines. The PO-2 came back at about fifteen hundred feet, flying across their line, and dropped a stick of bombs. Sergei heard them thud into the ground, the pop and hiss as they went off. Yellow smoke began to drift across their position.

Three Lisuvonov Li-2 transports came over and white parachutes blossomed in a line a mile away. They saw the small, dark shapes of the paratroopers moving, darting about. Detached parachutes drifted across the devastated ground, some for men, and large ones, for the supply canisters. Behind them they could hear the bark of Colonel Karpov deploying his forces, and the grumble of the Studebaker engines as the trucks moved into fire support positions.

'So what are they waiting for?' muttered Sergei.

Alexei cocked an ear. The grinding of the observation biplane was still evident.

'I'd say they were waiting for aircraft.'

Sergei was watching the treeline. He saw the puffs of smoke and the mortar shells went shush-shush-shush as they came down.

'*Forward*!' he bellowed, for you had to advance into mortar fire, it was axiomatic. You ran away, it pursued you, and blew you apart. The line came up off the ground, five hundred starved men who knew how to fight.

Alexei stayed where he was and Sergei thought he must have known what was coming. He heard the heavy drumming of the DSHks opening up, and the cracking of whips about his ears. The first Shturmovik came over his head with a howl, its cannon like ripping canvas. Mud, flesh and bone flew in the air and grit coated his teeth as he ran forward. He moved in bursts from hole to hole, trying to co-ordinate his rushes with the wheeling Shturmoviks, who were laying heavy fire down in the killing ground, the pilots coming over low, walking the rudders left and right.

Smoke was drifting across the battlefield and it was difficult to see, hard to hear what was happening against the background of the noise, the crackle of the small arms, the crump of the mortars and the whining of the aircraft engines. The fog suddenly glowed orange as one of the Studebakers went up. He had a feeling that Alexei was moving to his left. He heard the bark of command ahead of him, heard the thump of a mortar. He pulled a stick of gelignite from his tunic and lit it with his cigar. The commandant had had a fine supply and he had helped himself.

It went off with a crump that left him dazed. Bits of flesh rained down on him and pushed himself forward and went through the smoking crater. Some bastard was firing at him and something smacked into his side. He fired back until the sub-machine gun was quiet, and the noise stopped. He bumped into a tree.

It was quiet in there; the noise of the guns and the crying of the dying faded away as he went forward.

The Studebaker was burning and the pain of his scorching flesh brought him to. There was no noise of battle, but he could hear voices. Alexei pushed himself up and away from the crackling truck. Peering underneath he could see an NKVD officer, hands on hips surveying the scene from amidst some underlings.

Alexei could taste blood in his throat. The smoke had cleared and he could see the dead all over the rough ground. He twisted open his canteen of vodka, and took a huge pull at the liquor, feeling it fiery and wonderful in his throat. He had a stick of gelignite and he got to his feet in pain, and lit its fuse from the burning truck.

He stuffed it inside his tunic, and staggered around the front of the blazing vehicle. The fuse burned him as it hissed down.

He held his hands high and the look of alarm on the NKVD men's faces as they saw him vanished in a twinkling. Just one surviving, shuffling slave. They would prove their superiority to him by shooting him themselves.

He walked right into them, and wrapped his arms tight about the officer . . .

Sergei came down the railway line, the one that brought the coal down from Vorkuta, the coal he had dug, on the line the *zeks* had built, and that was where they found him. Border troops they were, heavily-armed. Down the line in the town he could see a train waiting.

They laughed to see him coming, bloody and staggering.

'Where might you be going?' the sergeant asked mockingly.

'To Moscow,' he said, surprised that they should have to ask.

'And what business have you there?'

'I'm going to kill Stalin, of course,' he said. 'He's responsible for it all.'

'Of course,' the sergeant said gravely. It was best to be polite, when dealing with madmen. 'Then I mustn't hold you up.'

He went through their ranks. Steam was drifting about the locomotive wheels.

He didn't hear the bang: the sleeper just came up and hit him. Fresh blood bubbled in his mouth.

The locomotive whistle wailed down the track.

'Wait,' Sergei whispered. 'Wait for me . . .'

30

Spasitel Mira

London, November 1948

THE strange woman was there again, sitting outside his delapidated old church in the cold. It would soon be dark, but it was the winter. He did not have to prepare for evensong until after tea, so he pulled on a coat over his cassock and went outside.

'May I sit down?' he asked politely.

He spoke in Russian, and she replied in the same way.

'It is your bench, Father,' she said mildly. 'You do not need my permission to sit on it.'

'You are wearing your medals today, I see.'

'They gave me a new one today,' she said. She pointed at the high wall across the road, where the bulk of the palace was just visible through the trees. 'The King gave it to me.'

'Which one?'

'This one,' she said, pointing.

'Won't you come in? I have seen you sitting outside before. My church is not in very good repair, I'm afraid, but you are welcome.'

'No, thank you.'

'What is your name? I am Father Vladimir and I came here after the civil war. I have been here ever since.'

'I am Ruth, Ruth de Gunzberg. I live in Bayswater, but I come and sit here sometimes, as you have noticed.'

'Won't you come to one of our services?'

'Oh, no. I couldn't,' she protested.

'Why not?'

'My friend Yelena says that when the people are there, in His house, that is when God comes. I am afraid to meet God. That is why I come to His house when He isn't about.'

'Why are you afraid?' he asked gently.

She reached into her handbag and took out a packet of cigarettes. 'Do you smoke? No? I must give up.'

She lit the cigarette, and blew smoke as the number six bus growled by.

'Why are you afraid?'

'Because of all the things I have done . . . And not done . . . I watched as they put them on the train, and drove away. That's why I'm here and they are there. I made my daughter righteous . . . I gave up Pavel . . . they made a great chain for Ebenezer Scrooge to drag with him when he was gone. When I go I shall have one of bones and skulls . . .'

'The medals – The Croix de Guerre I see, and the new one, the George Cross, I recognise them both. These are not given to evil people.'

She lifted the little cross sadly. 'Tiny momentos. But I like them. I'm trying to set the record straight.'

'If you will not come into God's house, then He must come out to you.' He stood over her. '*Spasitel mira*, saviour of the world. We trust not in Princes, they are but mortal . . .'

She sat on the bench, and she shivered in fear . . .

Moscow, December 1948

They crowded about the priest as he said the *Milebin* and performed the service of intercession. They were nearly all women and they filled the little church, making it warm with their bodies. In the crush, with all the people packed together, Yelena felt the presence of God. It was a very simple little church, a poor affair really, no fabulous icons, mirror glass or gilt pillars, and Father Valery was a simple village priest, but that was no matter. The people had come together in a mass and, with them all together, God had come, too, and He had forgiven her sins.

Father Valery had been with the partisans, offering spiritual strength to them while the war was on. The Party had encouraged him to do so. Now the war was won he offered the same service to those in need, and one day the Party would come round and close his little clandestine church and take him away.

Yelena could not bear to think of that day, because without the comfort of God she knew she would go mad. So she stood with the women in their headscarves and let the words wash away her guilt. And when it was over she went out with them into the snow-covered streets. Some of the women went straight away to the end of one of the many queues. It would take them much of the day to collect their family ration, so it paid to start early. In the square workmen were putting up a new portrait of Stalin. Underneath was the message: 'He lives, thinks and works for us.' A light was kept on all night in the Kremlin to encourage the belief. Yelena was one of the ones who knew he stayed nearly all the time in his Kuntsevo dacha, behind twin walls within which roamed savage dogs.

The legless veteran was in the little cart he had made, where the corner of the two buildings afforded a little shelter from the icy wind. Those with jobs lived in dugouts and drained water tanks, and counted themselves lucky. The colours of his medal ribbons contrasted with his blue pallor. She had seen him in the summer, sitting in the sun, for it was free. He had a portrait of Stalin tattooed on his chest but she doubted that she would see it again. One became expert at assessing the life expectancy of one's fellows in the camps and the knack had not deserted her. She dropped a few kopeks in the trolley, and he blessed her. She crossed the road and a hissing black party limousine in the Chaika lane spattered her with slush.

Ivan was waiting for her in their apartment. Her grandson, his namesake, was at school, it was not yet time for her to collect him.

'I wasn't expecting you,' she said, and kissed him.

'The telephones weren't working. I just got on the aircraft and came.' He went into the kitchen and came out with mugs of tea. 'Were you at the church?' he asked.

She nodded. 'You know, if only everybody came out and filled the streets with their masses then God would come too. His power would make the Kremlin walls fall, He would lead us out of this dark valley.'

'Yes,' said Akulov. 'But the MGB and the MVD would come too. They would machine-gun the people.'

'God is more powerful than they,' she muttered.

'My darling,' Akulov said quietly, 'I think the time has come for you to die.'

She looked sharply at him. They had discussed this and she knew what he meant.

'If we are to go, then we should both go. I do not want to live without you, Ivan.'

'I cannot be hidden,' he said evenly. 'I am a general. But you could be.'

She shook her head abruptly. 'No! I shall not do it.'

'For little Ivan Nikolayevich you must. If they come for us they will take him, too. They will put him in a children's *kombinat*. Some terrible prison like Akmolinsk or Ashkhabad, and, even if he lives, we shall never see him again. But you and he, you could be hidden.'

'But why now, Ivan?'

'I fear Rykov.'

'Rykov took Alexei from us, but he has not been able to attack us ourselves. You are powerful enough to protect us,' she protested.

'I still fear Rykov,' he said, stubbornly.

She looked up then. 'What has happened?' she asked steadily.

'I get letters . . . from men I served with. They still fold them up in triangles, without envelopes, as they did in the war. I got another, from someone else. It gave an address in Kirov and I was able to go there, not in uniform, I found Nikolai.'

'Nikolai is in the Gulag!' she whispered.

'He escaped. He walked out.'

'But how did he escape from the mines?' Fear was sweeping through her, making it difficult to speak.

'There was a revolt,' Ivan said quietly. 'The *zeks* rose up and killed their guards. Alexei, Sergei and Nikolai led them. But Nikolai chose to walk out. He dressed as a geologist and it took him two months, but he got to Kirov. The others marched on Kotlas and paratroopers and dive-bombers were sent against them. They died in a pitched battle.'

'Alexei Mikhailovich has died,' she said with certainty.

'He blew up a group of MGB men with dynamite.'

She closed her eyes. 'It is I, I who killed him,' she whispered, and he shook his head.

'Rykov will come at us. I am certain of it,' Ivan said.

'How are we to hide, little Ivan Nikolayevich and I?' she said sadly.

'With Nikolai, I think. Then little Ivan will be with his father, which is good.'

'You cannot arrange this,' she protested.

'No. One must have a man with real power, someone like Krivitskiy.'

She shuddered. 'Going to the Cheka for help is like asking for a death warrant.'

'Not necessarily,' he said. 'Krivitskiy might need me, too.'

She got up, looking blindly out of the window. Workmen were putting up a new slogan under another portrait of the man. '"There is nothing more precious in the world than man himself."'

'There must be a priest,' she said. 'Wherever it is, if there is a priest there will be the people, and *then* there will be God.'

Staritsa Woods

Akulov took the rifle from its case and slung it over his shoulder. Fresh snow had fallen from the pines lining the track on to the bonnet of the Chaika, and it was melting. The sprawl and dirty air of Moscow was eighty kilometres away and he was deep in the country.

Warmly clad, he went along the path, his boots crunching on the snow. He could smell woodsmoke on the air, and through the trees he saw a small, traditional wooden hunting lodge in a clearing. Poles ran alongside the path carrying cable and it was equipped with electricity and a telephone. Those who used it were men of influence – they needed both comfort and communications when enjoying rural pleasures.

He climbed up on to the verandah that ran along the front of the little house, stamping his boots to rid them of snow, and went inside. Standing in front of a log fire was Krivitskiy.

'I need a favour,' Akulov said. 'I need to make three people disappear.'

Krivitskiy smiled thinly. 'I have made a lot of people disappear in my time. Is that what you mean?'

'I have made plenty vanish as well,' Akulov said brutally. 'Soaked up without trace in bloody mud and sand from here to Berlin. But that is not what I mean. I want them hidden, alive and well.'

'Who?'

'My wife Yelena, my grandson Ivan and his father, Nikolai.'

'Why?'

'I have a particular enemy, Rykov.'

Krivitskiy turned to look into the fire. 'I know about Rykov. But what does he have to do with me?'

'Rykov is going to be your boss, one day soon. Maybe not this year, maybe not next. But one day. The Boss is going to kill Beria, because he kills all his chiefs of the Cheka, in the end. And then it will be Rykov.'

'Why Rykov?'

'Because the Boss needs him for what he can do. The Boss needs it. It is building up, the drumming in his head, that can only be purged by blood. A lot of blood. More than before. Not yet. Not next year. But soon.'

Akulov picked up his rifle, and slung it back over his shoulder. 'But I am a soldier,' he said. 'I cannot, it is known, deal in political affairs.'

He went outside on to the wooden verandah and Krivitskiy
followed him. As they stood on the other side of the clearing a
big buck came out of the trees and stood looking at them. Akulov
clapped his hands, and the beast bounded back among the trees.

'Why didn't you shoot?' Krivitskiy enquired.

'My profession is killing men, not animals,' said Akulov.

He went back down the path. The melted snow had frozen in
glassy rivulets on the bonnet of the black Chaika, just as it had on
the one that had drawn up beside it. A man got out as Akulov came
trudging through the snow, a small, stocky figure in a big coat. It was
Khrushchev.

'He's waiting for you,' said Akulov.

Moscow

As the black Chaika turned the corner into Bolshaya Lubyanka, the
artificial rubber tyres squealed. The noise sliced into Rykov's head
and the turning of the car as it went around the square to stop outside
Number Two increased the dizziness he had been feeling since he got
up. The affliction had bothered him for some time now. He had put it
down to the injuries caused by the bomb, but it seemed to be getting
worse, not better. He had tried to concentrate on his work, had even
taken time to go down to the interrogation rooms and assist with the
procuring of confessions from the constant stream of traitors spying
for the West, and sometimes he had found this to help. But the pain
in his head was always there, sometimes a dull ache, sometimes a
searing band of iron. He had thought of getting Western analgesic
tablets, but had rejected the idea as being too dangerous. A man had
many enemies, known and unknown. Kaledin, for instance. The man
had used his position to obtain advanced medicines from the West
for his sick daughter. Well, where was Kaledin now? In the Gulag,
was where, wearing a KRD number and sentenced under Article 58,
convicted of infection with decadent bourgeois Western values.

He certainly wasn't going to fall into the same trap. But the pain
remained. He became aware that the door of the limousine was open
and that his driver was waiting, looking at him, strangely, he felt. The
man smiled when he saw his boss move, and helped him from the car.

Rykov noted the attention. He, too, thinks I'm weak, he thought. He decided to have the man investigated.

The dizziness was bad as he went inside the Lubyanka and he had to hold on to the banister as he slowly climbed the stairs. Outside his office he heard a hurried rattle of a desk drawer closing. He knew it was his secretary hiding the picture of her family that she had: the picture she took out and looked at when he wasn't there. A wave of hatred for them all swept over him. He found being about them intolerable. Their presence was pain. In the street he saw them, stolid, patient, waiting in queues, heard the short, understood jokes, always about the system, heard the matching, understood chuckle. He hated them. It wasn't the way it should be.

He pushed open the door to his office and stepped in. As he did so the blood drummed inside his head and the room began to rotate about him. With a strange, snarling cry he fell to the floor.

When he awoke he was in a quiet, white-painted room, lying in bed. A man in a white coat was sitting in a chair watching him and he felt alarm. There was a strange taste in his mouth. He must have been drugged.

'Which prison is this?' he asked. The pain was still there, throbbing dully behind his eyes, but the dizzy nausea had gone. Now it was clear. Someone had succeeded in giving him chemicals. He had taken part in the new methods of interrogation they were developing for the psychiatric hospitals. His enemies must have given him something.

The man smiled reassuringly. It did not reassure Rykov. He, too, had smiled at people.

'I'm Doctor Feldman,' the man said. 'This is a hospital, General.'

A Jew. Jews were behind everything.

'A psychiatric hospital?' Rykov's eyes darted about the room. Fresh flowers were in a vase. That would be where the microphone would be. The orderlies would be waiting behind the door, with the syringe. Big men, to hold him down while the Jew injected him. Rykov knew how it was done.

Feldman's smile faded slightly, then became fixed. 'No, General. You were taken ill at your office and the MGB brought you here. This is an MGB hospital.'

Rykov relaxed, a little bit. 'I am free to go then.'

'Yes, but we would like to make you feel better first. Your secretary mentioned that you had been complaining of headaches, and of feeling dizzy. We have examined you and I have to say there seems to be nothing wrong with you physically. Apart from the injuries that you have received. An explosion, I take it. In the war?'

'In the war,' agreed Rykov, and his eyes looked inward.

'It is possible that the headaches and other symptoms are associated with that. Blast injuries take a long time to heal.'

'I worked very hard in the war,' Rykov said, ignoring him. 'Very, very hard. So many threats to the security of our country . . .'

'The war is over now,' Feldman said comfortingly.

It was. That was the problem.

'I think you may have overdone it. They say you came back to work as quickly as you could after the accident and it may be that you need a rest. Some sick leave.'

Rykov came out of his reverie. 'Yes,' he said. 'I'd like a holiday.'

Feldman looked relieved. 'I'll authorise it on medical grounds. A dacha at the Black Sea, perhaps.'

'I don't like hot weather. I like it colder.'

'Whatever you wish, General.'

'I have some friends in the north. They have a nice big house in the forest and I might do some hunting.'

'A good idea. Plenty of sunshine and fresh air. It will do you good.'

'Yes,' said Rykov, certainly. 'It will do me good.'

He came down the steps of the Lisunov as the big American propellers swung to a stop and a Major was waiting at the bottom to great him. The air was cold but dry; the flight had been long, but he was here. The man saluted smartly.

'Major Golubev, General,' he beamed. 'General Derevenko has asked me to make your stay as pleasant as possible so if there's anything you need, anything you want to do, just tell me and I'll arrange it.'

'Thank you,' Rykov murmured, and the ache in his head eased a little. It was good to be back in congenial company. A big truck, an American Studebaker was waiting.

'Excuse the transport, General, but you can't get about in a limousine up here.'

'Oh, don't worry about that,' Rykov said pleasantly. 'I was up here myself, you know, more than ten years ago. I ran a camp in Berelyakh.'

'I didn't know that, sir,' Golubev said respectfully.

They climbed up into the cab, where the driver was waiting. The seats were comfortable and the powerful heater easily able to combat the cold. Rykov settled back to enjoy the drive through the snow-clad trees and hills. As they drove along the road there were signs of the work going on further away from the road. Gangs of men, trucks laden with ore. The road was in good repair, he saw men attending it every other kilometre, dragging logs and stone by hand and it climbed up through the hills. As they rounded a corner he saw a strange sight, a straggling line of great poles walking up the side of the mountain. On and on they went, like sagging crosses in an old cemetery, towards the top. They seemed to have no purpose.

'What is that?' Rykov asked. Golubev signalled the driver to pull over.

'Quite an amusing story, sir. And an instructive one,' he added hastily.

'All these trucks that are passing, they're bringing the ore out of the mine up there. Output has been expanded tremendously and they're working on four levels, drilling new sections. The trucks are American – Diamond-Ts – and it was decided that it was unpatriotic to pay out dollars for their tyres and spare parts. They had a party meeting, and decided to build a funicular cablecar system to take it from the top to the bottom, flying right over the valley. They could put up the poles – there they are – they had the cars built. The only problem was the cable, the only place that makes it is in Leningrad, and they couldn't give them any for about ten years.

'Anyhow, the Party chief gets up and roars: "There are no fortresses a true Bolshevik cannot storm!" So they decide to *make* the cable. They find some cabinetmaker among the *zeks* and have him put together a big device, around which they twist the wire of the cable. In the end it was ready and they had a few thousand of the slaves carry it up the mountain and hang it from the poles. The day came when it all worked, and they sent down an empty car. It arrived at the plant at the bottom, and they sent a half-loaded one. Then a full one. Everyone was delighted, and so they had a celebration, put flags on the poles, brought in the *zek* band to play. The party committee got in a car and started off down from the top. And about *there* the cable began to snap.'

Rykov listened to Golubev with shining eyes, his mouth slightly open.

'Yes . . . go on.'

'The cablecar hung over the valley. The question was, what was to be done? Clearly, they couldn't hang up there for ever. A lot of money had been spent, so they had a quick board of inquiry. It was decided that it was plain that, since they had so dismally failed to storm their fortress, they were plainly *not* true Bolsheviks. In fact, quite the opposite: as they had wasted so much money and effort, they were clearly guilty of activities under Article 58, paragraph 14, counter-revolutionary sabotage, probably Trotskyist in nature. There was no point in spending *more* money bringing them down simply to shoot them. They thought of just leaving them up there, but then someone remembered the cabinet-maker, who was required to pay for his part in this sabotage.'

'Yes, yes?' Rykov said eagerly.

'Well, they sent him up the pole with a big hacksaw and told him to get cutting!'

A strange, hoarse gargling came from Rykov's throat. His eyes bulged, and his scarred face became suffused purple. Golubev stared at him in alarm, until he realised that the old Chekist was laughing.

After a while Rykov took a handkerchief from his coat pocket and wiped his face, and they continued on their way.

'General Derevenko is having a concert tonight, General. He has numerous artistes, you know. Many excellent performers. Clowns, dancers, musicians. He would be pleased if you would attend.'

'Delighted,' Rykov said. 'I like culture. When I ran my camp I had an orchestra. Professors of music.'

'We are passing one of the camps on our way. The slaves will be coming in soon. The old traditions have been kept up here and a band will be playing. Would you care to stop off for a few minutes?'

'Delighted,' said Rykov.

The truck turned off along a well-used track, and soon the camp came into view. Rykov eyed it expertly. Little had changed since his day. A wooden wall with corner watchtowers, surrounded by two barbed wire fences. They drove under a green-painted wooden arch, with its inscription "Labour is a matter of honour, courage and heroism" painted on it.

They pulled up by the large parade ground where, as Golubev had promised, a small orchestra of strange creatures wrapped in filthy rags were producing an uplifting tune. As he surveyed the interior of the camp, Rykov's leather-gloved cork hand beat against his knee in time. Rows of ragged tar board huts, prisoners coming in, attempting to break into a trot under the blows of their brigadiers. With an expert eye Rykov noticed the *urka* criminals in charge of the politicals, the *urka* supervisor readily distinguishable not only from his club and well-fed appearance but also by the dark, obscene tattoos that covered what was visible of his body.

'They strive to attain both the norms here?' he remarked.

'Not a bad camp, this, General,' agreed Golubev. 'I worked here myself. A high production of gold, and an excellent death rate. Not always easy to manage, that. When they die like flies you can't get enough work out of them and, of course, go easy on them, then not enough die.'

'*And* they don't produce the gold.'

'I can tell you're a *real* professional, General.'

A brigade coming in five wide through the gate caught Rykov's attention. They were actually running in step at the end of their day. He knew how hard it was to get men to move at all when they were as close to exhaustion-death as these. Their brigadier barked a command and they halted, in time, standing looking straight ahead, their chests heaving. In their eyes was fear. More than half a dozen carried the dead bodies of their comrades. The brigadier also intrigued Rykov. He was quite small and he was young, he moved well, seeming like a cat beside the staggering, faltering crew he commanded. He was warmly-dressed and he strolled casually about those he controlled and they feared him.

'Now there's another,' Rykov murmured. 'A professional. No shouting, no wasted effort. But he has them so terrified that if he tells them to cut their own throats they'll do it.'

'Steklov,' Golubev said immediately. 'An interesting customer. One of us, once. In the NKVD at the end of the war but fell foul of some internal politics, I believe, got broken and ended up here. Someone like him is pure gold, of course, and they put him to work immediately. He tops the norms all the time. Brings back gold and dead by the basket load.'

It was dark by the time they reached General Derevenko's villa. Rykov had stayed listening to the band while the prisoners shuffled by and now his headache had completely gone.

'Wonderful weather,' Rykov said jovially. The sun was shining and there was no trace of wind. Their rubber-soled felt boots crunched the snow underfoot as they walked down the path through the trees towards the carefully-camouflaged hide.

'Nice day,' said Steklov. The young brigadier assessed the ground with an expert eye. The hide had been well placed and the game would almost certainly come within range. 'Well-sited,' he approved.

'Derevenko enjoys his hunting,' commented Rykov.

He looked over the ground of the hunting preserve. The trees had been carefully thinned by logging teams and, from the hide, game driven from the thickets beyond would be visible as it ran.

Already, he could hear a dog giving out an impatient woof, eager to begin.

'What about you, Steklov?' he said casually. 'What are you doing here? You were one of us, they tell me. What did you do?'

'Well . . .'

'Don't say it was nothing,' said Rykov, smiling.

The younger man grinned. 'No, for nothing you only get ten years. It was at the end of the war in Berlin. I was working in this zone and I'd recruited this German to work with me, since he knew the local population so well. Franz, his name was, a really good sort – he'd worked for the Gestapo. And efficient? You should have seen him!'

'I worked with the Gestapo myself,' said Rykov. 'Before the war. Admirable types.'

'That's right. Anyhow, we fell foul of this bastard general, whose zone it was. A big bastard called Akulov.'

Rykov suddenly went very still. Steklov was looking over the *taiga*, and did not notice.

'He wanted Franz for war crimes. Now, if I'd known how slippery this Akulov was, I'd have handed Franz over no problem, but, frankly, I thought an NKVD captain, which I was, outranked a stupid soldier, even if he *was* a general, and I told him he could ram his war crimes up his backside. He didn't say any more, and I forgot about it until some SMERSH swine came and arrested me. I got twenty years on trumped up charges and here I am. SMERSH were the military secret police, put into terrorise the soldiers, but Akulov must have had something on the ones who came for me. He used them to get at me. They didn't mind – they were always ready for a swipe at us NKVD. Akulov got Franz and he had him shot.'

'How interesting,' Rykov murmured. 'We must talk about it a little more, later on. But I think I hear the beaters beginning.'

From the brush, in the distance, came the calling of men and the barking of dogs.

'I've put a few lads out in the middle, General,' said Steklov. 'We'll funnel the game your way.'

Rykov felt a prick of excitement in his chest as he heard the hunt getting under way. He was wearing a webbing harness over his jacket and he checked with his good hand for the pistol, lead-weighted club and sharp woodsman's axe it carried.

There! Something moving in the scrub. A strong bark as a dog picked up the scent. A loping figure coming down the hillside. It caught sight of one of Steklov's men and swerved away down the path that led past the hide. Good work, Steklov, Rykov thought approvingly.

The beast was coming. The dogs broke cover on the hillside and it looked desperately over its shoulder as the baying broke out. It would have been big, once, and it was still tall – Rykov had had Steklov pick for size. He could hear the frantic breath gasping in its diseased chest. As it came up, too late to turn, to stop, to run away, he rammed the point of his club into its abdomen, and it folded up, falling on to the snow-covered path on its face. Efficiently, measuring the blow, he cracked it across the back of the head as Steklov came running up.

'Good hunting, General,' he said admiringly. He grinned. 'Would you like it stuffed or just the head on a board?'

'Now I'll show you something we did when I was a young lad chasing escapees. Saves a lot of trouble and helps conserve the wildlife in the winter.'

He took his axe and, with two blows, severed the hands at the wrists. He held them up.

'See? Proof of capture, and you can leave the rest for the bears and wolves.'

Steklov produced a bag, and they strolled back up the path.

'That was the surgeon,' said Rykov. 'What have we next?'

'The writer. He's escaped in the wood up here.'

Rykov stayed in the new hide for some time while Steklov went off to organise the hunt. Then he saw him coming back through the woods.

'Sorry about this, General. We can't get the bastard to move. He's sitting on a tree stump.'

Konstantin looked up as Rykov came into the clearing. His chest heaved with the simple effort of dragging air into his lungs and his ragged, filthy clothes, charred from clustering about the stove, were wet. They hung stiff in the freezing air. His face was brick red from frostbite and congealed blood stuck to his skin where they had beaten him to get him to move. The young dog handlers stood about him, their wolfhounds panting. He could smell vodka on the air – it came from their breath, puffing like small clouds.

'Comfortable?' asked Rykov.

'It will do,' said Konstantin.

'Why are you here, Konstantin?'

'I am here because I cannot walk to my favourite café in Paris,' he said, and they could see that he simply did not care, any more.

'Why am I here?' he asked. 'What can such a dedicated crawler as myself, one with tongue as brown as the muddiest African river be doing here? Well, I'll tell you. I simply could not take it any more. The creative impulse will out, you know. Well no, you *don't* know. I thought it dead, after so many years, but I wrote a story. A short story.'

'We should like to hear it,' Rykov said.

'It's quite simple. A man escapes from a lunatic asylum. He spends the day going about Russia. At the end of the day he returns to the madhouse, and asks to be let back in. They ask him why, and he explains. It's insane, out there, he says. I sent it off as my entry for last year's prize.'

'You were the one who was insane,' said Rykov. 'Now, can we persuade you to your feet?'

Konstantin looked about him. 'Where are the swans?' he asked, and answered himself 'The swans have gone. But where are the ravens?' He looked at Rykov. 'The ravens have stayed. No, Rykov I will sit here.'

'You will die, if you sit there.'

'We all have to die.'

Rykov looked down at his feet. 'My boots are muddy. Come clean them for me, and I will let you live a little longer.'

'I shall sit here,' Konstantin said, his voice clear and young again.

'Feed the dogs,' Rykov said to the head handler and, as they slipped the leads, Konstantin fluttered his hands like a bird.

'Free . . .' he said.

Long shadows of trees were running across the icy ground when Rykov finally walked back through the park towards the magnificent villa of his host. Steklov was with him and the beaters followed with their dogs at a respectful distance. He was relaxed. Even the stump of his arm had stopped hurting.

In the dusk a man weaved his staggering way through the trees.

'What's that?' Rykov asked, puzzled.

'I don't know,' said Steklov. 'He looks drunk.'

They stood quietly as the man tottered towards them. His hands clutched his chest. Then they saw that he had no hands. He was pressing the stumps of his wrists against his body, to staunch the flow and his wadded coat and trousers, his shapeless cloth boots, were stained with black blood.

'It's the surgeon!' Steklov exclaimed delightedly.

Wide, mad blue eyes stared at the group of killers standing in the dusk and, with a hoarse cry, he crashed away through the undergrowth. The chief dog handler held his wolfhound by the collar.

'Sir?' he asked.

'Let the bears and wolves have a turn,' Rykov said genially. 'He's the one who operated on me. He cut me open.'

At the villa, the beaters made their way off to their quarters, while Rykov went inside with Steklov. He went to the study, where the General was at his desk, working on papers. Rykov sat down in a comfortable armchair, while Steklov stood at its side.

'Good day?' Derevenko asked affably.

'Excellent hunting. You have a marvellous preserve here.'

'I flew down to Vanino today,' Derevenko said. Found a couple of promising dancers in the new draft and they're performing tonight. Care to see if they're any good?'

'Delighted,' Rykov said politely. 'But can we sort out an administrative error first?'

Derevenko's little eyes looked warily out at Rykov from the folds of fatty skin about them. 'Yes . . .?'

'It's young Steklov here. There appears to have been a miscarriage of justice in his case.'

'There does?' Derevenko's eyes darted from one to the other.

'Yes. He's a fine young man, a devoted Chekist, a brass-hard Stalinist. While engaged in his duties in the German occupied territories he fell foul of a Red Army officer. This man brought these false charges against him.'

'You know something about this?'

'Yes,' Rykov said easily. 'His name's Akulov and I've had him under observation for some time. He's suspected of collaboration with decadent Western elements. Young Steklov has confirmed to me that his investigations in Germany uncovered this. That's why Akulov brought these false charges against him.'

'All right. You attend to it, then.'

'I will,' said Rykov. 'Indeed I will.'

It had been a wonderful day. After a fine dinner he went up to his room. It was lit by two candles, tall white tapers on each side of the bed. Steklov was waiting there, holding a young woman by the arm. She was wearing an old, stained white wedding dress, and she stared at the monster who had entered the room in terror.

'Here's the bride,' Steklov said softly.

Tbilisi, Georgia, April 1949

The church stood blond and unharmed in the warm spring sun, taking the best place in the nineteenth century square that had been built around it. Yelena came down the boulevard, past the market stalls of vegetables and fruit. From the little restaurant there came the smell of kebab.

When Krivitskiy had put them there she had thought it some strange, secret police joke, for along the road was Gori, a town with one inhabitant, and he had gone to Moscow. He was responsible for it all, Iosif Dzhugashvili, who preferred to call himself Josef.

But the point was not him, but where he came from: Georgia. The writ of the Russians did not run well there; the dark, bright Georgians thought the Russians fools and dullards, and made jokes about them that they found very funny. Such things as collectives did not work well here and, among a people devoted to trade, smuggling, sex and intrigue, the grim and boring implications of a dictatorship of the proletariat seemed ridiculous. Life, they felt, was for living. They had dutifully erected a statue of Lenin in the main square. They had heard that he strode, and declaimed, so there he was, shouting and marching into the future.

They had chickens, a garden and a tiny orchard of plum trees and olives. Ivan went to school in the old quarter, where houses on stilts walked on the edge of the dark, curving Kura river, and tin roofs filled in the gaps between old Persian courts and Tatar balconies. She took him in the morning while Nikolai Savinkov worked in the garden, and then she sat under the plane trees by the market and sold, an egg at a time, what she had brought. Sometimes a live chicken was there, and there was much haggling to be done over something of such value. She might have an onion or two, some garlic, later peppers and oily black olives. The Georgians did not believe in collective farming.

And they still believed in God.

The church was open and, her eggs sold, she went in. Father Zahari was there, attending to his crimson and gold robes in the dressing room. He nodded gravely, and she went down the long aisle. Turning along the short transept there was a door. She went in and there was a small office, with a telephone. She picked it up and dialled.

There was no reply. Over one and a half thousand kilometres to the north a telephone rang in an empty hunting lodge in the Staritsa woods. She replaced the receiver and then, picking it up, dialled again. This time it was answered quickly, but without acknowledgement.

'Yes,' said a flat voice.

'This is Blue Mist,' she said.

'Wait.'

The line hissed emptily, and then the receiver clattered as someone picked it up.

'Yes?' said a man, and she recognised Krivitskiy.

'You know who this is?' she asked.

'Yes.'

'He told me to call four times, and then if there was no reply, I was to call you. Where is he?'

There was a pause, and then Krivitskiy spoke.

'He is in the Gulag,' he said without emotion.

Elgen, Eastern Siberia

'You're a slave,' the man said. He sat at a fine desk covered with a white cloth, and was eating a late lunch. Outside the window a white horse stood, steam coming from its nosebag. Fine, polished boots protruded from under the desk.

'I'm a very expensive one,' observed General Ivan Akulov.

'You're free,' said the commandant. He speared a potato and lathered it with gravy. 'I go down to Magadan and pick up as many like you as I need.'

'I, and people like me, are more expensive than you could imagine. Out there you have engineers, doctors, physicists and soldiers. We have all been trained at great expense and trouble to become expert at our various jobs. Which we are now not doing. We are, instead, rather incompetent lumberjacks. Even the peasants you have out there are expensive, because if you set any one of them back on a piece of land a hundred feet square and told him it was his he would produce more for you than an entire collective of slaves up here.'

The commandant, whose name Akulov had noted from the door was Moroz, smiled. 'Yes, there's one advantage to being up here. Nobody minds what you say.'

He put his knife and fork together on his plate, and lit a real manufactured cigarette. A *pyechka* iron stove stood in the corner of the room and it was warm. 'I'm new here,' he said abruptly. 'The

MGB came last week and shot the previous commandant and half the staff. Now I'm in charge. Do you know why my predecessor was shot?'

'He couldn't fulfil the production norms he was given,' Akulov said positively.

'Right.'

'But you will.'

Moroz stared out of the window. 'If I don't want to be shot, too.'

'How will you do it?' Akulov asked.

'Strict linking of rations to output. If the slaves don't complete their norms, they don't get the food.'

'That might just work, if the prisoners got the full ration to begin with. Is this an Article 58 camp?'

'Only for politicals? No,' Moroz said.

'Then, in effect, it's run by the *urkas*, the criminals. All the good food, the fat, the pieces of meat, the cabbage, the potato, the eggs, the milk and so forth will be eaten by them. What is left has no nutritive value and that is what the prisoners eat. The *urkas* will have jobs within the camp that do not involve hard labour, and will keep warm. They will wear warm clothes. The prisoners, who have not had enough to eat to do their work, will be out logging or at work on the farm. They will lose even more of the few calories they have inside them because they are dressed in rags and the weather is sub-zero. The *urkas* will have stolen their warm clothes either to wear or to sell to the guards for food, tobacco or vodka.'

'The camps are not in the business of lowering the death rate,' Moroz said abruptly. 'They are designed to kill potential trouble-makers.'

'Well, then that they do with great efficiency. But they are also meant to contribute economically. They have to provide.' Akulov smiled grimly at Moroz. 'Norms are set,' he said. 'Those who cannot meet them join the troublemakers.'

Moroz sat in silence for a few moments. 'A man called Krivitskiy called me. He told me I had a new prisoner coming and he told me who you were. And that the MGB would be checking the norms in three months time.'

He got up and looked out of the window. Behind him Akulov bent briefly over the desk. Moroz had been eating steak. 'I don't care what you do,' Moroz said, 'provided the norms are met.'

*

The two men were playing *otchko*, seeing whose cards could get closest to twenty-one. They possessed recognisable features, pink in colour, and they cursed and laughed energetically as they won or lost. Two of their mates lounged by the corridor wall, watching. They were *urkas*.

Outside the window where Akulov stood patiently was a pile of corpses, stacked like logs, slowly appearing from under their pall of snow. It wasn't possible to dig in the permafrost to make graves until summer, so those who died throughout the long winter were piled up. The dead men and women were thin, emaciated as skeltons, thinly veiled with yellow skin. Their eyes were frozen open and they stared through the window at those inside who had killed them. They were *zeks*, prisoners.

A roar of triumph came from the box on which the two men were playing their card game. The winner squatted back grinning, as his partner cursed.

'Go on then, Louse,' he said. 'Get my winnings.'

The loser got up and came towards Akulov, looking surly. 'Get them off, then,' he snarled. 'Give me your clothes, if you don't want a beating first.'

'Go ahead,' Akulov murmured. 'Be my guest.'

The *urka* called Louse reached out to grab Akulov by his padded jacket. There was a swirl of movement in the corridor and the criminal tumbled through the air and there was a loud report. He screamed, and they could see his arm sticking out at right ankles, snapped like a dry branch.

The other card player came out of his squat, a short club suddenly in his hand. Akulov sidestepped him as he lunged and smashed his head into the wooden supporting beam of the door with a huge crash. He lay on the floor and blood began to pool under his face. Akulov bent down and picked up the club.

'Anyone else?' he asked menacingly, and the two hangers-on backed away.

'You'll be for it,' one said malevolently. 'You just wait until the Knout hears about this!'

The barracks was not quiet, but filled only with the sounds of men snoring, or moaning in troubled sleep. Occasionally there came the shuffling of a prisoner going to the stinking, twenty gallon latrine bucket in the corner. Through slitted lids Akulov watched them. Light from the moving searchlights outside leaked into the great barracks, reflected from the snow.

He had a bunk to himself, although many had to share. It had been allotted to him silently, the man about to die. Fear had been in their faces.

A board creaking, moving feet pausing to check their location . . . Akulov snored.

There was a whisper. Two voices. He could see them. His bunk was against the wall and he had purchase against it. He came out of the darkness like a wolf. He felt the blood suddenly hot on his hand and a man was scrabbling frantically to get away. He crashed into the other row of bunks and Akulov had him by the hair. He opened his throat with the commandant's steak knife, from ear to ear.

There was the cautious rustling of fearful men, awakened fresh into horror, and Akulov stood in the lane between the bunks, the knife still in his hand.

'Light,' he demanded, in a voice like gravel. 'Get a light, so that you all may see me.'

From close by there was the flickering of a pale flame, a wick in fat. Someone brought it over, a boy, perhaps sixteen years old. There was the noise of men shuffling close and Akulov stood up tall, huge in his padded clothing, and the starved creatures marvelled to themselves at his size.

'They're dead,' he said, and his deep voice carried through the barracks. '*Urkas.* Any of you know me? I'm General Akulov.'

'I do, General,' came a voice, and the throng parted to let him through. A pinched face looked eagerly at him in the small light.

'Kravechenko, General. Major Boris. I was with you in the attack on Berlin.'

'I know you,' Akulov said warmly. 'Any more army men?'

There was a thin chorus of voices.

'So what are you doing, letting these filthy criminals steal from you, take your very food and clothes, make you do their work, hey? Fine soldiers like you?'

'You know how it is, General,' said Kravechenko. Akulov remembered him as a fine infantry leader. 'When you get here you're not organised but they are. They're criminals. They stick together. By the time people like us have realised what's going on, it's too late.'

'Well, it's not too late now. I'm here.'

'What can you do, General?'

'Do? I fucking took Berlin, with Zhukov. I can certainly get rid of a few criminals!' He paused, and he could feel a current of hope running through the starved, ill men about him.

'Listen. Anyone who knows me knows that I am an honest man.

I tell my troops the truth. In turn, I expect honesty from my men. In my army, an NCO who cheats on his men gets sent to the penal battalion. If we are to survive we are all going to have to pull together. I find a man cheating on his mates here, he'll get sent logging till he dies. It is one for all and all for one.'

'Why, General, you sound like a revolutionary!' called a voice, and they all laughed softly.

'The commandant, Moroz is under a sentence of death. If the norms are not fulfilled in three months, he will be shot. He has told me I can do anything I want, provided we produce the goods.'

Kravechenko was looking down at the two dead *urkas* on the floor. He had a strange, savage smile on his face. 'I know what I want to do,' he said.

'There'll be better food,' Akulov said. 'I take it the *urkas* run the kitchen?'

'The cook's theirs.'

'Not any more. Anyone been a cook here?'

'Me, General. I was a cook in the army.'

'Any doctors?'

Two voices called out.

'Good. I take it the doctor here is theirs, too.'

'He's a *feldsher*,' a voice said in disgust. 'A vet's assistant. The *urkas* get all the sick chits, the whole quota, and the real ill get sent out into the forest. They come back dead, and we put them in the pile with the others, by the wire.'

'Well, that's all changing, too,' Akulov said softly. 'You two doctors, you'll carry out the sick inspection in the morning and I want the *urkas* split up among the logging brigades. The women, too. You know the *urka* women?'

'It's easy, General. They're the ones you can recognise as women. They eat the food of the others and they get their medical treatment.'

'Not tomorrow, they won't,' Akulov promised. 'Not any of them.'

That's the one they call the Knout,' Kravechenko said to Akulov. 'The *urka* boss. The other one's the *naryadchik*, the guard chief, Karpushko.'

The felling brigades were assembled in the square, male and female and the dogs that ran between the watchtowers, their chains screeching along the wire, snarled even more savagely than usual. They sensed something wrong, something not normal.

In the brigades the *zeks* looked sideways at the strangers in their midst. Those who, with shocked faces, felt the bruises on their arms and faces, whose tongues moved painfully on broken teeth. Ivanov and Krestinsky had done the medical inspection as soon as the reveille hammer pounded on the rail at dawn. They had had Akulov, Kravechenko and a picked team of the fittest of the ex-soldiers at their backs. Selection had been by means of the club.

The *urka* boss was a powerful man, with black hair and beard. He came out of his hut and passed something to the guard chief, Karpushko.

'They look of a kind,' said Akulov.

'No difference,' said Kravechenko.

Pushing whatever he had taken into his pocket, the *naryadchik* came into the square.

'Where's the *lekpom*, the medic?' he shouted.

'Here,' said Ivanov, stepping forward.

'You? You're not the medic. You've put sick men in the brigades!'

'No. *He* did that, the one I replaced. *I* have put in the ones who should be there.'

Karpushko pushed his face close up to the doctor's. 'I'll deal with you out in the woods, *zhid*.' He turned. 'Get this mess sorted out!' he shouted. 'Get the brigades as usual.'

Slow, unpleasant smiles appeared on bruised faces, and they all looked at Akulov.

'*Wait.*'

A voice cracked over the parade ground, and it was silent, except for the constant screeching of the wire as the dogs loped back and forth.

Moroz stepped down from the wooden platform outside the guardpost. He was in the full uniform of an NKVD Colonel and he had guards with sub-machine guns at his back. He walked across the ground to Karpushko and struck him in the face. Then he jerked a package from Karpushko's pocket; it was a full bottle of vodka.

'Accepting bribes from prisoners,' he said coldly. He motioned to his men. 'Take his rifle.'

They seized it.

'Take bribes from them, *be* one of them,' said Moroz. 'Get into the brigade.'

Karpushko stumbled, dazed with disbelief, into the rank next to Ivanov.

'*Zhids* only here,' the doctor said humorously. 'We're all Jewboys.'

Their guard was standing close by.

'That one's partner, too,' said Akulov, pointing at the Knout, and the man did as he bid. The gates creaked open like jaws, and the columns marched out.

'I know you,' Ivanov said to the man marching just ahead of him. 'You're the one they call "Hitler", aren't you? You and one of your mates got me alone in the latrine last winter. Still got your screwdriver? You took all my clothes and sold them to *him*, the *naryadchik* that was, Karpushko there. You got a loaf of real white bread for that and he let you and your mate into the women's section. I know, because my girl's in there and she told me. I got frostbitten toes and that's why I walk funny.'

They halted at their site. Spring was coming and the thin sun had melted a little of the ice on the pools. Brushwood was piled up and their guard got a fire going and turned his back on them.

'Let's go,' said Ivanov, who was brigadier. They marched towards the trees and he smashed the flat of his axe into the kidneys of the man who liked to be called Hitler. He collapsed, moaning, in the snow. By his side the broken guard boss Karpushko suddenly ran, breaking away into the trees.

'We'll get him later,' Ivanov grunted. He reached inside the *urka's* jacket and took out a screwdriver, sharpened to a razor edge and a needle point. The side of his face still ached where he had been sliced with it.

'Get his clothes off,' he said to his team, and they eagerly stripped the warm clothing from him.

'Hold him up high,' Ivanov ordered. He stood on a log, and the *urka* screamed as he drove the screwdriver through his hand, smashing it into the tree trunk with his axehand.

'That was my girl you took, in the women's camp,' Ivanov said, then, with measured strokes, he began to chop into the trunk.

Someone came panting down the path, a woman. She was fat, and her breath came in gasps as she struggled through the snow. Akulov saw her and also the fury that was pursuing her, a savage, rag-clad creature who caught her, slamming her face again and again into the ground.

When Akulov came up she was still thrashing her attacker with her knees on her neck and her hands in her hair, holding her face into a pool of unfrozen water. Bloody bubbles broke the surface, and the limbs went slack. Her killer looked up at Akulov with glittering eyes.

'They're *my* clothes,' she said savagely. She began to strip them from the corpse.

He heard a voice shouting through the wood and a prisoner came running through the trees. He recognised the young boy who had held the fat lamp for him in the barracks hut.

'General, the Knout's loose! He's with some of the other *urkas*. Major Kravechenko said to come quickly.'

The boy turned, hurrying back through the trees. 'I'll take you,' he called, and Akulov left the woman pulling on her warm, still-warm clothes, and hurried after him.

Only one set of footmarks were in the snow coming down the track; those of the boy as he had hurried down. In the clearing from whence they had come Akulov saw the snow rucked and stamped with feet and he turned suddenly as the boy ran off the path, and the axe meant for his head slashed through the branches of a pine. He whirled, and ran.

He heard a harsh voice shouting in the dialect of the *urkas*, and others reply to either side, and boots pounding down the path. He burst out on to the logging track. The body of the woman lay naked by the bloody pool of water and he could smell woodsmoke, heard the crackle of brushwood burning through the trees. They were shouting behind him.

The guard was standing warm beside his fire. He turned as he heard Akulov smashing through the trees. He ran by him and, at the last moment, lunged, knocking him flying into the snow. He took the rifle, and turned to face the running men.

He knew the weapon by its feel. It was the 1944 Mosin-Nagant, and his hand automatically went to his mouth to pull off his glove, because there was many a good Soviet soldier dead in a grave through trying to get the safety off with a gloved hand, and the enemy about to grenade the trench. The lug on the cocking piece extension was in its locking recess and he twisted it with finger and thumb as they bounded towards him in triumph. The guard chief, Karpushko, was with them, armed with an axe like the others, all six of them.

The bolt moved smoothly up, back, forward and down and Akulov shot the first *urka* at a range of ten feet. Blood sprayed into the air through his back and the body continued its forward rush to land in the fire. He got Karpushko with his second shot, and the three others with the rest of the magazine.

The rifle was empty, then. He stood up. The guard was still lying winded, gasping for breath, and six dead men lay on the snow.

He only had five bullets in the magazine. He folded out the fitted bayonet as the Knout leaped to his feet, his axe swinging. Akulov was by the fire and the dead man's hair was burning in the flames. The rifle was in his hand and he threw it like a spear.

The man writhed on the ground, the rifle rammed through his guts, the blade glittering bloodily out of his back. Akulov picked up the axe and buried it in his head. He put his foot on the man's chest and heaved, twisting the rifle to break the suction, and it came free. He went over to the guard, who was rasping on hands and knees, and helped him to his feet.

'You killed six men trying to escape', he said clearly. 'Six men. I shall tell Commandant Moroz this. Six. That will be one week's paid leave and a bonus for each.'

The outrage on the man's seamed face slowly cleared as the import of Akulov's words sank in, and a slow smile spread over his face. 'Six,' he said.

'Six,' Akulov repeated. 'I shall tell Commandant Moroz myself.'

The guard beamed and took his rifle. The *urka's* face was frying in the flames, with an unpleasant smell like charring pork and he bent down and dragged him out by one boot, then began to go through his pockets to see what he had on him.

Some men and women had appeared through the trees, drawn by the noise of the gunfire. Ivanov was there, and Kravechenko. A bloody axe was in one hand and he grasped the young boy by the elbow. He took in the scene as Akulov came over to them.

'This one went with them,' he said. He gave the boy a savage push so that he fell on his knees in the snow. 'He betrayed you.'

'I was afraid,' the youth sobbed. 'I was afraid of them.'

They were all watching intently.

'You were afraid of the wrong man,' said Akulov, and he swung the axe.

Tbilisi, Georgia, November 1952

He had been on the train a very long time. He had looked out of the window as it ground through Kursk but they had taken all the gutted steel carcases away to melt down and the only signs of the titanic battle were the war memorials. They were suitably dead and the land was still devastated.

There was little to see past Kharkov until the black lands gave evidence of their fertility, yellow lines of harvested hay standing a hundred yards long at a time. Past Rostov the line went through artificial mountains, black and dirty pink, piles of vomit spewed from the Don coal mines.

They gave way to real mountains, and the train had panted heavily up into the Caucasus. Green streams rushed down beds of black shale; cloud and rain whipped over ancient stone mausoleums, hundreds of years old. Nothing moved on the land. Their ancestors were gone. There were no Kalmyk nation, no Balkars, no Chechens or Ingush, the Karachai people were gone.

He had been on the train a very long time and he was glad to get off and walk along the boulevard from the station in the morning sunshine. The Georgians appeared to think it cold and they wrapped themselves in colourful shawls. He enjoyed the brightness of their costume, his eyes unused to things that expressed joy. He breathed in the air that seemed, to him, to be very warm.

He could see the square, and a church of blond stone. The boulevard was lined with plane trees and the leaves rustled in a blood-red tide at his feet.

A woman was sitting patiently on the pavement, a small basket at her feet holding, two eggs, jars of plums and olives, some sunflower seeds. A tethered chicken pecked in the earth. He stopped, and held out some roubles.

'I was told the best chickens in Tbilisi were for sale here,' he said.

Yelena looked up. 'This one is reserved. I have been keeping it for my husband to have with me, for dinner. I am going to cook it with mushrooms and onions and cream, and surround it with rice.'

He sat down with her on the pavement and she felt the strength of his arm about her. She took a plum from her jar.

'We have a tree,' she said, holding back the tears, 'Nikolai, Ivan and I.'

'I have to go to Moscow,' said Akulov. 'I have been given command of the *Kantemirovskaya* armoured division and I'm taking Nikolai with me.'

'Will you be gone long?'

'Not long. Then you can join me.'

'Why Nikolai?'

'It was his idea, too.'

31

Vozhd

Moscow, 1 March 1953

I T was coming again, he had been promised. The door of the Chaika
clunked closed and he settled back against the upholstery, buttoned
and padded like an antique sofa. The MGB driver got into the front,
and the limousine rolled across the courtyard to the inner gate. The
low, large dacha was behind him.

The gate glided back under the command of the *okhrana* guard
in his bullet-proof cabin, and they went through, halting between
the gates as one closed before the other opened. The dogs that ran
between the two sets of walls stared hungrily and thirstily through the
glass at Rykov, and he stared back. He was hungry and thirsty too,
and for the same things as they – twitching flesh and hot, spouting
blood, and for the screaming that accompanied it. But he would get
it before they would, because he had been promised it. The man in
the dacha behind him broke his word on almost anything, but not
that, for he needed it as much as Rykov did.

Now he was crippled, now he limped, and wore a leather glove
over his cork hand, now his scar tissue gleamed red in the light of
the corridors, and people would not look him in the eye when he
went down them. They were not so foolish, he knew, as to laugh
at him to his face, but they did so as he passed, not aloud, but to
themselves. *Ne sluchayno*, it was not accidental that people avoided
looking him directly in the eyes.

Rykov knew who they were, he had a list of each and every one.
Some great, some small. Men and women. The children who had
pointed at him in the street. He had a list of them all.

He was not afraid of hard work. No, he would be at the office
early and leave late. His men would find him a good master in the
months ahead.

The gate rolled back and the dogs watched Rykov moving away
with disappointment. Rykov sat tingling with anticipation as the

limousine pulled out on to the government road through the pine forest, and accelerated along the central lane. It had been too long . . .

The Chaika slowed as the driver applied the brakes, and Rykov came out of his dream. The road ahead was cluttered with tanks which had completely blocked it as they manoeuvred about, gouts of blue diesel smoke blasting from exhausts, tracks squeaking, engines roaring.

An officer stood in the middle of the road, holding up his hand, commanding them to halt, and Rykov snapped forward in his seat, his eyes as alert as a viper's. He would enquire as to the man's name and command, and add *him* to the list. Every day, the list became longer. Looking through the windscreen, past the curtains on the windows he could see that the man was tall. He wore an elite Guards uniform and he was handsome.

The rear-view mirror of the Chaika was dark and the bellowing of the tank engines filled his ears. The darkness was moving.

The thirty-four's right track bit into the rear of the limousine and hoisted the tank on top. Gunning the engine in low gear the driver rode along the entire length of the car, squashing it down in a cacophony of bursting tyres, splintering glass, crumpling steel and screams. He clambered back down on to the road, suspension rocking, and halted.

Rykov was trapped across the floor. The door had burst open and the roof pinned him to the chassis. He scrabbled like an animal in a trap.

The noise of the engines had died away and the smell of petrol filled his head like a monstrous perfume. He could hear boots, thudding down from the tank, coming towards him. They stopped, and he twisted his head to try to see the man.

It was Akulov, who was dead.

'Let me free!' Rykov whispered.

The big man took a cigar from the top pocket of his uniform and put it in his mouth.

'Let me go!' Rykov begged.

The match rasped on the box and there was the smell of good tobacco. The flame flicked high in the air, arcing down, and Akulov stepped back.

Rykov screamed.

Nikolai Savinkov was waiting, still standing where he had stopped the car, and Akulov signalled to him. With a few shouted commands, the tanks began shifting themselves to unblock the road.

Another Chaika was waiting, on the Moscow side. It came forward as the tanks parked themselves, slowing as it passed the burning wreck. In the flames a hand moved, like a spider caught on a burning log.

In the rear of the other Chaika Khrushchev looked at Akulov and nodded in grim approval. Then the limousine swept forward, taking him towards the dacha, to dine . . .

Beria and Malenkov were already there. Khrushchev assessed the situation in the time it took him to come into the room and sit down at the dining table, eyes moving shrewdly in the jolly peasant mask. The *vozhd* was alert and he had some papers in front of him. Only a waitress pouring tea was in the room with Stalin and his three henchmen.

The waitress's hand was unsteady and she spilled some of the tea into Khrushchev's saucer. Stalin was watching.

'Why are you afraid?' he asked softly. He looked at the tea. 'Drink it,' he ordered Khrushchev who picked up the cup. It was very hot and it burned his mouth but he smiled.

It's good,' he pronounced.

Stalin picked up his own cup, looking at it suspiciously, and then threw the contents into the face of Beria, sitting next to him. The waitress hurried from the room.

'You're all useless!' he said. He waved a file in the air. 'It's all here,' he said. 'Confessions from the filthy *zhids*. Blind as kittens, the lot of you . . . what will you do without me? The country will perish because none of you know how to recognise enemies.'

He turned to Beria, who was calmly wiping the tea off his face with one of his many handkerchiefs. 'That girl is a spy,' he said. 'Beat her until she confesses.'

'I'll see to it,' Beria promised.

People wanted to kill Stalin and he knew it. 'Find out who gave her the poison.'

'I will,' Beria said.

Blisters were forming inside Khrushchev's mouth. He opened the file that was passed down to him. The coming terror was sweeping down on the nation like a storm line; everyone could see the towering black clouds, lit from within by lightning, hear the crack and roll of the thunder. The Jews had confessed. Details of a vast Zionist conspiracy were there. Ben-Gurion in Israel had organised the conspiracy by Jews in the socialist countries at the behest of the American President, Truman. Throughout the Soviet Union Jews seethed like rats in the sewers, waiting to infect and kill the leading cadres of the nation.

'You're useless, all of you!' Stalin said again. 'I wish Hitler was here – he understood the problem . . . Ah, Hitler, what a lad! I wish he hadn't killed himself. He could have come here, worked for us. He liked us communists – the idealists of socialism, he called us. Ah, me. Pity. I'd have given him your job, Lavrentiy.'

Beria smiled through a red and stinging face.

'Ah, well,' Stalin sighed again. 'I'll have to make do . . . Very well, tell us what you've got.'

'We have the letters ready and signed by the leading Jewish communists,' said Beria. 'The lists are in the files. Broadly, the letters are the same. They say that the Jews who sign them understand the rightful hatred against their race that the Doctor's Plot has aroused amongst the people. The Jewish doctors we will try – they're ready to plead guilty – and hang publicly in Red Square on May Day.'

'What about that little rat, that *svoloch* Molotov?' Stalin said sharply. 'I want him there too, and his *zhid* wife. I want *all* those Jews swinging in the wind.'

'I have former Presidium member Molotov under surveillance,' Beria assured him.

'See how high treachery can reach? Is he still snivelling about his wife being in the camps?'

Yellow eyes, like a tiger's swept over the three men. Stalin smiled, showing discoloured teeth. 'Go on, then. We hang them in Red Square and I want a film of it, mind. It'll be something to watch before the Westerns.'

'We hang them on May Day', Beria said. 'And arrange for a spontaneous wave of uncontrollable hatred for the Jews to sweep the country. With a hundred thousand or so slaughtered in the pogrom, the letters of the Jewish communists are published, begging Comrade Stalin to resettle *all* Jews. We round them up, put them on the trains and dump them in Siberia with the rest we moved in the war.'

'Wonderful,' Stalin said dreamily. 'A world without Jews . . .' Then his features stiffened again. 'It should be possible to do something about the Ukrainians. I hate them almost as much as the Jews.' He sighed. 'Still one thing at a time. Comrade Khrushchev, let's have your report on the meeting of the Committee of Architectural Affairs.'

Khrushchev burst a blister with his tongue. The inside of his mouth was raw.

'The first stage of the rebuilding of Moscow under the tutelage and in the style of Comrade Stalin has been satisfactorily accomplished,' he said. 'The great buildings of the University, the Foreign Ministry, the Ukrainia Hotel and several others are all either complete or ahead of the planned schedule. It has been agreed that the full reconstruction of the city as a monument to Comrade Stalin shall now go ahead. I have the plans here for the newly-created area now occupied by Red Square and the Kremlin. All will be demolished to create Mausoleum Prospekt, leading up to the Monument to Victory, to be dominated by a statue of Comrade Stalin, personifying victory. The statue will be two hundred metres high, and visible from any point of the city. The order for five hundred tons of copper has been made.'

Stalin nodded. It was satisfactory. Khrushchev could dance; he could do the *Gopak*. He knew that if the dinner party guests included high-ranking foreign officials then there he would be, at some stage, squatting on his haunches with his arms folded, legs pumping and his heavy shoes pounding the floor, streaming with sweat and grinning like a maniac.

Malenkov couldn't dance, but he knew how to crawl. Stalin looked at him, the only one yet to speak.

'And you, have you any good ideas today?' he said harshly.

'Yes, Comrade Stalin. Firstly, of course, the name Moscow should be changed. To Stalinsk.'

Khrushchev and Beria beamed in approval.

'Secondly, why do we count the years from the mythical birth of the man called Christ? Surely the calendar should be counted from the birth of Stalin?'

Stalin smiled. His subordinates had done well! 'Very good, Matryona,' he approved.

It had been Zhdanov who had given Malenkov the nickname of a peasant-woman, simultaneously mocking his lack of education and his effeminate appearance. Zhdanov had been proud of *his* intellectual abilities.

It was Malenkov who had the last laugh, though. Zhdanov was found dead in his dacha, and the last man to see him alive, on his way to Leningrad to oversee the massacre of his organisation, was Malenkov who liked to see to things personally. Survival, in Stalin's court, was not an ordinary competitive sport.

'See to it, Matryona,' Stalin said. He pressed a button. 'Let's have some champagne. Get some prominent Christian to put forward the idea in *Pravda*.'

The hatch opened and Malenkov went over to fetch the tray. He poured champagne into a glass.

'Try it,' Stalin ordered.

Malenkov sipped it and nodded, pronouncing it good. He put it down in front of the man who ruled from the Arctic Ocean to the Caspian, from Berlin to Vladivostok. Stalin did not pick it up immediately. He would wait several minutes to see if Malenkov showed signs of poisoning. People were thinking of killing him, he was sure of it . . .

'Fill the other glasses,' he ordered.

Ghosts hung over the shoulders of the four men in the room, not simply the millions the *vozdh* had slaughtered, and the hundreds of thousands each and every one of the others was responsible for, for to serve was to share, but certain specific ghosts that they all knew personally. The millions were millions, their fate decided by an overworked NKVD man's need to clear the cells for a fresh batch, or by the *khanovey's* sword-sharp howl over the tundra. But there had been some who had had it done to them in the full light of the day, in a mocked-up courtroom.

Malenkov thought of himself as a theorist of Marxism. He had liked to talk with Bukharin, but he had assisted in his judicial murder. Yagoda and Yezhof had held Beria's job. Now you could look for their memory where you would and not find it, not in photographs, not in history books, glimmering only in the minds of those who had them killed.

Of course, it did not have to be done in a courtroom. Khrushchev had run the purges in Moscow, as Party Secretary. His counterpart in Leningrad, Kirov, had been assassinated. Dzerzhinsky died and Stalin had walked in his funeral. Malenkov had killed Zhdanov in his own home.

They all knew how it was done.

Khrushchev was standing at the end of the table. He had a book in his hand.

'What is it?' asked Stalin. He had still not touched his champagne, waiting to see what happened to Malenkov. There were people out there, who wanted him dead.

'*The Prince* by Machiavelli. I remembered you saying that your copy had become worn.'

A spark of interest showed. Stalin read the volume constantly, along with Nechaev's archive. 'Let me see. Lavrentiy, did you have the house checked for deadly vapours?'

'It is as you asked,' the secret policeman said soothingly. 'Only fresh air.'

Stalin knew that people were trying to kill him, he was certain of it . . .

Khrushchev passed the book over the table. Malenkov was by the sofa. As Khrushchev drew back his hand his sleeve dragged against one of the champagne flutes. It tumbled, shattering the goblet.

'I'm sorry, I'm sorry!' he apologised.

He picked up the stem. It had a long shard still attached, glittering in the light.

Then they all moved at once. Beria seized the left arm, Malenkov the right, pinning them fast to the arms of the chair. Malenkov had a thick, stuffed cushion from the sofa. He slammed it over Stalin's face, forcing his head against the back of the seat.

Khrushchev lunged forward, plunging the glass dagger into the centre of Stalin's body above the paunch. He was a strong man and it vanished up to the base. He pulled it out a little from the body and twisted. A hoarse, gargling came from underneath the cushion, and then the body slowly went slack. Beria and Malenkov released their grip and Khrushchev stepped back. Malenkov lifted the cushion from the face. Blood had gushed from the mouth and ran down the chin. His eyes stared, knowing and unmoving at them. People had wanted him dead, he had been certain of it . . .

Moscow, 26 June 1953

The limousine rolled quietly as a cat along the street and, with the window down and the warm summer night's air on his face, Beria allowed himself to muse on the frailties of human nature. Human beings found stress difficult to bear, sought relief from it. When he had had Yezhof arrested the man had known the torture and execution that was coming, for he had done the same to so many others. While waiting he had spent the time drinking, and making paper aeroplanes.

Drinking was not *his* vice. He was glad that the drunken, lugubrious affairs at the old man's dacha were over. He did not make paper aeroplanes, either.

There were a surprising number of people still on the streets though it was past midnight. Perhaps it was the presence of his MVD troops in the capital, he thought in amusement. He had moved two elite state security units in – the First Red Banner Dzerzhinskiy Motorised Infantry Division and the Second Motorised Infantry Division on the pretext of burglaries in the city. They had complete control.

There. A young woman was moving quickly along the pavement. He liked the way she hurried along, obviously anxious. Her legs were long, her breasts bouncing in her hurry.

'That one,' he murmured, and the limousine rolled to a stop. The bodyguard in the front seat came smoothly out of his seat.

'It is late for young ladies to be out,' he said. 'Let us give you a lift.'

The limousine hissed through the dark Moscow streets. When it stopped the building towered black above them, its wings stretching into the night . . .

'Where is this?' she said fearfully.

'This is the Lefortovo Prison,' he said. 'It's mine.'

There could be no one in the capital who did not know what the Lefortovo was. The Lubyanka was famous, and its operatives capable in their tasks, but the Lefortovo was where the experts were.

'Boris,' he said. 'Show the young lady around.'

They went inside. Beria did not need liquor for relief. He needed a victim. A woman, a fresh one each night, young, beautiful, and terrified . . .

He watched her go in the early light, stumbling away from the grim, star-shaped tower, tripping in her hurry, clutching her torn clothes about her. Just one more day. One more day and it would all be his . . .

He went out to where the limousine was waiting, and climbed in. He would go back to his dacha to bathe and take breakfast, as he always did. It was important not to do things out of the ordinary, not among people for whom nothing was coincidence if it could be seen as conspiracy.

Outside the metro station two vast, overalled stone women beat an anvil with giant hammers and tongs, and there was a tank.

The MVD owned no tanks . . .

The army commander in the turret stared coldly at the limousine as it hissed by and Beria looked frantically about him. The street was bare of his troops. He picked up the transmitter of the radio set carried in the big car.

'Krivitskiy.' His second-in-command's voice came through quickly and clearly.

'You're there!' Beria said in relief. 'Army units are on the streets and our troops are not to be seen.'

'They have not moved from outside the Lubyanka,' Krivitskiy said comfortingly. 'You are in the car? Get here quickly while I find out what is happening.'

The tyres squealed as the heavy limousine wheeled in the road, heeling over like a ship. The deep rasp of the engine at full power echoed from the buildings as it accelerated up to speed; as it passed, the tank commander spoke into his microphone, following the fleeing vehicle with his eyes.

Krivitskiy had a good view over Dzerzhinskiy Square from his office. As he stood there, he saw the hurrying black Chaika make for the entrance, gleaming in the sunshine. It vanished beneath him.

The door soon opened, bringing the man with the vulture face and a whiff of carbolic from the corridor. The Lubyanka was clean, there were no bugs.

'So what is up?'

Beria's face expressed his passions clearly. Krivitskiy had seen cunning, ambition, cruelty and lust pass over it in as many seconds, but now he saw something fresh – fear.

'Calm yourself,' he said. 'All is well.' He had a piece of paper on his desk, he passed it over.

'What is it?' Beria asked.

'The editors of the Great Soviet Encyclopaedia asked me, as your deputy, to write your entry for this year's edition.'

Beria scanned the sheet, distracted, anxious. 'What are you talking about? This is some crap about the Berents Sea.'

'It was as close as I could get to your name,' Krivitskiy said smoothly.

From outside in the square there came the sudden rattle of machine gun fire. The police chief hurried to the window. Below, a handful of MVD guards lay dead. Led by a section of tanks, armed army troops were fanning across the square. MVD men came out, their hands high. They were better with men who did not fight back, masterful with women and children. They dropped their weapons and lay face down as they were bid.

Beria suddenly bolted for the door but it slammed back on its hinges and the giant figure of Akulov filled the doorway. He grasped Beria with hands like kettles, and his men searched him. They found an automatic pistol which Akulov pocketed and then they took him away.

Krivitskiy stood at his window, watching as the army set up their blocking points. He stretched out his arms, feeling the extent of his domain, of his power.

There was a footfall at the door. He turned, alone in the room, and there was a tall Guards' officer standing there. He had a gun in his hand.

'You're dead!' he said, colour draining from his face and the warmth from his stomach.

'No,' said Nikolai Savinkov. '*You* are.'

They hustled Beria down the stairs, their boots thumping and clattering, and the MVD men in the great hall, standing with their hands high and their faces to the wall, peeped surreptitiously over their shoulders to see their boss being taken away. The soldiers guarding them smacked them with their rifle butts, none too gently. The secret police had preyed on the military for a long time. Too long a time . . .

The heavy BTR-152 *Bronetransporter* armoured personnel carrier was backed right up against the entrance, its twin rear doors open, the picked military police inside waiting for their charge. The big six-cylinder Zil engine grumbled, exhaust fumes leaking back into the building.

Akulov and the guards flung Beria inside and the doors clanged shut.

'Go!' Akulov ordered, and the vehicle crunched into gear, its six wheels rumbling on the road. The waiting tanks and APCs took up station, and the convoy growled across the square at speed.

Akulov's own BA-64 armoured command vehicle stood waiting outside. He was about to get in it when a picture came into his mind like a clip of film, something that he had seen as he had been hurrying Beria down the stairs. He turned abruptly and ran back up.

The door to Krivitskiy's office was open. He was kneeling in front of his desk, his arms along its length, held there by two soldiers. Behind him stood Savinkov, a heavy Makarov automatic pistol in his hand.

'No, Nikolai,' said Akulov.

'It won't take a moment,' said Nikolai, without turning round. Akulov came up behind him and lifted the muzzle of the gun from the back of Krivitskiy's skull.

'Why not?' Nikolai said passionately. 'We're killing Beria. This one's no better, no better at all.' His blue eyes glittered. 'Let's kill them all,' he said. 'Now we've got the opportunity.'

'We'll have to shoot all the party officials too, Nikolai. Shall we start with Malenkov, Bulganin, Molotov, Khrushchev?'

'Yes! Kill them, too.'

'Khrushchev only gave me a division. Bonapartism, it's called. I couldn't make myself Tsar if I wanted to. And when I'd lost, the Terror would be back, and more millions would die. This way, there's an end to it.'

Nikolai allowed the gun to drop to his side and Krivitskiy, his face dead white, cautiously got to his feet.

They went down the stairs again, out to the waiting command vehicle. They rolled through the streets, wary civilians eyeing all the soldiers.

'It's better this way,' said Akulov. He peered out of the viewing slot of his armoured shutter. 'We're here.' The white wedding cake of the military headquarters towered in tiers and spires above them. They went inside, leaving the concentration of troops and tanks all around. The steps led down into the basement.

Harsh, bright lights lit up the bare room. A number of men stood along one wall while others formed a crowd around the other three. In the line Nikolai saw Beria, and recognised some of his top henchmen, Merkulov, Dekanosov, Goglidze, Meshik. The crowd was thick with marshals and generals in full uniform, and politburo men in shapeless suits. He saw Zhukov and Konev, chest heavy with medals, saw the gleaming eyes of the victors, Malenkov, Bulganin, Khrushchev.

Assistants were spreading tarpaulin on the floor. By the wall, buckets of water stood, with mops.

'Are we doing this right, Lavrentiy?' Malenkov called mockingly.

'You know how it is done as well as I,' Beria muttered. 'You have done your share.'

Bulganin was cocking a military Makarov.

'Not with that,' Zhukov said warningly. 'The bullet will ricochet everywhere. Don't the *Chekisty* use some small pistol for the job?'

'Here,' said Khrushchev. He had an open box on the table. 'They use the TT.'

They had them kneel, as they had had so many others kneel, and as he got down on his knees Beria looked around at the ring of his killers.

'I would have slaughtered you all!' he said savagely.

The shots rang loud and metallic in the room. Gore and bloody fragments of bone spattered the tarpaulin.

'Burn them!' said Zhukov. Beria's NKVD had savaged his armies all the way to Berlin. 'We want no memory of *them*.'

'The Lefortovo has a crematorium,' said Malenkov, and the waiting soldiers took the bodies up to dump them into the BTR.

'Come on,' said Akulov. 'Let's get out of here.'

Outside in the sunshine they watched the armoured personnel carrier roll to the gates. It left a thin line of dripped red blood from its cargo.

Nikolai and Akulov got into the command car and followed the dead men out on to the street, into the warm morning sun . . .

Moscow, 25 February 1956

'I haven't been in here since Tsar Nicholas gave Mikhail his award,' said Yelena. 'It was only months before Kerensky came to power and seems so long ago.'

She led Akulov out of the great white vestibule of the palace state entrance and through the tall doorway, guarded by its golden doors. Above them was a bas-relief of St George slaying the dragon. The immense hall stretched before them, the high, gold-splashed coffered ceiling supported by lines of pilasters. Gigantic, glittering chandeliers cast a river of light down the highly-polished, inlaid and decorated floor. Besuited delegates shuffled about within, goggling at their imperial past.

'I wonder if they had time to put his name up before it all fell,' she said.

They made their way along the high, white and gold pilasters, upon which were inscribed name after name.

'The Order was established in seventeen sixty-seven. These are all the units and individuals who won the cross.'

'Here he is,' said Akulov. 'There is Count Mikhail.'

Yelena stood looking at where the names came to an end and then turned away. 'I just wanted to see if he was there. My grandfather, the general, is here somewhere too . . .'

As they were moving back down the lines, Akulov saw someone else, a small, bald man standing by one of the columns of victory, talking to two other men.

'Look over there,' he said. 'There's Rakosi. That's the man I'll be dealing with in Hungary. He's our boy.'

Yelena looked across the hall.

'I don't like him,' she said firmly, and Akulov smiled faintly. He knew his wife.

'He calls himself "Stalin's Hungarian Disciple." He has a statue of Stalin made out of bronze in Budapest, taller than the trees.'

Yelena looked at the Hungarian dictator with unfriendly eyes. 'A little man . . .' she said softly. 'What is it like in Hungary?'

'Bad,' he said shortly. 'The economy was bad in forty-eight when Stalin put him in and, by all accounts, it's got worse. The AVH is their KGB. Their *apparatchiks* are called *funkcionariusoks*, the funkies.'

'Don't tell me – they live in dachas and ride in chauffeured limousines.'

'Something strange happened after Stalin died. Nikita Sergeyevich demoted Rakosi and put in my old comrade, Imre Nagy. He and I were New Bolsheviks before there were any old ones,' Akulov said grinning! 'I was wounded from the front in Tsar Nicholas's army and he was captured there fighting in the army of the Habsburgs. I knew him in Moscow, just before the revolution. He was like Ruth – he was looking for a new and better world for the people.'

'And what did he do, when he had the power?'

'He gave it to them,' Akulov said quietly. 'People who'd been driven out of business opened up their shops again. Clubs and cafés sprouted up like spring flowers. The radio played music – some of it *American*. They say that Western books were on sale. A woman could go to a beauty parlour and there was food and drink on sale to anyone who wanted to buy it.'

'And where is Imre now, if the rat over there is in power again?'

'It was all too much.' Akulov inclined his head to indicate those all around them, the party delegates. 'Nikita Sergeyevich put Rakosi back in. Imre wouldn't confess to errors, and now he's a non-person.'

Somewhere in the hall, a bell began to ring.

'I must go and take my place,' he said. 'I used to think that sitting in a command car was uncomfortable, but compared to eight hours in a Congress seat . . .'

She straightened his tie a millimetre or two and brushed specks of dust from his lapel. 'When you're in the Tsar's house you have to look smart,' she said mischievously. 'I'll see you tonight, my darling. I have my pass and I'm going to wander around. I may never get in here again!'

They separated in the great vestibule, where Akulov joined the hundreds of others going into the *Zal Zasedaniy* meeting hall for the next session of the Twentieth Party Congress. Yelena stood to watch him go in. She remembered being there as a young woman, come to see Mikhail honoured by the Tsar. Two great halls, of St Alexander and St Andrew had been there then, richly decorated, now they had been knocked into one, as long as a playing field. It was austere and, at its end, an immense statue of Lenin stared down its length. At the long table beneath him she recognised Khrushchev, Malenkov and Molotov. She turned, and went up the wide staircase as the great doors shut for the closed session.

In the hall above she looked out. Nearby were the shining golden domes of the Cathedral. Over the Kremlin wall the skyline was punctuated by the high, inhuman white buildings of Stalin – fortresses, spired blockhouses. She turned away and, as she did so from the meeting hall beneath there came a huge, collective gasp. It died away and a single voice shouted out in shocked protest, and then there was quiet. A man was addressing the delegates.

Akulov found his place in the boxed rows of seats. He could see a number of people he recognised. Marshals Koniev and Zhukov, rivals to take Berlin were there together. They nodded to him. The Hungarian leader, Rakosi, sat not far away. Krivitskiy was there, too, looking self-assured.

The small, balding man in a baggy-trousered dark suit got up from the long table below Lenin's statue and went to the enclosed podium. He put down a sheaf of papers, placed his hands on the wooden walls at either side of him and began to speak. Like everyone else, Akulov composed his features into a suitably attentive expression to hear what Khrushchev had to say. Experts were known to be able to listen, applaud and even vote while actually asleep.

But nobody slept that morning.

'The title of my speech today is On the Cult of Personality and its Consequences,' he said. 'Who is it that I am referring to? Whose cult? Which person? What have been the consequences of that cult?'

Khrushchev looked about the great hall. There was a strange *frisson* of movement among the delegates as people shifted their position, attempting to see him better, for this was not how speeches to the Party Congress began.

'The man was Stalin,' Khrushchev said clearly. 'And the consequences of what he did we live with today – mass terror, poverty, murder, the ravages of war. Stalin had us believe he was a genius but he was not. He was an evil man.'

The gasp of pent-up breath boomed throughout the hall. From somewhere a man was screaming shocked abuse at Khrushchev. His companions restrained him, and Khrushchev went on.

'Someone knew Stalin well when our predecessors first founded our communist state. Who was that?' He turned to gesture at the huge statue behind him. 'Lenin, Lenin, whose principles should have been followed in building our new nation. They were not. Because of Stalin, and the cult of his personality. Lenin knew. Before he died, he wrote a Letter to the Party Congress. This letter has become known as his Testament. He knew that leadership of our great movement was about to pass away from him and he wished to guide those who followed. He discussed the merits and faults of six men. We know their names: Zinoviev, Kamenev, Bukharin and Pyatakov. And Trotsky and Stalin. If any of these men are present, would they care to stand?'

Khrushchev looked rhetorically about the hall.

'No, they are not here. Stalin we know is dead – but we also know that the others are dead, too. Shot by Stalin, axed to death by Stalin. As "enemies of the people". This was *wrong*. It was *Stalin* who should have been shot. *Stalin* who was the enemy of the people.'

Again, the stunned gasp of shock. Some looked about them, wondering if even now Chekists, or GPU, NKVD, MGB or KGB men would not descend mercilessly upon Khrushchev and drag him screaming from the hall, never to be heard of again.

'What did Lenin say of Stalin? He compared him to Trotsky, saying that they were "the two most able leaders of the present Central Committee." A correct assessment. It was Trotsky, who with Lenin, brought about the success of the Bolshevik Revolution. And a fool could not have gained such power over all of us.'

Somewhere, a man began to sob. It could not be so! All his life he had been told that the sun rose because of Stalin, that it set because he ordered it that way. And Trotsky had been an enemy of the Revolution, Stalin had said so!

'Of Stalin he said, "having become General Secretary, he has unlimited authority concentrated in his hands and I am not sure whether he will be capable of using that authority with sufficient caution." Caution. Even Lenin was not able to see sufficiently clearly into the future to see what Stalin was to do with his unlimited authority. But what else did he say? He said that he was *grub*. Crude, gross, a bully without normal social decencies. Vile. And he said that the comrades of the Party Congress should think about a way to remove Stalin from his post and appoint another man who in all respects differed from Comrade Stalin.'

Khrushchev looked at the shocked delegates, picking a few out by eye.

'Would that they had,' he said softly. 'Our nation, our Party, would have been a very different affair if they had. Stalin claimed to be the Brass-Hard Leninist, the best communist of all. He was *not* a communist. He abandoned the method of ideological struggle for that of administrative violence, mass repression and terror. Whoever opposed him – and this included many honest communists – was doomed to moral and physical annihilation.'

The delegates sat in the hall for a long time, for Khrushchev had a lot to say. The list of horror was very long. The people had been savaged, the Party leadership murdered. He had slaughtered the best military and civilian commanders and had supplied Hitler with war *matériel* up to the very day the Nazis invaded. He had refused to listen to warnings of the attack, and had not allowed the soldiers to prepare defensive positions. The immensely costly war which had followed had been made more so by his handling of it. It had been won by the men of the Red Army in spite of, not because of, Stalin's leadership, for the man who at its end had called himself *Generalissimus* had been an incompetent, mediocre commander whose only real talents lay in his ability to terrorise those subordinate to him.

Akulov was looking at Koniev and Zhukov, and saw them nod in profound agreement.

Like all the others not actually intellectually dazed by Khrushchev's litany of crime, Akulov was assessing what was said and not said. Stalin, with his henchmen Yezhof and Beria, were being held solely responsible for everything that had happened. Three individuals. Krushchev was being very careful to point out that it was they, and not the system, that was at fault. On the contrary, he made it clear that it was the three criminals who were responsible for "violations of socialist legality". Now that they were gone, he told the delegates, the unique relationship between the party and police had been reestablished, "as in the days of Lenin and Dzerzhinskiy", with the party and state in control of the police, the KGB their faithful servant, their "shield and sword", Leninist norms had been restored.

Akulov could see Krivitskiy. He sat relaxed, as Khrushchev assured the delegates that the organs of state security would be strengthened, that their "revolutionary vigilance" would be raised to even greater heights.

Akulov looked at the Central Committee members at Khrushchev's back. He could see Molotov and Malenkov. They looked unwell. They could have been live ghosts at Khrushchev's exhumation of the corpses.

He saw Rakosi, the Hungarian who had raised a bronze statue of Stalin in Budapest, higher than the trees. He sat, pale and sweating, like a man condemned to death.

At a distance of over a kilometre the German Mk IV tank was only a small dark block against the white of the gently-rolling, snow-covered countryside. Hidden in its firing position the barrel of the Soviet tank twitched minutely as the gunner lined up his sights. Nearby, Akulov and Piotr Sadovsky covered their ears.

They felt the blast of the overpressure as the 115 mm main armament fired. Akulov, whose eyes had not lost their precision, saw the black round skimming over the snow in a near flat arc. As it vanished into the target and he took his hands from his ears, he heard the clang of it striking home coming on the chill wind.

'Very good,' he said.

Noises were coming from the turret of the tank at its range firing position. The hatch raised and a man threw out a smoking shell case, holding it in gloved hands. It lay hissing on the dirty, caked snow and ice.

'We're still working on the automatic ejection system,' said Sadovsky. 'It's supposed to go into the chute once the gun elevates automatically after firing, and out of the hatch there in the turret rear, but it sometimes gets hung up. We'll sort it out. This is a T-55 with T-62 bits on, after all. It's not developed yet. But let's go look at the Mk IV.'

They got into the Jeep and drove along the road of the firing range towards the target.

'Fin-stabilised Armour-Piercing Discarding-Sabot,' Sadovsky recited. He held the steering wheel between his thumbs and the sides of his palms. The once-ragged row of stumps that had been his fingers had been trimmed by surgery.

'The sabot that holds the round in the barrel slips away in flight, while the fins open up to stabilise it. It'll pierce 300mm of armour at over a kilometre.'

'It's a clever concept,' said Akulov. 'I wish we'd had it when we were fighting these ones in the war. Who thought it up?'

'Some weapons team in America,' Sadovsky said.

'It's not our idea?'

'No. We got a complete set of their plans through GRU, Military Intelligence.'

'Why do we have to do that?' Akulov demanded. 'Don't we have our own designers?'

'Of course! You know that, Ivan. The military gets only the very best, whether it's material, scientists or engineers.' He waved a fingerless hand at the distant smoke in the pale, milky blue sky that was Moscow. 'They get the *brak*, the junk. Military quality is better than export quality – but it's still difficult to keep up.'

'Keep up?' Akulov queried.

There was no one else about, just the two of them and the old enemy tank on its target pad.

'With the *West*, Ivan Ivanovich. Over there the people don't put up with *brak*. They eat like the *nomeklatura* and the weapons are good. And so *many* of them.'

'I know. I have a relation, my uncle's daughter Tatyana. She is an economist in Nosovibirsk. She tells me about this. The Western economies can simply outspend us, while still giving the people what they want.'

'Never mind, Ivan Ivanovich, pure communism is on its way, and will provide everybody with everything, burying capitalism as it does so. We have Nikita Sergeyevich's word for it. And this tank will probably never see production, for Nikita Sergeyevich is putting all his money into rockets with nuclear warheads. H-bombs are in, tanks are out. Now, take a look at this. Here's the entry hole.' He pointed to a small, almost insignificant hole just below the turret of the tank. 'Now, if we get up here – '

They clambered up on to the deck, using the Jeep as a step, and peered inside the hatchless turret. The interior of the tank was a tangled mess.

'White-hot fragments macerate anything inside,' said Sadovsky. 'Namely, the crew.'

Akulov nodded in sober respect. 'A very effective weapon,' he said.

'The T-62 will also have night-fighting capability. It has infra-red driving lights and searchlights. Of course, this isn't even the proto-type, we are just trying out systems.'

'It will be very capable,' Akulov agreed. They climbed down and back into the Jeep, where they sat for a moment.

'But what have *they* got?' said Akulov. 'In the West?'

'Don't you know?'

'I'm a General. I get Red Tass. The public gets Pravda. Red Tass gives me about the same level of genuine information that in the West is delivered by the British *Times* or the American *Washington Post*. If I apply and sign for them I can get *spetskhrany*, numbered copies of Western military magazines and books – translated – which may then be read only by me. In the West they are available in the shops.

'So I know that if we go to war against them we can expect to fight Centurions or M48s. I even have some idea of their capability. But the men who will do the fighting have *no* idea, because they aren't allowed to. "Don't tell your best friend what your brother shouldn't know" is how it goes. In all units there's always a KGB crew around to enforce "secrecy". If they found one of my officers giving a lecture on current Western armour they'd arrest him as a spy!'

Sadovsky started the Jeep and drove away from the target. 'It doesn't matter, Ivan Ivanovich,' he said, laughing. 'They can never invade us because they will not be able to find their way, since we produce no maps!' He turned to look at Akulov, and his eyes glittered madly in his frost-scarred face. 'Is this not genius? To deny the enemy vital information? And should they stumble upon Moscow they will not be able to call anyone on the phone because there are no telephone directories!'

He roared with laughter.

'Do you want a drink, Piotr Pavlovich?' Akulov asked sympathetically.

'Yes,' Sadovsky said with heartfelt desire and they drove towards the new factory complex ahead of them. When he parked the Jeep, Sadovsky waved his maimed hand about him.

'Isn't it strange? When we worked at the providing grounds as *zek*-specialists, one mistake and we were back to the mines and death. Now it's assured expansion. And even if what you make isn't that good, they'll find a use for it. I spoke to Belyakov over at the MiG bureau the other day. His MiG-21 whipped the Sukhoi in competition, but Sukhoi's still making it. They've turned it into some kind of ground attack machine.' He put his face close to Akulov's, staring into his eyes. 'What about you, Ivan Ivanovich? What technical details did they apply to you? That bastard Vyshinsky hung poor Andrey on a meatbook in the van they took me away in, I found him in the dark . . . My daughter screamed for me as they dragged her out of her bed . . . Anna killed herself in front of me . . . I let them down, Ivan Ivanovich, I promised to keep, them safe . . .'

'None of us could promise that and keep it,' Akulov said gently. 'Let's have that drink, and I'll sign the stage papers.'

They went upstairs to Sadovsky's office and sat down at Finish bleached-pine furniture. A tray holding two shotglasses and a carafe, condensation frosting its sides, rested on a low table and Sadovsky poured.

'I'm truly fucked up, Ivan Ivanovich. I can't concentrate any more. I built a tank factory from nothing and we out-built the Germans and now I can hardly run a range trial out there.'

He drained his glass, and poured another. 'I can't concentrate, and the memories keep flooding in . . . not just memories, I'm *there* . . . I used to get the dreams, and I'd wake up and be in the real world.

But now I can be awake . . . *here* . . . and yet what's going round in
my head is more real . . .'

Akulov put his glass down on the table, untouched. It was ten
o'clock in the morning.

'You can talk to me, Piotr Pavlovich,' he said gently. 'I was
there, too.'

'Do you get it? Do these things happen to you?' Sadovsky asked.

'Not so bad, perhaps. But I cannot bear the sound of dogs barking
. . . those brutes they had in Kolyma, trained to savage any of us in
zek clothing, on command . . . that, and the noise of metal on metal.
It was the first thing we heard every morning, was it not, the guard
banging on the rail with a hammer in the dark, and one more day in
Hell ahead of you?'

'The dogs, yes . . . you remember Boris, who was on the train with
us? He and I looked after it with Andrey. We worked together in my
tank factory before we were arrested and Boris was with me in the
camp. We were on the logging teams.'

'I know,' said Akulov, and Sadovsky looked up.

'Have I told you before? I can't remember things like that, and yet
what happened then is on my mind all the time . . .'

'It doesn't matter,' Akulov said gently. 'Tell me what happened
to Boris.'

'The dogs were always well fed. Real meat . . . Something went
wrong with the supply – I think the rail line was blocked . . . the
dogs would have gone hungry, and they were talking about what
they should do. There were horses there, and cattle, but it was felt
that they were too valuable to kill. One of the guards suggested they
chop up some corpses of the *zeks* that were dead, the ones piled up
like logs, but of course they were frozen solid. We went out logging,
and the dogs came too. Boris was the first to go. They took his clothes
off out in the woods and had the dogs eat him. They cracked open his
skull with an axe and they ate his brains . . . They fed the dogs in the
morning and the afternoon until the supplies came . . .'

A film of sweat coated his face, he drank more vodka. 'Food
. . . you thought about it all the time. Had dreams about it.
Incredible, vivid dreams. More real than sex. There was this doctor, proper one, free on a contract, not a prisoner. A woman.
She liked mushrooms. They grew in a certain part of the forest.
We knew she went there to pick them. We were waiting for
her one day. She cried out and ran when she saw us because
she thought we were going to rape her. But we wanted her for
something much more important . . . We cut her up and roasted

her on a fire, Ivan Ivanovich, . . . She was fat, I can still smell the smoke . . .'

The sweat was running down his face into the collar of his shirt, turning it a spreading dark blue.

'The engines of the tanks,' he muttered. 'I *hate* the engines. They ran the trucks, revving the motors to hide the noise. *I* revved the truck, and they beat them to death with crowbars . . . The air in the sheds stank of blood and vodka, because they were always drunk. I drink vodka and I am back in the shed, ankle-deep in blood and brains and bits of bone. Range trials with half humanity . . .'

He looked up at Akulov with despairing eyes. 'I get you out here to see the tests, Ivan Ivanovich, and you come even though you know there is no need. I can talk to you and you understand. All the others are dead. Boris and Andrey. My wife and children. Nobody understands . . . I wake up in the night, and my daughter is screaming *Papa, papa*, and I cannot come to her help. They take her away, screaming, and I never see her again . . . If only she were alive, Ivan I would have something to live for. She would help keep the monsters away . . .'

On the couch Gaia's father swayed and slowly fell over. Akulov got up and settled him on his side. The carafe was almost empty. He went out. A secretary was outside at a desk.

'Keep an eye on him,' he said and she nodded, her eyes sympathetic.

He went back outside. His Chaika was parked near the edge of the proving ground, and he walked over to it. In the distance the evolutionary T-62 was manoeuvering on to a half mile test track of steep and changing ground, gullies and ridges. With the interest of a professional, he decided to watch it. There was a Thermos of coffee in his car and he poured a mugful while he was waiting, enjoying the warmth in his hands as he held it.

In the cold, it was ready to drink within a few minutes. A growl as the twelve cylinder diesel engine developed power signified the beginning of its run. He saw it pick up speed, and dip into the first gully, emerging on the other side with dirty snow spraying high into the air from its wide tracks. The crew had the hatches down, supporting themselves inside against the violent movements of the vehicle.

Someone was running out there, on the icy, muddy scrub. A staggering, weaving figure. It fell over, and picked itself up, and lurched onwards.

Akulov cursed, dropping his mug on to the ground. He began to run in pursuit.

'Piotr!' he bellowed. 'Piotr Pavlovich!'

Sadovsky looked behind him, wild, insane, and Akulov saw him wave an angry, desperate arm, pushing him away, saw his mouth screaming something, words lost in the roar of the approaching tank.

It went out of sight, smashing through the frozen puddles into the belly of the ravine. There was just the howl of machinery propelling forty tons of metal, and Sadovsky threw himself flat on the ridge line.

Akulov was behind him. He grabbed him with huge hands as the tank came over the hill. It was on them. Akulov fell flat next to Sadovsky, holding him next to him, and the tank came over them like an express train.

The noise ground on, going away down the track, and Akulov lifted his face from the icy mire. On each side of them, as straight as tram tracks, ran the great ruts of the tank tracks. Sadovsky lay next to him, weeping into the frozen grass.

'Now look what you've done,' Akulov said gently. 'We're all muddy.'

He picked Sadovsky up and cradled him in his arms as easily as a child would carry a pet cat.

'Now we'll have to go home and get changed,' he said. He began to walk across the ground towards his car. At the end of the run, the tank was pulling up.

'You'd better come home with me, Piotr Pavlovich. We can't leave you here. And when we get home let us call Nikita Sergeyevich. He is letting the *zeks* out of the camps. If Gaia is still alive, *he* will find her.'

32

Ruszkik Haza

Buda-Pest, Hungary, 23 October 1956

THE dawn light was beginning to fill the small room and Ruth blew out the candle she had been typing by. From her window she could see down from Buda into the business and shopping district of Pest on the other side of the curving Danube river. Spires and rococo buildings pushed up in the pale blue light and the patches of green that were the parks were turned russet and gold by the autumn. She opened the window to let the smoky air out. When she had finished her work she would go down to the café. She sat back down in front of the small black Remington typewriter and the thin metal fingers began to wave like the legs of a frantic spider, spattering the page with words.

'The people of Hungary are fighting to be free. Domination and tyranny are conditions they know well and so is armed resistance. Over the centuries the Hungarians have risen time and again against those who would subjugate them. And they have known freedom. And just recently enough for its taste to be still sweet in the mouths of the people outside the room where I write. When the Habsburg Empire fell in 1918, the Hungarians ruled themselves.

Freedom was once again extinguished by the forces of Adolf Hitler only two short decades later. At the war's end Hungary was 'liberated' by Stalin's Russia, and the people exchanged one black tyranny for another. Rakosi was the Russians' man here, the satrap and acolyte of Stalin. His secret police, the *Allamvedelmi Hivatal*, the Avo, arrested and tortured tens of thousands of innocent men and women. Life in Hungary became a grey existence of fear and poverty.

Then something wonderful happened. Stalin died. And his creature Rakosi was dismissed. A new man took over, Imre Nagy. A human being, who although a lifelong communist allowed life to begin again. Men and women could meet in the legendary cafés of Buda-Pest, could talk and joke, discuss politics without fear of arrest, for the jovial man talking at the next table at Gerbaud's might well be the premier himself, Nagy. The people knew how he had let his daughter marry a Protestant minister, how he loved the arts, painting, music, the theatre and good food and drink. They saw him when they went to the match to support the famous Honved national football team, their most enthusiastic fan.

It couldn't last. Life in Russia is grim, people might notice the Hungarians enjoying their new-found good time. Nagy was dismissed, Rakosi brought back.

But a second miracle occurred. The first was the long-overdue death of Stalin. The second was his denunciation by Nikita Khrushchev, in the now-famous "Secret Speech" to the XXth Party Congress. A new wind was blowing from the Kremlin and, for the first time in decades, it did not carry the stench of blood and fear. A fresh scent of hope was on the air.

The Russians got out of neighbouring Austria a year ago. Now the Austrians work 45 hours a week, not the Hungarians' 60, and for 230 per cent more wages. People notice what their neighbours do. If it can happen for Austria, it could happen elsewhere ... The first to test the new mood of the Russians were the Poles. Their soft-line leader Gomulka openly attacked the Stalinist policies imposed on his country earlier this very month. Students and workers took to the streets. And a third miracle happened. Khrushchev flew into Warsaw, saw Gomulka, and ordered the Soviet tanks to withdraw. The collective farms are to be junked. Cardinal Wyszynski is out of prison.

Here in Buda-Pest the people watched. Rakosi is gone, but the man who replaced him is another Soviet *apparatchik*, Ernst Gero, a former secret policeman. Soulless, Stalinist and humourless, he crawls to Moscow, even having renounced his Hungarian citizenship for that of the USSR. He is the most hated man in the country. The people want the most popular man in Hungary to have his job, the man from Kaposvar – Imre Nagy.

The verdict of the eastern European peoples occupied by the Russians, given bleak communist governments they did not vote for, is epitomised by the East Germans, the first to rise up in the riots of 1953, and the only ones able to leave – through Berlin. Hundreds of thousands flee to the West each year, from scientists to manual workers, from nurses to their patients. The entire law faculty of Leipzig university went across *en masse*.

The Hungarians can't go. Instead, workers and students have taken to the streets. They have been joined by officer cadets and members of the Communist Youth, all ripping the hated Soviet stars from their uniforms. Last night they pulled down the gigantic statue of Stalin and burned their Party cards on the corpse. All over the city you can hear their cry: "Death to Gero! Death to AVH! *Ruszkik Haza!*" That means "Russians Go Home."''

From the open window came a faint grinding and squeaking, the sound of metal moving on cobbles, the grunt of powerful diesel engines, and she got up. In the distance a group of mud-coloured tanks was moving along the embankment. They turned at the Margaret Bridge, crossing the river into Pest.

Ruth quickly sat down, and finished typing.

> 'In the dawn light on this Wednesday the 24th of October I have just seen a group of Soviet tanks moving in the city. Tanks went into Warsaw when the Poles stood up for de-Stalinisation, but they left again. As the Hungarians stand up as a nation once again they must hope that the tanks now moving into position do so as well – "*Ruszkik Haza!*"''

Ruth pulled the paper from the machine, adding it to the ones already typed, and folded it up in a strong brown envelope, licking and sealing the flap. From the street below came the parp of a car horn and she hurried down the stairs.

He was waiting nervously in the lobby, her British businessman, his little black Austin standing outside. She gave him the envelope and he quickly tucked it under his jacket.

'The *Reuter* offices in Vienna,' he said, and she smiled reassuringly at him.

'Come back soon,' she said. 'You know what they say. "Vienna is the city to live in, Prague the city to see, but Budapest is the place to have a good time in."'

'Maybe that's why the Russians are here,' he said dryly. 'To have a good time.'

She heard the sound of the little round car going up the street, and went into the café. Steam was coming from the ancient espresso machine and the air was scented with the smell of bread.

After she had had breakfast, she took some Zeiss lenses and a camera body from her room. She stowed away a fresh pack of Munkas cigarettes and, dressed in slacks, hiking boots and a strong blue windcheater, went out into the city.

She crossed the river by the elegant Chain Bridge and went into Pest. People were coming down Academy Street, some carrying the dead bodies of their relatives, the demonstrators killed by the AVH in Parliament Square during the night as they chanted for Nagy, and she took some photographs. A Russian T-34 stood on a street corner, strangely draped in a Hungarian tricolor. Some young men and women were talking to the crew. The young Russians seemed confused. They thought they were in Berlin and they wanted to know where the Nazis were. She took photographs of them, too.

Ruth moved further into the city. Machine gun fire could be heard. The tap of a rifle, the flat bang of a tank's gun. A little girl in a dirty white dress, about ten years old, came running down the street. She saw Ruth and crossed the road to get to her. She began speaking frantically in Hungarian.

'Your brother?' Ruth said. She spoke little Hungarian. 'Do you speak Russian?'

'Yes!' the girl cried. 'Come quickly, they are killing my brother and Sandor!'

Ruth ran with her the way she had come. In a small, lonely park there was a group of men by a tree. Three were Avo, secret policemen readily recognised by their blue collar markings. Drum-magazine Russian PPSh sub-machine guns were slung from their shoulders and they surrounded two youths. They had a noose about the neck of one and they heaved, swinging him up into the air from a branch. He flapped like a fish, his face turning purple.

'What do you think you're doing?' Ruth shouted, in Russian. They turned, surprised, letting go of the rope, and the boy fell to the ground.

'These are criminals,' one said. He pointed to a Soviet monument standing nearby. A heavy hammer lay on the grass and pieces of shattered stone littered the grass.

'They were breaking up State property. So we shall hang them.'

Ruth lifted her camera and took a photograph. 'Then I had better take pictures of your nasty faces, so the whole world knows what murderers look like,' she said. The Avo man darkened with rage, and he ran towards her.

'You give me that, or we'll hang you too!'

Then she was back at Arisaig, on the fighting mat at the Scottish country house with the big man. When he had finished teaching her she had known that she could hurt, maim or kill a man six stones heavier than herself with ease. Now it was as though she had never been gone. Her hands moved out to grip and she pulled him down, his shout of terror arrested in the dry snap of breaking bone. She rolled sideways on her knees and he lay beside her, his neck at a strange angle. His two partners stared in disbelief. As they clumsily began to unsling their weapons, she picked up the gun he had dropped. They had trained them at Arisaig to strip, rebuild, load and fire any one of two dozen weapons in the dark. The PPSh had been one of them.

The wood and metal were smooth and familiar in her hands. She fired two short bursts and the Avo men tumbled backwards like pheasants. She slung the gun over her neck and went to the two boys standing white-faced by the tree. The one they had been hanging had a livid rope burn about his neck. There was a lock knife in her pocket, she took it out and cut away the ropes. The little girl looked at her in delight.

'Who are you?' one of the boys whispered in awe.

'I'm a friend,' she said. 'You speak Russian?'

'We have to,' he said, and turned aside to spit. 'They make us.'

'I found her,' the little girl crowed.

Ruth bent down and took the guns from the dead men. 'You want these?' she asked casually. 'You can have them.'

'I am Sandor,' the first boy said. He looked no more than fourteen and his chin was smooth. 'This is Miklos.'

'He's my brother,' the little girl said. 'I'm Eva.'

The two boys took the weapons.

'Have fun,' Ruth said.

'No, no,' Sandor protested. He had red hair and he reminded her of Johnny Nichols in America. 'We are *your* men. You must show us how to use these.'

'Our father is in the Avo cells,' said Miklos. 'We will take you there, and you will show us how to get him out.'

As they went down the street together they were joined by a few other boys and girls.

'These are our friends,' said Sandor. 'We will *all* be your men.'

The little girl attached herself firmly to Ruth's side.

'But *I* found her,' she said, again.

Ruth distributed the hand grenades and Tokarev automatic pistols taken from the dead men, and the children held them in awe and delight.

'Keep the pins in,' she warned.

They could hear machine gun fire as they went down the road, and they began to see Hungarian flags spread out here and there, taken from doors and windows, placed to cover dead fighters. At the corner to the square they peered round.

'There!' said Miklos. 'There is the Avo building. That is where they hold my father.'

Wreckage strewed the square. A truck was burning near the gate to the police station and some students were firing a machine gun from behind it while others fired theirs from the shelter of the trees. The Avo men were firing back from the windows of the fortified building.

'This is no good,' Ruth said. 'You can't take a building like that with a machine gun. You need to be able to knock holes in it.'

The faces of the children brightened at the thought.

She led her troop back down the street and, from the shelter of an alleyway they looked across a wide junction where a Russian anti-tank gun commanded the approaches. Four soldiers were inside a sandbag emplacement.

'There,' said Sandor. 'That will knock holes in things.'

Ruth assessed the ground. 'Too far,' she said. 'They look alert and they're behind cover.'

They moved on. By the embankment she saw a parked tank and, nearby, an open-topped command car. A big figure was inside, talking to two other officers.

'Here,' she said, taking off her sub-machine gun, and handing it to one of the girls. She took the Tokarev pistol she had and put it in the waistband of her slacks, pulling the windcheater over it.

'You stay here,' she said. 'Come with me, Eva.'

She held the little girl's hand and came out across the road to the command vehicle. Some soldiers were nearby, but looked indifferently at the sight of a woman walking with her daughter. They stopped on the pavement and she looked up.

'Hullo, Ivan!' she called.

Akulov turned in surprise. 'Ruth!' he said, and beamed. 'What are *you* doing here?'

'Writing for Reuters,' she said. 'Don't stand up there – come down and say hallo to me, Ivan Ivanovich.'

Akulova said something briefly to the two junior officers and got out through the armoured rear doors. He embraced her, huge in his general's uniform.

'There's an anti-tank gun down there, Ivan,' she whispered. 'And I want it.'

He stiffened.

'I've got twenty armed soldiers covering you and I want you to walk down the road with me and get the gun.'

She stepped back, and he could see the Tokarev hiding under her windcheater.

'Just tell your colleagues you'll see them later.'

Akulov had been a soldier all his adult life; he understood the necessity of being able to make fast decisions when people were, in one way or another, threatening to kill him. He turned.

'This woman has important information for me,' he called up. 'I'll see you back at the headquarters.'

They saluted and the diesel belched blue smoke and moved off, its small tracks squeaking and clattering on the cobbles. Akulov looked down at the small girl.

'Is this one of your soldiers?'

'Yes,' Ruth said firmly, and she felt the little hand tighten with pride in hers.

They began to walk down the hill, and from the alleys and doorways the children assembled about them.

'Are these your soldiers too?' asked Akulov.

'As good as they come,' Ruth agreed, and Sandor and Miklos grinned in delight, repeating it to their friends.

'Hide the weapons,' said Ruth, and they crossed the open space of the junction, and walked up to the gun emplacement. The soldiers inside saluted Akulov.

'I have a target for the gun,' he said simply. 'Bring it.'

They put the wheels down and pushed it along the street towards the sound of firing, manoeuvering it by the trails. The soldiers looked slightly bemused by the children helping them, and pulling the ammunition cart.

'What are you shooting at?' asked Akulov.

'An Avo building,' said Ruth. 'Chekists.'

The gunner turned to her. 'You want us to shoot Chekists?' he said. They pushed the gun around the corner and settled it down with swift, practised movements. A shell slid into the breech and the gunner settled into his seat as machine gun fire pecked at his armour plate, he sighted the gun with smooth twirls of his controls.

'The *Chekisty* shot my brother in the war,' he said, and fired. The building shuddered, belching smoke and debris from a window. The case clanged, smoking, on to the cobbles and the layer slammed another into the breech.

'*Chekisty* took my parents from our village,' he remarked conversationally. 'I never saw them again.'

The gates blew apart, pieces tumbling over and over in the air.

After the third shell white cloths sprouted from the building, waving frantically.

'That do it, sir?' the gunner asked Akulov.

'Yes,' he said. 'You can take the gun back now.'

They rolled it back along the street as the students and workers

in the square emerged from behind their trees and barricades. From
the building a uniformed column emerged, making for the gates the
gun had blasted open. It was led by a uniformed Avo Major. He was
pushing a girl of seven or eight years in front of him.

'I won't harm her if you don't shoot,' he yelled. He saw Akulov
standing there, huge in his army uniform and his terror turned to
relief. Arrogance returned to his face.

'You help me with this lot,' he demanded.

Ruth was hiding behind Akulov's bulk. She aimed the Tokarev at
the Major's feet, kneeling and peeping from behind his jacket. She
fired twice, as she had been taught, and he crumpled to the ground.
A student quickly pulled the girl away.

They were angry, the young men and women, they dragged him
over to a tree in the square and tied his ankles and hung him up
from a low branch, upside down, so that he dangled two or three
feet from the ground. He flapped and kicked, trying to free himself,
and a fortune in paper money fell from his uniform like snow.

They lined the other Avo men up at pistol point and piled up
autumn leaves, twigs and branches, waste paper and every single
note of money. They opened his wallet and a girl extracted a piece
of paper. She held on to it and tossed the wallet into the first bright
flames of the fire they had lit.

'Come on, Ivan,' Ruth said. 'There are honest people inside that
building. Let's get them out.'

He didn't hesitate, and the strange alliance of children and adults
and students streamed through the shattered gates into the Avo
building. Behind them they heard the Avo man begin to scream.

Things of horror were in the basement. Dank, dark cells equipped
with chains, whips and sharp hooks, nail presses and metal devices
to crush joints and limbs.

There was a room with two baths, side by side.

'They fill one with ice water, the other with water that's nearly
boiling,' said Ruth. 'They put you in one to freeze, and then fling
you into the other. The Gestapo did it to me. The pain is quite
dreadful and they do it again and again and again . . .'

There was a small door, tightly locked. They could hear voices,
but no one had the key. Akulov seized a crowbar from the wall and,
with one immense heave, tore the door from its hinges. Cells lined
the long, narrow, damp corridor. Some were so small a prisoner could
not lie down or stand up. All were windowless and some were as
dark as night while others were lit, night or day, by a single powerful
bare bulb.

'You go blind, in the end,' said Ruth matter-of-factly. 'The Gestapo did that to people who irritated them.'

Akulov smashed the locks with a hammer and the stench of the suffering of years came out. With it came bent, emaciated, but smiling men and women. Ruth saw Miklos and Eva with their arms around a man shrunken to half his size. He was weeping.

Upstairs the students had broken into a huge room, set up like a telephone exchange. Banks of recording equipment lined the walls and there were shelves of tapes. On the floor were batteries of filing cabinets marked Suspicious Persons.

There were well-equipped bedrooms with carpets and curtains, and a well-stocked bar. They found pornographic magazines, and whips.

'The SS had a place like this in Ravensbruck,' said Ruth bleakly. 'How little things change, Ivan.'

They went outside and even the smoky air with its haze of propellant tasted fresh. In the square a girl was pinning something white to something charred hanging from a branch.

'It's his pay slip,' she said coldly. 'Look at it. The bastard earned a hundred times as much as a worker!'

Ruth stood in the smoky square with Akulov, and there was a sudden outburst of cheering.

'Nage! Nage!' voices shouted. 'He's Prime Minister! It's been on the radio!'

'Maybe Imre can sort this out,' said Akulov hopefully.

Ruth looked at him questioningly.

'I know him, Ruth. We were Bolsheviks together, before the Civil War.'

'You know him?' Ruth repeated. 'Then come with me, there's a man I want you to meet.'

They set off down the street, together with her small private army of children.

'Your collection is growing,' he said laconically.

'I'm going to give them some training this morning,' she said, and they cheered.

'This is a strange sort of way for a newspaper reporter to behave,' Akulov observed, but she did not reply.

They went back to the embankment and along the side of the great river towards Parliament Square. Behind it stood a fifteen-storey tall building of white stone, surmounted by a radio mast. Civil police guarded the entrance and the green lawns in front from strongposts equipped with heavy machine guns.

'I was due to interview the boss here today,' Ruth said. 'But there's no need now. I'll introduce you. He's Colonel Kopacsi and he's a good man – he hates the Avo.'

Someone came down to the fortified lobby. Ruth's children waited for her and she went up with Akulov. In an office on the twelfth floor Akulov met the Budapest police chief, a sandy-haired man in his thirties.

'Sandor, this is General Ivan Akulov. He and I know each other from a long time back. But he also knows Prime Minister Nagy. I thought that he might be of help. Nagy and the Russians are going to have to talk.'

Kopacsi eyed the big man opposite him. 'I'm trying to find the Prime Minister,' he said. 'No one can make contact with him and I fear that he is simply a prisoner of Gero, that Gero has only announced that he is Prime Minister to calm the people. What do you say, General?'

'It is probable. I can tell you that two senior Soviet officials are flying in today to talk with Gero. They are Suslov and Mikoyan. At a guess they have come to fire him for his bad handling of the situation. You should see Imre then.'

Kopacsi nodded thoughtfully, and then smiled. 'You're a useful man, General. I was at a meeting called by the Russians last night. One of their senior men is already here – he was introduced only as the Senior Adviser. He told me, and he emphasised every word, that "the Fascists and Imperialists are bringing out their shock troops into the streets of Budapest, and yet there are still comrades in your country's armed forces who hesitates to use arms!" I told him, and *I* emphasised every word, that "evidently the comrade adviser from Moscow has not time to inform himself of the situation in our country. We need to tell him that these are not 'Fascists' or other 'Imperialists' who are organising the demonstration; they come from the universities, the handpicked sons and daughters of the peasants and workers, the fine flower of our country's intelligentsia which is demanding its rights and wishes to show sympathy with the Poles in their similar struggle." He was very angry with me.'

'What did he look like?'

'Blue eyes – steel blue eyes behind metal-rimmed glasses. He was perhaps a Jew and he was your age.'

'Krivitskiy,' said Ruth, and Akulov nodded in agreement.

'Who is Krivitskiy?'

'Head of the KGB,' Ruth said succinctly, and Kopacsi nodded.

'He had the smell of the *Chekisty* about him.' He turned to Akulov. 'It would be very helpful to have a Russian general here while I am trying to find out what is happening,' he said. 'I have to tell you that I have joined the fighters for freedom, and have instructed all police stations in Hungary to do likewise, and to issue arms to them. Will you stay?'

'Do I have a choice?' Ivan asked.

'It would be helpful,' Kopacsi repeated, and Akulov smiled.

'Then I shall stay.'

Ruth got up. 'I must go and collect my troops. We have some training to do.'

'Ruth, what are you doing?' Akulov pressed. 'You told me you were working for a newspaper and in a few hours this morning you have kidnapped a Soviet general, stolen a piece of artillery and used it to attack a police station, helped execute the man in charge and freed all the prisoners. You are now going off to provide a bunch of schoolchildren with training in the arts of guerilla warfare. Why?'

'I'm trying to put the record straight,' she said. She turned to Kopacsi. 'I don't suppose you have any plastic? No. Nitroglycerine?'

'The warehouse on Zsilinszky Street,' the police chief said quickly. 'I'll send some policemen with you to get in.'

'They'll have liquid soap there too. Got a petrol pump here for the vehicles? Marvellous. We'll need some bottles for the bombs. Some people call them Molotov cocktails after that revolting little man of Stalin's. I prefer the name Worcester Sauce. You can feel it burn all the way down and it leaves a nice warm glow behind.'

She laughed merrily, and felt in her pockets for her packet of Munkas cigarettes. She lit one and went out, and down to the waiting children.

Akulov sat in his chair, thinking, then he looked up. 'Do you have a *vertushka* here? A special line?'

'The *Kozvetlen* telephone? Of course.' Copacsi indicted a green phone on his desk.

'Call the Kremlin. Say who you are, and that General Akulov wants to speak to Comrade Khrushchev.'

It took a little while, and then Akulov heard Khrushchev's voice.

'Ivan Ivanovich. You're with the Chief of Police there?'

'Yes, Nikita Sergeyevich. I have to tell you he's with the insurgents, the ones who call themselves Freedom Fighters.'

'What's going on with all these traitors?' Khrushchev demanded angrily. 'Why are they going over to the imperialists?'

'There are no imperialists, Nikita Sergeyevich. Just Hungarians.'

'So why are they fighting? Haven't we given them what they want? We dug up that man Rajk that Rakosi killed, gave him a slap-up funeral. They can have done with the collectives if they must. We got rid of Rakosi, too. What more do they want Ivan Ivanovich?'

'I think they want rid of us,' Akulov said dryly. 'But they're realists; they may settle for less. But you must get rid of Rakosi and put in Gero.'

'He's our man. He does what we say.'

'*They* know that. If you want the fighting to stop put in Nagy and have him broadcast to the nation. And pull out the troops like you did in Poland.'

There was silence on the phone, except for Khrushchev's breathing.

'It isn't easy to know what to do here. There is a strong feeling that a show of force will prove that the workers do not back the students who are making the trouble.'

'I was out on the streets this morning, Nikita Sergeyevich. It's not just the students. There are workers, former Communist Party officials, officers and cadets from the Kossuth Officer's School and the Rakoczy Academy, even Avo men. Regular Army officers like Colonel Maleter have joined. Policemen like Chief Copacsi here.'

There was silence again, and then Khrushchev spoke in a different tone of voice.

'What is taking place in Hungary is a fascist, capitalist and imperialist mutiny, and those supporting it must take the consequences.' Then he reverted to the manner he had used before. 'Stay with Copacsi, Ivan Ivanovich, and keep me informed.'

Akulov put down the phone. Copasci, who had been listening on an extension looked at him enquiringly.

'He's sending in tanks,' said Akulov. 'If your Freedom Fighters crack you'll be back to where you started, if not worse. If you don't, he'll think again.'

The two tanks came slowly down Karolyi Street, making for the big intersection at Kalvin Square. The boulevard was deserted and dark; only the old gas lamps on their ornate iron poles casting pools of lights through which flickered the jog-trotting infantry at the side of the two armoured vehicles.

On the rooftop, Sandor spoke, as he had been trained that afternoon.

'One,' he commanded, and his troop of children stuffed the

shirt cloth wicks into the bottles of petrol, holding them in with loose-fitting corks.

The tanks grumbled closer. Fifty feet above on the baroque roof they could hear the squeaking and clatter of the tracks on the cobbles.

'Two,' Sandor said, and they tipped their bottles so that petrol flowed into the cloth wicks. He lit a newspaper with the Zippo lighter Ruth had given to him.

The tanks were almost below, at the entrance to the square.

'Three,' Sandor ordered, and they dipped the wicks into the flame and threw the bombs down upon the infantry.

The street was suddenly illuminated by the blossoms of flame, and screaming men running about on fire, beating at themselves. As Sandor and his fighters ran along the roof to the corner of the street they heard the sudden drumming of sub-machine guns as the two tommy-gunners, Ruth and Miklos, opened up from the alley.

The two tanks had halted and the commanders had battened down.

Children came running, fleet and silent, out of the darkness, and little hands smeared jam over vision blocks. Then they were gone, as if they had never been, swallowed up by the night.

The two tanks jerked into motion, the drivers revving their engines to escape the trap. As they came into the square they skidded, in slow motion, slithering helplessly, their tracks churning. The whole road had been lined with silk cloth taken from the Party bosses' store off Szena Square, and lubricated with oil.

Above, the firebombers lit their weapons and the bottles rained down like comets on to the engine slats, and around the air intakes. Hatches were suddenly flung open as men escaping the flames struggled out. The sub-machine guns opened up again. Sandor carefully threw two grenades down on to the decks below and, as his crew escaped down the stairway, he heard the twin crump of the explosions.

As they slipped away through the maze of tiny streets and alleys that only they knew, behind them it was quiet, except for the crackling of the flames.

They emerged from one of the blocks of flats and crossed the twin tram tracks of Jozsef Avenue by the cinema to vanish into Corvin Passage, another of the twisting alleys. Nearby was the heavily-walled bulk of the Kilian Baracks, taken over by Colonel Maleter, the Hungarian army officer turned freedom fighter. When they tumbled down the steps into the cellar they found the others already there with Ruth. On a table were some of the spoils – the two heavy machine guns from the tank turrets, and a collection of *Automat Kalashnikov* assault rifles taken from the dead soldiers.

Ruth had something else: a bagful of tricolor armbands. As Sandor came down the stairs with his fighters she gave him one to put on.

'Well done!' she said. 'You're real Hungarian soldiers now. Here are your combat medals.'

The young people crowded about her. They ranged in age from Sandor's sixteen to Eva, who was ten and who become Ruth's runner. Not all had taken part in the fighting, – the little ones had been messengers and carriers of supplies. They had brought food and there was bread, cheese, sausage and milk.

As the supply of armbands dwindled, Eva looked anxiously at the bag. Finally, Ruth took one out and put it about the little girl's arm.

'There,' she said. 'You were my first soldier.' She turned to the others, and began to distribute food. 'Tomorrow won't be as easy,' she warned. 'It'll be daylight, and the Russians will be more alert, now that they've seen what can happen.'

Then she beamed at them. 'But they aren't as clever as we are! Tomorrow, we'll have new tactics – and new weapons. Eva has brought good news from Csepel.'

The little girl blushed with pride. 'We're getting an anti-tank gun. Big enough to take out a tank, small enough to wheel along alleys and courtyards where tanks can't go. We're fish, remember? We hide in the water of the city. We hit and we run.'

With all her troops munching, Ruth took two thick sandwiches up to the two guards above and, when she returned, ate herself.

'So tomorrow,' she said through a mouthful of cheese, butter and flat bread, 'I want some big saucepans, and some soup-plates.'

In the lead T-34 Georgy Svetlov peered through the armoured glass of his driver's compartment. The street was a mess, lined with the skeletons of burned out cars, the walls plastered with anti-Russian slogans. Dirty black smoke was streaming across from an alley. It was like fog as they went through it and he tasted it, acrid from burning tyres.

As he came out into the clearer air he cursed. In the smoke someone had slapped jam across his vision port. He knew better than to use his wiper and he peered desperately through the clearest part he could find. Big grey things like anti-tank weapons were hanging down in front of him from the tramcables. Beyond them he could see rows of broad, circular things like land mines nestling in the ripped-up boulevard. The commander, Lieutenant Chernyak, saw them at the same time and as Georgy was pulling on his steering lever he got the command to wheel right.

The rebels had put up a thick barricade of overturned yellow trams lined with paving stones and cobbles and he did not dare risk being trapped and pinned on it. From behind him came the crump of grenades, and the back of the tank rattled like a drum under machine gun fire.

The side street was clear, and he roared down it.

'Left at the end,' ordered Chernyak. 'We'll take them from the rear.'

The T-34 suddenly shuddered and the lever went slack in his hand as the tank slewed across the street to bury itself in the wall. There was a tremendous crash as the tank behind went into them and the moment of silence that followed was broken by the flat bang of a small artillery piece, and the almost immediate clang of its round slamming into armour at close range.

Chernyak threw back his batch and scrambled out across the rubble-covered deck. The tank track snaked along the ground like entrails and a small anti-tank gun was in the road behind them. A woman got up from the seat, and a swarm of children appeared, spiriting it away through an alley. The third tank was on fire.

The window of the house opposite was open. As the bottles rained down like comets and the road became filled with fire he ran towards it. But a boy with red hair was standing there with a sub-machine gun, looking at him. Petrol exploded next to him, licking him with flame, and the boy fired . . .

Akulov sat in his shirtsleeves on the camp bed that had been set up for him on the twelfth floor of Copacsi's police headquarters and, like the rest of Hungary, listened to the radio.

'The Hungarian Government has come to an agreement with the Soviet government whereby Soviet forces shall immediately withdraw from Budapest. Negotiations are underway with regard to the withdrawal of Soviet forces stationed in Hungary. There is to be a cease-fire. After the re-establishment of order we shall organise a new and single police force and we shall dissolve the organs of state security. No one who took part in the armed fighting need fear reprisals.'

Imre Nagy's rich, rolling country tones came to an end and were replaced by the sound of cheering from outside that did not seem as though it would ever end. Copacsi looked up at Akulov and there were tears rolling down his cheeks.

'Do you want me to translate?' he asked. Akulov got up and looked out of the window. In the shattered streets ragged men and women were capering in a thousand victory dances.

'No,' he said. 'You won and I understand that.' He looked at the Hungarian. 'Well done,' he said simply.

The K line rang, the direct link, and Copacsi picked it up.

'Khrushchev,' he said, handing it over.

Khrushchev sounded almost jovial. 'You've been a great help, Ivan Ivanovich,' he said warmly. 'In the morning I want you to go and join Premier Nagy. You know him. Help sort out the arrangements from the army's side.'

'Very good, Nikita Sergeyevich,' Akulov agreed.

'I'll have someone take you over in the morning,' said Copacsi, and Akulov swung himself wearily on to his bed as the noises of celebration gained in intensity in the dusk outside.

In the morning when Akulov came down to leave the building, an old American army Jeep from lend-lease was waiting outside. A huge Hungarian flag hung from a pole affixed to the side. It had a hole in its centre, like all the flags on show, where the red symbols of communism had been torn out. In the driver's seat was Ruth. By her sat the small girl of the day before with a tricolor armband on.

'Good morning, Ivan,' called Ruth. She looked tired and elated at the same time, sparkling eyes ringed with black. 'I'm to take you to Nagy. Have you heard the news? He's forming a multi-party government and he's going to hold democratic elections. Hungary's withdrawing from the Warsaw Pact. By the way, this is Eva. She has been fighting with me. She lost her parents in the war and I've told her that I lost my little girl, so I'm going to be like a mummy to her and she's going to be my little girl. We're going to help each other. Aren't we?'

The little girl looked at Ruth with ultimate faith. 'Yes,' she affirmed.

'This is General Akulov,' Ruth said. He's going to make the arrangements for the Russian troops to go away.'

The small eyes inspected him.

'I'm not a Russian,' said Akulov. 'I'm from the Ukraine.'

'That is good,' she said gravely. He got into the back and they set off with a jerk. The day was sunny and crisp.

'You're famous,' said Akulov. 'Everyone's heard about the White

Russian Countess who came out of nowhere. How many tanks did you get, Ruth?'

'Enough,' she said. 'With all the others. The people won.'

'Nikita Sergeyevich could have done it, if he'd been prepared to level the whole place,' Akulov observed. 'Like we did in Berlin. But he wasn't.'

'He made the speech,' said Ruth. 'Either Stalin was a terrible freak thrown up by communism or he was its entirely natural fruit, and communism inevitably leads to repression, lies and poverty of one degree or another whoever is in charge. By admitting defeat here, he is claiming the first.'

She twirled the wheel and the Jeep bounced over rubble. 'I'm going the long way around,' she said. 'Taking the pretty route.'

Akulov looked at the devastation of the war. Vast piles of debris were everywhere. Houses gaped and burned out Russian tanks and armoured cars littered the streets. Splashes of colour decorated the rubble where fallen freedom fighters lay covered by a flag. The Russians they had killed lay in the open. Sprinkled with lime, they looked like statues. Everywhere men and women moved among the dead, lifting the flags, looking for loved ones.

'Not that pretty,' he observed. She stopped on the corner of Stalin Avenue. The block of stone bearing his name had been prised out of the wall and lay among the rubble on the ground. The old enamel plate of Andrassy Street, hidden since 1948, had been re-affixed. Along the boulevard a steady stream of Soviet ammunition carriers, tanks and guns was moving. Trucks were there, drawing field kitchens, the little bright fires glowing, steam puffing gaily as they left the city.

'That's what people find pretty,' Ruth said. In the square they could see the great pink marble plinth with the boots that were all that was left of Stalin's statue. They were filled with Hungarian flags.

'They call it Boot Square now,' she said cheerfully.

On the corner an old man had set up an ancient wicker chair in which he sat, holding a glass of warm gold *barack*, rare, treasured apricot brandy, and he watched the Russians leaving. He was small and slight, like a sparrow, with the sharp nose and chin, the sucked-in cheeks of emaciation. From time to time he raised his glass and inhaled the fumes like an elixir. A truck full of armed freedom fighters passed and he raised the glass high, beaming with toothless gums, his milky blue eyes shining.

'*El jen!*' he cried, 'Long live!'

And then he drank.

Ruth turned the Jeep, and they went on. Along the street the old

Kossuth coat-of-arms adorned the government buildings, bright as bunches of flowers. Going towards the Hunyadi Square market they passed farm carts coming in loaded with bread, milk, meat and potatoes.

'They say it's like 1945. New beginnings after so much sorrow and blood. They'll get it right this time.'

The shop windows were shattered by the gunfire and the goods inside were on open display.

'There hasn't been one case of looting,' Ruth said fiercely. 'Not one! This is a holy city. They say even the thieves have given up their trade.'

In the square the café owners had worked hard to clear the debris. People were sitting outside in the sun on cracked and broken paving stones as though nothing had happened. Ruth pulled in.

'Let's have a coffee,' she said.

They sat down at a little table and a red-haired boy came bounding forward.

'My lieutenant, Sandor,' Ruth said proudly. 'His father owns his café again.'

As Sandor brought steaming, milky coffee a very frail man carefully got up from his table and bowed to Ruth. He was eating some bread, dipping it into a large cup of warm milk.

'This is Thomas,' Ruth said to Akulov. 'We liberated the Marko Street prison on the second day of the war.'

'Are your teeth loose?' Akulov asked sympathetically.

'Yes, General,' Thomas said, staring steadily at him.

'I was in the camps in Kolyma before the war,' Akulov said. 'Mine were loose, too. I made a grater by punching holes in a piece of a tin can, because I could not gnaw the raw potato.'

The former prisoner nodded at the shared experience.

'I'll pick you up in about an hour,' said Ruth. She turned to Akulov. 'We're going to view one of the new attractions of Budapest. Rakosi's villa on Fo Street. My dear, you should see it! Indoor, illuminated swimming pool. Luxury bathrooms with slimming equipment – slimming equipment! While the people were starving! Grand pianos, Hi-fi, cellars of French wine, American kitchens. Thomas wants to go and spit on his grave, but he's run off to Russia.'

'Piss!' Thomas said indistinctly, through milky bread. 'I would *piss* on his grave.'

'I'm being polite,' Ruth said cheerfully. In the distance, in Buda, people were swarming about the Liberty Monument on the hill. Next to the graceful female figure had been placed a dominating bronze Red Army soldier. Now ropes by the dozen encircled it and tiny, Lilliput figures heaved. It swayed, and slowly fell on to its face.

Akulov heard a small happy giggle, and turned to see Eva laughing.

A boy came along the square selling papers. He saw Akulov and held out a copy, grinning.

'*Igazsag*, General. That means *Truth*.'

Akulov fumbled in his pockets. 'I don't have a forint,' he said.

The boy handed it to him. 'Have a free copy. Take it home with you. You know what they say about your papers? *V Izvestiakh nyet Pravdi*. In the News there is no Truth, and *i v Pravda nyet Izvestii*, in the Truth there is no news.'

He went off laughing and people bought from him all the way round the square.

'Over twenty papers have come out since the people rose,' Ruth said happily. 'Passionate, idealistic, articulate and from the heart.'

Eva tipped up her mug of milk, letting the last drops slide down, and put it on the table with a sigh of pleasure. Ruth took a handkerchief and wiped her mouth then she finished her coffee and lit a Munkas, blowing the smoke in a grey stream in the sunshine.

'Are you ready, darling?' she asked Eva, and they got up. On the corner where their Jeep was parked a large box had been set up. A sign above it said: "For the Families of Those who gave their Lives for Freedom." It was stuffed with currency notes. Ruth reached in her pocket and put in some money.

Akulov looked around the square. A hundred pairs of Hungarian eyes stared at him. He took out his wallet and emptied it into the box.

Tokol Airfield, Budapest, 3 November

'I think this just about finishes it up,' said Akulov. He sat on one side of the long polished table with his team of technical officers, and the Hungarian Honved Army delegation sat on the other. Akulov faced Pal Maleter, former Hungarian Army Colonel, Freedom Fighter leader and now General and Defence Minister of the independent state of Hungary that he had helped to create. From outside the heavily-curtained room came the sound of the Tupolev and Antonov transport aircraft. Each time the rising screech of engines signalled the departure of an aircraft from the runway Akulov saw General Kovacs, Maleter's Chief of Staff, smile.

Akulov signalled to the stewards, who placed bottles of Giraffe beer, Szilvorium plum brandy and vodka on the table. They brought shotglasses and charged them.

'First, a toast to the new friendship between the Hungarian and Soviet peoples and their respective armies. May they never fight again.'

All stood up with a crash and downed their drinks, shouting in approval. Beer chasers were poured, and they retook their seats. Akulov picked up the papers in front of him.

'Very good. Let me summarise the points of our agreement. If we are all happy with it then I suggest a final working session tomorrow morning to finalise the technical details regarding units, and a detailed timescale.'

Akulov ran one large finger to the head of his sheet of paper and began. 'The Soviet Union agrees to withdraw all its forces from Hungarian soil.'

There was drumming of approval from the Hungarian side. Maleter smiled, but held up his hand for quiet.

'This withdrawal has already begun.'

Akulov gestured towards the curtains, and the noise of the aircraft. 'We have done our best, I don't think that the people of Budapest can see any soldiers on their streets. However, this leads to point two. There are a lot of troops in Hungary, with a lot of heavy equipment and stores, and to avoid the disruption of the transport network we propose that the withdrawal be a phased one. This is what we can sort out tomorrow, a detailed timetable. Point three, the Hungarian garrisons must now stop denying us food and fuel. Point four, this has caught us by surprise – ' Akulov looked up to smile at the Hungarians. 'We weren't expecting to leave so soon!'

They all laughed.

'The point being that we are not prepared for a winter movement of troops and that, consequently, the withdrawal may not be as swift as both sides might like. However, with goodwill on both sides this need not be a problem. The fifth and last point is one that is important to us. We are the Soviet Army. We smashed the Fascist Hitlerites and our honour matters to us. We propose that when our last units march out of Hungary, they do so to an appropriate colourful military ceremony. One suitable for two friendly countries. Bands, martial hymns, speeches and flags.'

'We shall be glad to do this,' Maleter affirmed and Akulov signalled for the glasses to be refilled.

With his glass in his hand, he paused. From without came the sudden noise of men shouting. The tall doors of the conference room crashed back and twenty green-capped KGB men ran into the room with sub-machine guns. They covered the Hungarians.

Behind them came a single figure in civilian clothes. He sauntered into the room with his hands in his pockets.

'You are prisoners of the Soviet Army,' he said.

It was Krivitskiy.

Maleter stood up and looked at Akulov in contempt. 'So that was it, was it? So much for the honour of the Soviet Army!'

The KGB men hustled the Hungarians from the room.

'What the hell have you done?' Akulov demanded angrily.

Krivitskiy spread his hands apologetically. 'I'm just the messenger boy,' he said. 'The bosses in Moscow have changed their minds.'

Akulov went to the window and tore back the curtain. Outside a four-engined Antonov had just taxied in. Its propellers were slowly swinging and down its loading ramp marched columns of armed soldiers . . .

7 November, 1956

From the smashed cellar they could see down the road to the Kilian barracks. Beneath them the tunnel they had used to leave lay destroyed. The ammunition they had fetched sat worthless in its boxes. Ruth, Sandor and Eva lay hidden in the rubble, their clothes and skin the same colour, and watched as the Russian officers walked down the devastated street to the gates. The old building was shattered from the shelling and the skeletons of burned out ambulances lay charred about. The firing had stopped. The defenders had held out for three days as the Russians destroyed Budapest and now it was all over.

There were tattered white flags poking from the places where shell holes had taken the place of windows. Now the gates where Maleter had placed his tank and joined the revolution creaked back. A Soviet colonel stood waiting as the last freedom fighters emerged.

They were a ragamuffin army, dressed in tatters. Seeping blood from their wounds made the only splashes of colour on them. They shuffled out, holding their heads up. From the cellar Ruth and the two children could see Miklos carrying a young girl. Thomas, even more frail than when they had freed him from prison, staggered wearily along the street, supporting himself with a crutch made from a window frame. There were about forty in all – all that was left of the resistance.

'Go down the street,' the colonel shouted. 'Ambulances are waiting for you.'

They moved slowly, past the ambulances, past the wrecked tanks, stumbling on the debris. Behind them soldiers shut the gates as others placed the bipods of their machine guns on chunks of rubble for support.

The colonel gave the order and when Ruth lifted her head, clutching Eva to her, bodies lay scattered all down the street. The troops moved out, pausing on their way to finish off the dying.

'It's all over,' Ruth whispered. 'We must get out.'

'Out where?' asked Sandor, lying next to her. His red hair was white with powdered stone and plaster.

'Out of the country. The Avo's back and they'll be searching for everyone who took up arms. Kadar's the new Rakosi and the Russians will have him make a clean sweep. We must go.'

They had seen the pitiful streams of people making their way down the wet roads out of Budapest, pushing prams and carts over the fallen beech leaves. They had gone the other way, to the Kilian barracks to fight, but now was the time to join the refugees.

'I have a British passport,' Ruth said. 'And money. I left them with Zoltan at the hotel, to put in his safe. If it's still standing, he'll have them. We'll go to the British Legation in Liberty Square and get documents for you.'

Dusk was falling and the soldiers were gone. Like wary animals they slipped from the ruins, leaving only the dead behind.

It was easy to get lost in the city. So many of the landmarks were gone; in the gathering dark they slipped from one great sweep of rubble to another, made their way from one street to another through entire houses gutted by shell fire. In the gloom beside a wall Ruth tripped and fell on to a pile of still-warm corpses. There was a faint smell of baking bread in the air and she realised she was amongst the dead of a bread-queue that had not moved in time when the tanks rounded the corner.

They retraced their tracks near the Franciscan Church, where lorry loads of soldiers were looting the big liquor store. Many were already drunk and fired their weapons at anyone in sight. They slipped away, passing under the black flags lining the road, the smell of stone dust and fire in their mouths.

When they came up near to the river, a moon had risen. It glinted on the water.

'You can't cross,' said Sandor. 'Your hotel is in Buda and the Russians have checks on the bridges. You are known, Ruth. They are looking for you – they call you a traitor.'

'Well, we can't go without my passport and money,' Ruth said practically.

'Let me go,' said Eva. 'I have run all over the city. They will not stop me and I know where the hotel is.'

'Bring it to my father's café,' said Sandor. 'We'll get some food there before we go to the Legation.'

'Wait,' said Ruth, but the girl was gone. 'Take care . . .'

The café in the square was still standing and inside there was some warmth, a bowl of hot water and a piece of soap, some bread and milk.

'I'm going to find Eva,' said Sandor soon after they arrived. 'I'll wait near the bridge for her.'

Deadly tired, Ruth sat dozing by a fire made of wood from the shattered buildings. She awoke suddenly, reaching for her gun. Sandor was standing there, his father behind him.

'They caught Eva,' he said. 'She was wearing her arm band and they have taken her away.'

Ruth sat thinking for a moment, trying to process the information.

'Ivan,' she said. 'Where are the Soviet officers staying? The Astoria Hotel, isn't it? I need a telephone that's working.'

'Ours still works,' Sandor's father said. 'There was less destruction at this end of town.'

She took the phone and dialled. 'General Akulov, please. Yes, his wife.'

In the quiet of the dark café they heard the deep voice come on the line.

'Yelena?'

'It's me, Ruth,' she said, and he was silent. 'Ivan, do you remember a small girl who was with me? Eva? She has just been arrested.'

'She is very young,' he said after a few moments. 'She will be released. The fighting is over and we will not be persecuting children. Things will get back to normal now, you'll see, Ruth.'

'They murdered our fighters in the Kilian barracks, Ivan,' she said. 'They shot them down after they had surrendered.'

'The fighting is over,' said Akulov. 'Your little friend will soon be free, you'll see. I must go now.'

There was a clatter as he put the phone down, and only the burr of the empty line.

23 November

'It's Nagy,' said Krivitskiy. He paused and pointed through the bare trees of the park to the white three storey building that overlooked it from the end of Andrassy Street. Fresh glass shone in its windows and men were repainting its outside.

'He's in there,' Krivitskiy said to Akulov, walking next to him. 'The Yugoslav Embassy. He's there with half the old cabinet and their families. We want him to come out but he won't.'

'Why do you want him to come out?' Akulov asked.

Krivitskiy pointed to a nearby statue from the days of the Habsburg Empire, miraculously unharmed by the fighting. Around an elegant stone neck someone had hung a sign:

LOST – THE CONFIDENCE OF THE PEOPLE. HONEST FINDER IS ASKED TO RETURN IT AT ONCE TO JANOS KADAR, PREMIER OF HUNGARY, AT 10,000 SOVIET TANKS STREET.

'You know the current joke going the rounds? "Except for nearly ten million counter-revolutionary landlords, factory owners, bankers, counts and cardinals, the Hungarian workers remain loyal to the people's democratic regime, and all six of them form the Kadar government." That's why we want Nagy out. The people still worship him. – They know Kadar's no more than our puppet. Nagy can come out, take over the government again. It'll be better for everyone. We're not going, we've made that plain. What we have, we hold. But let the Hungarians have Nagy – then things will work smoothly. It'll be better for everyone.'

'So walk up to the door and tell him,' Akulov said shortly.

Krivitskiy spread his hands wide in exasperation. 'He won't believe *me*. I suppose I can't blame him – secret policemen don't have the best of reputations. But this comes all the way from Nikita Sergeyevich. I'm only the messenger boy.'

'So why tell me?'

'He trusts *you*. Just tell him it's safe. He can come out with his family, go home to Orso Street and tomorrow we'll swear him in at Parliament Square.'

Akulov stared steadily at Krivitskiy. 'Do you promise *me* it's safe for him?'

'I give you my word, Ivan Ivanovich. On the name of the revolution. Nothing will happen to him.'

The door opened and Akulov went in. In his hand he bore a letter and he gave it to the Yugoslav Ambassador who was waiting formally. With him was Nagy, tired and worried, but with his moustaches still curling upwards.

'It's from Kadar,' said the Ambassador. He read from the formally-printed sheet of paper.

'The Hungarian Government repeats herewith the assurance already given several times by word of mouth that it has no desire to punish Imre Nagy and the members of his group in any way for their past activities. We therefore expect that the asylum granted by the Yugoslav embassy to this group be withdrawn, no longer being required, and that its members will return to their homes.'

The Ambassador turned to Nagy, whose face had creased with relief.

'I don't think you can get much plainer than that,' Nagy said.

'They want you to be premier again,' Akulov said to Nagy, smiling. 'Kadar's no good.'

'Well, perhaps we can save something from all this yet,' Nagy said, nodding his head.

Children and women were coming down the stairs, carrying bags. The other members of the cabinet gathered and from the doorway Akulov heard the rattle of a diesel engine, and the squeak of brakes.

'There's the bus,' he said. 'Come on, Imre, I'll take you home.'

'Back in time for supper,' Nagy said in a young girl close to him. They went out, and got into the bus, chattering happily.

As it moved off down Andrassy Street, a Soviet police car pulled away from the kerb in escort. Near Gorki Street one of the Hungarians, Haraszti, who had been President of the Journalists' Association, sat forward in his seat.

'We live along here, General,' he called.

'Slow up, driver,' Akulov ordered. As the bus maintained speed he walked forward and thumped the glass behind the man's seat.

'Did you hear me? Stop now.'

He looked back along the bus, and saw the police car turning off as an armoured car and a personnel carrier took up station. The

Hungarians saw it, too. Sensing the sudden tension, the children began to whimper, holding close to their mothers.

The bus stopped outside a building of the Soviet High Command and a lieutenant came forward and opened the door. Akulov barred the way and the young man raised his sub-machine gun.

'Superior orders, General. Everyone off! Anyone who tries to escape will be shot.'

They had to drag Nagy off. As they took him through the big oak doors he turned, casting one last, terrible glance upon Akulov . . .

The telephone rang in Akulov's room, the one they had given him in the hotel they had requisitioned, looking over the river. Snow was beginning to fall, covering the shattered buildings in a soft blanket.

'Your wife, General,' said the telephone operator. There was a click as she connected the line. 'Go ahead, caller.'

'Yelena?' Akulov asked.

'It's me,' said a quiet voice. There had been another click when the operator left the line so it was clear. He was speaking to Ruth.

'I'm looking for a small girl,' she said. 'Arrested three weeks ago for wearing a tricolor armband. Her name is Eva and she is ten years old, Ivan. They say the prisons are full.'

'I'll have to ask,' he said slowly.

'Come and have a coffee,' she said. 'At the same place.'

He came when it was dark, slipping into the dim, closed café in his long coat.

'We don't have any coffee,' she said quietly. 'It ran out some time ago.'

'Those who fought are being shipped out,' said Akulov. 'Young and old, wounded or not. Adult or child. By freight train to Siberia. The square of Vermezo is where they assemble them for deportment. Some sixteen thousand have already gone. Your Eva is scheduled to leave tomorrow. It is beyond my power to get her out because the KGB are in charge.'

'I still have some weapons,' Ruth said. 'And I have Sandor. I need a car, or a truck and a couple of Soviet uniforms. Oh, and papers.'

Akulov took out his wallet. 'Here are your papers,' he said. 'A truck is outside. Some uniforms are in the back.' He smiled faintly. 'I knew, you see, what you would need.'

The freight train was sixty trucks long. They were grey, slab-sided, windowless and their doors were locked. They were hauled by a steam locomotive and in the valley the sound of its grunting could be heard before it was seen.

It came into view through the pine trees, and the smoke from its stack diminished as the driver saw the signal commanding him to halt. The locomotive rolled slowly towards the sign. As it approached, a twig- and grass-covered bundle rolled over the rail from the trackside to lie on the sleepers, and the locomotive pulled the trucks above it, one after the other. When it stopped, the bunndle was lying close to the last two sections of the train, which were passenger carriages.

On the tracks, Ruth crawled towards the coupling that joined the carriages to the last freight car. She was wrapped in camouflaged sacking and on her back she wore her sub-machine gun. In her hand she had a crowbar, its end wound about with cloth tape.

She used it to get a silent purchase on the coupling and carefully disconnected the carriages from the train. Then she got back under and crawled under the trucks, unseen. She emerged by the locomotive and climbed up into the driver's cab. Sandor was standing there, his sub-machine gun covering two KGB men who were standing glowering beside the rails below. The driver stood waiting beside the controls.

'It's done,' Ruth said. 'Move on.'

The man in his blue boiler suit twirled the silver wheel and the train grunted as it moved forward. It slowly gained speed and, as they went around a curve in the forest, Ruth looked back, and saw small, frantic figures emerging from the abandoned carriages. A few miles further on they stopped the train and Sandor shinned up the telegraph pole beside the track. He cut the wires and, coming down, repeated the operation at the next.

When they came to the river, the train slowed and stopped. They got down and began to break open the locks of the freight cars. Thirsty, tired but suddenly elated people began to climb down from them, blinking in the light. Some of them helped to free the others. As each door rolled back, Ruth looked anxiously as the people came piling out.

'Eva?' she called. 'Eva?'

A little figure came running and hurled herself into her arms. Ruth held her tight, then looked at her, wiping at the tears that ran down her face.

'Darling,' she said, 'how dirty you are! We must get you some clean clothes, just as soon as we can.'

The people about them laughed and Ruth stepped from their crowd, clutching Eva by the hand.

'Listen now,' she called. She pointed down to the river bank, where an old, tarry black barge was moored.

'That barge will take us away from here. We'll get most of the way to the Austrian border, and then we'll have to walk over the mountain. Not far, about twenty kilometres. Shall we go?'

Sandor was waiting down there, and they began to stream down the side of the hill to the vessel. Ruth looked up at the driver in his cab.

'Take it down the line and dump it,' she said.

The man twirled his controls again, and it began to move. He jumped down on to the track side.

'Not me,' he said. 'I'm coming, too!'

Saarfold Village, Austria

Near dawn the *Berghofmeister* was wakened by his wife.

'Listen, Heinz. People. Many people.'

They weren't making much noise, but from below the windows of his bedroom in the wooden inn there came the sound of many voices, and the shuffling of feet coming up the road. He pushed back his plump duvet and went over to the window.

There they were, sitting on the ground outside, leaning up against walls, tired, huddling in corners against the cold.

'Refugees, Lily,' he said positively, turning back inside the room. 'From Hungary.'

'Are you sure? There have been none for some time, not since the Russians brought in their armies . . .'

'I am sure, woman,' he said impatiently, taking a coat from the peg on the door, and putting it on. 'See for yourself – there they are. Get down and light the big fire, they will be cold.'

As he went down and unlocked the wide wooden door he heard the first crackling of flames from the fireplace. Outside a dirty woman was standing, muddy to her knees, a small, even dirtier and muddier girl beside her. The woman had a sub-machine gun slung over her back and a wad of currency in her hand.

'Good morning, *Herr Hofmeister*,' she said politely. She held out the money and he waved it away, smiling. She beamed.

'Three hundred for breakfast!' she said, and they began to come into the warm.

Peredelkino

'I know what that is,' said Yelena.

Piotr Pavlovich Sadovsky held the little painted aeroplane between the thumb and palm of one hand, and began to wind its propeller with the thumb of the other.

'Do you remember?' he asked.

'It's a Nieuport scout. You made one for Ruth, and a Sopwith for me. When we were fifteen.'

'I know. I remember, too.'

The lawn of the dacha was bathed in sunlight. At the end was the drive, leading through the larches and pines.

'I'm back there now,' he confessed. 'I made this for the boy, because I thought he might like it. Help us make friends . . . He might want a MiG or a Sikhoi, but I can't think of those. I stop at about the year seventeen, Yelena, I don't move on any further. The revolution finished me and I can't live with it any more. Do you think Gaia will understand? She looked up to her daddy. Maybe she won't know me, just wonder who this crippled old fart is . . .'

'She'll know you,' Yelena said comfortingly. 'And she will understand. We *all* understand, all of us who endured it.'

He let the propeller go and it whirred into a blur, sending a blast of air over him.

'Two hundred turns, that's what it takes.' He looked anxiously at her. 'I don't smell of vodka, do I? A crippled, drunken old fart. That's not what you want from a daddy, is it? But I can't get through without it.'

'You don't smell of vodka.'

'I brushed my teeth . . . It's not what you need, is it? Here's Grandpa, darling, yes, him, the one in the corner with a bottle in his pocket . . .'

'It'll be all right, Piotr, you'll see. Ivan will be here soon and you'll be together.'

He began to wind up the elastic again, with short, nervous movements. 'She'll ask what I did, how I survived . . . here's Grandpa darling, don't go too near his cage, he eats people . . .'

'You must stop, Piotr! You are not to blame for anything you did. Blame the revolution, but not yourself.'

'She will hate me!' he cried. 'And the boy, too. I promised I would keep them safe, she and Anna. Krivitsky said to confess, but I was proud. So he put Anna in the *parilka*. She strangled herself as I watched . . .'

Tears were running down his cheeks and from the leafy lane there was the noise of a car. The Chaika pulled up and they could see Akulov at the wheel.

A woman got out and there was a boy with her. Sadovsky held up his arms in agony and the little, brightly-painted aeroplane flew from his hand, as colourful as a butterfly. They heard the little boy laugh in delight, scampering after it.

'*Daddy!*'

Gaia ran across the grass and into his arms . . .

33

Molot, Serp

1960

THE Ilyushin levelled off at cruise and the noise in the front of the passenger cabin settled down to a discreet whine as the pilot reduced power on the four Ivchenko turboprops. In the row of three seats Akulov, Yelena and Tatyana got themselves comfortable at the changed attitude, and the steward popped out of his little kitchen. The front compartment was small, but the seats big.

The steward was not Russian. He had olive skin, dark hair that curled in ringlets and bright eyes. He smiled as he deftly put their drinks down, showing very white teeth.

'What the hell is that?' said Akulov, peering out of the window. The clouds below were brown.

'It depends, Comrade General, sir, to what you are referring,' said the steward. He expertly drew the cork of the half bottle of French Chablis and poured it into crystal glasses for Yelena and Tatyana.

'The immense cloud of dust beneath our aircraft, or the land beneath the immense cloud of dust.'

Akulov looked at him in slight amusement. The steward poured three fingers of twelve-years old Scotch whisky into a crystal tumbler and set a small carafe of chilled water beside it.

'We have some way to go,' Akulov said, 'so I will take the answer to both.'

'The immense cloud of dust is the topsoil of untold hectares of land, and it is blowing from that land far away and falling upon my homeland. Here in the Soviet Union we are blessed. Everything we do is better and bigger than anywhere else in the world. Fifty million hectares of virgin land tilled at once! The biggest dust-storms in the history of the world! Truly we are fortunate. My people, were they beneath us as we fly, would, I am sure, after they had coughed the dust out of their lungs and swept it from their homes, be grateful to First Secretary Khrushchev for the free delivery of fresh soil. Perhaps with the soil has come the seeds of the maize that was planted, as another gift, although since the Comrade First Secretary believes that if you put spring wheat into a refrigerator it turns it into winter wheat who knows what form the maize will have taken by its aerial ride! Maize that feeds on air!'

'But why are your people not down there, coughing the free dust from their lungs?' asked Akulov.

'Which people are we talking about, Comrade General?'

'Your people.'

'With incredible foresight, Comrade General, sir, our enlightened leadership made sure that my people were moved, oh, some sixteen years ago, so that we should not have to suffer the consequences of breathing in this maize-ridden dust. Truly we are fortunate.'

Akulov drank some of his whisky. It was as smooth as butter. 'Your people,' he repeated. 'Who are they?'

'They do not exist,' said Yelena from beside him. She looked up at the steward. 'Am I not right? The Tatars of Crimea?'

'You are well informed, madam. As you say, we do not exist. Except, occasionally, when one of us is able to fly over our land, and look down upon it, on its fair orchards, its ripe vines, its sparkling rivers and grassy hills. But not today. Only a very large cloud of dust. Are you ready for some lunch? I will bring it.'

'How do you know about them?' demanded Akulov.

'Krivitskiy got drunk in the Washington Embassy, and told me about it. He was there and he moved them in trucks. In the war. Whole small nations. Stalin dumped them in the wilderness, where most of them died. Everything written and printed in their languages was burned, all efforts made to destroy their very memory. Once Russian princes paid them homage, now they are told they have never existed. They want to go home, but when they ask to go home, they are told that the Soviet Union *is* their home, that they should be content to stay within it wherever they have been put.'

'Empire,' Tatyana said unexpectedly. 'Imperial powers have always felt the right to treat their subject peoples as they see fit.'

'Is that what you are going to talk to Nikita Sergeyevich about?' asked Akulov. The Tatar steward reappeared, and began setting their tables with crisp white linen and silverware.

'It is, actually,' Tatyana said. 'Only, I'm going to start with a flag. Here, I've got it in my bag.'

She pulled out a soft bag from under her seat and opened it. Inside they could see scarlet and gold cloth.

'I brought it from Novosibirsk. It is very fine, as you can see, red with gold lettering, and a hand-stitched hammer and sickle, *molot* and *serp*.'

'Why do you want to show him a Party flag?'

'Because it *is*. The relevant piece of it is the hammer and the sickle. It has been the emblem of the Party and of the state since their inception. It appears on the Party flag as the symbol of its defence of the interests of workers and peasants. It is on the Soviet flag as the representation of the working class of the state. On the flags and banners of countries that have, under Soviet influence adopted the revolution, it appears to symbolise the worldwide community of Soviet and communist interests. It is, I say, an appropriate emblem for the Soviet Union to carry as it goes towards the end of the twentieth century.'

'You're a subversive, Tatyana,' said Akulov. 'I know you don't mean what you say.'

'No, I'm an economist,' she said equably. 'And I really do mean what I say. Professionally, I have no sense of humour.'

The steward brought a selection of little delicacies, round, glistening nodules of caviare on biscuits, smoked salom, rolled fillets of herring in sauce, hard-boiled quail's eggs.

'Go on, then,' said Akulov.

'A country that has incorporated into its own flag the symbol of the metropolitan power – in our case the hammer and sickle – may be considered to be, formally or informally, a part of that power's empire. The Russian Empire may be defined as the non-Russian republics of the Soviet Union acquired by the Red Army during and after the Civil War, plus the Baltic States taken after Stalin's deal with Hitler, and, very importantly, the Eastern European Empire acquired during and after the Great Patriotic War. This is the 'formal' empire, with the Soviet influences now being seen in such places as Cuba, Vietnam and Africa making an 'informal' empire.

'The Eastern European empire especially is seen as important to Russia. It acts as a security belt against the West and a beachhead for possible invasion; its armed forces are important additions to those of the USSR and its economies supplement the Soviet military and civilian sectors. The populations of the countries can also be used as hostages to moderate Western policies, most especially that of Eastern Germany. Both Party and people in Russia are proud of controlling the Eastern empire.'

'The same cannot be said in reverse,' Akulov said. 'I was in Hungary in fifty-six.'

'*Exactly*. The Communist governments of Poland, Hungary, Czechoslovakia, East Germany – the most important – are not seen by the people they rule as legitimate. For the governments to attain even a limited amount of popular support they would have to advocate the cause of national independence. As Hitler proved, nationalism is stronger than international socialism in the hearts of people. For Gomulka or Kadar or any of the others to champion national independence is simply to invite in the Soviet tanks once again. The people know their governments exist only by Soviet *fiat*. They are not legitimate. They lack both their traditional source, nationalism, and their legal one – free elections.'

Crumbs decorated the fine china plates and the steward took them away. From his little kitchen came enticing smells of cooking. They were the only three passengers in the cabin of *vlasts*.

'The problem goes further,' Tatyana went on.' Educated people in Russia are not generally opposed to the Kremlin, but the Eastern European intelligentsia is potentially or actually hostile to communist leadership. The people, as a whole, are immune to Soviet cultural influence. Throughout the bloc there is a deep contempt for Soviet culture, a deep attachment to religion and an affinity for Western values and traditions. The Communist leadership in the Eastern European countries is an alien, shallow and weak graft. The truth is that the border between East and West is not at the political boundary of the Elbe River, but on the cultural dividing line of the Bug River dividing Russia from Poland. The Eastern European nations are not Eastern at all, but Western.

'We produced an NKVD policy study in forty-four. We recommended treating them like Finland, in part because we saw the inherent problem. If, like Stalin, and now Nikita Sergeyevich, you proclaim the establishment of communism there to be irreversible, the victory of an inexorable trend for the future, then at all cost you have to hang on to them. If your trend becomes reversed, then the question will inevitably arise "why it may not be reversed in the Soviet Union, in Russia itself?" Which leads to the real point at issue, why Nikita Sergeyvich wishes to talk to me and why he has talked to other economic analysts. Empire is for the rich and powerful. Empires are like suits of very expensive and luxurious clothes. They increase the prestige of the wearer in a dramatic show of wealth, but leave him the poorer. Empires are expensive. They require demonstrations of genuine might. This the Russian empire has – the Soviet military forces are highly impressive.'

'We consider that we could, from a standing start, overrun Western Europe in seventy-two hours,' Akulov said.

'But also highly costly. We estimate – it has to be an estimate because there is no independent means of verifying official statistics – we estimate that out of a working population of around 100 million, between 30 and 40 million work for the defence sector, and that it is the only sector where real standards – meaning real cost – applies. As the managers say, "make a mistake producing something for the people, get your hand smacked. Make a mistake producing for export, get kicked. Make a mistake for the military, lose your head."

'But, if we can afford it, we can go against the trend of history. The trend of history is against formal empire. The biggest, that of Great Britain, is in the throes of disintegration. Which leaves the Rusian empire. Where is the money going to come from?'

'We're paying for the years when filthy elements like Stalin ruined the whole system. Now we're catching up,' said Akulov with certainty. 'We can afford it.'

The steward came from the kitchen, and bent down by him. 'Comrade General, sir. The pilot asks if you could come forward. There is a radio message for you.'

Akulov heaved himself from his seat. 'There isn't another country in the world where a simple peasant boy like me could become a general. Or Nikita Sergeyevich First Secretary. Only millionaires get to be president, in America.'

He disappeared into the cabin and when he came back a few minutes later fresh china plates were set out, bearing slices of pink beef, new potatoes and asparagus. Warm rolls and butter sat on side plates.

'That *was* Nikita Sergeyevich. They're putting me down in Poltava. There's rioting.'

'The Ukrainians are *rioting*?' said Tatyana. 'And Nikita Sergeyevich wants a *Ukrainian* general to sort it out?'

'That's it,' he said shortly.

'Why are they rioting?' she said sweetly.

'Something to do with an increase in food prices.'

'Food, yes. Under the last Tsar Russia was one of the two largest exporters of grain. Now we import millions of tons. There appears to be a constant and embarrassing association between socialism and food shortages. That the situation is easily remedied can be shown by the private plots of the peasants, which take up some four per cent of the land under cultivation and produce a quarter of the total crop output. The solution is clear – allow the farmers to farm their own land. Nikita Sergeyevich isn't going to, and nor will any other Soviet leader, because it would mean a reduction in centralised control over the population. Like losing the Eastern empire, it would imply failure of the system.'

'But what of your red banner, with its gold, hand-stitched hammer and sickle?' asked Yelena.

'Encourage her,' Akulov grumbled, and his wife smiled.

'One of the great historical symbols, surely,' said Tatyana. 'The sickle represents agriculture, the peasant. The hammer, industry, the worker. Yet in the Soviet Union the First Industrial Revolution, the creation of basic industries and infrastructure, is not yet complete. Between twenty and fifty per cent of the crops harvested rot because of inadequate storage, transport and distribution. Factories constructed from materials produced by excessive levels of investment take so long to build that by the time they work their products are obsolete. Because the pace of change in technology is increasing, not becoming slower.

'The Soviet Union has barely begun on the Second Industrial Revolution, that of mass consumption. But it appears that the west is embarking on the Third. Something strange is happening out there, a transformation in information and mass communications powered by electronics – computers. Our statistical office in Novosibirsk does not have a computer and as yet has no plans to acquire one. *Individuals* in the West have them, and can tap into information networks. In Novosibirsk we have some American photocopying machines. When we want to use them we have to apply to the KGB department which keeps them. They keep them safe against enemies of the people who might use them to print subversive material.

'The hammer and the sickle together form the symbol of a movement that claims to represent the future of mankind. *Molot* and *serp*. Hand tools that pre-date the first Industrial Revolution.'

'Clever words,' said Akulov. 'You wait and see. We are back to Leninist principles now. The new world is yet to come. I, too, can quote economics, Tatyana. Who said that in the final analysis the global competition between the socialist and capitalist systems would be resolved in favour of that system which manages to secure the higher long-range level of economic productivity?'

'Lenin. And who said that the loser would go into the trashbin of History?'

'That has to be Trotsky,' said Yelena. 'An unpleasant young man.'

The steward reappeared and beamed at them. 'We have a few minutes before landing. Some American raspberries? Or I have some ripe Camembert.'

'I would like some *Crimean* raspberries,' said Yelena.

'The finest in the world,' he agreed. 'But no one is there to harvest them.'

The whine of the Ivchenko turboprops sank to a dull growl and the nose of the airliner dipped, heading into Poltava. Akulov craned in his seat, looking down upon the approaching land. The Tatar steward beamed.

'See, Comrade General, sir. The Ukraine!'

'I know,' Akulov grunted, without looking round. 'I was born here.'

'So you have home here. So nice.'

'No, I live in Moscow.'

The steward looked at him sympathetically. 'Me as well, Comrade General, sir. They exile you, too, just like me.'

The crumbling white tower blocks lined the wide concrete boulevard like dead elephants, the people insects passing in and out of the bullet holes in their hides. They stopped to stare and glare as the two big limousines went hurtling down the central lane. Behind their car of guards Akulov braced himself on the jump seat as the Chaika leaped the join in the blocks every two seconds.

'If they're rioting I'd have thought you'd have a full military escort,' he observed.

One of the two men in shapeless grey suits on the back seat expectorated into a handkerchief.

'They're Ukrainian peasants,' he said contemptuously. 'My boys will soon find the ringleaders and we'll string them up by the balls.'

'*I'm* a Ukrainian peasant,' Akulov said menacingly. 'I took an army to Berlin.'

'Then you'll know how to handle troublemakers, General,' said the second. He was the city's Party boss. 'We just want you to get your troops out on the streets. Bayonet a few and the rest will come into line.'

'What's the problem? Why are they rioting?' Akulov asked.

'Food prices have been doubled and there are shortages. It's not our fault. Orders.'

'I know about the shortages. Bad harvest again. They're buying in from America. I want to know about *here*. Are you short of food *here*.'

'Well, *they* are, General. But don't worry, we've got plenty.' He wheezed and smiled in an oily fashion at Akulov. 'Don't worry, you can have anything you want. Plenty in the Party stores.'

'I'm glad to hear it,' said Akulov, suddenly bland. 'What about the grain stores?'

'Of course. We can honour our obligations to all entitled. White bread for the rest of the year, if we want.'

'Entitled?'

The KGB chief next to the Party boss looked at Akulov with bored eyes. 'Us,' he said succinctly. 'Rather than them.'

'I understand you,' Akulov murmured. The two limousines were passing through the suburban wasteland into the centre of town, where older, Tsarist buildings still stood.

'I used to come into market here with my father as a child. I was never hungry, do you know that?'

The two men said nothing, sitting indifferent.

'Right. Now I'll tell you what we're going to do. You are going to make yourself popular. When we get to the main square you get out on the balcony and announce free bread rations. Use military trucks to bring grain to the bakeries – '

The KGB chief stared at Akulov with the eyes of an adder. 'Free bread!' he spat, shocked. 'Let's give them free bullets!'

'Let's defuse this. I know these people because I'm one of them. They'll take a lot, put up with a lot. But get them angry, and you'll have a fight on your hands you'll wish you'd never started. So. *You*, the Cheka, stay out of sight. *He* gets the bread moving. Butter, cheese, sausage and milk, too, from the Party stores. People with food in their stomachs, with children who are fed, won't give you trouble. Tell them the price rises are cancelled until the end of the year.'

'You can't tell me what to do!' the fat man blustered.

'We in the Army got rid of the political commissars at our elbow years ago,' Akulov said coldly. 'If you want the whole place burned down with you in it, then keep going as you are. I will take no responsibility. I am here on the orders of Nikita Sergeyevich Khrushchev, and *I* am in charge. Now let's get to the main square and you do what I say.'

The cars came screaming down the street. Ahead, people were milling in dark, swirling masses of anger.

'Slow down,' Akulov ordered abruptly. 'Don't provoke them. Have you got a loudspeaker in this thing?'

Their Chaika slowed. They were in the old part of town. Tall, faded imperial buildings flanked them on each side, yellow and green and pink. In front the car full of guards was still racing ahead. Three small figures suddenly flew into the air, tumbling over and over to hit the ground.

'Oh, shit!' Akulov said softly. The car suddenly slewed, a wheel flying off, bouncing high across the open square, and the car vanished into a boiling mass of people.

'Get this fucking thing turned round!' Akulov bellowed, and the tyres screeched on the cobbles. People were running, spilling down the lane. A brick careened off the side of the car and fists thumped in fury at the back. A cobble came crashing through the windscreen and the Chaika hurtled into the wall at full power, a dead man's foot jammed on the pedal. Akulov smashed open the door and burst out. He knocked down the men who came at him with giant fists, like rocks. Someone screamed in agony, from the car behind. He fought his way up the steps of an old apartment building, throwing off those who would have pulled him down. On the steps he stumbled to one knee, but, with a titanic heave, pulled himself up, and got his back to the door. He kicked a man back down and cleared a space.

'*I'm one of you!*' he bellowed. Instinctively, he was speaking in the old tongue, that the Ukrainians understood. A boiling mass of them were working over what they had dragged out of the car.

'I was born here! I'm from the Ukraine. I am Ivan Ivanovich Akulov and I have come to get you food.'

They snarled, moving around the steps like wolves. He had his hand on his holster, but kept his pistol undrawn.

'*Wait!*'

A small figure had pushed her way up through the crowd. She stood looking up at him, a *babushka* wrapped up in black.

'I know you, Ivan Ivanovich. Do you know me?'

The breath was heaving in his chest. 'I know you, Masha, wife of Anatoly Andreyevich. I know you, and your four children.'

'Then let me come up.'

The woman came up, standing not as high as the scarlet and gold shoulder boards on Akulov's greatcoat. She looked down on her people below.

'This is Ivan Ivanovich Akulov, who was born in my village, and who is an honourable man.'

'Tell them if they take the Party boss to the headquarters he will authorise grain to be taken to the bakeries, on my orders. There will be free bread for all, this afternoon.'

There was a cheer, and some men dragged off the *apparatchik* in the direction of the square. Something like a butchered pig in bloody grey lay under the wheels of the Chaika. Akulov felt his face wet and he wiped it with his palm. It came away red with blood.

'See?' said Masha. 'He is an honourable man. He suffered as so many of us, suffered, when the Party men came from Russia, and stole from us. He, too, lost his family, when the men came from Russia, and murdered our own, or sent them away, to die in the cold of the north.'

'Where is your husband, Anatoly Andreyevich, and your four children, Masha?'

'See? He asks after my family. He is an honourable man. My husband Anatoly could not pay the tax, when they demanded it, the third time. He had to sell the house to Timofey Vasilyevich, Chairman of the Committee of Unwealthy Peasants, who led the grain confiscation squads. Do you remember Timofey Vasilyevich, Ivan Ivanovich?'

'Timofey Vasilyevich, the thief and drunkard?'

'That one. He paid fifty roubles. It was not enough and they took Anatoly from us and sent him to the north to the forests where he died. We stayed with my aunt. We lived on cattle bones that the children played *babki* with, boiled them with grass and bark and ground them up to eat. My Aunt Lydia said we should eat her if she died, but when she did we could not. In the winter I made a sort of bread from acorns we gathered from under the snow. Timofey Vasilyevich saw us there and accused us of being parasites and shirkers.'

A deep growl of hate ran through the crowd below, and Akulov knew that it was only the presence of the old lady that prevented them from moving on him again.

'We did not have enough to keep alive until the Spring. I chose the two strongest, my daughter Olga and my son Andrey. The two little ones I let starve, so that the others might live. I do not call them by name, so that I may try to remember them less.

'Timofey Vasilyevich liked to sing. When he broke into our houses with the other brutes to steal what we had he would sing the Communist song – *'Arise ye prisoners of starvation, Arise, ye wretched of the earth!'* I found him dying by a ditch that Spring, when the Party men had gone, and left him to his fate. I told the others and we all hurried as quickly as we were able, which was not very quickly, and we gathered about him and sang his song. Then we trampled on him, until he was dead. I see some here that were with me, that day.'

They bayed in approval, like wolves. Masha turned to Akulov.

'Ivan Ivanovich would have done what we did, for he is an honourable man. Did you not lose your own family in those times, Ivan?'

'Yes,' he said thickly. He could taste blood in his throat.

'Who killed them?'

'Chekists.'

'Yes. Chekists from Russia . . . Did you make them pay, Ivan?'

Akulov glared down at the mob below him. 'I did, in the end . . .'

'Of course. For you are an honourable man. This is the Ukraine. We did not like the Nazis when they came, but they let us proclaim an independent state of the Ukraine.' She put her arm on Akulov's, as light as a bird's wing. 'Ivan Ivanovich was not here; he was serving in the Red Army, for he is an honourable man. He fought the Nazis. When the Russians came to enslave us again when the Nazis were gone we fought. I see here some who fought with us. Olga fought and they captured her. They kicked her, big men in uniforms like the one Ivan Ivanovich wears, big men in heavy army boots. They kicked her until blood came from her mouth, and she died. But Ivan Ivanovich did not do that. He is an honourable man.

'Even though I had lost all the rest of my family, I still had my son, Andrey. He was very fond of the little ones. Before they murdered us and things were normal he would play with them, make himself a horse for them to ride upon. He was very upset when I stopped feeding them and I had to stop him from giving them his food. The following year he did not speak very much and I came out one morning to find him hanging from a tree.'

There was a burst of cheering in the distance.

'That will be the grain,' Akulov called. 'And food is to be taken from the Party stores.'

They stared up at him, thoughtfully, and he felt the old lady's hand on his chest.

'We have torn your fine uniform, Ivan Ivanovich. But no doubt your Russian masters will find you another, just as grand, just as bright. It will have scarlet stripes on the trousers and gold at the collar, as red as the blood of my Olga, as shiny as the coins they pay you with.'

She waved an old, dessicated hand to make the crowd part.

'Let him through. He has promised us some scraps from his table and, as we know, Ivan Ivanovich is an honourable man.'

34

Glavni Vrag

The Situation Room, The Kremlin, 18 October 1962

'IVAN Ivanovich!'
The lift doors hissed shut behind Akulov, and Khrushchev propelled himself out of his chair underneath the huge situation panel on the wall. Despite his sixty-eight years he moved quickly and energetically.

'Where the hell have you been?' he demanded.

Akulov towered over the diminutive Soviet leader. Cool, fan-driven air circulated over both of them. They were one hundred and fifty metres below ground.

'Minsk, Nikita Sergeyevich.' His eyes flicked over the board. America. The Caribbean. Cuba.

'What in the name of Lenin do you want to do there?' Khrushchev asked. 'It's an awful place. Flattened in the war, too.'

'I know. I went through it with an army. My daughter is buried there and I go regularly to tend her grave.'

'Oh. I'm sorry, Ivan. I didn't know.'

Akulov glanced around the room, trying to assess the crisis. He could see a lot of officers from the new prestige SRF strategic rocket forces. Vashugin, their new boss was there with them. They had probably walked over from their temple, the Dzerzhinsky Military Academy off Red Square, he thought sourly. Only three years in existence and the SRF outranked the other four services. With the possession of their nuclear-tipped missiles they claimed to have made all other forms of war obsolete and the halving of conventional strength that was taking place showed that Khrushchev believed them.

In a corner, Krivitskiy, their boss, was talking to a coven of senior KGB men. He recognised some GRU and army intelligence experts, specialists in America, some English-speaking translators. The crisis – for their occupancy of the new, nuclear-proof bunker below the

Military Central Executive Building indicated that it was such – was with the *glavni vrag*, the main enemy, the USA.

Khrushchev looked up at Akulov in squat, round-faced triumph.

'We're putting inter-continental rockets into Cuba. We'll have the *Yanquis* by the balls.'

Akulov looked up at the panel, seeing the island just ninety miles off the American mainland.

'Igor, give me the other picture,' Khrushchev called to an SRF technician, and the man adjusted controls at his console. The great panel changed to reveal the Soviet Union, and its neighbours. Ringed in scarlet all about were missiles, pointing into the heart of the USSR.

'See that?' Khrushchev demanded. 'The fucking Americans have their missiles on every border, threatening us. Like ... pistols, pointed at our head. The very oceans will soon be seething with their submarines, carrying these Polaris missiles of theirs. And we can't get at them yet. Our missiles only have a 3,200 kilometre range – the big ones aren't ready yet. But – '

He waved at the technician again. 'The other one back, Igor. See?'

Within Cuba, rockets with red stars pointed at the American mainland.

'Once we have our IRBMs – the intermediate-range first-strike SS-5 ballistic missiles – operational, we can devastate them from Phoenix to Halifax.'

The air was temperature controlled and moderate, but Akulov felt a chill running down his back. It was always a very bad sign when the civilian leaders began to use military terminology.

'What about the Americans, Nikita Sergeyevich? They will hardly sit back and allow us to do this.'

'They don't know!' Khrushchev crowed. 'They think we're just putting in SAMs – surface-to-air missiles against aircraft, you see. And once we have them working it'll be too late.'

'Their U-2s will see what's happening.'

'Ivan Ivanovich, the Americans are too liberal to fight. Did this new President of theirs, Kennedy, use his might to crush Cuba last year? *I* would have done. *He* didn't. He sent a few exiles over into the Bay of Pigs and didn't even give them air support! They were massacred!'

Khrushchev took Akulov's arm. 'He's gutless, Ivan,' he said confidentially. 'Young and pretty. Look about you, do you see anyone pretty in here? No, we have suffered, all of us here. The

Russian people have suffered. The First World War. The Civil War. The Second World War. All fought right here.'

The geniality of his expression was replaced by anger. 'We're paid for what we have! In blood. And the Americans surround us with military bases and nuclear weapons! They haven't suffered enough, Ivan. They don't know what it's like to earn your place in the world. *We* have. It's high time they learn what it's like to have their own land, their own people threatened.'

He glowered at the screen. 'They have their place in the world on the cheap. We're still paying for ours. What you pay for, you get. That's one capitalist lesson we'll be glad to teach them. They're gutless, Ivan. They won't fight. Were their cities razed in the war, like ours? Did they die? No! They paraded about in pretty uniforms and sent us spam, to do the fighting for them.'

'I know they haven't suffered, not as we have, Nikita Sergeyevich. But they don't like being threatened,' Akulov said thoughtfully. 'And they can fight. Look what they did to the Japanese. Slaughtered them in the islands. Burned tens of thousands alive in their fire raids. Atom-bombed two cities. I think they are *very* capable of wielding a big stick.'

'You leave the strategy to us, Ivan,' Khrushchev said shortly. 'War's changed since you drove to Berlin in a tank. Now it's all missiles. Listen, you don't think that with a pistol to a man's head he won't give you whatever you want? Our missiles in Cuba are like a pistol, cocked and ready to fire. We want West Berlin? It's ours. We want the NATO bases shut? It's done. You see if I'm not right.'

'Very good, Nikita Sergeyevich,' Akulov said formally. 'And what do you want this old tank driver to do?'

'Answer the telephone.'

'You need a *general* to answer the telephone?'

Khrushchev smiled, turning his charm back on. 'I need a general who knows how to negotiate, like you did in Hungary. I need a general with a voice like a tank in gear. I need a general who took an army all the way to Berlin. We know you, Ivan Ivanovich, – and they know you, too. We've set up a . . .'

Krivitskiy was walking by. 'Leon – what is this link for Ivan?'

'A back channel. Informal and quick.'

'That's it. A back channel. We leave it to Gromyko and this Dean Rusk it takes too long. We have to know. So we have this channel, a direct telephone link between us here and Kennedy's Excom.'

'What's that?'

'His Executive Committee,' said Krivitskiy impatiently. 'He's set up a special team.'

'I thought they didn't know what we're doing.'

'They don't,' said Khrushchev. 'And you'll help keep them that way. I'll get Vashugin to brief you.'

Akulov stood looking at the great presentation board. 'How did we get into Cuba?'

'We pay for it,' Krivitskiy said succinctly. 'Castro's on board, he's one of us. We set up his Party and secret police for him. We keep his economy afloat. He owes us.'

'He can't run his own economy?'

'You can have a secure regime or you can have a bunch of politically-suspect entrepreneurs running about making money, opposing your methods and threatening your rule. You can't have both. For what we get, an aircraft-carrier ninety miles off their shore, what we pay is good value.'

'Ivan Ivanovich!' Khrushchev called, from a desk. 'The Yanquis are on the line. The Excom. Want to introduce yourself?'

Akulov went over to the desk and sat himself down. 'This is General Ivan Ivanovich Akulov,' he growled, his voice like gravel crashing from a truck. Khrushchev smiled in approval.

'Hullo, Ivan,' said a voice, speaking in Russian. 'This is John Nichols, of President Kennedy's staff. We know each other, don't we, Ivan? It's good to talk with you again. If you hear me break off and speak in English, it's because I am translating to the President or his advisers. Now, about these missiles. The feeling here is that we're getting the mushroom treatment. What do you say?'

'The mushroom treatment – what is that?'

'You're keeping us in the dark and feeding us crap. Let's talk about these missiles.'

'SAMs,' said Akulov. 'Surface to air missiles for use against aircraft.'

'We know what a SAM is. I have pictures of the ones you're installing around San Cristobal right in front of me, as a matter of fact. They're SA-2s, like you have in the Soviet Union around your major air bases, IRBM complexes and other strategically important locations. We have pictures of them, too. So we ask ourselves, what is it in Cuba that you're so anxious to protect?'

Akulov thought quickly. 'The Revolution,' he growled.

Nichols chuckled. 'Listen. You're a general, so you'll understand what I say. All military organisations have to go by the book, right? You follow established procedures for the sake of maximum efficiency. But we've known you long enough to have a copy of your book, too. And we've looked up SA-2 missile sites in the shape of a trapezoid. Did I mention that the San Cristobal missiles are set up in the shape of a trapezoid? No? Well, they are. And our copy of your book says that SA-2s deployed in this formation are *always* used to protect medium and intermediate range ballistic missile complexes. So what do you say now, Ivan?'

'I say they are there to defend the Cuban Revolution.'

Nichols chuckled again. 'Save it for the mushrooms, Ivan. I'll talk to you again soon.'

Akulov put down the telephone. In a corner of the room Khrushchev was shouting into another one.

'Round the clock! Use flares if you have to. Get them finished!'

22 October

Akulov rubbed a hand over the stubble on his chin. Four days underground had left him feeling jaded and he longed to get out in the open air. He was worried about Natalia's grave because he had been called away only half way through his work of maintenance. He saw Khrushchev coming over to him with a file, and began to get up, but the little man waved him back, pulling up a chair.

'You were far away, Ivan Ivanovich.'

'I was thinking about my daughter. Her grave in Minsk, I have to go back and finish looking after it.'

'I'll have someone go over, if you want. I can pick up the telephone.'

'No . . . I go in old clothes and nobody knows I'm a general. That's the way I want it.'

Khrushchev looked puzzled, and was about to speak, when the telephone rang.

'Ivan? Johnny Nichols again. I thought that I'd let you know, we have some more photographs. Clearings near the SA-2 sites. You have a whole *raft* of stuff lying about. Missile trailers, control bunkers, oxidiser and propellant trucks, shelter tents and erector launchers. We are familiar with these, too. They are always – repeat, *always* – in the *immediate* vicinity of medium range ballistic missiles. So what do you say now, Ivan?'

Akulov looked at Khrushchev, with his palm over the mouthpiece. Khrushchev shook his head.

'We only need a few more days,' he whispered.

'Your technical analysis is mistaken,' said Akulov.

'Oh, no, it isn't. I forgot to mention, we can also see nuclear warhead storage sites. But not missiles, yet. So back to the mushrooms for you, and off to find the missiles for us. We take it that they're on board ships, coming to Cuba.'

Akulov put down the telephone.

'What would you do, Ivan Ivanovich, if you were Kennedy?' Khrushchev asked quietly.

'He has three options, that even this old tank driver can see. He can bomb the sites into dust, he can invade, he can declare a blockade to stop the missiles from arriving.'

Khrushchev opened his file and put down a selection of high-altitude photographs.

'We sent up two of our Cosmos surveillance satellites. They brought back these. Air Force bases in range of Cuba. Homestead, MacDill, Jacksonville Navy base.'

Akulov looked at the hundreds of armed fighter bombers lined up on the hard standings.

'The game's up,' he said. 'They're a hundred miles away, we're eleven thousand!'

Khrushchev angrily shoved the photographs back into their folder.

'He's bluffing! He's gutless, I tell you! The ships will be there in three days and he'll sing a different tune then. He's threatening to invade Cuba to take out our missiles? Then we'll invade Turkey and get rid of his. Two can play at this game!'

26 October

'Ivan? John Nichols. I thought I'd let you know your SA-2s are operational and you just shot down one of our U-2s. So we're going to take out the missile sites on Monday. Any freighter trying to break the blockade will be sunk.'

Khrushchev was standing close by, with Vashugin and Krivitskiy. Akulov indicated for him to pick up the extension.

'Any military action taken against the USA or any ally of the USA will be considered an act of general war. As of this moment we have one hundred and forty-four Polaris missiles, one hundred and three Atlas, one hundred and five Thor and Jupiter, fifty-four Titan missiles, six hundred IRBMs, two hundred and fifty MRBMs, one thousand six hundred long-range heavy bombers and thirty-seven aircraft carriers, all of which are ready to go. At any conservative estimate we can convert the Soviet Union into a radioactive heap of rubbish in thirty minutes!'

There was a long silence. Khrushchev was the colour of pale wax, his skin glistening.

'It's time to get out of the mushroom patch, Ivan,' said Nichols.

Akulov looked at Khrushchev, waiting.

'Tell him we'll take the missiles away,' he said huskily.

35

Shtrafnoy

Moscow, May 1968

THE woman with the grey hair which was arranged in a loose bun, sat quietly on the bench on the corner of the Alexandrovsky Gardens. In front of her was the high Armoury Tower and further along the picturesque orange Poteshnyy Palace behind which was the modern bulk of the Palace of Congresses. Closer by her bench was the Borovitsky Gate with its uniformed and armed KGB guards who checked the credentials of the shiny black Chaika and Zil limousines that bore personages of importance in and out of the Kremlin.

The guards had noted the presence of the woman, sitting in her raincoat, reading a book, but had given her little thought. From the bench she saw them move into activity, raising the barrier as a long, rare Zil came through the gate. She heard the big V8 engine burble as the driver pulled away, saw the nose dip on the soft springs as he slowed to negotiate the sharp turn that led down to the *Kremlyovskaya* embankment, and with a speed that belied her looks she jumped up and ran into the road.

There was a screech from the tyres of the limousine and it slid to a halt with her almost over the radiator. In the front, a guard in a short blue raincoat flung the door open.

'I wish to speak with Comrade Krivitskiy!' the woman shouted, and he grabbed her by the arm, pulling her away. Two guards from the gate were running down towards them.

The darkened glass of the Zil's rear compartment rolled down with a hum from its electric motor.

'Bring,' Krivitskiy said.

The door opened, and she got in. The guards stopped running.

'Drive on,' Krivitskiy said into his intercom, and the limousine hissed forward.

'Hello, Yelena,' he said then. 'Do you want to see me?'

'You know that I do! But you don't answer my letters and your secretary will not accept my telephone calls.'

'I'm a busy man,' he murmured. 'I have a lot to do. I have been with First Secretary Brezhnev, talking to the Czech leader, Dubcek. An interesting, if ultimately unintelligent man.'

'Why do you say that?'

'He doesn't read history. But what is it I can do for you, since we are sharing this limousine together?'

Yelena pulled a letter out of her bag. 'Two things. This letter – and a request from an old friend.'

'A friend?'

'Piotr Pavlovich Sadovsky. We were all at school together. He ran your armoured train and he built your tanks.'

'What does he want?'

'He and his family were taken away in the terror. His daughter Gaia survived, by a miracle. Ivan found her, reunited her with him and they lived together in an apartment near the Arbat, with her young son.'

'So?'

'Piotr Pavlovich is dead. He died of bronchitis because his lungs were scarred in the camps. Now the municipal authorities claim that she exceeds the maximum living space per person, and have ordered her to move. To a bad apartment in a poor part of town. The boy will have to move school, to a bad school. It will be hard for her to travel to work.'

'The law is the law,' he said, looking bored.

'Invalids and war disabled are allowed more room. Gaia spent eighteen years in the camps. She lost her youth there and she came back to no mother and a father mentally and physically crippled. She qualifies on both counts.'

'The fashion for rehabilitated people is now dead,' he said. 'What is the letter?'

'Just a word from you . . .'

'The letter.'

Yelena swallowed hard, biting down upon rage. 'It is from Ivan. In exile in Irkutsk. You may read it.'

Krivitskiy smiled faintly. 'I have already read it. I read it before you did.'

'Then you know what's happening to him!' she said hotly. 'He is being *persecuted*. KGB men steal his writing. Dogs are housed next to his apartment and they bark incessantly. From somewhere comes the noise of hammers beating on iron bars. They stop for a while, then they begin again. These are the sounds of the camps and

Ivan *hates* them. They upset him. Sometimes it is much worse and he actually thinks he is *in* the camps. When the feeling fades he has a strange taste in his mouth and he believes that chemicals, or drugs, are put into his water, or into the air, when he is asleep.'

'He is writing. What does he write?'

'You know what. First Secretary Khrushchev gave him permission to work on a book, one that would tell some of the things that happened, under Stalin. He met many people, heard many things.'

'Khrushchev is a non-person. We removed him. What he approved or did not approve is of no relevance now. And I have seen what Ivan Ivanovich has written. He used his position of power to talk to malcontents, to subversives, to nationalists and non-people.'

'We are all people. And our voices deserve to be heard. What happened to me, to him, to all the other millions under Stalin is important. The memory must be kept alive, for fear it might happen again. Ivan writes down what people told him, what happened to him. To keep the memories alive.'

'The past is an irrelevance. Things that were done in the past were necessary to make the future.'

'Unless the past is admitted, the future will *become* the past. Ivan is writing to keep the past in the past. And the KGB steal parts of his writing. And try to send him mad. And you could stop them. Why won't you? Weren't you comrades in the Civil War, friends?'

'My liking for someone is the same as my liking for coffee. If either get in the way of the revolution, I give them up.'

'Ivan stopped Nikolai Savinkov from killing you. He kept his side of the deal.'

'Ivan is simple-minded,' he complained.

'He is honourable.'

'I did warn him, just as I and First Secretary Breznev have been warning the little Czech, Dubcek. What more can men do?'

The Zil was cruising slowly along *Kropotinskaya*, by the river, not using the central Chaika lane down which the party limousines roared.

'Look, Ivan is in exile as an example. He was a general, he enjoyed privilege, he was one of the *vlasti*. The son of a peasant, we gave him everything – and he turned around and bit the hand that fed him. It's important that other powerful people don't get the idea that it's all right to criticise the system. So now anyone who thinks we're unkind to the Crimean Tatars or the Hungarians can look out to Irkutsk and see General Akulov in his *shtrafnoy izolyator* and think again.'

'People have to think correctly or be punished?'

'They can think what they want, just as long as they do and say what *we* want,' he said brutally. 'And that is what Ivan Ivanovich won't do. I'll let him come back to Moscow. All he has to do is give public confirmation of his total support for the government. But he's intransigent, unreasonable and I'll prove it. He's a general, a hero of the Great Patriotic War. I sent him a copy of the Memorandum the wretched Czech military has just produced, whining about our control over them. They've purged their army of our nominees, got rid of the political department. If Ivan Ivanovich had just written back condemning their actions and calling for the shooting of all responsible he could be on a plane to Moscow right now. But no. He supported them. He agreed that the military policy before this Dubcek was exclusively in Soviet interests, and that we plan in the event of war to sacrifice two-thirds of the Czech army in the first two days. And he recommends that we leave! His actions in Hungary were suspect – I should have known then. He knew where that bitch Ruth de Gunzberg was and didn't turn her in. Do you know she *fought* against us?'

'Ruth is a fine person. The daughter of a Count. Ivan is the son of a peasant. He joined the revolution to correct injustice, just like Ruth. For years and years he believed, even after the Bolsheviks murdered his family, tortured him, put him in a camp, took him out to fight for them to correct the mistakes they had made. And, in the end, he realised that the revolution was much worse than what it had replaced, that it cared for no one except the new ruling class, just as Ruth realised. And you ask him to stand up and tell lies for that ruling class? You are asking him to destroy his soul, to smash the principles he lives by. He will not do it.'

'Soul ... principles ...' Krivitskiy sneered. 'He is not Jesus Christ, nor are you Mary! You make yourself out to be so holy and clean but when it comes down to it you bend the knee. You're no different to me – we both have blood on our hands. You're a murderer, too.'

'You, yes. Not me,' she said steadily.

'Is your memory that bad?' he, jeered. 'I told you to shoot the White soldiers and you did – just like that!'

'I let them go. I had them line up six of their dead comrades and I fired six shots. I murdered no one.'

He looked at her, his old face suddenly white with fury 'Do you know who I am?' he whispered.

'I know who you *are*. You are the boy I went to school with who shouted: "We are believers. We do not believe in either God or men.

We manufacture gods and transform men. We will create a universe in our image." Well, here it is.'

She waved a hand about her, its small fist clenched in anger. 'Here it is, the universe you have created, a place through which shattered and demented people move like the survivors of a nuclear war.'

'You and your precious principles . . .' he said malevolently. 'I know how to change men's minds. Give me Lenin for a night and I'd have him chanting the Lord's Prayer by morning. Do you think you're different? I could *make* you like me.'

'This is it, is it?' she said steadily. 'Your new universe? And you, the torturer-in-chief, you are the supreme culmination of the species?'

Krivitskiy bent to speak into the intercom, and the limousine pulled into the side of the road.

'I have to get to Vnukovo airport. I'm going to Prague because Dubcek's as stupid as you are. What we have, we hold. You can get out here, Yelena.'

'Just let me be with Ivan,' she pleaded. 'We are no threat to you, whatever we believe. Let him come to Moscow, or I will go to Irkutsk. *Please.* Commit a good act so that on judgement day you can hold it up in front of God, to say your past was not all evil, to save yourself from your future, in Hell.'

The guard opened the door.

'As I said,' Krivitskiy said softly, 'the fashion for rehabilitated people is now dead.'

Poltava, The Ukraine, December 1968

It was daylight outside, but in the bare room curtains had been drawn across the windows, and it was illuminated by lamps. Behind them stood a man with a shoulder-held camera-recorder, and in their focus stood Johnny Nichols. The blazing red hair was silver and he wore a tweed sports coat and grey trousers. He was standing next to a coffin.

'There's a new word in Russia and its empire,' he said. 'The word is "dissent". The Prague Spring of Czechoslovakia has been replaced by Soviet winter and Alexander Dubcek's socialism with a human face lies crushed beneath Soviet tank tracks. The Kremlin is still Stalin's

Kremlin, a totalitarian tyranny as incapable of self-reform as of the squaring of the circle. Inside Russia there are those who applauded Dubcek's brave and principled attempt to bring democracy to his country, just as they applauded the attempt of Imre Nagy to bring it to his. Both efforts were brutally put down by force, and those who applauded Nagy, who applauded Dubcek, now stand up, brave men and women, and like Herzen, they cry: "*I am ashamed to be Soviet!*"

'Their ranks include the famous. Andrei Sakharov, nuclear physicist, and his wife, Elena Bonner. Sinyavsky and Daniel, victims of a show trial farcical even by Soviet standards, and who now languish in the camps. Aleksander Solzhenitsyn, author of *One Day in the Life of Ivan Denisovich*, its publication authorised by the now-fallen First Secretary Nikita Khrushchev, and perhaps the most influential book to circulate freely in Russia since the Revolution.'

Nichols put out a hand to touch the coffin lid, gently. 'Their ranks included this man, General Ivan Ivanovich Akulov. As a young soldier in the army of the Tsar, he became a Bolshevik while convalescing from wounds received fighting on the First World War Eastern front. His record of service to the world's first communist state was long and faithful. One of its star soldiers, he was caught up in the Terror of the late thirties, like so many millions of others, and rescued from the camps of the Gulag only in order to lead an army against the Nazis. His abilities as a general were such that by the war's end he had been awarded the highest honour the communists can bestow – Hero of the Soviet Union.

'Akulov survived another spell of incarceration in the Gulag in the post-war Stalinist Terror, and survived to be one of those who helped the former First Secretary Nikita Khrushchev to power. It was after Khrushchev's famous speech to the XXth Party Conference that the idealism that had led the young Ivan to join the Bolsheviks was finally allowed to flower. He was authorised by Khrushchev to write a book, chronicling both his own experiences in the Stalinist years and those of others.

'For five years he travelled. He found that the people he spoke to shared his own longings, that their story should be told, brought out into the open, freed from the vast pile of lies under which they had been entombed by the Soviet Communist government for so long. He became the champion of people who still suffered from wrongs done to them, their deep hurts still left unredressed, like the eight entire nations torn from their homeland by Stalin. His friendship with Imre Nagy, the hero of Hungary, went back to their youth. His sympathy for the free nations of Eastern Europe now enslaved by the Russians became clear. When First Secretary Khrushchev was ousted, General Akulov was arrested, charged with anti-Soviet activities and sentenced to exile in Irkutsk, a grim town in Siberia.'

Yelena was standing by Nichols and now the cameraman pulled the shot back to include her.

'That was in late 1964. Standing next to me is his wife, Yelena. She was once a Countess in the time of Tsar Nicholas. Like her husband, she was caught up in the Terror. She survived the horrors of the Gulag and was appointed to be a diplomat for the Soviets in Washington during the war. Like her late husband, she is a dissident. Two days ago she was told that her husband had died of a heart attack in Irkutsk. She asked for his body to be flown here, near to where he was born. In a few hours General Akulov is to be buried.

'She also asked for us to be here, as independent witnesses. Because Yelena Akulova believes that her husband was murdered.'

Nichols turned to Yelena.

'Yelena, who is it you accuse of having ordered Ivan to be killed?'

'His name is Krivitskiy. He is the Chairman of the KGB.'

'But isn't Chairman Krivitskiy something of a liberal, in Soviet terms? Unlike Beria, who was a psychopath? We know a little about Krivitskiy after all. Doesn't he speak good English, and collect Western big-band records? Doesn't he like to relax by reading American novels? Isn't it said that he holds frequent friendly discussions with dissident protesters?'

'His English is excellent, and he may in later years have taken to Western music and books. But his only interest in dissent is in its suppression and eradication. He was chosen for Lenin's secret police, the Cheka, as a young man, and he has remained a secret policeman ever since. If the name has changed, from Cheka through OGPU and NKVD to the KGB its function has not, and the qualities necessary to work for it have not.'

'You are in an unusually privileged position to be able to judge, aren't you?'

'Yes,' Yelena said. 'I went to school with him. And because both my husband and he rose to become powerful men in Soviet Russia, we remained in touch. I have been able to see what has happened to him. When I first knew that he had become a Bolshevik, just before the revolution, he was a very idealistic young man. He believed, like so many others of that time, that he was a part of a movement that was going to recreate the world, that was somehow going to recreate mankind itself into a supreme species of cosmic grandeur.'

'And what has happened to that idealistic young man?'

'Dostoevsky described it, in *House of the Dead*. "Whoever has experienced the power, the unrestrained ability to humiliate another human being . . . automatically loses power over his own sensations. Tyranny is a habit, it has its own organic life, it develops finally into a disease, the habit can kill and coarsen the very best man to the level of a beast. Blood and power intoxicate . . . The man and the citizen die with the tyrant forever; the return to human dignity, to repentance, to regeneration, becomes almost impossible." *That* is what has happened to him.'

'Why would he have Ivan killed?'

'For the same reason he sent him into painful exile. As an example to the others of the consequences of the refusal to acquiesce. The regime that rules the Soviet Union does not allow anyone to question that rule.'

'Why?' Nichols asked her. 'Western governments are questioned every day – in the papers, on the radio, the television, by the man or woman in the street. What is so special about the Soviet government?'

'Western governments are elected by the people. The people can criticise a government, too, change it at the next election if they do not like it. The government receives its authority from the people. The Soviet government seized power in a *coup* and it has never offered itself to the people in a free election. It couldn't. Because it would lose. The government of the Soviet Union represents itself, a tiny ruling class of party and government officials, perhaps half a million of them in an empire of two hundred and sixty million. It cannot, and will not, tolerate opposition, for its rule is not legitimate. It exiles, and finally kills, those who stand up for a better way of life for the people it controls. It killed my husband, Ivan, who was one such.'

Nichols looked back into the camera. 'We don't know, however, if what Yelena is saying is so. However badly treated he may have been, General Ivan Akulov may have died, in exile, of a heart attack, just as the KGB claim.'

Another man came forward. He had a hat on, and a scarf wound about his face.

'We have with us a doctor, a man who sympathises with the dissidents. For reasons that are possibly obvious, he prefers not to be shown.'

He turned to Yelena. 'You are sure you want us to open the coffin?'

Her face was unhappy, but set. 'Yes.'

Nichols took a screwdriver and began to undo the brass screws that held the lid down. When he was done, he lifted the lid, and Yelena stepped forward. As she looked inside she exclaimed, and lifted her hands up to her face.

'Ivan . . . Ivan darling . . . what did they *do* to you?'

When the doctor had finished, Nichols screwed the lid back down, and stood in front of the camera for the last time.

'What we have seen has proved Yelena Akulova correct beyond question. General Akulov died fighting. A man of nearly seventy, he was beaten by several others. The cuts, contusions and fractures to his fists show the injuries he inflicted upon them. The weals, wounds and broken bones of his body show how *they* killed him. It was murder, state-sponsored murder of a brave man who stood up in opposition. Here you have it. Real life in the land of freedom and happiness.'

When he had finished the cameraman began pulling his equipment apart. The lights were dimmed, the curtains drawn.

'Yelena, are you certain you want me to go ahead?' Nichols asked seriously. 'When this is shown on television there's going to be a lot of publicity. And the Soviets aren't going to take it lying down. They'll come for you with everything.'

'You must do it, Johnny. For Ivan, for all the people he wanted to help. For the memory of the dead.'

'You may be shot.'

'No. Krivitskiy's too sophisticated for that. The camps, or exile somewhere even worse than Irkutsk, Tomsk, perhaps, or Chita. Hell holes. Which will be your opportunity to create more publicity in the West, not just for me, but for all the others. You see, Krivitskiy understands something very well: he knows that for evil to triumph all that is necessary is for good people to do nothing. I count myself among the good. But it is no use simply sitting and thinking nice thoughts. You must stand up and be counted, you have to go out there and *fight*. It is a contest to the finish. I know that. And so does he.'

Moscow, March 1969

The door bell rang. Not the long sound of a heavy palm, accompanied by the kicking of boots that she had been expecting, but two short thumbings. They sounded almost polite.

The young man standing there when she opened the door was polite as well. He was smartly dressed in a dark suit and tie and held out his KGB identification for her to see in the palm of his hand.

'We wondered if you would mind coming down to headquarters for a chat, Mrs Akulova?' he suggested diffidently.

'You wondered? A chat? Do I have any choice?'

'You can tell me to go away, but my boss would like to talk to you. If I don't bring you along he'll probably send me out to be on the border guards or something, and I'd hate that.'

'Very well . . . Yuri, isn't it? I'll come.'

She had a thick wool overcoat on a peg by the door, together with a pre-packed bag. She wore, day and night, warm wool underclothes made for skiers and the clothes she put on in the morning were stout and warm. Survival in the camps had often depended upon what a man or woman was wearing when they were dragged out of their house . . .

She put on her coat and picked up the bag. The young KGB man looked at her, puzzled.

'You don't have to pack a bag,' he said. 'It's only a chat.'

'I think I'll take it,' she said wisely.

They went downstairs. Outside, a black Volga was waiting with a driver. Yuri held the door open for her and she got in.

'It is almost fifty years ago to the day that the Cheka took me away,' she said as the car pulled off. 'In a Black Maria. The floor was covered in blood. You knew where the Cheka were by the bloodstained path going up from the street to the house.'

Yuri smiled. 'We have carpets in here,' he said, pointing to the floor. 'We use American vacuum cleaners on them. For the dirt, not blood. Terrible things happened in the old days, so I've heard. I'm glad that's all in the past.'

She looked at him pityingly. 'You think it is?'

'Oh, yes,' he said, with certainty. They passed the shining glass façade of the Rossiya cinema complex at Puskkinskaya and the *Izvestiya* newspaper building, with its strange circular top floor windows.

'The old Convent was there,' she said. 'They turned it into the museum of atheism after the revolution. I see it's gone, now.'

'No need to convince people that there is no god, I expect.'

'There most certainly is, young man!' she said sharply. 'He rules all our lives, whether you choose to admit it or not.'

'Do you talk to your god, then?' he asked, seeming interested.

'Of course. I pray to God every day.'

They turned into the Marksa Prospekt between the bulk of the Moskva Hotel and the Gosplan building, staring at each other across the wide boulevard.

'Are we going to the Lubyanka?'

'Yes.'

'Are the parquet floors still down?'

'Yes, in the old building.'

'When they took you from your cell, if you'd been on the conveyor, you were disoriented. But if you felt the parquet under your feet you knew you were still in the Lubyanka. I think of the parquet and the smell of floor polish. And people screaming . . .'

'Terrible times,' he said, sympathetically.

The car swung into the curiously empty square.

'Nobody comes here still,' she said. 'It is the place of skulls, and they stay away.'

It had not changed. The very smell of floor polish brought a sweat to the surface of her skin. Walking down the polished corridors made the flesh under her toenails ache. They stopped outside a door, and she was certain that it was the same one. He opened it for her.

'Would you mind waiting inside, and I'll let him know you're here.'

She went in and her heart was thudding desperately, knocking against her ribs. The room was empty, simply furnished with a desk, a table and some chairs. She went to the window and below was the courtyard she remembered. It was empty. She wiped the palms of her hands against her coat.

'I'm sorry to have kept you.'

She turned, and a middle-aged man wearing glasses was standing there. She had not heard him come in. He was casually dressed in a Western-style sports jacket and slacks. He looked like a university lecturer.

'I'm Daniel Ermilov. Yuri was telling me you've been here before.'

'I'm sure you know that. What rank are you, Daniel Ermilov?'

'Oh, I don't exactly have rank,' he said vaguely. 'I'm a sort of adviser. I hope it isn't too upsetting for you.'

She pointed down into the courtyard.

'That's where they shot people. They made me stand up here and watch as they shot some people. I knew some of them.'

'Very distressing. Look, why don't you sit over here by the desk and we can have our chat.'

She sat down in the chair, still holding her bag.

'Do take off your coat. I know it's cold outside, but we have the heating on here.'

'I'll undo it,' she said cautiously. That was an old trick. They distracted you and when you looked round your warm clothes had gone. That could be a death sentence, if the *Khanovey*, the king of winds, was blowing.

'You *are* well-wrapped up.'

'After I left here they sent me to Kolyma. It doesn't pay to go there without warm clothes.'

'You have a bag packed and you're wearing a lot of clothing. Do you think you're going to Kolyma?'

'Don't play games with me, Daniel Ermilov! I am who I am, and this is what this is, the headquarters of the secret police. Nobody comes here with the thought of a holiday in mind.'

'The Gulag doesn't exist any more.'

'If you say so,' she said politely.

'Does it prey on your mind? All the things that happened to you, long ago?'

There was a gathering tension in the back of her neck, lights began to go off like flashbulbs behind her eyes.

'When people are subjected to very terrible events, those events leave scars on the mind just as much as on their bodies. They are more difficult to see for those outside, but not for those upon whom those events were inflicted. It is one of the reasons there should be free and open discussion of the past in the Soviet Union. It would greatly assist in alleviating the pain of millions.'

'What kind of discussion?' he asked. 'Do you feel talking to a psychiatrist might help?'

'Some people might find such a thing helpful. I feel that *any* open, free and unrestricted investigation into the past would be of immense benefit to the mental health of everyone. Including the people who work in this building.'

The first forked-lightning of pain sent its fingers through her head, and she grimaced.

'Is something wrong?' he asked, concerned.

'I have a headache. I get them sometimes.'

'Do you think that what happened to you here has anything to do with that?'

'I should not be surprised. I did not get them under Tsar Nicholas,' Yelena said pointedly.

'You think about the past a great deal.'

'The Soviet Union is *haunted* by its past. Until it is exorcised, the past will continue to destroy the present. The German people have had to come to terms with the fact that their government was responsible for the murder of millions, simply because of race. It has been very painful for them, but not as painful as living without doing it. Here we live with the knowledge that the government that murdered *millions*, simply on a class basis, is still in charge. The entire apparatus of terror, the fusion of party and secret police is still intact. The terror could be resumed at any time.'

'Do you compare Nazi Germany with Soviet Communism?' he asked.

'Where, in essence, are they different? They are, or were, both socialist; both paranoid, requiring hate objects; both needing to kill or maim any who stand in their way; both demanding public belief in things demonstrably insane, demanding worship of man-made gods; both based on the power of the lie.'

'You do not consider a communist country to be utopia, then?'

'I can think of no other form of government so certain to produce – slowly and steadily, like soil erosion, or the action of the tides – an erosion and corrosion of the human spirit. It cuts man off from all nourishment, from his metaphysical roots, from religious experience, from any feeling of belonging in and as one with the world. It produces a dehydration of the soul, spiritual death.'

Fluorescent battlements had begun to jerk across her eyes, dazzling her. Ermilov looked at her closely.

'Is your headache very bad?'

'It is not . . . pleasant,' she said.

'Would you like to go home? We can resume our conversation another time.'

'I would like to go home, yes.'

Ermilov went to the door. Yuri was sitting on a chair outside, waiting.

'You can take Mrs Akulova back to her apartment now.'

The car was outside. They got in and it drove away. She sat tense in the back seat, noting the route. It was different. It was the way to the Lefortovo.

'Is something the matter?' Yuri asked.

'Why are we going this way?'

'The traffic's bad on Gor'kovo,' the driver said casually. 'They're working on the road. Didn't you notice?'

'No.'

She could not help staring at the star-shaped prison as it came up but they swept by. A bead of sweat ran down from her temple, and she wiped it away.

'Did you think we were taking you there?' Yuri asked, sympathetically.

'I am familiar with the methods of breaking people down.'

They stopped outside her crumbling white apartment block. Yuri came up with her and waited while she opened the door.

'This isn't the best part of town,' he said. 'It's best if you have someone with you.'

'I did not always live here,' she said. 'I was sent.'

The door opened, and she went inside.

'Goodbye,' he said. 'Take care.'

She shut the door. She went inside and sat down on her bed, that served as a sofa. She sat, and waited for the pounding of the boots in the corridor, the noise of the sledgehammers smashing in the door . . .

36

Vyalotekushchaya

May 1969

THE doorbell rang, two short, polite thumbings. When she opened it, Yuri was standing there, together with another young man.

'Good morning,' he said cheerfully. 'Are you ready?'

She looked at them both. The other was red-haired, wearing Western jeans and jacket. He had a camera bag over his shoulder and a notebook in his hand.

'Ready for what?' she asked.

Yuri frowned. 'Why, for the trial, Mrs Akulova. When I called you yesterday I asked you to be ready this morning.'

'You made no call yesterday,' she said. 'But I am always ready to leave. That is something you learn, if you have been arrested by the KGB. Always be ready.'

Yuri looked at the man with him, and shrugged his shoulders faintly. 'This is Jurgen Deitrich, Mrs Akulova,' he said, speaking rather louder. 'He is a West German journalist. We have invited him along and he may report on the trial without hindrance.'

'You do not need to shout. I am neither deaf nor stupid.'

Yelena took her coat from the peg, and put her bag over her shoulder.

'May I carry that for you?' Deitrich asked politely.

'Thank you, but I prefer to hold on to my possessions. It is safer that way.' She turned to Yuri. 'After this trial, will I be coming back here? Or should I switch things off?'

'Mrs Akulova, how should I know?' he asked innocently. 'A trial is a trial and the judge must judge according to the evidence.'

She laughed. 'You mean the verdict is not already made out? You will clear my home out anyway, although there is nothing here of value. Your goons have taken all that was precious to me.'

'Mrs Akulova has a poor opinion of us,' Yuri commented. 'But you know that, you saw the programme.'

'Which programme?' Yelena asked.

'The one I told you about,' Yuri said patiently. 'The one you made with Mr Nichols, slandering the Soviet Union.'

'You told me nothing,' she said shortly. 'But if you have arranged this farce, let us get on with it.'

They went downstairs. A car was waiting, perhaps the same car. They got in, and it drove them away.

'For whom do you work, Herr Deitrich?' she asked with interest.

'I am a freelance journalist,' the German answered politely. 'I have sold articles to many publications and I speak both Russian and English.'

They crossed Pokrovskiye Square and stopped in a jam of traffic by a handsome aquamarine building, gloriously baroque. Ahead of them fire engines were roaring out on to the road.

'Do you know what that is?' she said to the journalist.

'It is the fire station,' he said, amused at the obvious.

'It is the Church of the Resurrection. The Bolsheviks cut it up into a fire station.'

'You do not approve?'

'Malicious destruction of the Lord's house is blasphemy. Let them have their fire station elsewhere. They have enough Stalinist piles about, like the courthouse, no doubt.'

'Ah, Stalin,' he said disinterestedly. 'You don't hear so much of him these days.'

At the end of the boulevard they drew around two gigantic statues of an armed peasant and worker, and stopped.

'As I said,' she remarked, getting out. 'A foul Stalinist pile.'

They went into the white slab-sided building and Yuri led the way. He opened a door to a windowless room, lit by fluorescent lights. It was recognisably a court room. A guard was standing inside.

'Mrs Akulova,' Yuri said. 'I must leave you. The guard will take you down to your lawyer.'

At one of the tables before the judge's bench a man was sitting, balding and in a grey suit. He stood up as she came down.

'Hello, once more,' he said. 'Well, here we are.'

'Once more? I am supposed to have met you?' she asked.

'We have met several times, as you know. It will not help, pretending not to know me,' he said severely, and she sat down.

At the other table was a woman, severely dressed in a dark suit with a high-necked blouse and red tie. The prosecutor. The judge's chair was as yet empty. Behind the rail sat some rows of people. She could see Yuri, and next to him his superior, Ermilov. Among some spectators was sitting the German journalist, Dietrich. The clerk at his table banged a gavel, and they all rose as the judge came in. Yelena remained sitting down.

She knew him. She was about to shout out in protest, and then she kept her mouth shut. He gathered his black robe round him, and sat down. He nodded at the prosecutor.

'You may begin, Comrade Lavritskaya,' he said, and, as the woman rose, Yelena added her name to the list in her head.

'This court hearing concerns the case of Yelena Nikolayevna Akulova, born in the year 1900, Russian. The acts of the accused Akulova are described by the indictment as crimes specified under Article 70 Part 1 of the criminal code of the RFSR.' She paused to clear her throat, and looked around. Everyone was paying attention. 'In the world arena today, the stormy growth of the material and spiritual forces of the Soviet Union and other socialist countries, the successes of the World Communist and Workers' Movement, have led to a propagation of the great ideas of communism on our planet unprecedented hitherto. There is no force which can restrain their revolutionising influence on the destinies of mankind.

'The course of the world revolutionary process evokes deep alarm amidst the imperialist reactionaries, and they permit themselves any means of struggle against the forces of social and national liberation, and against the world of socialism. The creative labour of the Soviet people and of the workers of fraternal socialist countries serves as an inspiring example for the peoples of all continents. Bourgeois propaganda is conducting a fierce struggle against the ideas of socialism, striving above all to defame the Soviet order and slander the historic achievements of our people. For a Soviet citizen to aid the agents of imperialism in their vile work is a crime against all oppressed peoples everywhere. It is just that which the criminal Akulova is accused of. You will hear – '

'How can I be a criminal if I have not yet been convicted?' Yelena called out, clearly. Lavritskaya paused, papers in hand, and spoke to her.

'As it happens, you still *are* a criminal. The accused was a convicted British spy in the 1930s, and although released for war work, never received a pardon. She simply failed to represent herself to the labour camp at war's end.'

'Like millions of others I was an innocent victim of the Terror! And my war work, as you call it, consisted of international diplomacy at the highest level.'

The judge spoke. 'If the accused cannot restrain herself from irrelevant interruptions she will be removed, and the trial continue without her. You may go on, Comrade.'

'The court will hear how the accused criminal Akulova organised and collaborated with a mercenary American television team to defame the very name of the revolution. This programme was shown recently in America, and the accused seen raving in front of the corpse of her husband, which she had had mutilated after his death. Among other vicious slanders, she accused senior government officials of having ordered the death of this man – himself another professional liar and slanderer of our people.'

'General Ivan Ivanovich Akulov, Hero of the Soviet Union, champion of the downtrodden . . .' Yelena said quietly.

Lavritskaya looked at her angrily, but once again the judge intervened.

'We can see that you have prepared your case with care, Comrade. However, before we become too involved with its technicalities it may be helpful to hear from the accused's lawyer, Comrade Rodov. How does the accused wish to plead?'

The man next to Yelena stood up. 'There can, of course, be no question but that my client is guilty as charged. She did, of course, commit the crimes she is accused of. But we have to ask ourselves why she did this. She publicly repudiated the revolution and this is not a rational act, not the act of a balanced mind. With the court's permission, two experienced medical men – a psychiatrist and a psychologist – examined the accused to assess her state of mind. The court may find it helpful to hear from them.'

'Let us do so.'

Yuri stood up, and came before the judge's bench.

'You are?'

'Yuri Selvinsky, I am a psychologist at the Serbsky Institute.'

'He is an officer of the KGB at the Lubyanka!' said to Yelena.

'They will take you away,' said Rodov, next to her.

'What is your judgement as to the state of mind of the accused?'

'I have written a full report, which is available to the court, but, to provide a summary, the accused lives in the past. She broods upon wrongs she believes were committed to her and her family decades ago. She believes that she is persecuted by the security agencies of the state – she has a fixation about it. Indeed, you have just heard that she thinks I work for them. To illustrate my point, please notice the way in which she is dressed. It is a warm and pleasant day outside, and yet she is heavily clad. She carries a bag with her everywhere she goes, containing supplies. You have heard how some thirty years ago she was convicted of spying. She spent some time in the labour camps, and this has affected her mind. She now believes that at any moment policemen will descend on her and take her away. Hence her obssession with warm clothes and the bag of supplies. She has acquired religious beliefs and has a manic certainty in the presence of some invisible god. She talks to this being constantly. I have communicated my findings to my superior, Professor Ermilov, who has been able to make the correct diagnosis.'

'May we hear from Professor Ermilov?'

Ermilov took the younger man's place and stood for a moment polishing his glasses with a handkerchief.

'This is a very sad case. No one disputes the vile crimes this woman has committed against the people of the Soviet Union – indeed, against oppressed peoples everywhere. Yet we should not let righteous anger at such horrors blind us to their cause, we should not seek justifiable revenge.'

Glancing over her shoulder Yelena could see Deitrich busy writing in his notebook.

'You have heard that the accused lives in, is *obsessed* by the past. That she suffers from religious delusions. Is that not the key? Her belief that the revolution is evil is delusion of the highest order. The truth is that we are not dealing with a criminal, but with one who is not of normal mind. The accused, Yelena Nikolayevna Akulova, is insane. Probably she has suffered from sluggish schizo-phrenia, *vyalotekushchaya*, for years. Now, however. I find a deep psychopathy, a malignant paranoia.

'Cerebral atherosclerosis indicates arriving senility and the medical judgement in these matters is clear-out. Schizophrenia is a disease in which patients are deemed not responsible for their actions. Yelena Nikolayevna Akulova cannot be tried here as a criminal, because she is not responsible for her actions. She requires treatment: not in one of our excellent prisons, but in one of our equally excellent mental hospitals.'

'Thank you, Comrade Ermilov. The court is inclined to accept your view. Does the prosecution have any objections?'

The prosecutor shook her head. 'Very well. The court rules that Yelena Nikolayevna Akulova is found not guilty of the charges made against her on the grounds of medical non-responsibility. It rules that she be sent to a suitable Special Psychiatric Hospital for the treatment of her illnesses. The court is adjourned.'

Yelena stood up and turned to the German journalist, still busy writing behind her.

'Herr Dietrich,' she called. 'If you have not recorded everything the KGB here will provide you with a transcript of the trial. They are *all* KGB, including the judge. I know him, and he knows me. His name is Steklov and he was the henchman of a state criminal named Rykov.'

London, England, June 1969

'We ought to call this the expatriates' club,' Nichols joked as he came into the flat.

'It is the Committee to Free Yelena Akulova,' Ruth said, 'and I have got some good British people to join, so there. We are not just a bunch of exiled Russians and Hungarians.'

'And an American,' Nichols said with a smile. 'Just rabble, really.'

The windows were open. On the warm Bayswater breeze came the sound of the Rolling Stones and the Beach Boys from the passing cars. The streets were colourful with psychedelia and Indian caftans.

'I've had the pub on the corner make us up some sandwiches.' Ruth said. 'I'm an old customer. I moved here when I came home on leave from SOE and found my lovely flat in Knightsbridge just a bomb hole. Now, Johnny, you never met my son Nikolai Sergeyevich, although you wrote about him in your marvellous book. He left – defected, is it? – after they killed Beria. Now he works for Amnesty International, so he's going to be very helpful to us. Joan, my lovely friend – we were in SOE together – is keeping the vigil over at the Soviet Embassy. I shall take over at ten. Fortunately, it is not far to walk. Eva is my daughter from Hungary. We left together, along with about three hundred people we let off a Russian prison camp train. We have been busy contacting them all, and so far every single one has agreed to help. We have manpower and we have special talents. You, Johnny, have contacts in politics and the press in America, and access to mass publicity. Boris is there, and will help, too. Eva is a qualified doctor, which in view of the revolting place Yelena is in will be very useful. Nikolai is a trained intelligence officer. I was in SOE and, if we need to make a firebomb or kill Krivitskiy silently, I can do it. And I do know *everybody*. So where do we start?'

They were sitting about the table, and Nichols held up a magazine, folded to show the inside pages.

'Here it is. A photograph of a suitably dressed up courtroom, and the article. The Soviets come across as advanced and sympathetic, Yelena as a deranged lunatic.'

'We need to discredit Deitrich, the author,' said Nikolai. 'He was the only Western journalist there and he was clearly their man.'

'He may not realise the extent to which they were using him, Ruth warned. 'Writers are among the easiest of intellectuals to subvert – Savinkov knew that. They're always short of money. Offer them syndication of their articles or books in the many – government – publications of the Soviet Union. Ladle praise over them. It always works. They always know that if they write anything truly critical they won't be allowed back in. We may not get anything overt on Dietrich. He's just one in a long line of Western hacks made use of by the Soviet regime.'

'Thank you, Ruth,' Nichols said dryly. 'I myself was once one of those hacks. But I agree.'

'We should try to get at Krivitskiy himself,' said Nikolai. 'Something personal that would, if made public, discredit him.'

'Good idea. Ruth, you actually knew him.'

'I'll work on it,' she promised. 'Eva, what about the official psychiatric organisations here, like the WPA?'

'I am not hopeful,' she said. The child of Budapest had grown up into a lovely young woman. She was in her early twenties, newly-qualified from St. Bartholomew's Hospital. 'They take the view that they are not concerned with political matters. I spoke to their secretary and he told me that in his view schizophrenia is the most important topic in psychiatry. He called it the scourge of the world. He said the Russians had over 200 highly-qualified doctors researching it and I was not able to convince him that these highly-qualified people are in the business of crushing dissent. He suggested, instead, that, as a Hungarian exile, I might myself be suffering from paranoia where the Russians were concerned.'

'We don't have first-hand evidence. No *samizdat* to show the world,' said Ruth. She picked up the magazine. 'We don't even know where she is, where they are holding her.'

Eva ran a finger along some lines of the article. 'That part worries me. First, they accuse her of schizophrenia, and then of impending senility. Their aim will be to destroy her will to resist. Torture of one kind or another will be used. I have never been tortured, but my training suggests to me that its effects could well be to make one unbalanced.'

'I have been tortured' Ruth said grimly. 'And seen it happen to others. Some it does send mad.'

'And if they fail to break her, after some period of time, they could simply destroy her mind, and release her as . . . senile.'

Leningrad Special Psychiatric Hospital, Arsenalnaya Street

Her cell was very small, with a stone floor and a wooden plank bed, and managed, in the middle of summer, to combine stuffy heat with a damp that came out of the walls. She sat on the hard bed in a rough cotton shift that looked as though it had once been white. It had not been washed for some time.

There was a clanking of metal in the door and it swung open. A fair-haired woman in her twenties came in. She wore a coverall and was carrying some clothes and a bag. She shut the door and sat down on the bed.

'All right. This is the Bolshoi Dom, and I'm Orderly Romachov. Let me tell you how it is here in the big house. *I'm* the one you'll deal with. If the doctor wants you to have an injection, I'm the one who holds you down. If the food gives you the runs – it will – I'm the one you have to call to get a non-regulation visit to the latrine. I'm the one who decides if you can have exercise.'

'You're very important,' Yelena said pleasantly. 'And you're from the Ukraine.'

The broad, but pretty face opened in surprise.

'My husband was from the Ukraine, too. How did you get this important job, Orderly Romachov?'

'I was sent, of course. I'm a prisoner, same as you. I live about the same as you, too. Rotten little room, lousy clothes, bad food, no liquor or tobacco. But I'm in charge, and so if you make my life better, I can make yours better.'

'I'm sure we can come to an understanding. What did you do. Orderly Romashov, to be put here?'

'You speak nice,' the girl said. 'I like listening to your voice. Why do you speak different?'

'I'm a Countess. From the time of Tsar Nicholas.'

'He machine-gunned the workers, didn't he?'

'No, he didn't.'

'The KGB machine-gunned *us*. Russian bastards. They always use Russians.' She looked at Yelena, holding the clothes and bag on her knees. 'We rioted,' she said proudly. 'We'd had enough. That prick Ognyov promised to double meat output in two years. And he did. They gave him the Order of Lenin. He'd slaughtered all the dairy cows to do it, and the next year we were starving. But we got the *svoloch*. We strung him up by the balls and he died. We set the Party headquarters on fire and they sent in the KGB troops and they machine-gunned us. Some they sent to the camps and me they sent here. I got a tenner.'

'We had a joke in my day, when I was in the camps,' Yelena said. 'One *zek* says to the other, how many years did you get? And he replies, "twenty". What did you do? "Nothing." That's ridiculous, says the first. For doing nothing you only get ten years.'

The girl smiled. 'You do speak nice. What did you do to get here?'

'Sort of the same as you. I wanted to set the Party Headquarters on fire.'

'It burned ever so pretty. Red, like their stupid flag. But look, let's get this sorted out.' She held up a thick overcoat, and the bag. 'You'll need a coat. And this bag's got things like soap and vitamin tablets in it.'

'I know. I put them there.'

'So it was yours, now it's mine. But you can buy it back.'

'I can do that. The bag also has paper, and a pen. I need to write a letter, and I need it to be posted. Can you do that?'

The shrewd peasant eyes narrowed. 'I might. But it would cost. What would be in it for me?'

In the letter I will tell someone to deliver some things to Leningrad – tobacco, chocolate, cheese, bacon . . . Anything else?'

'Knickers and socks. Mine are in holes.'

'All right.'

'I got a rash, too. I got it from the clothes. Some ointment.'

'This is a hospital, can't you get medicine here?'

The girl laughed shortly. 'Plenty. But it won't do good things to you.'

Yelena opened her mouth and levered at a tooth. A gold cap came away and she handed it to the girl. 'That'll pay for these, and to get the letter out. You tell me how you want the other things collected for you.'

The Ukrainian looked at the gold in admiration.

'I had a dentist fit it for me. It saves having to pull the whole tooth out.'

'You're a smart one,' the girl said, admiringly.

'Is it boring here?' Yelena asked.

'Boring? This is the most tedious place on earth.'

'Would you like me to tell you a story?'

Her face brightened, like a child's. 'What sort of story?'

'I know lots of stories. Would you like one about people, or animals?'

'Animals. I had a pet cat, when I was young. Lovely, she was.'

'This is a story about Mole and Ratty, Badger and Toad. Toad is rich, he lives in a fine house on the river.'

'He's one of the bosses. He's got a dacha.'

'No, this story is set in England, and they do things differently there. Toad owns his big house.'

'They machine gun the workers – I saw it on the television – and everyone's starving there. It's worse than here.'

'It isn't, you know. But, Toad. Toad has a very nice life. He spends a lot of time being silly. He rows his boat. He has a caravan, and goes about the country. He falls in love with a motor car. He spends much too much money, and Mole and Ratty and Badger who are his friends, have to watch over him. It isn't easy – '

'The others, they're narks, right? They're going to sell Toad to the real bosses.'

'No. They're his friends. Toad's foolish, but he's good at heart. They try to save him from getting into trouble.'

The girl was frowning, and suddenly her hand snaked out and she hit Yelena across the head.

'Don't spill all these lies! If Toad's got the dacha and the money they don't have to look after him! Why are they being nice to him? You're telling me stories like my mother told, and they aren't true.'

She jumped up, and went out of the door, crashing it shut behind her. Yelena unrolled her coat, and put it on. She opened her bag, and the smell of soap came out. She inhaled it like perfume. Then she took out some sheets of folded paper, and a pencil, and began to write, using a small, neat hand.

She was nearly finished, forty minutes later, when the lock turned in the door, and the girl came back in. She sat back down on the bed.

'I meant to tell you. Dr Kelchevskaya, the doctor who'll be in charge, she's back tomorrow.'

'Thank you.'

The girl produced a length of black sausage from her pocket and cut a piece off with a knife she carried. She gave it to Yelena.

'I got some vodka with the gold, too. I'll sleep tonight.'

'Shall I tell you a story about a rich man? He thought a great deal of himself, he was a very conceited man, and it led him to lose everything. He was sent to jail, and because he had lost everything, the good qualities he had came out. He escaped, he ran away from the police. He had many adventures, he found his friends again. They fought a civil war, and he recovered what was his.'

'My father said we would recover what was ours, in the Ukraine. He said we would fight a civil war, and get rid of the Russians. My mother told me so. He is dead now, they shot him. So that cannot be your story.'

'No. My story is the story of Mole and Ratty, of Badger and Toad.'

The girl looked wistfully at Yelena in the little cell. 'Tell me about Toad,' she said.

'The story begins with Mole. The Mole had been working very hard all the morning, spring-cleaning his little home . . .'

London

'Here it is,' said Ruth. She held up the sheets of closely-written paper in delight, as though they were icons. 'It came through this morning.'

'Fantastic,' said Nichols. 'How did she get it out?'

'She's got a sympathetic orderly, a Ukrainian girl. She took in gold in her teeth and she got this out by way of Tatyana in Novosibirsk. She's arranging for a supply of tobacco, chocolate and medicines to be taken up and smuggled in. But see what she says. This is a real *samizdat*, you can use it. The trial: the judge was Steklov, an old NKVD man, one of Rykov's protégés, one of the Stalin gang that joined Krivitskiy. The psychologist and psychiatrist were both KGB. She was interviewed at the Lubyanka, not the Serbsky, and the Leningrad SPH isn't run by the Ministry of Health but by the MVD. The MVD run the prisons. The boss of the Leningrad SPH isn't a doctor, but an MVD Colonel.'

'This is what we needed!' Nichols said joyfully. 'Now we have hard fact. Jerry Jacobs on *The Post* wants to work with us so I'll slip him this.'

In the street below workmen were painting a building, their shirts off in the sun. A small transistor radio was playing a song about love, and flowers in the hair.

'Nikolai's got Amnesty International ready. I've shown them this and they're going to begin pressing for an independent visit to verify the conditions.'

'Think they'll do it?'

'If we exert enough pressure. The Soviet regime is vulnerable to international opinion. It's not a legitimate government, so it craves acceptance and fears isolation. At the very least our pressure might have the effect of getting Yelena moved from the SPH to an Ordinary one.'

Nichols was skimming through Yelena's report. 'It's grim,' he agreed. 'Those who disagree with the regime are put in with those who are genuinely mentally ill . . . Some are kept in wards. If they try to avoid taking the medicine, or if they try to argue with the staff they are chained down to their beds and left there for three or more days. No bedpans or use of lavatories. The warders pass by at intervals and beat them.'

The telephone rang in the hallway of the flat and Ruth went out to answer it. Nichols stood with the document in his hand, looking out over the park, where people were walking, standing, looking at the flowers in their beds and smelling them, thinking about people being tortured thousands of miles away.

He suddenly heard Ruth's voice shouting in Russian. '*Yob tenya pereyob, nedoyobysh!*' she screamed. He heard the receiver clatter into its cradle. She came back into the room, and reached for a packet of cigarettes on the table, her hand shaking with anger.

'What on earth was that?'

'Someone speaking in Russian. I was very rude to him.'

Her face was pale and he saw tears standing in her eyes. From the radio in the street below came the guitar and voice of Joan Baez, singing about protest, and about peace.

'What did he say?'

She lit her cigarette, and smoke swirled across the room. 'He said we should stop making so much noise about Yelena. He said if we stopped the publicity, they would reduce the intensity of her treatment.'

Leningrad SPH

'Because you are insane, you have no rights,' the woman said. Orderly Romachov, who stood in an attitude of respect by the door had announced her as Dr Kelchevskaya. She wore a white coat, was in her forties and had her dark hair fashionably styled.

'Nobody in the Soviet Union has rights,' said Yelena. 'But I am sane.'

Kelchevskaya smiled. 'You reveal yourself immediately. Only someone suffering from mental illness would criticise the revolution. It is my task to make you well again.'

'As I have never believed that the revolution was anything but monstrous tyranny you will find this difficult,' Yelena said flatly.

'I am a Marxist, I am a psychiatrist. I deal with human minds according to his scientific laws. I have many aids to bringing a patient back to health. As you will see. The road back to sanity will be long and painful. And at times doubt enters your mind, remember that, because you are insane, you have no rights. You may not attempt legal redress against anyone. Any complaint about treatment that you may have in your madness will get no further than the walls of your cell. You are not a prisoner in gaol, nor one in a camp, you are a *patient*. The prisoner is sentenced to a definite term of years. You are here to get well. You will remain here for as long as it takes me to make you well. That can be months, years or decades. Do you understand me? You will leave here only when you are able to publicly recant your insane views. Only when I am certain that it is safe to release you into the society of good communists outside this hospital will you be released. Now, come, let me show you what people who do not believe in the revolution look like.'

She led the way out of the cell, and Yelena followed, with Orderly Romachov at her side. They went down a long, dirty corridor of cells. There was a vile, rotting stench in the air which came from the filthy doors at the end. Orderly Romachov unlocked them with the keys at her belt and they went in. The noise and the smell hit Yelena simultaneously. The floor was slippery with excrement and the foul mattresses of the beds were the same. She saw that Romachov and Kelchevskaya both wore short rubber boots, but that the occupants of the room, like herself, were barefoot.

The noise was a cacophony. Women of all ages swarmed everywhere, their hair straggling, dressed in filthy smocks. Nearby one lay on a bed, spittle foaming at her mouth, jerking in epilepsy. By her another was laughing, her eyes staring at nothing. As they went down the room she heard women talking to the air. One sat on her bed with her back to the wall. Every few seconds she crossed herself fearfully.

She saw them coming. 'Get it off, please, get if off,' she begged piteously.

Kelchevskaya paused, and turned to Yelena. 'This is Olga. She killed her mother with an axe. She believes that demons are coming to take her to Hell and that is why she crosses herself. She is insane, as you can see. She believes in God. She asks constantly for people to take off a great snake that the Devil has sent, and which is dragging her very slowly towards the gates of Hell.'

She looked closely at Yelena. Her eyes were brown and in the stench there was the incongruous scent of perfume from her body.

'Your insanity is not the same as hers, she said.' 'But let me assure you that if you do not make efforts to become sane, if you make me keep you here, you will, sooner or later, become like her.'

A woman stood, slack-faced, a chain holding her to her bed. As they came by she saw Kelchevskaya. Fear penetrated the dull mask and urine suddenly ran down her legs, raw with weeping sores.

'This is Vera,' said Kelchevskaya. 'Now she is closer to *your* form of insanity. A lecturer at a college, you would have said an intelligent woman. Yet what did she try to do? She tried to leave the Soviet Union! She was very critical of us when she first came, but we are taming her now.'

At the end of the room a bed was empty. A slimy, rotting mattress lay on the rusting wire springs. Chains hung down from each side, dark with old blood.

'This is for you.'

Orderly Romachov unlocked the manacles and put Yelena's wrists into them. To do so she had to lie on the foul mattress. Kelchevskaya produced a small bottle from one of her pockets and a syringe. She pushed the needle through the cap and began to suck up the contents.

'I am going to give you an injection of Sulphazin. It is a preparation of purified sulphur. Its effects last for around twenty-four hours and it will help you to come to terms with the wrongs you have committed against oppressed peoples everywhere. The great pain you will feel is the agony of your conscience.'

She pushed the needle into Yelena's arm, and thrust the plunger home. Yelena winced as the entering fluid tore at the fibres of her arm.

'I am familiar with this establishment,' Yelena said. 'And with doctors of your type. I have a friend who was made to work in one, once.'

'You have a friend who was treated here?'

'No, in the German concentration camp of Ravensbruck. The doctors there were SS doctors, conducting inhuman and insane experiments upon human beings.' Fearful pain wracked her body and her skin burned and itched, the light stabbed into her eyes. 'As such, they were the very essence of Nazism,' she gasped. 'Just as you and this torture chamber are the essence of the revolution.'

Kelchevskaya smiled. 'You think that now,' she said confidently. 'You will think differently once the madness has come out of your mind.'

Yelena's blood was on fire. Sweat gushed up from her skin, streaming in rivulets all over her body.

'See,' said Kelchevskaya. 'The drugs are driving the evil from you.'

The two walked back along the ward. Orderly Romachov turned and came back. She bent with her keys to check the manacles about Yelena's wrists.

'Think of Toad,' she murmured. '*He* got out.'

It was hot in the room and the pungent smell of slimy wet canvas filled her nostrils. The floor was hard, her elbows and knees, hip and chin, all the bony protrusions of her body were bruised as they rolled her over and over on it like a log, wrapping her up in the canvas.

As each dripping length was taken out of the bath and bound about her, Kelchevskaya checked it. Once she reproved Orderly Romachov for not making a length tight enough.

'It has to be taut the whole way around,' she said. The orderlies turned Yelena back the way she had come and, trussed and helpless, her nose smacked into the floor and began to bleed.

'The patient Stepanova died last month under this treatment, Doctor,' Romachov said. 'If you remember, we could not loosen the canvas in time. Of course, Stepanova did not matter, she was a mere border-crosser, but there are special instructions for this one . . .'

'Special instructions to get her to recant!' Kelchevskaya snapped. She cuffed Romachov on the face and, from the floor, Yelena could see the weal rising red.

'If there are special instructions,' the Ukrainian girl persisted, 'then there is someone special who will not be pleased if she dies . . .'

'I am watching,' Kelchevskaya said grudgingly, and it seemed to

Yelena that, as the remaining lengths were wrapped about her, they were marginally less tight than before.

The slight relief did not last long. The room was hot and the canvas that encased her like an embalmed mummy began to dry out. As it did so, it contracted, squeezing her whole body.

Breathing was difficult. As she strove to pull air into her lungs, the canvas resisted, pushing back.

'Can you move?' asked Kelchevskaya. Yelena could just see her. She was sitting on a stool where she could feel the pulse of Yelena's wrist, the only part of her except her nose and mouth to be left free.

'No, you cannot,' the inquisitor replied, answering her own question. 'You are helpless. The canvas is the iron grip of Marxist-Leninism and you can no more fight the scientifically-ordained laws of History than fly from this room. There you lie, while they squeeze you into the correct form.'

. . . it was pleasant, out in the garden, tending the flowers. Behind the biting ring of canvas Yelena closed her eyes. Out there the breeze was blowing, making the flowerheads bob, carrying their scent to her. The leaves were fresh, held out in the sun. Small birds stood on the slim branches, filling the little garden with song . . .

'Repent!' Kelchevskaya grated. 'Renounce your evil.'

. . . a little stream ran through the grass, clear and pure, splashing and gurgling over the little rocks, swirling slow as it ran into the pool where the fish darted by the willow. The children were playing, racing paper boats down the stream, running and laughing . . .

'Say after me: There is no god.'

. . . ducks there were in the pool, swimming and standing on their heads with their tails up, suddenly re-emerging with glittering beads of water rolling down their combed feathers . . .

In the gap between the two harsh bands of canvas about her face the swollen lips were slowly turning purple. From between them came a soft, rising and falling note. Kelchevskaya bent with Orderly Romachov to listen.

Orderly Romachov looked across the trussed body at the doctor with an expressionless face.

'She's singing,' she said.

. . . it had become dark in the little garden. Dusk had come as she sang to the children. Now she woke into light. She was in her cell, lying on the plank bed. A bare bulb was shining from a flex in the ceiling. Orderly Romachov was seated on a stool beside her and had covered her with her coat.

'She's gone,' said the girl. 'It's the middle of the night.'

From down the corridor there came the sound of someone howling in the chamber of the mad.

'She was very angry, when you were singing,' she said softly. Another long weal ran across the broad, pretty face, with its blonde hair. 'She kept you there too long. I told her we had to unwrap you, otherwise you would die.'

Yelena felt very weak, lying there. She could feel each binding where it had cut into her flesh.

'It was very pleasant in the garden,' she said. 'With all the children playing.'

Romachov bent forward. 'Your friend in Novosibirsk, Tatyana, she came through. There was someone waiting at the station where you said, with a suitcase. We had it picked up and we got it in. Everything you said.'

'Good! I'll need some paper and pencil, now.'

'You ought to rest.' Romachov was concerned.

'*She* will not rest. When she has woken up she will be back.'

'There was something for you.'

She held out a small, folded section of paper, and Yelena unwrapped it to its full size. On it she saw Ruth's neat handwriting.

'My darling Yelena,

Your *samizdat* came through. We are the Committee to Free Yelena Akulova! Everyone has joined whom you can think of. This morning two marvellous old boys walked in (I say old boys, but they are only our age. It's just that like you I don't think of myself as an old girl!) They are Russian expatriates, White soldiers from the Civil War and they say that you freed them from a firing squad with four of their friends. They live in London and are devoting themselves full time to the cause. One of the friends lives in New York and *he's* started a chapter there. All my Hungarians are working like beavers and so far we have two hundred and twelve cuttings in the newspapers. Nikolai has them up on a board in my sitting room – he calls it the war room – as soon as they come in. We have twenty-eight items on radio and Johnny is preparing to go on television both here and in the USA to publicise the case.

We will get you out.
Just survive, darling.
In the Lord's book it says:
Let God arise, and let his enemies be scattered: let them that hate Him, flee before Him.
Like the smoke vanisheth, so shalt thou drive them away: and

like as wax melteth at the fire, so let the ungodly perish at the
presence of God . . .'

Yelena read it twice, then carefully folded it up.

'Help me sit up,' she said, and the Ukrainian eased her up from
the mattress. There was a gap in the frame of her bed that she had
found, and she slipped the letter in there out of sight.

'Did they send some paper?'

Romachov had it ready, and for some while Yelena steadily covered
the sheets with her writing. Finally she folded them up.

'Get this out,' she commanded. 'I have given instructions for more
supplies to be sent, also money.'

Painfully, she lay back down on the hard wood bed, and the girl
helped her. She tucked the letter away.

'You were singing,' she said quietly. 'Singing in another language.
What was it?'

Yelena's face was criss-crossed with livid red and purple marks.
One eye was swollen almost shut and the blood from the burst vessels
had run down into her cheek. She smiled at orderly Romachov with
split lips.

'Mole and Ratty had been out on the river, hadn't they? They had
that most marvellous lunch from the hamper -coldtonguecoldham
coldbeefpickledgherkinssaladfrenchrollscresssandwiches – '

'It sounded so good, I wished I had been there,' Romachov
said wistful

'And Mole wanted to row, and fell in. And Ratty had to pull him
out. Mole spent many days with Ratty on the river after that, learning
to swim and to row, entering into the joy of running water; he learned
to listen in the reed stems to what the wind was whispering there.
And one day, they went to visit Toad. But before they did, Ratty
was teasing his friends, the ducks. He made up a song about them,
he called it the Duck's Ditty. Mole didn't think much of it, but Ratty
liked it.'

She moistened the cracked lips with a swollen tongue, and sang
softly.

> 'All along the backwater,
> Through the rushes tall,
> Ducks are a-dabbling.
> Up tails all!'

She looked at the prison orderly in the harsh light of the bare
bulb.

'It's much nicer to be down by the river with one's friends. Resting in the shade and talking. Watching the children play. I go there as much as I can, now.'

'You are a schizophrenic,' said Kelchevskaya. 'You suffer from schizophrenia and your disease is following the classical features categorised by Professor Snezhnevsky. You have deteriorated progressively. The development of the symptoms has been gradual, and only discernible to the trained eye. They include a slowly-evolving paranoia – you believe that you are being persecuted and you have become obsessional; you over-value your own importance, and exhibit grandiose ideas of reforming the world. You suffer from hallucinations and you believe in the presence of a god. Your disease, as a result of a mental derangement, paranoia and other psychological symptoms, has led you to anti-social actions which fall into the category of those that are prohibited by law. To the people around you, such mental cases as you do not seem obviously insane. It is your seeming normality that is dangerous, for a sick person such as yourself commits socially dangerous actions that are then exploited for the purposes of anti-Soviet propaganda by the West, and the Westerners then claim that you are normal, and not insane.'

'This is a difficult disease to diagnose,' said Yelena wickedly. 'Someone who is supposed to be mentally ill without any symptoms of mental illness. Wouldn't it be more honest simply to say that I, like others, objectively criticise specific acts and policies of the Soviet government, such as violations of its so-called Constitution, the total lack of rights for minority groups and behaviour towards other races unfortunate enough to be under its control, like the Hungarians and Czechs, and that the Soviet government is quite simply trying to crush me; that it is only because it craves acceptance from the legitimate regimes of the West, who would disapprove, that I have not simply been shot, hence the attempt to label me insane; and that you are, at best, a corrupt quack for going along with them, and, at worst, if you actually believe all this twaddle you talk, you are yourself mad?'

Two spots of colour appeared high on Kelchevskaya's cheeks. 'You have just exhibited some of the clinical criteria of your illness. You suffer from paranoid reformist delusional ideas.'

'I also have a black cat,' Yelena said dryly.

'You show poor adaptation to the social environment!'

'Were Lenin and Trotsky poorly adapted to their social environment when, in their struggle against the government of the Tsar, they were constantly subject to harassment and arrest? Possibly they, as I have been known to do, gathered herbs at midnight. Also frogs.'

'Your opinions have a moralising character,' she blustered.

'On All Hallow's Eve strange lights are to be seen inside my house.'

'What are you talking about?' Kelchevskaya snapped. 'Black cats and frogs. And what is All Hallow?'

'Halloween. I'm obviously a witch.'

'The state is powerful, and you are weak. It is not the act of a sane person for you to take on the state!'

'Jesus Christ took on the Roman Empire, and died for what he believed in.'

'You suffer from delusions of grandeur!'

'Lenin took on the government of the Tsar.'

'You believe yourself to be sane!'

'Believing that is probably one of your criteria of insanity.'

Kelchevskaya took a drug bottle from her pocket and began to suck up the contents with a syringe. 'We, however, know differently.' She squirted a little of the fluid into the air, holding up the syringe. 'We understand the severity of your mental illness. You are fortunate to be living in the Soviet Union, where medical care is the finest in the world. Our scientists have produced drugs which are of immense benefit in treating your disease.'

The needle went in and Kelchevskaya pressed the plunger home. 'Your psychotic symptoms will soon be gone. Soon you will be well.'

The lock turned and the door opened. Kelchevskaya looked at her, sitting slack on the bed. Yelena slowly looked up, her head shaking rythmically as it moved. Her lips and tongue moved involuntarily, purposelessly, without speech.

Kelchevskaya pulled up her sleeve and looked at her arm. It was pocked, dappled with fresh and old bruises from the constant injections. She dropped the sleeve. It was time to move on to the fresh arm.

She had brought in the apparatus for measuring blood pressure and placed it on the bed. She wrapped the cuff about Yelena's upper arm and began to squeeze the rubber bulb. The shiny line of mercury walked up the tube.

'What criticisms of the Soviet Union do you hold today?' she said. Very slowly, Yelena turned her dull eyes to her.

Kelchevskaya slipped her stethescope to her ears and began to release the air. As the sound of Yelena's heartbeat came through she frowned. She pushed the stethescope back about her neck, and pulled down one of Yelena's eyelids. The ball was deeply tinged with yellow.

Her hand was in her pocket and she had the syringe ready. For a few moments she hesitated. Then she shrugged to herself. The instructions for this one were most specific; they came from the highest level.

She administered the injection.

'Is there a god?' she asked. Yelena's mouth moved without speaking.

'Do you believe in your god?'

Some saliva appeared at the corner of Yelena's mouth, and dribbled down her chin.

'Good.' said Kelchevskaya. 'You are becoming well again.'

She went out, locking the door behind her.

Very slowly, Yelena began to move. She went to the small gap in the joint of the wooden bed, and clumsily, with difficulty took out the sheet of paper that rested, folded up in there. There was a small pencil stub.

She unwrapped the paper. The page was filled with Ruth's neat, joined up handwriting. Her lips moved as she read the final words.

> 'Let God arise, and let his enemies be scattered: let them also that hate Him, flee before Him.'

Very slowly, her hand moving jerkily, Yelena began to scrawl.

When Orderly Romachov opened the door her eyes were dull again. She held the paper in one hand on her lap and the pencil stub had fallen to the floor.

The Ukrainian girl quickly took the page and looked at the straggling letters. She picked up the pencil and began to write on the back of the paper.

When she had finished she put the paper away, and helped Yelena to sit back, folding up her coat for her as a cushion. She produced a small bottle of water, and held it up to her lips. When they were moistened, Yelena seemed to be trying to say something. She put her ear close to her, and stroked her hair.

'Yes,' she said. 'Toad.'

London

They sat around the table. Outside it was raining, the streets slick, the trees dark with reddening leaves.

'The Soviet government has agreed to allow a visit by Amnesty International,' said Ruth. 'It's clear that this is in response to the really high level of pressure we have been able to put on them by our publicity campaign.'

'I'm preparing a newsheet to send to all our members,' said Nikolai. 'And telling them not to relax their efforts.'

'They won't allow any cameras. You, Johnny, are specifically banned. I think they realise how effective your programme was – it was after it that this permission came through. We can have Eva and Nikolai in the Amnesty group, Eva for her medical knowledge, and Nikolai because Yelena knows him. They are claiming that Yelena has been held at the Municipal Hospital, the Golitsyn that was, in Moscow, just on Gorky Park, and not in the Leningrad SPH as we know. And they say that she is senile.'

Ruth unfolded a sheet of paper.

'This came through from Tatyana. It's the letter I first sent to Yelena. Here, by the sixty-eighth psalm, she has scrawled something. And here on the back Valeria Romachov, the Ukrainian orderly who has become Yelena's ally and friend has written some lines. She tells us what they have done to Yelena. After some weeks of what simply amounts to plain torture the use of mind-altering drugs began. Valeria Romachov describes two as being used, called Aminazin and Haloperidol.'

'Largactil and Haldol,' said Eva. 'Very powerful tranquillisers.'

'The effects of these drugs are very unpleasant. Valeria describes Yelena as saying that no sooner did she lie down than she wanted to get up; if she took a step she longed to sit down; if she sat down she wanted to walk. The maximum dosage has been administered to Yelena twice a day without relief for weeks. Valeria says that now she is almost completely withdrawn, and practically unable to speak. When she was being tortured she told Valeria that she went into herself, into a lovely mental world of gardens and streams, where children were playing. She writes that she hopes that she is able to do this now she is being filled with the chemicals. She says, very movingly, that Yelena has become like her own mother to her, that she tries to protect her, and cares for her. That she is good.'

There was a silence around the table.

'Bastards,' Nichols said shortly.

'There remains this scrawl of Yelena's. Valeria says Yelena tried to indicate that it was important. It's written by the sixty-eighth psalm: Let God arise, and let His enemies be scattered: let them also that hate Him, flee before Him. But what is she trying to say?'

She passed it around. When it got to Nichols he looked at it for a long time.

'Isn't the first word Where? No, Where's. Where is.'

Nikolai took it. 'Marthe!' he said. 'It says: Where's Marthe?'

'Marthe . . .' Ruth whispered. 'Of course!'

Moscow, October 1960

The morning was cold but sunny. They had put her wheelchair in a sheltered corner of the garden of the hospital. The building behind with its cupolas in the style of an old church effectively sealed off any noise from Leninskiy Prospekt but on the breeze came the music of the fairground and, in the sunshine, the big Ferris wheel glinted as it turned.

As they came down the path that led through the dormant flower beds they could see that she was carefully wrapped against the chill, a wool rug tucked in about her. A dark-haired woman with a high-necked green jersey showing under her white coat was standing with her. She smiled pleasantly at them as they came up.

'Good morning,' she said. 'I am Doctor Kelchevskaya, I have been looking after Yelena.'

Yelena did not move, except for the tremor of her head, and one hand that was visible.

There was just the two of them, Nikolai and Eva.

'Good morning. I am Nikolai Savinkov. This is my assistant, Eva. We are not medical people so perhaps you would tell us what Yelena's state of health is.'

'Of course. You are aware that early this year she was charged with various offences against the Soviet state. However, it was felt necessary to examine her medically, and at the Serbsky Institute here in Moscow, our premier psychiatric unit, she was found to be suffering from severe mental illness. She was a schizophrenic, but underlying cerebral atherosclerosis – a narrowing, a furring up of the arteries of the brain – was also found. It was judged that she was, in consequence, also suffering from incipient senility due to the consequent reduction in the oxygen supply to the brain.'

Kelchevskaya gestured towards the inert form in the wheelchair. 'I am afraid to say that this has turned out to be a most accurate diagnosis. When she came to me for treatment I was initially very hopeful that I could alleviate the symptoms of her schizophrenia – it is not itself a disease that is capable of cure – so that she could be released back into society. However, it quickly became clear to me that while I was achieving success in this area, the underlying senility of Yelena's brain was advancing at a great pace. I am afraid that now she is as you see her, no better than a vegetable.'

'Why does she shake like this?'

'That is Parkinson's Disease, which I expect you are familiar with. It is common in old people.'

'Is she, in your opinion, still suffering from schizophrenia?'

Kelchevskaya smiled tolerantly. 'Can a potato suffer from mental illness? There is little higher function left in her brain. So, no, she cannot be suffering from schizophrenia.'

'Even if she recovered from her senility.'

Kelchevskaya could not help herself from laughing derisively. 'You do not recover from senility, Mr Savinkov. The condition is irreversible.'

'It would require a miracle for her to talk again?'

'Miracles do not exist.'

'She can be no threat to the Soviet state, then.'

'None.'

'She could leave?'

'She cannot look after herself. So the Soviet state will do it for her. The state bears no grudge. It will care for her until she dies.'

'Nice place you have here,' said Ruth. The car had gone through the 'No Entry' sign, past the uniformed policemen and into the cul-de-sac in the pine woods. The finely-wrought gates had shut behind her and the car had motored along the gravel driveway that led up to the house. Now she stood inside, in the marbled hallway, and a fountain played.

'Thank you,' said Krivitskiy.

Ruth gestured about her as they went inside. Fine paintings hung on the walls and the carpet was soft under their feet. Split pine logs popped softly on the fire.

'Yes,' she said. 'You've done well for yourself.'

She looked sideways at him, and smiled maliciously. 'Tell me, Leon, what will you do if the Commies come back?'

Krivitskiy sat down on a sofa, ignoring what she had said. 'Shall we get on with it? It is best if you understand how it is, and then you can give up your pathetic attempts at publicity in the West.'

'Not so pathetic. They got you to permit an official visit from Amnesty.'

'All they will find is a cabbage,' Krivitskiy said brutally.

Ruth looked at him with a sudden hatred. 'Have you destroyed her mind?'

'No,' he said frankly. 'She would recover, if released. But she will not be. She will remain incarcerated until she dies.'

'Why do you hate her so, that you are being so cruel?'

'Emotion has nothing to do with it,' he said flatly. 'Yelena directly took on the state. Because of Akulov, and because she is who she is, her actions had widespread ramifications. We felt that it was essential that she be checked vigorously, and that perhaps, even more importantly, she be seen to be so checked. People are watching. You have organised an exceptionally powerful and well-run lobby in the West, campaigning for her release. Here in the Soviet Union the so-called "Human Rights" campaigners are spreading. They have links with nationalist dissenters in places like the Ukraine. We have opted for the most rigorous treatment to demonstrate the strength of our will to rule. You and your Amnesty will go home and they will say to you: "How is Yelena?" And you will say: "She does not exist. All there is is a dribbling, shaking cabbage." And campaigners in the West will become exhausted by beating on a door that will not open, and the dissenters here will be filled with fear and despair.'

They had asked to be left alone with Yelena for a while and, with an amused expression of contempt, Kelchevskaya had left them to sit on a bench in the sun a little way off. Nikolai slipped the rug from Yelena's arm and they could see the marks of the multiple injections.

Eva took the pre-loaded syringe from her bag and, looking as though she were tucking the rug about her, slid the needle into Yelena's arm. Gently, she pushed the plunger home.

They sat, one each side of her. Over at the park the music was playing. Steam was drifting from *Pl'zenskiy's* chimney, cooking the hot sausages. People were there, eating them with cold Pilsen beer.

The shaking of Yelena's head slowed and then ceased. A furled yellow rose was on a bush in front of her, caught by the cold of the coming winter before it could open, and her eyes focused upon it.

'We're more experienced than most, us on the Committee, when it comes to understanding things here,' said Ruth. 'Of course, we've lived through it all, which foreign observers haven't. We think you'll be aiming to take over, when Brezhnev's gone. Of course, he could last another ten years or more, but we think you have your plans laid. You haven't been boss of the KGB so long for nothing; you must know where all the bodies are buried. That's what we think.'

'Gnats in the woods may believe they know where a bear is headed as he passes. It is irrelevant to the bear what they think.'

'Wrong,' Ruth said quietly, triumphantly. 'We can stop you.'

Krivitskiy raised his eyebrows in disbelief. 'Really?'

'Yes. We have a television programme, called *This is Your Life*. It's very popular. The man who presents it ambushes a different person every week, and takes him or her to a studio where people who have known them during their life come on and talk about them. It's very popular.'

A wary expression had come over Krivitskiy's face.

'We've made our own version. Our story of *your* life. We have a number of people who know you, you see. I come on at the beginning, because I was at school with you, I was an Old Bolshevik, the same as you and we shared the same ideals. We were in at the beginning, but it passed away from me. Not you. You stayed in, you lasted the course. What did Conrad say about that? "Hopes grotesquely betrayed, ideals caricatured – that is the definition of revolutionary success." That must have happened to you. In a real revolution the best characters do not come to the front. Conrad knew. "Narrow-minded fanatics and tyrannical hypocrites. Then the turn of all the pretentious intellectual failures of the time." We knew them all, didn't we? I was married to one, you lived among them.

'You've done a lot of really vile things on your way to the monster you are today, Leon. But you could stand up, I suppose, and tell people you did it all for the good of the party, for the revolution, for freedom and happiness – you know, all that guff we used to spout, and people believed us. But there are some things that just disqualify you from membership of the human race. And if people get to know about them they're the kind of thing that make those people cross the road when they see you coming, make them leave the room as you come in.

'Nikolai is coming on. He's going to tell how he tried to kill you when they were getting rid of Stalin and Beria, and how Ivan Ivanovich stopped him, in order to keep his word to you. We have Yelena on film by his coffin, describing how you had Ivan Ivanovich murdered, of course. And we have a special guest star.'

Ruth patted her handbag.

'Have you got your own cinema here? I'm sure you have. All the bosses like to relax watching Western films. Stalin used to sign the death warrants and then go through and watch the latest from Hollywood, didn't he? I've got a clip from our film. Our special guest. Do you want to see her?'

'Who is it?'

'It's the woman who worked with you in Berlin, your closest aide. It's the woman who helped you escape when Hitler came to power. It's the woman you secretly married, here in Moscow. It's the woman you put on the train with her daughter Elisabeth, to be taken to the German concentration camps. It's the woman who loved you. It's *Marthe*, Leon. She survived Ravensbruck and we found her.'

Ruth took a small cinematic reel from her bag. 'You must be longing to see her again,' she said cruelly. 'Shall we put on the film?'

Krivitskiy stared at her stone-faced. 'So I put her on the train. I was following orders.'

'It didn't get them off at Nuremberg. But I agree, while *we* know what scum you are, it won't bother those who matter to you, your fellow-criminals on the Politburo. Most of them let Stalin send their wives to the camps without a murmur and you're just another member of the same slime club. No, what we've got on our film is something that *will* ruin you.

'Cast your mind back. It won't be difficult because you're already there. *I* was there too. Prinz Albrecht Strasse, May 1933. I came to get Marthe from the Gestapo. She had been flogged half to death by SA men and as I helped her down the corridor, a workman opened a door. For a moment I could see in. I saw you, talking to Manfred Liss. You had drinks in your hands and you were laughing.

'What Marthe says is that when the train arrived in Germany she and Elisabeth were taken off it and separated from the others. The man who took them off was Manfred Liss. But then, shortly afterwards, they were taken away, and sent to Ravensbruck after all. Liss had been in touch, hadn't he? *And you said to put them into the camp*. The only thing that went wrong was that they survived. When the camp was liberated they escaped to the West. Marthe says, and she knows, as one who was once an intelligence professional, that you and Manfred worked together. You gave him what he wanted, he gave to you and you both survived. Until after the war. When you shot him to keep him quiet.'

She smiled venomously. 'Is that enough for them to hang you, Leon? The man who is head of the KGB was a Nazi agent?'

'They were no different from us,' Krivitskiy said slowly. 'The Nazis and us, we thought the same. It is the West with its talk of rights that cannot be stomached . . . Rights for whom? Them, the rabble out there? Never!'

'We have two films,' she said clearly, icily. 'The first is the story of your life. We would plan a new ending in a month or two's time, when they shoot you. The second is the story of the campaign to free Yelena. One or other of them will be shown on television tonight. But we don't have an ending for the film on Yelena. We can only show it if we have live coverage of her coming down the airline steps at London Heathrow this evening.'

Nikolai cut the small, chilled yellow rose, he gave it to Yelena, and she sat looking at it. Someone came running from the hospital, a man, calling Kelchevskaya's name. They stood talking. Kelchevskaya became agitated.

'She's done it!' said Nikolai. 'Mama's done it!'

The psychiatrist came down the path and stopped some distance away, as though she could not bear to be close to them.

'You can take her,' she said thickly. 'You are to have her!'

Yelena looked up into her eyes. 'See,' she said. 'God *is* real . . .'

37

Perestroika

Kuntsevo Hospital, Moscow, September 1983

FROM the window of the room she could see out over the quiet pine forest where the dachas of those allowed into the hospital lay. It was quiet in the room too, with just a faint humming from the American machines with their silicon microchips, watching over the life of the man lying in the bed.

'I'm dying,' the General Secretary said. She allowed the door to shut quietly, automatically, behind her on its Japanese springs.

There was another man in the room. He stood up, short, stocky and balding, with a vivid birthmark on his head, where his hair had been.

'This is Tatyana Galina Serebryakova,' said Andropov. Tubes and wires connected him to the machines. His blood flowed out of him into a box at the side of the bed, and back again.

'This is Mikhail Sergeyevich Gorbachev.' Andropov said, and the two nodded politely at each other. She sat at the other side of the bed. Andropov's skin had a texture and colour like old church candlewax.

'I had intended Mikhail Sergeyevich to succeed me as leader of the Soviet Union,' said Andropov. 'However, the doctors say I shall shortly be dead. Chernenko will succeed me, but as he is but a dead man on furlough himself, Mikhail Sergeyevich Gorbachev will, within one or two years at most, be in charge.'

Andropov paused to catch his breath. Gorbachev stood up and held a glass of water to his lips. When he had sipped, he continued.

'Mikhail is the best of the younger generation. He will be a strong, energetic and innovative leader. He is fully aware of the enormous economic and technological problems that the Soviet Union faces. I fully expect him to solve them, and to lead the Soviet Union into the new millenium in a manner worthy of a great and prosperous power. The advisers he has – innovative men and women themselves

– also believe that this can be done. I did not think it right to pass on
the great burden of leadership to him, however, without making him
quite aware that there exists an entirely different viewpoint as to our
future, held by professionals in the Soviet Union. You are, as head
of the Economic Institute of Novosibirsk, the head of this faction,
and so I have asked you here today to give your views.'

'Thank you, Comrade General Secretary.'

Tatyana had a briefcase with her, she reached down and look out
a document.

'This is the Communist Party Programme. It was adopted by the
1961 Party Congress. It is a very important document of faith –
you could call it the Party Bible. It asserts that by the end of the
seventies, the Soviet state and economy would be so advanced that
the population would be assured of an abundance of everything.
Before 1980, it specifies, there will be so much food that everyone
will be fed free of charge. Housing, gas, water, electricity, heating
and transportation will all be free of charge. All citizens will have
two months free and luxury holiday a year, and will spend glorious
and long years of retirement tended for by free medical and social
services.'

Tatyana closed the document, held it up so that they could see it,
and put it back into her briefcase.

'It's difficult to get hold of these days. I had to go into our library
for it. It's not hard to see why. What are the realities of life in the
Soviet Union in 1983? The Communist Party has claimed from the
beginning to represent unique historical forces, and it has a unique
achievement to its credit. The Soviet Union is the only industrialised
nation where death rates are rising. The average Soviet male can
expect to live for only sixty years, six less than twenty years ago.
Equally unique is the rise in infant mortality – three times the rate
of the USA and increasing. If this continues, the Communist Party
will preside over the extinction of the Russian people.

'The Soviet Union, or if you prefer, as I do, the expression Russian
Empire, faces "contradictions" that are worse than grave. In Marxist
terminology the word "contradictions" is very specific, and refers to
the tensions which it is claimed inherently exist within the capitalist
system of production and which will, inevitably, cause its demise.
It may be worth commenting that in 1913 Tsarist Russia had a real
product per man hour that was three and a half times greater than that
of Japan. Capitalist Japan now out-performs us by a factor of four to
one. In my opinion the contradictions exist within communism, and
will within a decade cause *its* demise.'

An expression of shock, followed by anger, appeared on Gorbachev's face.

'Communism remains the most efficient system of both government and production,' he asserted flatly. 'The socialist system has immense untapped potential for improvement. What is required is *perestroika*, a reconstruction under strong and imaginative leadership.'

'The best and strongest driver in the world cannot win the Indianapolis 500 if he is driving a Model T Ford, to use an American example. He does not require a rebuilt Model T, but a proper racing car. The *only* area of communist industry and technology that can attempt to rival that of the West is the military. The high-technology revolution in the West is in the process of making our military obsolete *whatever* the investment, as the surrogate actions in the Middle East increasingly show.

'You will doubtlessly place heavy emphasis upon the need for each and every one in the Soviet Union to improve their performance, to work hard and give complete dedication. You will crack down on corruption and alcoholism. We have all been here before, of course. Lenin did the same things, calling them War Communism. The workers will not respond. Sixty-five years of communism has produced a total erosion of the work ethic and a desire to blot out the realities of the life it has produced by the totally excessive consumption of vodka, or, if that is banned, toilet water or the industrial alcohol in the systems of MiG 21 fighter aircraft.

'Your language, Comrade Gorbachev, will be dramatic, vigorous and satisfying. But you will not change the system, both because you still believe in it, and because it will not let you. The upper class of the Soviet Union is happy with the way things are. Scientific socialism has brought them, if nobody else, *enormous* benefits. Yet the noises you will make will seem to them to be a sufficient threat that you will face the possibility of removal by armed *coup*. Before the end of the decade the economic crunch will be so severe that there will be no question of competing with the West. Soviet strength will be insufficient to hold on to the Eastern empire, and withdrawal will take place. On my predictions, the beginning of the nineties will see famine requiring Western aid. By then, of course, the Soviet Union, and its revolution will have ceased to exist.

'I saw on television film of a Western jet airliner. Some accident had taken place aboard, and the controls did not work, with the exception of the throttles to the engines. The crew was using these in an attempt to guide the aircraft to a crash landing. They succeeded.

Although the aircraft was destroyed, most of the passengers survived. That is *your* task, Comrade Gorbachev. To attempt to manage things so that the people of the Soviet Union survive its fall, and can build their lives anew.'

He looked very determined, the short man with the livid birthmark on his head. Andropov lay propped up on his pillows, his eyes closed, his breath fluttering.

'He's recommended I take you on as one of my advisers,' said Gorbachev. 'Would you like the job?'

'Yes, please.'

'That's settled. We'll have you moved to Moscow. Are you married?'

'No.'

'Oh?'

She shrugged. 'I have seen too closely what happens to children in this world. I didn't want it to happen to mine . . .'

38

Revoliutsiia

Moscow, July 1991

YELENA put the old key into the lock and it turned. Behind them the two Englishmen in their jeans and training shoes began opening up the big yellow van, and the old ladies went inside.

'The children are still here,' Ruth said, looking up at the dusty fresco about the hall. 'The princess would be pleased.'

Yelena went past the stair and through the house, moving slowly with the aid of a stout rubber-tipped walking stick. The door was open and she stood on the step, looking at the little garden. An old rose climbed against the wall.

'She used to sit out here when it was warm, and dream about the old days, when it was all hers. And they still have the little plots we made – look! I shall be busy with the seed packets I've brought, I can see. And I do think that's the rose I put in, so many years ago.'

'It's a tough old vine, like us,' Ruth said.

The driver called from the hall, peering incredulously inside the ancient lift, wanting to know if it worked.

'Of course it works, young man,' Ruth said. 'Lukomskii and Shliapnikov made that in St Petersburg in nineteen ten. My father had one just like it. It's not Soviet *brak*, you know.'

The young man grinned, and began lifting in smartly-marked, polystyrene-wrapped boxes.

'Sorry,' he said. 'It just seems funny lifting high-technology satellite dishes and things in a lift about a hundred years old.'

'We both have relatives in the West,' Ruth said, as they, too, got in. 'We have no intention of relying upon the Moscow telephone exchange when we feel like a chat!'

She closed the lattice gate and pressed the brass button with a practised hand, and the lift hummed upwards under its old electric motor. When they got out Yelena found another old key and opened the dirty red door.

'My dear, this can't have been decorated since you left!' Ruth said. 'I'm glad I packed all that good Dulux paint. I shall have it looking like new in a few weeks.'

Yelena went through to the little kitchen and opened the window. From the building next door came the gentle notes of a piano.

'There's a box marked Kitchen,' she said to the driver. 'If you bring it up there's a kettle in it and we can have tea.'

He unloaded his boxes and went back downstairs. Yelena stood by the window for a moment, listening.

'Such comfort,' she said quietly, 'when things were very bad.'

The furniture began to come up, and the strong brown cardboard boxes. The box marked Kitchen arrived, and Yelena put a red kettle on the gas, and laid out mugs in a row. She made tea from bags, and gave some to the two boys. They had a table set up in the kitchen by this time, and wooden chairs, and she put a mug down for Ruth.

'I have got that right, haven't I?' she murmured. 'I gave you my herb tea once and you were horrified.'

'It was the *taste*, darling. Like drinking stewed hay.'

'It's very good for you. When I was working in the green-house in Magadan I had a tin pot and I used to boil up a con-coction of all the good ones I grew. People used to come by for a spoonful when they could and I'm sure it helped to keep us alive.'

'I'm sure, too. But tea, that was the thing . . . when you thought you couldn't chop another tree, haul another log, if there was tea, you could. Dreadful stuff it was, so strong it attacked the mug. Nothing like dear Fortnum and Mason, I assure you.'

Then the two men were done, and the small rooms were filled with chairs and beds, boxes and bookshelves, tables and cupboards. They went on their way, and the two old ladies heard the grumble of the big diesel engine going off along the Moscow street.

'We must make a start,' said Yelena. 'Have you got your knife, darling?'

She stood by a box and Ruth fished in her handbag. Her hand emerged holding a small flat leather case, and she took out a wickedly-hooked blade with a hole for her finger, and expertly slit the wide sticky tape that sealed the box.

'Dear Mappin and Webb,' she said. 'It still cuts like it did when they made it all those years ago.'

Yelena looked fondly at her old friend. 'So you always tell me, darling.'

Ruth turned to one of the boxes of electronics as Yelena began to unpack her box. With a wrapped picture in her hand she looked up to see what Ruth was doing.

'Those are for Tatyana,' she said. 'They aren't ours.'

'I know. But there are some things of mine in there.'

She felt inside the packaging and pulled something out in triumph. It was a small, rather ugly pistol, made largely out of stamped metal.

'You haven't brought that?' Yelena exclaimed.

'I certainly have. A jolly good device, at close range. You can't afford to miss, of course. You have to reload after each shot, and that takes about a minute. Did I ever tell you how I got Gestapo Colonel Frisch with one?'

'Many times.' Yelena looked sternly at Ruth. 'You haven't brought anything else?'

'Certainly!' she said unrepentantly. 'I knew if Tatyana had this stuff cleared we'd get it through with no trouble. Let's face it, if we're to spend our declining years here we may as well have *some* protection. Remember that nasty young man who broke into our flat in Bayswater? Snivelling, he was, when he saw the Sten.'

'You've brought the *Sten*?'

'Well, I couldn't very well leave it behind,' Ruth said, reasonably. She pulled the old sub-machine gun out from the wrapping and the sun coming through the window gleamed dully on the metal. 'Not under the circumstances. If some nasty Russian youth breaks in, I'll be the one who has to poke the gun up his nose. You'd be off dreaming somewhere and wouldn't notice he was there until it was too late.'

Yelena smiled. She had the box open, and began pulling things out, moving slowly because of her stiff legs.

'I know, darling. Well, if you've been a little sneaky and smuggled in your guns, I suppose I had better confess, too.'

A desk was in front of the window, where the boys had placed it, and she carried over a package and unwrapped it. An old black Remington typewriter appeared, its enamel shiny, a red and black ribbon snaking across its face. Yelena tightened it, the spool whirring.

'I knew there was more to coming out here than being buried with your ancestors,' Ruth said. 'What does this mean?'

'I've been thinking about it all for a while. About the past. Our past, what happened to us . . . I want to tell the story. Now they're gone . . . Our story, the one about you and me, about Ivan and Savinkov, about Rykov and Krivitskiy, about all of them, Pyotr Pavlovich and Verochka . . . our story, because we were there.

It matters and someone has to tell it. The people out there, they were never told, and if you don't know what happened then it can happen again.'

'And you had to come here to do it?' Ruth said gently.

'Yes,' Yelena said simply. 'Here the ghosts live; here they will gather round, and talk to me.'

Ruth rummaged in a box marked Cellar and came out with a dark green bottle. She carried it carefully over to the white Electrolux refrigerator humming faintly in the kitchen and put it inside.

'There', she said. 'When you've written the first chapter we'll open some Cliquot and you shall read it to me. I think it's a *wonderful* idea.'

'*Klikofskoe*, that was what Mikhail called it. We drank a whole bottle sitting in the bath together . . . so naughty.'

'What will you call it?' Ruth asked keenly.

'*REVOLUTION*. That's what they called it, wasn't it? The horrible thing they made. *Revoliutsiia*.'

'Where will you start?'

Yelena got up and went over to the wall. She had hung up an old, framed photograph on a hook. Fresh young faces smiled out from the yellowed print. A school photograph.

'Here,' she said. 'At the Lycée. That was where it all started.'

Ruth stood looking at the old class, and Yelena took a blue box of Croxley Script paper and put it by the elderly typewriter. Then she came to stand next to her.

'There's Krivitskiy,' she said. 'Darling, if I'm writing my book, don't you think you'd better tell me what happened to him?'

'Mm? You know what happened to him, darling. His friends on the Politburo had him in one day. He came in a Zil, and he went out in his shoes. They gave him a little two room apartment somewhere. That's where he shot himself, wasn't it?'

'I *know* that,' Yelena said patiently. 'But why did they break him?'

'Because he had been a spy, darling. He collaborated with the Nazis.'

'But how did they know that?'

Ruth beamed. 'Well, because I told them, darling. Once we had you out. I mean, you don't have to keep your word to people like him, do you?'

From outside they heard the soft hum of the lift.

'I wonder if that's Tatyana?'

There was a knock, and she came in smiling, her eyes bright behind her horn-rimmed glasses, a man in white technician's overalls and with a small toolbox in his hand behind her.

'So you're in! Wonderful. Is this it?'

Ruth pointed to the polystyrene-packed boxes, set aside in a pile. At a command from the economist the technician began to carefully unpack them. He went out with a grey microwave horn in one hand and a small satellite dish in the other and they heard him climbing the stairs to the roof.

Yelena had the kettle on for tea.

'May we ask why Mr Gorbachev wants a satellite phone?' she said, rinsing mugs. Tatyana was loking in her bag. She came out with a packet of Marlboro cigarettes.

'Do you mind?' she asked, 'No?'

She lit one with short, slightly nervous movements and blew smoke towards the half-open door. 'Mikhail Sergeyevich doesn't. Boris does.'

'Who?'

'Yeltsin.'

'I thought you worked for Gorbachev,' Ruth said.

'I did, but I'm with Boris now. Gorbachev can't go ahead with the reforms – he hasn't got it in him. He's a Party man and he's out of touch, as out of touch as Tsar Nicholas in the year seventeen . . .'

'That's not the picture we've been getting, back in Britain,' Ruth said, interestedly.

'No, they think Gorby's the great white hope, isn't that the expression? Because the Cold War's ending and the West won. And they're sending all this aid to bolster the economy because they think it'll be spent on hamburgers instead of missiles. I wish they'd keep it locked up in their banks at home.'

'But why?'

'Where do they think it's going?' Tatyana cried in exasperation. 'After all this time, and they still don't know how it works here . . . Who gets it? *The Party and the KGB*. Who keeps it?'

'The Party and the KGB,' Ruth said wearily.

It's just like all the money they raised for the poor starving people in Africa,' said Yelena. 'They gathered it all up and just gave it to the dictators and gangsters who were responsible for the famine to begin with. And the people went on starving.'

'That's the way it's always been. Here the Party exists to keep itself in existence, and the KGB supports it. They are symbiotic; they need each other . . . We can't change Russia until we get rid of both, and we can't get rid of them while the West is giving them billions.'

'Russia?' Yelena said shrewdly. 'What of the Soviet Union?'

Tatyana tapped ash into a saucer. From the roof came the grinding whirr of a drill.

'That's all gone,' she said quietly. 'There'll be a host of independent nations, any day now. And good luck to them. For Russia, it'll be a question of whether they can hang on to the Far Eastern republics . . . I doubt it, myself, I think they'll be better served going it alone. It's what's going to happen here that concerns me, that's why I'm with Boris. How to get rid of the Party and KGB *apparat*. It's not easy because they want to survive, they want to keep power.'

She stubbed out her cigarette and lit another. 'Broadly, they're split into two. The old guard, hardliners who'll settle for being a century behind the West in every way provided they can retain their power and privilege. Then the younger men. They see reform bringing them benefits. Make the old state industries into cooperatives. Adapt to the world market. Oil, minerals, timber. And who to run these new industries? Well, the only people who speak foreign languages, the only people with experience of working abroad, the only people who know how the markets work.'

'The Party and KGB,' said Ruth.

'That's it! Then, when the cooperatives are ready, privatise them, intact with capital. Privatise. A fine word that the West will approve of. Or, in Russian terms, a private monopoly without competition run by former Party and KGB *apparatchiks*.'

'You're leaning towards the latter.'

'I don't want to go with either, but that is the way I see it heading. Any anything is better than the old system. But it's not how you see it on your Western television screens . . . We need democracy, but when you've never tasted it, it has a funny flavour. There are too many Russians out there who'd accept a dictator again, provided he got bread in the shops and kept the liquor stores open.'

'Who got the money? The aid?'

'*We simply don't know where it's gone*. My guess is the old guard has most. Steklov's their man at the treasury.'

She saw Yelena look up, and nodded.

'Yes, *that* Steklov. Rykov's man. He went to the Party from the KGB and he's a more sophisticated gangster than Rykov ever was . . . I suspect him, but we can't get at him, he's too well protected.'

She stayed while the technician installed the telephone, smoking nervously and drinking tea, and, when it was working, she left. The two old ladies resumed their slow unpacking.

'Some of your ghosts aren't dead yet, darling,' Ruth observed. She put the small, pressed-metal 'Woolworths' pistol in a drawer of the desk. 'Your story may not have a neat ending.'

'Real stories never do. They always go on after everyone in the bit you write about is long dead.'

Ruth fished in her handbag and brought out another ancient piece of clandestine warfare equipment, a knife with several, strange blades. She inserted one under a section of gloss paintwork, cracked and raised like a mud flat, and lifted it up.

'Look at this frightful brown paint smeared everywhere. We must get some industrious young men in to remove it all. Then we can make it look nice. What do you think, darling? Look at this card. Ivory with a hint of pink? Yes?'

Yelena smiled. 'Ivory with a hint of pink,' she said . . .

August 21

Rapid-fire banging, of car doors, a hoarse shout of command. Men's feet running.

She heard them, and began to run herself, all about the apartment, down the long corridors, looking inside the rooms, gathering up the children.

Downstairs she heard the front door close. They were inside the building.

They were playing, she found Natalia and Nikolai and she scooped up her daughter and clutched Nikolai by the hand. The corridor was very long and their feet echoed on the bare floorboards. Ruth was somewhere in the apartment – she could hear her running, too – her voice shouting for the children, for up the stairs was coming evil.

She had Boris now as well. But where was Alexei? There, she could hear him coming, he was calling to her, to let her know.

Pounding boots on the landing, a heavy fist on the door. 'They must not go that way.' The children clustered about her, dozens of them. Her arms were not big enough, but there was the door, the one at the back that was secret, and safe, and she opened it.

Natasha stood there, grinning in her fitted blue NKVD skirt, a pair of bloody pliers in her hand. She snatched at Natalia and slammed the door in her face.

The sweat was streaming from her face, the breath heaved in her chest.

'*Yelena!*'

It was Ruth! Ruth must be at the other way out. The children swirled about her, a hundred of them, and she must not lose one.

There it was, the door. The way out to safety for them. She opened it wide and Steklov was there, smiling in his judge's robes as he spread out his arms for the running children. Sharp steel glittered in his hands. She ran forward, sweeping them back inside, and felt the gnashing of steel in her back.

They ran down the corridor, thousands of them. The floor was slippery with blood; it climbed uphill and they slipped, the little ones, she had to pick them up and carry them.

'*Yelena, are you there?*'

It was Tatyana! Her voice was coming from behind the door, so it was safe.

She had all the children in her arms and she pulled open the wide doors and went through.

They were in a yard with high walls. The blood that was flowing down the corridor came from the yard. Rykov was standing up on a platform. He had a pistol in his hand and he shot at the children as they floundered in the gore. He never missed.

She ran towards him, to stop him, but the more she ran, the farther away he became, and all about her the children screamed and died.

She opened her eyes. The bedside lamp was on and Ruth's bed was empty. In the room next door she could hear voices, and the sound of men's boots.

The door opened and Ruth came in, wrapped up in her wool dressing gown, carpet slippers on her feet.

'Tatyana's here, darling.'

The sweat was drenching her. It ran down her face and Ruth produced a handkerchief, wiping it away.

'You were having one of your dreams, a bad one. I couldn't wake you and I had to go and let them in.'

'Rykov was there. He was killing the children again.'

Ruth was fetching a fresh nightdress for her. The arthritis in her knees was very bad and flickering battlements began to march across her eyes.

'I'll go and get your special tea, darling. It will help.'

Ruth knew. She put on the clean nightdress, and lay back on the pillows. Ruth came in, accompanied by Tatyana. Fragrant herb tea steamed from the mug. Outside it was dark and she could hear someone talking on the telephone. In the room a burly figure was directing subordinates. He had a uniform, he was KGB.

'What is happening?' she asked. The tea was very good.

'I'm sorry we've broken in like this,' Tatyana said quietly. 'We had to use the phone. To talk to the West. That's why we put it in.'

'We?'

'Boris, Yeltsin. He's talking to Bush, to Thatcher, to NATO.'

'What are the *Chekisty* doing here?'

'They're General Kalmykov's men. He's one of us. He was sent to arrest Boris, but instead he got him out of his flat.'

'Sent by whom?'

'There's been a *coup*.' Ruth said softly. 'The Stalinists are back.'

It was quiet, the little apartment empty. Yeltsin had gone, hustled away by his team of KGB minders. The two old girls sat by the window in the morning light. Yelena's arthritis was painful; it and the terrible dreams came and went together; she sat in a comfortable wing chair where she could see out, and rest her swollen joints.

Something was in the air, the faint sound of mice, away in the distance. Ruth listened, her mug of tea half way to her mouth.

'Tanks,' she said.

Within a few minutes one was coming down the street. It parked itself on the corner, dominating the junction. Black smoke belched from its funnel and drifted away on the breeze as the driver cut the engine.

'Silly boy,' Ruth murmured absently. 'I could drop a jug full of burning petrol down his hatch from the roof up there.'

'How would you do that, darling?' Yelena murmured.

'Nasty things, tanks. Not nice for the people outside them, and horrid inside. Cramped, noisy and smelly. Dangerous, too. The crews like to get out of them. I'd wait until the commander wanted to come out – for some fresh air, or just to spend a penny. I'd torch him and the tank, and when the crew came out to get away from the flames, machine-gun them.'

'So efficient, my dear. But *before* you brush up on The Sten Gun – How to Massacre a Tank Crew, let's try making friends with them.'

Ruth looked at her thoughtfully. 'Hmm. Good idea.'

'Well, I wasn't married to a tank general for nothing. Ivan Ivanovich used to talk about the friction inherent in war. *One* of the problems a commander faces in keeping his troops moving forward is their inbuilt tendency to try to dig in, to make a home for themselves. A hole will do. Even a *bad* hole is better than going forward and being shot at and bombed upon. Once let them get settled, they begin to fraternise with the civilian population about them – bartering for milk and eggs, giving tinned meat for a live chicken, a bar of chocolate for fresh vegetables to make soup. Maybe helping with some medical supplies. Trying to make friends with the pretty girls. Playing with the children. Once this has happened, Ivan used to tell me, for all military purposes against those civilians, the troops are useless.'

Looking down from the window, they saw the turret hatch cover come up, and a young man clamber out. The driver pushed up his own cover. They looked around them, uneasily.

'See,' said Ruth. 'They don't like being inside.'

'They'll only be young. They probably don't know why they're on the streets of Moscow. Prague, Buda-Pest, yes. They'll have been told it's the West making trouble, but Moscow?'

Yelena looked down upon the tank, thoughtfully. 'Fill up the samovar, darling, and put it on the heat. I'll get some of those nice chocolate Olivers from Fortnums and put them on a plate. They'll probably be hungry. Then you go down and ask that nice young man sitting on the turret if he'd like to come up and get some tea for all of them.'

'They'll want to use the bathroom; they'll be embarrassed having to go in the street.'

'Good idea. I'll put out some hand towels and a new cake of the Crabtree and Evelyn soap. Young men like to smell nice.'

In a short while Yelena heard the whirring of the old lift and a young Lieutenant came shuffling through the door with Ruth, smiling and blushing.

'So cruel, darling,' Ruth exclaimed. 'These poor boys have been rousted out without any breakfast or anything.'

'Don't even know why we're here,' the young soldier mumbled.

'This is Lieutenant Petrichenko, darling.'

'Such a handsome young man!' Yelena said. 'But we can't call you Lieutenant all the time. What do your friends call you?'

'Dmitri Pavlovich,' he said, blushing anew.

'Dmitri Pavlovich, the samovar is hot. There is milk and sugar. Ruth, have you shown him where the bathroom is? And these boys will be hungry. We must make up some sandwiches. Cheese, yes? And chutney? So wicked, turfing them out without any explanation.'

'Officers we did not know came to give the orders,' he said.

'Best to be careful, if you don't know them,' Ruth said darkly. 'I shouldn't think they have your interests at heart.'

'It is true,' admitted the young man.

A few minutes later he was on his way back down in the lift, bearing a tray of mugs and a plate well filled with biscuits.

The two old saboteurs beamed conspiratorially at each other, then Ruth went to the refrigerator and, taking out fresh butter and yellow cheddar, began to make a pile of thick sandwiches.

'It's best to get it out,' Tatyana said. 'We used it, but now we've got our own. Boris is holed up in the White House, and talking to everyone from there.'

The technician in his white overall worked expertly, undoing the screws and connections he had put in only weeks before, putting the parts into an ordinary brown fibre suitcase.

'Just in case some nosy KGB man comes poking round. There are still plenty left who think possession of something made in the West is proof of counter-revolutionary activities.'

'This lot is,' said Ruth, and smiled.

'How are you taking it away?' Yelena asked.

'We'll just walk off, through the crowds, just like them.'

'Are the people on the streets?' Yelena said eagerly.

'Yes. Many. Demonstrating against the *coup*.'

'I wish I could be there . . .' Yelena said wistfully. She was seated by the window, in a comfortable chair, her knees and ankles puffed with arthritis. 'When many are gathered together, then God is there . . .'

The man finished packing the parts of the satellite telephone into the case. He took off his overall and folded it on top, before shutting the lid.

'I'll be off,' he said. They heard the lift whirr.

'Who does he work for?' Ruth asked.

'For us,' Tatyana said cryptically.

'If he knows about satellite phones he must be KGB,' Ruth said shrewdly.

'He is. He's Kalmykov's man. The *Chekist* you saw here. And he's *our* man. He's just persuaded the commander of the KGB Alpha Force to sit on the fence over this.'

'What's that?'

'Alpha Force? The KGB assault group. With the Army neutralised they wanted Alpha Force to go in to take out Boris, once they found him. They don't know he's in the White House yet.'

Tatyana reached in her bag and lit another cigarette. 'I must get back. Are you all right? Have you got enough food and drink? Just sit tight for a day or two, and it will all be over.'

'They're going to lose?' Yelena asked.

'Of course!' They're old guard. They didn't realise how power has shifted away from the palace. We'll have them out in a few days. Then we can get rid of Gorby. He's old guard, too. We'll have Boris in charge.'

She drew on the cigarette, and smiled through the smoke. 'Then the real fighting will begin. Who'll control Boris?'

'You?' suggested Ruth.

'With luck. The *parachutisti* and military-industrial KGB otherwise.'

'Ruth. Go with Tatyana a little way,' Yelena urged. 'See what the people are doing then you can come back and tell me.'

Tatyana bent and kissed her. 'I'll see you in a day or two. Once it's over.'

They went down in the lift and out on to the sunny street. People stood on the corners talking in groups. Young men and women clambered about the tanks, sitting on the turrets and gun barrels, and the equally-young crews fraternised with them. A group of *Afghansy* veterans harangued a KGB trooper, slowly pushing him against the wall. A few old men and women were sprinkled in the crowds like grains of salt, watching with a certain grim satisfaction.

'What do you see?' Ruth asked.

'People,' Tatyana said in surprise.

'No. I see the young, who were there in Hungary. I can see the veterans from the war. I can see a few tough old cranks like me, and I see the intellectuals and the politically-motivated. We'd all have been on our way to the camps, fifty years ago. I don't see the people. Not the ordinary, middle-aged. They're all at home, and afraid. They got broken years ago.'

They came to a park with summer flowers in bloom. A bench was there and Ruth sat down on it.

'I'll sit here for a while,' she said. 'I'll watch from here. The pilot dropped me twenty miles from my reception committee when I went to fight with the *Maquis* and I had to force march at night over the mountains to get to them. Loaded up like a mule, I was. But that was a long time ago. A gentle stroll down the street is more my cup of tea now.'

Tatyana bent and kissed her as she had Yelena.

'Take care,' she said.

Ruth watched her go, watched the crowds on the streets. She dozed in the dappled sunshine. When she woke some young men and women were draping a huge flag on a nearby tank, using its gun barrel as a flagpole. She blinked in the sun, before recognising something that had been gone from Russia for most of the century. It was the Imperial emblem . . .

Yelena will be pleased, she thought, and got up, walking back past the important tanks to the house.

She opened the door. The children of a long-dead princess smiled down upon her in the hall. She was tired now, her feet sore as she went to the lift, thoughts of a good drink and a hot bath on her mind.

Something shone on the stair, a dull gleam like the silver paper of a cigarette packet. She hesitated, weary, but her training took over, that said always to note anything out of the ordinary, and she climbed up, holding on to the banister.

A small pistol made of pipe and stamped metal lay there, shiny against the worn red carpet. She picked it up, and it smelled of propellant.

She turned and went back down the stair, hurrying to the lift. The old gates rattled smoothly across and, she pressed the brass of the button.

The door to the apartment was open and two soldiers were inside, kneeling on the floor. They were working with bandages. Yelena lay on the carpet that was dark with her blood.

One of the soldiers looked up. It was Dmitri, the commander of the tank.

'We were coming in to bring back the mugs . . .' He was very white. 'A man was coming down the stairs, one of the *vlasti*, a Party man. He went past us. We came up, and she was here . . .'

They had put a field dressing over Yelena's stomach.

'We have radioed for an ambulance . . .'

Ruth knelt down stiffly, taking Yelena's hand. Her eyes opened.

'Were the people there?' Yelena whispered.

'Darling, what happened?'

'Were they *there*?' she insisted.

'They were there. They filled the streets,' Ruth said.

A slight colour of happiness came into her pale face. 'Then God is here,' she said with joy.

Blood was tinging the edges of the dressing.

'It was Steklov,' she said. 'He was looking for Yeltsin and he knew me. He sent his men away to wait for him. He said he had time for what he had to do. I asked what grudge he held against me, and he said I had made him look foolish, because I had survived. Also, he said, when he had come to kill Ivan, Ivan fought, and knocked out some of his teeth. He wished me to pay.'

'They are all the same, his kind,' Ruth said savagely. Yelena's eyelids fluttered. 'Things you find if you lift a slab.'

Yelena opened her eyes again. Her voice was weak, but she smiled. 'Darling, you would have been so proud of me . . . I was standing by the desk, I reached in and took out the little pistol and pointed it at him.'

'Why didn't you shoot him?' Ruth cried, in agony.

'He jumped at me, and snatched it away. He knocked me down, and then he shot me . . .'

The breath was shallow in the old chest.

'Hold on, darling . . . the ambulance is coming . . .'

'No . . . he looked like Rykov, darling. He smiled . . .'

The eyes were closed now.

'Don't cry . . . God is here. He will take me with him. I shall be with Ivan, and have the children with me again. I shall sit by the river and watch them play . . .'

Ruth kissed her hand, holding it in hers, and her tears made it wet.

'Why didn't you shoot him?' she wept. 'All you had to do was pull the trigger.'

'I can't kill people,' Yelena whispered. Her voice rustled like dry leaves in the coming wind.

'I won't . . .'

Ruth knelt on the carpet, holding her hand, until they came, and took her away.

The key scratched in the lock and a bar of light filled the corridor as he came in. He shut the door and stood for a moment, his eyes adjusting to the gloom. The curtains were not drawn, and the apartment was lit by the street lamps below on Kalinin Prospekt. His breath rasped in the silence. He had been hurrying. Then he moved on, his shod feet padding on the thick Wilton carpet. He went into the bedroom, and opened a mirrored-fitted wardrobe. He took out an aluminium Halliburton suitcase, and laid it open on the king-size bed.

It was very quiet in the well-insulated apartment; even the noise of the traffic did not penetrate the double-glazing. The sound that made him stiffen, peering fearfully into the dark corner of his bedroom by the wall came from within. It was a metallic noise, the sliding of machined parts, the compressing of a spring.

'Why don't you put the light on?' Ruth asked.

She thumbed the switch in her hand and a small lamp on an

antique table came on, illuminating the room. Steklov stood by the bed, staring at her in horror.

'Don't you want people to know you're at home?'

She sat in a wicker chair. 'This is a Sten gun,' she said. She raised its barrel so that he could look down it. 'It's an old weapon, you know. Not state of the art. People criticised it when it was made, even. It's not very accurate but I never minded that. It's got a good rate of fire, you see. Five hundred and sixty shots a minute. Stick it round a door and pull the trigger and you had good hopes of seeing everyone inside lying on the floor when you went in. If I, sitting here, aim it somewhere in your vicinity, you being over there, I'd say I have as good a chance as any of seeing you blown into some of your component parts when I pull the trigger. Which I'm going to do in a minute.'

'No!' Steklov said hoarsely. He was pale in the yellow light.

'Why not? You killed Yelena, now I've come to kill you. I'm the accountant and I've come to see that the books balance.'

'No!' Steklov said again. He swallowed with difficulty, his mouth suddenly dry.

'Why not? You've lived a long time. Long enough.'

'Life is good,' he whispered. 'I do not want to die.'

'Well, *we* didn't want to die either. None of us. Life seemed good to us too. To all the millions you killed, you and your kind.'

'You are not dead!'

'Not officially, no. But I am not what I seem, either. The revolution, it broke everyone, smashed them up into sharp, agonising fragments and those who lived through it knitted back together into strange, crippled things. I'm one of those. What you made, you and your kind, broke me a long time ago. It broke everyone.'

Old eyes looked at him intently, the gun rested on her knee.

'That isn't quite right. It broke *nearly* everyone. Just a few were never broken, because they were special, they were good. Ivan Ivanovich wasn't broken. But he *was* killed. By you. And Yelena was never broken. She was pure sunlight. But she's dead now. Because *you* killed her.'

Ruth looked at the empty case. 'Where were you going, so secretly, and in such a hurry?'

'Vnukovo,' he answered, reluctantly.

'To catch a plane?'

'I have one waiting for me.'

'To take you where?'

'To Switzerland.'

'I thought you were back in charge, you and your kind?'

'Yeltsin is standing on a tank, addressing the crowd. Western television cameras are recording him. He should have been shot, but he has not been. *All* the people should have been shot, but they have not been. I know defeat when I see it and I do not wait for the arrival of the squad coming for my capture.'

'I was already here waiting for you. When you have to run, never go back. We were taught that, but then, we were the ones running. From people like you. You aren't used to it. Now, shall I shoot you where you stand? Do you have any preference?'

'You are mistaken about your friend.' A bead of sweat dripped off his chin, she saw it sparkle. 'I did not kill her.'

'You did!'

'Only in self-defence. You must have know how she hated me, because I was given the orders to execute her husband. She told me so. She fired her pistol at me. We struggled and it went off again by accident. That was how she died.'

'You do hang on to life, don't you?'

'Life is good,' Steklov said slowly, painfully.

'That's what Gestapo Colonel Frisch said to me. He tortured my friend Joan so that she could not even walk and I shot him. One shot, with the pistol you used to kill Yelena. I'm using the Sten today. I'm older, I might miss with just one shot. I can get you with a full magazine, though.'

'We can make a deal,' said Steklov. 'I can be useful to you.'

'How?'

'You need things. The best food and drink. An apartment like this. I have the files, I know who you can talk to, strip them of everything they have.'

'I have an apartment. And I can buy what I need, I have hard currency.'

His eyes flickered in the light. 'Money, then,' he whispered.

'What do you mean, money?' she said derisively. 'People are using roubles for wallpaper. I have pounds, marks and dollars.'

'So do I,' he said softly. 'Millions and millions of them.'

'How would someone like you get hold of that?'

'The West sent aid. For that fool Gorbachev. I am Party Treasurer and I know where it is because I put it there.'

'In Switzerland?'

'Yes. I'll give you some of it.'

'How much?'

'As much as you want. *Millions.*'

Ruth looked at him thoughtfully. 'But how could I trust you?'

'You can!' Steklov cried eagerly. 'There is so much that one man could never spend it all.'

'Prove I can trust you,' Ruth said coldly.

'You can . . . I am good to my kind . . . listen, I will tell you a story that will prove you can trust me. Do you remember General Rykov?'

'I remember Rykov.'

'It was Rykov who rescued me from the camp. I worked for him . . . There was a girl, in Moscow, a secretary, young and pretty, I was attracted to her. Rykov suggested we should be married. We had a private ceremony, out at his dacha on the Black Sea. He lent it to us for our honeymoon. She was radiant in her white wedding dress and, she kept it on. When we were alone she waited for me in our bedroom. But it was Rykov who went in.'

They stared silently at each other.

'Do you see?' Steklov said entreatingly.

'I see,' she said expressionlessly.

'It was necessary that I prove my loyalty to him. In blood. And I was rewarded. A lesser man might have felt resentment but I served him well, we understood each other. So you see, you can trust me.'

Ruth got up, slowly. 'Yes, I see. Very well, then. I'll come on the plane with you.'

Steklov's face suddenly flushed pink.

'I'll wait downstairs while you pack,' she said. She walked down the corridor and he stood looking after her, almost dazed with relief.

'How did you get in?' he said suddenly.

'I have a knife,' she said. 'With picks for opening locks.'

'Oh.'

She turned the latch on the door.

'But how did you get past the guard?'

She opened the door. 'General Kalmykov took me,' she said, and the big man came in, with his men.

She went outside. There was a bench there, down among the trees and shrubs. She slipped the magazine from the gun, hanging the weapon from its sling under her coat. She sat down on the bench. In her handbag she had a packet of Hungarian cigarettes and she took one out and sat smoking it, watching the cars go by.

As she was finishing it there was a terrible scream from the building above. It came down at her and something hit the paving with a noise like a sack of wet sand bursting from a height and the shriek was cut off. She got up, putting out her cigarette stub, and went over to the ground beneath the building. The wall was spattered with gore and Steklov lay on his back, as broken as a doll. His eyes still moved and he looked at her. His hand was bloody pulp and the fingers had no nails.

'The pistol,' she said quietly. 'It only fires once.'

She stepped around him, and walked away along the grey boulevard.